D1459670

Look who's reading Michael Palmer:

THE SISTERHOOD

"A suspenseful page-turner . . . jolts and entertains the reader."
—Mary Higgins Clark

"Terrific . . . a compelling suspense tale."   —Clive Cussler

SIDE EFFECTS

"Has everything—a terrifying plot . . . breakneck pace . . . vividly drawn characters."   —John Saul

FLASHBACK

"The most gripping medical thriller I've read in many years."
—David Morrell

THREE COMPLETE NOVELS

Michael Palmer

THREE COMPLETE NOVELS

Michael Palmer

THE SISTERHOOD

SIDE EFFECTS

FLASHBACK

WINGS BOOKS
NEW YORK

This omnibus was originally published in separate volumes under the titles:

The Sisterhood, copyright © 1982 by Michael Palmer
Side Effects, copyright © 1985 by Michael Palmer
Flashback, copyright © 1988 by Michael Palmer

This edition contains the complete and unabridged texts of the original editions. They have been completely reset for this volume.

201 East 50th Street, New York, New York 10022,

http://www.randomhouse.com/

Random House
New York • Toronto • London • Sydney • Auckland

Printed and bound in the United States of America

Library of Congress Cataloging-in-Publication Data

Palmer, Michael, 1942–
   [Novels, Selections]
   Three complete novels / Michael Palmer.
     p.   cm.
   Contents: The sisterhood—Side effects—Flashback.
   ISBN 0-517-14959-1 (hard)
   1. Physicians—Massachusetts—Boston—Fiction. 2. Hospitals—Massachusetts—Boston—Fiction. 3. Detective and mystery stories, American. 4. Boston (Mass.)—Fiction. I. Title.
PS3566.A54A6 1996
813'.54—dc20
                                   95-43724
                                      CIP

8   7   6

Contents

THE SISTERHOOD

*Dedicated with Love
to my sons, Matthew and Daniel
and
to my parents*

ACKNOWLEDGMENTS

The Sisterhood is the godchild of the very special people listed below. My gratitude to them goes much deeper than the words on this page could express.

- —To Jane Rotrosen Berkey, my agent and friend, for knowing I could long before I knew
- —To my editors, Linda Grey and Jeanne Bernkopf, for the style, wit, and wisdom they have injected into this work
- —To Donna Prince and Dr. Richard Dugas for critical reading after critical reading
- —To Attorney Mitchell Benjoya of Boston and Dr. Steven I. Cohen of Providence, Rhode Island for technical assistance
- —To Clara and Fred Jewett and the others who have taught me to live—and to write—one day at a time.

Finally a special thanks to Jim Landis, without whom, quite truthfully, none of this would have happened.

M.S.P.
Boston, 1982

⋀ PROLOGUE

"It's all right, Mama . . . I'm here, Mama . . ."

Fine fingers reached across the starched hospital sheet. Slowly, they closed about the puffy, white hand, restrained by adhesive tape and a leather strap to the side of the bed.

The patient, her other arm and both legs similarly bound, stared unblinking at the chipped ceiling. The rhythmic rise and fall of the sheet over her chest and sweep of her tongue across cracked lips were the only outward signs of life. Her gnarled, gray-black hair framed a face that had once been thought quite beautiful.

Now, skin clung tightly to bone, and dark circles of pain obscured her eyes. Although one could easily have placed her age at sixty-five, the woman was, in fact, only five months past her forty-fifth birthday— the day on which her terminal illness had first been diagnosed.

The girl seated to one side of the brass bed tightened her grip, but turned her head away as a tear broke free and glided over her cheek. She wore a heavy, navy blue coat and winter boots that dripped melting snow into a small pool on the linoleum floor.

Five motionless minutes passed; the only sounds came from other patients in other rooms. Finally, the girl slipped off her coat, moved her chair close to the head of the bed, and spoke again. "Mama, can you hear me? Does it still hurt as much? Mama, please. Tell me what I can do to help?"

Another minute passed before the woman answered. Her voice, though soft and hoarse, filled the room. "Kill me! For God's sake, please kill me."

7

"Mama, stop that. You don't know what you're saying. I'll get the nurse. She'll give you something."

"No, baby. It doesn't help. Nothing has helped the pain for days. You can help me. You must help me."

The girl, more confused and frightened than at any time in her fifteen years, looked up at the bottle draining clear fluid into her mother's arm. She rose and made several tentative steps toward the door before the older woman's renewed pleas stopped her short.

Haltingly, she returned to the bedside, stopping a few feet away. An agonized cry came from a room somewhere down the hall. Then another. The girl closed her eyes and clenched her teeth against the hatred she felt for the place.

"Please come over here and help me," her mother begged. "Help me end this pain. Only you can do it. The pillow, baby. Just set it down over my face and lean on it as hard as you can. It won't take long."

"Mama, I . . ."

"Please! I love you. If you love me, too, you won't let me hurt so anymore. They all say it's hopeless . . . don't let your mama hurt so anymore . . ."

"I . . . I love you, Mama. I love you."

The girl continued to whisper the words as she gently lifted her mother's head and removed the thin, firm pillow.

"I love you, Mama . . ." she said again and again as she placed the pillow over the narrow face and leaned on it with all the strength she could manage. She forced her mind back to the warm and happy times —long spring walks, baking lessons, steamy mugs of hot chocolate on snowy afternoons.

Her body was thin and light, with only hints at the fullness of a woman. Struggling for leverage, she grasped the pillow case and drew her knees up. With each passing scene she pressed herself more firmly against the pillow. Bumpy rides to the lake, picnics on the water's edge, races to the raft. . . .

The movement beneath the sheet lessened then stopped.

Her sobs mixing with the rattle of sleet against the window, the girl lay there, unaware of the fragment of pillow case which had ripped free and was now clutched in her hand.

After nearly half an hour, she rose, replaced the pillow, and kissed her dead mother's lips. Then she turned and walked resolutely down the hall, out of the hospital, into the raw winter evening.

The day was February seventeenth. The year, 1932.

CHAPTER I
BOSTON
October I

MORNING SUN SPLASHED into the room moments before the first notes came from the clock radio. David Shelton, eyes still closed, listened for a few seconds before silently guessing Vivaldi, *The Four Seasons,* probably the *Summer* concerto. It was a game he had played nearly every morning for years. Still, the occasions on which he identified a piece correctly were rare enough to warrant a small celebration.

A soothing male voice, chosen by the station to blend with the dawn, identified the music as a Haydn symphony. David smiled to himself. You're getting sharper. The right continent—even the right century.

He turned his head toward the window and opened his eyes a slit, preparing for the next guessing game in his morning ritual. Hazy rainbows of sunlight filtered through his lashes. "No contest," he said, squinting to make the colors flicker.

"What did you say?" the woman next to him mumbled sleepily, drawing her body tightly against his.

"Sparkling autumn day. Fifty, no, fifty-five degrees. Nary a cloud." David opened his eyes fully, confirmed his prediction, then rolled over, slipping his arm beneath her smooth back. "Happy October," he said, kissing her forehead, at the same time running his free hand down her neck and across her breasts.

David studied her face as she awoke, marveling at her uncluttered beauty. Ebony hair. High cheek bones. Full, sensuous mouth. Lauren Nichols was by all standards a stunning woman. Even at 6:00 A.M. For a moment, another woman's face flashed in his thoughts. In her own special way Ginny, too, had always looked beautiful in the early morn-

9

ing. The image faded as he drew his fingers over Lauren's flat stomach and gently massaged the mound beneath her soft hair.

"Roll over, David, and I'll give you a back rub," Lauren said, sitting up suddenly.

Disappointment crossed his face, but was instantly replaced by a broad grin. "Ladies' choice," he sang, rolling over and bunching the pillow beneath his head. "Last night was really wonderful," he added, feeling the thick muscles at the base of his neck relax to her touch. "You are something else, Nichols, do you know that?"

Out of David's field of vision, Lauren forced the smile of an adult trying to share a youthful enthusiasm she had long outgrown. "David," she said, increasing the vigor of her massage, "do you think you might be able to get a haircut before the Art Society dinner dance next week?"

He flipped to his back, staring at her with a mixture of confusion and dismay. "What has my hair got to do with our lovemaking?"

"Honey, I'm sorry," she said earnestly, "I really am. I guess I have a thousand things hopping around in my head today. It was beautiful for me, too. Honest."

"Beautiful? You really mean that?" David said, immediately regaining his élan.

"There's still a hell of a lot of tension in your body, doc, but less each time. Last night was definitely the best yet."

The best yet. David cocked his head to one side, evaluating her words. Progress, not perfection. That was all he could ask for, he decided. And certainly, over the six months since they had met, progress there had been.

Their life together was often an emotional roller coaster, quite unlike the easy, free-flowing years with Ginny. Still, their differences had not been insurmountable—her judgmental friends, his cynicism, the differing demands of their careers. As each crisis arose, was dealt with, and passed, David sensed their caring grow. Although there were things he wished were different, he was grateful just to feel the caring, and the willingness to try.

It was willingness David thought had died for him eight years before in screams and glass and twisted metal.

Realizing that Lauren had said all she was going to on the subject of their physical relationship, David flipped over once again. The back rub continued. Maybe you're finally ready, he thought. Maybe it's time. But for God's sake, Shelton, don't rush it. Don't push her away, but try not to smother her either. As he played the feelings through in his mind, the apprehension surrounding them faded.

"You know," he said after a while, "of all the bets and guesses I've ever made with myself, you've been the most striking loss."

"How's that?"

"Well, I think it's safe to tell you now. On our first date I bet myself a jumbo Luigi's special-with-everything-except-anchovies pizza that we would run out of things to say in a week."

"David!"

"I just couldn't imagine what an unsophisticated, stripes-with-plaids surgeon was going to find to talk about with a chic, jet-set newspaper reporter, that's all."

"And now you know, right?"

"What I know is that my body turned you on so much you couldn't resist trying to play 'enry 'iggins with the rest of me." He laughed, spinning around to give her a bear hug, a maneuver that usually led to an out-and-out wrestling match. When Lauren showed no inclination to join in, he released her and leaned back on his hands.

"Something the matter?" he asked.

"David, you started crying out in your sleep last night. Was it another nightmare?"

"I . . . I guess so." David answered uncertainly, testing the muscles in his jaw. Only then did he realize they were aching. "My face hurts, and that usually means I spent most of the night with my teeth clenched."

"Can you remember what it was this time?"

"One I've had before, I think. Fuzzier than other nights, but the same one. It doesn't happen so often anymore."

"Which one?"

David felt the concern in her voice, but her expression held something more. Impatience? Irritation? He looked away. "The highway," he said softly. "It was the highway." The tone and cadence of his words took on an eerie, detached quality as he drifted back into the nightmare. "All I see for a while is the windshield . . . the wipers are thrashing back and forth . . . faster and faster, fighting to keep pace with the rain. The center line keeps trying to snake under the car. I keep forcing it back with the wheel. Ginny's face is there for a moment . . . and Becky's, too . . . both asleep . . . both so peaceful. . . ." David's eyes had closed. His words stopped, but the memory of the dream was unrelenting. Out of the darkness and the rain, the headlights began coming. Two at a time. Heading straight for him, then splitting apart and flashing past, one on either side. Wave after blurry wave. Then, above the lights, he saw the face. The crazy drunken face, twisted and red with fire, eyes glowing golden in the flames. His hands locked as he prayed the oncoming lights would split apart like all the others. But he knew they wouldn't. They never did. Then he heard the brakes screeching. He saw Ginny's eyes open and widen in terror. Finally, he heard the scream. Hers? His? He could never tell.

"David?"

Lauren's voice cut the scream short. He shuddered, then turned to her. Droplets of sweat had appeared on his forehead. His hands were shaking. He took a deep breath, then slowly exhaled. The shaking stopped. "Guess I got lost there for a moment, huh?" He smiled sheepishly.

"David, have you seen your doctor lately? Maybe you should get in touch with him," Lauren said.

"Ol' Brinker the Shrinker? He tapped me dry—head *and* pocketbook—about three months ago and told me I had graduated. What are you worried about? It's only a nightmare. Brinker told me they're normal in situations like mine."

"I'm worried, that's all."

"Lauren Nichols, you're frightened that I might come apart in the middle of the Art Society banquet and get your life membership canceled!"

Lauren's laugh lacked conviction. After a few seconds, she stopped trying to pay homage to his sense of humor. "David, is there anything at all that you take seriously? In just one sentence you manage to poke fun at me for being concerned about your health and for caring enough about art to be active in the Society. What is with you?"

David started to apologize, but swallowed the words. The look in her eyes told him that some very basic issues were suddenly on the griddle. Something more than a simple "I'm sorry" was needed. For several interminably silent seconds their eyes locked.

Finally, he shrugged and said, "There I go again, huh? An ounce of flippancy is worth a pound of facing up to real feelings. I know I do it, but sometimes even knowing isn't enough. Look, Lauren, what I said wasn't meant maliciously. Truly it wasn't. The nightmares still scare me. It's hard for me to face that. Okay?"

Lauren was not yet placated. "You haven't answered my question, David. Is anything significant enough to keep you from joking about it?"

"As a matter of fact," he said, "most things are significant to me. Shit, you should know that by now."

"But only you know for sure which is which, right?"

"Dammit, Lauren, I'm a doctor—a surgeon—and a damn good one. Of course things are important to me. Of course I care. I care about people and pain, about suffering, about life. My world is full of injury and disease and no-win decisions. The day I lose my ability to laugh is the day I lose my ability to cope." He fought back the impulse to continue, sensing he was already guilty of attacking their morning spat with a sledgehammer.

"I'm going to take a shower," Lauren said after a few moments. She was already out of bed, pulling on a blue velour dressing gown.

"Want company?"

"I think it's the right time for a little space and some hot, soapy water. Go make some breakfast. I'll get myself squeaky clean and we'll give this day a fresh start over a cup of coffee."

David sat staring out at the glittering new day until he heard the sound of water against tile. The day, possibly the most important one for him in years, was not starting out the way he had planned. By now he was to have told Lauren about the exciting turn of events at the hospital. Events that might well mark the beginning of the end to so much of the frustration and disappointment that had colored his life. By now he was to have reaffirmed his desire to have her move in with him, and she was to have at last agreed that it was time.

"Just calm down, Shelton, and let things happen," he said, clenching his hands, then consciously relaxing them. "Everything is finally coming together. Nothing, no one, can mess them up again except you."

He selected a frayed, green surgical scrub suit from the half-dozen stuffed in a bureau drawer, dressed, and walked to the window. Four stories below, a few early risers were crossing the still-shaded islands of Commonwealth Avenue. He wondered how many of them were feeling the same sense of anticipation he was—the excitement of facing a new beginning. Beginnings. The thought brought a wistful smile. How many times had he, himself, felt that way? High school, college, medical school. Ginny, Becky. So many beginnings. Beginnings as promising as this one. David sighed. Was the morning the start of a page, of a chapter, or perhaps of a whole new story? Whatever it was to be, he felt ready. For of all the bright beginnings in his life since the accident and the nightmare year that had followed the deaths of his wife and daughter, this was the first one he completely trusted.

The apartment, though small, gave the illusion of roominess, born largely of tall windows and ten-foot ceilings—trademarks of many dwellings in the Back Bay section of the city. A long, narrow corridor connected the bedroom to a living room cluttered with near-antique furniture, a dining alcove, and a tiny kitchen that faced an alleyway at the rear of the building. The front and bathroom doors faced one another midway down the hall.

Humming an off-key rendition of the Haydn symphony, David shuffled to the kitchen. Usually, he would exercise and run before eating, but this morning, he decided, could be an exception. He was a muscular man, with broad shoulders and powerful arms that made him appear heavier than his 175 pounds. There were slivers of gray throughout his black, bushy hair. His wide, youthful eyes ran the spectrum from bright blue to pale green, depending on the light. Fine creases, once transient and now indelible, traversed his forehead and the bridge of his nose.

He stood in the center of the kitchen rubbing his hands together with mock professionalism. "Zo, ve crrreate ze brrreakfast." He swung open the refrigerator door. "Ze choices, zey are many, yes?" His voice echoed back from near-empty shelves.

Once, after hoplessly blackening two steaks, he had announced to Lauren, "I think I'll write a culinary arts book for the single man. I'm going to call it *Cooking for None*."

13

Selecting breakfast fare was not difficult. "Let us zee . . . ve could haf tomato juice or . . . tomato juice. Ze English muffin, eet looks nice, non? . . . And zee five ecks, zey beg to be scrrrambled, yes?"

Lauren breezed into the dining alcove as he was setting their meal on the table. "Nicely done," she said, surveying his work. "You'll make a wonderful wife for someone someday." A few strands of glistening hair fell from beneath the towel she had wrapped around her head. Her smile announced that, as advertised, she was starting the morning over again.

"So," David said deliberately, "what are your plans for this day?" He was pleased at having fought back the impulse to blurt out his good news. He would disclose it casually, in the same matter-of-fact way Lauren so often told him about the luncheon she had been to at the White House or the assignment she had won to cover thus-or-so senator's campaign.

"David, do you have something you want to tell me?" she said.

"Pardon?" He stretched for one last bit of insouciance.

Lauren smiled. "My college roommate once had a surprise party for me. Just before everyone jumped out and yelled, she had the same expression on her face as you do now."

"Well, I guess I do have a little good news," he said, his nonchalance now a parody. "Dr. Wallace Huttner—*the* Dr. Wallace Huttner— is leaving town tomorrow for a few days."

"And?"

"And . . . he's asked me to make rounds with him this evening and to take over his patients until he gets back."

"Oh, David, that's wonderful," Lauren said. "Wallace Huttner! I'm impressed. The most widely acclaimed pair of hands to come out of Boston since Arthur Fiedler."

"Well, now we know that he's smart enough to recognize true surgical talent when he sees it. I'm covering his practice until he gets back from a three-day conference on the Cape."

"And there you sit, trying to impress me with how blasé you can act about the whole thing. What a funny duck you are, David."

The scrambled eggs, none too appetizing to begin with, remained on her plate as Lauren fired one question after another at him.

"Huttner was written up in *Time,* do you know that?"

"So he's operated on a few sheiks and prime ministers. He still puts his scrub suit on one leg at a time, just like the rest of us."

"Be serious for once, will you? Could this mean more money for you?"

David's eyes narrowed. He studied her face for a few seconds, looking for more than superficial interest behind her question. Although his lack of a typical surgeon's salary came up infrequently, a battle of some sort was sure to follow whenever it did. Lauren seemed unable or unwilling to accept the fickle economic realities of a medical specialty that was dependent on referrals from other physicians, especially in a city like Boston with its surfeit of doctors.

Even after two years at Boston Doctors Hospital he realized that many of his colleagues still had reservations about him. Word had filtered back. "Shelton? Oh, yes, I suppose I could refer this woman to him. But she's not the easiest person to deal with and, frankly, I'm just not sure he could handle her. I mean that trouble he got into, going to pieces after his wife and kid died. I'd like to help him out, I really would. But what would *I* look like to my patient if I send her to a surgeon and he up and comes unglued?"

It wasn't easy. He had never expected it would be. Lauren's concern over his financial situation was understandable, albeit somewhat discouraging. It would take time, he tried to explain. That's all—just some time.

Her expression appeared nonjudgmental. Still, David tiptoed around the issue. "Well, Huttner is chief of the department. It should mean more acceptance from the doctors who refer patients to surgeons." Any acceptance from most of them would be an improvement, he reflected ruefully. He still appeared in the operating room so infrequently that the nurses sometimes stood around after he entered, waiting for the surgeon to arrive.

"Is he grooming you to be his partner?"

"Lauren, the man hardly knows me! He just saw the chance to throw a few crumbs in the direction of a doc who's struggling some, that's all."

"Well, Mr. Ice Water," she said, smiling, "you can act any way you want to. I'll stay excited enough for both of us. What time do you take over for him?"

"I'm meeting him at the hospital at six. We should be done by eight or nine and . . . God, that reminds me. The Rosettis invited us for dinner, either tonight or tomorrow. I told them we'd—"

"I can't make it," Lauren said. "I mean I have to work."

"You don't like them, do you?"

"David, please, we've been over this before. I think the Rosettis are very nice people." Her words were hollow. David's unsuccessful attempts to draw her into his long-standing friendship with the tavern owner and his wife remained a source of tension.

"Okay, I'll phone Joey and get a raincheck," David said, relieved that he was able to put the matter to rest without a major confrontation.

"That would be fine. Really." It was Lauren's way of thanking him for his restraint. "I do have to work. In fact, I'm flying to Washington this morning. The President's going to announce details of his latest economic program and the service wants me to cover it from the personal, human side. I'll probably be there for a couple of days."

"In that case, you'll need all the nourishment you can get." He nodded at her untouched breakfast. "Want seconds on the eggs?"

Lauren glanced at her watch, stood up, and stretched as high as she could reach. "Just leave them there until I get back from Washington." She walked halfway toward the bedroom before adding, "They can only improve with age." She giggled and dashed down the corridor as David sprang up to give chase. She waited until he had nearly reached the bedroom door before pushing it closed and flipping the lock.

"You'll live to regret this," David called out through the door. "Someday I'm going to become a famous chef and marry the Countess of Lusitania. Then I'll be lost to you forever."

Twenty minutes later, Lauren emerged from the bedroom, breathtaking in a burgundy suit and beige blouse. A silk scarf was draped loosely about her neck. "No caveman stuff, David," she said, anticipating his hug and blocking it with an outstretched hand. "This outfit has to last me at least a day. Listen, I almost forgot. You might be able to help me out."

"Only in exchange for caveman stuff."

"David, this is serious."

"Okay." He motioned that he was ready to listen.

"Senator Cormier's office announced that he's entering your hospital in the next day or two for an operation. Gall bladder, I think."

"You sure? Cormier seems more the White Memorial than the Boston Doctors type."

Lauren nodded. "Could he be coming in as Huttner's patient?"

"No chance. Huttner would never go away with that kind of prestige coming in on his service."

"Do you think you could get in to see him? Or even better, get me in to see him? His campaign for a stiff windfall profits tax against the oil companies has made him really big stuff. An exclusive interview would be an ostrich-sized feather in my cap."

"I'll try, but I can't guarantee any—"

"Thanks, you're a dear."

Lauren wished him luck with his new responsibilities, squeezed his hands, and kissed him lightly on the mouth. Then, with a final, "Be a good boy, now," she walked out of the apartment and down the hall to the elevator.

For several minutes David stood silently by the door, breathing in her perfume, but feeling only a strange emptiness. "At least she could have tasted them," he said as he began to clear the table. "In spite of what they looked like."

The night watchman was fat. Fat and agonizingly slow. From a recessed doorway, the nurse, a fragile-looking woman with hair the color of pale sun, watched and waited as he lumbered down the hallway. Now and again he stopped to poke at the door of a storage room or to check one of the bank of staff lockers lining the wall. B-2 West, the subbasement of the west wing of Boston Doctors Hospital, was, but for the two of them, deserted.

The nurse looked about at the grime, illuminated by bare ceiling light bulbs, and her skin began to itch. She was a petite woman, impeccably groomed, with makeup so meticulously applied it was almost invisible. Impatiently, she rubbed her thumbs across her fingertips. The watchman was taking forever. She glanced at her watch. Forty-five, maybe fifty minutes of safe time—more than enough, provided she could get moving and avoid any other unanticipated delays. A roach crawled over the tip of her shoe and for a moment she thought she was going to be sick. She forced herself to relax and waited.

Finally, the watchman was done. He keyed the security box, began whistling the "Colonel Bogey March," and, after a few in-place steps, strutted off to his own accompaniment. To some the man might have looked silly, or jovial, or even cute. To the delicate woman observing him he was, quite simply, repulsive.

She waited an extra few seconds, moved quickly down the row of lockers to number 178, then dialed the combination printed on the card Dahlia had sent her. The thin, half-filled syringe was right where she had been told it would be. She briefly held it to the light, then dropped it into the front pocket of her spotless uniform. Another check of the time and she headed for the tunnel leading to the south wing. She rode the elevator to Two South, then slipped into the rear stairwell and hurried up two more flights. Ducking into Room 438, she stopped, regaining her breath in soundless gulps. Through the gloom she could see John Chapman. The man was asleep, tucked in a fetal position, his face toward her. From beneath the sheet a catheter drained clear urine into a plastic collecting system.

Chapman's recovery following kidney surgery had been uneventful. The woman smiled at the thought. Uneventful . . . until now.

She checked the corridor. A nurse's aide—the first arrival of her day shift—had just stepped off the elevator. The fragile night peace was holding, but the nurse knew that within half an hour it would yield to the chaos of day. The time was now. Her pulse quickened. Anaphylactic shock! Almost fifteen years in hospital nursing and she had never even seen a full-blown case, let alone watched one from start to finish.

She moved to the bedside. There, on the nightstand, were the flowers. A glorious spray of lilies. Taped to the vase was the card.

"Best Wishes, Lily." She whispered the words without actually reading them. There was no need. They were her words.

On the table next to the vase lay Chapman's silver necklace and medic-alert tag. She illuminated the disc with her penlight. Again she smiled. It said:

DIABETIC
ALLERGIC TO PENICILLIN
ALLERGIC TO BEE STINGS

The small syringe in her hand held the bee venom concentrate used by allergists to desensitize their high-risk patients. Although practically speaking the dose was enormous, it was still minute enough to escape detection during a conventional autopsy.

John Chapman's cocoa face was loose and relaxed. Even asleep he seemed to be smiling. The nurse pulled over a straight-backed chair and sat. With one hand, she slipped the needle through the rubber stopper of his I.V. tubing. With the other, she gently shook him by the shoulder.

"Mr. Chapman, John, wake up," she cooed. "It's morning."

Chapman's eyes eased open. "Little Angel? Zat you?" His voice was a rich bass. A boyhood in Jamaica twenty-five years before still tinged the edges of his words. He focused on her and smiled. "My, but you are somethin' to gaze upon," he said. "Is it really morning or are you just one of my dreams?"

"No dream," she answered. "But I am a little early. My shift doesn't start for another half hour or so." She depressed the plunger, emptying the venom into the intravenous line. "I came in early just to see you."

"What?"

She didn't answer. Instead, she watched intently as a quizzical expression crossed Chapman's face, which quickly gave way to apprehension.

"I . . . I feel funny, Angel," he said. "Real funny." Panic crept into his voice. "I'm starting to tingle all over. . . . Angela, somethin's happening to me. Somethin' awful. I feel like I am going to die."

The woman looked at him blandly. You are, she thought. You are. At that instant the full force of the anaphylactic reaction hit. The lining of John Chapman's nose and throat swelled nearly shut. The muscles surrounding his bronchial tubes went into spasm. The nurse spun around to be certain the room door was closed. The reaction was more rapid, more spectacular than she had ever imagined it would be. In fact, she decided, it was more spectacular than anything she had ever witnessed.

"An . . . gel . . . please. . . ." Chapman's words were barely audible. His eyes had swollen shut.

Instinctively, she checked for a pulse, but she knew that vascular collapse had already occurred. A second later, the last sliver of air space in Chapman's respiratory passage closed. He rolled to his back and was still.

The nurse with pale sun hair held her breath during the final moments, then exhaled. Her faultless face glowed with a beatific smile, acknowledging that once again she had done her job well.

* * *

The Seth Thomas wall clock in his living room showed seven thirty when David finished stacking the dishes in the sink and changed into a navy blue sweat suit. He made a deliberate study of his small record collection before selecting Copeland's *Rodeo* and then began a series of slow-motion stretching exercises and calisthenics.

The Copeland was a perfect choice, he thought as he dragged a set of weights out from behind the couch. For ten minutes he lifted in various positions and angles, pushing himself harder than usual until the tension of Lauren's unemotional departure left him.

The weights had come to be as much mental as physical therapy—a morning ritual for almost five years, begun the day David had decided to return to surgery by repeating the last two grueling years of residency. That same day he smoked his last cigarette and ran his first mile. Within a few months he had more than regained the stamina lost during three years away from the operating room.

Glistening from the workout, he grabbed his stopwatch and keys, stuffing them into the pocket of his sweatpants as he stepped out the door.

He bypassed the narrow, rickety elevator in favor of the stairs at the end of the hall. Trotting down four flights and across the dimly lit foyer of the building, he pushed through the front doors and out onto Commonwealth Avenue.

The sunlight hit his eyes like a flashbulb. It was one of those days New Englanders boast about when they tell outsiders that there is nowhere else on earth to live. One of those days that renders February little more than a distant memory, and helps them forget the muddy drizzle of April and the oppressive, steamy heat of mid-August, at least for a while.

Stiffly at first, but with rapidly developing fluidness, he jogged the few blocks toward the esplanade. Elms and oaks flashed by, heavy now with reds and oranges and golds. The air, unwilling this day to succumb to commuters' exhaust fumes, tasted like mountain water.

David crossed over Storrow Drive and picked up his pace as he turned onto the tarmac path paralleling the river. For a time he ran with his eyes nearly closed, breathing in the day and taking increasing delight in the responsiveness of each muscle in his body.

He watched a lone oarsman sculling the Charles like some giant water bug. Even at such an early hour there were people scattered along the grassy bank reading, sketching, or just soaking in the morning. Cyclists glided silently past him in both directions. Dogs tugged their masters along. Intense-faced students, wearing their books on their backs like hair shirts, shuffled reluctantly toward classrooms where sterile fluorescence would replace the autumn sun.

David checked his stopwatch and glanced around him. Under six minutes to the bridge. He had won his first bet of the run. Sooner or later a Rolls Royce and an A-frame in the Berkshires would be his. Wiping sweat from around his eyes, he picked up his tempo a bit.

To his right a barefoot girl wearing jeans and a bright red T-shirt sent a Frisbee spinning toward her boyfriend. "Two Twinkies and a Big Mac says he catches it," David panted just before the disc spun sharply toward the river, hit the ground, and rolled down the bank. "Thank goodness," he laughed out loud.

At the three-mile mark he turned and headed back. "Everything is getting better," he said out loud, matching each syllable to the slap of his Nikes on the pavement. "Better and better and better."

Christ, it felt good to be alive again.

∿ CHAPTER 2

CHRISTINE BEALL EASED her light blue Mustang past the guard at Parking Lot C, forcing a thin smile in response to his wave. She cruised past several empty spaces without noticing them, then spotted one in the corner farthest from the gate and pulled in. Stepping onto the gravel, she adjusted her carefully tailored nurse's uniform and squinted up at the afternoon sun, but quickly gave up trying to absorb any of the magic of the brilliant autumn day. Her preoccupation with other thoughts, other issues, made it impossible.

Lot C was one of three satellite parking areas appropriated by Doctors Hospital to meet the needs of an ever-expanding staff. Christine started toward the minibus stop, then decided she needed the time and the three blocks' walk as a bridge between her outside world and the hospital. Up ahead, two other evening shift nurses waved her to join them, but after a few quick steps, she stopped and motioned them to go on. Pausing by the window of a secondhand furniture store, she studied her image in the dusty glass.

You look tired, she thought. Tired and worried . . . and scared.

She was not a tall woman, barely five foot four. Her sandy hair was tied back in a ponytail that she would pin up beneath her nurse's cap before starting work. Scattered freckles, still darkened by the summer sun, dotted the tops of both cheeks and the bridge of her nose.

"What are you going to do, kid?" she asked her reflection softly. "Are you really ready to start this whole thing in motion? Peg-whoever-she-is may be ready. Charlotte Thomas may be ready. But are you?" She pressed her lips together and stared at the sidewalk. Finally, with an indecisive shrug, she turned and headed down the block.

Boston Doctors Hospital was a massive glass and brick hydra with three tentacles probing north and west into Roxbury and another three south and east toward the downtown area. Over the one hundred and five years of its existence several wings had grown, decayed, and died, only to be replaced by larger and higher ones. Ongoing construction was as much a part of its being as the white uniforms scurrying in and out of its maw.

Never able to snare a benefactor generous enough to endow an entire building, the hospital's trustees had adopted the unimaginative policy of identifying the tentacles by the direction of their thrust. The sliding doors through which Christine entered the main lobby were located between Southeast and South.

She glanced at the large gold clock set in a marble slab above the information desk. Two thirty. It would be another twenty or twenty-five minutes before the day shift on Four South would sign out to her three-to-eleven group.

Christine leaned against a stone column and surveyed the activity around her. Patients and visitors filled every available seat, while dozens more crowded around the information desk or weaved their way across from one wing to another. Scattered wheelchairs punctuated rows of molded plastic chairs. The scene, one she had viewed hundreds of times over the past five years, still filled her with fascination and awe. There were days, certain special days, when she actually felt a physical merging of her body with the fiber of the hospital. Days when she felt its pulse as surely as if it were her own. Slowly, she crossed the lobby and joined the flow heading down the main artery of the South wing.

Christine's floor, Four South, like most of the other floors in the seven-story wing, housed a mixture of medical and surgical patients, each with a private doctor. A few residents, widely scattered throughout the hospital, served as emergency backup. On Four South, as on all other private floors in all other hospitals, nurses were the sole medical presence for most of each day.

Stepping off the elevator, Christine scanned the corridor, checking for an emergency "crash" cart or other equipment that might suggest trouble in one of the rooms. The floor seemed normally busy, but an instinct, developed over five years, whispered that something was wrong.

She was nearing the nurses' station when the cries began—pitiful, piercing wails from the far end of the hall. Christine raced toward the

21

sound. As she passed Room 412, she glanced in at Charlotte Thomas, who was sleeping, though restlessly, through the commotion.

The cries were coming from 438—John Chapman's room. At the doorway Christine stopped short. The room was a shambles. Candy, books, flowers, and shattered vases covered the floor. Seated in a chair, her face buried in her hands, was John Chapman's wife, a proud, stocky woman Christine had met at the time of his admission. The bed was stripped and empty.

"Oh my God," Christine murmured. She crossed the room and knelt by the woman, whose cries had given way to helpless whimpers. "Mrs. Chapman?"

"My Johnny's dead. Gone. They all said he would be fine, and now he's dead." She was staring through her hands at the floor, talking more to herself than to Christine.

"Mrs. Chapman, I'm Christine Beall, one of the evening nurses. Can I do anything for you? Get you anything?" Christine ached at the thought of John Chapman's death. The near-legendary fighter for blacks and other minorities had been up and doing well when she had left the hospital just sixteen hours before.

"No, no, I'll be all right," the woman finally managed. "I . . . I just can't believe my Johnny's dead."

Christine looked about. A few vases of flowers were intact, but most had been thrown to the floor or shattered against a wall. "Mrs. Chapman, who did this?"

The woman looked up. Her eyes were red and glassy, her features distorted by grief. "Me. I did," she said. "I came up to clean out Johnny's room. All of a sudden it hit me that he was gone. He's never coming back. The next thing I remember, the nurse was trying to keep me from smashing any more of Johnny's gifts. He even got a card and a book from the governor, you know. My God, I hope I haven't ruined it. I—"

"You didn't ruin it, Mrs. Chapman. I have it right here. And here's the orange juice you wanted."

Christine turned toward the voice.

Angela Martin nodded a greeting, then brought over the book and the juice. "I called your pastor, Mrs. Chapman," she said. "He'll be right over."

At the sight of Angela, immaculate and unruffled despite a difficult eight-hour shift, the woman calmed perceptibly. "Thank you, child. You've been so kind to me. And you were to my Johnny, too." She gestured at the mess. "I . . . I'm sorry about this."

"Nonsense," Angela said, "I've called Housekeeping. They'll take care of it. Come, let's wait in the quiet room until your pastor comes." She put a slender arm around the grieving woman's shoulders and led her out.

Christine stood alone amid the wreckage, remembering her initial surprise at John Chapman's humor and erudite gentleness. Was there anything else she could do now for the man's widow? Not really, she decided. As long as Angela Martin was with her, the woman was in exceptionally compassionate and skilled hands.

Christine started toward the door, then stopped and returned for the two undamaged vases of flowers. Mrs. Chapman might want to bring them home, she thought. She glanced at the note taped to the green glass vase. Lilies . . . from Lily? Good grief, what next? She shook her head. An unexpected death and bizarre namesake flowers. It all felt quite in keeping with a day that from its very beginning had seemed beyond her control.

Her roommates, Lisa and Carole, had both left for work when the phone began ringing. Christine had made a quick thrust at her alarm clock, then identified the true source of the insistent jangle. She had tried burying her head under the pillow. Eventually she had stumbled to the kitchen, certain that the ringing would stop as soon as she reached for the receiver. It did not.

"My name is Peg," the caller had said in a voice that was at once both soft and strong. "I am one of the directors of your Sisterhood. There is a patient on your floor in Doctors Hospital whom I would like you to evaluate and, if you see fit, present for consideration to your Regional Screening Committee. It is not possible for me to do so myself without an awkwardness that might well be noticed, since I no longer actively practice nursing."

Christine had put her hand under the faucet, then rubbed cold water over her face. Although mention of The Sisterhood had awakened her like a slap, she wanted to be sure. She stammered, "Well, no one has ever called and asked me to . . . what I mean is . . ."

The woman had anticipated Christine's concern. "Please, Christine, just hear me out," she said. "As is always the rule in our movement, you are under no obligation to do anything other than that which you believe in your heart to be right. I have known the woman about whom I am calling for many years. I feel certain that she would not want to survive the situation in which she now exists. She is in great pain and her condition, from what I have been able to learn, is without hope."

At that moment Christine knew, without being told, whom she was being asked to evaluate. "It's Charlotte, isn't it?" she said. "Charlotte Thomas."

"Yes, Christine, it is."

"I . . . I've thought about her a great deal lately, especially with the agony she's been going through these past few days."

"Were you planning to report her case yourself?" the caller asked.

"Last night. I almost called her in last night. Something stopped me from doing it. I don't know what it was. She is such a remarkable woman, I . . . ." Christine's voice trailed away.

"The path we have chosen to follow will never be an easy one," the woman said. "Should it ever become easy, you will know that somehow you have lost your way."

"I understand," Christine said grimly. "My shift begins at three this afternoon. If it feels right to me then, I'll call in her case report and let the Screening Committee decide."

"That is as much as I could possibly ask or expect, Christine. Perhaps sometime in the future circumstances will allow us to meet. Good-bye."

"Good-bye," she said, but the woman had already hung up.

Before falling asleep the previous night, Christine had drawn up an ambitious list of projects for the day. Suddenly, with a single phone call, none of them mattered. She carried a pot of tea to the living room and sank into an easy chair, totally absorbed in thoughts of The Sisterhood of Life. Over the ten months following her initiation into the movement a new meaning and purpose had entered her life. Now she was being asked to test that purpose. With Charlotte's life at stake, the test would not be easy.

Engrossed in thoughts of Charlotte Thomas and John Chapman, Christine wandered into the lounge to hang up her coat. Two of the day nurses had put aside the shift notes they were writing and were, instead, arguing about which of John Chapman's medications had most likely caused his fatal reaction. Christine had no inclination to join in. She greeted them with a nod, then said, "I'm going to see Charlotte for a few minutes. Send someone to get me in four-twelve if I'm not back by the time report is ready to start. Okay?" The women waved her off and resumed their conversation.

It had been nearly two weeks since Charlotte Thomas's surgery, two weeks during which Christine had walked into Room 412 dozens of times. In spite of the frequent visits, as she approached the door a strange image appeared in her mind. It was an image that came to her almost every time she was about to enter 412. Well, not exactly an image, Christine realized—more an expectation. It was quite vivid despite what she knew in the practical, professional part of her. Charlotte would be sitting in the vinyl chair next to her bed writing a letter. Her light brown hair would be piled carelessly on the back of her head, held in place by a floppy bow of pink yarn. The thin lines at the corners of her eyes and along the edge of her lips would crinkle upward in pleasure at the appearance of her "supernurse." She would look as healthy and radiant and alive at age sixty as she had probably looked at sixteen. A woman totally at peace with herself.

That was the way she had looked each day during her stay in August for diagnostic tests. The moment before she entered the room Christine imagined her voice, as clear and free as a forest brook, saying, "Ah, sweet Christine. My one-woman pep squad, come to bring some cheer to the sick ol' lady . . ."

At the foot of the bed Christine stopped and closed her eyes, shaking her head as if trying to dislodge what little remained of her imaginings and hope.

Charlotte lay on her right side, propped in that position by several pillows. White-lipped, Christine tiptoed to her bedside. Charlotte seemed asleep. Her coarse breathing, nearly a snore, was labored and unnatural. The oxygen prongs designed to fit in her nostrils had slipped to one cheek, exposing an angry redness caused by their continuous pressure. Her face was puffed and pasty yellow. Hanging from the poles on either side of the bed, plastic bags dripped their fluid into her through clear plastic tubes.

Christine was close to tears as she reached down and gently smoothed Charlotte's hair away from her face. The woman's eyes fluttered for a second, then opened.

"Another day." Christine said with cheer in her voice but sadness in her smile.

"Another day," Charlotte echoed weakly. "How's my girl?"

How typical, Christine thought. Lying there like that and she asks how *I* am. "A little tired, but otherwise all right," she managed. "How's *my* girl?"

Charlotte's lips twisted in a half-smile that said, "You should know better than to ask." She brought a bruised hand up and tugged lightly at the red rubber tube taped to the bridge of her nose and looping down into one nostril. "I don't like this," she whispered.

Christine shook her head. The tube had not been there when she had left last night. Her words were forced. "You . . . must have had some trouble with your stomach. . . . The tube is keeping it from swelling with fluid. It's attached to a suction machine. That's the hissing sound you keep hearing." She looked away. The tubes, the bruises, the pain—Christine felt them as if they were her own. She knew that with Charlotte more than with any patient she had ever cared for her perspective had gone awry. Many times she had wanted to run from the room—from her own feelings. To turn Charlotte Thomas's care over to another nurse. But always she had stayed.

"How's that boyfriend of yours?" Charlotte asked.

The change in subject was her way of saying she understood. There was nothing that could be done about the tube. Christine knelt down and with accentuated girlish embarrassment said, "Charlotte, if you're talking about Jerry, he's not my boyfriend. In fact, I don't think I even like the man very much." This time Charlotte did manage a thin smile —and a wink. "Charlotte, it's true. I'll have none of your sly winks. The man is a . . . a conceited, self-centered . . . prig."

Charlotte reached out and silently stroked her cheek. All at once, through the dim light, Christine fixed on her eyes. They held a strange, wonderful glow that she had never seen in them before. There was a force, a power in Charlotte's voice that Christine could almost feel. "The answers are all within you, my darling Christine. Just listen to your heart. Whenever you must really know, listen to your heart." Her hand dropped away. Her eyes closed. In seconds Charlotte was in exhausted sleep.

Christine stared down at her, straining for the meaning behind her words. She isn't talking about Jerry, she thought. I just know she isn't. Trancelike, she walked down the hall to shift report.

The lounge was filling up. Eight nurses—six from the outgoing group and two from Christine's shift—were seated around a table covered with papers, charts, coffee cups, ashtrays, and several squeeze bottles of hand lotion. One of the women, Gloria Webster, was still writing notes. Gloria was Christine's age, had bleached platinum hair, and wore thick, iridescent eye make-up. She looked up, took a sip of coffee, then returned to her writing. At the same time, she spoke. "Hi, Beall."

"Hi, Gloria, busy day?"

The blonde continued writing. "Not too bad. The same old shit. Just more of it than usual, if ya know what I mean." She put down her coffee.

"Report soon?" Christine asked.

"In a minute. As usual, I'm the last one to start these damn shift notes. I think what we should do is just mimeograph one set and paste 'em in each chart. They all say the same thing anyway, if ya know what I mean."

Christine's brief laugh was purely for the sake of the other woman. One of the other nurses had summed up Gloria's skills when she quipped, "She may be careless as hell doing meds and notes and things, but just the same she doesn't give a shit about the patients."

The last two nurses arrived and took their places at the table. Report began with a discussion of the new patients who had come onto the floor during the two shifts since the evening crew had last been on. They were discussed in more detail than the rest of the patients would be. Even so, most of the remarks from around the table were not about the patients, but about their doctors.

"Sam Engles, patient of Dr. Bertram . . ."

". . . Uh-oh, Jack the Ripper strikes again."

"Bert the Flirt, ten thumbs in the operating room but a dozen hands around the nurses."

"Stella Vecchione, patient of Dr. Malchman . . ."

"Good luck, Stella."

"Donald McGregor, patient of Dr. Armstrong . . ."

"She's nice, don'cha think?"

"Nice, but senile. She writes like my grandmother."

"Edwina Burroughs, patient of Dr. Shelton . . ."

"Who?"

"Shelton, the cute one with the frizzy hair."

"Oh, I know who you mean. Is he on drugs or something?"

"What?"

"Drugs. Penny Schmidt on three said she heard from one of the O.R. nurses that Shelton was on drugs."

"Good ol' Penny. Always a kind word for everybody. I'll bet she could find dirt in a sterilizer."

They went through the rest of the patients on the floor room by room. As she listened, Christine predicted to herself which of the nurses would limit her report to facts, lab reports, and vital signs, and which would make some comment on the appearance and activities of her patients. Three stressed the numbers, and three the people. Christine scored 100 percent, noting with some satisfaction that the human-oriented reports were given by the nurses whose work she admired the most. Gloria Webster was not among that group.

"Beall, I guess you're gonna take four-twelve again, like always," Gloria said as she doused a half-smoked cigarette in the bottom of a Styrofoam cup. She addressed all the floor nurses at her level by their last names, more out of a sense of camaraderie than any effort to display toughness. "Well, there's not much to report except that things are even worse than they were yesterday, and that includes the bedsore, if ya know what I mean. Her temp and B.P. keep bouncing up and down. Nasotracheal suction is ordered every two hours. I did the bedsore, so you won't have to do it again for four hours. Christ, does that thing smell. Nothin' much else, I guess. Any questions?"

Christine fought back the impulse to say, "Yeah, one. How can you talk like that about a woman who has more wonder, more magic in one cell than you have in your whole body?" Instead she bit back her feelings of disgust and anger and merely shook her head.

The remainder of the report took ten minutes. Then the six day nurses put on their coats and left. The torch of care had been passed.

After the lounge had emptied out, Christine sat with Charlotte's chart and began reviewing it a page at a time. The process was painful. Page after page of notes, reports, and procedures. The chronology of a medical nightmare. As she jotted significant items on a small pad, Christine's sense of resolve grew. It *was* enough. Just as Peg had said on the phone. Enough. She would present Charlotte's case to The Sisterhood.

She spent several minutes rewriting her notes and double-checking to insure she had omitted no important information. Satisfied, she opened her address book and copied a phone number on a scrap of paper. Then she hesitated. Her mouth grew dry. She sat, picking absently at a fingernail. Come on, lady, she urged herself. If you're going to do it, then do it. In the moment before she stood up, her mind saw Charlotte's eyes. The glow of peace, of infinite peace, was even clearer than before. ". . . Whenever you must really know, listen to your heart."

There was a pay phone at one end of the floor, partially shielded by a glass partition. The nearby corridor was deserted. Christine hesitated once more, sensing her resolve begin to crumble. Maybe the Committee won't even return the call. Maybe when they review the case they won't approve. Maybe . . .

With every muscle tensed, she set the scrap of paper in front of her and dialed. After two rings, a click sounded, then a short beep. A female voice, nearly neuter on the recording, said, "Good day. Ten seconds after my voice goes off, you will hear a tone. There will then be thirty seconds for you to leave your message, the time of your call, and a number where you can be reached. Your call will be returned as soon as possible. Thank you."

Christine waited for the tone. "This is Christine Beall, evening shift, Four South, Boston Doctors Hospital. I would like to submit a patient for evaluation. The number at this pay phone is five, five, five, seven, one, eight, one. It is now three fifty P.M. I'll be available at this number until eleven o'clock tonight. After that I can . . ." Before she could leave her home number there was a sharp click as the recording machine shut off. She moved to place the call again and finish her message. Then, overcome by renewed uncertainty, she returned the receiver to its cradle. If it's supposed to happen, it will happen, she thought.

Harrison Weller stared vacantly at the ceiling, unaware of Christine's entrance. The tiny Sony television suspended over his bed by a metal arm flashed the logo and closing music of "The Guiding Light." He took no obvious notice of it. He was seventy-five, but his narrow, craggy face had a serene, ageless quality.

"Mr. Weller, how are you doing?" Christine asked, crossing over to him. "Why do you have the drapes closed? It's just beautiful outside. The sunlight will do you good."

He looked at her and forced a smile. "Charlene, isn't it?" he asked.

"Mr. Weller, you know my name. I've been in here nearly every day since you arrived. It's Christine."

"Sunny out, you say?" Weller's creaking voice reminded Christine of a high school actor trying to imitate an old man. He had arrived on the floor following repair of a fractured hip and immediately had become a pet of the nurses. Although he never seemed to mind their endearments, neither had he responded to them. He often appeared confused or withdrawn, behavior that had led his orthopedic surgeon to label him senile.

Christine opened the drapes, flooding the room with late afternoon sun. She raised Weller to a sitting position and set herself down next to him so that he could see her face. The old man squinted at her for a moment, then broke out in a grin.

"Well, aren't you a pretty one," he said, reaching up and lightly pinching her cheek.

Christine smiled and took his hand in hers. "How's your hip feeling, Mr. Weller?" she asked.

"My what?"

"Your hip," she said more deliberately in a voice that was nearly a shout. "You had an operation on your hip. I want to know if you are having any pain."

"Pain? In my hip?"

She was about to try again when Weller added, "Nope. Not a twinge, 'cept sometimes when I move my foot over to the left."

Christine gasped. It was by far the most complicated response he had made to any question since she had met him. All at once realization sparkled across her face.

"Mr. Weller," she shouted. "Do you have a hearing aid?"

"Hearing aid?" Weller creaked. "Of course I have a hearing aid. Had one for years."

"Why aren't you wearing it?"

"Can't very well wear something that's in a drawer at home, now, can I?" he said, as if the conclusion should have been obvious to her.

"What about your wife? Can't she bring it in for you?"

"Who, Sarah? Her arthritis has acted up so bad, she hasn't even been able to get out of the house to come see me."

"Mr. Weller, I can send someone out to your house to get your hearing aid. Would you like that?"

"Why sure I would, Charlene," he said, squeezing her hand. "And while they're at it, tell 'em to fetch my glasses too. Sarah knows where they are. Can't see past the tip a my nose without 'em."

Christine's glow had blossomed to an excited smile. "Mr. Weller, who's helping Sarah at home while she's sick?" she asked.

"Don't know for certain. Annie Grissom next door helps out some when she can."

"I can send a nurse to your house, Mr. Weller. If she thinks your wife needs one, she'll arrange for her to have a homemaker."

"A what?"

She started to repeat herself, but stopped in mid-sentence and threw her arms around him. "Don't worry, I'll take care of everything," she said in a voice that was half shout and half laugh.

Suddenly, Christine shuddered, then slowly loosened her embrace. She felt the eerie sensation of eyes watching her from behind. She spun around. Standing there, filling the doorway, was Dorothy Dalrymple, director of nursing for the hospital. She was in her mid-fifties, with close-cropped hair and a cherubic face. Her uniform stretched like a snowy tundra, enclosing a bulk of nearly two hundred pounds. Puffy ankles hung over the tops of her low white clinic shoes. The fleshy folds around her eyes deepened as she appraised the scene.

Christine hopped off the bed, tugging her uniform straight. Although she had come to know Dalrymple professionally over the years, she had never felt completely at ease around the woman. Perhaps it was her imposing size, perhaps her lofty position. She had certainly been kind and open enough.

The director moved toward her, stopping a few feet away, hands on hips. "Well, Miss Beall," she said, reprovingly, but unable to completely conceal a wry smile, "is this some new nursing technique, or have I walked in on a budding May-December romance?"

Christine smiled sheepishly and turned back to Weller. "Harrison," she said softly, "I told you we'd be discovered. We simply cannot go on meeting like this." Christine squeezed his hands reassuringly, then followed Dalrymple out of the room.

Over the decade and a half she had headed the service at Boston Doctors Dotty Dalrymple had become something of a legend for her fierce protection of "her nurses." Never considered a brilliant thinker, she was nevertheless well known throughout the medical community not only because of her bearlike charisma, but also because her identical twin, Dora, was the nursing director at Suburban Hospital, located some fifteen miles west of the city.

The two were called Tweedledum and Tweedledee—though never to their faces. They were, to the best of anyone's knowledge, the only nursing directors in the area who still faithfully wore their uniforms to work. It was a gesture, however unaesthetic, that contributed to their popularity.

Dalrymple put a motherly paw on Christine's shoulder. "So, Christine, what was that all about?" she asked.

Briefly, Christine recounted her discovery of the likely causes of Harrison Weller's "senility." The nursing director shared her excitement.

"You know," she said, "I spend so much of my time buried in paperwork, labor negotiations, and hospital politics that sometimes I actually forget what nursing is all about." Christine nodded modestly. "The flare you show for your work reminds me that no matter how little respect physicians show us, no matter how much they demean our intelligence or our judgment, we are still the ones who care for the patients. The ones who really know them as people. I honestly believe that most patients who recover from their illnesses are nursing saves, not doctor saves."

What about those who don't recover? Christine wanted to ask.

They walked down the hall in silence for a bit, then Dalrymple stopped and turned to her. "Christine, you are a very special nurse. This hospital needs you and more like you. Always feel free to talk with me about anything that troubles you. Anything."

Her words should have been reassuring, but something about her expression did not seem to fit with them. Christine felt suddenly cold and uncomfortable. She was searching for a response when the pay phone at the end of the hallway began ringing. She whirled to the sound as if it had been a gunshot.

"Well, it doesn't look like that telephone is going to answer itself, Christine," Dalrymple said, starting toward it.

"I'll get it," she blurted out, racing past the bewildered director and down the corridor.

Christine slowed as she approached the phone, half hoping it would stop ringing before she could answer it, yet at the same time worried that it might. She hesitated, then grabbed the receiver, reaching in her pocket for the pages of notes on Charlotte Thomas. Somehow she knew with total certainty that the call was for her.

The voice was a woman's, stern with perhaps the hint of an accent. "I am calling Miss Christine Beall, a nurse on this floor."

"This is Christine Beall," she said, swallowing against the dryness that had reappeared in her mouth.

"Miss Beall, my name is Evelyn. I am calling in answer to your message of earlier this afternoon. I represent the New England Regional Screening Committee."

With darting, fawnlike eyes, Christine scanned the corridor. Dalrymple had gone. There were people, staff and visitors, but none within earshot. "I . . . I have a case I wish to present for evaluation and recommendation," she stammered, not quite certain she remembered the prescribed order in which their conversation was to proceed.

"Very well," the woman said. "I shall be taking notes, so please speak slowly and clearly. I won't interrupt unless I feel it is absolutely essential to do so. Please begin."

Christine's hands were shaking as she set the notes in front of her. Thirty seconds passed during which her thoughts and emotions were racing so fast she was unable to speak. Charlotte wants so much to have it end, she reasoned, it must be right. It has to be right. Somewhere deep inside her, though, a kernel of doubt lingered. She was able to begin only after convincing herself that, even if the case were approved, she could always change her mind.

"The patient in question is Mrs. Charlotte Thomas," she said in a slow, factual monotone that she hoped would mask the quiver in her voice. "She is a sixty-year-old white woman, a registered nurse. On September eighteenth she had a Miles's resection and colostomy for cancer of the colon. Since her surgery, she has not done well at all. I have known Mrs. Thomas since her diagnostic admission in August and have spent many hours talking with her both before and after her operation. She has always been a vigorous, active, athletic woman and has told me on several occasions that she could never face life as an invalid or crippled by pain. As recently as this past July, she was working full time for a home health agency."

Christine sensed that she was rambling. Her hands were wet and cold. She had known it wouldn't be easy. Peg had told her this morning that it shouldn't be. Still, she had not expected this kind of tension. And this was only the initial case report. What if they approved? What if she actually had to . . .

"Miss Beall, you may continue," Evelyn said. At that instant Christine heard footsteps close by. Panicked, she whirled to face the noise. "Miss Beall? Are you there?" Evelyn asked.

Dotty Dalrymple was standing a few feet away. My God, what's happening, Christine thought. Has she heard?

"Miss Beall, *are you there?*" The voice was more insistent.

Her knuckles whitened around the receiver. "Oh, ah, yes, Aunt Evelyn," she managed, "hold on for a minute, can you? My nursing director is here." She set her arm down on the counter of the booth. Even then she could feel it shaking.

"Christine, are you all right?" Dalrymple said in a tone that seemed too bland, too matter-of-fact. "You look a little pale."

How much explanation does she want? Christine wondered. How much of a lie? "Oh, no, I'm fine, Miss Dalrymple. It's my aunt. My Aunt Evelyn."

Dalrymple shrugged. "As long as you're all right. You nearly jumped out of your skin when the phone rang before. Then, when you didn't come back, I became concerned that perhaps something had . . ."

Christine cut her off with a laugh that felt far too forced. "No, everything is fine. It's . . . my uncle. He had an operation today and I was waiting to hear. Everything's fine." Lies, one after another. She couldn't remember the last time she had lied.

"Tell your aunt I'm glad everything is okay."

"I'll just be another couple of minutes, Miss Dalrymple." She could barely speak.

"No problem, take your time." Dalrymple gave her a perfunctory smile and headed down the hall. Christine felt as though she were going to be sick. The notes on Charlotte Thomas were a crumpled ball in her fist.

"Evelyn, are you still there?" she said weakly.

"Yes, Miss Beall. Can you continue now?"

Christine thought, No, but said, "Yes . . . yes, I'm okay. I mean, just a second while I arrange my notes." Her fingers felt stiff, unwilling to respond. First Peg's phone call, then the agony of John Chapman's wife, then Charlotte, and now Miss Dalrymple showing up on this, of all days, and seeming to be watching her more than any of the other nurses. Barely connected or unconnected events, yet suddenly she was nearly paralyzed, her imagination braiding a cord of panic that tightened around her chest and throat. Awkwardly she smoothed the notes on the counter, fighting to regain control.

"The . . . the home health agency. Did I tell you about the home health agency?" The sound of her own voice began to loosen the fear.

"Yes, you did," Evelyn said patiently.

"Oh, okay. Let's see. Oh, yes, I was here." The words blurred in and out of focus. "Mrs. Thomas has been on hyperalimentation through an in-dwelling subclavian line for nearly two weeks and is still on intravenous antibiotics, hourly pulmonary therapy, and continuous oxygen." At that moment she realized that she had skipped a whole page. In fact, she was not certain what she had already covered. "Evelyn, I . . . I seem to have passed over some things. Is it all right to go back?"

"It's all right to do anything, dear. We'll be able to figure things out. Now just relax and give me what other information you have."

The woman's first warm words had an immediate effect. Christine took a deep breath and felt much of her tension vanish. "Thank you," she said softly. Evelyn's reassurance had reminded her: she was not functioning in isolation. She was part of a team, a movement committed to the highest good. If her role was difficult, at times frightening, so were those of the rest of her sisters. For the first time a note of calm appeared in her voice. "What I left out was that shortly after her surgery she had to be operated on again for drainage of an extensive pelvic abscess. One week ago she developed pneumonia, and last night a nasogastric tube was inserted because of the possibility of an intestinal obstruction."

She was still shaking, but now the words came more easily.

"Recently she developed a large, painful sacral pressure sore and is now requiring around-the-clock Demerol as well as the usual local therapies. The physician's notes in her chart as of yesterday state that her pneumonia is worsening. Despite all her problems, she has been designated a full resuscitation should she arrest." Almost done, she thought. Thank God. "Mrs. Thomas is married, has two children and several grandchildren. That is the end of my presentation." She sighed deeply.

"Miss Beall," Evelyn asked, "could you please tell me if there is documented evidence in her record of the spread of her tumor to other organs?"

"Oh, yes, I'm sorry. I missed part of a page. There was one thing. An X-ray report. It's a liver scan dated last week. The report from the radiologist says, 'Multiple filling defects consistent with tumor.' "

"When was the last case that you handled?"

"The *only* case. Nearly a year ago. Mrs. Thomas would be my second." It wasn't like this the last time, she thought. That was beautiful, not an ordeal. Her legs felt boneless. Instinctively she looked about for a chair.

"Thank you for your call," Evelyn said, "and for your excellent case presentation. The Sisterhood of Life Regional Screening Committee will evaluate this patient and contact you within twenty-four hours. In the meantime, as you know, you are to take no action on your own."

"I understand." It was almost over.

"Oh, one more thing, Miss Beall," Evelyn added. "The name of this patient's physician?"

"Her physician?"

"Yes."

"It's Dr. Huttner. Wallace Huttner, the chief of surgery here."

"Thank you," Evelyn said. "We'll be in touch."

⋀CHAPTER 3

DAVID SHELTON drummed impatiently on the arm of his chair and leafed through a three-month-old issue of *The American Journal of Surgery.* His excitement and anticipation at making evening rounds with Wallace Huttner had been dulled by a wait that had now grown to nearly three quarters of an hour. Huttner must have encountered unexpected difficulty in the operating room.

For a time David paced through the deserted surgeons' lounge, closing locker doors—a gesture that seemed, inexplicably, to restore some order to the situation. Forty-five minutes in an empty locker room had hardly been part of his scenario for the evening.

With mounting concern that Huttner might have forgotten their appointment altogether, he took off the suit he had resurrected from the recesses of his closet for the occasion and changed into a set of scrub greens, then slipped paper shoe covers over his scuffed loafers and tucked the black electrical grounding strip in at the back. He considered putting on his own green canvas O.R. shoes, but rejected the notion, fearing that the shoes, a clean, new pair, might give the impression, however accurate, that he had not spent much time in the operating room of late.

The ritual of dressing for the O.R. had an immediate buoying effect on his flagging morale. Donning a paper mask and hair guard, he began absently humming the opening bars of "La Virgen de Macarena," a melody he had first heard years before, heralding the arrival of the matador at a Mexico City bullfight.

Suddenly he realized what he was singing and laughed out loud. "Shelton, you are really off the wall. Next thing you'll do is demand two ears and a tail for a successful appendectomy." Stopping before a mirror, he stuffed several protruding tufts under his cap, then stepped onto the surgical floor.

The Dickenson Surgical Suite, named after the first chief of surgery at the hospital, consisted of twenty-six rooms, devoid of windows, and occupied the entire seventh and eighth floors of the East building. Ubiquitous wall clocks provided the only hint of what life might be doing outside the hospital. In atmosphere, politics, social order, even language, the surgical suite was a world within a world within a world.

From his earliest days as a medical student, and even before, David had dreamed of being a part of that world. He loved the sounds of machines and hushed voices echoing down the gleaming hallways, the tension in hours of meticulous surgery, the seconds of frantic action in a life-or-death crisis. Now, for the second time in his life, the dream was becoming reality.

Scanning the lime-tiled corridor, he saw signs of activity in only two of the operating rooms. The others had been scrubbed down and set up for the first cases of the next morning, then darkened for the night.

He bet himself that Huttner would be working in the room on the right and lost a weekend in Acapulco with Meryl Streep.

"Can I help you?" The circulating nurse met David at the doorway. She wore a wraparound green scrub dress that fell short of concealing her linebacker's build. Turquoise eyes appraised him from between a paper mask and a cloth, flower-print hair cover.

Assert yourself, David thought. Show some nice, crisp consternation at not being recognized. He was trying to formulate an intimidating response when Huttner looked over from his place at the right side of the table.

"Ah, David, welcome," he called out. "Edna, that's Dr. Shelton. Will you get him a riser, please. Put it, ah . . . over there behind Dr. Brewster." He nodded toward the resident who was assisting from across the table.

David stepped onto the riser and looked down into the incision.

"Started as a simple oversew of a bleeding ulcer," Huttner explained, unaware—or, at least, not acknowledging—that he was late for their rounds. "We encountered a little trouble when we got in, though, and I decided to go ahead with a hemigastrectomy and Bilroth anastomosis." David took note of Huttner's choice of pronouns and filed the insight away in the back of his mind.

Within a few seconds the rhythm in the room, disrupted by David's arrival, was reestablished. It became rapidly apparent to him that Huttner's concentration, deftness, and control were extraordinary. No wasted words or motion. No outward evidence of indecisiveness. Although others in the room were playing their parts, he was clearly both conductor and principal soloist.

Suddenly a pair of scissors slipped off the side of Huttner's hand as the scrub nurse passed them to him. They hit the floor with a clatter that might have been a small explosion. The surgeon's gray-blue eyes flashed. "Goddammit, Jeannie," he snapped, "will you pay attention!"

The nurse stiffened, then muttered an apology and carefully handed over another pair. David's eyes narrowed a fraction. From his vantage point the pass had seemed quite adequate. He glanced at the wall clock. Seven thirty. Huttner, he realized, had probably been operating for the better part of twelve straight hours.

A minute later, Huttner surveyed his results then rotated his head to relieve the tightness in his neck. "Okay, Rick, she's all yours. Go ahead and close," he said to the resident. "Standard post-op orders. I don't think she'll need the unit, but use your judgment when she's ready to come out of the recovery room. If there are any problems, contact Dr. Shelton. He'll be covering for me while I'm down at the vascular conference on the Cape. Any questions?"

David thought he saw a flicker of heightened respect and interest appear in the eyes of the scrub nurse. Real or imagined, the look immediately rekindled his excitement about what the next three days held in store for him.

Huttner stepped back from the table, stripping off his bloodstained gown and gloves in a single motion, and headed for the lounge with David close behind. Rather than collapsing in the nearest easy chair, as David expected, Huttner walked casually to his locker, withdrawing his pipe and tobacco pouch. He filled, packed, and lit the elegant meerschaum before settling into a thick leather couch. With a wave of his pipe, he motioned David to join him on the sofa.

"Turnbull should have referred that woman for surgery two days ago," he said, commenting on the internist who had failed to stop the bleeding ulcer. "I'll bet I wouldn't have had to take her stomach if he had." Huttner closed his eyes and massaged the bridge of his nose with carefully manicured, porcelain fingers.

In his early sixties, a tall, angular man an inch or two over six feet with dark hair appropriately gray at the temples, Huttner appeared every bit the patrician depicted by his press clippings.

"I've been hearing some nice things about your work from the nurses in the O.R., David," Huttner said in his well-cultivated New England accent.

Nice things. David spent several seconds evaluating the compliment. It was a reflex reaction, born of nearly eight years of condescending interviewers and pseudo-solicitous colleagues. David disliked the trait, but had come to expect it. Huttner's flattery was genuine, he was sure.

"Thanks," he said. "As you saw tonight, some of them don't even know me yet. I mean, one major case every week or two is hardly the best basis for judging." His words were not bitter—merely a statement of fact. David knew that Huttner might perform fifteen or more major operations for each one of his own.

"Patience, David, patience," Huttner said. "I recall telling you that when you first came to see me about applying for staff privileges. You must remember that, just as physicians are constantly hoisted up on pedestals, so are they also under continuous, magnified scrutiny." He tapped his fingertips together, carefully selecting his words. "Problems such as . . . ah . . . have befallen you are not quickly forgotten by the medical community. They are a threat, pointing up a vulnerability that most doctors don't want to admit they have. Just keep doing good, conscientious work the way you have been, and the cases will come." He sat back pontifically and folded his hands around the meerschaum.

"I hope so," David said, his smile a bit forced. "I want you to know how grateful I am for your trust and acceptance. It really means a lot to me personally."

Huttner brushed the compliment off with his pipe, although his expression suggested that it was expected and would have been missed. "Nonsense, I'm the one who is grateful. It's a relief to know that my patients will have a bright young Turk like you looking after them while I'm gone. As I recall, you trained at White Memorial, didn't you?"

"Yes, sir, I was chief resident there once upon a time."

"I never could seem to get accepted into that program," Huttner said, shaking his head in what might have been wistfulness. "And it's 'Wally.' I get enough 'sirs' every day to fill King Arthur's Court."

David nodded, smiled, and stopped himself at the last possible instant from saying, "Yes, sir."

Huttner bounced to his feet. "A quick shower, then I'll sign out to you on the floors." He tossed his scrub suit into a canvas hamper, then took a journal from his locker and handed it to David. "Take a look at this article of mine on radical surgery for metastatic breast disease. I'll be interested in what you think."

With that, he strode into the shower room, calling out just before he turned on the water, "You play tennis, David? We have to get together and hit a few before the weather closes in on us."

"It's often hard to distinguish between my tennis and my weight lifting," David said softly enough to be certain Huttner couldn't possibly have heard. He thumbed through the article. Printed in a rather obscure journal, it advocated radical breast, ovarian, and adrenal surgery for patients with widespread breast cancer. The concept was nothing revolutionary. In certain instances it was accepted. However, as horrible as the disease was, seeing the radical surgical approach laid out in print, scanning the tables of survival, brought a tinge of acid to David's throat. Survival. Was that really the bottom line? He slapped the journal shut and shoved it back in Huttner's locker.

The page operator was announcing the eight o'clock end to visiting hours when the two surgeons started making rounds on the floors in the West building. Earlier David had seen the patients he had in the hospital—a ten-year-old boy in for repair of a hernia and Edwina Burroughs, a forty-year-old woman whose factory job and four pregnancies had given her severe varicose veins, gnarled and twisted as the roots of a Banyan tree.

Wallace Huttner had more than twenty-five patients scattered over three different buildings. Almost all of them were recovering from major surgery. On every floor Huttner's arrival had immediate impact. Horseplay around the nurses' station stopped. Voices lowered. The charge nurse materialized, charts in hand, to accompany them on their rounds. Replies to Huttner's occasional questions were either stammered monosyllables or nervous outpourings of excess information. Throughout Huttner maintained an urbane politeness, moving briskly from one bedside to the next without so much as a hint of the fatigue David knew he must be feeling. The man was absolutely one of a kind, he acknowledged to himself. A phenomenon.

Before long, a comfortable pattern had evolved to their rounds. Huttner allowed the charge nurse to lead them to the doorway of a room. Then he took the patient's chart from her and proceeded to the bedside. David, the charge nurse, and often the staff nurse on the case followed. Next, Huttner handed the unopened chart to David, introduced him to the patient, and gave a capsule history of the initial problem, operative procedure, and subsequent course of treatment, couching details in medical jargon that no one except a physician or nurse could possibly have understood.

Finally he conducted a brief physical examination while David flipped through the record, using a spiral-bound pad to record pertinent lab data as well as Huttner's overall approach and plan for the case. For the most part, he tried to remain inconspicuous, speaking when addressed, but keeping his questions to what seemed like an intelligent minimum.

From time to time he glanced at Huttner. As far as he could tell, the man seemed satisfied that his charges were being left in capable hands. Before long, though, David began feeling uneasy. Despite the legends, the backup residents, and the unquestionable—perhaps unparalleled—surgical skills, Wallace Huttner was sloppy: progress notes were brief and often lacking some piece of information; some abnormal laboratory results went undetected for several days before they were noticed and a recheck ordered. Small things. Subtle things. But the pattern was there, unmistakable. It was not the kind of carelessness that would affect every case, but inevitably it would be manifest somewhere —in a prolonged hospital stay, a second operation, even a death.

He must know, David thought to himself. He knows, but so far he just hasn't found any way of dealing with the problems. It wasn't lack of pride or caring or skill—Huttner clearly possessed all three. The man was simply spread too thin, David decided. Too many cases. Too many committees, panels, and teaching obligations. How much could a man do in one day? Sooner or later he must either draw lines or make compromises or . . . get help. Maybe Lauren was right, he realized excitedly. Maybe Huttner *was* looking for a partner. Or maybe, David laughed to himself, Huttner had chosen him to cover the practice believing that of all the surgeons in the hospital he was the least likely to notice these inadequacies. No matter. The oversights and omissions were small ones. He would go through the charts the next day and fix it all up.

Just keep your mouth shut, he told himself. Only a few cases to go, then you're on your own.

Minutes later, David's decision to keep silent was challenged. The patient was a man in his late fifties, a commercial fisherman named Anton Merchado. He had been admitted to the hospital several weeks earlier for an abdominal mass. Huttner had drained and excised a cyst on the pancreas and Merchado was recovering nicely when he developed symptoms of an upper respiratory infection. In a telephoned order, Huttner had put the man on tetracycline, a widely used antibiotic.

The condition must have improved, David thought, because there was no further mention of it in Huttner's brief notes. However, the tetracycline order had never been rescinded. It had been in effect for nearly two weeks.

Anxious to speed up rounds, Huttner was giving his capsule review of the man's history while he examined his heart, lungs, and abdomen. David stood off to one side, his attention focused more on the chart than on what the older surgeon was saying.

On the day before Merchado was to be discharged from the hospital, he had developed severe diarrhea. Huttner's initial impression was viral enteritis, but over a few days the condition worsened beyond what a simple viral infection would cause. The early signs of dehydration began to appear.

David flipped from the progress notes to the laboratory reports and back. Huttner's mounting concern was mirrored each day in an increasing number of orders for laboratory tests and diagnostic procedures, all unrevealing. Efforts intensified to keep pace with Merchado's deteriorating condition, but there could be no doubt that the man was on a downhill slide.

As David read, the germ of an idea took root. He scanned page after page of laboratory reports, looking for the results of the stool cultures that had been ordered on several successive days.

"Well, what do you think?" Huttner said, turning to David. "David? . . ."

"Oh, sorry." David looked up. "I noticed the man was still on tetracycline and was just looking to see if he might have somehow developed staph colitis secondary to the treatment. It doesn't happen often, but . . ."

"Tetracycline?" Huttner interrupted. "I called in a stop on that order days ago. They're still giving it to him?"

Behind Huttner, in David's line of vision, the charge nurse nodded her head in vigorous confirmation.

"Well, no matter," Huttner said, hesitating slightly. David could almost hear him asking himself whether he had actually called in the stop order or had just meant to. "The culture reports have all been negative. Why don't you write an order to take him off tetra. Go ahead and get another culture if you want to."

David was about to comply when he noticed a culture report at the bottom of the lengthy computer printout that listed all results obtained on the patient to date. It read

"9/24, STOOL SPEC:
MODERATE GROWTH, S. AUREUS,
SENSITIVITIES TO FOLLOW."

Staph aureus, the most virulent form of the bacteria. David closed his eyes for a moment, hoping that when he looked at the sheet again the words would be gone. He took several seconds in making the decision to say nothing about his discovery and to correct the problem later. The hesitation was too long.

"What is it, David?" Huttner asked. "Have you found something?"

"Dammit," David cursed to himself. A dozen possible responses poured through his mind, were evaluated and rejected. There was going to be no comfortable way around it. No place to hide. Out of the corner of one eye he saw the two nurses standing motionless at the end of the bed. Did they know that in the next few moments the success of the evening and possibly of David's career might vanish?

The whole scene became strangely dreamlike for him. The hand slowly passing Merchado's chart to Huttner, the finger pointing at the offensively impersonal line of type—they were someone else's, not his.

The look David had last seen directed at the O.R. scrub nurse sparked in Huttner's eyes. They locked with his for a fraction of a second, then turned on the nurses. He thrust the chart at the charge nurse.

"Mrs. Baird," he growled, "I want you to find out who is responsible for failing to call my attention to this report. Whoever it is, nurse or

40

secretary, I want to see her in my office first thing Monday morning. Is that clear?"

The nurse, a stout veteran who had engaged in her share of hospital wars, looked at the page, then shrugged and nodded her head. David wondered if Huttner would actually follow through with what seemed so obvious an attempt to produce a scapegoat.

"Come along, Dr. Shelton," Huttner said curtly. "It's getting late and we still have several more patients to see."

It was nearly ten o'clock when they arrived on Four South to see the last of Huttner's patients, Charlotte Thomas. For the first time all evening Huttner deviated from the routine he had established. Taking the chart from the charge nurse, he said, "Come and sit down in the nurses' lounge for a bit, David. This next patient is by far my most complicated. I want to take a few minutes to go over her with you in some detail before we see her. Perhaps someone could bring us each a cup of coffee." The last remark was transparently addressed to the nurse, who managed a faint smile of acquiescence. "Light, no sugar for me, and for Dr. Shelton . . . ?"

"Black," David answered. For a split second he had almost said "bleak."

"Here you go, Doctor," Huttner said, sliding the chart across to David. "Leaf through it while we're waiting for coffee."

Before reading a word, David could tell that Charlotte Thomas was in trouble. Her hospital record was voluminous. He thought back to his residency and a tall, gangly New Yorker named Gerald Fox, who was one year ahead of him. Fox had achieved immortality, at least in White Memorial Hospital, by Xeroxing a three-page list of cynical maxims and definitions entitled, "Fox's Golden Laws of Medicine." Among his axioms were the definition of Complicated Case ("When the combined diameters of all the tubes going into a patient's body exceeds his hat size"), Gynecologist ("A spreader of old wives' tails"), and Fatal Illness ("A hospital chart more than an inch thick").

Coffee arrived just as David had begun to scan the admission history and physical examination. He heard Huttner say, "Ah, Miss Beall, thank you. You're an angel of mercy."

He looked up from the chart. It was not the nurse with whom Huttner had placed their order, but a far younger woman David had never seen, or at least had never noticed before. For several seconds his entire world consisted only of two large, oval, burnt umber eyes. He felt his body flush with warmth. The eyes met his and smiled.

"So, are you with our lady Charlotte again?" Huttner asked, oblivious to the silent meeting that was taking place.

"Huh? Oh, yes." Christine broke the connection and turned to

Huttner. "She's not looking too well. I asked to bring the coffee in because I wanted to talk to you about . . ."

"How rude of me," Huttner interrupted. "Miss Beall, this is Dr. David Shelton. Perhaps you two have met?"

"No," Christine said icily. She was well acquainted with Huttner's lack of regard for the insights and suggestions of nurses. Over the years she had given up even attempting to share hers with him. But Charlotte's situation was distressing enough for her to try. If Huttner would only agree to let up on his aggressive treatment, to cancel the resuscitation order, she might not intervene even if the Screening Committee approved her proposal. So she had tried, and predictably the man had cut her off—this time with an inane social amenity. Still, she felt determined to speak her mind. It was *his* tube that was sticking into Charlotte's nose. *His* order to prolong her suffering no matter what. He could play puppet-master with his other patients, but not with Charlotte. He would listen or . . . or have his strings to her cut. Christine swallowed the bone of anger that had begun sticking in her throat.

Huttner took no note of the chill in her voice. "Dr. Shelton will be covering all my patients, including Mrs. Thomas, for a few days," he said.

Christine nodded at David and wondered whether he might have the authority to back off on Huttner's overzealous approach to Charlotte, then realized there was no chance the surgical chief would permit that. "Dr. Huttner," she said flatly, "I would like to talk to you about Charlotte for a few minutes."

Huttner glanced at his watch. "That would be fine, Miss Beall," he said. "Why don't you let us finish reviewing Charlotte's case and examining her. Then you can go over things with Dr. Shelton here. He'll know exactly what I want for this woman." Huttner looked away before the first of the daggers from her eyes reached him. David shrugged his embarrassment, but Christine had already turned on one heel and left the room.

Huttner took a sip of coffee, then began speaking without so much as a word or gesture toward the nurse who had just left. "Mrs. Thomas is a registered nurse. In her late fifties, I think." David glanced at the birthdate on the chart. She was nearly sixty-one. "Her husband, Peter, is a professor at Harvard. Economics. She was referred to me by an internist because of a suspected cancer of the rectum. Several weeks ago, I performed a Miles's resection on the woman. The tumor was an adenocarcinoma extending just through the bowel wall.

"However, all the nodes I took were negative. I feel there's a very good chance that my clean-out may have gotten the whole thing."

David looked up from the coffee stain he was absently erasing with his thumb. The five-year survival rate after removal of a rectal cancer with such extension was under 20 percent. A chance? Certainly. A "very good chance"? He leaned back and wondered if it was worth asking Huttner to clarify the reasons for his optimism. It would not, he decided, be wise to question him about anything.

Comfortable in the blanket of his own words, Huttner continued his presentation. "As always seems to happen when we work on nurses or doctors, everything that could have gone sour postoperatively seems to have done so. First, a pelvic abscess—I had to go back in and drain it. Next, a pneumonia. And then a nasty decubitus ulcer over her sacrum. Yesterday she developed signs of a bowel obstruction and I had to slip down a tube. That seems to be correcting the problem, and I have a feeling that she may have turned the corner."

Huttner folded his hands on the table in front of him, indicating that his presentation was done. An almost imperceptible tic had developed at the corner of his right eye. He must be absolutely exhausted, David thought. Uncomfortable and anxious to do anything other than stare, David returned to the chart. "If she needs to be operated on for the obstruction?" he asked, already praying it would not happen.

"Then you go ahead and do it if that's your judgment. I'm leaving you in complete charge," Huttner said somewhat testily.

No more questions, David resolved. Whatever you want to know, figure it out for yourself. Just get through this night.

But already another potential problem was becoming obvious. He tried to reason it through, but quickly realized that only Huttner could supply the answer. His resolve stretched, then snapped.

"If she should arrest?" he asked softly.

"Dammit, man, she's not going to arrest," Huttner snapped with startling vehemence. Then, sensing the inappropriateness of his outburst, he took a deep breath, exhaled slowly, and added, "At least, I hope she doesn't arrest. If she should, I want a full Code Ninety-nine called on her, including tracheal intubation and a respirator if need be. Clear?"

"Clear," David said. He looked down at the chart again. Whatever criticisms might be leveled at Wallace Huttner, undertreating Charlotte Thomas certainly could not be one of them. Thousands of dollars in laboratory work, hospital care, and radiologic studies had already been done. Still, at least on paper, the woman appeared far from "turning the corner."

"Shall we go see the patient?" Huttner's tone was more order than request.

David was about to comply when he noticed the report of Charlotte's liver scan. The words burst from the page: "Multiple filling defects consistent with tumor." Numbness crept over him as he stared at the reading. Rarely had he heard of a patient surviving long with the spread of rectal cancer to the liver. Certainly, with this kind of disseminated disease, there could be no way to justify the aggressive therapy being given Charlotte Thomas. If, as in the Merchado case, this report had somehow been overlooked, whatever remained of his relationship

43

with Huttner was about to disappear with the finality of a nuclear explosion.

"What is it this time, doctor?" Huttner asked acidly.

"Oh . . . probably nothing," David said, wishing he were anyplace else. "I . . . ah . . . I was just reading this liver scan report."

"Hah!" Huttner's exclamation cut him short. "Multiple defects consistent with tumor, right?" He suddenly looked happier than he had all evening. "Look at the name of the radiologist who gave us that report. G. Rybicki, M.D., the living Polish joke of radiologic medicine. He read the same thing on a scan that we did preoperatively, so I checked her liver out carefully in the O.R. Even sent off a biopsy. They are cysts, David. Multiple, congenital, totally benign cysts.

"I even went to the trouble of sending Rybicki a copy of the pathology report," Huttner continued. "He probably never even looked at it, as witnessed by this repetition of his initial misreading. Maybe we'd better just tear the report out of the chart." He crumpled the sheet in a ball and tossed it into the wastebasket. "Now, if you have no further questions, shall we go in to see the woman?"

"No further questions, your honor." David shook his head in amazement and smiled, grateful to be allowed off the hook. There was something about Huttner's broad grin that went far toward dispelling the misgivings David had developed about the man.

Shoulder to shoulder, they walked down the corridor of Four South and into Room 412.

CHAPTER 4

THE ONLY LIGHT in Room 412 came from a gooseneck treatment lamp directed at an area just above Charlotte Thomas's exposed buttocks. Huttner strode to that side of the bed with David close behind and moved the lamp back a foot. He stiffened, then forced a more relaxed pose. Bewildered and somewhat amused, David stifled a smile at the man's reaction; then he looked down at the reason for it. The bedsore Huttner had described as "nasty" was far worse than that. It was a gaping hole six inches wide. The walls of the cavity were raw muscle, stained white by a drying poultice. A quarter-sized eye of sacral bone stared sightlessly outward from the center.

Huttner gave the kind of shrug that said, "Nothing worse than other things we've dealt with, right?"

David tried to respond, but could manage only a shake of his head. He had seen sores and wounds countless times from every conceivable source. But this . . .

"It's Dr. Huttner, Charlotte," Huttner announced as he flicked off the lamp and turned on the dim fluorescent light set in a cornice over her bed. He drew the sheet up above her waist and stepped to the other side of the bed. David followed, glancing at the I.V. bags and the restraints that held her on her side, at the urinary catheter snaking from beneath the sheet, at the oxygen and suction tubes. He understood the need for them and accepted their presence without a second thought. They were all as much tools of his trade as were the giant saucer lights and variegated steel instruments of the operating room.

However, in those first few seconds the one thing he noticed most about Mrs. Thomas was the emptiness in her face—a static soulless aura centering about her eyes, which were watching him through the dim light with a moist flatness. Even the sound of her breathing—soft, rhythmic cries—was empty.

Charlotte Thomas had The Look, as David had come to label it. She had lost the will to live, lost that extra bit of energy essential to surviving a life-threatening illness. The spark that was often the single difference between a medical miracle and a mortality statistic was gone.

David wondered if Huttner saw the same things he did, felt the same emptiness. Then, as if in answer to his question, the tall surgeon knelt by the bed, slipping his hand under Charlotte's head and cradling it to one side so that she could look directly at his face. For nearly a minute they remained that way, doctor and patient frozen in a silent tableau. David stood several feet away, swallowing against the heaviness that was building in his throat. Huttner's tenderness was as genuine as it was surprising—another facet had shown itself in this strange kaleidoscope of a man.

"Not exactly feeling on top of the world, huh?" Huttner said finally.

Charlotte forced her lips together—an unsuccessful attempt at a smile—and shook her head. Huttner smoothed the hair from her forehead and ran his hand over her cheek.

"Well, your temperature is down near normal today for the first time in a while. I think we might be getting on top of that infection in your chest." He went on, carefully mixing encouraging news with questions that he knew would be answered negatively. "Is the pain in your back any less?" Another shake. "Well, if things settle down the way I expect them to, we should be able to get that tube out of your nose in a day or two. I know what an annoyance it is. While I have you rolled over like this, let me take a listen to your chest, then I'll put you on your back and see if there are any new noises in your belly."

He examined her briefly, then glanced at the fluid levels in the intravenous bags and catheter drainage cylinder before kneeling beside her again. "You're going to make it, Charlotte. You must believe that," he said with gentle intensity.

This time Charlotte did manage a rueful smile to accompany her negative response.

"Please, just be patient, have faith and hang on a little longer," Huttner implored. "I know the pain you're going through. In many ways it's as awful for me as it is for you. But I also know that bit by bit you're turning the corner. Before you know it, you'll be putting on lipstick and getting ready to see those beautiful grandchildren you've told me so much about." He paused. In the silence David studied the man's face. His brows were drawn inward, his jaw taut as a bow string. He seemed to be trying, through sheer will, to transfuse the energy of his words and hope. The woman showed no reaction. "My goodness, I almost forgot," Huttner said at last. "Charlotte, you are in for a treat. I know how tired you must be getting of seeing my smiling mug every day. Well, you're going to get a break from that.

"I'm going off to a conference on the Cape for a few days. This handsome young doctor will be covering for me. He was the chief resident a few years ago at White Memorial. I couldn't even get accepted for an internship there. His name's David Shelton." Huttner motioned David over to the head of the bed.

David took Huttner's place, setting his arms on the sheet and resting his chin on them, six inches away from Charlotte's face. It seemed to take several seconds for her to focus on him.

"I'm David, Mrs. Thomas. How do you do?" he said, realizing at the same instant that she had already answered his ill-conceived greeting several times. "Is there anything you need right now? Anything I can get for you?" He waited until he felt certain no response was forthcoming, then made a move to stand up. Suddenly Charlotte Thomas reached out a spongy, bruised hand and grasped his with surprising force.

"Dr. Shelton, please listen to me," she said in a husky, halting voice that had its own unexpected strength. "Dr. Huttner is a wonderful man and a wonderful doctor. He wants so much to help me. You must make him understand. I do not want to be helped anymore. All I want is to have these tubes taken out and to be kept comfortable until I go to sleep. You must make him understand that. Please. This is torture for me. A nightmare. Make him understand."

Her eyes flashed for an instant, then closed. She took several deep breaths and settled heavily back on the pillow. Her breathing slowed. It seemed to David that it might stop altogether, but within a minute a coarse, rhythmic stertor developed and held.

All David could manage was a whispered, "You're going to be all right, Mrs. Thomas," as Huttner took him by the arm and led him out of the room.

In the hallway the two men faced one another. Huttner was first to break the silence.

"Quite some night we've had for ourselves, yes?" he said, smiling his understanding.

"Yeah," David answered. He pawed at the floor with one foot. He would have said more but for a persistent sliver of fear that he was about to come apart in front of the man.

Huttner scrutinized his face, then said, "David, never forget that many times patients with serious illness express the wish to die when they're in a stage of weakness and pain. I've been around for a long time. I've seen many patients as sick or sicker than Charlotte Thomas recover. This woman is going to make it. She is to get total, aggressive treatment and, if necessary, a full-scale Code Ninety-nine resuscitation. Understand?"

"Yes, sir . . . I mean, yes, Wally," David said mechanically, although he was searching his memory for the last time he had seen a sixty-year-old patient recover from the sort of severe, multisystem disease that beset Charlotte Thomas.

"We're in agreement, then," Huttner said, beaming with pleasure at having successfully made his point. "Let's go write a few orders on this woman, then we can call it a day."

As they approached the nurses' station, David bet himself a guitar and six months of introductory lessons that the last critical moment of the hectic evening had passed.

An instant later, a portly man dressed in a turtleneck sweater and tweed sportcoat emerged from the visitors' lounge at the far end of the hall and headed toward them. He was still thirty feet away when David knew with certainty that another wager had been lost. The anger in the man's jaw-forward stride was mirrored in his reddened face and tight, bloodless lips. His fists were suspended several inches away from his body on rigid arms.

David glanced over at Huttner, who showed a flicker of recognition but no other emotion.

"Professor Thomas?" David whispered.

Huttner nodded his head a fraction, then moved forward. David slowed and watched as the two men closed on one another like combatants at a medieval joust. The grandstand for their confrontation was the nurses' station, where several nurses, an aide, and the ward secretary fell silent, fascinated spectators.

"Dr. Huttner, what the hell is going on here?" Thomas lashed out. "You told me there would be no more tubes and I get here to find a red rubber hose coming out of my wife's nose attached to some goddamn machine."

"Now, Professor Thomas, just calm down for a minute," Huttner said evenly. "I tried to call you last night to let you know what was going on, but there was no answer. Let's go down to the visitors' lounge, and I'll be happy to go over the whole thing with you."

Thomas was not a bit mollified. "No, we'll have this whole business out here and now with these people as witnesses." He gestured at the gallery. "I came to you with Charlotte because our family doctor told us you were the best. To me the best meant not only that you would be the best in the operating room, but that you would be the best at treating my wife—as a human being, not just as some unfeeling piece of . . . of *carrion.*"

The intensity and pain in Peter Thomas's voice was startling. Behind the nurses' station, Christine Beall cautiously turned her head toward Janet Poulos, the evening nursing supervisor. Poulos met her gaze impassively, then responded with an almost imperceptible nod. She was a slender woman, a decade older than Christine. Her coal-black hair was coiled in a tight bun, accentuating her narrow features and dark, feline eyes. A thin scar paralleling her nose gave even her warmest smile a slight sneer and undoubtedly contributed to her reputation among the nursing staff as being uncompromising and humorless.

Christine saw her in a far different light, for it was Janet who had supervised her initiation into The Sisterhood of Life. The secrecy of the movement was such that Janet remained the only Sisterhood member whom she knew by name and face. The nod acknowledged that Poulos, too, was assessing the drama unfolding before them.

"All right, Professor," Huttner said, a thin edge appearing in his voice. "If it is what you wish, we shall discuss matters right here. Do you have more to say or do you want to know exactly what is happening with Charlotte?"

"Go on," Thomas said, relaxing his fists and leaning one elbow on the high counter in front of a totally bewildered ward secretary.

With the condescending patience of one who has learned that sooner or later he will carry the day, Huttner systematically reviewed the developments that had led to his decision to insert an intestinal drainage tube in Charlotte Thomas. Then, more gently, he said, "It may not be obvious to you right now, but I believe that our treatments are starting to take hold. Charlotte could turn the corner any time now."

Peter Thomas looked down and retreated half a step. At that moment it seemed to David as if Huttner had, in fact, won the man over. Then, as though in slow motion, Thomas brought his head up, shaking it back and forth as he spoke. "Dr. Huttner, I believe my wife is dying. I believe it and I even accept it. I also believe that because of what you call *treatment,* she is dying by inches, without so much as a flicker of dignity. I want those tubes pulled out."

Behind the counter, a nurse whispered something to the woman next to her. Huttner silenced her with a look that could have frozen a volcano.

With an instantaneous, almost theatrical change in expression, he turned back, smiling calmly, to Peter Thomas. "Professor, please know that I understand how you're feeling, I really do," he reasoned. "But you must understand my position and my responsibility in this thing. We talked about it when you first brought Charlotte into my office, and you agreed that I was to be in complete charge. I offered to arrange for a second opinion, but you felt back then that none was necessary. Now here you are questioning my judgment. I'll tell you what. We have a built-in second opinion right here." Huttner motioned David over. "This is Dr. Shelton. He's an excellent young surgeon who was chief resident in surgery at White Memorial. We've just examined Charlotte in great detail because Dr. Shelton will be covering my patients for the next few days. David, this is Peter Thomas. Tell him what our feelings are about Charlotte."

David reached out his hand and Thomas shook it uncertainly. During the seconds they stood appraising one another, Thomas seemed perceptibly to calm down.

"Well, Dr. Shelton," he said finally, "what *do* you think of my wife's chances?"

David looked down momentarily and closed his eyes. Somewhere in a remote corner of his mind a voice kept telling him that if he could just stall for a few minutes his clock radio would go off, waking him up. With consummate effort he brought his eyes up until they connected once more with Thomas's.

"Mr. Thomas, I just reviewed your wife's hospital record and met her for the first time," he said deliberately. "It really is impossible at this time for me to assess her whole situation accurately."

Thomas opened his mouth to object to what he considered an inadequate answer, but David stopped him with a raised hand. "However," he continued, hoping that his tone would not give away the fact that he had no desire to continue at all, "I will tell you that I see her as a critically ill woman whose chance of surviving this illness rests not only with receiving the best possible medical and nursing care—which, incidentally, she has been receiving—but also in having the will to make it through. This is the part I cannot assess yet. That strength comes not only from inside her, but from you, from Dr. Huttner, and from the rest of those who love and care for her.

"I know you'd like to hear a more clinical evaluation of her prospects, but right now I'm just not in a position to give you that."

Out of the corner of his eyes he saw Huttner beaming his approval. Holy shit, I got out of it! was all David could think. Then, even before Thomas responded, he felt a spark of anger at himself. He had not given even a hint of his true, bleak feelings about Charlotte's chances. As Thomas spoke, the spark grew white hot.

"You really don't see it, do you?" Thomas said, looking wildly around him. "None of you do. Charlotte and I have been married for over thirty years. Thirty full and happy years. Don't you feel we should have some say as to what kind of tortures she must be put through to prolong the agony of what has until now been a totally rich and fulfilling life?"

This time David did not look away. For several seconds a painful silence held. Finally he spoke. There was anguish in his voice, but also the power of conviction. "Dammit, I do feel that way. Exactly as you do, Mr. Thomas. I feel that very strongly."

Again there was an agonizing silence. David felt Huttner's eyes and sensed the world sinking beneath him. His tone mellowed. "But you must understand," he said. "I am not your wife's primary physician, Dr. Huttner is. And he is more experienced than I am in every aspect of medicine and surgery. It is his final say as to what kind of treatment your wife will or will not receive. I intend to carry on his therapies to the absolute best of my abilities."

Thomas glared at Huttner, then snapped, "I understand, all right. I understand completely." Spinning so fast that he nearly lost his balance, he stalked down the corridor toward his wife's room.

His outburst was the last straw for Huttner. It had been a long and trying day. He stepped back so that David and everyone at the nurses' station was included in his gaze. "I am going to say this one time and one time only." His voice was dry ice. "Charlotte Thomas is to be treated as aggressively as necessary to save her life. Have I made myself clear? Good. Now all of you get back to your jobs. Dr. Shelton, perhaps you had better go home and get some rest. Straightening out my practice could prove an exhausting experience for you."

With that, he marched down the hall and followed Peter Thomas into Room 412.

David stood alone in the center of the corridor. The group behind the nurses' station some fifteen feet away was frozen and silent. He glanced about with the sheepishness of a janitor sweeping center stage when the curtain suddenly opens before a packed house. For an instant he had the impulse to break and run. Then, out of the corner of his eye, he saw Christine Beall push herself off the counter and head in his direction. It was hardly the triumphant moment he would have picked for a second encounter with the woman.

As she neared, he looked away, inspecting a heelmark by his shoe. He sensed her eyes measuring him. When they first met, he had been captivated by their gentle power and determination. Now, before their umber stare, he felt vaguely discomforted.

Moments before she spoke he breathed in her perfume—a muted suggestion of spring. "Dr. Shelton, we're all very proud of the way you stood up for what you believe in," she said softly. "Don't worry. Things have a way of working out."

Her words. The way she spoke them. Not at all what David had expected. He repeated them in his mind but could not seem to grasp the feelings behind them. "Thanks . . . thanks a lot," he managed, preparing himself for the eyes before he looked up. By the time he did, Christine was gone. Activity behind the nurses' station had returned to normal, but she was not there.

David elected to go and write new orders on Anton Merchado before putting the whole ghastly evening to rest. In the morning he would be on his own. As he shuffled away, thoughts of the day to come, of regaining control of his life, sweetened the distasteful events of the past five hours.

"Things have a way of working out." He said Christine's words out loud as he pushed through the door to the stairway.

CHAPTER 5

HIDDEN IN A DOORWAY, Christine watched David leave Four South. She waited until she was certain he would not return before stepping into the dimly lit corridor. Her shift was nearly over. In the nurses' lounge, as in similar rooms on every floor in the hospital, the evening staff was compiling notes in preparation for the 11 P.M. to 7 A.M. crew—the graveyard shift.

In less than an hour 263 nurses would leave the hospital and head for diners or bars or home to mates who would, as often as not, be too tired to respond as lovers. They would be replaced by 154 others, each struggling to maintain biologic equilibrium in an occupation that demanded life-and-death decisions during hours when most of the world was sleeping.

For a time Christine stood in the deserted hallway listening to the clamorous silence of night in the hospital. The sighs and coughs. The moans and labored, sonorous respirations. Oxygen gurgling through half a dozen safety bottles. The obedient beep of a monitor in duet with the mindless hiss-click of a respirator. And in the darkened rooms, the patients, thirty-six of them on Four South, locked in their own struggle —a struggle not for riches or power or even happiness, but merely to return to the outside world. To return to their lives.

At night more than any time Christine felt the awesome responsibility of her profession. Like any job, nursing had its routine. But beyond the drudgery and the complaints, beyond the scut work and the deprecating attitude of many physicians, there were, above all, the patients. At times, it seemed, a silent conspiracy existed among physicians, administrators, and nursing organizations whose sole purpose was to expunge from nurses any notion that their primary purpose was the care of those patients. It even included the nurses themselves, many totally drained of the sense of caring and kindness that had first brought them into the profession.

Christine gazed down the corridor toward Room 412. Silently she renewed a vow that she would never give in to the confusion and the negativism. She would never stop caring. If a commitment to The Sisterhood of Life was the only way to honor that vow, so be it. Somehow she knew that as long as she was part of The Sisterhood, she was safe from the frustrations and heartache that had driven so many out of hospital nursing.

For Christine the commitment had begun on a Sunday. Outside Doctors Hospital a winter storm raged. Inside the nurses' lounge on Four South another kind of storm was brewing. Much of its fury emanated from Christine and all of it was directed against a physician named Corkins who had just ordered an emergency tracheotomy on an eighty-year-old woman, the victim of a massive stroke that had left her paralyzed, partially blind, and unable to speak. Christine had spent countless hours caring for her. Although the old woman was unable to move or talk, she had communicated with her eyes. To Christine the message was clear: "Please, let me go to sleep. Let this living hell end." Now, with the operation, hell would continue indefinitely.

For nearly an hour Christine had sat in the nurses' lounge sharing her tears and her anger with Janet Poulos. Carefully, gradually, Janet had introduced her to knowledge of The Sisterhood of Life.

Over the two days following the old woman's tracheotomy, Christine had spent many hours discussing her dismal condition with Janet, while at the same time learning more and more about The Sisterhood. Throughout her nursing career she had been able to find joy in even the most distasteful aspects of daily patient care. But with each minute spent helping to prolong the agony of the old woman, Christine's frustration grew. Disconnecting the respirator to suction the tube each hour. Frequent turnings. Urinary catheter changes. Deep intramuscular injections. Frantically trying to keep abreast of one incipient bedsore after another. And always the eyes looking at her, looking through her, their message even more desperate than before.

Finally the commitment was there. Christine followed the direction given to her by Janet Poulos and reported the old woman's case to the Regional Screening Committee. A day later, she received their approval and instructions.

Toward the end of her shift she slipped quietly into the woman's room. The drone of the respirator blended eerily with the howling winter wind outside. In the darkness she felt the woman watching her. She bent over the bed, pressing the tears on her cheek against the woman's temple. After a few moments, she felt her nod—once and then again. She knew! Somehow she knew. Christine gently kissed her forehead.

She brought her lips close to one ear and whispered, "I love you."

Reaching up, she disconnected the respirator, then waited in the darkness for five minutes before reconnecting it.

Nearly four hours into the next shift a nurse reported that she was unable to feel a pulse or obtain a blood pressure on the woman. A resident was called and, after finding a straight line on her electrocardiogram, pronounced the woman dead. Later that morning her two sons, much relieved at the end of their mother's suffering, had the body brought to a local funeral home. By 11 A.M. her bed was filled by a young divorcée in for elective breast augmentation. Like the waters of a pond, disturbed momentarily by a pebble, the hospital appeared as it always had, the last ripples of the old woman's existence gone from its surface.

"Christine?"

She spun toward the voice. It was Janet Poulos.

"You okay?"

Christine nodded.

"It looked like you were posing for the cover of *Nurse Beautiful.*"

"More like *Nurse Troubled.*"

"That scene with Huttner and the Professor?"

"Uh-huh."

"Want to talk about it?"

"No. I mean maybe a little. I mean you're the only one who . . ."

Janet silenced her with a raised hand. "The visitors' lounge is empty." She nodded toward the nurses' lounge. "From the looks of things in there, you've got about ten minutes before report. It's been sort of crazy up here tonight, hasn't it? I heard there were some problems after that Mr. Chapman was found dead," Janet added.

As they walked to the small visitors' lounge, Christine described the reaction of John Chapman's grief-stricken widow. Janet shook her head in disbelief.

"Why do you think she picked on the flowers to throw around the room?" she asked.

"Oh, she threw other things, too. Not just flowers." Christine dropped onto a sofa and Janet took the chair across from her.

"So she wrecked everything?"

"Almost. We managed to salvage two vases."

"Oh?" Janet shifted in her chair.

"Yes, and even one of those was a little strange."

"How do you mean?" The question was asked matter-of-factly, but Janet's posture and expression suggested more than passing interest.

Christine glanced at her watch impatiently. They had only five minutes before report. "Oh, it was nothing, really. Just that the flowers in the last vase were lilies, and the card attached to them said something like 'Best Wishes from Lily,' that's all."

"Oh," Janet said with a flatness not mirrored in her eyes. She scratched absently at the scar beside her nose, then suddenly changed the subject. "Are you thinking about submitting this Thomas's wife to the Screening Committee?"

"I've already done it." Christine felt off balance.

"And?"

"And nothing, Janet. I haven't heard yet whether she's been approved. You see, Charlotte and I have grown very very close to one another—"

"Well, I say, 'Bravo for you,'" Janet broke in.

"What?"

"I hope she's approved."

"Janet, you don't even know the woman . . . or the situation. How can you possibly say . . ."

"I may not know her, but I know Huttner. Of all the pompous, conceited, self-righteous bastards who ever hid behind a goddamn M.D., Huttner is the worst."

Janet's outburst was totally unexpected. For a time Christine was speechless. Certainly it was the overzealous, at times ego-based aggressiveness of physicians that had spawned The Sisterhood, but to Christine it had always been a conflict of philosophies, not personalities. "Wh . . . what has Huttner's conceit got to do with Charlotte?" She felt confused and strangely apprehensive.

Janet calmed her with a wide smile. "Whoa, slow down," she said, patting her on the knee. "I'm on your side. Remember?" Christine nodded, but uncertainty remained. "I believe in The Sisterhood and what we're doing the same way you do. Why else would I have recruited you? All I was trying to say is that in cases like this Mrs. Thomas we get a . . . double benefit. We get to honor the wishes of the woman and her husband by reestablishing some dignity in her life, and at the same time we get to remind a person like Huttner that he's not God. Yes?"

Christine evaluated the notion, then relaxed and returned the smile. "Yes, I . . . guess we do." She rose to leave.

"If support is what you need," Janet said, "you've got mine. I think you did the right thing in presenting this woman, and now it's up to the Screening Committee to do its part."

Christine nodded her acknowledgment.

Janet continued as she reached the door. "You know, Christine," she said, pausing to study the younger woman's face, "it's quite all right to benefit from doing something you believe in. The goodness of any work isn't diminished by the fact that you might, in some way, profit from it. Do you understand?"

"I . . . I think so," Christine lied. "Thanks for talking with me. I'll let you know what the Committee decides."

"Do that, please. And Chris? I'm here if you need me."

Still uneasy, Christine hurried to the nurses' lounge. She paused outside the door, trying to compose herself. Janet's explosion on the subject of Wallace Huttner had been startling, but it wasn't as disturbing as it had at first seemed. Janet had been part of The Sisterhood for years; surely she had handled a number of cases. Proposing and carrying out a death, even a euthanasia death, was an emotionally charged, gut-wrenching business. Over the years the necessity of facing the same decisions again and again was bound to take its toll in some way. In Janet's case, Christine decided, it was a bitterness toward those who made such awesome choices necessary.

She glanced down the hall in time to see Janet step into the elevator. The woman was an excellent supervisor and, even more important, a nurse dedicated to the truest ideals of the profession. In the moment before she entered the nurses' lounge, Christine felt a resurgence of pride at the secrets she shared with her "sister."

CHAPTER 6

CARL PERRY steeled himself against the pain he knew would knife through his throat, then, as gingerly as possible, swallowed. Pain, almost any pain, was better than the goddamn drooling he had been doing since the polyps or growths or whatever they were had been snipped off his vocal cords. It would be two more days of bed rest, intravenous fluids, and writing notes in order to communicate before the danger of his vocal cords swelling shut would be passed. At least, that's what Dr. Curtis had told him.

He reached over and tugged at the band of adhesive tape that held the intravenous line in place on his right forearm. Several hairs popped free from his skin and he hissed a curse at the I.V. nurse who had neglected to shave the area clean.

"I.V. tape—complain to Drs. Hosp. Admin.," he scribbled on a pad, tearing the note off and stuffing it in a drawer that was rapidly filling with other, similar reminders.

He flipped up the small mirror in his Formica hospital tray and took stock of himself. Even with the scratches Curtis's instruments had made on the corners of his mouth, he liked what he saw. Deep blue eyes, tanned skin just leathery enough, square jaw, perfect teeth. He looked the way most other men of forty-eight could only dream of looking. The women saw it, too—even the young ones. They fought for the chance to spend a few hours with him in the suite he kept at the Ritz. They all went home satisfied, too.

What a perfect idea it had been to start the rumor around the singles bars that each year the girl who gave him the best lay would get a free Porsche courtesy of Perry's Foreign Motors. He might actually do it too, if the day ever came when his looks gave out on him.

Bored and uncomfortable on the sweaty sheets, he flipped on the television, then just as quickly turned it off. Nothing but the eleven o'clock news starting on every channel. He massaged the front of his blue silk pajama pants and felt the stirrings of an erection. No, not yet, he decided. Wait until you're really ready to go to sleep, then have at it.

At that moment a nurse stepped into his room, closing the door carefully behind her. She was the same one who had sat on his bed and talked to him the night before the operation. A little old, maybe forty, he thought, but with a body that just wouldn't quit. Perry felt an immediate surge in the limp organ beneath his hand and again began massaging himself under the sheets, picturing the shapely nurse lying nude on his hotel suite bed, waiting for him.

"How are you doing, Mr. Perry?" she asked softly. She was standing less than a foot from him. Inviting him, he just knew it.

For a moment Perry was torn by the dilemma of having to release himself in order to write a note. Finally, he scribbled. "Fine, sweetheart, how're you?"

"Is there anything I can get for you before I call it quits for the night?" she asked, moving an inch closer.

Perry checked her left hand for a wedding ring. There was none, but that added little to his already mushroomed fantasy. "That depends . . ." he wrote.

"On what?"

Teasing him, tantalizing—that's what she was doing. He decided to chance it. "Whether we make it now or after I get out!"

He debated writing about the free Porsche, but rejected the notion as unnecessary.

"Do we do it alone or invite your wife along with us?"

His new, giddy abstraction had her legs stretched upward, heels resting on the wall over his bed. "Wife doesn't understand me," he wrote, playing along and adding a little smile face to the bottom of the page.

"Well, we'll see about everything when you're a little better," she said. "I'll admit that the idea of spending some nice time with you had crossed my mind." She toyed with the top button of her uniform and for a moment Perry thought she actually might undo it for him.

"You say when," he scribbled, slipping his free hand around her thigh.

"Soon." She smiled and stepped out of his grasp. "First, I have two presents for you. One is from your doctor and one is from me. Which do you want first?"

Perry deliberated, then wrote "Yours."

The woman left the room and returned holding something behind her back. Perry inhaled sharply at the way her uniform pulled tightly across her breasts. A C for sure, he thought. Absolutely. Thirty-four C. He looked up at her beaming face and noticed, for the first time, a thin scar running almost parallel to one side of her nose. A minor flaw, he decided. Candlelight, a little makeup, and, *poof,* no more scar.

After giving him what seemed like a deliberately prolonged look at her, the nurse theatrically drew her hands from behind her back. She held a bouquet of flowers. Bright, purple flowers.

"Beautiful," he wrote.

"They're hyacinths," she said.

After a brief search for a vase, she set the flowers in the empty urinal that rested on his bedside table. Perry winced at her somewhat crude break with the romantic mood of the moment. Maybe she's into kinky sex, he thought, not at all certain he was ready to play someone else's game.

"Second present?" he wrote.

"Just some new medicine." She moved inches from his face as she produced a syringe full of clear liquid from her pocket and injected it in the tubing of his intravenous line.

He reached out and again grabbed her by the back of the thigh. This time she made no attempt to move away. Suddenly he felt a strange tightness in his chest. His grip weakened, then, in less than a minute, disappeared all together. With difficulty and mounting panic, he turned his head upward and looked at the nurse. She was standing motionless, smiling benevolently down at him. He tried to scream, but only a soft hiss emerged from beneath his swollen, paralyzed vocal cords.

The air became as thick and heavy as molasses. No matter how hard he tried, he could not force it down into his lungs. His left arm dangled uselessly over the side of the bed.

"It's called pancuronium," the nurse said pleasantly. "A rapid-acting form of curare. Just like on poison darts. You see, your wife understands you much better than you realized, Mr. Perry. She understands you so well that she is willing to share a large portion of your insurance with us in order to eliminate you from her life."

Perry tried to respond, but could no longer manage even a blink. A dull film seemed to cover all the objects in the room, as gradually his panic yielded to a detached sense of euphoria. Through now immovable eyes and the mounting film, he watched the nurse carefully unbutton the top two buttons of her uniform, exposing the deep cleft between her breasts.

"Don't worry about the flowers, Mr. Perry. I'll see to it that they get some water," were the last words that he heard.

Janet Poulos set Perry's arm on the bed, checked the darkened corridor of Three West, and calmly left the floor. As the stairway door closed behind her, she gave in to the smile that had been tugging at her mouth from the moment the last of the pancuronium was injected. It had been an incredibly profitable day for The Garden. Just as Dahlia had promised it would be. First, a masterful performance by Lily, and now she, Hyacinth, had done at least as well. She laughed, and listened to her echo reverberate throughout the empty stairwell.

In her office on One North, Janet settled behind her desk, then closed her eyes and relived the scene in Carl Perry's room. The sense of power—of ultimate control—was at least as thrilling as it had been at the bedside. It was an excitement that she, like all the others in The Garden, had first discovered through The Sisterhood of Life. The Sisterhood, with its high-flown nobility, was fine for some, Janet reflected, but Dahlia's creation of the Garden had been sheer inspiration. That they could be paid, and paid well, for their efforts only sweetened the game. Janet blessed Dahlia for bringing Hyacinth to life.

Then, as so often happened after she handled a Sisterhood or Garden case, Janet began thinking about the man—the first man who had ever taken her, the only man she had ever loved. Was he a professor of surgery now as he had planned? Why had he never called again after that night? Well, he would certainly see her in a different light now. She had power, too. As much as the most powerful surgeon in the world. If he could only see her he would . . . Janet shrugged. "Who cares," she said out loud. "Who the hell cares anyhow."

She picked up the telephone. It was time to share the excitement of the day with Dahlia.

CHAPTER 7

IT WAS AFTER eleven thirty when the evening shift on Four South completed their report and the eleven-to-seven group took over for the night. Christine Beall rode the Pinkerton minibus to Parking Lot C. Exhausted, she declined an invitation for a nightcap from the four nurses riding with her and headed home.

Twenty miles away, in the bedroom suburb of Wellesley, Dr. George Curtis downed two fingers of brandy and shuffled back to bed from his oak-paneled study. His wife, who had turned on the bedside lamp and propped herself up on several pillows, looked at him anxiously.

"Well, how did it go with Mrs. Perry?" she asked.

Curtis sank down on the edge of the bed and sighed his relief. "She's pretty shaken up, but all things considered, she seems to be holding together all right. I offered to go over there and talk with her, but she said it wouldn't be necessary, that she had people. Best of all, she didn't say anything about wanting an autopsy."

His wife was concerned. "What do you mean 'best of all'? George, is something the matter?"

"Well, from what the resident on duty told me, Perry must either have had a coronary or bled into his vocal cords where I did the surgery. Either way, his wife could try and make a case for negligence by saying he should have been cared for in the I.C.U. Without an autopsy, she's got no definite findings, so she's got no grounds for a suit, and I say 'Amen' to that."

"Amen," his wife echoed as she turned off the light and rolled over next to him.

Christine drove slowly, steering by rote, unaware of the traffic around her. On the gaslit sidewalks the night world of the inner city was in full cry. The hookers and the hustlers, the junkies and the winos, and the clusters of young men milling outside tavern doorways. It was a world that usually fascinated her, but this night the people and the action went unnoticed. Her mind had begun playing out a far different scene.

It was a tennis match. Two women on a grassy emerald court. Or perhaps it was only one, for she never saw them both at the same time. Just a bouncing figure in a white dress, swinging out with energetic, perfect strokes.

Totally immersed in the vision, she cruised through a red light, then onto a wide boulevard leading out of the city.

All at once, Christine realized why it seemed like a match. With each swing, each stroke, the woman's face changed. First it was Charlotte Thomas, radiant, laughing excitedly at every hit; then it was the drawn, sallow face of her own mother, a stern Dutch woman whose devotion to her five children had eventually worn her to a premature death.

The strokes came faster and faster, and with each of them a flashing change in the competitor's face until it was little more than a blur.

Suddenly Christine glanced at the speedometer. She was going nearly eighty. Seconds later, a route sign shot past. She was traveling in a direction nearly opposite to her house.

Shaking almost uncontrollably, she screeched to a stop on the shoulder and sat, gasping as if she had just finished a marathon. Several minutes passed before she was able to turn around and resume the drive home.

It was after midnight when she reached the quiet, treelined street where she and her roommates had lived for two years. The decision to search for an apartment in Brookline had been unanimous. "An old town with a young heart," Carole D'Elia had called it, referring to the thousands of students and young working people who inhabited the quaint duplexes and apartment buildings. After a three-week search, they found—and immediately fell in love with—the first-floor apartment of a brown and white two family. Their landlady, a blue-haired widow named Ida Fine, lived upstairs. The day after they moved in, a large pot of soup outside their door heralded Ida's intention to adopt the three of them. Christine had resented her intrusion in their lives at first, but Ida was irrepressible—and usually wise enough to sense when she had overstayed her welcome.

Christine, Carole, and Lisa Heller were quite different from one another, but tailor made for living together. Carole, an up-and-coming criminal lawyer, handled the bills, while Christine took care of the shopping and other day-to-day essentials of cooperative living. Lisa, a buyer for Filene's, was the social chairman.

With a groan of relief and fatigue, Christine eased her Mustang up the driveway and into its customary spot next to Lisa's battered VW. The two-car garage was so full of the "treasures" Ida was constantly promising to throw out that there had never been room inside for more than their bicycles. As she walked around to the front, Christine noticed for the first time that lights were blaring from every room. A party. The last thing in the world she wanted to deal with. "Lisa strikes again," she muttered, shaking her head.

The unmistakable odor of marijuana hit her as soon as she opened the door. From the living room the music of an old Eagles album mixed with the clinking of glasses and a half-dozen simultaneous conversations. She was searching her thoughts for somewhere else to sneak off to for the night when Lisa Heller popped out from the living room.

Three years younger than Christine and six inches taller, Lisa was dressed in what had become the unofficial uniform of the house—well-worn jeans and a baggy man's shirt pirated from some past lover. Her face had a perpetually intellectual, almost pious look to it that seemed invariably to attract men who were "into" Mahler and organic food, both of which Lisa abhorred.

"Aha! The prodigal daughter returneth to the fold." She giggled.

There was something disarming about Lisa that had always made even Christine's blackest moments seem more manageable. "Lisa," she said, smiling around clenched teeth, "how many people are in there?"

"Oh, eight or ten or twelve or so. It's hard to count because some of them aren't really people, you know."

"Do me a favor, please," Christine pleaded, "Go get some rope and your raccoon coat and see if you can sneak me past the door as your pet Irish wolfhound or something. I just want to go to bed."

"Ah, bed," Lisa said wistfully, steadying herself against the wall. "Soon all that Gallo Chablis and fine Colombian dope in there will have us all in bed. The only question remaining is who will be bedded down with whom. Speaking of which . . ."

"Lisa, is *he* in there?"

"Big as life. It's his dope, doncha know."

Christine grimaced. Jerry Crosswaite was hanging on like a bad cold. She shook her head. "It's my fault," she added with theatrical woe. "My cardinal rule, and I broke it."

"What rule is that?" Lisa punctuated the question with a hiccup.

"Never date a man more than once who has vanity plates on his car with *his* name on them." The two friends laughed and embraced.

Although seeing Jerry still had its pleasant moments, they were becoming fewer and farther between. Ever since his unilateral decision that they were "made for each other," Jerry had mounted an all-out campaign to make Christine "The Wife of the Youngest Senior Loan Officer in Boston Bank and Trust History." For weeks he had barraged her with roses, gifts, and phone calls. To Christine's mounting chagrin, Lisa and Carole had become so swept up in the romantic adventure that they had undermined her efforts to discourage his ardor.

"Chrissy, will you stop complaining." Lisa said now. "I mean you're past thirty, and he's a nice man with an Alfa. What more could a girl want?"

Christine wasn't totally certain she was being teased. "Lisa, he has fewer sides than a sheet of paper . . ."

"Well, babe, I wouldn't kick 'im out of bed," Lisa said.

"Stick around, Heller, you may get the chance to find out if you mean that." Christine brushed past her and into the living room.

Jerry Crosswaite set down his wine and began a piecemeal effort to rise from the couch and greet her. Christine forced a grin and waved for him to stay where he was. There were twelve others in the room, many of them looking even more gelatinous than Jerry.

"Brutal," Christine muttered, at the same time smiling irrepressibly at Carole D'Elia, who was engrossed in a game of her own creation called 'Scrabble For Dopers.' In this version, to be played only with the aid of marijuana, any word, real or invented, would be counted as long as it could be satisfactorily defined for the other players.

Carole called her over. "Hey, Chrissy, you're the only one with any sense around here. Come and arbitrate this. Is or is not Z-O-T-L the noun for a decorative arrangement of dead salamanders?"

"Absolutely," Christine said, giving her a hug from behind. None of the women sharing the house smoked marijuana regularly, but from time to time parties simply materialized, and as often as not, pot was a part of them. Despite the relative inactivity around the room, there was a sense of vitality that Christine felt every time she was around her roommates. She decided that their company might be just the tonic for her trying day. Even if it meant dealing with Jerry Crosswaite.

"By the way," Carole said. "You had a call a little while ago. Some woman. Said she'd call back. No other message."

"Old woman? Young?" Christine asked anxiously.

"Yes." Carole nodded definitively, polished off the rest of her wine, and wrote down her thirteen points.

Crosswaite had negotiated his way across the room and come up behind Christine, putting his hands on her shoulders. She whirled around as if struck with meat hooks.

"Hey, easy does it, Christine, it's only me," he said. He had discarded the jacket of his Brooks Brothers suit and had unbuttoned his vest—a move that for him was tantamount to total relaxation. Only the fine, red road maps in his eyes detracted from the Playboy image he liked to project.

"Hi, Jerry," she said. "Sorry I missed the party."

His gesture swept the room. "Missed it, hell. It's been waiting for you. Lisa said you like the necklace. I'm glad."

Christine glanced around for Lisa so that she could glare at her. "Jerry, I really wish you would stop sending me things. I . . . I just don't feel right accepting them."

"But Lisa told me . . ."

She cut him off, trying at the same time to keep her voice calm. "Jerry, I know what Lisa told you, and Carole, too. But neither of them is me. Look, you're a really nice man. They think a lot of you, so do I, but I'm getting very uncomfortable with some of the gifts you've been sending and with a lot of the assumptions you've been making."

"Such as what?" Crosswaite said, an edge of hostility appearing in his voice.

She bit at her lower lip and decided that she was simply not up to a confrontation. "Look, just forget it," she said. "We can work the whole thing through another time when we have a little more privacy and a little less wine."

"No, Chris, I want to discuss it now." Crosswaite's control disappeared completely. "I don't know what your game is, but you've led me along to the point where this relationship is really important to me. Now, all of a sudden, you've gone frigid." His tone was loud enough to break through to even the most somnolent in the room. Embarrassed looks began to flash from one to another as Carole and Lisa rose to intervene. The banker continued. "I mean you were never any tiger in bed to begin with, but at least you were there. Now, all of a sudden, you're a fucking glacier around me. I want an explanation!" The room froze.

Christine took a step backward and brought her hands, fists clenched, tightly in against her sides.

The ring of the telephone shattered the silence.

Carole rushed to the kitchen. "Chrissy, it's for you," she called out after a few seconds. "It's the woman who called before."

Christine loosened her fists and lowered her arms before breaking her gaze away from Crosswaite.

There were three people in the kitchen. With a single look Christine sent them scurrying to the living room. Then she picked up the receiver.

"This is Christine Beall," she said, sharpness still in her voice.

"Christine, this is Evelyn, from the Regional Screening Committee. Are you in a position where you can talk uninterrupted?"

"I am." Christine settled onto a high rock maple stool she had found at a Gloucester flea market and later refinished.

"The Sisterhood of Life praises your deep concern and your professionalism," the woman said solemnly. "Your proposal regarding Mrs. Charlotte Thomas has been approved."

In the quiet kitchen, Christine began, ever so slightly, to tremble, as each word fell like a drop of water on hard, dry ground.

The woman continued. "The method selected will be intravenous morphine sulfate, administered at an appropriate time during your shift tomorrow evening. An ampule of morphine and the necessary syringe will be beneath the front seat of your car tomorrow morning. Please be certain the passenger side door is left open tonight. We shall lock it after the package has been delivered.

"We request that you administer the medication as a single rapid injection. There will be no need to wait in the room afterward. Please dispose of the vial and the syringe in a safe, secure manner. As is our policy, after your shift at the hospital is completed, you will please call the telephone recording machine and tape your case report. We all share the hope and the belief that the day will arrive when our work can become public knowledge. At that time reports such as yours—already nearly forty years' worth from nurses throughout the country—can be properly honored and receive their due praise. In transmitting your report there will be no need to repeat the patient's clinical history. Have you any questions?"

"No," Christine said softly, her fingers blanched around the receiver. "No questions."

"Very well, then," the woman said. "Miss Beall, you can feel most proud of the dedication you show to your principles and your profession. Good night."

"Thank you. Good night," Christine replied. She was speaking to a dial tone.

With a glance at the closed door to the living room Christine pulled on a green cardigan of Lisa's that had been draped over a chair. Quietly she slipped out of the back door of the apartment.

The night sky was endless. Christine shivered against the autumn chill and pulled the sweater tightly about her. On the next street a car roared around a corner. As the engine noise faded, a silence as deep as the night settled in around her. She looked at the stars—countless suns, each one a mother of worlds. She was a speck, less than a moment, yet the decision she had made seemed so enormous. Pressure through her chest and throat made it difficult to swallow. Panic, uncertainty, and a profound sense of isolation tightened the vise as she moved slowly to her car and unlocked the passenger side door.

Christine walked around the deserted block once, and then again. Hidden, she sat on a low rock wall across the street from her apartment and watched until the last of the partygoers finally left and the lights in the windows winked off. With a prolonged, parting gaze at the jeweled sky, she sighed and headed home. All that remained in the living room were a few half-filled glasses and a single, dim light, left for her by her roommates.

Christine flipped off the lamp. She was undressed even before reaching her room. Standing by the bureau, she unpinned her long, sandy hair, shook it free, and began slow passes with her brush, softly counting each one.

"Whenever you must really know . . ." Charlotte's words dominated her thoughts as she stepped across to her bed.

It was not until she turned the covers that she saw the envelope resting on her pillow.

She read the note inside, stiffened, then crumpled it into a tiny ball and threw it on the floor.

It said, "Christine, I've left. Maybe for good. Feel free to call, but only when you have something significant to say. Jerry."

CHAPTER 8

DAVID BEGAN his first day as Wallace Huttner's replacement by identifying a Berlioz piece as Mendelssohn, but bounced back moments later by correctly sensing that outside his window a day of change was developing.

There was a dry chill in the air that kept him from working up the heavy sweat he liked during his run by the river. To the east an anemic sun was gradually losing its battle for control of the morning to an advancing army of heavy, dark clouds, each with a glossy white border. The day mirrored his mood: the difficult evening rounds with Huttner had left him with a vague sense of discomfort and foreboding that neither a night of fitful sleep nor his morning workout had totally dispelled.

He had planned to make morning rounds along the same route he and Huttner had taken the previous night, but once in the hospital, he succumbed to a growing impatience to see how Anton Merchado was doing on his new treatment regimen.

The fisherman's bronzed, weathered face broke into a wide grin as soon as David entered his room. With that single smile David's apprehension about the day evaporated.

"I had a turd, Doc!" Merchado's gravelly voice held all the pride of a mother who had just given birth. "This morning. One beautiful, plop-in-the-water turd. Doc, I can't thank you enough. I never thought I'd ever have one again."

"Well, don't get too excited yet, Mr. Merchado," David said, barely able to control his own enthusiasm. "You certainly look better than you did last night, but I don't think the diarrhea is gone for good. At least, not just yet."

"My fever is down, too, and the cramps are almost gone,"

Merchado added as David probed his abdomen for areas of tenderness and listened for a minute with his stethoscope.

"Sounds good," David said, placing the instrument back in his jacket pocket, "but still no solid food. Just sips of liquids and several more days of the new antibiotic and intravenous fluids. You can tell your family that you'll be in the hospital for another week if things keep going well. Maybe even a little longer than that."

"Will you be my doctor when I get out?" he asked.

"No, only for a few days, then Dr. Huttner will be back. You're fortunate to have him, Mr. Merchado. He's one of the finest surgeons I've ever seen."

"Maybe . . . and then again, maybe not." Merchado's squint and wise smile said that he would push the matter no further. "But you leave your card with me just the same. I have a bunch of relatives that are gonna be beating down your door to get you to do some kind of operation on them. Even if they got nothing wrong."

With a grin that understated his delight, David left the room, then looked at the list of patients he had to see that morning. The names filled both sides of the file card on which he had printed them. Joy sparkled through him. For so many years he had not allowed himself even to daydream of having such a case load. As he neared the end of the hallway, he gave a gleeful yip and danced through the stairway door. Behind him, two plump, dowager nurses watched his performance, then exchanged disapproving expressions and several "tsks" before heading pompously to their charges.

David's rounds were more exhilarating than anything he had done in medicine in years. Even Charlotte Thomas seemed to have brightened up a small notch, although simply seeing her with the benefit of daylight may have had something to do with that impression. Her bed was cranked to a forty-five-degree angle and an aide was spoon-feeding her tiny chips of ice, one at a time. David tried several ways to determine how she was feeling, but her only response was a weak smile and a nod. He examined her abdomen, wincing inwardly at the total absence of bowel sounds. No cause for panic yet, but each day without sounds made the possibility of yet another operation more likely. For a moment David toyed with the notion of stopping even the ice chip feedings, then, with one last look at Charlotte, he decided to leave things as they were.

At the nurses' station he wrote a lengthy progress note and some orders for maneuvers he hoped might improve her situation. By the time he finished it was nearly one o'clock. He had twenty minutes for coffee and a sandwich before he was due in his own office. Five and a half hours had passed in what seemed almost no time at all. He tried to remember the last time it had been like this and realized it had probably been eight years. Not, he reflected ruefully, since the accident.

Even his afternoon office hours, at times embarrassingly slow, were made pleasantly hectic today by frequent phone calls from the hospital nurses to clarify orders or discuss problems.

At precisely five o'clock, as the door closed behind the last patient, David's office nurse, Mrs. Houlihan, yelled, "Dr. Shelton, there's a call for you from Dr. Armstrong. Her secretary is putting her on. You can pick up on three."

"Very funny," David shouted back from his office. He had only one telephone: its number happened to end in three. It was good to see Houlihan enjoying the unaccustomed busy day as much as he was.

"I'm off to cook up some hash for my brood. Good night, Doctor," she called out.

"Good night, Houlihan," David answered.

Moments later, Dr. Margaret Armstrong came on the line. As the first female chief of cardiology at a major hospital, Armstrong had earned nearly as much of a reputation in her field as had Wallace Huttner in his. Of all those on the medical staff of Doctors Hospital, she had been the most cordial and helpful to David, especially during his first year. Although she referred her patients to cardiac surgeons almost exclusively, or, where appropriate, to Huttner, she had, on several occasions, sent a case to David, taking pains each time to send him a thank-you note for the excellent care he delivered.

"David? How are things going?" she asked now.

"Busy today, but enjoying every minute, Dr. Armstrong." Perhaps it was the regal bearing, the aristocratic air that surrounded the woman, perhaps it was the twenty or so years difference in their ages—whatever the reason, David had never once had the impulse to address Margaret Armstrong by her first name. Nor had he ever been encouraged to.

"Well, I'm calling to see if I can make it busier for you," Armstrong said. "To be perfectly honest, I called Wally Huttner's office first, but I was pleased to hear that you're covering for him."

"Thanks. Fire away."

"It's an elderly gentleman named Butterworth—Aldous Butterworth, if you will. He's seventy-seven, but bright and spry as a puppy. He was doing fine for a week following a minor coronary until just a little while ago, when he suddenly started complaining about tingling and pain in his right leg. His pulses have disappeared from the groin on down."

"Embolus?" David asked, more out of courtesy than any uncertainty about the diagnosis.

"I would think so, David. The leg is already developing some pallor. Are you in the mood to fish us out a clot?"

"Happy to." David beamed. "Have you gone over the risks with him?"

"Yes, but it wouldn't hurt for you to do it again. David, I'm a bit worried about general anesthesia in this man. Do you think it might be possible to . . ."

David was so excited about capping his day with a major case that he actually cut her short. "Do him under local? Absolutely. It's the only way to fly."

"I knew I could count on you," Armstrong said. "I am most anxious to hear how things go. Aldous is a dear old friend as well as a patient. Listen, there's an Executive Committee meeting in an hour, and as chief of staff in this madhouse I have to attend. Could I meet you somewhere later this evening?"

"Sure," David said. "I have several patients to see before I head home. How about Four South? I've got a woman to see there with total body failure. Maybe you can even come up with some ideas."

"Glad to try," Armstrong said. "Eight o'clock?"

"Eight o'clock," David echoed.

Hands scrubbed and clasped protectively in front of him, David backed into Operating Room 10, then slipped into a surgical gown and began making preparations to orchestrate and conduct his own symphony. Aldous Butterworth seemed small and vulnerable stretched out on the narrow operating table.

David ordered Butterworth's right foot placed in a clear, plastic bag to keep it visible without contaminating his operative field. The foot was the color of white marble.

Using small injections, he deadened an area of the man's right groin. With no pulse to guide him, he knew that the femoral artery could be an inch or more away from his incision. A miscalculation, and he faced an operation so difficult that a second incision might be the only solution. Focus in, he thought. See it. Hidden beneath his mask, the corners of his mouth turned up in a thin, knowing smile. He was ready.

"Scalpel, please," he said, taking the instrument from the scrub nurse. He paused, closed his eyes, and breathed in the electricity of the moment. Then he opened them and surveyed the expectant faces watching him, waiting for him. With a slight nod to the anesthesiologist and a final glance at Butterworth's bloodless foot, he made his incision. The taut skin parted, immediately exposing the femoral artery. "Bull's-eye," he whispered.

In minutes the artery, stiff and heavy with clot, was isolated and controlled with two thin strips of cloth tape placed two inches apart. David made a small incision in the vessel wall between the tapes. Gently he eased a long, thin tube with a deflated balloon at the tip down the inside of the artery toward the foot. When he determined that the tip was in position, he blew up the balloon and carefully drew it back through the incision. Two feet of stringy, dark clot pushed out before David lifted the balloon free. Repeating the procedure in the opposite direction, he removed the thicker clot that had caused the obstruction in the first place. An irrigation with blood thinner, and he was ready to close. He tightened the cloth tapes to prevent blood flow through the artery, then closed his incision in the vessel with a series of tiny sutures.

For the second time in less than twenty minutes David shared a momentary gaze with each person in the room. He then took a silent, deep breath, held it, and released the tapes. Instantly, Butterworth's foot flushed with life-giving color. A cheer burst out from the team. Textbook perfect. The whole case, textbook perfect. In absolute exhilaration, he called out the good news to Butterworth, who had slept through the entire procedure.

"That was *really* fine work, Dr. Shelton. That was really *fine* work, Dr. Shelton. That *was* really fine work, Dr. Shelton." David repeated the words of the veteran scrub nurse over and over, trying to reproduce her inflection exactly. "Maybe you should give her a call and ask her to say it again so you can get it just right," he advised himself. He had dictated an operative note, showered, and dressed. Now he was headed down the corridor of Four South to share the news of Butterworth's successful operation with Dr. Armstrong.

He glanced at his watch. Ten of eight. His second straight late evening in the hospital. A first for him since joining the surgical staff more than eighteen months before.

Margaret Armstrong had already arrived on the floor and was seated at the nurses' station sharing coffee and relaxed conversation with Christine Beall and the charge nurse, Winnie Edgerly. As David approached the group, his eyes were drawn to Christine. Her eyes and her smile seemed to be saying a thousand different things to him at the same time. Or maybe they were his words, his thoughts, not hers. Lauren's jewel-perfect face flashed in his mind, but faded as the tawny eyes tightened their hold.

Dr. Armstrong's voice pulled him free. "Yo, David," she called out merrily. "Word is sweeping the hospital about my little man's new foot. Bravo to you. Come, we shall toast your successful operation with a cup of this coffee." She glanced in her cup, grimaced, then added, "If, in fact, that is what this is."

She wore a black skirt and light blue cashmere sweater. A simple gold butterfly pin was her only jewelry. Her white clinic coat, unbuttoned, was knee length—the type reserved unofficially only for professors or those with sufficient seniority in the teaching community. Her dark wavy hair was cut short in a style perfect for her bright blue eyes and finely carved features. There was an air about her, an energy, that commanded immediate attention and respect. An article written six years before about her contributions to her field had dubbed her the

Grande Dame of American Cardiology; she had been only fifty-eight years old at the time.

As David took in the scene at the nurses' station, he couldn't help but reflect on the easy, animated relationship that existed between Armstrong and the two nurses. Quite the opposite from Dr. Wallace Huttner, even allowing for the fact that Dr. Armstrong was a woman. The contrast became even more striking when she got up and poured him a cup of coffee.

She introduced him to the nurses as the "hero of the day," and, with a mischievous wink at Christine, added that David was, to the best of her knowledge, single. He blushed and covered his eyes in genuine embarrassment, but realized at the same time that he was carefully avoiding any further eye contact with Christine. Seconds later, Armstrong had him describing Butterworth's operation in detail. For the moment the danger had passed.

Rona Gold, a practical nurse, joined the group as David used red and blue pens to sketch pictures of the procedure he had done.

It seemed clear to David that Armstrong already knew the details, probably from one of the O.R. nurses. Still, she encouraged him at every chance to continue.

"Well," she said finally, "I stopped by the recovery room to see Aldous and he doesn't remember a thing. Snoozed his way through the whole ordeal. Here he is in danger of losing a leg or worse and he sleeps through the procedure. That is my idea of good local anesthesia, what?"

"I think I put him to sleep while I was trying to explain what I was going to do to him," David said.

Armstrong shared an appreciative laugh with the three nurses, then said, "David, you mentioned something about having a complicated patient here on Four South. Charlotte Thomas?"

"Why, as a matter of fact, yes," David said. "Are you a mind reader as well as a cardiologist?"

"Nothing that exotic. The nurses and I deduced that she was the only one on the floor who fit the bill, so I took the chance and went over her chart."

"And?"

"And you're right. She is rapidly developing total body failure. In fact, I have only one observation to add to the excellent note you wrote this morning outlining her many problems. Your Mrs. Thomas has, on top of everything else, definite signs of coronary artery disease on her electrocardiogram. At least, in my interpretation of her electrocardiogram," she added modestly. "I really have nothing dramatic to contribute to what is already being done. Does it seem as though the bowel obstruction will require reexploration?"

"God, I hope not," David said. "It would mean her third major operation in less than three weeks."

"Dr. Shelton, I have a question," Christine said.

He responded quickly. "It's five, five, five-two, oh, one, six."

"What is?"

"My phone number!" David said, immediately realizing that he should have learned more about Christine Beall before exposing her to his sense of humor.

Gold and Edgerly laughed briefly, but Christine did not crack the slightest smile. "That's not funny," she said. "Neither is a woman as sick and in as much pain as Charlotte Thomas."

David muttered an apology, but she ignored it.

"What concerns me," Christine continued, "is why, if she has so many seemingly incurable problems, Dr. Huttner has made her a full Code Ninety-nine. Especially after what happened last night."

"Last night?" Armstrong asked. "What happened last night?"

David paused, uncertain which of them she was addressing. Christine sat back, looking expectantly at him for his version.

"Well," he said finally, "Mrs. Thomas's husband and Dr. Huttner got into a discussion about the aggressive approach Huttner has elected to take in her treatment. The husband was frustrated and more than a little angry. Understandable, I guess, and certainly something we're all used to encountering."

"How did Wally handle it?" Armstrong leaned forward with interest, absently rolling her coffee cup back and forth between her hands.

"As well as could be expected under the circumstances, I think," David said. "He may have overreacted a bit. He stuck by his philosophical guns. Refused to alter his treatment plan regardless of what Thomas, who was under obvious strain and pressure, demanded him to do. Finally Huttner drew me into the whole thing. I'm afraid that my opinion and the way I expressed it were not quite what he wanted to hear in that situation." David managed a rueful grin at his own understatement.

"And how do you feel about the whole thing, David?"

Dr. Armstrong's voice was soft. There was an openness in her expression that made him certain there would be no recrimination from her.

"I think it's a bitch of a situation, if you'll pardon the expression," he said. "I mean it's always harder to decide *not* to use treatment on a patient than it is to just go ahead and employ every medicine, machine, and operation you can think of. That's why we end up with so many patients who drag on as little more than vegetables.

"Personally," he continued, "having watched several of my own family members die prolonged, painful deaths, I think there are times when a doctor must make the decision to hold off and let nature take its course. Don't you agree?"

Hold off . . . Let nature take its course. . . . There was something about the words, the way they were said. Margaret Armstrong closed her eyes as they echoed in her mind, then yielded to other words. Other words and the voice of a young girl.

"It's all right, Mama. . . . I'm here, Mama."

"Don't you agree, Dr. Armstrong?"

"Mama, tell me what I can do to help. . . . Does it still hurt as much? Tell me what I can do to help. . . . Please, tell me what I can do. . . ."

"Dr. Armstrong?"

"Oh, yes," she said. "Well, David, I'm afraid I agree much more with Dr. Huttner's approach than with yours." How long had she drifted off? Were they expecting an explanation?

"How do you mean?"

No, she decided. No explanations. "The way I see it, following your philosophy, a physician would constantly be confronted with the need to play God. To decide who is to live and who is to die. A medical Nero. Thumbs up, we put in an intravenous. Thumbs down, we don't."

David responded with an emotion and forcefulness that momentarily startled even him. "I believe that the major responsibility of a physician is not constantly to do battle against death, but to do what he can to lessen pain and improve the quality of patients' lives. I mean," he went on, less vehemently now, "should every treatment, every operation possible be used on every patient, even though we know there's only a one-in-a-million or even a one-in-ten-thousand chance that it will help?" In the silence that followed, he sensed that once again he'd used a verbal cannon where a slingshot or perhaps even a velvet glove had been called for.

At this point, Winnie Edgerly, a straightforward if somewhat plodding woman of about fifty, felt moved to enter the discussion. "I cast my vote with Dr. Armstrong," she said earnestly. "I wouldn't want any tubes pulled out of me if there was even the slightest chance. I mean, who knows what might happen or what might come along at the last minute to help. Right?"

"Now don't get me wrong, Mrs. Edgerly," David said, carefully minimizing the intensity in his voice. "I am not advocating pulling out any tubes from anyone. I'm arguing that we should all think twice—or more than twice—before putting the tubes down someone in the first place. Sure they can help, but they also can prolong hopeless agony. Does that help make my feelings any clearer?"

Edgerly nodded, but her expression suggested that she did not agree.

Finally Dr. Armstrong said, "So, David, how does all this apply to your Mrs. Thomas?"

"It doesn't," he said shortly. "The treatment program for Mrs. Thomas has been clearly spelled out by Dr. Huttner. It's my responsibility to carry those plans out to the best of my ability. That's all there is to that."

Armstrong seemed about to say something further when the overhead page sounded, summoning David to the emergency ward. "When it rains, it pours." He smiled expectantly at Dr. Armstrong.

"But I'll bet you don't mind getting wet like this at all," she said. "I'm very happy for you, David."

"Thank you, Dr. Armstrong." He swallowed the last of his coffee. "Thank you for everything."

With a nod to Edgerly and Gold, and a longer look at Christine, David headed off toward the emergency ward.

Christine sat silently behind the nurses' station as the others dispersed to go about their business. There was a puzzled, ironic expression on her face. She slipped her right hand into the pocket of her sweater and, for a minute or two, fingered the syringe and ampule of morphine that she had wrapped in a handkerchief and stuffed inside. Then she rose and walked with forced nonchalance down the hall toward Room 412.

CHAPTER 9

"DO YOU DO HANDS, Dr. Shelton?" Harry Weiss, the hawk-nosed resident who had called David to the emergency ward, could easily have won the role of Ichabod Crane in a production of *The Legend of Sleepy Hollow*.

"Show me what you have," David said.

The emergency ward was in its usual state of mid-evening chaos. Two dozen patients in various stages of discomfort and anger at the hospital sat in the crowded waiting room. Litters glided past like freighters in a busy port, bearing their human cargo to X ray or the short-term observation ward or an in-patient room. Telephones jangled. A dozen different conversations competed with one another. David caught snatches of several of them as the resident led him to Trauma Room 8. "What do you mean you can't have the results for an hour? This man is bleeding out. We need them now . . ." "Mrs. Ramirez, I understand how you feel, but I can't help you. There is simply no Juan

Ramirez on the emergency ward at this time . . ." "Now, you're going to feel a little pinprick . . ."

The patient David had been called about was a forty-year-old laborer who had lost a brief but unmistakably furious encounter with his power saw. The top halves of two fingers were gone completely, and a third was held together at the first knuckle by a sliver of tendon. Another no-win situation, David thought to himself as he evaluated the damaged hand. He spoke briefly with the man, who had stopped his profuse sweating but was still the color of sun-bleached bone. Then he guided the overwrought young resident into the hallway. It was David's decision whether to do the repair himself or to spend the extra time to take the resident through it. He chose to take the time, remembering the many late nights when other surgeons had made the extra effort to teach him. It was nearly half an hour before he felt confident that Weiss could complete the repair on his own.

Four South was unusually quiet as David stepped off the elevator and started down the corridor toward Room 412. A burst of laughter from the nurses' lounge suggested that it was coffee break time—at least for some of the staff. He thought about Christine Beall, half hoping that she might step out of one of the rooms as he was passing.

Just the image was enough to rekindle an uneasy warmth. So, she's interesting looking and has strange eyes, David thought. Lauren is beautiful and has incredible eyes. You're reacting like this because she's away, that's all. Face it, with Lauren you have everything you've ever wanted in a woman—beauty, brains, independence. Right? Right. The logic was all there, black and white and irrefutable. But somewhere in the back of his mind a small voice was saying, "Think again . . . think again . . ."

The lights in Charlotte Thomas's room were off. David stood at the doorway, staring across the darkness toward her bed. The gastrointestinal drainage machine, set for intermittent suction, whirred, stopped, then reassuringly whirred again. Bubbles of oxygen tinkled through the water of the safety bottle on the wall. He debated whether or not to disrupt her sleep in order to check findings he knew would be unchanged at best. Finally he stepped across the room and turned on the fluorescent light over her bed.

Charlotte was lying on her back, a tranquil half-smile on her face. It took David several seconds to realize that she was not breathing.

Instinctively, he reached across her neck and checked for a carotid pulse. For an instant he thought he felt one, but then knew that it was his own heart, pounding through his fingertips. With both fists he delivered a sharp blow to the center of Charlotte's chest. Then he gave two deep mouth-to-mouth breaths and several quick compressions to her breastbone. Another carotid check showed nothing still.

He raced to the doorway. "Code Ninety-nine four-twelve," he

screamed down the deserted corridor. "Code Ninety-nine four-twelve."
He ran back inside and resumed his one-man resuscitation.

Thirty seconds passed in what seemed like a year before Winnie
Edgerly burst into the room pushing the emergency crash cart. At the
same instant the page operator, alerted from the nurses' station, announced, "Code Ninety-nine, Four South. Code Ninety-nine, Four
South. Code Ninety nine, Four South."

Seconds later, Room 412 began to fill with people and machines.
Edgerly inserted a short oral airway into Charlotte's mouth and began
providing respirations as best she could with a breathing bag. David
continued the external cardiac compression. An aide rushed in, then
wandered meekly to one side of the room, waiting for someone to tell
her what to do. Two more nurses raced in, followed by Christine, pushing an electrocardiograph machine. Leads from the machine were
strapped tightly to Charlotte's wrists and ankles.

A resident appeared, then another, and finally the anesthesiologist,
a huge Oriental who introduced himself as Dr. Kim. He replaced Edgerly at the head of the bed and looked over at David, who had turned
the job of cardiac massage over to one of the residents and had moved
to man the cardiograph.

"Tube her?" Dr. Kim asked. David nodded his answer.

As the room filled with still more people, including the inhalation
and laboratory technicians, Kim set about his task. He picked up a steel
laryngoscope and inserted its right-angle, lighted blade deeply into
Charlotte's throat, lifting up against the base of her tongue to expose
the delicate silver half-moons of her vocal cords.

"Give me a seven-point-five tube," he said to the nurse assisting at
his side. The clear plastic tube, with a diameter of three quarters of an
inch, had a deflated plastic balloon wrapped just above the tip. Skillfully, the giant slipped the tube between Charlotte's vocal cords and
down into her trachea. He used a syringe to blow up the balloon, seal-
ing the area around the tube against air leaks. Next he attached the
black Ambu breathing bag to the outside end of the tube, connected
oxygen to the bag, and began supplying Charlotte with breaths at a rate
of thirty per minute.

Christine stood just to David's right and watched as he tried to
center the needle on the cardiograph. All at once, her eyes riveted on
the slashing up-and-down strokes of the stylus. There was a rhythm—a
persistent, regular rhythm. *Oh, my God, he's bringing her back!* Her
thoughts screamed the words. The one possibility she had never considered, and now it was happening. With every beat a new horrifying
image occurred to her. Charlotte, hooked to a respirator. More tubes.
Day upon endless day of wondering if the woman's oxygen-deprived
brain would awaken. *What had she done?*

The finely lined paper flowed from the machine like lava, forming a
jumbled pile at David's feet. The rhythmic bursts continued.

"Hold it for a second!" David called for the resident to halt his thrusting cardiac compressions in order to get a true reading from the machine.

Instantly the pulsing jumps of the needle disappeared, replaced by only a fine quiver. The pattern had been artificial—a response to the efforts of the resident.

Christine had misinterpreted the cardiograph. She felt near collapse.

"Her rhythm looks like fine fibrillation. Please resume pumping." David's voice was firm but calm. Christine sensed a measure of control return. "Christine, please get set to give her four hundred joules."

The order registered slowly. Too slowly.

"Miss Beall!" David snapped the words.

"Oh, yes, Doctor. Right away." Christine rushed to the defibrillator machine. Was everyone staring at her? She couldn't bring herself to look up. Turning the dial on the machine to 400, she squirted contact jelly on the two steel paddles and handed them to David.

David motioned the resident away. Then he quickly pressed one paddle along the inside of Charlotte's left breast and the other one six inches below her left armpit.

"Everyone away from the bed," he called out. "Ready? Now!"

He depressed the red button on the top of the right-hand paddle. A dull thunk sounded as 400 joules of electricity shot through Charlotte's chest and on through the rest of her body. Like a marionette's, her arms flipped toward the ceiling, then dropped limply to the bed. Her body arched rigidly for an instant, then was still. The cardiograph tracing showed no change.

The resident resumed his pumping, but soon motioned to the medical student standing nearby that he was tiring. The two made a smooth change.

Immediately David began ordering medications to be given through Charlotte's intravenous lines. Bicarbonate to counteract the mounting lactic acid in her blood and tissues, Adrenalin to stimulate cardiac activity, even glucose on the chance that her sugar may have dropped too low for some reason. No change. Another Adrenalin injection followed closely by two more 400-joule countershocks. Still nothing. Calcium, more bicarbonate, a fourth shock. The cardiogram now showed a straight line. Even the fine fibrillation was gone. The resident again took his place over from the student and the pumping continued. At the head of the bed, the mountainous anesthesiologist stood implacably squeezing the Ambu bag, which seemed like little more than a pliant black softball in his thick hands.

"Hook an amp of Adrenalin to a cardiac needle, please," David ordered. Although an injection through the subclavian intravenous line should end up in the heart, perhaps the tip had somehow become dislodged. He put his hand along the left side of Charlotte's breastbone and used his fingers to count down four rib spaces. Holding the ampule of Adrenalin in his other hand, he plunged the four-and-one-half-inch needle attached to it straight down into Charlotte's chest. Almost immediately, a plume of dark blood jetted into the ampule. A direct hit. The needle was lodged in some part of the heart. Behind him, Christine held her breath and looked away.

David shot in the Adrenalin. For a moment the cardiograph needle began jumping, and with it his own pulse. Then he noticed that the medical student was rocking back and forth, inadvertently bumping into Charlotte's left arm each time. He motioned the student away from the bed. Instantly the tracing was again a flat line.

Christine felt the tension in the room begin to dissolve. She stared at the floor. It was almost over.

David looked at the anesthesiologist with a shrug that asked, "Any ideas?"

Dr. Kim stared back placidly and said, "Will you open her chest?"

For a few seconds David actually entertained the thought. "How are her pupils?" He was stalling, he knew it.

"Fixed and dilated," Kim replied.

David gazed off into one corner of the room. His eyes closed tightly, then opened. Finally he reached over and flicked off the cardiograph. "That's it. Thank you, everybody." It was all he could manage.

The room began to empty. David stood there for a time looking down at Charlotte's lifeless form. Despite the tubes and the bruises and the circular electrical burns on her chest, there was something beautifully peaceful about the woman.

At last, peaceful.

All at once, some of the impact of what had happened began to register. His hands and armpits became cold and damp with sweat.

As he walked out of Room 412 to call Wallace Huttner, David was shaking. Deep inside him was the chilly feeling that somehow he had just struck the tip of a nightmare. He glanced at the wall clock. How long had they worked on her? Forty-five minutes? An hour? "What the hell difference does it make," he muttered as he sat down at the nurses' station to write a death note in Charlotte Thomas's chart.

"You all right?" Christine asked softly as she set a cup of muddy coffee in front of him.

"Huh? Oh, yeah, I'm okay. Thanks," David said, resting his chin on the counter and studying the Styrofoam cup at close range. "Thanks for the coffee."

"I'm sorry she didn't make it through for you," she said.

David continued staring at the cup, as if searching for the answer to some kind of cosmic mystery.

"Potassium!" he exclaimed suddenly.

Christine, who had moved to leave the uncomfortable silence, turned back to him. "What about potassium?"

He looked up. "Something wasn't right in there, Christine. I mean over and above the obvious. I'm probably wrong, but I can't remember handling a cardiac arrest where I couldn't get a flicker of cardiac activity back—even when quite a bit of time had elapsed between the arrest and the Code Ninety-nine. Shit! I wish there had been time to get a potassium level on her. Potassium, calcium—I don't know what, but something felt like it was out of whack."

"Can't you get a potassium level done now?" Christine asked.

"Sure, but it won't be much help. During the resuscitation and after death potassium is released into the bloodstream from the tissues, so the levels are usually high anyway." He clenched his fists in frustration.

Christine felt an ache building inside her. "How could her potassium level have gotten out of line in the first place?"

"Lots of ways." David was too distracted to notice the change in her expression. "Sudden kidney failure, a blood clot, even a medication error. It makes no difference now. I'm probably way off base anyway. Dead is dead." He realized the anguish that she was feeling. "I . . . I'm sorry," he said. "I didn't mean that. I'm afraid the pleasant task of calling Dr. Huttner on the Cape has me a little rattled. I don't think this is the sort of news he'd be too happy about having me save until he gets back. Look, maybe sometime we can sit and talk about Mrs. Thomas. Okay?"

Christine looked away. "Maybe sometime . . ." she whispered to herself.

David fished out the number Huttner had given him. After the usual hassles with the hospital switchboard operator, his call was put through. Huttner's hello left no doubt that he had been asleep.

"Great start," David muttered, looking upward for some kind of celestial help. "Dr. Huttner, this is David Shelton," he said into the receiver.

"Yes, what is it, David?" Even his first words held an edge of impatience.

At that moment David knew that he should have waited until the next day to call. "It's Charlotte, Dr. Huttner, Charlotte Thomas." He felt as though his tongue was swelling rapidly and had already reached grapefruit size.

"Well, what about her?"

"About an hour and a half ago she was found pulseless in her bed. We worked on her, a full Code Ninety-nine for nearly an hour, but nothing. She's dead, Dr. Huttner."

"What do you mean you worked on her? What in the hell happened, man? I checked on her before I left this morning and she seemed stable enough."

David had not anticipated an easy time of it with Huttner, but

78

neither had he expected a war. His tongue passed grapefruit and headed toward watermelon.

"I . . . I don't know what happened," he said. "Maybe hyperkalemia. She had a brief period of fine fibrillation on her cardiogram, then nothing. Flat line. No matter what. Absolutely nothing."

"Hyperkalemia?" Huttner's tone was now more one of bewilderment than anger. "She's never had problems with her potassium in the past."

"Do you want me to call Mr. Thomas?" David asked finally.

"No, leave that to me. It's what he wanted anyway." Huttner's voice drifted away, then picked up with renewed intensity. "What you can do for me is to get in touch with Ahmed Hadawi, the chief of pathology. Tell him there's going to be a postmortem on this woman tomorrow. I want to know exactly what happened. If for some reason Thomas won't consent, I'll notify Hadawi myself that it's off. You tell him we'll be at the Autopsy Suite tomorrow morning at eight sharp with a signed permission from Peter Thomas. Good night."

"Good night," David said a minute or so after Huttner had hung up. He set the receiver down, then added, "Good grief."

The nurses' station was quiet—deserted except for David and a ward secretary who was painfully trying not to notice him. Eyes closed, he sat, rubbing his temples, struggling to sort out the unpleasant emotions swirling within him. Confusion? Sure, that was understandable. Depression? A little, perhaps. He had just lost a patient. Loneliness? Dammit, he wished Lauren were home.

But there was something else. It was hazy and diffuse. Difficult to focus on. But there *was* something, some other feeling. Several minutes passed before David began to understand. Underlying all his reactions, all his emotions, was a vague nebula of fear. Trembling for reasons that were not at all clear to him, he dialed Lauren's number, hanging up only after the tenth ring. Even though he had unfinished business in the hospital, he felt the urgent need to get out. He would call Hadawi from home, he decided.

Christine leaned against a doorway and watched David leave. She had no qualms about the rightness of what she had done, but his discouragement was painful for her.

Later, she excused herself from shift report and walked down the deserted corridor to the pay phone. The number she dialed was different from the one she had used the previous day. God, had it only been a day? No voice answered this time—only a click and a tone.

"This is Christine Beall of Boston Doctors Hospital," she said in a measured monotone. "In the name of compassionate medical care and on instructions of The Sisterhood of Life, I have, on October second, helped to end the hopeless pain and suffering of Mrs. Charlotte

Thomas with an intravenous injection of morphine sulfate. The prolongation of unnecessary human suffering is to be despised and to be terminated wherever possible. The dignity of human life and human death are to be preserved at all costs. End of report."

She hung up, then on an irrepressible impulse picked up the receiver and dialed Jerry Crosswaite's number. With the sound of his voice, the impulse vanished.

"Hello," he said. "Hello . . . Hello?"

Christine gently set the receiver back.

In the shadows at the far end of the hall, Janet Poulos observed Christine as she left report and made the call that Janet felt certain was her case report on Charlotte Thomas.

"Sound her out about The Garden," Dahlia had urged. "Be careful what you say, but sound her out."

Janet countered with her belief that Beall was far too new in The Sisterhood to be ready for The Garden, but Dahlia insisted.

"Just remember," she said, "what would have happened to you three years ago had I decided *you* weren't ready. As I recall, you were thinking about taking your own life before I phoned."

In fact, Janet had passed beyond the thinking stage. At the moment of Dahlia's call she had more than a hundred sleeping pills laid out on her bedspread. Self-loathing and a profound sense of impotence had pushed her to the brink of suicide.

For years she had lived on hatred—hatred toward physicians in general and one in particular. She had joined The Sisterhood to use the organization in order to put certain M.D.'s in their place. Where necessary, she had even manufactured data on patients to get the Regional Screening Committee's approval and recommendations.

However, after six years and nearly two dozen cases, what little sustenance she had gained from such activities had disappeared.

Then, with a single phone call, everything had changed. Somehow, Dahlia knew about the falsified laboratory and X-ray reports, about Janet's hatred for physicians and their power, about many intimate details of her life. She knew, but she didn't care.

In the course of the year after she joined The Garden Janet was brought along slowly. Every few weeks Dahlia would transmit the name of a patient in the northeast who had been approved by The Sisterhood for euthanasia. Janet would arrange a meeting with the distraught family of the patient and offer a merciful death for their loved one in exchange for a substantial payment. The contract, once made, was then unwittingly honored by The Sisterhood nurse who had initially proposed the case.

It was a wonderful, lucrative diversion, but The Garden had much, much more in store for Hyacinth. Other flowers blossomed within Doctors Hospital. One of them, Lily, was transplanted from the ranks of The Sisterhood by Janet herself. Soon both women were given other responsibilities, primarily in the area Dahlia referred to as "direct patient contact." They were no longer bound to Sisterhood cases—euthanasia was not a concern; the new cases had proven more rewarding in every sense. John Chapman and Carl Perry were just two of them.

As Christine rang off, Janet moved toward her. Dahlia had reasoned that after handling a case as traumatic as Charlotte Thomas's, Beall might be ready. Hyacinth still had strong doubts. She would talk with the woman, but only until her own suspicions were confirmed. Beall would need a few more years of tongue lashings from physicians who, as often as not, were deadly weapons in their own right. She would need a few more thankless Sisterhood cases.

Then she might be ready.

Christine spotted Janet coming and waited.

"It's done?" Janet asked solemnly. Christine nodded. "Talk for a few minutes?" Again a nod. In silence they walked to the visitors' lounge. Christine dropped onto the sofa and this time Janet sat next to her.

"It's never easy, is it?" Janet folded one leg beneath her and watched as Christine picked at a sliver on the edge of the coffee table.

"I'm okay, Janet. Really. I know what I did—what we're doing—is right. I know how badly Charlotte wanted it to end. Cancer throughtout her liver, and Dr. Huttner wanted to keep sticking tubes in her. It was right." Her voice was strained but under control.

"You'll get no arguments from me, kid," Janet said, reaching over and squeezing her hand reassuringly. Christine squeezed back. "It's just too bad that we're the ones who have to shoulder all the darn responsibility, that's all." Christine responded with a nod and a rueful shrug.

Perhaps Dahlia was right. Janet elected to push a bit further. "All that responsibility, and what do we have to show for it? Nothing."

Christine spun toward her, eyes flashing. "Janet! What on earth do you mean, nothing?"

Time to retreat, Janet decided. For once in her life, at least, Dahlia had misjudged. Beall's naive, idealistic flame had not yet been doused. She took pains to meet Christine's gaze levelly. "I mean that after all these years, after all the hundreds, and now I guess thousands, of Sisterhood recruits, nothing has changed in the attitude of the medical profession."

"Oh." Christine relaxed.

"So until things change, we do what we have to do. Right?"

"Right."

"Listen, Christine. Let's have dinner sometime soon. We have a lot in common, you and I, but this is hardly the place to discuss our mutual interests. Check your schedule and I'll check mine. We'll set something up in the next few days. Okay?"

"Okay. And, Janet, thanks for your concern. I'm sorry I snapped at you. This day's been a bitch, that's all."

Janet smiled warmly. "If you can't snap at your sister, who can you snap at? Right?"

"Right."

Janet rose. "I've got to get Charlotte taken care of. Her husband left word he won't be coming in to see her. Call me at home anytime you need to talk." With a wave she left. At least Dahlia would know she had tried. Beall simply wasn't ready. Too bad.

Christine returned in time for the end of report. Restless and saturated with nursing and with Boston Doctors Hospital, she stood against a wall until the final patient had been discussed, then left before any of the others. Ahead of her, waiting for the elevator, were Janet and an orderly. Between them, on a litter, lay the sheet-covered body of Charlotte Thomas.

Held fast by the scene and her reflections on it, Christine watched as the litter was maneuvered onto the elevator. Not until the doors had closed was she able to move again.

⅄ CHAPTER 10

Fox's GOLDEN LAWS of Medicine defined *pathologist* as "The specialist who learns all by cutting corners to get straight to the heart of the matter, leaving no stone unturned (gall or kidney)."

As usual, the recollection of one of Gerald Fox's immortal definitions forced a smile out of David. This despite his discomfort at the prospect of having to observe the autopsy on Charlotte Thomas.

He was already ten minutes late, but he knew that nothing would be completed except perhaps the preparation of Charlotte's body and the first incision. Although Fox's observations were usually right on the mark, David had never felt that his cynical maxim about pathologists was totally accurate. He thought back to his first exposure to forensic pathology, a lecture given by the county coroner just before David's group of second-year medical students was ushered in to view their first autopsy.

"Cause of death, ladies and gentlemen," the old pathologist had said, "that is what we in forensic medicine are asked to determine for our medical and legal colleagues. In fact, nobody other than God himself knows what causes a person to die. Nobody. Rather what we can determine is the condition of each organ in a patient's body at the time of his or her death. From this knowledge, we can deduce with some accuracy the reason for cessation of cardiac, cerebral, or pulmonary function—the only true causes of death.

"For example. If a patient is killed by a gunshot wound through the heart, we may say quite safely that death was due to cardiac standstill from a penetrating wound to the heart muscle itself. But what of the patient with a disease like cancer? We might be able to locate cancerous tissue in the liver, brain, lungs, or other organs and certainly, in one respect, may say that cancer is the cause of death. Determining the immediate cause, however, is nigh impossible. Did the heart stop because it was poisoned by some as yet unknown substance secreted by the cancerous cells? Or did lack of sufficient fluid volume, for reasons perhaps unrelated to the cancer itself, cause such an impairment in circulation that the heart could no longer function and simply stopped?

"You must keep this in mind whenever you read such diagnoses as 'cancer,' or 'emphysema,' or 'arteriosclerosis' as the cause of a patient's death. They may have been a cause leading to death, but as to the direct cause of death—that, my friends, remains a mystery in the vast majority of cases."

A mystery. David hesitated outside the two opaque glass doors labeled AUTOPSY SUITE in gold-leaf letters. A sleepless night and chaotic morning had left him tense and uneasy. The prospect of Charlotte's autopsy only aggravated those feelings.

Then there was Huttner. Cape Cod was only seventy miles away, close enough for him to make the drive up that morning without much difficulty. Whether or not he would choose to return there after witnessing the autopsy was a different story. David bet himself a long-overdue and much-feared trip to the dentist that Huttner would elect to stay in Boston and resume control of his practice. He had given some thought to turning the bet around so that at least he wouldn't have to face the Novocain and drill if he lost the last two days of his adventure. In the end, however, he decided that if he lost he would be able to submerge the misery of a visit to the tooth merchant in other, more substantial miseries.

Needles of formalin vapor jabbed deep into his nostrils as he entered the suite. It was a long room, nearly twenty-five yards from end to end. High ceilings and an excess of fluorescent light obscured, in part, the fact that there were no windows. Seven steel autopsy tables, each fitted with a water hose and drainage system, were evenly spaced across the ivory-colored linoleum floor. In addition to the hose, used for cleaning organs during an autopsy and the table afterward, every station had its own sink, blackboard, and suspended scale. A large red number, from 1 to 7, inlaid in the floor, was the only characteristic individual to each one. That is, except for Station 4.

On either side of that table six tiers of wooden risers had been built, identical to those in high school gymnasiums. At certain times the risers were filled with students in various stages of distress or fascination. At other times the stands held groups of residents in pathology or surgery, craning to study the dissecting skills of a senior pathologist. Station 4 was the center court of the Doctors Hospital Autopsy Suite.

At 8:15 on the morning of October 3, Stations 1, 4, and 6 were in operation, and a sheet-wrapped body rested on the table at Station 2. Wallace Huttner was standing, arms folded, at Station 4. The risers were empty but for a resident scheduled to post the body on table 2 and three medical students. As David approached, he caught sight of Charlotte's open-mouthed, chalk-colored face. He bit at his lower lip, swallowed a jet of bile, and decided that it would be best to concentrate on the rest of her anatomy. He could deal reasonably well with autopsies as long as he viewed them as examinations of parts of a body. The nearer he allowed himself to get to the human aspect, the more unpleasant the procedure became for him.

Ahmed Hadawi, a quick, dark little man with disproportionately huge hands, had made his initial incision and was elbow-deep in the chest cavity, busily separating the chest and abdominal organs from their attachments to the neck and body wall. He made a soft clucking noise with his tongue as he worked, but otherwise seemed without emotion or expression. Occasionally he bent over and murmured a few words into a pedal-operated Dictaphone.

Huttner nodded coolly in response to David's greeting. His stance and manner bore no hint of the relaxed, interested, almost fatherly physician who had sat with David in the surgeons' lounge just thirty-six hours before. After the nod, he returned his attention to the dissection, carefully avoiding further eye contact. David looked at the man helplessly. Then, as so often happened in difficult situations, the macabre portion of his humor took over. If he hugs himself any tighter, he thought, maybe he'll just break into little pieces and I can cover his practice until someone glues him back together.

At that moment he caught another glimpse of Charlotte's face. "Stop it, Shelton!" he screamed at himself. "This isn't funny. Just stop it!" The mental slap was enough. He shifted his weight several times from side to side, then settled down, his attention focused on the pathologist.

"Now, then, we are ready to take a look at some things," Hadawi said. The resident stepped down from the risers to get a better view and

Huttner tightened his autoembrace a notch as the pathologist began pointing out the anatomical status of each of Charlotte's organs as they existed at the instant of her death.

"The heart," he began, "is moderately enlarged, with thickening of the muscle and dilatation of all chambers. There is a small, fresh puncture wound through the anterior left ventricle, which I assume is the result of Dr. Shelton's commendably accurate intracardiac injection."

David thought that the moment might be right for a modest smile and nod, but then realized that no one was looking at him. He smiled and nodded anyway.

The little pathologist continued speaking as he dissected. "There is fairly advanced narrowing of all coronary arteries, although there is no gross evidence of recent damage such as might be caused by a myocardial infarction." Margaret Armstrong's interpretation of Charlotte's electrocardiogram had been right on the button, David noted. "Keep in mind," Hadawi added, "that evidence of an acute infarction—say, less than twenty-four hours old—is often seen only in microscopic examination of the heart muscle itself, and then only if we happen to catch just the right section."

"I want to be notified as soon as those slides have been examined," Huttner ordered, more, it seemed to David, out of a need to make some kind of statement than anything else. Hadawi glanced up at him and, with no more acknowledgment than that, turned his attention to the lungs. Immediately his stock as reflected in David's eyes rose several points. Both lungs were more than half consolidated by the heavy fluid of infection. Even if there had been no other problems, it seemed entirely possible that Charlotte would have been unable to survive her extensive pneumonia.

The remainder of the examination was impressive mainly for what it did not show. Pending, of course, microscopic examination of the abdominal lymph nodes, Hadawi announced that he was unable to find any evidence of residual cancer in the woman's body. The liver cysts, which had been misdiagnosed by the radiologist, Rybicki, were scattered throughout the organ, and similar fluid-filled sacs were found in both kidneys. "Polycystic involvement of hepatic and renal parenchyma," Hadawi said into his Dictaphone.

Finally the pathologist stepped away from the table. "I have a few remaining things to do on this body," he said, "but they will have no bearing on my findings. To all intents and purposes, Wally, we are done. Most significant of what I have to tell you is that this woman's pressure sore was extending beneath her skin to the point where I doubt that even with multiple grafts it ever would have healed. Infection of the sacral bones had already begun and would have been almost impossible to treat.

"She has enough coronary arteriosclerosis so that I feel her final event was probably a cardiac one. I intend to sign her out as cardiovascular collapse secondary to her pulmonary and bedsore infections. An additional stress undoubtedly came from her partial small bowel obstruction, which, as you saw, was due to adhesions from her recent surgery."

David said, "Dr. Hadawi, Dr. Huttner, if we could sit down over here, there are a few questions that I have." He could not bear the thought of having to discuss Charlotte's case over her dissected body. Hadawi responded with a brief, understanding grin and took a seat on one of the risers. Huttner, who still held his arms around himself, followed reluctantly. David gauged the expression on his face as somewhere between disgust and fury. Nowhere in his eyes or manner was there a hint of disappointment or sympathy. Regardless of her underlying disease, Charlotte Thomas had walked into the hospital as Huttner's patient, had been operated on, and had died. That made her a postoperative mortality. Her operation and the many complications that ensued would be discussed in depth at Surgical Death Rounds. Hardly a prospect that would sit well with this man, David realized. He was far more accustomed to asking the questions than to answering them.

"Now, David," Hadawi said, "just what is it that troubles you about what you have seen?"

"Well, most of my concern centers about her heart, which seemed so unresponsive to everything that I tried during her Code Ninety-nine. It may have been simply that too much time elapsed between the moment of her cardiac arrest and the time I started working on her, but it just doesn't feel like that. I wonder if perhaps her potassium could somehow have risen too high and caused a fatal cardiac arrhythmia."

"That is always a possibility," Hadawi said patiently. "I've saved several vials of blood. I'll be happy to have her potassium level checked. However, you must keep in mind the limits of accuracy of such a measurement done in a postmortem patient—especially one who has received prolonged external cardiac compression."

Finally Huttner spoke. It was no surprise to David that he was unwilling to surrender without a fight. "Look, Ahmed," he said. His second and third fingers bobbed up and down at the man, but Hadawi showed no outward hint of being offended by the gesture. "I'm not totally satisfied with all this. Dr. Shelton here has a point. Since there's nothing obvious on gross exam to explain this woman's sudden death, then we should look further before signing her out as something so nonspecific as cardiovascular collapse. Maybe some nurse made a medication error on her and caused an allergic, anaphylactic reaction of some kind. She was known to be allergic to penicillin."

Hadawi was obviously used to dealing with Huttner's ego. He merely shrugged and said, "If you wish, I shall be happy to order a penicillin level on her blood. Is there anything else you would like?"

Huttner seized the chance to avoid a Surgical Death Rounds presentation as a drowning sailor might grasp a passing chunk of drift-wood. A medication error would provide him with instant absolution.

"Yes, there are some other things I think should be done," Huttner said with a professorial tone that included several significant pauses. He seemed actually to be savoring his own words. "I think she should have a complete chemical screen. Antibiotic levels, electrolytes, toxins—the works."

"With no specific idea of what we're searching for, that will be quite expensive," Hadawi said softly, as if anticipating the eruption that would follow even this mild objection.

"Damn the money, man," Huttner fired, his fingers jabbing even faster than before. "This is a human life we're talking about here. You just do the damn tests and get me the results."

"As you wish, Wally."

Huttner nodded his satisfaction, then started to leave. As he passed David, he snapped his fingers. "I almost forgot, David," he said over his shoulder. "The Cape Vascular Conference really wasn't all that it was cut out to be. I've decided not to go back. Thank you for your help yesterday. I think there's a meeting in January I might want to attend. Perhaps we can work out another coverage arrangement then."

His voice, David thought, held every bit as much sincerity as Don Juan saying, "Of course I'll respect you in the morning."

CHAPTER 11

IN HIS SELECTION of a hospital, as in all the other affairs in his life, Senator Richard Cormier was his own man. While many Washington politicians considered it a status symbol to be cared for at Bethesda Naval or Walter Reed, Cormier overruled the objections of his aides and insisted that he be operated on by Dr. Louis Ketchem at Boston Doctors. "Always trust your own kind," he said. "Louie's an old war-horse just like me. Either he does the cutting or I don't get cut."

The walls of Cormier's room were covered top to bottom with cards, and cartons containing several hundred more were stacked neatly in one corner. In addition to a nurse and the senator, the presence of a secretary and two aides helped to create an atmosphere almost as chaotic as that perpetually found in his Washington office.

"Senator Cormier, I must give you your preop meds, and these people will have to leave your room." The nurse, an ample matron named Fuller, projected just the right amount of authority to get the senator to comply with the request.

Cormier ran his fingers through his thick, silver hair and squinted up at the nurse. "Ten more minutes."

"Two," she said firmly.

"Five." The bargaining brought a sparkle to his eyes.

"All right, five," she said. "But one minute longer and I use the square needle to give you this medication." She bustled out of the room, turning at the doorway to give Cormier a glare that said she was serious. The senator winked at her.

"Okay, Beth, time to get packed up," he said to his secretary. "Remember, I want a thank-you sent to everyone who put a return address on his card. I signed what seemed like a thousand of them yesterday, but if you run out, have some more printed up and I'll sign them after the operation. Gary, call Lionel Herbert and tell him to fly up here for a meeting the day after tomorrow. Tell him to be prepared to make some concessions on that energy package or, by God, it's back to the drawing board again for his boss and those oil people he's so damn friendly with. Bobby, call my niece and tell her I'm fine, not to worry, and, most of all, not to be upset that she couldn't leave the kids to fly here. I'll call her myself as soon as they let me back near my phone. Oh, and Bobby, have you got all the names of people who sent flowers? I want to send each of them a personal note. Do you think it would hurt anyone's feelings if I told them to send candy next time? This place looks like a funeral parlor and smells like a bordello."

Bobby Crisp, a young lawyer as sharp and eager as his name, smiled over at his boss. "You must be getting more confidence in me, Senator," he said. "This is only the fourth time you've told me to do the same thing. Back when I first started working for you, it was seven. Everything's taken care of. I'll have the list ready for you as soon as you're ready to write, which will probably be half an hour after you come out of the anesthesia, if I know you. By the way, do you know someone named Camellia?"

"Who?" Cormier asked.

"Camellia. See those pink and white flowers over there on the table? They came this morning with a note that just said 'Thank you for everything. Camellia.' "

"Men," Beth said scornfully. "Those pink and white flowers, as you call them, *are* camellias. Let me see that note." She read it and shrugged. "That's what it says, all right."

"Thanks for checking," Crisp said. "I got low marks in reading throughout law school."

"Now, now, settle down, you two," Cormier said. He rubbed his chin. "Camellia's a strange enough name so that I should remember it. Camellias from Camellia, eh? . . ." His voice drifted off as he tried to connect the name with a person. Finally he shook his head. "Well, I guess a little memory lapse here and there is a small price to pay for the frustration I'm able to cause on The Hill with the rest of my senility. Whoever she is, she'll just have to live without a thank-you note."

At that moment Mrs. Fuller reappeared at the door. "I said five minutes, and it's already more than that," she said. "I swear, Senator, you are the most obstinate, cantankerous patient I've ever had."

"Okay, okay, we're done," Cormier said, waving the other three out of his room. "You know, Mrs. Fuller, if you don't sweeten up soon, you're going to move from the sleek cruiser class into the battle-ax category." He smiled at her and added, "But even then you'll still be my favorite nurse. Go easy with that needle, now."

The nurse swabbed at a place on Cormier's left buttock and gave him the injection of preoperative medication. Fifteen minutes later, his mouth began feeling dry and a warm glow of detachment crept over him. Like the beacon from a lighthouse, the corridor ceiling lights flashed past as he was wheeled to the operating room.

Louis Ketchem was a towering, slope-shouldered veteran of more than twenty-five years as a surgeon. Over that span he had performed hundreds of gall bladder operations. None had ever gone any smoother than Senator Richard Cormier's. The removal of the inflamed, stone-filled sac was uneventful except for the usual amount of bleeding from the adjacent liver. As he had done hundreds of times, Ketchem ordered a unit of blood to be transfused over the last half hour of the operation.

The anesthesiologist, John Singleberry, took the plastic bag of blood from the circulating nurse, a young woman named Jacqueline Miller. He double-checked the number on the bag before attaching it to the intravenous line. To speed the infusion, he slipped an air sleeve around the bag and pumped it up. Cormier, deeply anesthetized and receiving oxygen by a respirator, slept a dreamless sleep as the blood wound down the tubing toward his arm like a crimson serpent.

At the instant the blood slid beneath the green paper drape, Jacqueline Miller turned away. The drug she had been instructed to use, the drug she had injected into the plastic bag, was ouabain, the fastest acting and most powerful form of digitalis—a drug so rapidly cleared from the bloodstream, so difficult to find on chemical analysis, that even the massive doses she had used were virtually undetectable. Three minutes were all the ouabain required.

Without warning the cardiac monitor pattern leapt from slow and regular to totally chaotic. John Singleberry glanced at the golden light slashing up and down on the screen overhead and spent several seconds staring at it in disbelief.

"Holy shit, Louis," Singleberry screamed. "He's fibrillating!"

Ketchem, who had not encountered a cardiac arrest in the operating room in years, stood paralyzed, both hands still inside Cormier's abdomen. His orders, when he was finally able to give them, were inadequate. But for the work of the nurses, including Jacqueline Miller, several minutes might have passed with no definitive action. Sterile drapes were quickly stuffed into the incision and two unsuccessful countershocks were given. Seconds later, the monitor pattern showed a straight line.

Without warning Ketchem grabbed a scalpel, extended his incision, and slashed an opening through the bottom of Cormier's diaphragm. Reaching through the opening, he grasped the man's heart and began rhythmically squeezing. A nurse ran for help, but everyone in the operating room already knew it was over. Ketchem pumped, then stopped and checked the monitor. Straight line. He pumped some more.

For twenty minutes he pumped, with absolutely no effect on the golden light. Finally he stopped. For more than a minute no one in the room moved. Ketchem bit down on his lower lip and peered over his mask at the body of his friend. Then two nurses took him by the arms and helped him move away from the operating table, back to the surgeons' lounge.

Off to one side, Jacqueline Miller closed her eyes, fearing they might reflect the excited smile beneath her mask. The greatest adventure in her life was ending in triumph. Oh, Dahlia had told her where to go and what to say, but *she* had been the one to actually pull it off. Little Jackie Miller, ordering around one of the richest, most powerful oilmen in the world.

She tingled at the irony of it all: from girlhood in a squalid tenement to a secret meeting in Oklahoma with the president of Beecher Oil. What would Mr. Jed Beecher have said if he knew that the woman who was giving him instructions, the woman who was taking his quarter of a million dollars, the woman who was dictating his every move had just taken her first airplane flight.

Jacqueline silently cheered the good fortune that had brought Dahlia and The Garden into her life. She still knew little about either of them, but for the present she really didn't care. When Dahlia was ready to disclose her identity, she would, and that was all there was to that. As long as the excitement and the monthly payments were there, Camellia would do what she was asked and keep her eyes and ears open for cases that might be of interest to The Garden. As for The Sisterhood of Life, they would simply have to survive without any further participation from Jackie Miller. No more free rides.

Mexico. Jamaica. Greece. Paris. Jacqueline ticked the places off in her mind. One more case like this one, and she would be able to see all of them. The prospects were dizzying.

Behind her on the narrow operating table, covered to the neck by a sheet, Senator Richard Cormier looked as he had throughout his operation. But his dreamless sleep would last forever.

⋀ CHAPTER 12

"LADIES AND GENTLEMEN, if you would all find seats, we can get started and hopefully make it through this inquiry in a reasonable amount of time."

Like an aging movie queen, the Morris Tweedy Amphitheater of Boston Doctors Hospital had handled the inexorable pressure of passing years with grace and style. Although undeniably frayed around the edges, the cozy, domed lecture hall still held its place proudly atop the thrice-renovated West Wing. There was a time when the seventy-five steeply banked seats of "The Amphi" had accommodated nearly the entire hospital staff—nurses, physicians, and students. However, in 1929, after almost fifty years of service, it had been replaced as the hospital's major lecture and demonstration hall by a considerably larger amphitheater constructed in the Southeast Wing basement.

Hours upon hours of heated argument on the pros and cons of demolishing the jaded siren ended abruptly in 1952 when the state legislature designated the structure an historic landmark. Her stained glass skylights, severe wooden seats, and bas-relief sculptures depicting significant events in medical history were thus preserved for new generations of eager physicians-in-training.

But, despite a century of continuous service, never had the Morris Tweedy Amphitheater entertained a session such as the one for which this milling group of fifty men and women was assembled. It was eight o'clock on the evening of Sunday, October 5—two days after the postmortem examination on Charlotte Thomas.

As hospital chief of staff, Dr. Margaret Armstrong sat behind a heavy oak table facing the arc of seats. Beside her, attempting to bring some order to the room, was Detective Lieutenant John Dockerty.

Dockerty was a thin, rumpled man in his late forties. He wore a gabardine suit that appeared large for him by at least two sizes. His limp green eyes scanned the hall, then turned to a sheaf of papers on the table in front of him. As he looked down, an errant wisp of thinning, reddish brown hair dropped over one eye. He absently swept the strands back in place, only to repeat the ritual moments later.

His languid, almost distracted air suggested he had encountered most of what there was in life to see. In fact, he had spent more than fifteen years on the Boston police force carefully cultivating that demeanor and learning how best to utilize it.

He looked over the hall again, then spoke to Margaret Armstrong out of the corner of his mouth. "This group is obviously much more adept at giving orders than they are at taking them."

Armstrong laughed her agreement, then banged a notebook on the table several times. "Would you all please sit down," she called out. "If we can't show Lieutenant Dockerty cooperation, at least we can show him manners." In less than a minute, everyone had found a place.

The hospital administrator sat to one side of the hall surrounded by his assistants. He was a paunchy, foppish man who had run away from his Brooklyn home at age seventeen and changed his name from Isaac Lifshitz to Edward Lipton III. For years he had kept his job by pitting his enemies against one another in a way so skillful that none of them ever had the unified backing needed to push for his ouster.

On the other side of the room were clustered the men and women who comprised the hospital board of trustees. The men, a homogeneous, patrician lot, were vastly more concerned with the impact that their trustee position might have on their Who's Who listings than with the influence that they might have on Boston Doctors Hospital. The token black on the board was distinguishable from the others only by color, and the four women were not distinguishable at all. The inquiry marked the first time in recent memory that the entire twenty-four-member board was present for a meeting.

Midway up the center aisle, Wallace Huttner sat with Ahmed Hadawi and the other members of the Medical Staff Executive Committee. Joining that group, occupying the chair just to Huttner's right, was Peter Thomas.

The back of the amphitheater was the domain of the nurses. Eight of them, all in street clothes, formed a rosette around Dotty Dalrymple, who appeared volcanic in a plain black dress. Janet Poulos was there, along with Christine Beall, Winnie Edgerly, and several other nurses from Four South, including Angela Martin.

On the right-hand side of the hall, several rows behind Edward Lipton III, sat David. He sat alone until the very last minute, when Howard Kim, the anesthesiologist who had helped with Charlotte's unsuccessful resuscitation, lumbered down the stairs and squeezed into the chair next to him.

John Dockerty had drawn up the guest list for the evening. Dr. Armstrong had made the arrangements.

"I want to thank you all for coming," Dockerty began. "You must believe me that inquiries such as the one I have requested tonight occur much more frequently on *Columbo* and in Agatha Christie novels than they do in actual police work. However, I want to move forward as quickly as possible on the matter of Charlotte Thomas, a matter involving all of you in one way or another. Theatrics have never been my bag, so to speak, but this meeting seemed like the most effective way for me to gather the preliminary information I need, while at the same time keeping all interested parties informed. In the next few days I'll be contacting some of you for individual questioning." He looked down at Margaret Armstrong, who nodded her approval of his opening remarks. Then, sweeping his hair back in place, Dockerty called Ahmed Hadawi and motioned him to a seat angled across from the oak table, so that the pathologist could look at him without completely turning his back to the audience.

"Dr. Hadawi, will you please review for us your involvement in the case of Charlotte Thomas?" Dockerty asked.

Hadawi spread a few sheets of notes in front of him, then said, "On October third I performed a postmortem examination on the woman in question. The gross examination showed that she had a deep pressure sore over her sacrum, moderately advanced coronary artery narrowing, and an extensive pneumonia. It was my initial impression that she had died from sudden cardiac arrest caused by her infections and the generally debilitated condition resulting from her two operations."

"Dr. Hadawi, is that your impression now?" Dockerty asked.

"No, it is not. The patient's physicians, Dr. Wallace Huttner and Dr. David Shelton, were present at the autopsy. They requested a detailed chemical analysis of her blood."

"Help me out here, Dr. Hadawi," Dockerty cut in. "Don't you do these chemical analyses routinely on each—er—patient?"

Hadawi smiled sardonically and folded his hands on the table. "I wish that were possible," he said. "Unfortunately, the cost of postmortem examinations must be borne by the institution involved, and it is hardly an inexpensive proposition, what with sophisticated tissue stains, clerical help, and all else that is required. While we would never knowingly omit a critical stain or test, we of the pathology department must nevertheless temper our zeal with judgment that will enable us to stay within our budget." He paused for a moment and gave a prolonged, hostile look at Edward Lipton III.

"Please proceed," Dockerty said, scribbling a few words on the pad in front of him.

Hadawi referred to his notes. "Of the many chemical analyses that were done, two came back with abnormally high levels. The first of these, potassium, was seven-point-four, where the upper limit of normal is five-point-zero. The second was her blood morphine level, which was elevated far above that found in a patient receiving the usual doses of morphine sulfate for pain."

"Dr. Hadawi, would you please give us your impression of these findings?" Dockerty's voice was free of even the slightest hint of tension.

"Well, my impression of the potassium elevation—and please keep in mind that it is an opinion—is that it is artificially high, a reflection of events occurring in the tissues during and just after the cardiac arrest. The morphine elevation is an entirely different story. Without question, the level measured in this woman was critically high. Easily, although not necessarily, high enough to have caused cessation of respiration and, ultimately, death."

Dockerty spent a few seconds distractedly combing his hair with his fingers. "Doctor, you imply that death was caused by an overdosage of morphine." Hadawi nodded. "Tell me, do you think an overdose of this magnitude could have been accidental?"

Hadawi drew in a short breath, looked at the detective, then shook his head. "No," he said. "No, I do not believe that is possible."

There was not a whisper or movement in the amphitheater. For several seconds Dockerty allowed the eerie silence to hold sway. Then he said softly, "That, ladies and gentlemen, makes Charlotte Thomas's death murder. And her murder is why we are assembled here." Again silence. This time, Hadawi shifted uncomfortably in his seat, anxious to be done with his part.

"Thank you for your help, Doctor," Dockerty said to him. As Hadawi stood to go, the detective added, "Oh, one more small thing. You mentioned that the chemical tests were ordered by Mrs. Thomas's doctors, ah"—he glanced at his notes—"Dr. Huttner and Dr. Shelton. Do you remember specifically which one of them actually asked for the tests?"

Hadawi's dark eyes narrowed as he searched Dockerty's face for some hint of the significance in his question. Finally, with a bewildered shrug, he said, "Well, as I recall, Dr. Shelton requested the potassium level. The rest of the tests were ordered by Dr. Huttner."

Dockerty nodded the pathologist back to his row, whispering another "Thank you" at the same time. He searched the hall for a moment and was facing away from David when he said, "Dr. Shelton?"

Howard Kim reached up a massive paw and patted David on the back as he inched sideways past the giant and into the aisle. David had known for a day about the abnormal blood tests, had even heard the wildfire rumor around the wards that some kind of police investigation was under way. Although Dr. Armstrong had not told him that he would be asked to make a statement, he was not at all surprised to be called by the detective.

Dockerty smiled, shook his hand firmly, motioned him to the seat vacated by Hadawi, and then, seeming at times disinterested, led him minute by minute through the events that followed Charlotte Thomas's cardiac arrest. Gradually David's statements became free-flowing and animated. Dockerty's style made it easy for him to talk. Soon he was sharing information with the disheveled lieutenant in the relaxed manner of two friends in an alehouse. Then, without changing the pace or tone of their conversation, Dockerty said, "Tell me, Dr. Shelton. I understand that shortly before Mrs. Thomas was found by you to be without pulse or respiration, you had a discussion about her and about seriously ill patients in general with Dr. Armstrong here and some of the nurses—namely, ah"—he consulted his notes—"nurses Edgerly, Gold, and Beall. Do you mind telling me what you had to say in that discussion?"

For five seconds, ten, fifteen, David was unable to speak. The question didn't fit. It made no sense unless . . . His mind began spinning through the implications of Dockerty's question to Hadawi as to which doctor had actually ordered the test that had disclosed the high morphine level. The indefinable sense of fear, so vague among his feelings that night on Four South, now thundered through him. His temples began to throb. His hands grew stiff and numb. *Holy shit, he's going after me! He's going after me!*

At that moment he realized that Dockerty's eyes had changed from liquid to steel and were locked on him, probing, gauging, boring in. David knew it had already taken him too long—far too long—to react to the question. He inhaled deeply and fought the panic. Loosen up and stop reading so much into this, he thought. Just tell the man what he wants to know.

"Dr. Shelton, do you recall the incident I'm asking about?" The elaborate patience in Dockerty's voice had a cutting edge.

Even before he answered, David sensed that his words would be stammered and clumsy. They were. Expressing his thoughts around "er's" and "ah's," he said, "I simply told them . . . that a patient who is . . . in great pain with little hope of surviving his illness might . . . might be treated with some temperance. Especially if the therapy planned is . . . particularly painful or . . . dehumanizing . . . such as being put on a respirator." He battled back the urge to say more, consciously avoiding the panicked talking that comes with trying to explain an explanation.

Dockerty ran his tongue slowly over his teeth. He bounced the eraser end of his pencil on the table. He scratched his head. "Dr. Shelton," he said finally, "don't you think that withholding treatment from a sick patient is a form of mercy killing? Of euthanasia?"

"No, I don't think it's a form of any kind of killing." Molten drops of anger began to smolder beneath his fear. His voice grew strained. His words came too rapidly. "It is good, sensitive clinical judgment. It is what being a doctor is all about. For God's sake, I've never advocated shutting off a respirator or giving anything lethal to a patient."

"Never?" Dockerty delivered the spark softly.

David exploded. "Dammit, Lieutenant, I've had more than enough of your insinuations!" He was totally oblivious now to all the others in the amphitheater. "If you have an accusation to make, then make it. And while you're at it, explain why I was the one who kept saying that something wasn't right during the resuscitation. Why I was the one who requested the potass . . ." The word froze in his mouth. He realized even before Dockerty spoke, what the detective was driving at. "Damn," he hissed his frustration.

"I have had the chance, Dr. Shelton, to speak briefly with some of the other physicians and nurses who were with you in Charlotte Thomas's room. Like you, several of them were concerned that something was not completely right. Apparently the problem was obvious enough for others besides you to pick up on it. Whether or not they would have gone so far as to ask for blood tests on this woman, we'll never know because you did. At least, for the potassium you did."

"And you're trying to say I did that to cover myself and to insure that nobody thought about anything like morphine?" Dockerty shrugged. "This is ridiculous! I mean this is really crazy," David cried.

"Dr. Shelton," Dockerty said calmly. "Please get hold of yourself. I am not accusing you or anyone else of anything."

"Yet," David spat out.

"Excuse me?"

"Nothing. Are you finished with me?"

"Yes, thank you." Once again Dockerty appeared as mechanical as he had throughout most of the inquiry. As David stalked back to his seat, he noticed that halfway up the center aisle. Wallace Huttner sat staring at him with icy, metallic eyes. Involuntarily, he shuddered.

Dockerty whispered with Dr. Armstrong for several seconds, then called Dorothy Dalrymple. The nursing director extracted herself from her seat with the side-to-side movements of a cork coming free from its bottle. Once released from her chair, she glided down the aisle steps with paradoxical grace. A feminine handshake with Dockerty, then she adjusted herself on the oak chair and smiled that she was ready.

Dockerty led her through a description of Charlotte Thomas's appearance over the day prior to her death as summarized in the nurses' notes. "The nurses' notes are generally written at the end of each shift," Dalrymple explained. "Therefore, the notes from the October second evening shift were not done until after the patient's death. However, the nurse who cared for Mrs. Thomas that night, Miss Christine Beall, saw her at seven o'clock, approximately two hours before her death. Her excellent note states that the patient was—and I quote now—'alert, oriented, and somewhat less depressed than she has been recently.' Miss Beall further writes that her vital signs—pulse, respiration, temperature, and blood pressure—were all stable." Dalrymple swung her massive shoulders and head toward the audience and peered up to where the nurses were grouped. "Miss Beall," she called out, "do you have anything to add to what I have told the lieutenant?"

Christine, who had been totally depressed and distracted since David's outburst, was not paying attention. She had learned about the discovery of morphine in Charlotte's body less than twenty-four hours before. The information had come via a telephone call from Peg, the nurse who had asked her to evaluate Charlotte Thomas in the first place. "Christine, I want to keep you abreast of as much as we know of what is going on here without worrying you unduly," the woman had said. "There is going to be some kind of inquiry on the case tomorrow night, I've been told. A policeman will be there. However, your Sister, Janet Poulos, has reviewed your notes in the patient's chart. There is nothing there, she feels, that will in any way implicate you. It is our belief that the investigation will be a short-lived and fruitless one, and that Charlotte Thomas's death will be attributed to the work of an individual whose name and motives will never be discovered. All Sisterhood operations at your hospital will be curtailed indefinitely, and before long the entire matter should just blow over. You are in no danger whatsoever, Christine—please believe that."

Christine, lips pressed tightly together, was staring up into the blue and gold dome when Dalrymple addressed her.

Several seats away, Janet Poulos watched helplessly, every muscle tensed by the prospect of Christine leaping to her feet, shouting her confession to the hall, then crying out the only other Sisterhood name she knew: Janet's. God, she wished there had been enough warning to call Dahlia. Dahlia would have known exactly how to handle things.

Janet's gaze moved past Christine to where Angela Martin sat, cool blue eyes fixed on the scene below, golden hair immaculately in place. The woman was absolutely nerveless. Even if it had been her name that Christine Beall knew, Janet doubted that Angela would have been ruffled. Almost ten years as members of The Sisterhood and they had never even known one another. Now they were best friends, sharing the excitement and rewards of The Garden and speculating about the mysterious woman who had brought them together.

Janet scanned the hall and wondered if Dahlia had eyes and ears present other than Lily's and Hyacinth's. Quite possibly, she acknowledged. The woman remained only a whispered voice on the telephone, but time and again Janet had been impressed with her cold logic and endless sources of information. Because of her The Garden was growing steadily—in other hospitals as well as in Boston Doctors. Anywhere there was a Sisterhood of Life member, there was a potential flower. Dahlia believed that more than anything else. The bottom line of both movements was the same: nurse and patient alone in a room. She had, perhaps, been hasty about Beall, but she remained a woman of near-perfect judgment whom Janet wanted desperately to know.

Powerless for the moment, Janet slid back in her seat and watched.

"Miss Beall?" Dalrymple called again. Winnie Edgerly nudged Christine. "I asked if you had anything to add to what I have told the lieutenant."

Christine swallowed. Once, then again. Still, when she tried to speak only a sandpaper rasp emerged. She cleared her throat and tightened her grip on the arms of her seat.

"I'm sorry," she managed. "No, I have nothing to add."

Janet sighed relief and closed her eyes. Beall had come through.

Christine looked down to where David sat, head resting on one hand, staring vacantly at Dalrymple and Dockerty. She could feel as much as see his isolation. In fact, she realized, she too was isolated. Despite the calls from Peg, despite the words from Janet and the knowledge that the vast Sisterhood of Life was behind her, Christine felt marooned. At that moment she wanted to run to him and somehow reassure him. To tell him that she, above all people, knew he had nothing to do with Charlotte's death. "Everything will be all right," she told herself over and over again. "Just leave things alone and they will be all right." She forced her concentration back to the scene being played out below her.

"Miss Dalrymple," Dockerty continued, "you have a list of the medications given to Mrs. Thomas?"

Dalrymple nodded. "She was receiving chloramphenicol, which is an antibiotic, and Demerol, which is an analgesic."

"No morphine?"

"No morphine," she echoed, shaking her head for emphasis.

"No morphine . . ." Dockerty let the word drift away, but his voice was nonetheless loud enough for all those present to hear. "Tell me," he said, "is it possible for one of the nurses or other hospital personnel to have gotten his hands on morphine sulfate in the quantities Dr. Hadawi has suggested were given Mrs. Thomas?"

Dalrymple thought the question through before answering. "The answer to your question is, of course, that anyone can get his hands on any drug if he has enough money and is willing to go outside the legal channels to do so. However, I can state that it would be virtually impossible for one of my nurses—or anyone else for that matter—to get away with more than a tiny quantity of narcotics from the hospital. You see, only a small amount of injectable narcotic is kept on each floor, and that is rigidly counted by two nurses at each shift change—one from the group that is leaving and one from the group that is coming on. The night nursing supervisor has access to the hospital pharmacy, but even there the narcotics are locked up securely and only the hospital pharmacists have keys.

"So," she concluded, shifting her bulk in the chair and folding her hands in a large, puffy ball, "assuming a legal source, only a pharmacist or a physician could obtain a sizable amount of morphine at a single time."

Dockerty nodded and again conferred in whispers with Dr. Armstrong. "Miss Dalrymple," he said finally, "do the nurses' notes indicate whether or not there were any visitors to Charlotte Thomas's room on the night of her death?"

"Visitors to a patient's room, other than physicians, are not usually recorded in nurses' notes. However, I can tell you that none were mentioned."

"Not even the physician who found Mrs. Thomas without pulse or respiration?" Dockerty asked.

Dalrymple's expression suggested that she did not at all approve of the detective's oblique reference. "No," she said deliberately. "There was no mention of Dr. Shelton entering the patient's room. However, I hasten to add that most of the nurses were on break at the time of the cardiac arrest. There was no one on the floor at the time to see him arrive."

Dockerty seemed to ignore her last point. "That will be all, thank you very much," he said. As he nodded the woman back to her seat, David again ignited.

"Lieutenant, I've had just about enough of this!" He stumbled to his feet and braced himself against the seat back in front of him. To his left Howard Kim's moonface looked up at him impassively. "I don't understand why you think what you do or even what you are driving at, but let me state here and now that I would never administer a drug or any treatment to a patient for the express purpose of harming him in any way." In the seconds that followed David heard his tiny mental voice telling him that, once again, he was sailing on his own words toward a maelstrom.

"Sit down, for Christ's sake," the voice kept saying. "He can't hurt you, dummy. Only *you* can hurt you. Sit down and shut up!"

Mounting rage and panic snuffed out the voice. His words were strangled. "Why me? Surely there are others—her husband, relatives, friends who were in that room before I was. Why are you accusing me?"

"Dr. Shelton," Dockerty said evenly, "I have not accused you of anything. I said that before. But since you brought it up, Professor Thomas was teaching a seminar that evening. Twenty-three students. Seven to ten P.M. And, as far as he knows, no other visitors were scheduled to see his wife. Now, if I've answered your questions, we can proceed with—"

"No!" David shouted. "This whole inquiry is a sham. Some kind of perverse kangaroo court. A first-year law student could conduct a more impartial hearing than this. If you want to railroad me into something, then do it in court, where at least you have to answer to a judge." He stopped, grasping for some morsel of self-control. Inside him, the voice resumed. "Don't you see, dummy, this whole inquiry was a setup to get you to do exactly what you have gone and done. I tried to tell you to keep cool, but you don't even know how, do you?"

"Very well," Dockerty said. "I think we've heard enough for now. I'll be contacting some of you individually in the near future. Thank you all for coming." He whispered some final words to Dr. Armstrong, then packed his notes together and left the hall without so much as a glance at the pale statue that was David.

By the time David had calmed enough to release the wooden seat back and look around, the Morris Tweedy Amphitheater was nearly empty. Christine and the other nurses had gone. So had Howard Kim. As he scanned the back of the hall, his gaze met Wallace Huttner's. The tall surgeon's eyes narrowed. Then, with a derisive shake of his head, he turned and strode out, arm in arm with Peter Thomas.

David stood alone, staring up at the glowing red EXIT sign over the rear door, when a hand touched his shoulder. He whirled and met the concerned, blue eyes of Margaret Armstrong.

"Are you all right?" she asked.

"Yeah, sure, great." He made no attempt to clear the huskiness in his voice.

"David, I am so sorry for what just happened here. If I had known how heavily Lieutenant Dockerty was going to pounce on you, I never would have allowed the whole thing to happen. He said he wanted to check the spontaneous reactions of several people. You were just one of them. All of a sudden you erupted, and there wasn't even a chance for me to . . ." She gave up trying to explain. "Look, David," she went on finally, "I like you very much. Have since the day you got here. Just give me the benefit of a hearing. After what's just happened to you, I know that won't be easy, but please try. I want to help."

David looked at her, then bit back his anger and nodded.

"How about an hour or so at Popeye's?" Her smile was warm and sincere.

"Popeye's it is," David said, picking up his jacket. Together the new allies left the hospital.

Popeye's, a local landmark, had seen nearly thirty years of doctors and nurses bringing their problems and their lives to its tables. Outside the tavern an animated neon sign, the pride and joy of the management, depicted characters from the comic strip chasing Wimpy and his arm-load of hamburgers across the building. As they entered, David caught sight of four of the nurses who had been at the inquiry. Neither Dotty Dalrymple nor Christine was among them.

"I haven't been here in years," Dr. Armstrong said after they had settled at a rear table. "My husband and I courted in some of these booths. Nothing has really changed except for that garish sign outside."

David noted that she wore no wedding ring. "Is your husband living?" he asked.

"Arne? No, he died eight, no, nine years ago."

"Oh, yes, how stupid of me," David said, remembering that he, like everyone else at Doctors Hospital, knew she was the widow of Arne Armstrong, a world famous neurophysiologist and a possible Nobel laureate, had he lived long enough to complete his work. "I'm sorry."

"Don't be silly . . ." Dr. Armstrong said, stopping in midsentence as a shapely blonde in a black miniskirt and skintight red sweater arrived to take their order. "I'll have a beer, a draft. And my date here?" She smiled over at David.

"Coke," he said. "Extra large, lots of ice."

The waitress left and Armstrong looked at David. "Not even with all that's happened to you tonight?"

She knew. Of course she knew. Everyone did. But she wasn't testing him. There was, David realized, admiration in her voice.

"It's been nearly eight years since I touched a drop of alcohol. Or a pill," he added. "It's going to take a hell of a lot more than Dockerty could ever dish out to get me back there. Even though I'm sure my teeth will finally vaporize from all the cola I consume." His voice drifted away. Thoughts of John Dockerty staring placidly through him were followed by images of other confrontations he had been forced to endure over the years since Ginny and Becky were killed.

As if reading his thoughts, Armstrong said, "David, you know that I'm aware of much that has happened to you in the past." He nodded. "You should be aware, then, that Lieutenant Dockerty also knows. I am not sure how he learned so much so quickly, but he is very good at his job, I think. And you know what a giant glass house a hospital is. Everybody's life is everybody else's business and what people can't gossip about with certainty, they usually contrive simply to fill in the gaps."

David gave a single, rueful laugh. "I've been the center of hospital rumor before," he said. "I know exactly what you mean. This time, though, it's not just harmless speculation. I would never set out to hurt anyone, let alone murder him."

"No need to tell me," she said. "I'm already a believer. As I said before, I think Lieutenant Dockerty is very thorough and very good at his job. I'm sure that will be in your favor. He just doesn't seem the type who will stop until his case is airtight."

Their drinks arrived, and David welcomed the chance to break from the conversation for a few minutes. "Maybe I should voluntarily take myself off the staff until this whole thing blows over," he said at last.

Armstrong slammed her stein on the table, splashing some of its contents and startling the couple in the next booth. "Dammit, young man," she said, "never in all my days have I run into anyone who was more his own worst enemy than you are. Based on what I heard tonight and what I believe to be true, our lieutenant friend had better come up with a great deal more in the way of incriminating evidence before I'll allow anyone, including you, to move for your suspension. And if you don't think I have that kind of power around here, then just watch."

David's smile came more easily than it had all evening. "Thank you," he said. "Thank you very much."

"Well, now." She glanced at her watch. "This old bird has a full day at the office tomorrow, so I suggest we call it quits for the night. We'll talk again. Meanwhile, you've got to make yourself relax. Be patient. People like Lieutenant Dockerty, and also your friend Wallace Huttner, can't be told much of anything. They have to find out for themselves." She smoothed a five-dollar bill on the table and, without waiting for change, walked with him to her car.

As she got in and rolled down the window, David said, "I've repeated myself so many times, I feel like a broken record, but . . . thank you. I guess there just aren't any better words. Thank you."

"Just take care of yourself, David," she said, "and get through this in good shape. That will be all the thanks I need."

He watched until her car had disappeared around the corner, then walked numbly to the adjacent lot where his was parked. The car, a yellow Saab he had owned for less than a year, rested on its rims. All four tires had been viciously slashed. Across the driver's side, in crudely sprayed red paint, was the word MURDERER.

"A big glass house," David muttered as he stared at the sloppy cruelty. "You said it, lady. A big, fucking, animal of a glass house."

CHAPTER 13

BARBARA LITTLEJOHN had waited outside the TWA terminal only a minute before a cab arrived. That was long enough for the raw New England evening to penetrate her clothing, stiffen her joints, and draw her skin so tightly that it hurt. The flight from L.A. had been punishing enough, she thought, but this . . . She was still shivering when the cab passed through the toll booth and inched down, in heavy traffic, into the Sumner Tunnel—the dank, exhaust-filled tube connecting East Boston with Boston proper. By the time they broke free on the downtown side it had begun to rain.

Barbara insisted the driver work his way as close as possible to the entrance of the Copley Plaza. She dashed into the lobby wondering how she could once have thought New England weather whimsical and charming.

She was an attractive woman in her late forties, tall, tanned, and nearly as thin as in the days when she'd worked her way through nursing school as a fashion model. The desk clerk, though at least ten years her junior, undressed her with his eyes.

"I'm with the Donald Knight Clinton Foundation," she said, ignoring his leer. "We have a board-of-directors meeting here?"

"Oh, yes, ma'am. Eight o'clock, room one thirty-three. Across the lobby to the elevators, one floor up." He glanced at her overnight bag. "Will you be registering with us tonight?" Again the leer.

"No, thank you. I'll be staying with friends." She walked away, leaving the man with his fantasies.

Two women, one from Dallas and the other from Chicago, spotted Barbara as they entered the lobby and caught up with her at the elevator. A brief but warm exchange, then the three rode up together.

It was Monday, not yet twenty-four hours after the inquiry at Boston Doctors Hospital. The women, sixteen of them in all, had hastily rearranged their schedules and traveled to the Copley meeting from all parts of the country—New York, Philadelphia, San Francisco, Miami. They came because Peggy Donner had sent for them and because of their commitment as regional directors of The Sisterhood of Life.

Room 133 was plush—forest green crushed-velvet wall covering, lithographs of elongated horses at the Punchestown Races of 1862, conference table in the center, serving table to one side, and an overstuffed green leather couch beneath the lone window.

Barbara shook hands with the earlier arrivals and made a quick count. Twelve. The four from Boston, including Peg, were late. "No coffee?" she asked no one in particular as she opened her briefcase, extracted a thick folder marked "Clinton Foundation," and set it at the head of the glossy walnut table.

"The chief orderly was just here," one of the women answered. "He said the crash cart would be up shortly." Her humor dented the tension in the room, but only transiently. The emergency meeting was unprecedented, and of those present only Barbara knew its purpose in detail. She checked her watch. Eight ten. Their regular quarterly meetings seldom started late. But this was Boston's show, and although she had some other business to transact, she would wait.

Around the room, in small groups and muted voices, the women shared news of their families, their nursing services, and their institutions. They had come together from worlds where each of them held title, power, and influence. Susan Berger, nursing coordinator for the Hospital Consortium of San Francisco, chatted with June Ullrich, field investigations administrator for the largest pharmaceutical house in the country. They knew, as did all the others, that their lofty positions were due, in part, to their involvement with The Sisterhood of Life. Functioning through its visible arm, the Donald Knight Clinton Foundation, the movement published a monthly newsletter updating the status of various philanthropic Sisterhood projects and outlining available upper-echelon nursing positions for which members would receive special consideration.

As coordinating director of The Sisterhood, Barbara Littlejohn was also administrator of the Clinton Foundation and of half a million dollars in voluntary contributions made each year by Sisterhood nurses. Although the titles were hers, the influence and much of the power still rested with Peggy Donner. Barbara checked the time again and spread her notes on the table. Five more minutes and she would begin, with or without Peg.

At that moment the bell captain, a ferretlike man with petroleum hair, marched in with the coffee cart. He floated a tablecloth over the serving table and arranged the cups, sterling, and coffee urn with a flourish. As a finale, he stepped outside the room, returned with a large floral centerpiece, and ceremoniously placed it between the neat rows of cups.

"Flowers," Susan Berger remarked. "Now this is a first. Peggy must be softening us up for another of her schemes. God, but they're lovely."

The bell captain smiled, as if taking the compliment personally. He spent a few, final center-stage moments straightening the arrangement, then backed out of the room, still smiling. Despite his efforts, the vase still seemed to be overflowing with dahlias. The Garden would be watching and listening, they warned; the offspring appraising the parent. It was a warning that only one at the meeting would understand.

Ruth Serafini, the robust, dynamic dean of the nursing school at White Memorial Hospital, was the first of the Boston group to arrive. Peggy Donner had spawned the movement in Boston, and although it had spread rapidly to hospitals throughout the country, the Boston representation was still by far the largest. Three directors, including Ruth, were needed to oversee activities in the New England states. Peggy herself was no longer involved with day-to-day operations.

"Are the rest coming soon?" Barbara asked after a brief handshake.

"No idea. I got caught in traffic." Ruth poured a cup of coffee, then took a place at the table.

"Sorry for the delay, everyone," Barbara said finally. "I think we should start and get through the Foundation business. It's only been six weeks, so there won't be a financial report tonight." Those standing took seats. Barbara surveyed the group one at a time and smiled. How far they had come from the small cadre of nurses who had once met in Peggy's basement to share their visions and ideals and to form The Sisterhood. As she moved to begin, the final two arrived. The first, Sara Duhey, was a striking young black woman who held a master's and Ph.D. in critical-care nursing. The second was Dotty Dalrymple.

"Welcome," Barbara said warmly. "Nothing like being twenty minutes late for your own party."

"Not ours, Barb," Dalrymple said. "Peggy's. She'll be here soon. Wants you to go ahead with whatever business you have."

"Very well." Barbara glanced at her agenda. "Meeting's in order. First, we've gotten progress reports from our rural health centers. Patient visits are up almost one hundred percent in both the Kentucky and West Virginia clinics. The nurses administering them assure us that within the year both places will be flying on their own." The directors applauded the news, and the two seated closest to Tania Worth of Cincinnati patted her on the back. The centers had been her brainchild and had been approved largely because of her commitment to them. Tania beamed.

Discussion moved quickly through other projects: daycare centers for children of actively working nurses, modern equipment for under-financed hospitals, scholarships for work toward advanced degrees in nursing, efforts to upgrade the function and image of hospital nurses. Susan Berger gave a brief report on efforts around the country to establish living wills, giving each person the right, ahead of time, to limit the life-preserving measures employed on him. To date the efforts, conceived long ago by Peggy Donner, had met with little success.

"Last but not least," Barbara said, "we've gotten a letter from Karen. Some of you never met her, but she was on the board for several years before her husband received an appointment to the American Embassy in Paris. She sends love and hopes that we're all well. In less than two years she's made it all the way up to assistant director of nursing at her hospital." Several of the older women applauded the news. Barbara smiled. "It seems," she went on, "that Karen has located five Sisterhood members from a list I sent her of those who have moved to Europe. She says they are close to organizing a screening committee, but can't agree on whether the European branch should name itself in English, French, Dutch, or German."

"Perhaps we should find out what Sisterhood of Life would be in Esperanto," one woman offered.

The directors were laughing at her suggestion when Peggy Donner entered. Instantly the room quieted.

In the silence Peggy made deliberate, individual eye contact with each woman. Almost grudgingly, it seemed, the gravity in her expression yielded to pride. These were the most beloved of her several thousand children.

"Seeing you all once again lifts my spirit as nothing else ever could. I'm sorry to be late." She moved toward the head of the table, but stopped by the huge spray of dahlias. Her lips bowed in an enigmatic smile. Then she lifted a pure, regal white blossom and cradled it pensively in her hands. Finally, with a glance at Barbara, who confirmed that it was time, Peggy took over the meeting.

"It has been nearly forty years—*forty years*—since four other nurses and I formed the secret society that was to grow into our Sisterhood." Her voice was hypnotic. "Recently one of those four nurses, Charlotte Thomas, died at Boston Doctors Hospital. She was Charlotte Winthrop when we first met—only a senior nursing student—but so vital, so very special. She remained active in our movement for only a decade or so, but during that time she was responsible, as much as anyone, for our remarkable growth.

"She had a terminal illness, complicated by a cavernous bedsore, and expressed to me her desperate desire for the freedom of death. She expressed that wish to her physician as well, but as too often happens in his profession, he turned a deaf ear and was using the most aggressive methods to prolong her hopeless agony.

"Several days ago, I called an exceptional young nurse in our Sisterhood, Christine Beall, and asked her to evaluate Charlotte for presentation to our Regional Screening Committee. For many reasons, personal and professional, it was impossible for me to do so myself. The Committee approved and recommended intravenous morphine. Through a series of unforeseeable and unfortunate circumstances, an unusually thorough autopsy was performed and a critically high blood morphine level was found."

The nurses sat in stunned silence as Peggy outlined the investigation that followed and John Dockerty's session in the Tweedy Amphitheater. She paced as she talked, absently using the flower as a prop. Her tone was even and calm, her presentation purest fact. Only when she discussed David Shelton did emotion appear in her words. She described his background in great detail, stressing the difficulties he had encountered through his use of alcohol and drugs. There was disgust in her face and her voice. "A disturbed young man," she said categorically. "One who would be doing the medical profession a great service by leaving it."

Peggy's pacing became more rapid as she searched for words. "My sisters," she said gravely, "it has been over twenty years since our system of Regional Screening Committees was established. Over those years more than thirty-five hundred cases have been handled without the slightest hint of our—or anyone's—involvement. There is every reason to believe that the situation that has developed in Boston will never occur again. Unfortunately, it has this once. I have been close to Lieutenant Dockerty since the very beginning of his investigation. Although he suspects this Shelton is guilty of Charlotte's death, he is not convinced. More and more, he is learning of a special relationship that existed between Christine Beall and Charlotte. He has even mentioned the possibility of requesting her to submit to a polygraph test. I will not allow that to happen!"

For the first time several at the table exchanged concerned glances. None had ever seen her so close to losing control. The atmosphere in the room became increasingly uncomfortable.

Peggy continued. "We are a Sisterhood. Our bond is as sacred and immutable as if it were blood. When one of us suffers, we must all share her pain. When one of us is threatened with exposure, as Christine is now, we must all fly to her aid. I, and each of you, should expect as much from our sisters. We must protect her!" The woman's voice had risen to a strangled, desperate stridency. For a time there was silence, save for pulses of leaden rain clattering across the window behind her. Around the room uneasiness gave way to strain and, for some, an icy foreboding. Petals dropped from the flower, mangled in Peggy's hands.

Barbara Littlejohn moved to reestablish control. "Peggy, thank you," she said, struggling to blunt the tension in her voice. "You know that we all feel as you do about the movement. We are certainly committed to giving Christine Beall all the support we can." She hoped against hope that her reassurance would have some impact on what she knew Peggy was about to demand. The woman's vacant stare told her otherwise.

"I want that man found guilty." Peggy's words, barely audible, were spoken through clenched teeth.

The women gaped at her in disbelief. Dotty Dalrymple buried her face in her hands.

"What are you talking about?" Susan Berger was the first to react. There was incredulity and some anger in her voice.

Peggy glared at her, but Susan did not look away. "Susan, I want the pressure off Christine Beall. There is no telling what might happen to her or to our Sisterhood if the police try to break her down. I've worked too hard to allow anything like that to happen. Our work is too important. I want the Board's approval to take whatever steps are necessary to protect Christine and our interests. With a little ingenuity, I'm sure we can convince the police of Dr. Shelton's guilt. Considering his background, the most that would happen to him is a few months in some hospital and a year or two away from medicine. That seems a small price to pay for—"

"Peggy, I can't go along with this." Ruth Serafini spoke up. "I don't care what this Shelton has done. Something like this works against the dignity of a man's life, against everything we stand for." Her plea brought mutters of agreement and support from several others. Serafini glanced around the table. Of the fifteen women, seven would support

Peggy no matter what she asked of them. The others? A vote would be very close. Ruth pushed forward. "What if we just let things be and see what happens? If necessary, we can supply Christine Beall with money, lawyers, anything she needs. At this point it's not even a certainty that—"

"No!" The word was a slap. Ruth Serafini backed away from Peggy's eyes as if they were lances against her chest. Peggy pressed her assault. "Don't you understand? A piece at a time, no matter how hard she resists, Christine will tell them about us.

"Can't you see the distortions that would appear in the press? It would ruin us. It would end forever our dream. I will never allow that to happen!" She hurled the mutilated flower on the table and turned to the window. Her shoulders heaved with each rapid breath. For a time the only sounds were her breathing and the eerie music of the autumn storm. Yet when she turned back Peggy was smiling. Her voice was soft. "My sisters, a year ago I presented a plan by which I felt we could at last inform the public of our existence and of the holy task we have undertaken. With several thousand taped case reports from the finest, most respected nurses in the world, I felt we could mount a campaign for acceptance so intense that those opposed to our beliefs would have no choice but to acquiesce. It would have been the culmination of a life's work, for me and for all of you.

"As is our way, I submitted my belief to a vote. I was defeated. As is my way, I accepted the wishes of our Sisterhood. I promise you now that if we do not act tonight to protect this woman from the threats against her, I shall move ahead with that plan rather than risk a debasing, distorted, sensationalist disclosure by the police and the press. I will release the tapes. I have them—all of them—and *I will do it.*"

Looks darted from one to another around the table. The reports were the blood oath that bound them together. Once given—once the first report was completed by a nurse—there could be no turning back from her commitment to the movement. Since the very beginning it had been that way. Reports at first in writing and later by voice. All of those present had made them—some many times—and now Peggy would make them public. What defiance remained among the directors melted.

Peggy turned to Barbara Littlejohn. "Barbara, I would like a vote giving me authority to do whatever is necessary to insure the guilt of Dr. David Shelton and to protect the interests of Christine Beall and The Sisterhood of Life."

Barbara knew that further argument was fruitless. The expressions around the table echoed her feelings. With a shrug she called the question. To her left, Sara Duhey slowly lifted her hand. In order Barbara's eyes called on each one, and like a ripple their hands came up. The vote of support was unanimous.

Breaking the silence that followed, Dotty Dalrymple cleared her throat and spoke for the first time. "Peggy, as you well know, Christine Beall is a nurse on my service. I have come to know her fairly well, although I have not yet chosen to tell her of my commitment to The Sisterhood. She is, as you have described, a remarkable nurse, devoted to the ideals we all share. Can we be certain she'll allow this man to answer for what she has done, regardless of our decision here tonight?"

The question had been on everyone's mind.

"That, Dorothy, must be our responsibility—yours and mine. When the time is right, you must go to her. Explain the situation as only you can. I know that you will make her understand. You may have to share your secret with her, but I think she has earned that confidence. If necessary, I and the rest of those here will share our secret with her as well. Is that acceptable to you?"

Dalrymple smiled. "I've known you far too long and too well to ask if I have a choice. I'll talk to her."

Peggy nodded and returned the smile.

Dorothy Dalrymple did indeed know Peggy well. From the beginning Dotty had followed her rise—had even been party to her decision to enter medical school at a time when it was difficult enough for a woman, let alone a nurse, to do so. She had followed Peg's astounding success in the field of cardiology and her marriage to one of the most famous scientists and human rights advocates in the world. She had watched her assume the leadership of the medical staff of one of the largest hospitals in the country.

She knew, as surely as she knew sunrise, that Margaret Donner Armstrong could accomplish anything. The sentence they had voted for David Shelton was as good as carried out.

With a few parting words Barbara Littlejohn dismissed the meeting. As she said her good-byes, Dotty paused by the lavish bouquet, bending to inhale its strong perfume and briefly touch a feathery petal. Then, with a final glance at Peggy, she left.

The room emptied quickly. Soon only two remained—Peggy Donner, gazing serenely out the window, and Sara Duhey, who paused outside the doorway, then returned. She was still ten feet away when, without turning, Peggy said, "Sara, how nice of you to stay. We so seldom get a chance to talk."

The willowy black woman froze, then noticed her own reflection in the glass.

"So this is how Peggy Donner earns the reputation for having eyes in the back of her head."

"One of the ways." Margaret Armstrong turned and smiled warmly. Sara had been a personal recruit of hers. "I see a troubled look in those beautiful eyes of yours, Sara. Are you concerned about what happened here tonight?"

"A little. But that's not what I stayed to talk to you about."

"Oh?"

"Peggy, a few days ago Johnny Chapman died at your hospital of a massive allergic reaction—probably to some medicine, they're saying. Had you heard of him and the work he's done?" Armstrong nodded. "Well, I've known Johnny for years. Served on so many committees with him I've lost count."

"And?"

"Well, I've talked to a few people about his death—you know, people from my community. At least one of them felt there was nothing accidental about it. You can probably guess that Johnny's been a thorn in the side of a lot of important people over the years."

"My dear, every time an important or influential person dies, someone has a theory about why it couldn't have been a natural or accidental occurrence. Invariably their theories are nonsense."

"I understand," Sara said, "and I hope you're right in this case. We'll never know for certain, because Johnny's church forbids autopsies. His wife told me that. She had it written in big red letters on the front of his chart, along with a list of the things he was allergic to."

Armstrong shifted uncomfortably. "Just what is it you're driving at?"

"Peggy, this man told me he had heard ahead of time that Johnny Chapman would not leave Doctors Hospital alive. He didn't. Then, two days after Johnny suddenly goes into anaphylaxis and dies, Senator Cormier has a fatal cardiac arrest on the operating table. The papers said it was a heart attack, but they also said that because the attack was instantly fatal there was no definite cardiac damage on his autopsy."

"Sara, I still don't see what—"

"Peggy, two of the cases I have handled through The Sisterhood involved intravenous ouabain. Both of them looked like heart attacks. The drug is impossible to detect. Isn't it possible that someone could be—"

"Young lady, I think I've heard enough. Your insinuations are in poor taste and way off base. Worse than that. They come at a time when our movement needs total unity."

Sara Duhey stiffened. "Peggy, please. Don't lash out at me. I don't want to stir up any hornet's nest. All I'm asking is whether it's possible that someone in your hospital is using our methods. There are still more Sisterhood members on the staff of Boston Doctors than at any other single hospital."

"And I know every one of them personally," Armstrong said. "They are all superb nurses and completely honorable human beings. Now, unless you have something much more concrete than what you have presented me here, I would suggest—no, I will insist—that you keep your farfetched notions to yourself. We have much more pressing concerns, you and I, starting with the man who is posing a threat to our entire movement." Armstrong sensed the impact of her outburst and softened. "Sara, after this Shelton business is cleared up, we can discuss your concerns in more detail. All right?"

Sara Duhey studied the older woman, then nodded. "All right."

"Thank you," Armstrong whispered.

The two women left Room 133 together. Outside, the storm had intensified and wind gusted with a fury that shook buildings.

CHAPTER 14

"A CRACK THAT HAD the habit of looking like a rabbit . . ." David repeated the words over and over as he studied the series of thin lines that gerrymandered his living room ceiling.

". . . had the *funny* habit of looking like a rabbit." Where had he read that? What were the exact words? No matter, he decided. None of the cracks looked anything like a rabbit. Besides, the super had promised they would be plastered over, so it was a fruitless exercise anyhow.

He rolled to one side, tucked an arm under his head and stared out the window. The outlines of buildings across the alley undulated through a cold, driving rain.

It had been nearly two days since the nightmarish session with Dockerty. The morning after the inquiry David had tried to conduct his affairs at the hospital as usual. It was like working in an ice box. No virus could have spread through the wards faster than news of the tacit indictment brought against him. Most of the nurses and medical staff took special pains to avoid him. Some whispered as he walked past and one nurse actually pointed. Those few who spoke to him picked their words with the deliberateness of soldiers traversing a mine field.

By early afternoon he could take no more. Aldous Butterworth and Edwina Burroughs were the only two patients he had in the hospital. Butterworth was essentially Dr. Armstrong's problem again. The circulation in his operated leg was better than in his other one. Edwina Burroughs was anxious to go home and probably as ready for discharge now as she would be in the morning. David wrote a note in Butterworth's chart instructing Dr. Armstrong to arrange for his sutures to be removed in three days; then he made out a list of directions for Edwina Burroughs and sent her home.

He was walking, head down, toward the main exit when he collided with Dotty Dalrymple. They exchanged apologies, then Dalrymple said, "Heading to the office?"

David fought the impulse to brush aside her courtesy with a lie. "No," he said. "I've canceled the rest of the day. Actually, I'm going home."

He was surprised at the interest and concern in her eyes. Although the two of them were acquainted, they had never talked at length.

"Dr. Shelton, I want you to know how distressed I am about last night." She was, David realized, the first person all day who had openly said anything to him about the session.

"Me too," he muttered.

"We haven't had the chance to get to know one another very well, but I've heard a great deal about your work from my nurses—all of it highly complimentary." David's face tightened in a half-smile. "My praise plus a dime gets you a phone call. That's what you are thinking, isn't it?" she said. David's smile became more open and relaxed. Dalrymple rested a fleshy arm against the wall. "Well, I'm afraid I don't have much in the way of cheery news for you, but I can tell you that Lieutenant Dockerty was in to see me this morning. Your name came up only briefly and, for what it's worth, I think he is not at all convinced of your guilt despite that circus last night."

"From the reaction around the wards this morning, Miss Dalrymple, I'd say that if that's the case he's in a tiny minority. All of a sudden, I feel about as much control over my life as a laboratory mouse. At the moment Lieutenant Dockerty is very low on my list of favorite people."

"I guess if I were in your position I'd probably be feeling the same way," Dalrymple said. She paused, as if searching for words to prolong their conversation. Finally she shrugged, nodded a "Good day," and headed off.

She was several steps down the hall when David started after her. "Miss Dalrymple, please," he called out. "If you can spare another minute, there is something you might be able to help with." The nursing director slowed, then came about like a schooner, smiling expectantly. "You had Charlotte Thomas's chart last evening," David said. "If it would be possible, I'd like to borrow it for a day. I have no idea what to look for, but maybe there's something in there that won't read just right to me."

Dalrymple's expression darkened. "I'm sorry, Dr. Shelton," she said. "The chart I had last night was only a copy. The lieutenant has the original." She hesitated. "Now, I don't even have the copy." David looked at her quizzically. He felt uneasy with the way she was weighing each word. "I . . . ah . . . gave it away, Doctor . . . this morning . . . Wallace Huttner and the woman's husband . . . and a lawyer.

They came to me with a court order for my copy of the chart. Apparently it was the only one the lieutenant would allow to be made."

David's hands went cold. A damp chill spread from them throughout his body. He had little doubt as to what they were doing: malpractice. No other explanation made sense. He carried a million dollars in liability. Peter Thomas wanted to be prepared to move as soon as any action was taken against him. David shuddered. On top of everything else, Thomas was going to sue him for malpractice. And his own chief of surgery was helping him do it.

Dalrymple reached out to touch his shoulder and then seemed to change her mind. "I'm sorry, Doctor," she said coolly. "I wish I could make it better for you, but I can't."

David tightened his lips against any outburst. "Thanks," he mumbled, then hurried toward the exit.

By the time he arrived home his emotions were blanketed by a pall of total frustration. He paced the apartment several times. Then, overwhelmed by feelings of impotence, he threw himself across his bed and grabbed the telephone. He would call Dr. Armstrong, or Dockerty, or even Peter Thomas. Anyone, as long as it felt as though he was doing something. Indecision kept him from dialing. His address book lay on the bedside table. He opened it and flipped through the pages, hoping halfheartedly that someone's name would leap out at him. Anyone's who might help.

Most of the pages were blank.

His brothers were listed—one in California and one in Chicago. But even if they were next door, he wouldn't have called them. After the accident, after the alcohol and the pills and, finally, the hospital, they had quietly separated him from their lives. Christmas cards and a call every six months or so were all that remained.

A few associates from his days at White Memorial were listed. From time to time over the past eight years some of them even invited him to parties. He was fun to be around . . . as long as he was fun to be around. The more he had chanced talking about the course his life had taken, the fewer the invitations had become. There would be no real help from any of them.

In a doctor's life, fragmented by college and medical school and internship and residency and marriage and children and setting up a practice, firm friendships were rare enough. For David, having to retrace so many steps had made close ties impossible.

The shroud of isolation grew heavier. There was no one. No one except Lauren, and she was five hundred miles away, probably having lunch with some congressman and . . . Wait! There *was* somebody. There was Rosetti. For ten years, whenever he was down or needed advice, there had always been Joey Rosetti. Joey, and Terry, too. Over the months with Lauren he hadn't seen them very much, but Joey was the kind of friend to whom that really didn't matter.

Excited, David looked up the number of Joey's Northside Tavern and dialed. Even if Rosetti didn't have any advice—which was doubtful, since he had advice for everything—he would have encouragement, probably even a new story or two. Just the prospect of talking with him was cheering.

A curt, gravelly voice at the Northside Tavern informed David that Mr. Rosetti was not available. The cheer immediately vanished.

"This is Dr. Shelton, Dr. David Shelton." David emphasized the title in the manner he reserved only for making dinner and hotel reservations or for working his way past the switchboard operator at an unfamiliar hospital. "I'm a close friend of Mr. Rosetti's. Could you tell me when he'll be back or where I can reach him?"

The voice called someone without bothering to cover the mouthpiece. "Hey, some doctor's on the phone. Says he's a friend of Mr. Rosetti's. Can I tell 'im where he's gone?"

In a few moments it spoke to David. "Ah, sir, Mr. Rosetti and his wife've gone to their house on the North Shore. They'll be back late tonight."

David heard the voice ask, "Any message?" but he was already hanging up. In less than a minute the silence and inaction were intolerable. Purely out of desperation, he called Wallace Huttner. When the ringing began, he fought the urge to hang up by pressing the receiver tightly against his ear. The ear was throbbing by the time Huttner came on.

"Yes, Dr. Shelton, what is it?" The distance in the man's voice could have been measured in light-years.

"Dr. Huttner, I'm very concerned and upset about what happened last night and with some things I've learned today," David managed. "I . . . I wondered if I might talk to you about them for a few minutes?"

Huttner said, "Well, actually I'm quite far behind in the office and—"

"Please!" David cut in. "I'm sorry for raising my voice, but, please, just hear me out." He paused for a moment, then sighed relief when Huttner made no further objection. Struggling to keep his words slow and his tone more composed, he said, "Dr. Huttner, I know that you helped Mr. Thomas and his lawyer get a copy of Charlotte's chart. Somehow you must believe that I had nothing to do with her murder. I may have given you and some of the others the impression that I favor mercy killing, but I don't. I . . . I need your help—someone's help— to convince Peter Thomas and the lieutenant of that. I . . ." At that instant David realized how ill conceived his call had been. He really had no clear idea of what he wanted to say or ask. Huttner sensed the same thing.

"Dr. Shelton," he said with cool condescension, "please understand. In no way have I judged your guilt or innocence. I assisted Peter this morning as a favor to a distraught old friend. Nothing more."

Old friend? David nearly laughed out loud. A few days ago Peter Thomas had made it clear they barely knew one another. Now they were old friends. He clenched the receiver more tightly and forced himself to listen as Huttner continued. "The lieutenant was by to see me earlier today, and it seems as if he's conducting a most thorough inquiry into the whole matter. Let us just wait and see what direction his investigation takes. If, as you say, you had nothing to do with Charlotte's death, I'm sure the lieutenant will be able to prove it. Now if you've no further questions . . ."

David hung up without responding.

When he awoke still dressed at five thirty the next morning, the muscles in his jaw were aching.

David amused himself for nearly an hour by counting the seconds between a flash of lightning in the alley and the subsequent clap of thunder. Three calculations in a row agreed exactly—the electrical discharge was a mile and a half away. Measured against the disappointments of the past two days, his mathematical triumph was like winning an Olympic medal. Fifteen minutes reading a mindless paperback. Two with the weights. Another few with the book. They were, he realized, the random, anxious movements of someone with no place to go. The same sort of restlessness that had characterized his first few weeks of hospitalization in the Briggs Institute.

He stared at the phone and considered trying Lauren again. He had tried earlier in the day—her home number and even the hotels in Washington where she usually stayed. She'll be here soon, he told himself. If not today then tomorrow. Their only contact after she had left had been a brief conversation just before the hideous session with Dockerty in the Amphi. Lauren had called to explain that she would be on the move, covering reaction to the death of Senator Cormier. In fact, she confessed, her main reason for calling (other than "just to say hi," she said) was to see if David could talk to people at his hospital and get some inside information on the sudden tragedy. At the time he'd felt certain he could learn something. Of course, there had been no way of knowing that within a few hours he would become a pariah at Boston Doctors.

David went to the kitchen for some water, then to the bathroom for some more.

She'd said she'd be in Springfield today covering the funeral. Possibly for a day or two after that. Perhaps she would call and they could meet in Springfield. Maybe they could even drive to New York or . . . or maybe up to Montreal.

Random movements, random thoughts.

He reopened the mystery novel, read for a time, then discovered that the last ten pages of the tattered paperback were missing. He barely reacted—just shrugged—and shuffled off to take a shower—his second of the day. As he turned on the water, the telephone rang.

David skidded into the hallway and raced to the bedroom. "Hey, where have you been?" he panted. "I've been worried. I didn't even know for sure what city you were in."

"David, it's Dr. Armstrong. Are you all right?"

"Huh?" Oh, damn. "I'm sorry, Dr. Armstrong. No, I'm fine. I was expecting a call from Lauren and . . . uh . . . she's a woman that I . . ."

"David? Take a minute and relax. Do you want me to call back?"

"No, no, I'm fine. Really." He stretched the phone cord to reach his bureau and pulled on a pair of scrub pants. Then he sighed and sank to the bed. "Actually, I'm not fine. I've been sitting around here all day. Half the time I wait, and the other half I try to figure out what I'm waiting for."

"But you haven't . . . ?" She let the question drift.

"No, not even close," he said, forcing a laugh. "Not a pill or a drop of anything. I told you the other night that nothing was going to get me back there." Actually, the urge had been there several times—fleeting, but unmistakable. It never lasted long enough to pose a major threat, but after so many years, any sense of it at all was frightening.

"Good. I'm glad to hear it," Armstrong said. "I'm truly sorry to have taken so long to get back to you."

"I understand." He cut in, hoping to spare her any uncomfortable explanations of the turmoil he knew was surrounding him—and her—at the hospital. "Any news?"

"Not really. Our friend the lieutenant has been present on and off since Sunday. He checks in with me or Ed Lipton to let us know he's around, but that's about it."

"Well, I bumped into Miss Dalrymple yesterday and asked for her copy of Charlotte Thomas's chart. I thought perhaps I could get some brainstorm from studying it."

"And did Miss Dalrymple give it to you?"

David missed the chord of heightened interest in her voice. "No. I think she would have, but she didn't have it anymore." Briefly, he reviewed the conversation with Dotty Dalrymple and his subsequent call to Huttner.

"So," she said after a moment's pause, "the buzzards circle."

David smiled ruefully at the image. "Circle and wait," he said. "I feel so damn helpless. I want to do something to show them all I'm still alive and fighting, but I can't even find a stick to wave."

"I understand," she said. "If I were you, I would just sit tight and see what develops."

"You're probably right, Dr. Armstrong, but unfortunately passivity has never been one of my strong suits. If I don't do something to sort this whole mess out, who will?"

"I will, David."

"What?"

"I told you the other night I would do what I could."

"I remember."

"Well, I have a friend in personnel who's checking the hospital computer for any former mental patients or drug problems or prison records. That sort of thing."

David became excited. "That's a great idea. How about past employment at Charlotte Thomas's nursing agency?"

"We could try that."

"And graduates of her nursing school. And . . . and activists supporting patients' rights, living wills, things like that. And . . ."

"Whoa! Slow down, David. First things first. You just stay where I can get in touch with you, and fight that self-destruct impulse of yours. I'll do the rest—don't worry. Are you coming back to work?"

"Tomorrow. I thought I'd try tomorrow. Anything would be better than sitting around like this waiting for the other shoe to drop. Thanks to you, it'll be much easier to concentrate on my job knowing at least that something's being done."

"Something's being done," Armstrong echoed.

Margaret Armstrong set the receiver down and glanced through her partially open office door at the patients in her waiting room—half a dozen complex problems that she would, almost certainly, unravel and deal with. Even after so many years, her own capabilities awed her.

"Mama, please. Tell me what I can do to help."

She understood now. She had the knowledge and the power and she understood. But how could she have been expected to know then what was right? She had been still a girl, barely fifteen years old.

"Kill me! For God's sake, please kill me."

"Mama, please. You don't know what you're saying. Let me get you something for the pain. When you feel better, you'll stop saying such things. I know you will."

"No, baby. It doesn't help. Nothing has helped the pain for days. Only you can help me. You must help me."

"Mama, I'm frightened. I can't think straight. That lady down the hall keeps screaming and I can't think straight. I'm so frightened. I . . . I hate this place."

"The pillow. Just set it over my face and lean on it as hard as you can. It won't take long."

"Mama, please. I can't do that. There must be another way. Something. Please help me to understand. Help me to know what to do. . . ."

Margaret Armstrong's receptionist buzzed several times on the intercom, then crossed to the office door and knocked. "Dr. Armstrong?"

The door swung open and the receptionist knew immediately that she should have been more patient. It was just one of those times when the cardiac chief was totally lost in thought. One of those times when she sat fingering a small strip of linen, staring across the room. They came infrequently and never lasted long.

The receptionist eased the door closed and returned to her desk. Minutes later, her intercom buzzed.

The talk with Margaret Armstrong and their plan of action, however ragtag, injected a note of optimism into David's day. Some Bach organ music and twenty minutes of hard, almost vicious lifting nurtured the mood. He was showered, dressed, and stretched out, thumbing through a journal, when a key clicked in the front door. He charged down the hall and was almost to the door when Lauren entered. She was carrying her raincoat and a floppy hat, but otherwise looked as if she had just come in from a garden party. Her light blue dress clung to her body, more out of will, it seemed, than design. A thin gold necklace glowed on the autumn brown of her chest.

In those first few moments, standing there, looking at her, nothing else mattered. Then, as he focused on her face, she looked away. Suddenly David felt frightened even to touch her. "Welcome home," he said uncertainly, reaching a tentative hand toward her. She took it and moved to him, but there was no warmth in her embrace. Her coolness and the scent of her perfume—the same fragrance she had worn the morning she left—filled him with a sense of emptiness and apprehension. "I had no idea when you'd be coming back," he said, hoping that something in her response would dispel the feelings.

"I told you when I called the other day that I'd be tied up with the Cormier story," she said, settling into an easy chair in the living room. David noted that she had avoided the couch. "What a shitty thing to have happen," she went on. "Of all the people I ever interviewed in Washington, Dick Cormier was the only one I really trusted. Everyone did. His funeral was very moving. The President spoke, and the Chief Justice, and . . ."

David could no longer stand the tension inside him and in her nervous chatter. "Lauren," he said. "There's more, isn't there? I mean it's not just the senator. Something else is eating at you. Please talk to me. I'm . . . I'm very uncomfortable with the feeling in this room right now. There's a lot I have to tell you, but first we've got to clear the air a little." Another man, he thought. Lauren's met another man. There was nothing in her face to discourage that notion. She stared out the window, biting at her lower lip. For a moment David thought she was about to cry, but when she finally spoke, her voice held far more irritation than sadness.

"David," she said, "a policeman was waiting for me when I arrived home. I spent more than two hours at the police station answering questions from Lieutenant Dockerty—some of them very personal—about you, and about us."

"Did Dockerty tell you what it was all about?" he asked, relieved that he'd been wrong about another man.

Lauren shook her head. "Only briefly. He was nice enough at first, but his questions got more and more pointed—more and more offensive. Finally I just stalked out and told him I wouldn't talk to him again without a lawyer. He made it sound like you were really sick and I was protecting you in some way. David, I can't have—"

"Damn that man!" David shouted. "When this is all over, he's going to answer for this shit. I've had about all I can take." His fists were white and tight against his thighs. "Lauren, this is a nightmare. The man's on some kind of vendetta. Ever since he came on the scene he's gone after me like he had blinders on. I didn't do anything. He's taken a pile of circumstantial horseshit, and he's been trying to mold it into some kind of case against me." His control was disappearing. He sensed it, but was unable to back off. One after another, his words tumbled out, each louder and higher pitched than the last. "I could handle the crap he's been laying down at the hospital. That I could handle. But hauling you in . . . The bastard's gone too far." He was pacing now, thumping his fist against his side.

"David, please!" Lauren screamed. "You're acting crazy. Please get hold of yourself. It frightens me to see you like this."

He stopped in his tracks and forced his hands open. A deep breath, then he said, "I'm sorry, babe. I am. First it's too much joking, then too much crazy." He managed a thin smile. "I guess I'm just . . . too much, huh?" He sank numbly into the couch. "Lauren, could you hold me for a minute?" he asked, reaching his hands to her.

Lauren's lips tightened. She looked at the floor and shook her head. "David, we've got to talk."

"So talk." He folded his hands in his lap.

"My wire service has people all over, David. Including the police department here. Business like this—being questioned at the police station and all—my boss is very straight and very conservative. If he gets wind of this—"

"Jesus Christ!" David exploded. "You make it sound as if I'm doing all this to give you a black eye. Can't you understand that I haven't done anything? My God, here I am being harassed up and down by some monomaniac, in danger of losing my career—or worse—and my girl friend is worried about being embarrassed in front of her bureau chief. This is insane. Absolutely insane!"

"David"—Lauren's voice was low and measured with anger—"I've told you over and over again how much I dislike the label 'girl friend.' Now please calm down, and try to understand my position in this thing, too."

Speechless, David could only look at her and shake his head.

Lauren straightened her dress, sat rigidly upright, and met his incredulity with defiance. "I know you'll be pleased to hear," she said, "that of all the things you have to worry about, having to endure the Art Society dinner dance Thursday will not be one of them. After the lieutenant brought me home, Elliot May called and asked if I was planning on going. I knew how little you were looking forward to the affair, so I took the opportunity of relieving you of the burden." The wildness in his eyes was frightening. She forced her lips into a proud pout and turned toward the window.

He rose and took a step toward her. In that frozen, terrifying moment, he sensed his self-control slipping away. Fists clenched, he took another step.

Suddenly, the buzzer from the downstairs foyer sounded. David whirled and half stalked, half stumbled to the intercom in the hall.

"Yes?" he shouted.

"It's Lieutenant Dockerty, Dr. Shelton." The policeman's voice crackled from four floors below. "May I come up, please?"

"Do I have a choice?" David said as he pressed the door release.

For the next half-minute the only sound was David's breathing—bitter, frantic gulps, gradually slowing as he fought for composure. He had been expecting a visit from Dockerty for the past two days. Typical of the man to pick a time like this to show up. He heard the clank as the gears of the rickety elevator engaged. Standing by the door, he shook his head disdainfully at the groan from the straining cables. The antiquated box took more than a minute to make the four-floor trip. A second clank, and the rattle of the automatic inside gate signaled its arrival. David stepped from his apartment just as Dockerty pushed open the heavy outside door of the elevator. He was accompanied by a tall uniformed officer.

"Dr. Shelton, this is Officer Kolb," Dockerty said. "May we come in, please?" It was an order. David thought for a moment about Lauren, then shrugged and led them into the living room.

"Miss Nichols." Dockerty nodded, but made no move to introduce Kolb to her.

Lauren stood and picked up her raincoat. "If you'll excuse me," she said formally, "I was just leaving."

She had taken one step toward the door when Dockerty said, "I think perhaps you had better stay, Miss Nichols." Lauren's eyes narrowed at him. She stiffened, then strode back to her chair.

Inside David confusion and panic began to build.

Dockerty stared at the floor for a few silent seconds, then reached into his coat pocket and produced a manilla-covered pad. The forms inside it were green. "Dr. Shelton," he said, handing the pad to David, "do you recognize these?"

David flipped through the sheets, then stammered, "Yes, they're my C two-twenty-two order forms. But I don't see what . . ."

"For ordering narcotics?" Dockerty asked.

"Yes, but . . ."

"They're preprinted with your name, aren't they?"

"Enough!" The word shot out. "I've had enough of this. Would you tell me what you want, or . . . or leave." He was nearly screaming. Inside his gut, inside his chest huge knots formed and began to tighten.

"Dr. Shelton, I sent notice to all the pharmacies in the city, asking for the names of everyone who purchased injectable morphine in the last month." He produced a single green form from his breast pocket. "This form C two-twenty-two was used to purchase three vials of morphine sulfate from the Quigg Pharmacy in West Roxbury. It's dated October second, the day Charlotte Thomas was murdered. It's your form, Dr. Shelton. There's your name printed right on it."

David snatched the form away. "That's not my signature," he said automatically. He stared at the writing, then closed his eyes. For years he had been kidded—had himself made jokes—about the scrawl that was his signature. "An unscrupulous chimp could prescribe for my patients," he had once quipped. The signature on the C222 would have passed his desk without a second notice.

"Perhaps," Dockerty responded tonelessly. "But I suspect that it is. You see, Doctor, there's more. The warrant I obtained to search your office allowed me to remove not only your forms, but this." He reached in his pocket again and produced a small, gold-framed photo. "Mr. Quigg at the pharmacy has positively identified you from this photo as the one who purchased the morphine from him."

David stared down at the picture. It was one he had never been able to put away. The whole family—David, Ginny, and three-year-old Becky—posing by the swan boats in Boston's Public Garden. It had been taken only two months before the accident.

For a time Dockerty seemed unable to speak. Finally he shook his head. "David Shelton, I am placing you under arrest for the murder of Charlotte Thomas."

The words fell on David like hammers. An uncomfortable, high-pitched buzzing noise began swelling in his head. He tried to shake the sound loose as the tall policeman read him his rights from a frayed, cardboard card. The man's words seemed jumbled and slurred. David watched, a detached observer, as uniformed arms reached out and handcuffed his wrists behind him. Dockerty's apology for having to use the restraints was nearly lost in the mounting buzz.

David was disoriented, frightened almost beyond functioning. He tried to pull away. Without a flicker of expression, the patrolman tightened his grip.

Bewildered and mortified, Lauren backed away as David, needing support to stand, was led out the door.

Dockerty moved to follow, then turned to her. "He's going to need a lawyer, Miss Nichols," he said grimly. "If I were you, I'd make sure it was a damn good one." With a nod, he headed down the corridor.

The wind had died off, but a cold, heavy rain was still falling. Dockerty threw a windbreaker around David's shoulders and zipped it up the front. Even so, by the time they dragged him the short distance to the squad car he was soaked to the skin. Through bizarre, disconnected scenes, David watched the events of his own arrest. The eerie blue light, a strobe atop the squad car . . . tiny, perfect diamond shapes in the metal screen . . . pedestrians bundled against the downpour, frozen through the screen and the front windshield. David saw them all in stop-action. A grotesque slide show.

The station house . . . the lights . . . the uniforms. Then it was the voices. "Empty your pockets . . ." ". . . son, can you hear me? Son? . . ." ". . . here's his wallet. Get the shit you need from his license . . ." "Give me your right hand, thumb first . . ." "Over here, stand over here . . ." ". . . the other hand now . . ." "Look, fella, it's just a number. Let it hang there . . ." "Face straight ahead . . . now turn . . . no, this way, this way . . ." "Three's empty. Put him in there . . ."

Next it was the noises. Scraping of metal on metal . . . a loud clang—the elevator?—no, not here. Can't be the elevator . . . music . . . from where? . . . where is the music coming from? . . . More voices . . . ". . . here, boss, over here . . ." ". . . a light, I need another light. My fucking cigarette's soggy . . ." "When the fuck's dinner? Don't we even get fed here? . . ."

Finally, the wide, blurry bands . . . up and down in front of him. Gradually the blurs narrowed and darkened. . . . Bars! They were bars!

Again the buzzing crescendo. Images of other bars, other screens exploded through his mind.

"No! Please, God, no!" he screamed. He whirled and dropped to his knees by the toilet, retching uncontrollably into water already murky with disinfectant.

Barely aware of the bile singeing his nose and throat, David crawled across the stone floor and pulled himself onto a metal-framed cot. He descended into a cold, unnatural sleep long before his sobs had faded.

CHAPTER 15

"TIME TO MOVE OUT, son. There's some Listerine in this cup. Splash some cold water on your face and swish this stuff around in your mouth for a minute. It'll help you wake up."

David worked his eyes open a crack. His first sight of the morning was the same as his last the night before. Bars. This time the narrow blue and white bars of the sweat-stained pillow beneath his face.

The officer was a plethoric man, fifty or so, with a belly that hung several inches over his belt. He leaned against the doorframe of the cell and watched patiently while David pulled himself up and wiped sooty sleep from his eyes. "Are you able to talk, son?" he asked.

David nodded, squinted at the man, then took the mouthwash. The officer seemed in no great hurry, so David took a minute to stretch the ache from the muscles in his neck and back, trying at the same time to get some sense of himself. For the moment, at least, the terror and confusion of the past night were gone. In their place was a strange but quite comfortable feeling of well-being. Knees locked, he bent forward and put the tips of all ten fingers on the floor. Peaceful, he thought. This shithole, all the madness, and here I am feeling peaceful.

Then he remembered. It was at summer camp. He was eleven—no, twelve—years old. A sudden stomach cramp while swimming far from the raft. In an instant he was on the bottom, pain strangling his gut and water forcing its way into his lungs. Then, as suddenly as it had started, the pain and the terror had vanished. In their place, the same detached peace. He was dying—then and now—helpless and dying.

The sergeant's radish cheeks puffed in a grin. "Glad to see you're feelin' better," he said. "The night boys were worried. Said you weren't even able to hold a dime, much less make the phone call they tried to give you." When David didn't answer, he added, "You are feelin' better, aren't you?"

"Oh, yeah, I'm okay, thanks," David said distantly, still testing his body and his feelings for pain. "Wh . . . where am I, anyway?"

"District One," the man answered. He looked at David with renewed concern. "You're in the jail at District One in Boston. Do you understand that?" David nodded. "We have to go now. You've got to go to court. The judge and the people at the court will help you. Don't you worry."

David watched with bemused curiosity as the policeman clicked a handcuff on his right wrist and led him out of the cell. He smiled politely at the black, silver-haired prisoner who was snapped into the other cuff. Calmly, fuguelike, he focused on the manacled hands—black and white—and followed them into the back seat of a squad car.

"Name's Lyons," the black man said as the car pulled away. "Reggie Lyons." His wise face held countless thin lines, etched by years of hard living, and several thicker ones, clearly carved by more tangible items.

"David. I'm David," he answered.

"You ain't never been this route before, David, have you?" Lyons asked. David shrugged, looked out the window, and shook his head. "Well, you is in for *a* treat. The tank at Suffolk is the worst, man. I mean the pits." David stared at a motorcycle cruising next to them and nodded. "Hey, you all right? Well, it don't matter much one way or tuther. Crazy's prob'ly better. You just stick close to ol' Reggie. He'll take care of you."

The tank was, in fact, a cage. The holding room for prisoners awaiting court appearances. Twenty men, all "presumed innocent" were packed inside—rapists, drunks, vagrants, murderers, flashers. Around the outside, half a dozen lawyers were vying to be heard over one another and over the din inside. "Perkins, which one of you is Perkins? . . ." "Frankly, Arnold, I don't give a flying fuck if the kid is guilty or innocent. He either cops the first charge and saves us a trial or he ends up going down for both and spending three to five in Walpole . . ." "Look, kid, I know what you've seen on *Perry Mason,* but that just ain't the way it works. Today we don't talk guilty or not guilty. Today we talk money. If you have some or can get some, we bail you out. Otherwise you wait for your trial in Charles Street. Nobody cares about your story today. This is just for bail. Understand? Just for bail . . ."

David wedged himself in one corner of the tank and stared through the chain link at a high window that was opaque with grime. Bit by bit, reality—and the terror—was returning. He thought about the hospital. The operating rooms would already be on their second cases of the day.

"Hey, David, you got a lawyer?" Reggie Lyons stood next to him, leaning against the cage. A cigarette, wrinkled and bent, popped up and down at the corner of his mouth as he spoke.

"Ah, no, Reggie, I don't," David said absently. "At least, not that I know of." An uncomfortable pressure grew beneath his breast bone. He tried to remember when he had last eaten. When he had last run by the river. He looked about the cage, awareness growing every second and with it an abysmal despair.

"Shelton? David Shelton. Which one of you is Shelton?" The bailiff was a dumpy man in his late fifties. There was an air about him—a look in his eyes—that suggested his favorite pastime outside of court might be pulling the wings off insects.

Reggie Lyons leaned over and whispered, "David, don't you be scared now. Jes' go in there an' think about the beach or your favorite broad or somethin'. All the uniforms an' robes is jes' dress-up. A game they play to impress one another an' scare the shit out of us."

David turned and looked at Reggie's aged, ageless face. "Thanks," he said hoarsely. "Thanks a lot."

The man stared at him curiously, then took one of David's hands in both of his. His palms were thick with calluses. "Good luck, man," he whispered. "Don't give in to 'em."

The paunchy bailiff snapped handcuffs on David as he stepped out of the tank. Moments later, he was seated in the prisoners' dock. The three-foot-high, four-foot-square pen was a wooden island, separating him from the rest of the courtroom. Told to stand, he braced his legs against one low panel as new words, new voices and scenes worked their way into his nightmare.

The clerk who read the charges was a spinsterish woman who looked as if she had been born into the ornate old courtroom.

"As to complaint number three one nine four seven, your complainant, John Dockerty, respectfully represents that in the City of Boston in the County of Suffolk in behalf of said Commonwealth, David Edward Shelton of Boston in the County of Suffolk on the second day of October, in violation of the General Laws, chapter two six five, section one, did wrongfully murder one Charlotte Winthrop Thomas with intent to murder her by injecting into her body a quantity of morphine sulfate.

"The court has entered a plea for the defendant of not guilty."

David leaned more heavily against the panel as the district attorney, a slick young man with two rings on each hand, briefly outlined the case against him. Disconnected words and phrases were all that registered. ". . . premeditated . . . unconscionable misuse of his skill and knowledge . . . clandestine injection . . . positively identified as . . . murder, as heinous as any committed in passion. . . ."

"Dr. Shelton, do you understand the charges that have been brought against you?" the judge said mechanically. David nodded. "Speak up, please. Do you understand the charges?"

"Yes," David managed.

"And do you have a lawyer?"

For several seconds there was total silence in the room. Then a voice called out from the last row of seats. "Yes, yes, he does, Your

Honor." A thin man, dressed in a three-piece pinstripe suit, rose and walked briskly down the aisle toward the judge.

"You're representing this man, Mr. Glass?"

"Yes, Your Honor."

"Let the record show the defendant is represented by Mr. Benjamin Glass."

David's eyes narrowed as he studied the man who had come forward to champion him. Black hair . . . thinning . . . strands combed carefully across the top . . . scuffed brown leather briefcase . . . broad gold wedding band, intricately carved.

Glass walked to him and smiled encouragement. "You okay?" he asked softly. David managed a nod. "You're white as a ghost. Do you need to see a doctor or anything?" This time a shake. The lawyer's face was dark, nearly olive colored—unlined and youthful, yet at the same time seasoned and assured. Dark circles underscored the intensity in his eyes. "Sorry I'm late. Lauren didn't connect with me until this morning. Let me get you out of here, then we'll talk."

Ben Glass approached the judge. "Your Honor, I would like to move for bail and petition for a probable-cause hearing." He looked slight to David, almost frail. But his stance, the tilt of his head exuded confidence.

It was his world, David realized, his operating room. "Thank you, Lauren," he whispered. For the first time the flicker of hope appeared in his nightmare.

"On what grounds?" the judge said.

"Your Honor, Dr. Shelton is a respected surgeon with no criminal record and no recent history that would suggest the need for psychiatric observation and evaluation."

"Very well. Fifty thousand dollars cash."

"Your Honor," Glass said with just the right incredulity, "this man may be an M.D., but I assure you, he is no millionaire. Please save us a trip this afternoon for review by a supreme court justice. Make it a hundred thousand, but let me pay a bondsman."

The judge tapped his fingertips together for a few seconds, then said, "All right, Mr. Glass. One hundred thousand dollars bail it is."

"Thank you, Your Honor."

Ben took David by the arm and, with the bailiff close behind, led him from the courtroom. "You're almost home, David," he said. "My friend the bondsman will want ten thousand dollars. Have you got it?"

"I . . . don't think so," David said.

"Family. Can you get it from your parents or someplace?"

"My parents are dead. I . . . I have two brothers and . . . a . . . oh, an aunt who might help. What if I can't come up with the money?"

"Believe me, you don't want to have that happen. The place you stayed last night is a palace compared to Charles Street, where they'll send you now. Tell you what. Maury Kaufman, the bondsman, has gotten so fat off my clients that he owes me. He'll agree to cuff this one for a day rather than risk losing my trade. Today is Wednesday. I'll get you until Friday morning to come up with the cash. Okay?"

"Okay," David said as the bailiff removed his handcuffs and motioned him back into the tank. "And Mr. Glass—thank you."

"David, I hope this doesn't shake your confidence too much, but while you were taking Godliness one-oh-one in medical school, I was one of those hippie weirdo flower children getting pushed around at antiwar demonstrations. It's Ben. You can only call me Mr. Glass if it makes it easier for you to come to grips with the fee you're going to have to pay me." He turned and headed down the hall as the bailiff clanged the tank door shut.

"Hey, David, is that Glass dude your lawyer?" A toothpick had replaced the cigarette in the corner of Reggie Lyons's mouth.

"I . . . I guess he is," David said, pleased with the bit of animation that had returned to his voice.

"Well, then. I guess I can stop gettin' all worked up 'n' worried about you. He don't look like much, but I seen him prancin' around in court a few times. The dude's a tiger. I mean he is *the* man."

"Thanks for telling me, Reggie. It helps." David actually grinned. "You've really been great to me. Say, what are you here for anyway?"

Lyons smiled and winked. "Jes' bein', pal," he said. "I is here jes' for bein'.'"

The sign over the bar said, "Paddy O'Brien's Delicatessen: Home of the world's best chopped liver, and the most famous Irish Jew since Mayor Briscoe."

"I've never even heard of this place." David smiled as he slid onto the wooden bench across from Ben. Shamrocks and Stars of David were everywhere. On the wall over their booth the photograph of a ragamuffin group of Irish revolutionaries hung side by side with one of a spit-and-polish Israeli tank unit.

"Are you Jewish?" Ben asked.

"No."

"Are you Irish?"

"No."

"I rest my case. It's no wonder you've never found your way here. Sooner or later, though, most people do. And here you are."

"Thanks to you."

"It's what I do," Ben answered matter-of-factly. "If my appendix bursts someday, then I might end up here savoring the chopped liver, thanks to *you*. That's the way it all works, right?"

"Right," David said. He knew that the easy talk they'd shared since leaving the courtroom had been as carefully orchestrated by Ben as his choice of this gritty, vibrant restaurant. He also knew they were wise choices. Bit by bit, he was relaxing. Bit by bit, he sensed the resurgence of hope.

Ben ordered a "sampler of delights" that easily could have fed ten. They ate in silence for a while, then he said, "It's probably unfair to have waited until after you've eaten to discuss my fee, but it is how the wee ones at home get fed. It's ten thousand dollars, David."

David startled momentarily, then shrugged and took a sip of water. Suddenly finding himself $20,000 in debt was little more than a gnat on his nightmare. "I don't have it," he said flatly.

"I'm a bit more lenient in my payment schedule than Maury the Bondsman," Ben said, "but I expect to get paid."

David's lips tightened. "I guess that after being accused of murder and spending the night in a cell, there's really not much place for false pride. I'm sure I could borrow the money if I can just sit on my vanity long enough to ask. My brothers would probably be willing to help. And I have this friend who owns the Northside Tavern—"

"Rosetti?"

"You know Joey?"

"Not well, but enough to know that he's a good kind of friend to have. Somehow Rosetti's always been able to straddle the fence between the North End boys and the establishment without falling off on either side. If he's your friend, I say give him a call."

"If it comes to that, I will."

"Well, like I said, I expect to get paid." David nodded. "We're in business, then," Ben said, reaching over to shake his hand. "Now I can tell you what you get for your money—and what you have to do to keep me. You get everything I can give you, David. Time, friends, influence, sweat—whatever you need. In exchange I want only one thing from you —besides the fee, that is." He paused for emphasis. "Honesty. I mean total, no-crap, no-bullshit honesty. There are no second chances. If I catch you in even a tiny fib, you find yourself another lawyer. There are enough unpleasant surprises in this job as is without constantly worrying about whether I'm going to get one from my client."

"We're still in business," David said.

"Fine. Why don't you start by giving me some background on yourself. Assume I don't know anything."

At that moment a sprightly little man with freckles and graying red hair bounced over and leaned on the table. He wore a grease-stained apron with a large green Star-of-David on the front. His high-pitched brogue made every word a song. "Benjy, me boy. Openin' the annex to your office again, I see."

"Hi, Paddy. It's been a while." Ben shook his hand. "Place looks good. Listen, this is my friend, David. He's a surgeon, so you'd best keep this rowdy crowd quiet while we're working or I'll have him graft your precious parts to your dart board."

Paddy O'Brien laughed and patted David on the shoulder. "Go

ahead, if it'll make 'em work any better. Benjy here's the best there is at lawyerin' *and* at bummin' the check, so watch out. You boys go on about your business. I'll have two pints sent over—courtesy of the house."

"Make that one, Paddy," Ben said. His eyes met David's for an instant. "For me."

"One pint and one Coke comin' up," the little man said without batting an eye.

"So, assume you don't know anything, huh?" David was smiling.

"I was late this morning because I was talking to John Dockerty," Ben explained. "I didn't stay long enough to learn too much, but I will tell you he hasn't put this thing in a drawer. Please, humor me and just assume I know nothing, okay?"

"Okay." David shrugged. "How far back?"

"It's your story," Ben said.

"My story . . ." For a moment David's voice drifted away as pieces of events, bits of people flashed through his thoughts. "Began innocently enough, I guess." He shrugged. "Two older brothers. Decent, loving parents. White picket fence. The works. When I was about fourteen, the whole thing unraveled. Mother got cancer. It was in her brain before anyone even knew she had it. Even so, she lived for almost eight pitiful months. My dad owned a small store. Appliances. He ended up selling it so he could nurse mother—in between her hospitalizations, that is. A few weeks before she died, *he* had a coronary. Dead before he hit the floor, they told me.

"I'm still not sure why, but from that time on all I wanted to be was a doctor. A surgeon, too. Even back then."

It had been years since David had sat and gone through the whole thing. He felt surprise at how easily the words came. "Is this the kind of stuff you want to know?" he asked. Ben nodded.

"My aunt and uncle took care of me until college, then I was essentially on my own. I was never any great genius, but I knew what I wanted and I clawed and scraped to get it. Scholarships and jobs all the way through medical school. I'd find what I thought was my limit, then I'd push myself past it. By the middle of my internship it was starting to get to me. I was sort of a wunderkind in the hospital, but outside I was coming unglued. Smoking too many cigarettes, sleepless nights, depressions that didn't want to go away. I fought the problem the only way I knew how. I pushed myself even harder at work. Looking back, I feel sure that if it weren't for a stop sign some kids had stolen, I would have gone off the deep end."

Ben startled at the strange association, then he smiled. "A woman?"

David nodded. "Ginny. Her car and mine smacked together at an intersection. The sign her way was missing. The irony is still really painful. I met her through an auto accident, then . . ." For the first time, words became difficult.

Ben raised a hand. "David, if this is too hard for you right now, we can do it another time. Sooner or later, though, they are things I have to know."

David toyed with his glass, then said, "Nope, I'm okay. Just stop me if it gets too maudlin—or too boring." Ben grinned and waved him on. "We got married six months later. She was an interior decorator. A rare and gentle person. My whole life changed just by having her there. Over the next four years there was magic in everything I did. The head of the surgical department at White Memorial asked me to stay on an extra year as chief resident. That job is about the only way a surgeon can get a staff appointment at WMH. So it was all there. For a little while at least.

"We had a little girl, Becky. I finished the residency and started in practice. Then there was the accident. I was driving. I . . . well, I guess the details aren't important. Becky and Ginny were dead. Just like that. I had scrapes and cuts, but really nothing. Except that in my own way I died too. I never really got back to work. I went from being a social drinker—almost a teetotaler—to being a drunk. One long bender. Thank God, I had enough sense to stay away from the operating room.

"I tried seeing minor cases at the office, though. That's when the pill cycle started. My version of changing seats on the *Titanic*. Ups to get started, downs to sleep. You know the story. At first my associates were tolerant. Helpful, even. One at a time, though, I managed to work over their faith brutally enough to drive them away. It went on like that for almost a year. In the end, I was removed from the staff. I didn't even know it had happened because I was lost in another bender."

"It's a bitch of a cycle to break out of," Ben said.

"Alone it is. That's for sure. Well, one morning I woke up in a cage. My last friend couldn't stand it anymore. Actually, it was a hospital he brought me to. Briggs Institute?" Ben nodded that he knew the place. "It turned out to be a great place for me, but not those first few weeks. No handle on the door. Bars on the windows. The whole scene . . . Are you still awake?"

Ben managed a short laugh. "I got snatches of your story from Lauren and Dockerty," he said, shaking his head, "but not like this. Getting locked up last night like you did . . ."

David shuddered. "I don't have classic claustrophobia. At least, I don't think I do. It's just that ever since those early weeks at Briggs the thought of being locked up or trapped in a small place gives me this awful, gnawing sensation in my gut, and sometimes a chill that . . ." He stopped and managed a smile. "It really does sound like claustrophobia, doesn't it?"

"I don't like labels," Ben said.

"Well, no matter." David swallowed against the dusty dryness in his mouth, then drank half a glass of water. "Let's see. . . . There's not much left to tell. Several months at the institute and I was ready to go back to medicine. But not to surgery. I spent almost three years as a G.P. in one of the inner-city clinics, then went back and repeated the last two years of my surgical residency. I made the staff at Boston Doctors nearly two years ago. It hasn't been easy, but things have been picking up. At least until a week ago they were."

"David, this is much more than I ever hoped you would be able to tell me at this point," Ben said. "I'm grateful to you for doing it. Makes my job much easier."

David looked at him quizzically. "I'm curious," he said. "Why is it you haven't asked me whether or not I'm guilty of murder?"

Ben grinned and set his chin in his hands. "I have, my friend. A dozen different times in a dozen different ways. You've hauled yourself too far for me not to move hell and earth to keep you from getting bloodied anymore."

"Thank you." David whispered the words. "Ben, when you talked to Lauren, did she . . . ? Well, what I mean is we had a fight and . . ."

"David, I don't want to get in the middle of anything like this, but I do have something to say. I've known Lauren Nichols for years. She's a bright, incredibly beautiful woman who, by choice or circumstance, has not had to face too much adversity in her life. She . . . ah . . . she asked me to give you this." He pulled out a pink envelope—Lauren's stationery—and handed it to David.

"Not much doubt what it says, is there?" David folded the envelope and stuffed it in his pocket as he spoke.

"No, I guess not," Ben answered softly. "Are you all right to go home? I mean, if you need a place to stay for the night . . ."

"No thanks, Ben. I'll be okay. Really."

"I'll call you tomorrow," Ben said.

"Tomorrow," David echoed.

The steely afternoon sky was threatening, but the steady rain of the past several days had let up. The walk from Paddy O'Brien's to his apartment was about two miles and, with nothing to hurry home for, David forced a leisurely pace, stopping once to wander through the old cemetery where Paul Revere was buried. He reasoned that the graveyard would be an appropriate place to read Lauren's letter.

He needn't, he decided afterward, have bothered. The note was what he expected—semiformal—one-third thank-you-for-everything and two-thirds just-doesn't-seem-like-things-will-work-out-for-us. "I guess she took me for better or for better," David said as he tore the note into tiny pieces and ceremoniously tossed the pink petals over an ancient grave. He was surprised at how little hurt he felt. Perhaps it was because the loss of the relationship was just another brick in the wall that was closing him off from life. Then, as he trudged toward Boston Common, he began to realize that he had rarely been totally at ease around Lauren. It was largely his fault for trying to force her into the spaces Ginny had filled in his life. Even before it had started, he had doomed the relationship with his hopes.

The advance unit of the rush home had begun filling the walkways of the Common. Haggard businessmen, giggling groups of secretaries, and stylish career women—all crossing the grassy park on the way from their day to their evening. For a while David amused himself by trying to make eye contact with each person who passed. In the first few minutes the score was zero connections for twenty-five or thirty tries. He looked down at the pavement wondering if perhaps there was something there he was simply missing. Finally he bet himself that if one absolute, unquestionable eye contact could be made before he arrived home, the nightmare that followed the death of Charlotte Thomas would soon end.

By the time he reached Commonwealth Avenue, a light, misty rain had started falling again. He squinted upward and picked up his pace.

A block ahead of him a thin, elderly gentleman sat on a bench reading the early evening edition of the *Boston Globe*. He gauged the rain with an outstretched palm, and decided there was time to finish the last paragraphs of the article about the mercy killing at Doctors Hospital.

It was on page three, a two column spread describing in some detail David's arrest and arraignment. Unable to find a picture of him in time, the court reporter had resurrected one of Ben Glass from the newspaper's morgue.

The dapper little man finished the article, folded his paper beneath his arm, and started his walk home. Lost in thoughts of the story he had just read, the man failed to notice David's attempt at eye contact.

CHAPTER 16

"CHRISSY, CHECK the bathroom out. Does it look okay?" Lisa called out as she pulled on a skirt and zipped it up the side.

"Lisa, the bathroom looks fine. I told you, don't worry about the place. I've got an hour before she's due. That's plenty of time to clean up." Christine dropped a record into its jacket and replaced it on the shelf, taking a moment to straighten the row of albums. She had felt increasingly jittery and apprehensive since Dotty Dalrymple's late-afternoon call and now wished her roommates would head off for the evening so she could have some time to herself before the woman arrived.

The nursing director had given no hint as to why she wanted to stop over, but it was hard for Christine to believe the visit related to anything other than the death of Charlotte Thomas. She had given thought to calling the Regional Screening Committee for advice on how to handle the situation, but decided it was foolish when she wasn't at all certain of what, exactly, the situation was.

Lisa popped into the living room naked from the waist up. "Carole, bra or no bra for this guy?"

"He's a *blind* date, Lisa," Carole shouted from her room. "Just don't let him touch you and he'll never be able to tell whether you have one on or not."

"What do you think, Chrissy? Bra or no bra?"

Christine appraised her for a moment. "It's been a dull season," she said. "I think you should go for it." Her voice held far less cheer than she intended.

Lisa shrugged and slipped on a blouse. "You seem tight as a drum. Anything you want to talk about?"

"Believe me," Christine said, "if I had something to talk about, I would. I've never had Miss Dalrymple visit like this, that's all. She could want to promote me, she could want to fire me. I just have no idea.

Listen, you guys have fun. I hope he's nice. And thanks for helping me tidy up the place."

"Ooh, wait a minute!" Lisa snapped her fingers and dashed to her room, talking as she ran. "These came earlier this afternoon. I guess while you were out." She returned with a vase of flowers. "I think they'll be the perfect touch over here by the window . . . no, on the table . . . no, I think perhaps over the . . ."

"Lisa, those are lovely. Who sent them?"

"The mantel. Yes. They're perfect for the mantel."

"Lisa, *who?*"

"Oh, they're from Arnold. Arnold Ringer, the office heartthrob. The fool believes these are a shortcut to my body. And you know what?"

"He's right!" The two of them said the words in unison, then laughed.

Christine was straightening the kitchen when the doorbell rang. Moments later, Carole and Lisa called their good-byes and she was alone.

Her solitude lasted a sigh and one pace to the living room and back. With a purely symbolic knock Ida Fine slipped in the back door. Folded under her arm was a copy of the evening *Globe.* She started talking before Christine could explain that her visit was ill-timed.

"So where are my other two? Gone for the evening? So why not you?" Ida seldom asked a question without answering it herself or at least following it with another, often unrelated query.

"They've got dates, Ida," Christine said, hoping that the flatness in her voice would get the message across without being offensive.

"And you, the prettiest of the three, have none? You're sick, is that it? You're not feeling well. I have some soup upstairs. I know you nurses are too sophisticated to believe in such things, but . . ."

"No, Ida, I'm fine." There was no stopping the woman short of a frontal assault. "I'm just busy tonight. My nursing supervisor is coming over soon, so I've got to get ready. Maybe tomorrow or even later tonight we can talk, okay?"

Ida slapped the newspaper on the table. "I'll bet it's about that doctor who murdered the woman at your hospital," she said. "A doctor yet. My mother always wanted me to marry a doctor, but no, I had to be pigheaded and marry my husband, God rest his soul . . ."

Christine's eyes widened and fixed on Ida, who just kept talking. ". . . not that Harry was a bad man, mind you. He was a very good man. But sometimes—"

"Ida, what are you talking about?"

"The murder. David somebody. Must be Jewish. No, he can't be Jewish. A Jewish boy murdering a patient? I can't—"

"Ida, please!" Christine's shout produced instant silence. "What on earth are you talking about?"

"It's right here. In the *Globe*. I thought you knew. Here, keep the paper. Just leave me the TV section. I forgot to get a *TV Guide* while I was at the market."

She talked on, but Christine no longer heard her. The newspaper rustled in her hands even after she had folded back the page. "SURGEON CHARGED WITH MERCY KILLING; RELEASED ON BAIL," she read.

Color flashed in her cheeks, then drained. "Oh, my God," she said softly as she read the account of David's arrest and arraignment. "Oh, my God . . ."

Ida's verbal onslaught continued for another minute, then slowed and finally stopped. Christine read the article one word at a time, unaware that her landlady's gaze was now riveted on her.

Ida brought a chair from the kitchen table and Christine sank down numbly as she read the last few lines.

Reliable Globe sources report that Shelton filled prescriptions for large quantities of morphine on the day of Mrs. Thomas's death. Attorney Glass declined comment on the evidence, but reasserted his confidence in the innocence of his client. "When all the facts are in," he said, "I am sure the truth will be learned and my client will be vindicated." Dr. Shelton has been released on $100,000 bail. No date for trial has been set.

Ida rushed to the sink, wet a washcloth, and rubbed the cold compress over Christine's forehead. For almost a minute Christine made no move to stop her. Finally she nodded and gently pushed Ida's hand away.

"I guess you hadn't heard?" Ida said. "You know this David?" Miraculously, she stopped at two questions.

"Yes. I . . . know him," Christine said. David Shelton had been in and out of her thoughts since the day they'd first met on Four South. Nothing persistent or overwhelming—or even well defined—but he was there. Dockerty's inquiry had given her reason to talk about him with other nurses without seeming too obvious or interested.

Ida Fine rubbed her hands together anxiously. "Chrissy, your face is the color of my Swedish ivy. You want me to help you to bed or . . . or to call a doctor?"

Christine shook her head. "Ida, I'm all right. Really. But I have got to be alone for a while. Please?"

"Okay, I'm going. I'm going," Ida said. The pout invaded her voice more by reflex than by intention. "If you need me, I'm right upstairs. Also food, if you need food . . . keep the paper . . ." She was still talking as she backed out the door.

Christine read the article a second time, then wrote Ben Glass's name and law firm in her address book. Why had David purchased so much morphine? And on the day Charlotte died. A coincidence? Perhaps, but certainly not an easy one to accept. Maybe the hospital rumors were true this time. Maybe he does use drugs. Or deal them. Possibly both. But her sense of the man, however hazy, would not permit her to believe that was true.

She pressed her fingers against her temples as a dull, pulsing ache began accompanying each heartbeat. It really made no difference, she realized, why David had purchased morphine. She knew what she had done with the vials left her by The Sisterhood, and there was simply no way she could allow him to suffer for that. It had seemed so right, she thought. Damn it, it *was* right. Charlotte wanted it. The Committee approved. She hadn't acted alone. She closed her eyes tightly against the pulses, which had become hammers. Every tiny movement of her head made the pounding worse.

"Lie down," she told herself. "Find some aspirin, some Valium—something—and lie down." She blinked at the kitchen light, which had suddenly grown sun bright, then pulled herself to her feet. At that instant the doorbell rang.

She moved awkwardly to the stove. Tea, must make her some tea, she thought. The bell sounded again, more insistently.

With a groan Christine turned and raced through the hallway to the front door.

Dotty Dalrymple, wearing a purple overcoat, looked more imposing than usual. She smiled warmly from beneath a broad-brimmed purple rainhat and stepped inside. "This is wet," she said, holding her black umbrella like a baton. "Is there somewhere I can store it?" She seemed totally at ease.

The pounding in Christine's head began to recede as she set the umbrella by the door and hung up the tent-sized coat. "Tea," she said, forgetting to invite the woman in. "Would you like some tea?"

"Tea would be fine, Christine." Dalrymple's smile broadened as she motioned at the hallway. "In the living room?"

Christine calmed down a bit more. "Oh, I'm sorry, Miss Dalrymple," she said. "I didn't mean to be so impolite. Come in. I . . . I'm sorry for the mess the place is in but . . ."

"Nonsense." The director cut her off. "It's a lovely apartment. Please, Christine, relax. I promise not to bite you." She surveyed the living room briefly, selected an armless, upholstered chair across from the couch, and set herself down. "You mentioned tea?"

"Oh, yes, there's water on the stove. Let me heat it up."

"Lemon, if you have it," Dalrymple called out. "Otherwise plain."

"It'll only be a minute," Christine said, bustling about the kitchen. She bit into a biscuit from the only box she could find. "Damn," she hissed, spitting the stale cookie into the trash.

In the few minutes it took to arrange two cups of tea and some lemon slices on a tray, Christine singed her forearm and put a thin cut in the corner of one thumb. Two steps into the living room she froze, barely preventing the cups from toppling over. Dotty Dalrymple had a copy of the evening *Globe* unfolded on her lap.

"I assume from your reaction that you have read this evening's paper," Dalrymple said.

Christine closed her eyes and inhaled sharply. If her nursing director had made the connection between her and Charlotte, something was very wrong. Now she wished she had called The Sisterhood Screening Committee for advice. "I . . . my landlady showed it to me a little while ago," she stammered. "It's awful."

"Do you know Dr. Shelton well?" Dalrymple asked, motioning her to the couch.

"No, not really. We've barely even talked. I . . . I just met him for the first time last week." Too many words, she thought. What could she want?

"Do you know his background?"

His background? The question caught Christine off guard. Why would Dalrymple ask about that? Does she suspect? Was she trying to cover for her somehow? Christine decided to continue the verbal joust until the woman's purpose was clearer. "His background? Well, not much really. No more than some hospital rumors."

"The man is a known drug addict and probably an alcoholic," Dalrymple cut in bluntly. "Did you know that?" Christine was too shaken by the nursing director's statement to answer. After a moment the woman continued. "Several years ago he was removed from the staff at White Memorial. His appointment to the staff of our hospital was made over the loud protests of many of the other physicians. David Shelton is not a credit to his profession."

David's face formed in Christine's thoughts—gentle and intense, with kind, honest eyes. Dalrymple's words made no sense next to that picture. "I . . . I don't know what to say."

Dalrymple leaned forward in her chair and stared at her intently. "Obviously I am here sharing these facts with you for a reason." Her voice held a strange, mystical quality. "Christine, we are sisters, you and I. Sisters." Christine gasped. "I wanted so much to tell you that afternoon on Four South, but our rules forbid it. I have been part of The Sisterhood of Life since my earliest days in nursing. In fact, I represent the Northeast on our board of directors."

"I never would have thought . . . what I mean is, I never suspected . . ."

Dalrymple laughed. "There are several thousand of us, Christine. All over the country. The very best nursing has to offer. Joined by ideals and our pledge to forward the cause of human dignity."

"Then you know about Charlotte?"

"Yes, my dear, I know. All the directors know—the New England Screening Committee knows—and, of course, Peggy knows. I am here representing all of them. I am here to help."

"Help me?"

"Yes."

Christine shook her head. "Who's going to help Dr. Shelton?" she asked sullenly.

"My dear, you don't seem to have understood what I said." Dalrymple leaned forward for emphasis. "The man is a . . ."

Christine cut her off with a raised hand and a finger to her lips. She stared toward the side of the house. Dalrymple looked at her quizzically, then followed the line of her sight to the spot.

"I heard something," Christine whispered. "Out there by the window."

Dalrymple cocked her head to one side and listened. "Nothing," she said softly.

Christine wasn't convinced. She tiptoed to the side of the window and peered out at the night. The driveway and as much of the street as she could see were quiet. She stood there pressed against the wall for several minutes. Still nothing. Finally, with a shrug, she pulled the blinds and returned to the couch. "There was a noise out there," she said. "Some kind of a thunk."

"Probably a cat," Dalrymple said.

"Probably." There was little certainty in her voice. Dalrymple sipped patiently at her tea, waiting for Christine's concentration to return enough to continue their discussion.

"I'm . . . I'm sorry," Christine said at last.

Dalrymple smiled. "I understand what you're going through, dear," she said. "We all do, even though a situation such as yours has never before arisen and probably never will again. Ours is not an easy task. Everywhere along the way there are choices to make, and few if any of them are painless." There was an edge in her voice that Christine found unsettling.

"Just what are you suggesting I do?" she asked.

"Why nothing, dear," Dalrymple said. "Nothing at all."

Christine stared at her with disbelief. "Miss Dalrymple, I can't let that man suffer for something I've done. I could never live with myself."

Dalrymple looked back impassively and shook her head. "I'm afraid, Christine, that many more would suffer if you made any attempt to clear him."

Foreboding tightened in Christine's gut. "Wh . . . what do you mean?"

"Peg—the woman you spoke to—is Peggy Donner. Almost forty years ago, she founded The Sisterhood of Life. She has dedicated her entire life to its growth."

"And?"

"Christine, she will not allow you or any other sister to be hurt for doing what is right. She fears that your exposure will sooner or later lead to the exposure of the entire movement."

"But that's not true!" Christine cried. "I would never disclose anything about . . ."

"Please. What matters is not what you think would happen, but what Peggy thinks would happen. You see, before she would risk having the public learn of us through a sordid police investigation and sensationalist press, she will move to inform them herself." Dalrymple's expression was grave. "She has our tapes, Christine. All of them. If you move to go to the police, she has promised the board of directors that she will make them public in her own fashion. For several years now she has wanted to do so anyway. Only pressure from the rest of us has kept her in check. We did not feel it was time."

The throbbing in Christine's head began anew. "This . . . this can't be happening," she murmured. "It just can't."

"But it is, Christine. And the careers of all those in The Sisterhood hang by the thread that you hold. I'm not at all happy with the situation, despite my personal dislike for degenerate physicians such as Dr. Shelton. However, you must believe me, as one who has known Peggy for many years. She will do it."

Christine could only shake her head.

"We would like you to take a vacation from the hospital," Dalrymple continued softly. "I'll have no trouble granting you a leave for, say, three or four weeks. When you return, a shift supervisor's slot will be waiting for you. Perhaps Greece? The islands are beautiful this time of year. A month in the sun for you and the whole matter will have blown over."

"I . . . I don't think I could do that."

"For all our sakes, Christine, you must. Please believe me, Peggy's threat is not an idle one. With our number and the positive image she would project, she feels certain that The Sisterhood can now withstand exposure. If you go to the authorities, nothing, no one will be able to stop her. She may even be right, but I for one do not wish to risk my career and life on that chance."

"There would be chaos," Christine said.

"At least."

"I need time. Some time to think."

"The sooner you take your trip, the better," Dalrymple said. "I promise that getting away from this city will make the whole process much easier on you." She stood up, withdrew an envelope from her purse, and handed it to Christine. "This should help you do what you must. Please call me if I can be of any further help. It is a difficult situation, Christine, having to hurt one to avoid hurting many. But the choice is clear."

Christine followed her to the hallway and stood numbly to one side as she put on her coat. "Your sisters," Dalrymple said, "all of us, are grateful for what you are doing." She reached out and squeezed Christine's hand, then turned and let herself out.

The blue sedan, parked in an islet of darkness between two streetlights, was virtually invisible. Slouched behind the wheel, Leonard Vincent kept his attention fixed on the house as he struggled to catch his breath. The close call beneath the window and his dash to the car had left him winded and, despite the chill night air, soaked with sweat. On his lap his right hand moved in continuous circles, working the blade of a knife over a whetstone with the loving strokes of a concert violinist. The blade was eight inches long, tapered and slightly curved at the tip. The handle, carved bone, was nearly lost in his thick fist. The knife was Leonard Vincent's pride—the perfect instrument for close work.

The front door opened. Vincent snickered at the sight of the huge woman maneuvering herself down the concrete front steps. As she crossed the street to her car, he amused himself by planning the description he would use in his report. "At precisely five thirty a blimp floated into the house." Vincent's sallow face bunched in a mirthless grin. "She rolled out of the house and bounced down the stairs to her car. At precisely six fifteen she started getting behind the wheel. At six thirty she made it."

Distracted by his own wit, Vincent was slow to react when the woman made a sudden U-turn and came toward him. An instant before her headlights flashed by, he dove across the front seat, striking his forehead on the passenger door handle. He cursed the handle, then the door, and then the fat bitch who had made him hit it. But mostly he cursed himself for taking a job without knowing exactly who was hiring him or even what he was expected to do.

It had started with a call from a bartender friend. "Leonard," he had said, "I think I may have something for you. There's this broad in here askin' me if I know of anyone who's interested in makin' some big bucks. She says that whoever it is will have to be able to keep his mouth shut and do what he's told. I tried to find out some details, but she just gives me this fucking look, shoves a fifty across the counter, and says that there'll be more if I can get her someone who asks less questions than I do. You interested? I'll tell you, Leonard, the broad's weird, but I think she's on the level. Also, she's got great tits."

Right away, Vincent hadn't liked her or the setup. The name she had given him, Hyacinth, was a phony, he was sure of that. But no matter. Except for setting up the job, all she would do is deliver the money.

So he had ended up with twenty-five hundred bucks up front, a phone number, and a name—Dahlia. Another phony.

Vincent rubbed at the egg that had started forming over his left eye. He cursed Dahlia, who was responsible for his sitting out in a hurricane, bumping his head on a goddamn door. "Face it, Leonard," he told himself, "you've really hit bottom this time, no matter how good the fucking money is."

He watched the house until he was reasonably sure Christine Beall was not coming out, then he shoved the knife into a hand-tooled leather case and drove around the corner to a phone booth. A woman answered on the second ring.

"Yes?"

"This is Leonard." His voice was a toneless rasp.

"Yes?"

"You wanted a report on everyone who talks to this Christine."

"And?"

"Well, a big fat woman just left. She got here about forty-five minutes ago."

"Mr. Vincent, your instructions were to call as soon as she met with someone, not to wait until they had left."

"Hey, you don't sound like Dahlia. Is this Dahlia?"

"Mr. Vincent, please. When Hyacinth paid you, she told you to call this number and report. Now you will either do exactly as instructed or I promise you trouble. Big trouble. Is that clear?"

The threat was effective. Leonard Vincent feared nothing that he could see, but an icy, disembodied voice was something else. He cursed himself again for taking the job. "Yeah, it's clear," he said.

"All right. How long did you watch the house after the woman left?"

"Ten, fifteen minutes. I don't know exactly. Long enough, though. She's staying put."

"Very well. Return to your post, please."

"What about sleep?"

"You are being paid, and paid well, to watch that woman and report on her movements, Mr. Vincent. Now return to your post. And remember, we wish to know the minute she talks with anyone—not after they have already left. Call this number at two o'clock, and we shall discuss your sleep. Oh, one last thing. Before she paid your advance money, the woman who hired you did some checking around. She learned of your tendency to hurt people, sometimes without provocation. No one is to be touched without our say-so. Is *that* clear?"

Vincent shrugged. "Like you said, it's your money." He hung up the phone, stared at it for a moment, then spat on the receiver. A reflex check of the coin return and he drove back to watch the house.

The only lights in the apartment shone through the blinds of the living room window. Every few minutes Christine's silhouette appeared, then vanished. Leonard Vincent picked up his whetstone and began clucking a one-note melody as he withdrew another knife from the glove compartment.

* * *

Christine had been unable to sit since Dotty Dalrymple's departure. She paced from room to room, tapping the unopened envelope against her palm. Suddenly she looked down, as if noticing it for the first time. Then she tore it open.

Inside were five neatly banded packets of hundred dollar bills—ten in each.

"The choice is clear," she said out loud, testing her nursing director's words. Again the image of David's face formed in her mind. She stared at the packets, then threw them on her bureau.

"The choice is clear," she whispered.

CHAPTER 17

ON THURSDAY, the ninth of October, as on the previous three days, Boston forecasters predicted an end to the tenacious low pressure system and the rain. For the fourth straight day, they were wrong.

In Huddleston, New Hampshire, ninety minutes north of the city, a one-hundred-fifty-year-old covered bridge washed away before Crystal Brook—little more than a trickle in August.

Accidents on frenetic Route 128, never a rarity, more than tripled.

On David Shelton, however, as on most in the area, the effects of the unrelenting downpour were even more insidious. It was more than a mile from his apartment to the financial district and the law offices of Wellman, MacConnell, Enright, and Glass. Irritable and frustrated by inactivity, he chose to defy the storm and walk to his appointment with Ben. Within a block he was soaked beyond the consideration of turning back. "Wet is wet," he pronounced testily, trudging head down into the wind.

The suite of offices occupied most of the twenty-third floor of a mirror-glass building whose name and address were both One Bay State Square. "No wonder he charges $10,000," David muttered as he approached the reception area. Three women were handling traffic with practiced calm in a space nearly as big as David's whole office.

He looked and felt like a drowned rodent. For a moment he thought of asking the severe receptionist for some towels and a change of clothes, but nothing in her expression encouraged that kind of frivolity. "Mr. Glass," he said meekly, "I have an appointment with Mr. Glass?" The woman, struggling to mask her amusement, motioned him to a bank of leather easy chairs. Discreet chimes sounded, signaling Ben.

Whatever the goals of the interior decorators, David decided, making clients who looked like drowned rodents feel less conspicuous was not one of them. The sterile opulence featured thick gold carpeting, original oils on the walls, and a jungle of bamboo palms and huge ferns. A well-stocked library was prominently displayed behind glass walls. Even more impressive to him was the fact that several people were actually using it.

Ben popped around a corner, smiled at David's appearance, then extended both hands. "Either you walked over or this is autumn's answer to the Blizzard of Seventy-eight," he said.

"Both." He took the lawyer's hands in his and squeezed them tightly. Ben was a thin break in the clouds—an island in the madness and confusion.

"Had lunch yet?" he asked as they walked to his office.

"Yesterday. But please, nothing for me. You go ahead if you want."

"Meatloaf à la Amy?" He produced a brown bag from his desk. "There's plenty here. You sure?"

David shook his head. "No thanks. Really." He looked around the room. Ben's cluttered office was in sharp contrast to the rest of the austere suite. Books and journals were everywhere, many of them open or marked with folded sheets of legal paper. The walls were overhung with framed photographs and pen-and-ink drawings. "Your partners let you get away with all this earthiness?" he asked, gesturing at the disarray.

"They think I'm camp." Ben grinned. "One of my partners once called my office 'funky.' A thousand a month just for this room and he calls it funky." He took a bite of sandwich, then spoke around chews. "Even soaked, you look better than yesterday. Are you holding up all right?"

David shrugged. "I got suspended from the staff at the hospital," he said flatly.

"What?"

"Suspended. I had a visit this morning from Dr. Armstrong—she's the chief of staff and the only one at that place who really seems to give a shit about what happens to me. Anyhow, she called and asked to stop by. I knew what she had to say and suggested she tell me over the phone, but she insisted on doing it in person. That's the kind of woman she is."

"So?"

"So, last night the executive committee voted, over her objection, to ask me to voluntarily suspend my staff and O.R. privileges until this whole business is cleared up."

Ben shook his head. "Not ones to waste any time, this executive committee of yours."

"According to Dr. Armstrong, Wallace Huttner, the chief of surgery, led the push. He's also helping the murdered woman's husband put together a malpractice case against me. If I'm found guilty, they want to be ready to move right in and sue. Dr. Armstrong said they made my suspension voluntary as a favor to me—to keep me from having an enforced suspension on my record. I think they did it because it's less paperwork for them."

"Shit," Ben muttered.

"It's probably just as well. Even before I was arrested the place became instant iceberg the minute I set foot in the door. It's all crazy. I . . . I don't know what the hell to do. I'd fight back if I had even a faint idea of who or what I was fighting, but . . ."

"Hey, easy," Ben urged. "The fight's just starting. For now I'll throw the punches, but you'll get your chance. This afternoon we share ideas about who and why. Tomorrow we'll start planning what to do. Somewhere out there is an answer. Just be patient and don't do anything rash or crazy. We'll find it."

David nodded and managed a tense smile. "Hey, I almost forgot this." He pulled a soggy envelope from his pants pocket. "Good thing pencil doesn't run," he said, passing it over. "Dr. Armstrong didn't want me to get into any more trouble at the hospital, so in exchange for my promise to stay put, she did some checking for me. There are four names on the sheet inside. She got them from the hospital personnel computer. Two orderlies with prison records, a nurse with a drug-use history, and another nurse who is pressuring the hospital to post a Patient's Bill of Rights. I don't know any of them. It's not much, but Dr. Armstrong said she would get the names to Lieutenant Dockerty."

Ben cut him off. "She already has, David."

"What?"

"The lieutenant called a short time ago. I talked to him for half an hour. He wants you—and Dr. Armstrong—to quit playing Holmes and Watson and let him do his work."

"Do his work?" David's voice was incredulous. "Ben, the man has spent almost a week tar-and-feathering me. He's the other side. He's one we should be fighting."

Ben shook his head. "No, pal, he's not," he said firmly. "He's a damn good cop. I've known him for as long as I've been in practice. Whether you believe it or not, he doesn't want to see you fall."

"Then why the fuck did he arrest me?"

"Had to." Ben shrugged. "Pressure from all sides and a ton of circumstantial evidence. Motive, opportunity, weapon—you know all that."

David clenched his fists. "I also know that I didn't kill that woman," he said.

"Well, John Dockerty's not one hundred percent convinced you did either. Otherwise he wouldn't be trying to work on Marcus Quigg, the pharmacist who—"

"Dockerty told me who he is," David broke in. "But, Ben, I never met the man. Why would he want to do this to me?"

"One of the big three," Ben said. "Vengeance, fear, money."

David shook his head. "Ben, until Dockerty said his name, I'm sure I never heard it before. Marcus Quigg isn't exactly John Jones, you know. If I took care of a Quigg . . . no, vengeance doesn't make any sense at all."

"Unless it was a sister or daughter," Ben said. "Different name."

"I guess." David slapped the desk in exasperation. "But there are just too many unpredictable events to believe anyone could have planned to frame me. Way too many."

"David, right now it can't do anything but harm to try and overthink this thing. There simply isn't enough information . . . yet." Ben paused, twisting his wedding band as he searched for words. "David," he said finally, "I wasn't going to bring this up today, but maybe it's best that I do. I told you yesterday that I wanted complete honesty from you, yes?" David nodded. "You didn't mention to me that you were once accused of deliberately overmedicating a cancer patient of yours. Is that true?"

David stiffened. Disbelief widened his eyes. "Ben, I . . . this is crazy," he stammered. "That was at least nine years ago. I was completely exonerated. I . . . how do you know about it?"

"Lieutenant Dockerty knows. I don't know who, but someone tipped him off."

"The nurse, it must have been that goddamn nurse. How in the hell . . . ?"

"What happened?"

"It was nothing. Really. I ordered pain medicine on a dying old lady —every four hours as needed. And believe me, she had plenty of pain. Well, I found that this one nurse was too damn lazy to check on whether she needed it. So I changed the order to every two hours, lowered the dose, and took out the 'as needed' part so the woman had to receive it. The next day the nurse reported me. There was an inquiry and I think *she* ended up getting censured."

"Well, now it seems she's getting even," Ben said. "Listen, David, you must tell me everything. No matter how insignificant it might seem to you. Everything. This nurse coming forward after nine years may be yet another coincidence. There *was* the article in last night's paper. But if someone put her up to it, we've got even more problems than we realized. And maybe, just maybe, you have the answer inside you without even knowing it."

"Maybe . . ." David's voice drifted off. For a few seconds he squinted and scratched above one ear.

"What? What is it? Do you remember something?"

David shook his head. "I could swear something popped in and out of my mind. Something someone said about Charlotte Thomas. I . . ." He shrugged. "Whatever it was—*if* it was—is gone."

"Well, go home and take it easy, pal. We'll meet again tomorrow. Same time?"

"Same time," David said weakly.

"Say, listen, if you're free tomorrow night, why don't you plan on coming here at four. We can talk, then you can come home and have dinner with us. You can meet Amy and the kids and get a good meal in the bargain. She'd love to get to know you. Would even if I hadn't told her you were paying for little Barry's orthodontia."

"Sounds fine," David said with little enthusiasm.

"Do you good," Ben added. "Besides, Amy has this sister . . ." He smiled, then suddenly the two of them were laughing. David couldn't remember the last time he had.

"You're losing it, Shelton," David said as he paced through the apartment. "You're losing it and you know it." The two hours following his departure from Ben's office had seemed like ten.

Outside, the steady rain continued, punctuated now and then by the muted timpani of distant thunder. One minute the three rooms felt like an empty coliseum, the next like a cage. It was becoming harder and harder to sit, more and more difficult to concentrate—to focus in on anything. Call someone, he thought. Call someone or else ignore the rain and go run. But stop pacing. He picked up his running shoes and stepped to the window. Sheets of rain blurred the somber afternoon sky. Then, as if in warning, a lightning flash colored the room an eerie blue-white. Seconds later, a soft rumble crescendoed and exploded, reverberating through the apartment. He threw the shoes in his closet.

This is how it felt; he recognized it. After the accident. This is how it all started. Still the restlessness increased.

Is there anything in the medicine chest? Didn't Lauren always keep something here for her headaches? Just in case the pacing won't stop. In case the loneliness gets too bad. You don't need anything, but just in case. In case the sleep doesn't come. In case the night won't end.

He paced from one end of the hall to the other, then back. Each time he paused by the bathroom door. Just in case . . .

All at once he was there, reaching for the mirrored door of the medicine chest. Reaching, he suddenly realized, toward himself. He froze as his outstretched hand touched its reflection. His eyes, glazed with fear and isolation, locked on themselves and held. A minute passed. Then another. Gradually, the trembling in his lips began to subside. His breathing slowed and deepened. "You're not alone," he told himself softly. "You have a friend who has learned over eight hard years to love you—no matter what. You have yourself. Open that door, touch one fucking pill, and lose him. All those years, and he'll be just . . . gone. Then you *will* be alone."

His hand dropped away from the mirror. Resolve tightened across his face, then pulled at the corners of his mouth until he was smiling. He nodded at himself—once, then again. Faster and faster. He saw the strength, the determination grow in his eyes.

"You're not alone," he said as he turned from the mirror and walked to the living room. "You're not alone," he said again as he stretched out on the sofa. "You're not . . ."

Twenty minutes later, when the phone rang, David was still on the sofa. He skimmed over the last few lines of the Frost poem he was reading, then rolled over and picked up the receiver.

"David, I was afraid you hadn't gotten home yet." It was Ben.

"Oh, no, I'm here," David said. He smiled, then added, "I'm very much here."

"Well, enjoy your free time while you have it," Ben said excitedly, "because I think within a day or two you'll be back to work."

David felt an instant surge. "Ben, what's happened? Talk slowly so it registers."

"I just received a call, David, from a nurse at your hospital. She said that she can positively clear you of the murder of Charlotte Thomas. I'm meeting her at a coffee shop in a couple of hours. I think she's for real, pal, and if I'm right, the nightmare's over."

David glanced down the hall in the direction of the bathroom. "Thank God," he said, half to the phone and half to himself. "Ben, can I come? Shouldn't I be there?"

"Until I know what this woman has to say, I don't want you involved. Tell you what. Expect me at your place at nine—no, make that nine thirty—tonight. I'll fill you in then. With luck, our dinner tomorrow night will turn out to be a celebration."

"That would be wonderful," David said wistfully. "Tell me, who's the nurse?"

"Oh, she said she's met you. Her name's Beall. Christine Beall."

At the mention of her name David felt another momentary surge. "Ben, that's what I was trying to think of in your office. Remember? When something popped in and out of my head?"

"I remember."

"Well it was something *she* said. Christine Beall. Right after I shot my mouth off to Charlotte's husband. She whispered to me that she was proud of the way I stood up to Huttner, and . . . and then she said, 'Don't worry. Things have a way of working out.' Then all of a sudden she was gone. Ben, do you think . . . ?"

"Listen, pal, do us both a favor if you can. Try not to project. A few hours, then we'll know. Okay?"

"Okay," David said. "But you know I will anyway, don't you?"

"Yeah, I know," Ben said. "Nine thirty."

"Right." David checked his watch. "Will you at least synchronize with me so I don't go too nuts waiting for you?"

Ben laughed. "Five of five, pal. I have five of five."

"Four fifty-five it is," David sang. He set down the receiver.

His elation was brief. Over the past few days, conscious thoughts of Christine had been submerged in the nightmare. At that moment David realized they had never been far from the surface.

"It wasn't you, was it?" he said softly. "You know who did it, but it wasn't you."

His concern for Christine faded quickly as the impact of Ben's call settled in. He clenched his fists and pumped them up and down. A grin spread over his face, then a giggle, then a laugh. He rushed to his record collection. Seconds later he was bouncing through the living room, throwing jabs and uppercuts at the air. The music from *Rocky* filled the apartment.

Fanfare still in his ears, he walked down the hall and into the bathroom. He stood before the medicine cabinet and looked at himself. "You made it, buddy," he said to his reflection. "Stronger than ever now. I'm proud of you. Really."

Out of curiosity, not need, he reached up and pulled open the door. The shelves were empty.

A shower and long-overdue letters to his brothers killed an hour and a half. Feasting on spaghetti with Ragu sauce did in another thirty minutes. The seven o'clock news made it two hours until Ben.

David paced impatiently for a while, then pulled his chess set from the closet along with his copy of *Chess Openings Made Simple*. Within a short time he gave up. Renewed thoughts of Christine made it impossible to concentrate. Somehow, in the short time they had talked, in their brief contacts, she had touched him deeply. There was a disarming, innocent intensity about her—an energy he had seldom seen survive the years in medical or nursing school. Then, too, there were her eyes—wide and warm, inviting and exploring one moment, flashing with anger the next. More and more, he found himself hoping, even praying, that she had no direct involvement in the death of Charlotte Thomas. By nine o'clock he had convinced himself that there was no way she could have.

For a time he entertained himself by measuring what he knew of the woman against Lauren. Quickly he realized that, as typically happened, he was attributing qualities to Christine that he *wanted* to be there. "When are you going to learn, Shelton?" He chastised himself loudly, then returned to the chessboard.

By nine fifteen he was pacing again. Once he heard the elevator gears engage and raced out into the hall. Then he remembered that he would have to buzz Ben through the downstairs foyer door. Still, he waited out there just in case. The elevator stopped one floor below.

He returned to the apartment and spent five minutes playing out a conversation with Wallace Huttner in which the surgical chief apologized for jumping to such misguided conclusions and suggested that they might explore the possibilities of a partnership. David practiced a refusal speech, then, in case Huttner was truly contrite, one of acceptance.

At precisely nine thirty the downstairs buzzer sounded. David leaped to the intercom.

"Yes?"

"David, it's me." The excitement in Ben's voice was apparent despite the barely functional intercom. "The woman is for real. Sad, but very much for real. It's over, pal, it's over."

The word *sad* stood out from all the others. "Come on up," David said as he pressed the door release. His voice held surprisingly little enthusiasm.

Thirty seconds later the elevator clattered into use. Shit, David thought, it *was* her. He stood in the open doorway and listened to the groaning cables. Turning his nightmare over to Christine Beall was not the way he had wanted it to end, no matter what her actions had put him through. He was halfway to the elevator when the car light appeared in the diamond-shaped window of the outside door. A second later, the car crunched to a halt. The automatic inside gate rattled open.

David stopped several feet away and waited for Ben. Five seconds passed. Then another five. He took a tentative step forward. The door remained closed. Finally he peered through the grimy window. Ben stood to one side, leaning calmly against the wall.

"Hey, what's going on?" David asked, swinging open the heavy door. The lawyer's eyes stared at him, moist and vacant. His face was bone white. Suddenly the corners of his mouth crinkled upward in a half-smile.

"Ben, not funny," David said. "Now cut the crap and come on out of there. I wanna hear."

Ben's lips parted as he took a single step forward. Crimson gushed from his mouth and down his chin. David caught him halfway to the floor. The back of Ben's tan raincoat was an expanding circle of blood. Protruding from the center was the carved white handle of a knife.

Sticky, warm life poured over David's hands and clothes as he dragged his friend from the elevator.

"Help!" he screamed. "Someone, please help me!"

He pulled the knife free and threw it on the carpet, then rolled Ben's body face up. The lawyer's dark eyes stared unblinkingly at the ceiling. David checked for a carotid pulse, but knew that the blood, now oozing from one corner of Ben's mouth, was the sign of a fatal wound to the heart or a main artery.

"Please help." David's plea was a whimper. "Please?"

The stairway door at the far end of the hall burst open. Leonard Vincent stood there, his massive frame darkened by the light behind him. Almost casually, he reached to his waistband and withdrew a revolver. The ugly silhouette of a silencer protruded from one end.

"It's your turn, Dr. Shelton," Vincent rasped, certain he was facing the man Dahlia had described. He had followed Christine Beall to a coffee shop and recognized the criminal lawyer with whom she was meeting. Dahlia's response to his call was immediate: Glass first, then Shelton, and later the girl. Now, thanks to the lawyer, he could handle the first two almost at once.

David stumbled backward and tried to straighten up, but his hand, covered with blood, slid off the wall and he spun to the carpet. Inches away was the knife. He grabbed it by the tip and hurled it at the advancing figure. It fell two yards short. Vincent picked it up and calmly wiped the blade on his pants. He was less than fifty feet away. Between them, Ben's lifeless body stretched across the corridor. Light from an overhead bulb caught the huge man's face. He was smiling. His smile broadened as he raised the silenced revolver.

David scrambled backward, his mouth open in a soundless scream. His mind registered a spark from the tip of the silencer at the instant the doorjamb beside his ear exploded.

He dove head first into his apartment, flailing with his feet to close the solid wood door. The latch clicked shut moments before a soft crunch and the instantaneous appearance of two dime-sized holes by the knob.

David looked wildly about, then clawed himself upright. He raced to the living room. The fire escape! Opening the window, he looked down at his stockinged feet. For a moment he thought about the closet and his running shoes. No chance, he decided. With a groan of resignation, he stepped out onto the metal landing. There was a crash from inside the apartment as the front door burst open. An instant later David was racing down toward the alley, four flights below.

The night was tar black and cold. The metal steps, slippery in the driving downpour, hurt his feet, but the discomfort barely registered. Just beyond the third floor, his heel caught the edge of a step and shot out from under him. He fell hard, tumbling down half a flight. Several inches of skin ripped from his right forearm. Above him, there was a loud clank as Leonard Vincent stepped onto the fourth-floor landing. At that moment David had the absurd notion that he should have opened the window to the fire escape, then hidden in the closet.

I'll bet it would've worked, he thought, as he scrambled, panting, toward the second-floor landing. He slipped again, electricity pulsing up his spine as he slid the final few stairs. Through the metal slats overhead, he saw the man, a faint dark shadow moving against the night sky.

On his hands and knees, David struggled to release the ladder from the second-floor landing to the alley. Through his soaked shirt needles of rain stung his back. The metal slats dug into his knees. The ladder release would not budge.

With a glance above him, David grabbed the side of the landing and rolled off. He hung there for a moment, trying to judge the distance to the pavement, then dropped. He felt and heard the crunch in his left ankle as he hit. The leg gave way instantly. He screamed, then bit down on the edge of a finger so hard that he drew blood.

Lying on the wet pavement, he heard the clanging footsteps and grunting breaths of the man overhead. The killer was nearing the second landing.

David stumbled to one foot, then hesitated. If the ankle were sprained, there would be discomfort, but he could move. If it was broken, he was about to die. Teeth clenched, he set his left foot down. Pain seared through the ankle, but it held—once, then again and again. Suddenly he was running.

At the end of the alley he looked back. The man had lowered the ladder and was calmly stepping off the bottom rung.

Clarendon Street was nearly deserted. David paused uncertainly, then decided to try for heavily trafficked Boylston Street. At that instant he saw a figure half a block from him walking in the opposite direction toward the river. Instinctively he ran that way. His gait was awkward. Every other stride was agony. Still, he closed on the figure.

"Help," he called out. "Please help." His cry was instantly swallowed by the night storm. "Please help me."

He was ten feet away when the figure lurched around to face him. It was an old man—toothless, unshaven, and drunk. Water dripped from the brim of his tattered hat. David started to speak, but could only shake his head. Gasping, he supported himself against a parked car. Without sound or warning, the rear window of the car shattered. David spun around. Through the gloom and the rain he saw his pursuer's shadow, down on one knee in position to fire once more. He was running when flame spit from the silencer. Running when the bullet meant for him slammed into the old man, spinning him to the pavement.

He pushed himself forward, through the pain and the downpour.

Pushed himself harder than ever in his life. His heels slammed down on small stones, sending dagger thrusts up each leg. Still he ran—across Marlborough Street, across Beacon Street, and on toward the river. It was his route, his run—the path he had jogged so many promising sunlit mornings. Now he was running from his death. Behind him, the huge killer gained ground with every stride.

Traffic on Storrow Drive was light. David splashed across without slowing down—onto the stone footbridge and over the reflecting basin. Ahead of him, the lights of Cambridge shimmered through the rain and danced on the pitch-black Charles.

Double back, he thought. Double back and help Ben. Maybe he needs you. Maybe he's not really dead. For God's sake, *do something*.

He risked a glance over his shoulder. The man, delayed by several cars on Storrow Drive, had lost some ground, but not enough. David knew the chase was almost over. With fear his only rhythm and flailing strides, he was near collapse. He scanned the deserted esplanade for somewhere to hide. The killer was too close. His only hope was the river. Stones along the bank tore away what was left of his socks as he scrambled over them and plunged into the frigid oily water.

He had little capacity left for more pain, yet icy stilettos found what places remained and bore in. Behind him, Leonard Vincent crossed the footbridge and neared the bank. As deeply as he could manage, David sucked in air and dropped below the surface. He was twenty feet from shore, pushing himself along the muddy bottom. His clothes became leaden, at first helping him stay down, then threatening to hold him there. He broke once for air. Then again. Still he drove himself. The water stung his eyes and made it impossible to see. Its taste, acrid and repugnant despite years of waste- and pollution-control, filled his nose and mouth.

All at once his head struck something solid. Dazed and near blind, he explored the obstacle with his hands. It was a dock—a floating wooden **T**, laid on the river to tether some of the dozens of small sailboats that spent the warm months darting over reflections of the city.

For a minute, two, all was silent save for the spattering of rain on the dock and on the river. David crouched by the dock in four feet of water, rubbing at the silt in his eyes. His feet and legs were numb. Then he heard footsteps—careful, measured thumps. The killer was on the dock! David pressed the side of his face against the coarse slimy wood. The footsteps grew louder, closer. He slid his hand under the dock. Did it break water? Was there room enough to breathe? If he ducked under he might be trapped without air. If he didn't . . .

He inhaled slowly, deeply, realizing the breath might be his last. Eyes closed tightly, he pulled himself beneath the dock. His head immediately hit wood. Terror shot through him. He was trapped, his lungs near empty. Pawing desperately overhead, his hands struck the side of a beam. An undersupport! He pushed to one side and instantly his face popped free of the water. There were four inches of air. A thin smile tightened across his lips, then vanished. The footsteps were directly over his face. Through the narrow slits between timbers he could have touched the bottoms of the man's shoes, now inches from his eyes. The pacing stopped. David bent his neck back as far as he could and pressed his forehead against the bottom of the dock. Through pursed lips, he sucked in air slowly, soundlessly.

Above his face, the shoes scraped, first one way and then another, as Vincent scanned the river. Then, with agonizing slowness, the man headed toward the other arm of the **T.**

In the icy water David began to shake. He clenched down with all his strength to keep from chattering and wedged himself more tightly between the river bottom and the dock. All feeling from his neck down was gone. The footsteps receded further and further, then disappeared. The closed space began to exert its own ghastly terror. Is he just sitting up there? David wondered. Sitting and waiting? How long? *How much longer can I stay like this?*

He counted. To one hundred, then back to zero. He sang songs to himself—silly little songs from his childhood. Gradually, inexorably, he lost control over the soft staccato of his teeth. Still he did not move. ". . . This old man he played two, he played knick-knack on my shoe . . ." ". . . I knew a man with seven wives and seven cats and seven lives . . ." ". . . Red Sox, White Sox, Yankees, Dodgers, Phillies, Pirates . . ."

The chill reached deep inside him. He could no longer stop the shaking. How long had it been? His legs seemed paralyzed. Would they even move? ". . . Red Rover, Red Rover, come over, come over . . ." ". . . I'll bet you can't catch me, betcha can't betcha can't . . ."

"I'll bet . . . I'll bet . . . I'll bet I'm going to die."

⋀CHAPTER 18

JOEY ROSETTI closed his eyes and breathed in the fragrance of Terry's excitement. That scent, her taste, the way her dark nipples grew firm beneath his hand—even after twelve years the sensations were as fresh and arousing as they were warm and comfortable.

He rubbed his cheeks against the silky skin between her thighs, then drew his tongue upward between her moist folds.

"It's good, Joey. So good," Terry moaned, drawing his face more tightly against her. She smiled down at him and dug her fingers through the jet-black waves of his hair.

Shuddering, she brought his mouth to hers. Her heels slid around his body as the hunger in their kiss grew. He entered her with slow, deepening thrusts.

"Joey, I love you," Terry whispered. "I love you so much."

She sucked on his lips and caressed the fold between his buttocks. The heavy muscles tensed as her fingers worked deeper.

Joey's thrusts grew quicker, more forceful. It would be soon, they knew, for both of them.

Suddenly, the telephone on the bedside table began ringing. "No," Terry groaned. "Let it ring." But already she felt a let-up in Joey's intensity. "Let it ring," she begged again. Six times, seven—the intrusive jangling was not going to stop. The pressure inside her lessened. An eighth ring, then a ninth.

"Damn," Joey snarled, popping free of her as he rolled over. "This better not be a fucking wrong number." He mumbled a greeting, listened for half a minute, then said the single word, "Where?" A moment later, he kicked the covers off and scrambled out of bed.

"Terry, it's the doc," he said. "Doc Shelton. He's hurt and he needs help." He flicked on the bedside light and raced to the closet.

"I'm coming with you," Terry demanded, pulling herself upright.

"No, honey. Please." He held up a hand. "He's like crazy. I could barely understand him. But he did say there was trouble. I don't want you there. Call the tavern. See if Rudy Fisher's still working. If he is, tell him to get his ass over to the esplanade by the Charles River. The Hatch Shell. I'll meet him there."

"Joey, can't you call someone else? You know how I feel about that m—"

"Look, I don't have time to debate. Rudy's been with me longer than y—for a long time. If there's trouble, I want him around."

Twelve years had taught Terry the uselessness of arguing with her husband over such matters. Still, his insistence on Rudy Fisher, a giant who doted on violence, frightened her. "Joey, please," she urged. "Just be careful. No rough stuff. Please promise me. If he's hurt, then just get him to a hospital and come home."

"Baby, the man saved my life," he said, pulling on a pair of pants. "Whatever he needs from me he gets."

"But you promised . . ."

"Listen," Joey snapped, "I'll be careful. Don't worry." He forced a more relaxed tone. "I'm a businessman now, you know that. If he's hurt, I'll get him to the hospital. Don't worry. Just do what I asked you to." He grabbed a shirt from the closet.

Terry sat on the edge of the bed, admiring him as he dressed. At forty-two he still had the cleanly chiseled features and sinewy body of a matinee idol. There was a calm, unflappable air about him that gave no hint of the deadly situations he had survived in his life. Reminders were there, though, in the burgundy scars that criss-crossed his abdomen. One, an eighteen-inch crescent around his left flank, was a memento from his days as a youth gang leader in Boston's North End. Intersecting it just above his navel was another scar—ten years old—the result of a gunshot wound sustained while thwarting a holdup at the Northside.

Rosetti had been one of David's first private patients at White Memorial—a twelve-hour procedure that some of the operating room staff still spoke of reverently. During Joey's convalescence, a friendship had developed between the two men.

"Terry, will you stop gawking and make that call," Joey said tersely as he stepped into a pair of black loafers. He waited until her back was turned, then snatched his revolver and shoulder holster from beneath the sweaters on his closet shelf.

He was headed toward the door when Terry said, "Joey, don't use it, please."

Rosetti walked back and kissed her gently. "I won't, honey. Unless I absolutely have to, I won't. Promise."

Terry Rosetti waited until the door slammed shut, then sighed and picked up the phone.

* * *

David sat on the ground of the esplanade, hanging on to the dangling pay phone receiver to keep from falling over. He shook uncontrollably, fading in and out of awareness as the driving rain splattered him with mud. Squinting through the downpour, he could see the Hatch Shell Amphitheater. The mountainous half-dome, looming several hundred yards away, was the only landmark he'd been able to think of to give Joey.

Slowly, painfully, he released the phone, rolled over in the muddy puddle, and began crawling toward a night-light at one side of the dome. For ten minutes, fifteen, he clawed his way over the sodden ground. The tiny bulb, at first a beacon, soon became his entire world. It seemed farther away with each agonizing inch. Again and again he tried to stand, only to crumple beneath the pain in his ankle and the overwhelming chill throughout his body. Each time he got to his hands and knees and pushed on. Twice he doubled over as spasms knotted his gut, forcing fetid river water and bile out of his nose and mouth. The taunting light grew dimmer, more distant.

"It can't end like this." David said the words over and over, using them as a cadence to force one hand, then one knee in front of the other. "It can't end like this . . ."

Suddenly the grass turned to concrete, then to smooth slick marble. He was on the stairs at the base of the Shell. His shivering gave way to paroxysmal twitches of his hands, shoulders, and neck—the harbingers of a full-blown seizure. Blood dribbled from the corner of his mouth as his teeth, chattering like jackhammers, minced the edges of his tongue. Overhead, the night light flickered for a moment, then went black. David felt the incongruous peace of dying settling within him. He fought the sensation with what little strength, what little concentration, he had left. Christine knows, he thought. She knows why Ben is dead and now she'll die, too. Must hang on. Hang on and help her. It can't end like this. . . . It can't.

The emptiness had set in only minutes after Christine had declined Ben's offer of a ride and started home. It was as if a tap had opened, draining from her every ounce of emotion and feeling. She had abandoned her attempt to shelter herself beneath the overhangs of buildings and wandered along the center of the sidewalk, oblivious to the downpour.

The session with Ben had been easy—at least, easier than she had anticipated. In his comfortable, nonjudgmental manner, he had assured her again and again that her decision to confess was the right thing, the *only* thing to do. He had accepted the explanation she chose to give— one in which she, acting alone, had honored the wishes of a close, special friend who was dying painfully. The most difficult moment had come when he brought up the forged C222 order form.

"The what?" Christine asked, stalling for even a little time.

"The form. The one Quigg, the pharmacist, claimed Dr. Shelton filled at his store."

Christine's mind raced. Clearly, Miss Dalrymple or one of the others had used the form to protect her. With no forewarning of what had transpired, she had no ready response. "I . . . I used it and . . . and then I bribed the pharmacist."

"How did you come by it in the first place?" Ben asked. There was no trace of disbelief in his face.

"I . . . I'd rather not say just yet." Christine held her breath, hoping the lawyer would push no further. With a few days she could think of something. If Miss Dalrymple still wished to protect The Sisterhood, she would have to do whatever she could to insure that the pharmacist did not contradict her. She would also have to convince Peggy that Christine was determined to keep the movement out of her confession.

Ben studied her for a moment, then nodded. "Very well, then," he said. "Let's talk about how I believe you should handle things. That is, if you want my advice."

"I'd like more than that, Mr. Gl . . . I mean, Ben. If it's possible, I would like you to represent me."

"I'll have to think it over, Christine. Just to be sure there wouldn't be any conflict of interest involved." He smiled. "But off hand, I don't think there would be. You meet me Monday morning at my office. Nine o'clock. I'll see to it that Lieutenant Dockerty is there. Don't worry. I'll tell you ahead of time exactly what to say to him. Monday, okay?"

Christine nodded.

Monday. Christine repeated the word over and over again as she scuffed through the rain. Three days before her life would, to all intents, come to an end. Hell, she realized, it had ended already. A bus careened past, spraying her boots and trench coat with muddy street water. She did not even break stride. In a rush of images, she pictured what was to follow for her: the arrest . . . the judge . . . Miss Dalrymple . . . her brothers and sisters . . . the newspapers . . . her father, already confined to a nursing home . . . the nicknames— Death Angel, Mercy Murderer . . . her roommates and their families. . . . But most punishing of all, perhaps, were the images of David and the hatred she knew he would feel for her.

She walked past the turnoff for her street. Little by little, the great black hole within her grew. The relief and the peace she had felt while talking with Ben were gone. Tears of rain supplanted the tears she was too empty to cry. Monday.

Unseeing, she studied the windows of shops and stores as she passed. All at once, she was standing in front of a pharmacy—her pharmacy. The elderly pharmacist knew her, knew all three roommates, in fact, and liked them all. Dreamlike, she entered, exchanged a few forced pleasantries, then asked the man for a refill of the Darvon she occasionally took for cramps. Her last prescription, filled six months ago, was at home in her bureau, the vial still nearly full. After a brief check of her file, the man refilled it for her.

On the walk home Christine began to compose the note she would write.

"Rudy, he's up here!" Joey cried out. "Mother of God, what a mess! I think he's dead."

David's motionless form lay face down in a puddle to one side of the amphitheater steps. He had crawled up the stairs and wedged himself behind a marble slab, hidden from the sidewalk below. Gently Joey rolled his friend over to his back. The driving rain splattered filth and blood from David's face. At that instant, he moaned, a soft whine, nearly lost in the night wind.

"Jesus, go get a blanket!" Joey screamed. "He's breathing!" He cradled David's head in one hand and began patting his cheek—faster and harder. "Doc, it's Joey. Can you hear me? You're gonna be all right. Doc? . . . ."

"Christine . . ." David's first word was an almost indistinct gurgle. "Christine . . . must find Christine." His eyes fluttered open for a moment, strained to focus on Joey's face, then closed. Rosetti set a hand on David's chest. He nodded excitedly at its shallow, rhythmic rise and fall.

"Hang on," he said. "We'll get you to the hospital. You're gonna be all right, Doc. Just hang on." He looked up and muttered a curse at the downpour. In moments the wind died off. The heavy rain gave way to a light, misty spray. Joey stared overhead in amazement, then nodded his approval.

"First thing in the morning You get a raise in pay." He grinned.

David heard Rosetti's voice, but understood only the word *hospital.* No, he thought. Not the hospital. He struggled to hang on to the thought, to put it into words, but his consciousness weakened, then let go, and he plunged into darkness.

Five minutes later, he was bundled in a blanket, propped against Joey on the back seat of Rudy Fisher's Chrysler. His uncontrollable shaking continued but, moment by moment, he was regaining consciousness. Joey ordered Fisher to the Doctors Hospital emergency ward. Like echoes down a long tunnel, David heard his own words— disconnected, tinny whimpers. "Ben is dead . . . Christine is dead. No hospital, please . . . Must find Christine. . . . I'm cold . . . so cold. Please help me get warm . . ."

Several ambulances were lined up in front of the emergency entrance, their lights flashing in hypnotic counterpoint. Joey jumped out and returned moments later with a wheelchair.

"Place is a fucking zoo," he said as they eased David out of the car.

"Must be the rain. Looks like a scene from some war movie. Rudy, wait for me in that space over there. You all right, Doc?"

David tried to nod, but the lights and the signs and the faces spun into a nauseating blur. He was retching as Joey pushed him through the gliding doors into the artificial brilliance of the reception area. The atmosphere and action were reminiscent of a battleground infirmary. A constant stream of patients—some bleeding, some doubled over in pain —flowed in through several doors. Litters were everywhere. Joey took in the scene, then pushed his way through the crowd surrounding the triage nurse.

The woman, a trim brunette in only her second month of screening duty, listened to him incredulously and then rushed over to David. He was moaning softly, his head rolling from side to side as he struggled to steady it. "My God, he's cold as ice," she said, holding a hand beneath his chin. "Keep his head still while I get an orderly. What happened to him?" She rushed away before Joey could answer. A matronly intake clerk, clipboard in hand, arrived seconds later and began firing questions at him.

"Name?"

"Joseph Rosetti."

She looked at David. "That's not Joseph Rosetti, that's Dr. Shelton."

"Oh, I thought you meant my name. If you already know his, why did you ask?"

The clerk flashed him an ugly look and tore off the top sheet on her clipboard. "Name?" she said in the identical voice as before.

Joey fished out David's soggy wallet and found some of the information the woman requested. He came near to losing control several times, but held his temper for fear that she would rip off another sheet and start over again. In answer to "Name and address of next of kin," he was about to say he had no idea, but thought about the chaos his answer might cause and gave his own.

"Religion of preference?" the woman asked blandly.

Joey looked down at David, whose skin now had a pea-green cast. "Look," he snapped, "this man is hurt. Can't the questions wait until a doctor sees him?"

"I'm sorry, sir," she bristled, "I don't make hospital policies, I only carry them out. Religion of preference?"

Joey fought the impulse to grab the woman by the throat. The dark-haired nurse returned at that moment with an orderly, sparing him a final decision. "I've emptied out Trauma Twelve," she said. "Take Dr. Shelton there. Sir, if you'll finish signing him in, you can wait in one of those seats. I'll let you know as soon as someone has evaluated him." She looked at Joey's face and realized for the first time how very handsome he was. Her smile broadened. "Any questions?"

"No," Joey said. "But could you tell this—ah—nice lady here that I do not possess the knowledge of Dr. Shelton's religion of preference?" He winked at the young nurse, whose cheeks reddened instantly, then took the intake worker by the arm and led her back to the reception desk.

In the feverish emergency ward only one pair of eyes followed attentively as the orderly wheeled David away. They belonged to Janet Poulos. Only her ears heard and understood the single word he moaned: "Christine."

With multiple accidents and two gunshot wounds tying up personnel, Janet had agreed to work overtime until the crush of patients lessened. Now, she realized, that decision might be paying off in unexpected ways. Her mind raced as she tried to sort out the significance of what she had just witnessed and heard.

Leonard Vincent had been hired by The Garden to watch Christine Beall and to intervene only if it looked to Dahlia as if the woman had decided to confess and expose The Sisterhood. That much Janet knew. Dahlia had made the decision to protect The Garden at all costs; and every flower was also a member of The Sisterhood, whether they were active in that movement or not.

Beall and Shelton must have connected, Janet reasoned. She must have gone to him. Must have spoken with him about The Sisterhood. Why else would he be here in this condition calling out her name? Dahlia had turned Leonard Vincent loose, but Shelton had somehow escaped. It was the only explanation that made any sense. If it were true, then it was Hyacinth's good fortune to be in just the right place at just the right time. Janet began to tremble with the excitement of it all. The opportunity had been laid in her lap. If she handled things well, made the proper decisions, Dahlia might see fit to involve her in the innermost workings of The Garden. The rewards would be enormous.

Janet glanced about. The police, always present in the emergency ward, were occupied with the gunshot and accident victims. She sensed she could move through the chaos unnoticed, but only if she moved quickly. Was there time to call Dahlia? She checked the hallway to Trauma Room 12. The area outside the room was deserted. There might not be another chance.

Adrenalin. Potassium. Insulin. Digitalis. Pancuronium. Janet ticked off the possibilities as she hurried to the nurses' station. She wondered about Christine Beall. Had Vincent already accounted for her? No matter, she decided. The only problem she could do anything about at the moment was waiting for her in Trauma 12.

"Dr. Shelton, my name is Clifford. Can you lift up your bum so I can pull these pants off you?" The pudgy orderly was past thirty, but looked like he had yet to shave for the first time.

David grunted his reply but, with consummate effort, was actually able to do what the man/boy requested. Gradually, ripples of warmth washed over the deep chill inside him. As his awareness grew, so did the throbbing pain in his ankle and arm, along with lesser aches above his right ear and on the soles of his feet.

"You look like you've had quite a time of it," Clifford said cheerfully, spreading David's sodden pants over the back of a chair.

"The river . . . I . . . was in the river." David's voice was distant and flat. "Ben is dead . . ."

"Can you hold this under your tongue?" the orderly asked, shoving a thermometer into David's mouth. "Who's Ben?" David mumbled and struggled to reach the thermometer. "No, no, don't touch that," Clifford scolded. "Doctor will be in shortly to check you over. You just keep that under your tongue until I get back."

Never take an oral temp on someone who's freezing to death, idiot! The unspoken disapproval flashed in David's eyes as the corpulent orderly left the room. Then his lips tightened in a half-smile. He was coming around. Bit by bit his random thoughts were connecting. Suddenly Ben's face appeared in his mind, blood pouring from his mouth. Renewed terror took hold. Desperately, he pulled himself up, first on one elbow, then to an outstretched hand. "Christine," he gasped, spitting the thermometer out. "I've got to get to her." As his head came upright, the walls began to turn, slowly at first, but with rapidly building speed.

David fought the spinning and the nausea, and forced himself to a sitting position. Sweat poured from his forehead and dripped down his sides. The floor blurred beneath him. As he leaned forward, the room began to dim, and he knew that he was falling. For an incredible moment he was weightless, floating in a sea of brilliant light. Then there was nothing.

Janet Poulos caught David by the shoulders as he toppled forward and eased him back onto the litter. His respirations were rapid and shallow, the pulse at his wrist thready. Briefly she thought about sitting him up again. The precipitous blood-pressure drop from such a maneuver might well remove the need for the syringe full of Adrenalin in her pocket. Too chancy, she decided, pulling his feet up on the litter. She made a final check of the corridor. There was a crisis of some sort several rooms away and the crash cart was being rushed in. Perfect, she thought, stepping back into the room and closing the door behind her. Everyone just stay where you are for a little while.

"Dr. Shelton, can you hear me?" she asked. "I'm going to put a tourniquet on your arm to draw some blood. It will only take a minute."

David moaned and pulled his arm away as she looped the rubber tubing around it. "Now, now, David," she said sweetly. "Just hold still. This isn't going to hurt a bit." She slapped the skin over the crook of his elbow and looked for a vein. The area was blanched and cold, every skin vessel constricted to the maximum. Janet groaned and slapped more frantically, cursing herself for forgetting about the body's response to hypothermia and shock.

David's head lolled back and forth as his consciousness began to return. Panicked, Janet jammed the needle into his arm, hoping for a chance hit in a vein. At that instant Clifford burst into the room. The syringe popped free and slipped from her hand as Janet whirled to the sound. A drop of blood appeared at the puncture site.

"Well, Doctor, I'm back. Sorry to have . . ." Clifford stopped short, confronted by Janet's withering glare.

"Damn you," she hissed, ripping off the tourniquet and quickly retrieving the syringe. Shielding Clifford from view, she squirted the Adrenalin beneath the litter, then turned back to him. "Don't you know to knock when doors are closed? I was in the middle of drawing blood on this man and you just screwed it up."

"I . . . I'm sorry." The orderly shifted nervously from one foot to the other and stared at the floor.

"You'll be hearing from me about this," she spat. Her mind was swirling with thoughts of what to do next. Then she froze. Harry Weiss, the surgical resident, was standing in the doorway.

"Is everything all right?" he asked calmly.

Janet nodded. "I . . . I didn't know when someone was going to get in to see Dr. Shelton, here, so I thought I'd draw some bloods on him just to get things started."

"Thank you. That was good thinking." Weiss smiled. "If you haven't drawn them yet, why don't you wait until I've finished taking a look at him."

"Very well, Doctor." Janet managed another icy glance at Clifford, then walked from the room before racing to the telephone.

"Dr. Shelton, it's me, Harry Weiss." The hawk-nosed resident David had guided through the difficult hand case looked at him anxiously. David's eyes were open, but he was having obvious difficulty focusing. Weiss leaned closer. "Can you see me all right?"

David squinted, then nodded. Moments later he was struggling to sit up. "Christine. Let me call Christine," he heard himself say. The dizziness began anew, but he battled it, flailing with both hands.

Harry Weiss grabbed his wrists and pushed him back. "Please, Dr. Shelton, I don't want to have to tie you down," he begged. He looked about for Clifford as David's thrashing increased, but the man had left. "Nurse," he called out, "would someone please get an orderly and a set of four-point restraints in here on the double."

In less than a minute David was lashed to the litter by leather arm and ankle cuffs. His efforts weakened, giving way to sobs. "Please . . . just let me find her . . . just let me call." His words were unintelligible.

Weiss looked down at him and shook his head sadly. "I think we're all right now," he said to the small group who had rushed in to help. "Leave us alone so I can examine him. Call the lab and tell them I want a complete screen and CBC. Have them do a scan for drugs of abuse as well. When I'm finished, start an I.V.—normal saline at three hundred cc's an hour—at least until we know what's going on. One of you find out who's on for psych tonight and let me know. If it's a good one, we might call him down. If it's one of those turkeys who's sicker than the patients, we probably won't." The group smiled at his remark, but only the orderly laughed out loud. Harry Weiss shot him a momentary glare, picked up a piece of the shattered thermometer, then said, "And Clifford, when are you going to learn that we never take oral temperatures on someone with hypothermia. It's too inaccurate. Rectal temps only. I don't want to hear of your doing that again." He nodded that his orders were complete and the room quickly emptied.

"Atta boy, Harry," David wanted to say, but he was unable to get words out. The terror, shock, and hypothermia were taking their toll. Even had the orderly used a rectal thermometer, David's temperature would not have registered. Still, his eyes were open. He watched as the tall resident began examining him. Tell the man, David thought. Sit up and tell him that you don't need a fucking shrink. Tell him that Ben is dead. Tell him that you must find Christine. That she might already be dead. Tell him you're not crazy. But . . . but maybe you *are* crazy. Maybe this is how it is. How it feels. There he is, poking and grabbing all over you, and you can't even talk to him. Maybe this is what crazy is. I mean people don't suddenly have a neon sign appear on their chests saying, "THIS PERSON HAS LOST HIS MIND: THIS PERSON IS MAD." Where the hell is Joey? Joey was here a while ago. Where the hell is he now?

Pain shot up his leg from where Weiss was examining his ankle. David groaned and fought to sit up. The leather restraints held fast. "Sorry," Weiss said gently. "I didn't mean to hurt you. Dr. Shelton, can you understand me? Can you tell me what happened?"

Yes, yes, David thought. I can tell you. Just give me a minute. Don't rush me. I can tell you everything.

Harry Weiss saw him nod and waited for more of a response. Finally he said, "Well, you're beginning to feel warmer. I've ordered some tests. We're going to get X-rays of your ankle, your arm, and, just in case, a set of skull films. I think everything's okay, but I can't say for sure about your ankle. Understand?"

"Joey," David said. "Where is my friend Joey?" For a moment he was unsure of whether he had actually said the words or only thought that he had said them.

The resident's face brightened. "Joey? Is he the one who brought you here?" David nodded. "Great, well, it sounds like you may be coming around. I'll go talk to your friend. Then I'll send him in to stay with you until X-ray is ready. We're very busy tonight, so there'll probably be a bit of a wait. I'm going to turn off the overhead light. Try to get some rest and don't shake this blanket off."

"Thank you," David whispered. "Thank you." Weiss looked down at him briefly, shook his head, and left the room, flipping the light off on his way.

David tested the restraints one at a time. No chance. He took a deep breath, exhaled slowly, then settled back. The shaking had stopped and much of the deep chill had disappeared. There was something soothing about the dim quiet of the room and the familiar clamor from outside. "Time to rest," he told himself. "Rest and get your strength back. When Joey gets here we'll go after Christine. When Joey gets here . . ." Slowly his eyes closed. His breathing became more shallow and regular.

Through a peaceful, twilight sleep David heard his friend enter the room. Don't wake me up, Joey, David thought. Give me another minute or two, then we'll get going. Well, okay, I know you're worried about me. I can sleep later. His eyes blinked open an instant before Leonard Vincent's massive hand clamped down over his mouth, pinning him roughly against the litter.

Dressed in the orderly's whites Hyacinth had provided, Vincent had encountered no problem in making his way from a rear entrance to Trauma 12. He grudgingly acknowledged Dahlia's wisdom in ordering him to wait by a phone near Doctors Hospital. "A hunch," she had called it. He had balked at the prospect of strolling into the emergency ward, but assurances that the emergency ward police were all occupied and the promise of a bonus had convinced him to try. Now he silently applauded himself for the decision.

"You've been a great pain in the ass, Dr. Shelton," he growled. "I have half a mind to make this hurt more than it should. But because at least you tried, I'm gonna make it quick and easy."

David watched helplessly, his eyes spheres of terror as Vincent raised a knife over his face, giving him a clear view of the ugly tapered blade.

With his hand still pressed over David's mouth, the killer hooked two thick fingers beneath his chin and pulled up. "One slice, just like a surgeon," he whispered, drawing the dull side of the blade slowly across David's exposed neck.

"For God's sake, wait! I didn't do anything," was all David could think of in that final moment. Eyes closed, he listened for his own death scream. Instead, he heard a loud thud and the clatter of Vincent's knife on the floor. His eyes opened in time to see the killer's body lurch sideways, then crumple over. Behind him, Joey Rosetti lifted the heavy revolver he had used as a club, preparing, if necessary, for another blow.

"Nice place you run here, Doc," Joey said, quickly undoing the restraints. "If I ever need another operation, remind me to go back to White Memorial."

"He's the man," David blurted excitedly. "The man who killed Ben. He . . . he was going to . . ."

"I know what he was going to do," Joey said, unbuckling the restraints. "Leonard an' me have met before. He does it for a living. The shit. If he's after you, my friend, then you are into some serious business."

David sat up. This time the dizziness was bearable. Instinctively he rubbed his hand over his throat. The rush of terror had done more to bring him around than had anything else. "Joey, get me out of here," he begged. "Shoot that animal, then get me out of here. We've got to find Christine."

Joey glanced at Vincent, who was lying on one side, his face contorted by the tiled floor. "We'll let the cops take care of Leonard," he said. "I promised Terry I wouldn't use my gun—at least, the other end of it—unless I had to. Someone will find him here. Can you walk? Where the hell are your pants?"

"There, over there on the chair. I . . . I think I can walk with a little help." David slipped off the table and steadied himself against Joey's arm. His ankle throbbed but held weight as he wriggled into his damp, muddy jeans. "Joey, there's this woman, Christine Beall. She's the only one who can straighten out the mess I'm in. We've got to find her." He sighed relief at the realization that, at last, his thoughts were coming out intelligibly.

"Okay," Joey said, "but first we've got to drift out of this place with as little commotion as possible. I saw this gorilla here dressed up like a doctor or something heading for your room. Nobody else even looked twice at him. I figured he wasn't going in to give you a checkup. Now listen—my manager's parked by the front door. Let me get a wheelchair. We'll go as far as we can with that, then run like hell. It's a red car, an Olds or Chrysler or some ox like that. Do you remember it?"

David shook his head. "I'll find it, Joey, don't worry. Let's just get the hell out of here."

Rosetti helped him into a wheelchair, then casually pushed it down the trauma wing corridor and across the reception area. As the electronic front doors slid open, a woman's voice behind them called out, "Hey, you two, where are you going?"

David scrambled out of the chair and hung on to Joey's arm as they raced the last few yards to the Chrysler. "No rubber," Joey panted as they dove into the back seat.

Rudy Fisher nodded and eased past two parked cruisers down the sweeping circular driveway and off toward Boston's North End.

* * *

Janet Poulos stood helplessly to one side of the reception area and watched them go. She had told Dahlia nothing of her abortive attempt to handle matters. Now she had another decision to make—whether or not to see if Leonard Vincent was alive and needed help. Since she was the only person the man could identify if he were arrested, the decision was not difficult.

She stopped by the crash cart, took several ampules of pancuronium, and dropped them into her pocket. The respiratory paralysis caused by the drug helped maintain respirator patients. Well, now it would help her, too, provided she had the chance to use it. If not, she would have to find a way to help the man escape. Perhaps she could still salvage some heightened prestige in Dahlia's eyes.

Janet cursed her rotten luck and David Shelton for causing her so much difficulty. Then she stalked down the hall to Trauma 12, hoping she would find Leonard Vincent dead.

"Ouch! What is that stuff?" David winced as Terry Rosetti scrubbed at the dirt embedded in the deep gouge along his arm.

"Just something I use to clean the windows," she said. "Now sit still and let me finish."

The Rosettis' North End apartment was old, but spacious and newly renovated. Terry had decorated the place with grace, making full use of a collection of family furniture that would have been welcome in any of the posh antique shops on Newbury Street.

David lay stretched out on the large oak guest bed, savoring the smell and texture of fresh linen and wondering if he would ever feel warm again. He was weak, lightheaded, and aching in a half-dozen different places. Still, he could sense his concentration improving as the mental fog brought on by his hypothermia began to lift. He silently thanked Joey for reasoning him out of an immediate search for Christine in favor of a hot shower.

Terry Rosetti, a full-breasted, vibrant beauty, expertly wrapped his arm in gauze. "Fettuccini and first aid," David said. "You are truly the complete woman."

Terry's smile lit up the room. "Tell that to your friend out there. I think he's starting to take me for granted. Do you know he was actually able to stop in the middle of making love to me to answer the phone when you called?"

"No wonder it seemed to be ringing forever," he said. "I almost hung up."

"It's a lucky thing you didn't," Terry said. "David, Joey didn't *kill* that man, did he?"

The fear in her eyes left no doubt of the importance his answer held for her. "I wanted him to pull the trigger back there, Terry. I really did. That animal killed my friend. But Joey said he'd promised you and backed off."

Terry Rosetti swallowed at the lump in her throat.

At that moment, Joey marched into the room, carrying a load of clothes, a pair of crutches, and the Boston phone book. "I think this must be the woman," he said. "C. Beall, 391 Belknap, Brookline. I checked the other books and this is the only name that fits. By the way, the clothes and shit are courtesy of the North End Businessman's Association."

"What's that?" asked David.

"Oh, just some simple business types like me who like to help poor, unfortunate folks that get chased into the river by a gorilla." Joey smiled conspiratorially at Terry and winked. He failed to notice her lack of reaction. "You feel up to traveling, Doc?" he asked.

"Yeah, sure. What time is it anyway?"

"Twelve thirty. It's a new day."

"Three hours." David shook his head in amazement. "It's only been three hours . . ."

"What?"

"Nothing, hand me the phone, please. I only hope she's all right."

Joey squinted down at him. "You positive *you're* all right?" he asked.

"Sure, why?"

"Well, you're the one with the education an' the degrees an' shit. All I got goin' for me is my street smarts. Just the same, I can think of at least six or seven good reasons why we would want to tell this C. Beall what we have to tell her face to face, not over the phone. Remember, you've already been arrested for murder. Right now that woman's your only hope of gettin' off."

David understood instantly. If Christine had nothing to do with Ben's death, the news could panic her into a hasty, possibly fatal move. If she was somehow involved or had knowledge of who might have hired Leonard Vincent . . . He wouldn't allow himself to complete the thought. "When this is all over," he said, "I'm going to write my medical school and tell them to bring you in as a guest lecturer. You could teach medical students about making it in the real world. Let's go find her."

Ten minutes later, they were back in Rudy Fisher's car headed toward Brookline. "Don't push it too hard, Rudy," Rosetti ordered. "We don't want to get stopped. If Vincent already got paper for the woman, all the fancy driving in the world isn't gonna help." David grimaced and looked out the window.

After a mile of silence, Joey said, "Doc, there's somethin' I want to tell you. Call it a lesson if you want, since you're gonna make me a teacher."

David turned toward his friend, expecting to see the wry glint that usually accompanied one of his stories. Joey's eyes were narrowed, dark, and deadly serious. "Go on," David said.

"Leonard Vincent may not be the slickest operator in the world, but he is a pro. And as long as he or someone like him's in the picture, you're gonna be playing by his rules. Understand?" David nodded. "Well, we don't have much time, so I'm gonna make the lesson simple for you. There's only one rule you gotta know. One main rule for survival in Vincent's game. I didn't follow it back there in the hospital because Terry made me promise not to. But you got no Terry, so you pay attention and do what I say. If you even think someone's gonna do it to you, you damn well better do it to him first. Understand?" He slipped his gun into David's pocket. "Here. Whatever happens, I got a feelin' you're gonna need this more than me. Terry'll make you something real special when she hears you got it away from me."

John Dockerty knelt by the door to David's apartment and watched as the medical examiner's team finished working around Ben's body and wheeled it into the elevator. He looked up at the patrolman who had been making inquiries in the other apartments on the floor. The man shrugged and shook his head. "Nothing," he mouthed.

The news came as no surprise to Dockerty. Survival in the city meant hearing, seeing, and reporting as little as possible. He picked at the bullet holes in the door-jamb, then retraced the steps it seemed the action had taken. There was blood smeared on the hallway floor and wall of David's apartment and along the bottom of the open bedroom window. He made a note to check David's military and health records for mention of his blood type.

A fatal knife wound, bullet holes, blood all over, an old drunk shot to death two blocks away, and not one witness. Dockerty rubbed at the fatigue stinging his eyes and tried to re-create the scenario. There were several possibilities, none of which looked good for Shelton. He had little doubt the man was dead.

At that moment David's phone began ringing. Dockerty hesitated, then answered it.

"Hello?"

"Lieutenant Dockerty, please."

"This is Dockerty."

"Lieutenant, it's Sergeant McIlroy at the Fourth. We just got a call from one of our people at Doctors Hospital. Apparently this David Shelton—you know, the one you busted for that mercy killing?"

"Yeah, I know, I know."

"Well, this Shelton showed up a little while ago on the emergency ward all smashed up. I called your precinct and they said you'd want to know about it right away."

"Tell your people to hold him at the hospital," Dockerty said.

"Can't. He's gone. Took off with some guy a few minutes after he arrived. No one realized it until too late. Our men were off taking statements from two assholes who had a shoot-out at the High Five Bar."

"Who the hell was the guy?" Dockerty's head began to throb.

"Don't know."

"Well, isn't it on Shelton's emergency sheet?"

"That's just it. There is no emergency sheet. The clerk swears she typed one out, but now no one can find it."

"Jesus Christ. What in the hell is going on?"

"Don't know, sir."

"Well, tell the men at the hospital I'll be right over. They're not to let anyone leave who saw Shelton. No one. Got that?"

"Yes, sir."

"Jesus Christ." Dockerty dropped the receiver in place and swept some strands of hair off his eyes and back under his hat. It was going to be a long goddamn night.

Rudy Fisher made three passes along Christine's street before Rosetti felt certain there were no "surprises." He directed the giant to wait half a block away, then helped David up the concrete steps to the house. "Old Leonard's probably having a time of it right now." Joey laughed. "I can just imagine him trying to weasel his way out of that situation in the hospital with the only ten or twelve words that he knows."

David braced himself on his crutches and peered through the row of small panes paralleling the door. He moved gingerly, but even a slight turn or drop of his head brought renewed dizziness and nausea. The prolonged hypothermia, he realized, had somehow impaired his balance center or perhaps his body's ability to make quick blood-pressure adjustments.

The house was dark, save for a dim light coming from a room on the right—the living room, David guessed. He glanced at his watch. Nearly 1:00 A.M.

"I guess we ring the bell, huh?" David asked nervously.

"Well, Doc, given the options, I'd say that was your best bet. I'm glad you're not this tense in the operating room."

David managed a laugh at himself, then pressed the bell. They waited, listening for a response. Nothing. David shivered and knew that the chill reflected more than the fine, wind-driven mist. He rang again. Ten seconds passed. Then twenty.

"Do we break in?" he asked.

"We may have to, but I'd suggest trying the back door first." Joey walked to the street and motioned to Rudy Fisher that they were going around to the back. David gave the button a final press, then fought through a wave of queasiness and followed.

It was that third ring that woke Christine. She was stretched across her bed, careening through one grisly dream after another. On the floor, shards of torn notepaper were strewn about two pill bottles. Both of them were full.

"Wait a minute, I'm coming," she called out. Could both her roommates have forgotten their keys? Knowing them, a likely possibility. She pushed herself off the bed, then stared at the floor. The shredded note, the bottles of gray-and-orange death—how close she had come. She threw the pills into a drawer, then swept up the scraps with her hands and dropped them in the basket. By the end of the terrible dark hour that had followed her return home, Christine had resolved that nothing ever would make her take her own life. Nothing, except perhaps a situation such as Charlotte Thomas's. She would face whatever she had to face.

Again the doorbell sounded. This time it was the buzzer from the back door. "I'm coming, I'm coming." She rushed through the kitchen and was halfway down the short back staircase when she stopped dead. It was him, David, propped on crutches and peering through the window. She reached down and flipped on the outside light; then she gasped. His face was drawn and cadaverous, his eyes totally lost in wide, dark hollows. A second man, his back turned, was standing behind him. Christine's pulse quickened as first confusion, then mounting apprehension gripped her.

"Christine, it's me, David Shelton." His voice sounded weak and distant.

"Yes . . . yes, I know. What do you want?" She felt frightened, unable to move.

"Please, Christine, I must talk to you. Something has happened. Something terrible . . ."

Joey grabbed his arm. "Are you crazy?" he whispered, working his way in front of the window. "Miss Beall," he said calmly, "my name is Joseph Rosetti. I'm a close friend of the Doc's. He's been hurt." He paused, gauging Christine's expression to see if any further explanation was necessary before she let them in.

Christine hesitated, then descended the final two stairs and undid the double lock. "I . . . I'm sorry," she said as they entered the hallway. "You took me by surprise and . . . Please, come up to the living room. Can you make it all right? Are you badly hurt?"

For the next fifteen minutes she did not say another word as the two men recounted the events of the night. With each detail a new emotion flashed in her eyes.

Surprise, astonishment, terror, pain, emptiness. David studied them as they appeared. He wondered if she were even capable of a successful lie. Whatever she might have done, he was now certain that in no way was she responsible for Ben's murder.

Still, she was somehow involved. That reality pulled David's attention from her face. "Christine, what did you tell Ben?" She seemed unable to speak. "Please, tell me what you said to him." There was a note of urgency and anger in his voice.

"I . . . I told him that it was me. That I was the one who . . . who gave the morphine to Charlotte."

David's heart pounded. His arrest, the filth and degradation of his night in jail, the unraveling of everything he had regained in his career, Ben Glass's death—*she was responsible.* "And the forged prescription?" There was bitterness in his words now. "Were you responsible for that, too?"

"No! . . . I mean, I don't know." The muscles in her face tensed. Her lips quivered. The only explanation she could think to give him was the truth; but what was the truth? The Sisterhood had sacrificed David to protect her, she felt certain of that. But why Ben? It was hard enough to accept that they would choose to send an innocent man to prison, but murder? "Oh, my God," she stammered. "I'm so confused. I don't know what's happening. I don't understand."

"What?" David demanded. "What don't you understand?" His eyes flashed at her from their craters.

Christine began to cry. "I don't understand," she sobbed. "So much is happening and nothing makes sense. It's horrible. The pain I've caused you. And Ben—they've killed Ben. Why? Why? I . . . I need time. Time to sort this all out. It's crazy. Why would they do it?"

"Who're *they?*" David asked. Christine didn't answer. "Dammit," he screamed, "what are you talking about? Who're they?"

"Now just hold it a minute." Joey put up a hand to each of them. "You're both gonna have to calm down or we could all find ourselves in trouble. Leonard Vincent's probably out of the picture, but there's no guarantee he was working alone. The longer you two spend goin' at one another like this, the more chance there is that some goon's gonna crash in here and do it good to all three of us." He paused, allowing the thought to sink in, and watched until he sensed an easing in the tension. "Okay. Now, Miss Beall, I don't know you, but I do know the doc here, and I know the shit he's been through. The way I see it, you're both in hot water until this whole business is straightened out. I can see that the news we've brought has shaken you, but this man here deserves an explanation."

"I . . . I don't know what to say." She spoke the words softly, as much to herself as to them.

Joey could see that she was coming apart. He glanced at David, whose expression suggested that he sensed the same thing. "Look," Joey said finally, "maybe what we should do is just call the cops and—"

"No!" Christine blurted. "Please no. Not yet. There's so much I don't understand. A lot of innocent people could be hurt if I do the wrong thing." She stopped and breathed deeply. When she continued, there was a new calm in her voice. "Please, you must believe me. I had nothing to do with Ben's death. I liked him very much. He was going to help me."

David leaned forward and buried his face in his hands. "Okay." He looked up slowly. "No police . . . yet. What do you want?"

"Some time," she said. "Just a little time to work this whole thing through. I'll tell you everything I know. I promise."

David sensed himself soften before the sadness in her eyes and turned away.

"Look, Doc," Rosetti said impatiently, "I meant what I said before. We're just not smart stayin' here any longer than we have to. If it's no police, then it's no police. If it's some time to talk, then it's some time to talk. Only not here."

David heard the urgency in Rosetti's voice and saw, for the first time, a flash of fear in his eyes. "Okay, we'll get out," he said. "But where? Where can we go? Certainly not my apartment. How about the tavern . . . or your place? Do you think Terry would be upset if we went there?"

"I have a better idea. Terry and me have this little hideaway up on the North Shore. I think if you two can keep from rippin' each other apart without me for a referee it would be a perfect place. Doc, you can't see yourself, but let me tell you, you look about ready for an embalmer. Why don't you go on up there tonight and get some sleep. Tomorrow you can take all the time you need to talk things out." David started to protest, but Rosetti stopped him. "This ain't the time for arguin', pal. You're my friend. Terry's friend too. So I know you'll understand that I don't want her mixed up in anything this messy. It's the North Shore or you're both on your own. Now what do you say?"

David looked over at Christine. She was slumped in her chair, staring at the floor. There was an innocence about her—a defenselessness —that was difficult to reconcile with his pain and the hell she had caused him to live through. Who are you? he thought. Exactly what is it you've done? And why?

"I . . . I guess if it's okay with Christine, it's okay with me," he said finally.

Christine tightened her lips and nodded.

"It's decided, then," Joey announced. "There's food in the house. This time of year, there's not too many folks on Rocky Point, so you shouldn't be bothered. I'll draw you a map. Take Christine's car. We'll follow you to the highway just in case. It's nice up there. Especially if the rain is through for good. There's an old clunker jeep in the garage. The keys are in the toolbox by the back wall. Use it if you want. Okay?"

"Give me a minute to pack a couple of things," Christine said. "And to leave a note for my roommates that I won't be home tonight."

"Okay, but not too long," Joey replied. "And, Christine? Tell your friends to keep the door locked—just in case."

"Mr. Vincent, you have bungled things badly. Possibly beyond repair. Hyacinth took a great risk helping you escape that mess in the hospital, but never again. This time I want results. The girl first, then Dr. Shelton. Understand?"

"Yeah, yeah, I understand." Leonard Vincent slammed the receiver down, then rubbed at the thin mat of dried blood that had formed over the stitches in his head. That twit Hyacinth wasn't his type, but for being cool in a crunch he had to hand it to her. After regaining consciousness, he had been unable to keep his feet. He remembered her helping him to a stretcher. Seconds later, a doctor arrived. It was then that the woman really put on her show, explaining how this poor orderly had slipped and smacked his head on the floor, and how she would take care of all the paperwork if the guy would just throw some stitches into the gash.

Yes, sir, Vincent thought, he certainly did have to hand it to ol' Hyacinth. Then he remembered the way she had looked at him just before she sent him out of the hospital—the hatred in her eyes. "You asshole," she had said. "You absolute asshole."

The memory triggered a flush of nausea and another siege of dry heaves—his third since leaving the hospital. Vincent held on to a tree until his retching subsided. "People are gonna die," he spat, fighting the frustration and the pain with the only weapon he knew. "People are gonna fuckin' die."

Carefully, he eased himself behind the wheel of his car and drove to Brookline. He turned onto Belknap Street just as another car, heading away from him, neared the corner at the far end. Vincent tensed as he peered through the darkness, trying to focus on the car before it disappeared around the corner. It was red—bright red. The killer relaxed and settled back into the seat. He stopped across from Christine's house and scanned the driveway. The blue Mustang was gone.

Muttering an obscenity, he reached inside the glove compartment and pulled out the envelope Hyacinth had given him. "Well, Dahlia, whoever the fuck you are," he said, "I guess you get the doctor first whether you want it that way or not."

He tore open the envelope and spread David's emergency sheet on the passenger seat. Across the space marked "Physician's Report" the words ELOPED WITHOUT TREATMENT were printed in red. The information boxes at the top were all neatly typed in. With an unsteady hand, Vincent drew a circle around the line of type identifying next of kin.

CHAPTER 19

THE WHARF WAS DARK, quiet, and even more eerie than usual. John Dockerty backed inside a doorway and listened until the echo of his footsteps had been absorbed by the heavy night. It took several minutes to sort out the random sounds that surrounded him. Clinking mooring chains. Gulls caterwauling over a midnight feast. The lap of harbor swells against thick pilings. The reassuring drone of a foghorn.

Gradually the tension in his neck relaxed. He was alone on the pier.

Through the silver-black mist he scanned along the row of warehouses, ghostly sentinels guarding the inner harbor. Then he crossed the narrow strip of pavement and ducked into a small alley. At the far end a slit of dim light glowed from beneath an unmarked warehouse door. Dockerty knocked softly and waited.

"Come in, Dock, it's open." Ted Ulansky's voice boomed in the silence.

Dockerty slipped inside, closing the heavy metal door quickly behind him. "Christ, Ted," he said. "I spend twenty fucking minutes sneaking around to be sure I'm not followed, and you bellow at me louder than the foghorn out there."

"Just goes to show what confidence I have in you, Dock. Come on over and park your duff." Ulansky pumped Dockerty's hand, then motioned him to a high-backed oak chair beside his desk. He was an expansive man with a physique that bore only a faint resemblance to the All-American linebacker he had been at Boston College two and a half decades before.

"Nice place," Dockerty said sarcastically, looking around the large, poorly lit office. "Is this it?"

"This is it," answered Ulansky with mock pride. "The fabled Massachusetts Drug Investigation Force headquarters. Want a tour?"

"No, thanks. I think I can manage to take it all in from here."

In fact, the MDIF, while not publicized, had gained an almost fabled reputation for quiet efficiency and airtight arrests. Ulansky, as head of the unit, was gradually acquiring a superhuman reputation of his own. The office, however, was hardly the stuff of which legends are made. It was stark and cold. Bare cement walls were lined with filing cabinets—more than two dozen of them—all olive-green standard government issue. Inside the metal drawers, Dockerty knew, was virtually every piece of information available on illegal drug traffic in the state.

In one corner of the room, partially covered by Ulansky's carelessly thrown suit coat, was a computer terminal connected through Washington with drug-investigation and -enforcement agencies throughout the country.

Ulansky lowered himself into his desk chair. "A drink? Some coffee?" Dockerty shook his head. "Must be serious business for you to come out here in this rat's-ass weather, then refuse a drink."

"I guess," Dockerty said distractedly, reopening his battle with some obstinate strands of hair. "I appreciate your coming out."

Ulansky buried a shot glass of Old Grand-Dad in a single gulp. "Believe me, with the Czernewicz fight on live from the coast tonight, you're about the only one of the precinct boys who could have gotten me out of the house. Jackie Czernewicz, the Pummeling Pole. You follow the fights?"

Dockerty shook his head again. "Too much like a day at the office for me."

Ulansky smiled. "Tell me, then," he said, "what prompts a visit from you to this Hyatt Regency of law enforcement?"

"I'm involved in a really weird case, Ted." Dockerty scratched the tip of his nose. "An old lady got murdered while she was a patient at Boston Doctors Hospital. Morphine. So far I've narrowed the field of suspects down to about three dozen. Even made one arrest."

"Yeah, I read about that," Ulansky said. "A doctor, right?"

"Right. A ton of circumstantial stuff against him, but way too neat, if you know what I mean. The captain, that pillar of justice, got pressure from some fat cat at the hospital and insisted that I bust the doctor. I did it, but I've never been convinced. Now the guy's lawyer has been murdered. Ben Glass. You know him?" Ulansky grimaced and nodded. "Well, he was knifed. Outside the doc's apartment door, no less. There are bullet holes all over, and the apartment door's smashed in. There's blood in the hallway and even on the wall.

"A little while ago the doctor gets brought to the emergency ward at the hospital soaked and freezing and half crazy. Then, before he can get any treatment, he splits with another guy. By the time I hear about it and get to the hospital, there's no record he was ever even there. For all I know he may be dead by now. I've got the usual lines out for him, but I'm at a stone wall with the rest of the case. I feel like the whole fucked-up mess is partly my fault for letting the captain talk me into arresting him."

"How can we help?"

"My only hope of breaking something open is a pharmacist named Quigg. Marcus Quigg. Owns a little drugstore in West Roxbury. He swears that this Dr. Shelton filled a big prescription for morphine the day this woman was OD'ed."

Ulansky's moon face crinkled as he worked the name through his memory. "We've got something on the man someplace," he said. "I'm almost sure of it. What about a C two twenty-two?"

"Quigg's got one. The doctor claims it was stolen from his office, that he never ordered any morphine."

"Signature?"

"Only a maybe from the guys at ident. They tell me Shelton's signature is a scrawl. Easy to duplicate."

"So maybe it *is* his," Ulansky said.

"Maybe." Dockerty shrugged. "My hunches have been wrong before."

"Sure, about as often as a solar eclipse."

Dockerty accepted the compliment with a tired grin. "I need a handle on that pharmacist, Ted," he said. "The man bends, but he won't break. I figure if he'd take a payoff to do something like this, he must have dirtied his hands on something else at one time or another."

"Well," Ulansky offered, "we can go through the files and check the computer for you. I have a feeling something's down on paper about him." He paused, then continued in a softer voice. "Dock, you know that if we can't find anything on him we can easily set something up that will work just as well. Maybe better. You want that?"

Dockerty tensed, then rose and walked slowly to the far side of the room. Ulansky moved to add something, then sat back and let the silence continue. Dockerty rested one arm on a filing cabinet. For more than a minute he studied the blank wall. "You know, Ted," he said finally, "in all these years on the force I've never once purposely set anyone up. If I did it this time, I know it would be to make up for mistakes I've already made." He shook his head and turned back to Ulansky. "I don't want to do it, Ted. No matter what my fuck-ups may have put that doctor through, I don't want to do it." Ulansky nodded his understanding. "Look," Dockerty added, "check everything you can to dig something up on Quigg. Call me first thing tomorrow. If I've got nothing and you've got nothing, we'll talk."

"Don't worry, Dock," Ulansky said stonily. "If Marcus Quigg has so much as pissed on a public toilet seat, I'll find out. Don't worry your ass about that at all."

"That was it, that was the exit. I told you one twenty-seven and you just breezed right past it." David, bundled in an army blanket, sat wedged against the passenger door. He glared at Christine, but turned away before she noticed.

"Sorry," she said flatly. "My mind was on other things." She took the next turnoff and doubled back. Traffic was light, but her difficulty concentrating was such that she kept their speed below fifty. For a time they drove in silence, each aware that the tension between them was building.

Finally Christine could stand no more. She pulled into the dirt parking lot of a boarded-up diner and swung around to face him. "Look, maybe this wasn't a good idea—maybe we should go back."

David stared out the window, struggling to comprehend the existence and the incredible scope of The Sisterhood of Life. Christine had given him only the roughest sketch of the movement, along with the promise of more details in the morning. Still, what she had told him already was awesome. Several thousand nurses! Dorothy Dalrymple one of them! He had listened, his eyes shut, his head close to exploding, as her factual, curiously dispassionate voice divulged secrets that could easily decimate the hospital system to which he had dedicated so much of his life.

Now he felt sick. Tired and angry and sick.

Christine sensed his mood, but could not contain her own growing frustration. "Dammit, David," she said, "I've been trying to explain to you as best as possible what has happened. I didn't expect a reward, but I didn't expect the silent treatment either."

"And just what did you expect?" Irritation sparked in his voice.

"Understanding?" she said softly.

"My God. She kills one of my patients, gets me thrown in jail for it, causes my friend to be murdered almost in my arms, and wants me to understand. And . . . and that Sisterhood of yours. Why of all the presumptuous, insane . . ."

"David, I told you about The Sisterhood of Life because I thought you deserved to know. Back there at my house you seemed willing to listen and at least try to understand. Instead all you've done is pull into a shell and come out every few miles to snap at me. I'll tell you one last time. I did not cause you to be arrested. I didn't even know it had happened until I read it in the papers. I imagine The Sisterhood is responsible, and that sickens me. I joined the movement because of its dedication to mercy. Now I discover it's involved in despicable crimes— against you, against Ben, and God knows whom else. If I had known ahead of time, I would never have allowed any of this to happen. Why else do you think I went to Ben to confess?"

She paused for a response, but David was staring out the window. "I thought you might be able to help me work things out," she continued, "but that was foolish of me. You have every right to be angry. Every right to hate me. I'm going home."

She turned and started the engine. David reached across and shut it off. "Wait, please. I . . . . I'm sorry." His speech was halting and thick. "I've been listening to my own bitterness and anger and trying to understand where they're coming from. I thought it was my pain talking, or frustration, or even fear, but I'm starting to know better. I liked you —maybe more than I would allow myself to accept. That's what's doing it. I didn't want to believe you were any part of this. Now you tell me that you *were* part of it, but you ask me to believe you didn't know what your Sisterhood was capable of doing. Well, I want to believe that. I do. It's just that . . ." He gave up fumbling for words. How much of what she had told him had actually sunk in? "Look," he said finally, "I'm absolutely exhausted. I can't seem to hold on to anything. Please. Let's call a truce for the night and just get up to Rosetti's place. We'll see what things are like tomorrow. Okay?"

Christine sighed, then nodded. "Okay, truce." Hesitantly, she extended her hand toward him. He clasped it—first in one, then both of his. The warmth in her touch only added to his confusion. Why did it have to be her? Why? The question floated through his thoughts like a mantra, over and over again, easing his eyes closed and smothering the turmoil within him. He heard the engine engage and felt the Mustang swing onto the roadway in the instant before he surrendered to exhaustion.

"David? . . . I'm sorry, but you have to wake up." Christine pulled the blanket away from his face and waited as he pawed his eyes open. "Are you feeling better?"

"Only if there are degrees of deceased," he mumbled. He pushed the blanket to his lap and peered through the windshield. They were parked on the shoulder of a narrow pitch-black road. "Where are we?"

"We're in lost," she said matter-of-factly.

Her humor, unexpected, nearly slipped past him. He glared at her for a moment, then stammered. "But . . . but we weren't going there. I think we should take the next right, or at least the next left."

"At least . . ." They both laughed.

"What time is it?"

"Two. A little after. We were right where the map said we were supposed to be, then all of a sudden, about fifteen or twenty minutes ago, the landmarks disappeared." She handed him Joey's drawing.

David opened his window and breathed deeply. The air, scrubbed by four days of rain, was cool and sweet with the scents of autumn. An almost invisible mist hung low over the roadway. Within a few breaths he could taste the salt captured in its droplets. Then he heard the sea, like the thrum of an endless train, up through the woods to their right. "Have we passed Gloucester?" he asked.

"Yes, just before I got lost."

He smiled. "You did fine, Christine. The ocean's over there through the trees. It sounds as if we're pretty high above it. I'll bet a Devil Dog we're near this place Joey marked as 'cliffs.' "

"Bet a what?"

"A Devil Dog. You see I . . . never mind. I'll explain tomorrow. Assuming I'm not too foggy to figure out what this map says, and if there are no other roads between us and the ocean, we should be close to the turnoff for Rocky Point. I vote straight ahead."

She eased the Mustang back onto the road and into the darkness.

After a quarter of a mile, the pavement rose sharply to the right. Moments later, they broke free of the woods. The sight below was breathtaking. The steep slope, dotted with trees and boulders, dropped several hundred feet before giving way to the jet black Atlantic. Overhead, a large gap had developed in the clouds, exposing several stars and the white scimitar of a waxing moon. Christine pulled to the side and cut the engine.

"Even if we had no idea where we were, we wouldn't be lost," David said gently. "See that dark mass on the other side of the cove? I think that's Rocky Point."

Christine did not respond. She stepped from the car and walked to the edge of the drop-off. For several minutes she stood there, an ebony statue against the blue black of the sky. When she returned, tears glistened in her eyes. The rest of their drive was made in silence.

The little hideaway, as Joey had called it, was splendid—a hexagonal glass and redwood lodge suspended over the very tip of the point.

"David, it's just beautiful," she said.

"You go ahead and open the place up," David said. "I'll be along."

"Do you need help?"

David shook his head, then realized he was not at all sure he could make it on his own. He pushed himself out of the car and onto the crutches. Immediately the dizziness and nausea took hold. He struggled to the bottom of the short flight of steps leading to the front door. For hours tension and nervous energy had helped him overcome the pain and the aftereffects of his hypothermia. Now, it seemed, he had nothing left. He grabbed the railing, but spun off it and fell heavily. In seconds Christine was beside him, supporting him, guiding him inside.

The huge picture windows and high beamed ceilings were little more than hazy, whirling shapes as she helped him past a large fieldstone fireplace to the bedroom. As she lowered him onto the bed, the telephone in the living room began ringing.

"Go on and answer it, I'll be all right," he said, eyes closed. "It's probably Joey."

He heard her leave, and for several minutes he battled encroaching darkness and waited. By the time she returned, he was losing.

"David, are you awake?" A single nod. "You were right, that was Joey. He wanted to make sure we got here in one piece. Please nod if you understand what I'm saying, okay? Good. He called some friends of his on the police force. David, no one knows anything about Leonard Vincent being picked up tonight. Everyone in Boston is looking for you, but Vincent must have escaped the hospital before he was noticed. Joey said he would keep checking around and call us later today or else Saturday morning. We're okay as long as we're up here, but he said to be careful if we drive back to the city. David?"

This time he did not acknowledge.

Hours later, David's eyes blinked open in misty wakefulness.

He was undressed and under the covers, his torn, swollen ankle propped up on pillows. Nestled beside it was a plastic bag of water—the remains of an improvised ice pack.

He lifted himself to one elbow and looked out through the ceiling-to-floor windows. An endless sea of stars now glittered across the clearing night sky.

A cry came from outside the room. David grabbed his crutches and limped toward the sound. Christine was asleep on the living room couch. She cried out again, more softly this time. David moved to rouse her. Then he stopped. He could wake her for a minute or ten or even an hour, but it would make no difference. He knew the resilience of nightmares.

CHAPTER 20

THE SIZZLE AND AROMA of frying bacon nudged David from a dreamless sleep and kept his first thoughts of the morning away from the horror of the past night.

Sunlight, isolated from the ocean breeze by the wall-sized windows, bathed him in an almost uncomfortable warmth. Sun! David opened his eyes and squinted into the glare. For nearly a week the world had been a damp, monotonous gray. Now he could almost taste the blue-white sky.

His forearm was throbbing beneath Terry's bulky dressing, but not unbearably so. He dangled his legs over the edge of the bed and flexed his ankle. A numb ache, also tolerable. In fact, he realized, there was a strange, reassuring comfort about the pain—perhaps an affirmation that in order to hurt, in order to feel, he must still be alive. The notion brought with it a fleeting smile. How many times had he encountered patients who seemed to be actually enjoying their pain? Next time he would be more understanding.

He heard Christine moving about the kitchen, then suddenly there was music from a radio. Classical music! Telemann? Absolutely, he decided. A jumbo pizza and six mindless hours of uninterrupted T.V. said it was Telemann. For a time he listened, thinking about the woman and the fantastic story she had told him. Last night he had been furious. As angry and frustrated as he could ever remember. But now, in the sunlight and the music, he realized she was in many ways as innocent, as caught in the nightmare, as he was. True, she had given the morphine to Charlotte Thomas, but in no way could she have anticipated the events to follow. He had to believe that. For his own sanity he had to believe that.

He closed his eyes, savoring a few final seconds of the promise of a new day. Then he picked up one crutch and hobbled out of the bedroom.

The kitchen, separated from the living/dining area by a butcher-block counter, was on the west side of the hexagon. Christine stood by the sink, working a wire beater through a bowl of pancake mix. The sight of her triggered a warm rush through David's body. No afternoon sun could have brightened the room as she did that moment. Her hair, a loose, sandy braid, dangled halfway down her back. A light blue man's shirt, knotted at the bottom, accentuated the curve of her breasts and exposed a band of honeyed skin at her waist. Below that, faded jeans clung to her hips and buttocks.

As he watched, David sensed the hammering in his chest and tried to will it to stop. "Mornin'," he said casually, wondering if he looked more at east than he felt.

She turned. "I couldn't decide whether to wake you or to wait and risk ruining breakfast, so I took the coward's way out and turned on the radio. Did you get enough sleep?"

David searched her expression. Was she asking for their truce to continue, to be allowed to bring things up in her own time and her own way? "I slept fine," he said. "Thanks for putting me to bed."

"I was afraid you'd be upset about my doing that." Christine set the beater down and walked to him.

"Only that I wasn't conscious when you did," he said. Her laugh gave him his cue. He would keep things light until she was ready to talk. "Listen, can I help in there? I'm a wonderful cook . . . for any type of meal whose main ingredient is water."

"I think things are under control. You could light a fire. It's a little chilly on this side of the house. There's wood already laid in the fireplace. This afternoon, if you want, you can be in charge of lunch."

"Fair enough." He headed for the hearth.

As Christine returned to the sink she heard him mumble, "Maybe some Cup-A-Soup and instant mashed potatoes . . . or perhaps beef jerky in white wine sauce . . ." Silently she thanked him. A rueful smile tightened across her face as she remembered Dotty Dalrymple's assessment. "A degenerate," she'd called him. And just what does that make us? Christine wondered. We who have taken it on ourselves to weigh the value of a human life. We who can believe so mightily in our commitment to end it whenever we think appropriate. What does that make us?

She glanced into the living room. David was sitting by a low fire, his swollen ankle propped on a hassock. "Show me how to make it, David," she whispered. "Show me how you survived the hell I helped put you through. I know it's a lot to ask, but please, please try."

Joey Rosetti's jeep was antique in body and spirit, if not in years. From the passenger seat David watched with admiration as Christine maneuvered the snorting beast around rocks and muddy puddles on the steep grade to the ocean.

Talk throughout the morning had been light, with only oblique references to the horrors that had brought them together. When Christine suggested a picnic by the water, David started to object—to insist that they confront the issues facing them. Quickly, though, he acknowledged that he too wanted the respite to continue. There would be time enough to talk after lunch.

The stony dirt track they had chosen wound through a tangled fairy-tale forest of beach plum, wild rose, and scrub pine. After several hundred yards, it deteriorated into a series of partly overgrown hairpin turns.

"Maybe we should back up and try to find another road," David said.

"Maybe . . ." She bounced through a vicious loop that he had felt certain would be impassable. "But I'll bet you a . . . a Fruit Pie we make it on this one."

Moments later, the thick brush fell off to either side. A final hairpin and the road spilled onto a sandy oval scarcely thirty yards long, a perfect white-gold medallion resting on the breast of the Atlantic. Christine skidded to a dusty stop. The engine noise faded. They sat, feeling the silence and the colors.

"A penny . . . ?" David asked finally.

"For my thoughts?"

"Uh-huh."

"You'll want change."

"Try me."

"Well, I was just deciding which spot would be best to spread the blanket and set our lunch."

"That's it?"

"That's it." She took the bag of food and the blanket, then kicked off her shoes and hopped onto the sand. "After we eat, we can talk, okay?" He nodded. "Well, are you coming?"

"In a minute. You go ahead."

Concern darkened her face, then vanished. With a delighted whoop, she raced across the beach.

David sank back in his seat, aware of a heavy, husky discomfort across his upper chest. In the minutes that followed the feeling intensified. He struggled to pin it down, to label it. Gradually he understood. He was being drawn into her world, her life. He was caring more almost every minute. Caring for the woman whose actions, whose hubris, had triggered his nightmare and had somehow led to the death of his friend. Caring for a woman who had confessed to murder, for a woman whose situation was . . . hopeless.

This is crazy, he thought. Absolutely insane. This woman is headed nowhere—except possibly to jail. She has no career now. No future beyond the turmoil of an arrest and trial. Lauren had so much—talent, beauty, direction, self-assuredness. What has Christine Beall got?

"David?" Christine's voice startled him, and for a moment he couldn't locate her. Then, through the windshield, he saw her, elbows resting on the hood of the jeep, studying him. "Are you all right?"

"Huh? Oh, sure, I'm fine," he lied.

"Good. I couldn't tell if you were in a trance or just in a snit because I forgot to let you put lunch together. It's ready whenever you are."

David smiled thinly, lowered himself from the jeep, and limped across the sand to the partly shaded niche where she had spread their blanket.

Silence settled in as they picked at the mélange of foods Christine had found—sardines, marinated artichoke hearts, Wheat Thins, boiled eggs, black olives, string cheese, and Portuguese sweet bread.

"That was delicious," David said finally. "Want to flip for rights to that last artichoke?"

"No, thanks, I'm full. You go ahead." She paused, then continued with almost no change in her tone. "Charlotte wasn't dying of cancer, was she?" It was a statement more than a question.

So much for Camelot, David thought. With a deliberateness that he hoped would help him form a response, he set his fork in an empty jar, then swung around to face her.

"You mean the autopsy findings," he said. She swallowed hard and nodded. "Well, then, the simple answer to your question is probably not. On autopsy there was no obvious cancer. For sure it could have popped up again in six months or a year, or even two. But for now that's your answer."

Christine started to reply, then bit at her lip and turned away. Without the slightest warning, even to himself, David snapped at her. "Damn it, Christine, don't do this to yourself. If you're going to work this whole business through—and I think you should—then do it from all sides—not just the ones that will heighten your guilt. Either we take a hard look from every angle or we might as well go back to small talk. Understand?"

Christine nodded. Her eyes were glazed and vacant. "I . . . I just feel so damn lost," she said hoarsely. "So frightened, so . . . so hopeless."

That word again. This time it was David who looked away. He could not shake the feeling that she was right. What *did* she have to look forward to? Then he thought of Lauren. For better or for better. That was how he had described her commitment to him. Now it was his turn to decide.

In that instant he felt a renewed spark of anger. Christine Beall had made choices and because of those choices people had gotten hurt—and killed. Now she was feeling hopeless. Wasn't she getting just what she deserved?

What she deserved. David shook his head. How many of his colleagues thought that getting arrested, then suspended from the Doctors Hospital staff was just what *he* deserved. Did he have any more right to pass judgment than they did?

He reached out and took Christine's hand. Her fingers tightened about his. He could feel her despair.

All at once, he folded his arms in a rigid professorial pose. "Just where do you get off thinking you have the right to make that diagnosis?" he asked haughtily.

"What diagnosis?"

"Hopelessness. Here you are in the presence of perhaps the world's greatest expert on the subject, and you have the temerity to diagnose yourself without asking for a consultation? That is unacceptable. I am taking over this case." The emptiness in her eyes began to lift. "We must take an inventory," he said. "First the basics. I see ten fingers, ten toes, and two of all the parts there are supposed to be two of. Are they all in working order, miss?" She suppressed a giggle and nodded. "So far, this sounds very unhopeless. Are you perchance aware of the classic Zurich study on the subject? They measured hopelessness on a scale of zero to ten in over a thousand subjects, half of them living and half dead. A hopelessness index of ten was considered absolute. Can you guess the outcome of that research?" She was laughing now. "Can't guess? Well, I'll tell you. A marked difference was found between the groups. In fact, those in the deceased group invariably rated ten, the rest invariably zero." He rubbed his chin and eyed her up and down. "I'm sorry, miss. I really am, but I'm afraid that no matter how much you want to be, you are simply not hopeless. Thank you very much for coming. My bill's in the mail. Next?"

She threw her arms around his neck. "Thank you." Her lips brushed his ear as she spoke. "Thank you for the consultation." She drew her head back to look at him. Their kiss simply happened—a gentle, comfortable touching that neither of them wanted to end or change. A minute passed, and then another. Finally she drew away.

"It all went wrong," she said softly. "It seemed so right, and it all just went . . . crazy. Why, David? Tell me. How the hell can I ever trust my feelings again when something I believed in so very much turned out so sour?" She sank down to the sand and stared out at the Atlantic.

"You want to know why?" he said, dropping next to her. "Because you're not perfect, that's why. Because nobody's perfect, that's why. Because every equation involving human beings is insolvable, or at least never solvable the same way twice. I believe in euthanasia just as much as you do. I always have. It's an absolutely right idea as far as I'm concerned. The difference is that somehow I have come to understand that while it is an absolutely right idea, there is simply no way to do it right. Sooner or later, the human element, the unpredictable, uncontrollable X factor rears its ugly head, and *wham,* things come apart."

"And innocent people die," she said.

"Chris, as far as I'm concerned, when it comes to dying, we're all innocent. That's the problem. Someone in your Sisterhood—possibly this Peggy woman—has snatched up the good, honest beliefs of some wonderful, idealistic nurses and has run away with them. Again, the human element. Money, greed, lust, fanaticism. Who knows what will pluck that special string hidden within someone and set him off? You were about to expose The Sisterhood, or at least that's what somebody thought. That string gets plucked and crazy, insane decisions get made.

"There's this riddle I once heard," he continued. "It asks a person what he would do if he was presented with a healthy newborn infant and promised that by slaying that infant he could instantly cure the ills of all mankind. Someone in your Sisterhood has answered that riddle for herself. Ben, you, me—none of us is as important to them as their ideals. The individual sacrificed for the greater good. It happens all the time."

"That's horrible," she said.

"Maybe. But more important, it's human. You can shoulder the burden of responsibilities for my suffering or even Ben's death, if you want to, but that's being awfully tough on yourself for just doing what you believed in and for trusting that other human beings were just as constant, just as pure in their belief as you were.

"You have decisions to make, Chris. Huge, crunching, God-awful decisions. If you want, I'll help. But don't expect me to stand by holding the matches while you pour gasoline over yourself. I . . . I care too much."

Slowly she turned to him. Her eyes held him as they had during their first moments together. Her hands caressed the sides of his face. Their kiss, this time warm and deep and sweet, carried them to the sand. Moment by moment, as they undressed one another, the world beyond their beach drifted away. David kissed her eyes, then buried his lips in the soft hollow of her neck. Her hands flowed over his body, capturing new excitement for herself as she created it in him.

With every kiss, every touch, the loneliness and fear inside them lessened. With each new discovery the sense of hopelessness ebbed.

Christine's face glowed golden in the late afternoon sun as she pulled herself on top of him. He stroked her firm breasts, first with his hands, then with his tongue.

She was smiling as she reached down and guided him inside her.

"Barbara, just stop fretting and give me the names. I'll take care of it."

"But . . ."

"The names, please." Margaret Armstrong snapped the words, then balled the small piece of fabric in her fist and forced herself to relax.

Barbara Littlejohn hesitated. A throbbing in her head, which had begun during the flight from Los Angeles, intensified. Finally she opened a manilla folder and passed one letter at a time across the cardiologist's desk. "Ruth Serafini," she said. "Resigned from both the board of directors and the movement. Says that she understands you are doing what you think is right, but that she cannot, in all good conscience, go along with it."

"Not even a copy to me," Peggy muttered, scanning the letter, then tossing it aside.

"Susan Berger," Barbara continued. "Says essentially the same thing as Ruth, but goes on to state that until matters are resolved she intends to curtail all Sisterhood operations in northern California. No approval for new cases, and also her recommendation that all contributions to the Clinton Foundation be held up."

Peggy set the letter on top of the other without reading it. "Susan will listen to reason," she said evenly, weighing the possibility of doctoring the half-dozen tapes of Susan's that were locked in her basement vault. Without any reference to The Sisterhood of Life, the tapes would constitute a chilling confession. "She's far too ambitious a woman not to listen to reason." Peggy unraveled the square of linen and absently rubbed it between her fingertips.

Barbara Littlejohn, appearing gray and drawn despite her carefully applied makeup, passed across the third letter. "This is the one that upset me the most," she said. "It's from Sara."

Damn! The expletive was thought more than spoken.

"She says that she will reconsider her resignation if we conduct a careful investigation into involvement of The Sisterhood or its members in the deaths of John Chapman and Senator Cormier—both at this hospital. Peggy, we didn't have anything to do with—"

"Of course not," Peggy said. "John Chapman was a friend of Sara's.

She's just upset. Senator Cormier was autopsied and has already been thoroughly discussed at a death conference. I made it a point to attend. He had extensive coronary artery disease and simply had a fatal heart attack during surgery. That's all there is to that."

"I'm glad." There was genuine relief in Barbara's face and voice. "Peggy, I don't know what I would have done if you hadn't been available to discuss this. Everything seemed to be coming apart."

"Nonsense. You're doing a wonderful job. Our Sisterhood has not only survived forty years, it has grown. A situation like this Shelton business may dent our solidarity, but it won't break it. Just leave these letters with me. By day's end I'll have the whole matter under control."

"Thank you," Barbara said, taking Peggy's hand. "Thank you." She let herself out.

"The pillow, baby. Just set it over my face and lean on it as hard as you can. It won't take long." They're trying to destroy me, mama. They're trying to destroy our Sisterhood. Margaret Armstrong's eyes were closed even before the outside door of her office clicked shut behind Barbara. The sense of that evening so many years ago, of the hospital room, of the pain on her mother's face—suddenly they were real once again.

"Mama, I . . . Please, mama. Please don't make me do it."

"I love you. If you love me too, you won't let me hurt so anymore. They all say it's hopeless. . . . Don't let me hurt so anymore. . . ."

"I love you, Mama. I love you." Peggy Donner whispered the words over and over again as Margaret Armstrong watched and listened, the piece of linen gliding continuously across her fingertips.

"I love you, Mama . . ." Peggy said as she placed the pillow over the narrow face and leaned on it with all the strength she could manage.

Margaret watched the movement beneath the sheet lessen, then stop. She was shaking as the girl replaced the pillow and kissed her dead mother's lips. She looked at the square of fabric as if discovering it for the first time.

Once again, the ordeal was over.

John Dockerty paced from one side of the cluttered back room of Marcus Quigg's pharmacy to the other. Off to one side, Ted Ulansky watched, his broad face an expressionless mask. They had been grilling Quigg for nearly two hours, after finding enough improprieties in his records at least to have his license suspended. Dockerty's hunch had been right. There was no need to manufacture evidence against the squirrelly pharmacist. In just a few hours of work, checking his prescriptions and calling a few doctors, they had gained the kind of clout that should have brought Quigg to his knees begging for some kind of a deal. However, the little man had proved surprisingly resistant—or frightened.

"Mr. Quigg," Dockerty said irritably, "let's start all over again." The detective snapped a small stack of Quigg's bogus prescriptions against the palm of his hand. He and Ulansky had agreed ahead of time that Dockerty would assume the role of tough, threatening villain during the interrogation and Ulansky would wait until he felt the tension was right, then ride to Quigg's defense like a knight errant.

"Whatever you say," Quigg mumbled. He was maintaining what composure he had left by chain-smoking and avoiding any eye contact. However, from his vantage point, Ted Ulansky noticed that, for the first time, Quigg's hand was shaking. It would not be long.

"I've laid it all out for you," Dockerty spat. "These prescriptions tell me that you are at least a crook. At worst, you're a fucking dope pusher who is putting bread on his table by dealing pills to kids. Now either you tell us what we want to know, either you tell us who paid you to finger David Shelton, or I'll see to it that your pharmacy license is chopped up and stuffed down your throat as your first prison meal. Got that?"

Quigg bit at his lower lip. The shaking increased.

From the corner of his eye Dockerty saw Ulansky nod. Time for the finale. He tightened his jaw and spoke through clenched teeth. "I want a name, Quigg, and I want it now. Otherwise there's a cell waiting for you at Walpole. And believe me, a cute little fellow like you is dog meat to those guys. After a week, your asshole is going to be so wide from getting screwed that you'll shit in your pants every time you take a step." His voice was booming now. "The name, Quigg—I want the name."

"Enough!" Ulansky cracked the word like a whip. Quigg's ashen face spun toward him. The narcotics investigator inserted himself between the two men like the referee in a prizefight. He put a calming hand on Dockerty's chest, only to have it slapped aside. For an instant he wasn't certain the Irishman was acting. "John, calm down. Just calm down. That temper of yours has gotten you in enough hot water with Internal Affairs as is, so just get a hold of yourself." He turned benevolently to Quigg, noting with satisfaction that a trace of color had returned to the man's cheeks.

"Marcus, I want to help you out, I really do," he said, reassurance flowing from every word. "But you've got to realize what you're up against. You're sitting here balancing your career, your freedom, and your health against a name. Just a name. That's all the lieutenant is asking for. I know you're frightened about what will happen if you give it to us, but just think about what will happen to you if you don't. At least the detective here can offer you some hope. Can the name we want offer you that?"

Ulansky scrutinized the man's face. He saw fear and uncertainty, but not defeat—not the capitulation he had expected by now. He looked at Dockerty and shook his head.

"I . . . I want to speak to my lawyer," Quigg said.

Dockerty shot across the room, grabbed the man by his lapels, and pulled him to his feet. "You get nothing until I get some answers." Reluctantly, he released his grip. "We're taking you with us, Quigg," he said. "I want you to see firsthand what jail is all about. We still have business, you and me. Come on, creep, let's go."

Marcus Quigg felt the knifelike pain beneath his breastbone and thought for a moment that it was all going to end right there. The wafer-thin aneurysm that had replaced much of the muscle of his heart was stretching. He had wanted to tell them at the outset that he was no crook. He wanted to tell them now that the illegal prescriptions were strictly nickel-and-dime stuff—Band-Aids to try and hold together his failing business and his failing health and his wife, terrified of being left alone with four children. He wanted to tell them, but he couldn't.

What difference did it make anyway? He asked himself the question over and over as Dockerty snapped handcuffs on him and led him from the store. So this Shelton was in trouble because of what he was doing. Well, he was in trouble, too. Big trouble. The goddamn balloon in his chest was stretching and his doctor had said it could be a year or a month . . . or an hour. She had said there was nothing that could be done for him. Would Dockerty understand? Would he understand that, after a whole life of trying to do what was right, all he had to show for it was a frightened wife, four kids who needed to eat, and a ball of blood in his chest that could explode at any time?

Quigg felt the knot in his gut and tasted acid percolating in his throat. He wanted to tell them and just go home to his own bed. But he knew what would happen. He knew the money would stop. He knew the additional thousands of dollars he had been promised when the whole mess was over would never come.

As he was shoved into the back seat of the detective's car, Marcus Quigg silently cursed Dr. Margaret Armstrong and the misery she had brought him.

A pot of coffee, a shower together, and suddenly the evening had passed into crystal night. A birch log fire had transformed Joey's living room into a musty womb. Stretched on the couch, David and Christine alternated brief conversation with prolonged gazes at the velvet sky.

"Red silk," David said, fingering the robe he had borrowed from Rosetti's closet. "I never thought of myself as the silk dressing gown type, but it sure do feel fine."

Christine sat up, then pulled an edge of her robe across her lap. "David, I want you to know how much this day has meant to me." His eyes narrowed. "You know I didn't plan it this way, don't you?" He nodded. She saw the tightness in his face and the moist film over his eyes. "All of a sudden I feel . . . sort of selfish—even cruel."

"That's nonsense."

"No, it's not. I've allowed this to happen, knowing every minute it was going to end."

"You haven't exactly been alone," he said huskily.

"No, I guess not. . . ." Her voice trailed away. "David," she said at last, "I'm going back in the morning."

"One more day." His response was so quick that they both knew the thought had already been in his mind.

Christine shook her head. "I don't think that would be fair—to either of us. I know what you're feeling. I've been feeling it too. All day. My mind keeps flip-flopping from fantasies of what I want to have happen to the reality of what I know is going to. Staying here—even another day—will only make it hurt more when I go. I've caused you enough pain already."

"I don't want you to leave." He was battling the truth in what she had said. He knew it. Still, he was unable to stem the torrent of words. "It . . . it just isn't safe. Joey told you that last night. Vincent is loose somewhere in Boston. He's looking for me, and, as likely as not, he's looking for you, too. If we go back, we'd have to go straight to Dockerty. And what would we tell him? We can't go back yet. Hell, Chris, we don't have to go back ever. We could take off. Right now. Tonight. We could go to Canada or . . . or to Mexico. I speak some Spanish. Maybe we could open a little clinic somewhere. Practice together. What good would it possibly do to go back now?"

She kissed him lightly. "It wouldn't work, David. You know that as well as I do. My Sisterhood has done some terrible things. I couldn't live with myself if I didn't try to stop them. I only hope I can find a way to do it without hurting all those nurses like me who believed—"

"Dammit, there must be another way!" David stiffened, then muttered an apology for the outburst and sank into the cushion. She was right. The rational, logical part of him understood that. If their circumstances were reversed, he knew, he would be saying the same things. But at the moment the rational, logical part of him was not controlling his tongue.

"Look," he said, "maybe there is another way. Maybe we could go off somewhere safe and you could send what information you have to Dockerty or . . . or to Dr. Armstrong. Sure, that's it—Dr. Armstrong. She's been a friend and a help to me since this whole nightmare started. If anyone could help us convince the authorities about The Sisterhood's existence, she could." In spite of himself, the idea actually began to take hold. "Chris, the woman would be perfect. You heard it yourself that night on Four South. She's absolutely set against euthanasia. For all we know, if someone of Dr. Armstrong's stature comes out against them, the Sisterhood people might decide it was time to fold up the organization all together. We could write to her and she could—"

"David, please. Don't do this."

"No, wait, hear me out. Just let me finish. Charlotte Thomas wanted to die. As far as we can tell, she was going to die no matter what. Oh, maybe another day of misery or a few agonizing weeks, but she was going to die." Inside, David's mental voice began begging him to listen to the thoughtlessness of what he was saying, to the pressure he was putting on her. The pleas went unheeded. "From what you know of the woman, do you think she would want you, want us, to have our chance together snuffed out because you helped her accomplish what she simply didn't have the strength to do herself? Just another day or two to think things over. That's all I'm asking. We'll find another way, or we'll go back and face things together. At least let's wait until we hear from Joey. Maybe he'll find out Vincent's in jail somewhere after all."

She closed her eyes and held him with all her strength. In the silence that followed, the scene David had started to paint grew in her thoughts. It was a dusty village nestled in a horseshoe of craggy mountains. She even saw their clinic—a white clay building at the end of a sunbaked dirt street. She could feel the warmth and serenity of their life. She sensed the peace that would come from devoting herself to such a place and such a man.

Christine pressed her lips together and nodded. "Okay. Another day. But no promises."

"No promises." He felt only momentary joy at his victory before he began to acknowledge what he had known all along: unless they could find a truly satisfactory option, he would never allow her to run.

They made love in soft, unhurried harmony. For nearly an hour their eyes and mouths and fingertips explored one another. At last, when it felt as if neither of them could tolerate another touch without exploding, he entered her.

Marion Anderson Cooper was tough. Not only a tough cop, although he was that, too. He was tough in ways that only boys growing up on the streets of Roxbury with a feminine-sounding name could be tough. His toughness had been forged by rat bites as he lay on the shabby mattress he shared with his two brothers and tempered by two years in the mud and death of Vietnam. It was tested again and again by situations encountered as one of the first black sergeants assigned to the Little Italy section of Boston—the North End.

In the early morning hours of October 11 Cooper was making his second pass through the largely deserted streets of his patrol. From time to time he stopped the cruiser to shine his light in the window of a store or restaurant where he sensed something out of the ordinary.

Each time he identified the source of his uneasiness—a new product display or repositioned table—and moved on.

The purple Fiat, parked inconspicuously by a dumpster in one of the back alleys, had not been there on his earlier swing through the area. Cooper blocked the alley with the patrol car, flashed his spot on the license plate and radioed the dispatcher.

"This is Alpha Nine Twenty-one," he said, "requesting stolen check and listing on a purple Fiat, Massachusetts license number three-five-three, Mike, Whiskey, Quebec. Any backup units available?"

"Negative, Alpha Nine Twenty-one. Repeat license, please."

Cooper repeated the number and waited. The car was hot—he felt certain of that. In fact, he was surprised there hadn't been other redistributed vehicles on the first night of decent weather in over a week. If it were stolen, it was kids, not the pros. Had it been the pros, the little Fiat would have already been painted, supplied with new numbers, and on its way to fill an order in Springfield or Fall River or someplace.

The delay seemed longer than usual. Cooper drummed impatiently on the wheel. He flipped on his walkie-talkie and was stepping out of the car when the radio crackled to life.

"Alpha Nine Twenty-one, I have information on nineteen seventy-nine Fiat sedan, Massachusetts license three-five-three, Mike, Whiskey, Quebec." The woman's voice, sensuous and tantalizing, was one Cooper recognized as belonging to a hundred-and-seventy-pound mustachioed mother of five.

"This is Alpha Nine, Gladys," he said. "What have you got?"

"So far the car is clean as your whistle, Alpha Nine—no wants, no warrants. Registered to Joseph Rosetti, twenty-one Damon Street, Apartment C."

"Alpha Nine out," Cooper said. As he entered the alley, he instinctively unsnapped the flap of his service revolver.

The driver's side door of the Fiat was open. Cooper shined his flashlight on the seats, then the floor. Nothing. Suddenly he tensed. The thick, nauseating scent of blood—the perfume of death—filled his nostrils. Wedged behind the seats, covered by a scruffy tan blanket, was a body. He took a quick breath and pulled the blanket aside. At that moment all the toughness, all the gruesome battles in the rice paddies and the jungles and the city streets did not help at all.

Marion Anderson Cooper spun away from the car and puked on the pavement.

Joey's hands and feet were bound. He had been stabbed dozens of times before he died. Arranged neatly on his chest were one of his ears and parts of three fingers. The morning papers would dismiss his grisly death as "a probable gangland slaying."

Twenty miles north of the city, the real reason, a crudely sketched blood-smeared map, extracted after an hour of torture, rested on the passenger seat of Leonard Vincent's sedan.

CHAPTER 21

MOVING SOUNDLESSLY, Christine set her suitcase by the front door and returned to the bedroom. Through eyes reddened by nearly an hour of crying, she peered across the pale early morning light at David. He was sleeping peacefully, his bushy hair partly buried in the pillow clutched to his face. With a painful glance at the letter wedged alongside the dresser mirror, she tiptoed out of the house.

The morning was chilly and still. Her breath, faintly visible, hung in the air. Far below, a thick mantle of silver covered the ocean as far as she could see. With movements as dreamlike as the world around her she took the key from the jeep, dropped it in an envelope, and walked slowly to her own car. Any moment she expected to hear his voice calling to her from the deck. The sight of him, she knew, would snap her resolve like a dry twig.

Without a backward look, she slid onto the driver's seat of the Mustang and rolled it down the drive before starting the engine. At the end of the turnoff to Rocky Point, a quarter of a mile from the house, she stopped and set the envelope with the key in a small pile of rocks. A final check to be certain David would have no trouble spotting it, then she turned left onto the winding ocean road, heading south to Boston.

The thoughts and feelings whirling inside her made it impossible to concentrate. She took no notice of the dark sedan that cruised past her in the other direction, nor of the huge, featureless man behind the wheel. No notice, that is, until the car suddenly appeared in her rear-view mirror only a few yards behind.

Leonard Vincent maneuvered his car close to the smaller Mustang. Christine's momentary anger at being tailgated changed to terror as their bumpers made contact. At first, it was just a scrape, then a crunch. Suddenly Vincent sped inside her on the right and began forcing her across the road. Christine's knuckles whitened on the wheel as she strained to keep from spinning out of control. She searched to her left for an escape route and instantly broke into a terrified, icy sweat.

Not ten feet away was the edge of a drop-off—the high slope of rocks and trees where a thirty-six-hour lifetime ago she had stood and gazed for the first time at Rocky Point. Several hundred feet below stretched the Atlantic.

Another crunch, louder than before. Christine's head spun to the right. The front of Vincent's car was even with her passenger door. Beyond him, a shallow gully, then a sheer wall of sandstone. The Mustang vibrated mercilessly as its tires bounced sideways. Christine slammed on the brake. The acrid smell of burning rubber filled the car.

Leonard Vincent's expression looked bland, almost peaceful as he forced her closer and closer to the dropoff. Less than five feet remained between the Mustang and the edge of the road when Christine released the brake and floored the accelerator. Her car shot forward. Out of the corner of her eye, she saw the sedan slip away. Then the bumpers of the two cars locked.

In an instant they were both out of control, spinning in a wild death dance across the road. Christine fought the wheel with all her strength, but it ripped from her hands. Her right arm slammed down against the gear shift and shattered just above the wrist. At the moment the white-hot pain registered, Christine's car hit the sandstone wall. Her head shot forward, smashing into the windshield just above her left ear. The glass exploded and instantly her world went black.

She did not hear the scream of tearing metal as the two cars separated. She did not see the wide-eyed terror in Leonard Vincent's face as his car snapped free of hers like a whip, then catapulted toward the ocean, hitting nose down on the steep slope and bouncing off trees and boulders over and over again until it disappeared in the thick fog. She did not see her own car ricochet off the rock face, spin full circle, then roll toward the drop-off.

She was unconscious on the seat when the rear wheels of the Mustang dropped over the embankment. The car stopped, its chassis teetering on the soft dirt. Then it slid over the edge.

David felt the emptiness even before he was fully awake. He opened his eyes a slit, then closed them tightly, trying to will what he knew was true not to be so. She's in the living room, sitting quietly, looking out at the ocean. A dollar says she's in the living room. He held his breath. The silence in the house was more than the simple absence of sound. It was a void, a nothingness. There was no movement of air, no sense of energy, no life.

She's gone for a walk, he reasoned desperately. A little morning walk and immediately the great surgeon panics. He rolled toward the window, blinking at the sunless glare. The sky was a thin sheet of pearl —the sort of overcast that would miraculously disappear by midmorning, opening like a curtain on the extravaganza of a new day. A morning walk, that's all.

He pushed himself to one elbow and scanned the room. The realization that her clothes were gone sank in only moments before he saw the envelope wedged alongside the mirror. It was the scene from countless grade B movies, only this time inexorably real. Sadness as flat as the morning sky swept over him.

"Shit," was his first word of the day. Then his second and third. He pulled himself out of bed and walked purposefully past the dresser into the bathroom. He peed, then washed, then shaved. He limped to the kitchen and put on water for coffee. The ankle was stiff and slow, but almost free of pain. His nurse had done her job well.

He tidied the living room and waited for the water to boil. In one final jet of hope he checked the driveway. The Mustang was gone. Christine was gone. Mexico and any chance for a new, unencumbered life together were gone.

Numbly, he shuffled back to the bedroom.

His name was printed in the center of the plain white envelope. He watched his hands tear it open. Another note. The second one in less than a week. This time, though, he felt the anguish in every word—as it was written and as it was read.

Dear David,

I couldn't chance waiting for you to wake up and talk me out of doing this. I tried all night to make myself believe there was another way. God, how I tried. In the end, though, all I could think of was how much pain and sadness I've caused you. It's all so very crazy. Something that seemed so good, so right. And now . . . I am going to see Lt. Dockerty to make a full confession regarding Charlotte. Before I do, I am going to meet with Dr. Armstrong. What you said last night made so much sense. I know she can help me. Despite what has happened, I know in my heart that most of us are only following principles we believe in. With luck, Dr. Armstrong can help put matters to rest with as little public disclosure as possible. I have three names to give her for starters, plus some phone numbers and a few Clinton Foundation newsletters. That's not much, but it's a start. Maybe, we can find a way of getting inside the secrecy. Then there is the matter of who is responsible for hiring Ben's killer. I'll do what I can to find out before involving the police.

Finally, there is you—a special, magic man. In so short a time, you have reached places inside me that I'm not sure I even knew existed. For that, and much more, I owe you. I owe you a life free from running, from constantly looking over my shoulder. I owe you a chance to fulfill the dreams you've worked so hard and endured so much for. If the circumstances were any different, sweet, gentle David

—any different—I would have risked it. Gone wherever we decided. I honestly believe you would be worth the gamble.

But circumstances are not different. They are what they are. Don't worry about me. I'll go straight to Dockerty after I see Dr. Armstrong. Just be careful yourself.

Please understand, be strong, and most of all, forgive me for causing you so much hurt.

Love,
Christine

P.S. *The key to the jeep will be at the end of the turn off for Rocky Point. It's in an envelope like this one.*

The jeep. David laughed in spite of himself. From an even start it was doubtful the jeep could stay with Christine's Mustang for more than a few yards. She was certainly determined not to be dissuaded. Well, he would not be dissuaded either. He could not change the situation, so he would simply change his expectations. Whatever she had to face he would face with her, as long as she wanted him there.

David dressed, playing through in his mind the situations the two of them might encounter in the days and weeks ahead. He noticed the bulky sweater he had worn on the ride to Rocky Point. Christine had placed it, neatly folded, on a chair by the bureau. David grinned. Perhaps he could return it to Joey as a contribution toward the wardrobe of the next man chased into the Charles River. As he picked it up, Rosetti's heavy revolver fell out. David had completely forgotten about it. He hefted the revolver in one hand and felt the queasy tension that he had come to expect when handling guns of any kind. He tried to recall when Christine said Joey would call again. Last night? This morning? A moment of reflection and he went to the phone. Rosetti's Boston number was printed on a small card taped to the receiver.

The woman's voice that answered his call was older than Terry's.

"Hello, is this the Rosettis' residence?" he asked.

"Yes. Can I help you?"

"Well, could I speak with Mr. or Mrs. Rosetti, please?" For a time there was silence on the other end.

"Who is this, please?" the woman asked finally. Her voice was ice.

David began to shift nervously from one foot to the other. "My name is David Shelton. I'm a friend of Joey and Terry's, and I'm stay—"

"I know who you are, Dr. Shelton," the woman said flatly. Again there was silence. David felt an awful sinking in his gut. "This is Mrs. D'Ambrosio. Terry's mother. Terry can't come to the phone. The doctor's given her some medicine and . . . ." Suddenly the woman began to cry. "Joey's dead . . . murdered," she sobbed. David dropped to the couch and stared unseeing across the room. "Terry hasn't been able to talk to the police, but she talked to me, and she said it's because Joey helped you that he's dead." She broke down completely, any pretext of anger at him lost in her grief.

"But that's . . . impossible," he mumbled, his mind whirling. It was Leonard Vincent. It had to have been. He pressed his eyes, trying to stop the spinning. First Ben, now Joey . . . and Christine out there somewhere. "When did this happen?" His voice was lifeless.

"Early this morning. They found him in his car, stabbed and cut and . . . Dr. Shelton, I just don't want to talk to you anymore. Joey's funeral is Tuesday. You can speak with my daughter after that."

"But wait . . ." The woman hung up.

For several minutes David sat motionless, oblivious to the bleating of the receiver in his lap. Then he grabbed the sweater and the revolver, along with his crutches, and raced from the house. Hoping against hope, he checked the jeep. There was no key. He threw the gun on the seat and pushed himself down the road in long, swinging arcs. Still, by the time he returned, nearly half an hour had passed. He was soaked with perspiration, gasping for air. His ribs, battered by the unpadded arm supports, screamed as he pulled himself up behind the wheel. Then he stopped.

"Will you calm down," he panted. "She's fine. She's all right." He started the motor. She was probably in Dr. Armstrong's office right now, or even with Dockerty. All he had to do was cool down and get to Boston in one piece.

He glanced over at the revolver and thought about Rosetti's admonition to him. How had he put it? Do it unto others if you even think they're gonna do it unto you? Something like that. David shuddered, then cradled the gun in his hands. Had Joey died because he didn't have the revolver when he needed it? The possibility drained away what little spirit David had left. All that remained was anger. Anger and a consuming hatred. He would find Vincent, or whoever had murdered Joey. He would find them and either kill them or die trying. He clenched one hand, then squeezed it with the other until it hurt. Finally he worked the jeep into reverse and started down the driveway.

Concern for Christine diluted his anger with a sense of urgency. He tried accelerating, but the carburetor, choked on dust and sand, flooded. The idea occurred to him that a perfect thank-you gift for Joey would have been a tune-up and alignment for the jeep.

Would have been. David shook his head helplessly, then glanced at the watch Joey had given him. It was after nine. Above, the frail overcast was showing the first signs of surrender to the autumn sun. He forced himself to loosen up and restarted the engine. By the time he reached the ocean road, he had mastered a rhythm of shifting and acceleration that was acceptable to the relic. His thoughts returned to Christine. Perhaps he should have called the police. If she didn't have too great a start, at least they could detain her long enough for him to catch up. But who—the state police? Would she be upset if he involved them before she was ready? He turned the notion over in his mind. He had decided to stop at the first phone booth when he saw the flashing lights and barriers of a roadblock ahead.

A battered maroon pickup truck in front of him was struggling through a U-turn, its grizzled driver mouthing obscenities. David leaned out of the jeep and called to him.

"Hey, what's going on up there?"

"Eh?" The man stopped the truck obliquely across the road, still several maneuvers from a complete U.

"Up ahead, what's happened?" David tried again, this time shouting.

"Accident. Bad one too, damn it." The old man's tone left no doubt that he was taking the inconvenience personally. "Two cars over the side. One they just hauled up. One's comin' from way at the bottom. Fifteen, twenty minutes more, they said. Probably be an hour, the way Mac Perkins works that old tow rig of his."

Uneasiness took hold as David strained to see past the truck. "Did you see either of the cars involved?" he asked too softly.

"Eh?"

David groaned. "The cars," he yelled. "Did you see either . . . Oh, never mind. Could I get by, please?"

"Sure, but you ain't goin' nowhere. An' there's no need for you to go snappin' about it neither." All at once David's questions registered. "The cars, you say? Did I see the cars?" Totally exasperated, David nodded. "Only the little blue one," the man called out. "Smashed to smithereens it is, too."

David's hands knotted on the wheel. A sinking terror deepened inside him. He closed his eyes while the old man worked his pickup out of the way. In that instant the photolike image of another accident appeared in his mind. The rain, the lights, Becky's and Ginny's faces, even their screams. He wanted to open his eyes, to end the horror, but he knew that when he did only a new nightmare awaited. He had no doubt that the blue car the old man had seen was Christine's.

"Mister, road's closed. I'm afraid you'll have to turn around."

David whirled toward the voice. It was a state trooper, tall and thin, with a high schooler's face that made him look slightly ridiculous in his authoritative blue uniform. Before David could respond, his gaze swung past the spot where the truck had been to the cluster of police cars, tow trucks, and ambulances ahead. In the midst of them, resting on flattened tires, was the shattered, twisted wreck of Christine's Mustang.

"Mister? . . ." The young trooper's voice held some concern.

David's face was ashen. "I . . . I know the woman who was driving that car," he said in a remote, hollow voice. "She was my . . . friend."

"Mister, are you all right?" When David did not answer, the trooper called down the road, "Gus, send one of the paramedics over here. I think this guy's gonna pass out or something." He opened the door of the jeep. As he did, David pushed past him and began a hobbling run toward the car, oblivious to the salvos of pain from his ankle. He stumbled the last five yards and hit heavily against the door. Gasping, he stretched his arms across the roof and held on. The car was empty. The windshield was blown out, and the engine had been smashed backward, nearly to the front seat. An ugly brown swatch of blood stood out against the soft blue seat cover.

"God damn it," he cried softly. "God damn it . . . God damn it!" Louder and louder until he was screaming.

Several men rushed toward him just as the trooper took his arm.

"Mister, please calm down," he said in more of a plea than an order. He led David to the side of the road and helped him lean against the trunk of a half-dead birch.

After a minute, David managed to speak. "Wh . . . where's her body?" he stammered.

"What?"

"Her body, damn it," he screamed. "Where have they taken it?"

The young man broke into a relieved grin. "Mister, there isn't any body. No dead one, I mean. Not from this car anyway."

David sank to one knee and stared up at him.

"Passerby found the lady wanderin' down the road," the trooper explained. "Pretty battered up, with a nasty cut or two, and probably a broken arm, but nowheres near dead. Now, can you calm down enough to tell me who you are?"

Kensington Community Hospital, a twenty-minute drive according to the trooper, took thirty-five in the jeep. David had stayed at the accident scene for a short while, learning what he could. Christine's survival was miraculous. A couple had come upon her, bloodied and incoherent, wandering along the road. Later the rescue team found her Mustang wedged upside down against a tree fifty feet down the rocky slope and nearly half a mile from where she was picked up.

David remained long enough to watch with total dispassion as Leonard Vincent's mangled corpse was pried from his car and transferred to an ambulance. He left during the commotion that followed discovery in the wreckage of a silenced revolver and a variety of knives. Throughout his drive to the hospital he sensed renewed hatred building —hatred no longer directed at Leonard Vincent, but at those who had hired him.

The hospital was fairly new and very small—fifty beds or less, David guessed. He paused momentarily inside the front door, trying to develop some feel for the place. The lobby was deserted save for the ubiquitous salmon-coated volunteer behind the desk, rearranging the contents of her purse. To her right an impressive brass board listed the two dozen or so physicians on the hospital staff. Beside each name was a small amber bulb that the physician could switch on when he was "in the house." Only one had a glowing amber light. No one could accuse Kensington Community Hospital of being overstaffed, he thought sardonically.

The emergency wing was labeled with black paste-on letters above a set of automatic doors. As they slid shut behind him, David heard the volunteer say, "Can I help you, sir?" He shook his head without bothering to look back.

The physician on duty, an Indian woman with dark, tired eyes, met him halfway down the corridor. She wore a light orange sari beneath her clinic coat and had a White Memorial Hospital name tag that identified her as Dr. T. Ranganathan.

"Excuse me," David said anxiously, "my name is David Shelton. I'm a surgeon at Boston Doctors. A friend of mine, Christine Beall, was brought in here a short time ago?"

"Ah, yes, the automobile accident," she said in sterile English. "I saw her only briefly before Dr. St. Onge arrived and . . . ah . . . took over the case. She has a fractured wrist and possibly some fractured ribs on the left side. Also two scalp lacerations. However, at the time Dr. St. Onge dismissed me she seemed in no immediate danger. You will find her in there." She pointed at one of the rooms.

In addition to St. Onge, three others were in the room with Christine—an orderly, the lab technician, and a second nurse. David ignored them all and rushed to the examining table. "Dr. St. Onge, I'm Dr. David Shelton," he said looking only at Christine. She was lying on her side, sterile drapes over her head. A large patch of hair had been shaved away from her left ear. The drapes surrounded an ugly, three-inch gash that was nearly sutured shut.

"David?" Christine's voice was the empty whimper of a lost child.

He knelt by the table a safe distance from the sterile field. "Yeah, hon, it's me." The reassurance in his voice belied the anger and sadness inside him. "You're doin' fine. A few dents, but you're doin' just fine."

"We're a pair, aren't we?" she said weakly. The few words were all she could manage.

"And who the hell are you?" St. Onge was obviously not satisfied with David's introduction. He was a heavy man, barrel-chested with thick hands. His tan was still midsummer dark and his clothes custom made. David guessed him to be about fifty.

"Oh, I'm sorry," he said, backing off a step. "My name is Shelton, David Shelton. I'm on the surgical staff at Boston Doctors. Christine is a . . . close friend."

"Well, right now she's my patient," St. Onge growled. "I'm sure you wouldn't take too kindly to someone barging in on your work. Even if he was a fellow surgeon."

David swallowed what he really wanted to say, backed off another step, and mumbled, "I'm sorry. Could you tell me how she is?"

St. Onge rummaged through his set of instruments, found a needle holder, and returned to the cut.

"She has another gash I've already closed above this one. She's got a busted arm that Stan Keyes will probably have to reduce in the operating room. That is, providing he doesn't capsize and drown in that stupid regatta he's racing in today."

David tightened. "Is he the only orthopedist available?"

"Yup. But don't worry. Fortunately, he's a damn sight better orthopedic surgeon than he is a sailor." St. Onge chuckled. "The arm will keep until he gets back."

David turned his attention to the bank of four X-ray view boxes on the wall across from the litter and studied the views taken of Christine's chest, abdomen, ribs, forearm, and skull. The forearm fracture was a bad one, with multiple fragments, but fortunately did not involve the joint space. The function of her hand would likely be unimpaired. He thought about the superb orthopedic staff at Boston Doctors and began wondering if a transfer there would be possible.

St. Onge finished suturing the laceration as David was snapping the four films of Christine's skull into place. The man whipped off his gloves with a flourish, letting them fall to the floor. "Use one of my standard head-injury order sheets, Tammy," he said. "Keyes will probably want to transfer her to his service anyway when he does the wrist. Any questions, Dr. . . ."

"Shelton," David said icily, brushing past him and kneeling by Christine. The sterile drape had been discarded and David could appreciate for the first time the extent of the battering she had absorbed. Despite some attempt to clean her up, patches of dried, cracking blood still remained over her face and neck. Almost the entire left side of her scalp had been shaved, exposing the two angry gashes. Tiny diamonds of glass sparkled throughout what hair remained. Her upper lip was the size and color of a small plum.

"Christine," he said softly. "How're you holding up?"

"Oh, David . . ." Her words were agonized, tearless sobs. David's fists tightened against his thighs.

"Dr. St. Onge, has a radiologist gone over her films?" He rose with deliberate slowness and turned toward the man.

"Why, no. The radiologist has left for the day. On call, if necessary, but I didn't see any reason to call him in for findings as obvious as . . ."

"Excuse me, miss," David cut in, "could I have an otoscope please. And, while you're at it, an ophthalmoscope." The woman had a bemused expression on her face as she handed the instruments over. St. Onge was speechless.

David slipped the otoscope tip in Christine's left ear. At that moment St. Onge found his tongue. "Now you just wait one goddamn minute," he said. "That woman is still my patient, and if you . . ."

"No!" David snarled the word. *"You* wait one goddamn minute. This woman is being transferred to Boston."

"Why you have your fucking nerve!" St. Onge was crimson. "I'll have you up before the medical board for this, big city credentials and all."

"Do that, please," David begged. The marginal control he had maintained disappeared completely. "And while we're there, we'll ask why you were too arrogant to call in a radiologist to look at these films. We'll ask why you missed the basilar skull fracture in two of the views. We'll also ask how you overlooked the blood behind her left eardrum caused by that fracture. Okay?" The silence in the room was painful. He lowered his voice and turned to the nurses. "Could one of you call an ambulance for us, please?"

The nurse, Tammy, hesitated, then with an unmistakable glint in her eye said, "Yes, Doctor," and rushed out. St. Onge looked apoplectic.

David turned to the remaining nurse. "I'm going to need some meds and equipment for the trip. I'll send the stuff back with the ambulance. Meanwhile, could you hang a Ringer's lactate I.V., please? Fifty cc's per hour."

"I'll have your ass for this, Shelton." St. Onge hissed each word, then stalked away.

David used the phone at the nurses' station to call Dr. Armstrong. As he was dialing, he heard giggles and a muted cheer from the staff in Christine's room.

"David, I've been worried sick about you," Dr. Armstrong said. "What's going on? Are you all right?"

"I'm fine, Dr. Armstrong. Really," he said. "But Christine Beall isn't. Do you remember her? A nurse on Four South?"

"I think . . . yes, of course I do. A lovely girl. What's wrong?"

"She's had an accident. Automobile. We're at Kensington Community Hospital now, but I'm on my way with her to the Doctors Hospital E.R. Could you meet us there and take over her care? She's got a fractured arm, a basilar skull fracture, and some chest trauma, so you'll probably end up being traffic cop for a three-ring circus of consultants. Will you do it?"

"Of course I'll do it," Dr. Armstrong said. "Are you sure she can handle the trip?"

"Sure enough to try. Any risk is worth taking to get her out of here. Especially with you there waiting for her. I have a lot to talk to you about, but all of it can wait until you get Christine taken care of. We'll be there within an hour."

"That will be fine," Dr. Armstrong said softly. "I'll be waiting."

CHAPTER 22

AT DAVID'S INSTRUCTIONS the ambulance ride was made at a steady fifty. No lights, no sirens. The fifty-five-minute drive seemed interminable, but what little time they might save by a dramatic dash to the city was hardly worth the catastrophe of an accident.

Throughout the trip Christine slipped in and out of consciousness. David, seated at her right hand, systematically checked her pulse, respiration, blood pressure, and pupil size, looking for changes that might indicate a sudden rise in the pressure against her brain. Any significant increase, either from bleeding or swelling, and he would have only minutes to reverse the process before permanent damage began.

The tension inside him was suffocating. He had acted decisively in dealing with St. Onge, but had he been too hasty? The thought ate away at him. Any crisis in the moving ambulance would be immeasurably more difficult to handle than in the hospital. It was the sort of decision he had spent years in training to be able to make—the sort of decision he had unflinchingly made many times over the years. But this was different.

"Christine?" He squeezed her hand. There was no response. "Let's go over the equipment again," he said to the paramedic riding alongside him. Out of David's field of vision, the man, a former corpsman in Vietnam, shook his head in exasperation. Granted it was the first time he had ever carried instruments for drilling cranial burr holes, but this was the third check David had asked him to make.

On an off chance Christine could hear, David turned his back to her and whispered the list of instruments and medications. The paramedic held each one up or signaled that he knew exactly where it was. Scalpels, drill bits, anesthetic, laryngoscope, tubes, breathing bag,

Adrenalin, cortisone, suction catheters, intracardiac needle—they were prepared for the worst.

Reluctant to take his eyes off Christine again, David began asking their location fifteen miles from the hospital without even trying to digest the information.

"Pulse: one ten and firm; respiration: twenty; B.P.: one sixty over sixty; pupils: four millimeters, equal and reactive." The words became a litany, every two minutes. Dutifully, the paramedic repeated then charted them. There was no banter between the two men. No communication at all, in fact, other than the numbers, every two minutes. Pulse . . . respiration . . . B.P. . . . pupils.

As they entered the outskirts of Boston, the tension grew. David, constantly moving, checking, rechecking, rousing Christine. The paramedic, nervous in spite of himself, fingering the instruments of crisis. The driver, a burly young man with thick brown curls, growled a few words into the two-way radio and toyed with the control switches for the lights and siren. They were close enough now. Any sign of trouble in back and he would make a run for it, doctor's order or not.

Suddenly the trip was over. The ambulance swung a sharp U-turn and backed up to the raised receiving platform. The rear doors flew open. A nurse burst into the ambulance and, with a glance at Christine, went straight for the intravenous bag. Right behind her, an orderly grabbed one side of the collapsible litter. A quick nod from the paramedic and they were gone, the nurse, running to keep up, holding the I.V. bag aloft.

David moved to follow, then sank back on the seat. He caught a brief glimpse of Margaret Armstrong as she met the team halfway across the cement platform and began her examination even before they reached the entrance. Her white clinic coat, unbuttoned, swung behind her like a queen's cape. Her every movement, every expression exuded control and competence.

They had made it. They were home. The decision to move, however hasty, had held up. As relief swept through him, David began to shake.

He weaved his way across the busy receiving and triage area and headed straight for the trauma wing. Real or imagined, it felt as if everyone—staff and patients—was staring at him. Phoenix, rising from the ashes; Lazarus from the dead.

Pausing outside Trauma Room 12, he glanced inside. The room was empty. He shuddered at the memory of Leonard Vincent's knife gliding across his throat. Then he thought about Rosetti. As soon as Christine was out of immediate danger and he had finished speaking with Dr. Armstrong, he would go see Terry.

As David approached Trauma 1, Armstrong emerged and beckoned him inside. Christine was awake. Through a sea of white coats—residents, technicians, and nurses—her eyes—sunken shadows—met his. For a moment all he saw was pain. Then, as he drew closer, he saw the sparkle—the flicker of strength. Her swollen, discolored lips pulled tightly as she tried to smile.

"We made it," she whispered. David nodded. "Now you won't have to do burr holes on me."

David's eyes widened. "You were awake during the trip?"

"Awake enough," she managed. "I . . . I'm glad we're here."

Her eyes closed. A reed-thin surgical resident moved in, swabbed russet antiseptic over her right upper chest, and prepared to insert a subclavian intravenous line. As the man slipped the needle beneath Christine's collarbone, David grimaced and turned away. He came face to face with Margaret Armstrong, who was standing several feet behind him, watching quietly.

"David, I'm so relieved to see that you're all right," she said. "The stories that followed your brief visit here the other night were quite frightening."

"There's some trouble in this hospital—in a lot of hospitals, in fact. I have a great deal to talk about with you, Dr. Armstrong," David said. He glanced over his shoulder at the resident, who was calmly suturing the plastic intravenous catheter in place with a stitch through the skin of Christine's chest. "What about Christine?"

"Well," said Dr. Armstrong, leading him out of the room, "I'll examine her more carefully as soon as the crowd in there has finished. My initial impressions add little to yours. She has a definite skull fracture and some blood behind that drum, but so far she seems neurologically stable. I have both a neurosurgeon and an orthopedic man waiting in the house, but I think we'll hold off on the wrist until we've had a chance to watch her. Ivan Rudnick is the neurosurgeon. Do you know him?" David nodded. Rudnick was the best on the staff, if not in the city. "Well, Ivan will see her and do a CAT scan as soon as possible. If there's no evidence of active bleeding, we'll wait and hope."

"What about her chest trauma?" David asked.

"No problem as far as I can see. EKG shows no cardiac injury pattern. My more extensive exam should help confirm it."

"Dr. Armstrong, I'm really grateful to you for handling this."

"Nonsense," she said. "I can't tell you how flattered—and pleased —I am that you would ask me. By the way," she added, "there is one small problem."

"Oh?" David's eyes narrowed.

"Nothing critical, David, but there are no ICU beds. Not a one. We're checking on one postop patient now, but he's been very unstable and I doubt we'll be able to move him. I've decided we'll be all right putting Christine on a floor. There's a private room available on Four South. I know the girls up there will give her closer attention than she would ever get anywhere else, including the ICU. She'll be moved up there as soon as possible."

"That sounds fine," David said. "If the nurses don't mind, I'll hang around and do what I can to help monitor her. That is, after you and I have had our discussion."

"Yes," said Dr. Armstrong distantly.

"Well, you go ahead and finish. I'll wait in the doctor's lounge until you're free to talk. By the way, which room will she be going to?"

"Excuse me?"

"The room," David said. "What room is she going to?"

"Oh, ah, I have it right here. It's Four twelve. Four South Room Four twelve." The cardiologist smiled, then disappeared into Trauma 1.

Four twelve! David swallowed against the sudden fullness in his throat. Charlotte Thomas's room! Step one on the bloody brick road that had led through one land of madness after another. He fought his sense of superstition and tried instead to focus on the irony. Room 412 would serve as the first command post in their battle to bring The Sisterhood of Life to an end. The exercise worked well enough, at least, to keep him from racing back to Dr. Armstrong to demand a room change. He wandered across the triage area to the doctors' lounge and stretched out with a copy of the monthly periodical *Medical Economics.* The lead article was entitled "Ten Tax Shelters Even Your Accountant May Not Know." Before he had settled into shelter number one, David was asleep.

An hour later, the phone above his head jangled him free of a frightening series of dreams—Charlotte's cardiac arrest and the bizarre events that followed, replayed with all of the characters interchanged—all, that is, except Christine, who died again and again in one grisly manner after another.

His clothes were uncomfortably damp and the sandpaper in his mouth made it difficult to speak.

"On-call room. Shelton here," he said thickly.

"David? It's Margaret Armstrong. Did I wake you?"

"No, I mean yes. I mean I wasn't exactly . . ."

"Well," she cut in, "our Christine is safely in her room. Nothing new for me to add to what we already know. I think she'll be all right."

"Wonderful."

"Yes . . . it is." Armstrong paused. "You said you wanted to talk with me?"

"Oh, yes, I certainly do. That is, if you . . ."

"This would be an excellent time," she interrupted again. "I'm in my office—not the one in the office tower, the one on North Two."

"I know where it is," said David, at last fully awake. "I can be there in five minutes."

The cardiac exercise laboratory doubled as Margaret Armstrong's "in house" office.

David knocked once on the door marked STRESS AND EXERCISE TEST-

ING, then walked in. The small, comfortable waiting room was empty. He hesitated, then called, "Dr. Armstrong? It's me, David."

"David, come in." Armstrong appeared at the door. "I was just making some coffee."

As he passed where she had been standing, David breathed in the distinctive odor of liquor.

Instinctively he checked his watch. It was not yet one. He ran through a number of explanations as to why the chief of cardiology might be drinking under such circumstances, especially at such an hour. None were totally acceptable. Still, the woman seemed quite in control. For the moment, at least, he forced the concern to the back of his mind.

The lab was spacious and well equipped. Several treadmills and Exercycles, each with a set of monitoring instruments, were lined up across the room. The required emergency equipment and defibrillator unit were placed inconspicuously to one side—an effort, David knew, to avoid additional apprehension in patients already nervous over their cardiac testing.

One end of the suite had been set aside as a conference area, with a maple love seat and several hard-backed chairs encircling a low, round coffee table. Armstrong motioned David to the love seat, then brought a percolator and two cups. She seemed more subdued than David could ever remember.

"You seem tired," he said. "If it would be better for us to talk later, I could . . ."

"No, no. This is fine," she said too sharply. "Hospital politics, you know. But for a change I get to sit back and listen. Let me pour us some coffee, then you can fill me in on what has been going on."

She pushed a carton of cream toward him, but he shook his head. "Where to start," he said, using a few sips to sort out his words.

"The beginning?" She encouraged him with a comfortable smile.

"The beginning. Yes. Well, I guess the beginning is that I didn't give the morphine to Charlotte Thomas, Christine did." He sipped some more. "Dr. Armstrong, what I've got to tell you is incredible, potentially explosive stuff. Christine and I have decided to share it with you because . . . well, because we hoped you might use your position and influence to help us."

"David, you know that I'll put myself and whatever influence I have at your disposal." She leaned forward to give him a closer view of the reassurance in her eyes.

In minutes he was totally immersed in the story of Charlotte Thomas and The Sisterhood of Life.

Initially Armstrong encouraged his narrative with a series of nods, gestures, and smiles, interrupting occasionally to clarify a point. Soon, though, her posture grew more rigid, her gaze more impassive. Gradually, subtly, the warm blue invitation in her eyes turned cold. Still, David talked on, relieved at unburdening himself of the awesome secrets that, until now, he was the only outsider to hold. Nearly half an hour passed before he first sensed the change in her.

"Is . . . is something the matter?" he asked.

Without responding, Armstrong rose and walked unsteadily to a telephone resting on a small desk at the opposite end of the lab. After a brief, hushed conversation, she worked her way back and settled heavily into a chair across the table from him. All at once, she seemed frail, and very much older.

"David," she said gravely, "have you discussed all this with anyone other than me?"

"Why, no. I told you that earlier. We were hoping you could help us without involving—"

"I'd like you to start over. There are some points you must clarify for me."

"Chris, are you awake? Can you hear me?"

The voice seemed to be echoing from a great distance. Christine opened her eyes, then blinked several times, straining to focus. She recognized the woman as a nurse, though her features remained uncomfortably blurred. She tried to turn toward the side. Pulses of nausea and an excruciating pressure in her head made it impossible. The room was dark, but even the light from the hallway was unbearable. "I'm awake," she said. "The light hurts my eyes." Slowly she closed them.

"Chris, Dr. Armstrong ordered your pupils to be checked every hour. I'll do it as quickly as I can."

Christine felt the nurse's fingers on her right eye, then a searing pain as the beam from the penlight hit her pupil. A brief respite, then a second stab on the left. She tried to lift her hands, but they would not move. Was she restrained? Her right arm, especially, felt heavy and numb. For a moment, she worried that it was gone. Then she remembered being told by Dr. Armstrong that it was broken. She settled back on the pillow and forced herself to relax.

"Listen, I'm going to let you sleep for a while," the nurse said. "You're due for a new I.V. in about twenty minutes. I'm going to wake you up then and we'll try to get some more of this glass out of your hair. Okay?" Christine nodded as best she could. "Hey, I almost forgot. Only a few hours in the hospital and already you're getting flowers. These were delivered a couple of minutes ago. They're beautiful. I'm going to put them on the table here. I know you can't see them, but maybe by tonight you'll be able to. There's a card. Do you want me to read it?"

"Yes, please," Christine said weakly.

"It says best wishes for a speedy recovery, Dahlia."

Dahlia? The pain and the swelling in her brain made it difficult to concentrate. "But . . . I . . . don't . . . know . . . any . . . Dahlia," she said.

The woman had already left.

"David, this killer, this . . . this Vincent—you must tell me again how you think he found you on the emergency ward and then was able to locate your friend."

David toyed with the cover of a magazine, then dropped it on the coffee table and rubbed at his eyes. What had started as a comfortable, long-awaited unburdening had mutated into a tense interrogation as Dr. Armstrong probed for every possible detail. He felt off balance, bewildered, and threatened by the persistence of her questions and the strain in her voice.

"Look," he said, no longer trying to conceal his mounting apprehension, "I've told you everything I know. Twice. My theories about how Vincent found Ben and me and then Joey are just that—theories. Dr. Armstrong, I know something is going on here. Something that I've said has upset you. I'm not going to tell you any more until you level with me. Now, please, what is the matter?"

The look in her eyes was glacial. "Young man, much of what you have told me is impossible. Preposterous. A series of sick, misguided conclusions that can only cause pain and suffering to many good, innocent people." David stared at her in disbelief. "You are stirring flames of a fire whose scope you do not understand. This so-called killer you have described—it is impossible that he is connected in any way with The Sisterhood of Life."

"But . . ."

"Impossible, I say!" She screamed the words.

"Just what is impossible?" Their heads spun in unison toward the door. Dotty Dalrymple stood calmly watching, her hands buried in the pockets of her uniform. David's skin began to crawl at the sight of her.

"Oh, Dorothy, I'm glad you could make it down this quickly." Armstrong's voice was tense, but composed. "I phoned you because Dr. Shelton here was just telling me a preposterous tale about The Sisterhood of Life and hired killers and—"

"I know what he was telling you," Dalrymple said, her face puffed in a half-smile. "I know very well what he was telling you." She lifted her right hand free. Nearly lost in the fleshy ball of her fist was a snubnosed revolver.

"The light . . . please turn it off." Christine felt the glare even through tightly closed eyes.

Two women—a nurse and an aide—were picking fragments of glass from her hair with tweezers. "All right, Chris," one of them said. "I guess we've tortured you enough for now. I have to rouse you in forty minutes. We can do a little more then. Okay?" She shut off the overhead light. "Wait a minute. I'm sorry, but I have to turn it back on. Just a few seconds to adjust the flow of your new I.V.

"Prime rib of beef and pheasant under glass were on your little menu sheet, but since you didn't circle anything we decided to serve you the specialty of the house: dextrose and water."

A ten-second explosion and again the room dimmed. Christine tried to ignore the throbbing in her skull.

"By the way," the nurse said. "Ol' Tweedledum was on the floor a few minutes ago. She herded all of us into the conference room just to make it clear that heads would roll if you didn't get first-class service from everyone. As if we would give you anything else. Well . . . see you later."

Christine heard the woman leave. Tweedledum. For a time she wrestled with the name. Then she remembered. Dalrymple! Suddenly bits and pieces of information were swirling about in her head. Dalrymple condemning David. Dalrymple offering a bribe. Her mind, working sluggishly through bruised, swollen tissues, struggled to understand. Deep within her apprehension took hold and fueled the already unbearable pounding in her head. Dalrymple! Could she have been responsible? Nothing made sense. Nothing except that she had to find David. Had to talk to him. She tried to move, to reach the bedside phone. Her free hand touched it, then knocked it, clattering, to the floor.

She searched for the call button. They had pinned it somewhere. Where? Where had they said it was?

From the darkness over her bed drops of intravenous fluid flowed inexorably from the plastic bag, through the tubing, and into her chest.

Christine was fumbling through the bedclothes for the call button when her pain began to lessen. Deep within her an uncomfortable warmth took hold and spread. Thirty seconds alone at the nurses' station were all Dotty Dalrymple had needed.

David . . . call David. Christine battled to maintain her resolve. Her eyelids closed, then refused to open again. So much to do, she thought. David . . . Sisterhood . . . so much to do. Her head sank back on the pillow. Her hand relaxed and fell to her side. Suddenly nothing seemed to matter. Nothing at all.

She listened for a time to the strange hum that filled the room. Then, with an inaudible sigh, she surrendered to the darkness.

Dalrymple motioned Armstrong to the chair next to David. Her brown eyes flashed hatred at both of them. Her sausagelike finger moved nervously against the trigger.

"Dorothy, please," Armstrong begged. "We've come so far. Shared so much. You're just overtired. Perhaps . . ."

"Oh, Peggy, just sit back and shut up," she snapped.

David looked at Armstrong. "Peggy? You? But you're a . . ."

"Doctor?" Armstrong filled in the word. "A few more years of studying, that's all. Believe me, nursing school was easily as difficult." She turned back to Dalrymple. "Dorothy, you know I'm on your side."

"Are you? Are you really on anyone's side but your own? It wasn't you who went to see Beall. It's not your name she associates with The Sisterhood. It's not you whose life goes down the drain as soon as she talks to the police. I have much too much going for me to sit back and let that happen."

"Then . . . then you really did it? You hired a killer?" Dalrymple nodded once. "Dorothy, how could you do a thing like that?"

"Don't start getting high and mighty with me. Killing's our game, isn't it? You taught it to me. Now you draw your line one place and I draw mine another. You were perfectly willing to forge prescriptions and sacrifice Shelton here to save your precious Sisterhood. I'll bet if *you* had gone to see Beall—if it had been your neck on the block—you would have done the same things to protect yourself as I did."

Armstrong started to protest, but Dalrymple silenced her with a flick of the gun. She reached into her pocket and, smiling, withdrew a large syringe, filled to capacity. Then she checked her watch. "Two o'clock," she said. "If my nurses are as efficient at their jobs as I have trained them to be, the I.V. you ordered on young Miss Beall should be up and running."

Christine's death sentence! David stared at Dalrymple with sudden panic. "What did you give her?" He shifted his feet for better leverage and began searching for an opening, however slight.

Dalrymple sensed the change and leveled the revolver at his face. "It would be useless to try anything." She glanced again at her watch. "Besides, it's too late." She set the syringe on the table in front of him. "The two of you will be a murder/suicide," she said calmly. "I really don't care which is which, as long as the police are satisfied there are no loose ends. Doctor, I give you the choice. The needle or a bullet. Astute clinician that you are, I'm sure you can deduce that one will be considerably more painful than the other."

"Dotty, please, you don't know what you're doing," Armstrong begged, moving off her chair to grab at Dalrymple's free hand. Before David could react, the nursing director pulled her arm free and swung a full backhand arc, catching the woman flush on the side of the face. With an audible snap, Armstrong's left cheekbone shattered. Her slender body shot across the room and slammed against the wall fifteen feet away.

Her revolver still leveled at a spot between David's eyes, Dalrymple glanced over her shoulder at Armstrong's crumpled form. "I've wanted to do that for so long." She smiled. "Now, Doctor, you have a choice to make." She moved around the table, pushing it back with a trunklike leg to allow herself room. The muzzle of the revolver was only a foot from David's forehead as she offered him the syringe. "Please decide," she urged softly.

David was staring at her face when, out of the corner of his eyes, he saw motion. Margaret Armstrong, on hands and knees, was inching across the floor. Desperately David forced his eyes to maintain contact with Dalrymple's.

"Well?" said Dalrymple. "My patience is running thin."

David took the syringe and studied it. "I . . . I don't think I can get this in without a tourniquet," he said, stalling. In the moment Dalrymple looked down he was able to catch another glimpse of Armstrong. The cardiologist was drawing closer. Then he noticed her hands. Each one held a small metal shield. The defibrillator! Armstrong had activated the machine. The paddles, connected to the unit by coiled wires, carried 400 joules.

David rolled up his sleeve and pumped his fist several times. The wires were almost out straight and Armstrong was still ten feet away. Dalrymple's hand tightened on the revolver.

"Now," she demanded.

"Dotty!" Armstrong yelled.

Dalrymple spun to the sound at the instant David made his lunge. He threw his shoulder full against her vast chest. The woman stumbled backward, catching the low coffee table just behind her knees. She fell like a giant redwood, shattering the table. As her bulk touched the floor, Armstrong was upon her, jamming one paddle on either side of her face, and, in the same motion, depressing the discharge button.

The muffled pop and spark from the paddles were followed instantly by a puff of smoke. Dalrymple's arms flew upward as her huge body convulsed several inches off the floor. The odor of searing flesh filled the air. Vomit splashed from her mouth as her head snapped back. At the moment of her death the sphincters of her bladder and bowel released.

For several seconds David stood motionless, staring at the two women—one battered, one dead. Then, with resurgent terror, he broke from the room in an awkward, painful dash toward Four South.

Margaret Armstrong, rubber-legged, leaned against the sink, patting cold water on her face. She felt drugged, unable to sharpen the focus of her mind. Behind her lay the mountain of death that had, moments before, been Dorothy Dalrymple.

With great difficulty she forced her concentration to the situation at hand. If Christine were dead, she realized, David Shelton was all that stood against the continuation of her Sisterhood. Could he be eliminated? Should he be? Peggy Armstrong knew she would gladly confess to murder—sacrifice herself—to save the movement. But was she capable of killing an innocent person?

She walked unsteadily toward the door, then turned and looked back in disgust at Dalrymple. If a woman she thought she knew so well, trusted so implicitly, could have tried to buy her own security at such a price, how could she be sure that in a time of crisis there wouldn't be others? Trembling, more from her thoughts than her injury, Armstrong supported herself against a wall. Was it over? After so many years, so many dreams, was it all over?

She slipped out of the office and locked the door. The janitor would not be in until sometime the following morning. Less than twenty-four hours. If she wished to salvage The Sisterhood, she had only that long to plan, to prepare, to act. Questions, one after another, raced through her mind. Was it worth the price of another life? Could she do it? Was there an explanation that would hold up? At that moment the answers were not at all apparent.

CHAPTER 23

USING THE BANNISTER for leverage, David vaulted down the stairs from North Two to North One. Pulses of adrenaline muffled the screams from his ankle. He exploded through the doorway to the central corridor, scattering a trio of horrified nuns.

The main lobby was in its usual midday chaos. David weaved and bumped his way across it like a halfback in open field, leaving two men sprawled and cursing in his wake.

"Hang on, baby, please hang on," he gasped, scrambling up the stairs in the South Wing. Even two at a time they seemed endless, doubling back on themselves between each landing. "Fight the bitch. Fight her fucking poison. Please . . ."

His feet grew leaden. His legs gave way between the third and fourth floors, then again as he stumbled onto Four South.

The corridor was empty except for one aide struggling to tie an old man safely in his wheelchair. In the seconds she spent staring at the apparition limping toward her, the patient, a stroke victim, squirmed free and fell heavily to the floor. The aide, sensing the emergency, waved him past. "Go on," she urged. "Clarence does this all the time."

David nodded and raced to the nurses' station. "Code Ninety-nine Room Four twelve," he panted. "Call it and get me some help. Code Ninety-nine Room Four twelve."

The astonished ward secretary froze for a moment, then grabbed the phone.

For David the scene in Room 412 was the rerun of a horrible dream. The dim light, the bubbling oxygen, the intravenous setup, the motionless body. He flicked on the lights and raced to the bed. Christine, lying serenely on her back, was the dusky color of death. Through the hallway speaker the page operator began calling with uncharacteristic urgency, "Code Ninety-nine, Four South . . . Code Ninety-nine, Four South . . ."

For a second, two, his fingers worked their way over Christine's neck, searching for a carotid artery pulse. He felt it. The faint, rhythmic tap of life against the pad of his first and second fingers. His own pulse or hers? At that moment, as if in answer to his uncertainty, Christine took a breath—a single, shallow, wonderful whisper of a breath. With the first sound, the first minute rise of her chest, David was in motion. He clamped the intravenous tubing shut, then bent over and gave two deep mouth-to-mouth breaths.

Before he had finished, a nurse burst into the room, pulling the emergency cart behind her. Over the minutes that followed, the two of them, surgeon and nurse, functioned as one. The young woman was a marvel—a controlled whirlwind, providing a needed drug or instrument almost before the words were out of his mouth.

Confronting an unknown poison, David's approach was shotgun: a fresh intravenous solution opened wide to dilute the toxin and support Christine's blood pressure; an oral airway and several breaths from an Ambu bag to maintain ventilation; bicarbonate to counteract lactic acid buildup.

Christine's color darkened even more. He risked a few seconds away from the breathing bag and lifted her eyelids. Her pupils were tiny black dots, nearly lost in the brown rings that constricted them—the pinpoint pupils of a narcotic overdose. God, let it be morphine, David thought. Let it be something reversible like morphine. He ordered naloxone, the highly effective antidote for all narcotic drugs. Within seconds the nurse had injected it.

A few more breaths and David stopped again. This time to recheck Christine's carotid pulse. With a deep sinking sensation he realized there was none.

"Slip a board under her, please," he said, lifting Christine's shoulders free from the bed. "You'll have to forget about the meds and just do closed chest compression until we get some more help. Christ, where is everyone?" His speech was rushed and anxious.

"One nurse went home sick." The woman said the words in rhythm to the downward thrusts of her hands against Christine's breastbone. "Two more are at lunch. They'll be here."

David continued the artificial breathing. "We need someone on the cart," he muttered. "We need someone on the goddamn cart." With the nurse unable to stop her cardiac massage, the trays of critical medications might as well have been on the moon.

An orderly wandered in. David snapped at him to take a blood pressure. The man tried twice. "Nothing," he said.

"Can you do CPR?" David asked, hoping he might free the nurse to return to the emergency cart. The man shook his head and backed away. "Shit!" David hissed.

He looked down at Christine. There were no more spontaneous respirations, no signs of life. Her body was covered with deep blue mottling. Unless he could get help very soon—one more pair of skilled hands—Christine would slip beyond resuscitation. For five seconds, ten, he stood motionless. The young nurse watched him, her eyes narrowed in mounting concern.

Suddenly a woman's voice called out, "Whatever you need, Doctor, just order it."

Margaret Armstrong stood poised by the emergency cart. Her left eye was swollen nearly shut by a huge bruise covering the side of her face. Blood trickled from one nostril. Still she held herself regally, unmindful of the stares from around the room.

David's decisiveness, already dulled by Christine's lack of response, became further blunted by fear and uncertainty. "You . . . you can take over the cardiac massage," he said, wishing the woman were not standing so close to the medication cart. There were any number of drugs there that could serve as lethal weapons.

Armstrong shook her head. "No, no. You're both stronger than I am. Besides, I'm a nurse, and a good one. I'll handle meds. Now, dammit, let's get on with it!"

David hesitated another moment, then shifted into high gear, calling out for antidotes to the substances Dalrymple would have been most likely to use. The crunching blow Armstrong had absorbed had no apparent effect on her reactions or efficiency. She was, as she had claimed, an incredibly good nurse. Adrenalin, concentrated glucose, more naloxone, calcium, more bicarbonate—she drew them up and administered them with speed and total economy of movement.

More help arrived. Another nurse offered to relieve Armstrong, but was directed to the blood pressure cuff.

"She's still not breathing on her own," David said. "I think we should intubate."

Armstrong reached up and pressed her fingers against Christine's groin, searching for a femoral artery pulse. She looked at David grimly and shook her head. "Nothing," she said.

"All right. Give me a laryngoscope and seven-point-five tube."

"Hold it!" Armstrong's eyes began to smile. "Wait . . . wait . . . It's here, Doctor," she said. "It's here."

Seconds later, the nurse operating the blood pressure cuff sang out, "I've got one! I hear a pressure! Faint at sixty. No, wait, eighty. Getting louder! Getting louder!"

David rechecked Christine's pupils. They were definitely wider. Another fifteen seconds and she began to breathe. The young nurse who had helped from the beginning gave David a thumbs-up sign and pumped her fists exultantly in the air.

The final concern in everyone's mind disappeared when Christine moaned softly, rolled her head from side to side, then fluttered her eyes open. They fixed immediately on David.

"Hi," she whispered.

"Hi, yourself," he answered.

Around the room people congratulated one another.

"I . . . I feel much better. My headache's almost gone." Her expression darkened. "David, Miss Dalrymple. I think she might be the one who . . ."

He silenced her with a finger against her lips. "I know, hon," he said with soft reassurance. "I know everything."

She strained to see inside his words, then calmed perceptibly. "I do feel better. Much better, David. Dr. Armstrong is a miracle worker."

David glanced over at Armstrong. "Yeah," he said stonily, "a miracle worker."

Margaret Armstrong met his gaze and, for a few moments, held it. Then, one at a time, she whispered a thank-you to those in the room and motioned each to leave.

The young nurse was the last to go. Armstrong walked her into the hall, then said, "You did wonderful work in there. I'm very proud of you."

The nurse flushed. "You . . . you've been hurt. Can I get you anything?"

"I'll be fine," Armstrong said. "You go on along and get back to your patients." Then she turned and reentered Room 412. She knew that at the moment she had stepped to the emergency cart and had drawn up the correct medication, she had sealed the fate of The Sisterhood.

Christine was asleep. Across the room, David had opened the drapes part way and was looking out at the hazy afternoon. His hands hung heavily by his sides, his stance reflecting none of the victory he had just won. Armstrong walked quietly to his side. He would not look at her.

For a time the only sounds in the room were the gurgle of oxygen through the safety bottle and the steady sighs of Christine's breathing.

"That's a hell of a bruise you've got," David said, his gaze still fixed on the city below. "I think you should have someone look at it."

"I will," she said. "Later."

"That woman, that . . . that beast lying in your office—she was your creation. Your monster."

"Perhaps. I suppose that in some ways she was. Does it matter that I still truly believe in the good of what The Sisterhood of Life has been doing? Does it matter that the struggle for dignity in human death is just?"

"Sure." David snorted the word. "It matters. Like it matters to the fracture in Christine's skull. Like it matters to the crap she faces when —if—she recovers. Like it matters to the fucking judge and the prosecutor and the newspapers who are going to try her for murdering Charlotte Thomas. Like it matters to my friends who are dead just because . . ." His frustration and fury choked off the words.

A silent minute passed before Armstrong said, "David, I know how you are feeling. I really do. I know my help with Christine and what I did to Dorothy can't take away the pain you both have suffered. But I also know something else. Something that will do much to soothe your wounds." She hesitated. "I know that Christine will never have to stand trial for murder."

David whirled and stared at her. "What did you say?"

"Christine did not murder Charlotte Thomas." Her eyes leveled at his, her gaze and expression deadly serious.

"How . . . how can you say that?"

"She didn't," Armstrong said flatly, "because I did. And I can prove it."

CHAPTER 24

ARMSTRONG CLOSED the door to Room 412 as David first checked Christine's blood pressure, then slowly raised the head of her bed. He had listened to the woman's story for only a minute or two before realizing the importance of having Christine hear it for herself.

Sitting on the edge of the bed, he slipped a hand beneath her head. The room was dark, save for a spattering of pale sunlight through the partially closed drapes. David shook with excitement as he reached up and stroked her bruised, swollen face. "Chris, wake up, honey," he said. "Wake up."

Armstrong pulled a chair by the head of the bed.

Christine opened her eyes, smiled at David, then closed them again. "I'm awake," she said weakly. "It just hurts less with my eyes shut. I'll be okay, though. A few days and I'll be okay."

"You bet you will," he said. "Chris, Dr. Armstrong is here. She has something to tell you. I . . . I thought you would want to hear."

"Christine? Can you hear me? It's Margaret Armstrong." Christine turned toward the voice and again opened her eyes. For several seconds, the women looked at one another. Then Armstrong said softly, "Christine, I am Peg. Peggy Donner."

Christine studied her through the dim light, then reached out and grasped her hand. "The Sisterhood . . . is it over?"

"Not yet, dear. But . . . but soon."

David searched Christine's face for anger, or even surprise, but neither was there. A bond was forming between the two women—a connection that was beyond his understanding. He watched in silent fascination, transfixed by the scene.

"Christine," Armstrong said, forcing each word, "after I leave here, I am going to begin the dissolution of The Sisterhood. It will be done in such a way that none of the members will be hurt. That is, provided you and David can live with the secrets we share. Do you understand?"

Christine managed a nod. "I understand. But the reports—the tapes . . . ?"

"They will all be destroyed. All, that is, except one. That one I shall send to you. It was made by me after I injected Charlotte with a fatal dose of potassium. Christine, the morphine you gave her was not enough. She was stronger, far stronger, than anyone suspected. Charlotte was my friend. She was . . . she was our sister. I had promised her a peaceful death. After you left her room, I went in to say good-bye. One last good-bye. She was breathing easily. I waited, but she only seemed to get stronger. Once she actually opened her eyes. I had promised her. I loved her as . . . I loved her as I did my mother. I . . ." Armstrong could go no further. For the first time in almost fifty years she wept.

Christine loosened her fingers and brushed them across the older woman's tears. "I love you, Peggy," she said haltingly. "For what you tried to do, I love you."

A minute passed before Armstrong continued. "After I've done what is necessary for our Sisterhood, I'll go to see Lieutenant Dockerty and take full responsibility for Charlotte's death. Believe me, Christine, I *was* the one who did it." She turned to David. "I shall also take responsibility for Dorothy and for the deaths of your friends. I think there would be fewer questions if there is no suggestion of more than one person involved in all this."

David saw the concern in Christine's face at the word *friends*. "I'll explain later, Chris," he said. "Dr. Armstrong, I do appreciate what you did during the resuscitation. For that, I promise that as long as you do what you've said, there will be no interference from me."

"Thank you." Armstrong studied the coldness in his eyes, then bent down and kissed Christine on the forehead. Moments later she was gone.

David knelt by the bed. The scant light in the room glinted off the moisture in Christine's eyes. "When you get out of here," he said, "we're going to take a trip to some dusty little village in Mexico."

"But we get to come back?" There was joy and sadness in her smile.

"We get to come back."

She closed her eyes. For a moment, it seemed she had fallen back to sleep, but as he moved away she grasped his hand. "David, could you tell me one more thing now?" she asked.

"What's that?"

"Do you have vanity plates on your car?"

John Dockerty gulped at what remained of the stale coffee in his mug and sank back in his chair. It had taken the entire night and most of the morning, but at last Marcus Quigg had broken and had given him the

219

name. The triumph—if that is what it was—felt hollow. Images of the frightened, sick, little man would haunt him possibly forever.

That it was Margaret Armstrong who was responsible for the murders and the mistakes and the pathetic pharmacist only made things worse. She was someone he respected and, even more depressing, someone he had trusted.

"John Dockerty, master sleuth," he said sardonically. "Danced around the barn by a lady who turns out to be another goddamn Ma Barker." Well, at least he had gotten the pleasure of telling the captain —though not in so many words—what an ass the man had been to order the hasty arrest of David Shelton.

Dockerty checked his watch. It had been nearly an hour since the captain had promised to get a magistrate's probable cause warrant for Armstrong's arrest. He rubbed at the stubble on his face and was deciding whether to shave or not when the phone rang.

"Investigations. Dockerty," he said. ". . . Yes, Captain . . . that's fine, sir . . . I'll be down to get it right away. . . . Yes, sir, I know he looked guilty as sin. If I were in your position, I would have made the same decision. . . . Thank you, I'll be down in five minutes. . . . Turkey." Dockerty delivered the last word to the dial tone. He combed his hair with his fingers and pushed himself out of his chair. At that moment, with a soft knock, Margaret Armstrong stepped into his office.

"Lieutenant Dockerty, I have some things to talk with you about," she said.

"Yes," he replied, settling on the edge of his desk, "you certainly do."

Within thirty minutes, Dockerty had heard enough of Armstrong's confession to call in a stenographer. As a final act of defiance, he rang the captain and asked him to witness the proceeding. The man, a silky half-politician, half-policeman with bottle-black hair, listened in dumbfounded silence as Armstrong calmly admitted responsibility for the murders of Charlotte Thomas and Dotty Dalrymple, as well as for hiring the killer of Ben Glass and Joseph Rosetti. It was a story she had rehearsed carefully before driving to Station 1—an explanation she hoped would leave Dockerty satisfied that she had acted totally on her own. It disgusted her to have to paint Dalrymple as a heroine who had died because she had stumbled onto the truth, but any hint of a conspiracy would have risked exposure of the movement. She knew what policemen like Dockerty could do. Besides, Margaret was sure that up until the end Dotty had been just as dedicated to The Sisterhood as she was. The woman was frightened of losing her position and her influence, that's all.

Armstrong's confession held together well enough, but there was a vagueness about the details that made Dockerty uncomfortable. He attempted to pin her down, but was silenced by the captain, who found his tongue in time to say, "Now, Lieutenant, I'm sure the doctor will fill in some of these details in good time. As you can see, she's had a rather rough go of it."

Armstrong thanked him, adding a look that clearly made Dockerty an outsider in the exchange between two people of stature.

Dockerty decided to push his luck. "Just one thing," he ventured. "Exactly how did you go about hiring a killer like Leonard Vincent?"

"I shall cover that in a moment," she said, giving him her most withering, patrician stare, "but first, if you would direct me to your ladies' room?"

"If you'll wait," Dockerty said, "I'll get a matron to go . . ."

"Nonsense," the captain cut in. "Dr. Armstrong has been officially charged with nothing as yet. The . . . ah . . . ladies' room is just down the hall to the right. You can't miss it."

Armstrong again favored the captain with a look and carefully adjusted her skirt before striding from the room.

The ladies' room was a sty. The institutional mosaic floor was stained and cracked. What paper towels there were overflowed the metal wastebasket to one side of the sink. The air reeked of urine and disinfectant.

Margaret Donner Armstrong did not notice the filth. She scanned the room, then went directly to the toilet stall, hooked the plywood door shut, and sat down.

She felt pleased at the way she had manipulated Dockerty and the captain. If David and Christine were true to their word, The Sisterhood of Life would die with dignity. The irony in that realization brought her some solace.

After leaving the hospital, Armstrong had gone home and honored her promise. The tapes—all but one—she had incinerated, stopping now and again to listen to a particular report or to reflect on her friendship with a particular woman. Her dream—her ultimate dream—had nearly been fulfilled. If only Dorothy hadn't come apart.

Barbara Littlejohn had agreed that it was no longer possible for the movement to continue. At times during their telephone conversation the woman had actually sounded relieved. Armstrong wondered if Barbara would have reacted the same way as Dalrymple had her own reputation and career been on the line. The painful fact was that she simply did not know for certain—about Barbara or any of them.

So it had been decided. Barbara would make the calls and write the letters, then do what she could to continue the Clinton Foundation projects. And as the receiver dropped to its cradle, Armstrong knew that, after forty years, it was over.

Now, she sat looking at the sordid messages and primitive drawings on the door in front of her, remembering back fifty years to the last time she had been in such a place. She had felt frightened then. Frightened and dirty. She had feared the detectives and the way they stared at her breasts. She had taken her mind to special hidden places to keep from telling them what they wanted her to say. Hour after hour she had resisted their control, at one point choosing to wet herself rather than ask to leave the room. And in the end she had won. And with her victory had come the chance to strike out on a holy mission—a journey she had come close—oh, so close—to completing.

Now it was time to embark on another.

Armstrong reached inside her blouse to the waistband of her skirt and withdrew the syringe Dotty Dalrymple had almost forced David to use. For a few moments she fingered the deadly cylinder. Then she rolled up one sleeve and skillfully slipped the needle into a vein. She rested her head against the wall and closed her eyes. With a fine, slim finger, she depressed the plunger.

"It's all right, Mama . . . I'm here, Mama," she said.

∿ EPILOGUE

THE BREEZE, which had been little more than a zephyr all day, picked up suddenly, sending noisy flocks of dry leaves swirling about the gray stones.

Dora Dalrymple paused on the narrow path to pull her greatcoat tightly about her. She was, in face, size, manner, and dress, a virtual mirror of her late twin. Her incongruously tiny feet handled the steep downgrade with a sureness born of having taken the same walk each evening for three weeks.

The grave, still a fresh mound of dirt, was encompassed by a ring of pines. In the same grove a small, uncarved block of marble marked the plot where someday she herself would be buried. Ritually, she picked up the metal folding chair she had left there the first day and positioned it next to the dark soil. Then she placed a single flower over the spot where she knew her sister's heart to be.

"It's a mum, Dotty," she said, "sort of rust colored. I know mums aren't one of your favorites, but this one's so pretty and so like autumn. You're not upset by my choice today, are you?" Dora paused, as if listening to her sister's reassuring voice. "Good, I thought you'd understand," she said finally.

"People at the hospital are being very nice to me now. I think they've even stopped calling me Tweedle-dee behind my back . . . yes, I know. Well, it's out of respect for you that they don't, I think. Dotty, you got a call today from Violet in Detroit. I told her you were out for the afternoon and to call back later. I . . . I don't think I can continue The Garden without you. I mean, I helped and all, but you were the one who started it and kept it growing. . . . But The Sisterhood is finished. All of the nurses, including our flowers, have been notified.

223

None of them wants The Garden to die, but to survive we must grow. How will I find new nurses to join us? . . . Perhaps. Perhaps you're right. You always understood human nature better than I did. . . . So, I could cook better than you—what does that prove? It's apples and oranges as far as I'm concerned . . .

"I checked today with Mr. Stevens. Your stone is almost ready. It's beautiful. You'll love it, I know you will. . . . Okay, okay, so I'm changing the subject. I'm frightened of making a wrong decision, that's all. You were always so confident, so decisive . . . . Is that a promise? . . . Good. In that case I think I'll follow your suggestion and ask that lovely Janet to move in with me. . . . Dorothy, are you sure you know what you're saying? Forever is a long time to stand by anyone. . . . Well, all right. I'll call Hyacinth today. But remember, we'll both be counting on you every step of the way."

The conversation over, Dora placed the chair to one side of the grove and returned to her car, oblivious to the light rain that had begun falling.

Inside the Tudor mansion she and Dotty had purchased shortly after the inception of The Garden, she brewed a pot of tea and settled into an oversized easy chair, one of a pair they had designed themselves. Fifteen minutes later, the telephone rang.

"I'm calling Dahlia," the young woman's voice said.

"I'm sorry, but Dahlia is not readily available," Dora said, assuming the whispered tone she had heard Dotty use on so many occasions. "However, this is her sister . . . Chrysanthemum. You may, if you wish, confide in me just as you did in Dahlia."

"Well . . . all right, I guess," the woman said uncertainly. "This is Violet calling again from Detroit. Saint Bart's Hospital. A situation has come up here that I think could use some further research."

"Go on," Dora said reassuringly.

"It's a woman named Agnes Morgan. Her husband is Carter Morgan, one of the executive directors at Ford. She's only forty-two, but is drying out in our hospital for the third time this year. The scuttlebutt has it that her husband's been trying to get a divorce for several years so he could marry his secretary. Apparently Mrs. Morgan won't let him have one without bleeding him dry and doing what she can to ruin his career."

"Sounds very promising," Dora said, doodling the picture of an automobile on a yellow legal pad and overlaying it with an ornately inscribed dollar sign. "I'll do some checking up on the situation and call you. Meanwhile, dig up as much information as you can on this Mr. Morgan and his wife. It sounds like the benefits in this case would be quite substantial, assuming the gentleman decides to do business with us."

"I think he just might," Violet said. "When can I expect to hear from you?"

"Within a day or so, I think," Dora answered. "As you know, we'll take care of any business dealings. You'll have all the help you need."

She replaced the receiver and picked up a gold-framed photo of Dotty from the table. The likeness to herself was such that she might have been holding a looking glass.

"Well, love, we're still in business," she said, resting the picture on her massive lap. "I can't do it without your help, though, so you'd better not forget your promise. Anyhow, that's what sisters are for, aren't they?"

SIDE EFFECTS

SIDE EFFECTS

To Jane Rotrosen Berkey,
my agent, my friend, my muse;
and, of course, to Danny and Matt

ACKNOWLEDGMENT

A novel is hardly the sole endeavor many believe. I am both grateful and fortunate to have had Jeanne Bernkopf, my editor, and Linda Grey, editorial director at Bantam, in my writing life.

PROLOGUE
MECKLENBURG, GERMANY
August 1944

WILLI BECKER leaned against the coarse wood siding of the officers' club and squinted up at the late afternoon sun, a pale disk rendered nearly impotent by the dust from a hundred allied bombings of industrial targets surrounding the Ravensbrück concentration camp for women. He closed his eyes and for an instant thought he heard the drone of enemy planes somewhere to the south.

"Not a moment too soon, Dr. Becker," he muttered. "You will be leaving this hellhole not a moment too soon." He checked the chronometer his brother, Edwin, had sent him from "a grateful patient" in the Dachau camp. Nearly fifteen-thirty. After months of the most meticulous preparations there were now only hours to go. He felt an electric excitement.

Across the dirt courtyard, clusters of prisoners, their shaved heads glistening, worked on bomb shelters, while their SS guards jockeyed for bits of shade beneath the overhangs of barracks. Becker recognized two of the women: a tall, awkward teenager named Eva and a feckless Russian who had encouraged him to call her Bunny. They were but two of the three dozen or so subjects whose examinations he was forced to omit in the interest of escape.

For a minute, Becker battled the urge to call the two scarecrow women over and tell them that fate had denied them their parts in the magnificent work that scholars and generations to come would hail as the start of the Beckerian population control. Beckerian. The word, though he spoke it daily, still had a thrilling ring. Newtonian physics, Shakespearean drama, Malthusian philosophy; upon so very few had human history bestowed such honor. In time, Becker was certain, this immortality would be his. After all, he was still six weeks shy of his

233

thirtieth birthday, yet already acknowledged for his brilliance in the field of reproductive physiology.

Adjusting the collar on the gray-green SS uniform he was wearing for the last time, the tall, classically Nordic physician crossed the courtyard and headed toward the research buildings on the north edge of camp.

The Ravensbrück medical staff, once numbering more than fifty, had dwindled to a dozen. Himmler, bending to the cry for physicians in military hospitals, had suspended the experiments in gas gangrene and bone grafting, as well as those on battlefield cauterization of wounds using coals and acid. The doctors responsible for those programs had been transferred. Only the sterilization units remained, three of them in all, each devoted to the problem of eliminating the ability to procreate without impairing the ability to perform slave labor. Becker strode past the empty laboratories—another sign of the inevitable—and turned onto "Grünestrasse," the tarmac track on which the officials and research facilities of his Green Unit were located. To the east, he could see the camouflage-painted chimney tops of the crematorium. A gentle west wind was bearing the fetid smoke and ash away from the camp. Becker smiled thinly and nodded. The Mecklenburger Bucht, fifty kilometers of capricious Baltic Sea between Rostock and the Danish island fishing village of Gedser, would be calm. One less variable to be concerned about.

Becker was mentally working through the other incalculables when he glanced through the windows of his office. Dr. Franz Müller, his back turned, was inspecting the volumes in Becker's library. Becker tensed. A visit from Müller, the head of the Blue Unit and director of reproductive studies, was not unusual, but the man was considerate to a fault and almost always called ahead.

Was Müller's visit on this of all days a coincidence? Becker paused by the doorway to his office and prepared for the cerebral swordplay at which the older man was such a master. He congratulated himself for holding back the documentation, however scant, of Blue Unit's deception. Müller's blade might be as quick as his own, but his own had poison on its tip. Müller, he felt certain, was a sham.

The Blue Unit work concerning the effect of ovarian irradiation on fertility looked promising on paper. However, Becker had good reason to believe that not one prisoner had actually been treated with radiation. The data were being falsified by Müller and his cohort, Josef Rendl. Whether they had gone so far as to assist prisoners in escaping, Becker was unsure, but he suspected as much. His proof, though skimpy, would have been enough to discredit, if not destroy, both men. However, their destruction had never meant as much to him as their control.

In an effort to gain some tiny advantage, Becker opened the outside door silently and tiptoed up the three stairs to his office door. Not a sound. Not even the creak of a floorboard.

Becker opened the door quickly. Müller was perched on the corner of his desk, looking directly at him. "Ah, Willi, my friend. Please excuse the brazenness of my intrusion. I was just passing by and remembered your mentioning that Fruhopf's *Reproductive Physiology* was among your holdings." First exchange to the master.

"It is good to see you, Franz. My library and laboratory are always yours, as I have told you many times." A perfunctory handshake, and Becker moved to his seat behind the desk. "Did you find it?"

"Pardon?"

"The Fruhopf. Did you find it?"

"Oh. Yes. Yes, I have it right here."

"Fine. Keep it as long as you wish."

"Thank you." Müller made no move to leave. Instead, he lowered himself into the chair opposite Becker and began packing his pipe from a worn leather pouch.

Not even the formality of a request to stay. Becker's wariness grew. Hidden by the desk, his long, manicured fingers undulated nervously. "Sweet?" he asked, sliding a dish of mints across the desktop. It was Müller's show, and Müller could make the initial move.

"Thank you, no." Müller grinned and patted his belly. "You heard about Paris?"

Becker nodded. "No surprise. Except perhaps for the speed with which Patton did the job."

"I agree. The man is a devil." Müller ran his fingers through his thick, muddy blond hair. He was Becker's equal in height, perhaps an inch or so more, but he was built like a Kodiak bear. "And in the east the Russians come and come. We wipe out a division and two more take its place. I hear they are nearing the oil field at Ploesti."

"They are a barbarous people. For decades all they have done is rut about and multiply. What our armies cannot do to them, their own expanding population will eventually accomplish."

"Ah, yes," Müller said. "The theories of your sainted Thomas Malthus. Keep our panzers in abeyance, and let our enemies procreate themselves into submission."

Becker felt his hackles rise. Cynicism was the finest honed of Müller's strokes. An irritated, angry opponent left openings, made mistakes. Calm down, he urged himself. Calm down and wait until the man declares himself. Could he know about the escape? The mere thought made the Green Unit leader queasy. "Now, Franz," he said evenly, "you know how much I enjoy discussing philosophy with you, especially Malthusian philosophy, but right now we have a war to win, yes?"

Müller's eyes narrowed. "*Quatsch,*" he said.

"What?"

"I said *Quatsch*, Willi. Absolute nonsense. First of all, we are not going to win any war. You know that as well as I do. Secondly, I do not believe you care. One way or the other."

Becker stiffened. The bastard had found out. Somehow he had found out. He shifted his right hand slightly on his knee and gauged the distance to the Walther revolver in his top left drawer. "How can you impugn me in this way?"

Müller smiled and sank back in his chair. "You misunderstand me, Willi. What I am saying is a compliment to you as a scientist and philosopher. *Surtout le travaille.* Above all the work. Is that not how you feel? On second thought, I will have that sweet, if you please."

Becker slid the dish across. Here he was, bewildered, apprehensive, and totally off balance, and still with no idea of the reason for Müller's visit. Inwardly, and grudgingly, he smiled. The man was slick. A total bastard, but a slick one. "I believe in my research, if that is what you mean."

"Precisely."

"And *your* research, Franz, how does *it* go?" Time for a counterthrust.

"It goes and it stops and it goes again. You know how that is."

Sure, sure, but mostly it doesn't exist, Becker wanted to say. Instead, he nodded his agreement.

"Willi, my friend, I fear the war will be over anytime now. Weeks, days, hours; no one seems to know. I have no notion of what will happen to us—to those in our laboratory—after that. Perhaps our research will be made public, perhaps not. I feel it is crucial for each unit, Blue, Green, and Brown, to know exactly the nature and status of the work being done by the others. That way, we can be as well prepared as possible for whatever the future brings." Becker's eyes widened. "I have decided to start with your Green Unit," Müller went on. "A meeting has been scheduled for twenty-one hundred hours this evening in the Blue Unit conference room. Please be prepared to present your research in detail at that time."

"What?"

"And Willi, I would like time to study your data before then. Please have them on my desk by nineteen hundred hours." Müller's eyes were flint.

Becker felt numb. His data, including the synthesis and biological properties of Estronate 250, were sealed in a dozen notebooks, hidden in the hull of a certain Rostock fishing boat. His mind raced. "My . . . my work is very fragmented, Franz. I . . . I shall need at least a day, perhaps two, to organize my data." This can't be happening, he thought. Nineteen hundred hours is too early. Even twenty-one hundred hours is too soon. "Let me show you what I have," Becker said, reaching toward the drawer with the Walther.

At that instant, Dr. Josef Rendl stepped inside the office doorway. Rendl's aide, a behemoth whom Becker knew only as Stossel, remained just outside in the hall. They had been somewhere out there all the time. Becker felt sure of it. Rendl, a former pediatrician, was a short, doughy man with a pasty complexion and a high-pitched laugh, both of which Becker found disgusting. Becker's information had it that Rendl's mother was a Jew, a fact that had been carefully concealed. For a frozen second, two, Becker sized up the situation. Müller was but two meters away, Rendl three, and the animal, Stossel, perhaps five. No real chance for three kills, even with surprise on his side, which, it seemed now, might not be the case. The battle would have to be verbal . . . at least for the moment.

Becker nodded at the newcomer. "Welcome, Josef. My, my. The entire Blue Unit brain trust. What a pleasant honor."

"Willi." Rendl smiled and returned the gesture. "Leutnant Stossel and I were just passing by and noticed the two of you in here. What do you think of the meetings? A good idea to present our work to one another, no?"

You smarmy son of a Jew whore, Becker thought. "Yes. Yes. An excellent idea," he said.

"And you will honor us by presenting the Green Unit biochemical studies tonight?" Rendl, though an oberst, exactly the same rank as Willi, often spoke with Müller's authority dusting his words.

Becker, fighting to maintain composure, sucked in an extra measure of air. "Tonight would be acceptable." Both of the other men nodded. "But," he added, "tomorrow evening would be much better." Because, he smiled to himself, I intend to be a thousand kilometers away from here by then.

"Oh?" Franz Müller propped his chin on one hand.

"Yes. I have a few final chemical tests to run on Estronate Two-fifty. Some loose ends in the initial set of experiments." As Becker scrambled through the words, searching for some kind of purchase, an idea began to take hold. "There's an extraction with ether that I was unable to complete because my supply ran out. Late yesterday, several five-gallon tins arrived. You signed for them yourself." Müller nodded. Becker's words became more confident. "Well, if you would give me tonight to complete this phase of my work, I shall gladly present what I have tomorrow. You must remember that what I have is not much. Estronate Two-fifty is far more theory than fact. A promising set of notions, with only the roughest of preliminary work on humans."

Müller pushed himself straighter in his chair and leveled his gaze across the desk. "Actually, Willi, I do not believe that what you say is true." The words, a sledgehammer, were delivered with silky calm.

"Wh . . . what are you talking about?" The question in Becker's mind was no longer whether Müller knew anything, but how much. His trump card—Blue Unit's falsified data—would have to be played. The only issue now was timing.

"What I am talking about is information that your work on Estronate Two-fifty is rather advanced."

"That's nonsense," Becker shot back.

"Further, that you are lacking only stability studies and the elimination of a troublesome side effect—some sort of bleeding tendency, is it?—before more extensive clinical testing can be done. Why, Willi, are you keeping this information from us? You have here, perhaps, the most awesome discovery—even the most awesome weapon—of our time, yet you claim to know nothing."

"Ridiculous."

"No, Willi. Not ridiculous. Information straight from a source in your laboratory. Now either we receive a full disclosure of the exact status of your work, or I shall see to it that Mengele or even Himmler receives the information we have."

"Your accusations are preposterous."

"We shall judge that after you have presented your work. Tonight, then?"

"No. Not tonight." It was time. "My work is not ready for presentation." Becker paused theatrically, drumming his fingertips on the desktop and then stroking them bowlike across one another. "Is yours?"

"What?"

Becker sensed, more than saw, Müller stiffen. "Your work. The Blue Unit radiation studies. You see, the two of you are not the only ones with—what was the word you used?—ah, yes, sources, that was it. Sources."

Rendl and Müller exchanged the fraction of a glance. The gesture was enough to dispel any doubt as to the validity of Becker's information.

"Willi, Willi," Müller said, shaking his head. "You try my patience. I shall give you until tomorrow night. Meanwhile, we shall organize our data and present them at the same time."

"Excellent," Becker said, reveling in being on the offensive at last. "And, please, do try to have some of your human subjects available for examination. It would lend so much to the understanding of your work." This time, Müller and Rendl shared a more pronounced look.

"You don't really care, Willi, do you?" Müller said suddenly.

"I . . . I'm afraid I don't know what you mean, Franz."

"You see only yourself. Your place in history. The here and now mean nothing to you. Germany, the Reich, the Jews, the Americans, the prisoners, your colleagues—all are the same to you. All are nothing."

"You have your mistresses, and I have mine," Becker said simply. "Is immortality so homely that I should throw her out of my bed? You are right, Franz. I do not concern myself with petty day-to-day issues. I have already reached planes of theory and research that few have ever even dreamed of. Should I worry about the price of eggs, or whether the Führer's hemorrhoids are inflamed, or whether the prisoners here at Ravensbrück are pathetic inside the wire or without, on top of the dirt or beneath it?"

"Willi, Willi, Willi." Müller's voice and eyes held pity rather than reproach.

Becker looked over at Rendl, and there, too, saw condescension, not ire. Don't you dare pity me, he wanted to scream. Revere me. The children of your children will prosper because of me. The *lebensraum* for which so many have fought and died will be attained not with bullets, but with my equations, my solution. Mine!

Müller broke the silence. "We are all with the same laboratory. We all stand to lose much if we fall into disfavor—either now with the Reich or soon with the Allies. I expect a full disclosure of your work with Estronate Two-fifty, Dr. Becker."

Becker nodded his acquiescence and silently prayed that his portrayal of a beaten man would be convincing.

Minutes later, the three men from the Blue Unit were gone. Becker closed his eyes and massaged the tightness at the base of his neck. Then he poured three fingers of Polish vodka from a bottle Edwin had sent him, and drank it in a single draught. The encounter with Müller and Rendl, triumphant though it had been, had left him drained. He fingered his chronometer. Was there time for a nap? No, he decided. No sleeping until this filthy camp with its petty people and skeleton prisoners was a thing of the past.

He walked briskly from his office to the low, frame, barracklike building that housed the Green Unit's biochemical research section. With glances to either side, he backed through the rear door and locked it from the inside. The wooden shutters were closed and latched, creating a darkness inside that was tangible.

The flashlight was by the door—where he had hung it that morning. Using the hooded beam, Becker counted the slate squares making up the top of his long central workbench. Reaching beneath the fifth one, he pulled. The cabinet supporting the slate slid out from the others. Beneath it, hidden from even a detailed search, was the circular mouth of a tunnel.

"And the rockets red glare, the bombs bursting in air. . . ." Alfi Runstedt sang the words as he dug, although he had no idea of their meaning. The song, he knew, was the American anthem, and this day, at least, that was all that mattered. As a child in Leipzig, he had spent hours beside his family's new Victrola memorizing selections from a thick album of anthems of the world. Even then, the American "Star Spangled Banner" had been his favorite.

239

Now, he would have the chance to see the country itself and, even more wonderful, to become an American.

"Oh say does that star spangled ba-a-ner-er ye-et wa-ave. . . ." With one syllable, he rammed the spade into the sandy soil. With the next, he threw the dirt up to the side of the grave. The trench, three feet deep, was better than half done. Lying on the grass to Alfi's left, two meters from him, were the corpses of the peasant woman and her son, which would be laid inside as soon as the proper depth was reached. Alfi Runstedt paid them no mind.

He was stripped to his ample waist. Dirt, mingling with sweat, was turning his arms and walrus torso into a quagmire. The thick, red hair on his chest was plastered into what looked like a fecal mat. His SS uniform pants were soaked and filthy. ". . . and the home of the brave. O-oh say can you see. . . ."

"Alfi, take a break if you need one. We cannot make any moves until dark. I told you that." From his perch atop a large boulder, Willi Becker gazed down into the narrow crypt.

Alfi stopped his digging and dragged a muddy wrist across his muddy forehead. "It is nothing, Herr Oberst. Believe me, nothing. I would dig a thousand such holes in the ground for the honor you have done me and the reward you have promised. Tell me, do you know if many American women are thin like Betty Grable? One of the men in the barracks at Friedrichshafen had her picture by his cot."

"I don't know, Alfi." Becker laughed. "Soon, you shall be able to see for yourself. If we meet the boat in Denmark and if my cousin has made all the arrangements, we should be in North America with valid papers within a few weeks."

"Big ifs, yes?"

"Not so big. The biggest if anyplace is money, and hopefully we have enough of that. We'll need some luck, but our chances of making it out undetected seem rather good."

"And you do not think me a traitor or a coward for wanting to leave with you?"

"Am I?"

"You are different, Herr Oberst. You have research to complete. Important research. I am just a junior officer in an army that is losing a war."

"Ah, but you are also my aide. My *invaluable* aide. Was it not you who informed me of the old system of drainage pipes running beneath Ravensbrück?"

"Well, it was just my fortune to have worked with the sanitation department when I was younger and—"

"And was it not you who chose to keep that information our little secret and to help me with the connecting tunnel?"

"Well, I guess—"

"So don't say you are not deserving, Unteroffizier Runstedt. Don't ever say that."

"Thank you, Oberst. Thank you." And at that moment, Alfred Runstedt, the man who had overseen or assisted in the extermination of several thousand Ravensbrück prisoners, the man who had, not an hour before, calmly strangled to death a woman, her young son, her husband, and her father, wept with joy.

Hollywood, New York, baseball, Chicago—now just words, they would soon be his life. Since the June invasion at Normandy, and even more frequently since the abortive July attempt to assassinate the Führer at Rastenburg, in eastern Prussia, he had been forced to endure the recurrent nightmare of his own capture and death. In one version of the dream, it was execution by hanging; in another, by firing squad. In still another, ghostly prisoners, totally naked, beat him to death with sticks.

Soon, the nightmares would stop.

The grave was nearly deep enough. The wooded grove which was serving as an impromptu cemetery accepted the evening more quickly than did the adjacent field and was nearly dark when Becker pushed himself off the rock. "So, just a few more spadefuls, is it?" he said.

"I think so," Alfi answered. He had donned a windbreaker against the chill of dusk. His uniform shirt, hanging on a branch, would be kept clean for a final display.

"Cigar?"

"Thank you, Herr Oberst." Alfi paused to light the narrow cheroot, one of a seemingly endless supply possessed by Becker.

"I think you are deep enough now," Becker said after a half dozen more passes. "Let me give you a hand."

Alfi scrambled from the grave. One with the arms, and one with the legs, the two men unceremoniously tossed the bodies of the woman and the boy into the pit. Alfi replaced the dirt with the spade. Becker helped, using his foot.

"Forgive me if I am out of line, Herr Oberst," Alfi said as he shoveled, "but is there any possibility of notifying my sister at the munitions plant in Schwartzheide that, contrary to the reports she will receive, I am alive and well?"

Becker chuckled and shook his head. "Alfi, Alfi. I have explained to you the need for secrecy. Why do you think I waited until only a few hours ago to tell you of my escape plan? I, myself, have been measuring every word for weeks, afraid I might give it away. For now, and for the foreseeable future both of us must remain among the lamentable casualties of the war. Even my brother, Edwin, at the camp in Dachau will not know."

"I understand," Alfi said, realizing that he did not—at least not totally.

"By the morning, you and I shall be both free and dead." Becker stamped on the topsoil of the grave and began throwing handfuls of dusty sand and pine needles over the fresh dirt.

The idea of using the bodies of the farmer and his son-in-law was sheer genius, Becker acknowledged. Originally, he had planned to have the two farmers supply him with transportation to Rostock. Their lorry would now run just as well with him at the wheel. The other refinements in his original plan were dazzling. When all was said and done, Müller and Rendl would be left to face the music with little or no suspicion that he was still alive.

". . . and the home of the brave." Becker joined the startled Runstedt in the final line.

Both Runstedt and Becker groaned repeatedly with the effort of dragging first one body and then another through the sewage pipe to the false cabinet in the biochemical research building. Intermixed with the sounds of their effort were the scratching and scraping of countless rats, scurrying about in the pitch darkness.

The young farmer was, in height and frame, a virtual twin of Becker's. The older man, like Runstedt, was heavy, but taller than Runstedt by several centimeters.

"Don't worry about the difference in your heights, Alfi," Becker had reassured him. "By the time the explosion and fire are through with these bodies, no one will want to get any closer to them than it takes to remove our watches, rings, identification medallions, and wallets."

With Becker pushing from below, Runstedt hauled the corpses through the base of the cabinet and stretched them out on the wooden floor.

"Perfect, perfect," Becker said, scrambling through the hole. "We are right on time."

"Oberst," Alfi said, "I have one question, if I may."

"Of course."

"How will we keep the tunnel from being discovered after the fire and explosion?"

"Hah! An excellent point," Becker exclaimed. "One, I might add, that I am not at all surprised to have you make. I have kept the steel plate you removed to make the opening in the pipe. It fits perfectly, and stays in place with several small hooks I have welded on. With ashes and debris piled on top, I doubt the pipe will ever be discovered."

"Brilliant. Herr Oberst, you are a truly brilliant man."

"Thank you, Unteroffizier. And now, we must check. Have you said anything to anyone which might suggest you are planning to leave tonight?"

"No, sir."

"Good. And have you told the men in your barrack that you will be working late in the laboratory with me?"

"Yes, Oberst."

"Wonderful. We are ready to arrange the ether, to set the charge and the timer, and to exchange clothes with our friends here."

"Then it is off to hot dogs and Betty Grable," Alfi said.

"Hot dogs and Betty Grable," Becker echoed. "But first a toast to our success thus far. Amaretto?"

"Cheroots! Amaretto! My God, Oberst, how do you keep coming up with these things?" Alfi took the proffered glass, inhaled the wonderful almond scent, and then drained the liqueur in a gulp. The cyanide, its deadly aroma and taste masked, took just seconds to work.

Becker was removing his uniform and jewelry as Runstedt, writhing and vomiting on the floor, breathed his last.

With some effort, Becker dressed the young farmer in his own uniform, adding a ring, billfold, identification necklace, and, finally, Edwin's watch, an elegant piece which many in the camp associated with him.

Next, he stepped back and, with the use of the hooded flashlight, surveyed the scene. Everything, everyone had to be perfectly placed.

He undressed the farmer who was to have served as Alfi's double, tossed the clothes to one side, and then dumped the naked body down the tunnel. "Now, Alfi, my most loyal of servants, we must find a place for you." He shone the torch on the contorted, violet face by his feet.

In minutes the arrangement was complete. The young farmer's body lay in the center of the laboratory, his face resting beside a laboratory timer and a five-gallon tin of ether. Several other tins were spaced throughout the dry, wooden building. Alfi's body lay near the door, as far from the explosive vapors as possible. It would be the validity of Runstedt's face which would assure acceptance of Becker's own demise.

The simple elegance of the whole plan was as pleasing as a major research success, and Becker felt ballooned with pride as he made a final survey of the scene.

He checked the small ignition charge and set the timer for ten minutes.

Willi Becker was grinning as he dropped into the tunnel and pulled the workbench cabinet back in place. He sealed the drainage pipe opening, and without a glance at the farmer's body, crawled toward the exit beyond the camp's electrified fence.

He was behind the wheel of the lorry, a quarter mile from the camp, when the peaceful night sky turned red-gold. Seconds later, he heard the muffled series of explosions.

"Good-bye, Josef Rendl," he said. "I shall enjoy reading in *The New York Times* of your trial and execution. And as for you, Dr. Müller, it is game and match between us, eh? A shame you shall never know who really won. Perhaps someday, if you survive, I will send you a postcard."

His wife and son were waiting for him in Rostock. As Becker bounced down the road, he began humming the "Star Spangled Banner."

THE PRESENT
CHAPTER 1
Sunday 9 December

THE MORNING WAS typical of December in Massachusetts. A brushed aluminum sky blended into three-day-old snow covering the cornfields along Route 127. Dulled by streaks of road salt, Jared Samuels's red MGTD roadster still sparkled like a flare against the landscape.

From the passenger seat, Kate Bennett watched her husband negotiate the country road using only the thumb and first two fingers of his left hand. His dark brown eyes, though fixed on the road, were relaxed, and he seemed to be singing to himself. Kate laughed.

"Hey, Doc," Jared asked glancing over, "just what are you laughing at?"

"You."

"Well, that's a relief. For a moment there I thought you were laughing at *me*. . . . Tell me what I was doing that was so funny, I might want to write it down."

"Not funny," Kate said. "Just nice. It makes me happy to see you happy. There's a peacefulness in you that I haven't seen since the campaign began."

"Then you should have turned on the bedroom light last night at, oh, eleven-thirty, was it?"

"You didn't just pass out after?"

"Nope. Five minutes of absolute Nirvana . . . then I passed out." He flashed the smile that had always been reserved for her alone.

"I love you, you know," Kate said.

Jared looked at her again. It had been a while since either of them had said the words outside the bedroom. "Even though I'm not going to be the Honorable Congressman from the Sixth District?"

"Especially because you're not going to be the Honorable Congressman from the Sixth District." She checked the time. "Jared, it's only nine-thirty. Do you think we could stop at the lake for a bit? We haven't in such a long time. I brought a bag of bread just in case."

Jared slowed. "Only if you promise not to poach when goddamn Carlisle starts hitting to my backhand."

"Once. I stole a ball from you once in almost two years of playing together, and you never let me forget it."

"No poaching?"

Was he being serious? It bothered her that after almost five years of marriage she couldn't always tell. "No poaching," she vowed finally, wary of making a response that would chip the mood of the morning. Lately, it seemed, their upbeat moods were becoming less frequent and more fragile.

"The ducks bless you," Jared said in a tone which did nothing to resolve her uncertainty.

The lake, more a large pond, was a mile off 127 in the general direction of the Oceanside Racquet Club. It was surrounded by dense thickets of pine and scrub oak, separated by the backyards of a dozen or so houses—upper-class dwellings in most communities, but only average in the North Shore village of Beverly Farms. At the far end of the ice cover, hockey sticks in hand, a trio of boys chased a puck up and down a makeshift rink, their bright mufflers and caps phosphorescing against the pearl-gray morning. Nearer the road, a spillway kept the surface from freezing. Bobbing on the half-moon it created were a score of ducks. Several more rested on the surrounding ice.

The couple stood motionless by their car, transfixed by the scene.

"Currier and Ives," Kate said wistfully.

"Bonnie and Clyde," Jared responded in the same tone.

"You're so romantic, Counselor." Kate managed a two-second glare of reproach before she smiled. Jared's often black sense of humor was hit or miss—"kamikaze humor," she had labeled it. "Come on, let's duck," she called.

Her runner's legs, objects of the fantasies of more than a few of her fellow physicians at Metropolitan Hospital of Boston, brought her easily down the snowy embankment, her auburn hair bouncing on the hood of her parka.

As she approached the water, a huge gander, honking arrogantly, advanced to get his due. Kate eyed the bird and then threw a handful of bread over his head to a milling group of smaller mallards and wood ducks. A moment later, from atop the bank, Jared scaled an entire roll precisely at the feet of the gander, who snatched it up and swaggered away.

Kate turned to him, hands on hips. "Are you trying to undermine my authority?"

"Always side with the overdog. That's my motto," he said brightly.

"I even voted for Mattingly in the Sixth Congressional race. I mean who would want to waste his vote on a sure loser like the other guy?"

"A two-point defeat when you started out twenty-two behind? Some loser. Slide on down here, big boy, and I'll give you our traditional Sunday morning kiss."

"We have a traditional Sunday morning kiss?"

"Not yet."

Jared surveyed the embankment and then chose a safer, albeit much longer, route than Kate had taken.

She stifled a smile. *Never lift up your left foot until your right one's firmly planted* was a favorite saying of Jared's father, and here was the scion—the disciple—embracing the philosophy in its most literal sense. Someday, Jared, she thought, you are going to lift up both of your feet at the same time and discover you can fly.

His kiss was firm and deep, his tongue caressing the roof of her mouth, the insides of her cheeks. Kate responded in kind, sliding both her hands to his buttocks and holding him tightly.

"You kiss good, Doc," he said. "I mean *good.*"

"Do you think the ducks would mind if we started making dirty snow angels?" she whispered, warming his ear with her lips.

"No, but I think the Carlisles would." Jared pulled free. "We've got to get going. I wonder why they keep inviting us to play with them when we haven't beaten them once in two years."

"They just love a challenge, I guess." Kate shrugged, tossed out the remaining bread, and followed him along the safe route to the road.

"Did someone call this morning?" he asked over his shoulder.

"Pardon?"

"While I was in the shower." Jared turned to her as he reached the MG and leaned against the perfectly maintained canvas top. "I thought I heard the phone ring."

"Oh, you did." A nugget of tension materialized beneath her breastbone. Jared hadn't missed hearing the phone after all. "It . . . it was nothing, really. Just Dr. Willoughby." Kate slid into the passenger seat. She had wanted to choose carefully the moment to discuss the pathology chief's call.

"How is Yoda?" he asked, settling behind the wheel.

"He's fine. I wish you wouldn't call him that, Jared. He's been very good to me, and it sounds so demeaning."

"It's not demeaning. Honestly." He turned the key and the engine rumbled to life. "Why, without Yoda, Luke Skywalker would never have survived the first *Star Wars* sequel. What else could I possibly call someone who's three feet tall, bald with bushy eyebrows, and lives in a swamp? Anyway, what did he want?"

Kate felt the nugget expand, and fought the sensation. "He just needed to discuss some twists and turns in the politics at the hospital," she said evenly. "I'll tell you about them later. How about we use the little time we have to plan some kind of strategic ambush for the Carlisles?"

"Don't poach. That's all the strategy we need. Now what was so important to ol' Yoda at eight-thirty on a Sunday morning?"

Although the words were spoken lightly, Kate noted that he had not yet put the car into gear. From the beginning of their relationship, he had been somehow threatened both by her career and by her unique friendship with her aging department head. It was nothing he had ever said, but the threat was there. She was certain of it. "Later?" She tried one last time.

Jared switched off the ignition.

The mood of the morning shattered like dropped crystal. Kate forced her eyes to make and maintain contact with his. "He said that tomorrow morning he was going to send letters to the medical school and to Norton Reese announcing his retirement in June or as soon as a successor can be chosen as chief of the department."

"And . . . ?"

"And I think you know already what comes next." Deep inside her, Kate felt sparks of anger begin to replace the tension. This exchange, her news, her chance to become at thirty-five the youngest department chief, to say nothing of the only woman department chief, at Metro—they should have been embraced by the marriage with the same joy as Jared's election to Congress would have been.

"Try me," Jared said, gazing off across the lake.

Kate sighed. "He wants my permission to submit my name to the faculty search committee as his personal recommendation."

"And you thanked him very much, but begged off because you and your husband agreed two years ago to start your family when the election was over, and you simply couldn't take on the responsibility and time demands of a department chairmanship—especially of a moneyless, understaffed, political football of a department like the one Yoda is scurrying away from now—right?"

"Wrong!" The snap in her voice was reflex. She cursed herself for losing control so easily, and took several seconds to calm down before continuing. "I told him I would think about it and talk it over with my husband and some of my friends at the hospital. I told him either to leave my name off his letter or wait a week before sending it."

"Have you thought what the job would take out of you? I mean Yoda's had two coronaries in the last few years, and he is certainly a lot more low key than you are."

"Dammit, Jared. Stop calling him that. And they weren't coronaries. Only angina."

"All right, angina."

"Do you suppose we could talk this over after we play? You're the one who was so worried about being late."

Jared glanced at his watch and then restarted the engine. He turned to her. There was composure in the lines of his face, but an intensity—perhaps even a fear—in his eyes. It was the same look Kate had seen in them when, before the election, he spoke of losing as "not the end of the world."

"Sure," he said. "Just answer me that one question. Do you really have a sense of what it would be like for you—for us—if you took over that department?"

"I . . . I know it wouldn't be easy. But that's not what you're really asking, is it?"

Jared shook his head and stared down at his clenched hands.

Kate knew very well what he was asking. He was thirty-nine years old and an only child. His first marriage had ended in nightmarish fashion, with his wife running off to California with their baby daughter. Even Jared's father, senior partner of one of Boston's most prestigious law firms, with all the king's horses and all the king's men at his disposal, couldn't find them. Jared wanted children. For himself and for his father he wanted them. The agreement to wait until after the election was out of deference to the pressures of a political campaign and the newness of their marriage. Now neither was a factor. Oh, yes, she knew very well what he was asking.

"The answer is," she said finally, "that if I accepted the nomination and got the appointment I would need some time to do the job right. But that is the grossest kind of projection at this point. Norton Reese has hardly been my biggest supporter since I exposed the way he was using money budgeted for the forensic pathology unit to finance new cardiac surgery equipment. I think he would cut off an arm before he would have me as a department chief in a hospital he administrated."

"How much time?" Jared's voice was chilly.

"Please, honey. I'm begging you. Let's do this when we can sit down in our own living room and discuss all the possibilities."

"How much?"

"I . . . I don't know. A year? Two?"

Jared snapped the stick shift into first gear, sending a spray of ice and snow into the air before the rear tires gained purchase. "To be continued," he said, as much to himself as to her.

"Fine," she said. Numbly, she sank back in her seat and stared unseeing out the window. Her thoughts drifted for a time and then began to focus on a face. Kate closed her eyes and tried to will the thoughts, the face, away. In moments, though, she could see Art's eyes, glazed and bloodshot; see them as clearly as she had that afternoon a dozen years before when he had raped her. She could smell the whiskey on his breath and feel the weight of his fullback's body on top of hers. Though bundled in a down parka and warm-up suit, she began to shiver.

Jared turned onto the narrow access drive to the club. To Kate's

249

right, the metallic surface of the Atlantic glinted through a leafless hardwood forest. She took no notice of it.

Please Art, don't, her mind begged. *You're hurting me. Please let me up. All I did was take the test. I didn't say I was going to apply.*

"Look, there are the Carlisles up ahead of us. I guess we're not late after all."

Jared's voice broke through the nightmare. Dampened by a cold sweat, she pushed herself upright. The assault had taken place the day after the second anniversary of her previous marriage, and only an hour after her husband, a failure first in a pro football tryout, then in graduate school, and finally in business, had learned that she had taken the Medical College Admission Test, and worse, that she had scored in the top five percent. His need to control her, never pleasant, had turned ugly. By the evening of that day she had moved out.

"Jared," she pleaded quietly, "we'll talk. Okay?"

"Yeah, sure," he answered. "We'll talk."

The ball rainbowed off Jared's racquet with deceptive speed. A perfect topspin lob.

From her spot by the net, Kate watched Jim and Patsy Carlisle skid to simultaneous stops and, amidst flailing arms, legs, and racquets, dash backward toward the baseline.

The shot bounced six inches inside the line and then accelerated toward the screen, the Carlisles in frantic pursuit.

"You fox," Kate whispered as Jared moved forward for the killing shot they both knew would not be necessary. "That was absolutely beautiful."

"Just keep looking sort of bland. Like we don't even know we're about to beat them for the first time ever."

Across the net, Patsy Carlisle made a fruitless lunge that sent her tumbling into the indoor court's green nylon backdrop.

Kate watched the minidrama of the woman, still seated on the court, glaring at her husband as he stalked away from her without even the offer of a hand up. Husbands and wives mixed doubles, she thought: games within games within games. "Three match points," she said. "Maybe we should squabble more often before we play." A look at Jared's eyes told her she should have let the matter lie. "Finish 'em with the ol' high hard one," she urged as he walked back to the service line. Her enthusiasm, she knew, now sounded forced—an attempt at some kind of expiation.

Jared nodded at her and winked.

Kate crouched by the net. Eighteen feet in front of her, Jim Carlisle shifted the weight of his compact, perfectly conditioned body from one foot to another. A successful real estate developer, a yachtsman, and club champion several years running, he had never been one to take any kind of loss lightly. "You know," he had said to her on the only attempt he had ever made to start an affair between them, "there are those like you-know-who, who are content to tiptoe along in Daddy's footsteps, and those who just grab life by the throat and do it. I'm a doer."

The reference to Jared, even though prodded forth by far too many martinis, had left an aftertaste of anger that Kate knew would never totally disappear. When Carlisle sent the Samuels for Congress Committee a check for five hundred dollars, she had almost sent it back with a note telling him to go grab somebody's life by the throat. Instead, out of deference to her husband, she had invited the Carlisles over for dinner. Her hypocrisy, however honorable its purpose, continued to rankle her from time to time, especially when Carlisle, wearing his smugness like aftershave, was about to inflict yet another defeat on team Samuels/Bennett.

At last she was beating the man. Not even a disagreement with her husband could dull the luster of the moment.

Through the mirror of Jim Carlisle's stages of readiness to return serve, Kate pictured Jared's movements behind her. Feet planted: Jared had settled in at the line. Hunching over, knees bent: Jared was tapping ball against racquet, gaining his rhythm. Just before Carlisle began the quick bouncing which would signal the toss, she heard Jared's voice. "The ol' high hard one," he said.

Kate tensed, awaiting the familiar, sharp *pok* of Jared's serve and Carlisle's almost simultaneous move to return. Instead, she heard virtually nothing, and watched in horror as Carlisle, with the glee of a tomcat discovering a wounded sparrow, advanced to pounce on a woefully soft hit. The serve was deliberate—vintage Jared Samuels; his way of announcing that by no means had he forgotten their argument.

"Jared, you bastard," Kate screamed just as Carlisle exploded a shot straight at her chest from less than a dozen feet away.

An instant after the ball left Carlisle's racquet, it was on Kate's, then ricocheting into a totally unguarded corner of the court. The shot was absolute reflex, absolute luck, but perfect all the same.

"Match," Kate said simply. She shook hands with each of their opponents, giving Jim's hand an extra pump. Then, without a backward glance, she walked off the court to the locker room.

The Oceanside Racquet Club, three quarters of an acre of corrugated aluminum box, squatted gracelessly on a small rise above the Atlantic. "Facing Wimbledon," was the way the club's overstuffed director liked to describe it.

Keeping her hair dry and moving quickly enough to ensure that Jared would have to work to catch up with her, Kate showered and left the building. The rules of *their* game demanded a reaction of some sort for his behavior, and she had decided on taking the MG, perhaps stopping a mile or so down the road. As she crossed the half-filled parking lot, she began searching the pockets of her parka for her keys. Almost immediately, she remembered seeing them on the kitchen table.

"Damn!" The feeling was so familiar. She had, in the past, slept through several exams, required police assistance to locate her car in an airport parking garage, and forgotten where she had put the engagement ring Art had given her. Although she had come to accept the trait as a usually harmless annoyance, there was a time when visions of clamps left in abdomens concerned her enough to influence her decision to go into pathology rather than clinical medicine. This day, she felt no compassion whatsoever toward her shortcoming.

Testily, she strode past their car and down the road. The move was a bluff. Jared would know that as well as she. It was an eight-mile walk to their home, and the temperature was near freezing. Still, some show of indignation was called for. But not this, she realized quickly. At the moment she accepted the absurdity of her gesture and decided to turn back, she heard the distinctive rev of the MG behind her. There could be no retreat now.

It was a game between them, but not a game. Their scenarios were often carefully staged, but they were life all the same; actions and reactions, spontaneous or not, that provided the dynamics unique to their relationship. There had been no such dynamics in her first marriage. Put simply, Arthur Everett decreed and his dutiful wife Kathryn acquiesced. For two destructive years it had been that way. Her childhood programming offered no alternatives, and she had been too frightened, too insecure, to question. Even now there were times, though gradually fewer and farther between, when dreams of the farmhouse and the children, the well-stocked, sunlit kitchen and the pipe smoke wafting out from the study, dominated her thoughts. They were, she knew, nothing more than the vestiges—the reincarnations—of that childhood programming.

Unfortunately, much of Jared's programming was continually being reinforced, thanks largely to a father who remained convinced that God's plan for women was quite different from His plan for men.

"You have a wonderful behind, do you know that?" Jared's voice startled her. He was driving alongside her, studying her anatomy through a pair of binoculars.

"Yes, I know that." She stiffened enough to be sure he could notice and walked on. Please don't get hurt, she thought. Put those silly binoculars down and watch where you're going.

"And your face. Have I told you lately about your face?"

"No, but go ahead if you must."

"It is the blue ribbon, gold medal, face-of-the-decade face, that's what."

"You tried to get me killed in there." Kate slowed, but did not stop.

"It was childish."

"And . . . ?"

"And it was dumb."

"And . . . ?"

"And it didn't work."

"Jared!"

"And I'm sorry. I really am. The devil made me do it, but I went and let 'im."

He opened the door. She stopped, hesitated the obligatory few seconds, and got in. The scenario was over. Through it, a dram of purulence had been drained from their marriage before it could fester. Energy no longer enmeshed in their anger would now be rechanneled, perhaps to a joint attack today on the pile of unsplit wood in the yard and later to a battle with the *Times* crossword puzzle. As likely as not, before the afternoon was through, they would make love.

Eyes closed, Kate settled back in her seat, savoring what she had just heard. *I'm sorry.* He had actually said it.

Apologizing has been bred out of Samuels men was yet another teaching from the philosophy of J. Winfield Samuels. Kate had suffered the pain of that one on more than one occasion. She thought about Jared's vehement reaction to the possibility of her taking over the chairmanship of her department. The morning, she had decided, had been a draw: Dad 1. Wife 1.

"Now, Dr. Engleson, you may proceed with your report."

Tom Engleson's groan was not as inaudible as he would have liked. "Your patient is still bleeding, sir. That's my report." During his year and a half of residency on the Ashburton Service at Metropolitan Hospital of Boston, Engleson had had enough dealings with D. K. Bartholomew to know that he would be lucky to escape with anything less than a fifteen-minute conversation.

Dr. Donald K. Bartholomew held the receiver in his left hand, adjusted the notepad in front of him, and straightened his posture. "And what is her blood count?"

"Twenty-five. Her crit is down to twenty-five from twenty-eight." Engleson pictured the numbers being shakily reproduced in black felt tip. "She has had a total of five units transfused in the last twenty-four hours, two of whole blood, one of packed cells, and two of fresh frozen plasma." He closed his eyes and awaited the inevitable string of questions. For a few seconds there was silence.

"How many fresh frozen did you say?"

"Two. The hematology people have been to see her again. Her blood is just not clotting normally." He had decided to keep the complicated explanation for Beverly Vitale's bleeding problem out of the conversation if at all possible. A single request from Bartholomew for specifics, and the phone call could drag on for another half hour. In fact, there was no good explanation even available. The hematologists knew *what*—two of the woman's key clotting factors were at critically low levels—but not *why*. It was a problem the surgeon should have at least identified before performing her D and C.

"Have they further tests to run?"

"No, sir. Not today, anyhow." Getting D. K. Bartholomew to come into the hospital on a Sunday morning was like getting a cat to hop into the tub. "They suggested loading her up with fresh clotting factors and perhaps doing another D and C. They're afraid she might bleed out otherwise."

"How long will it take to give her the factors?"

"We've already started, sir."

There was another pause. "Well, then," Bartholomew said at last. "I guess the patient and I have a date in the operating room."

"Would you like me to assist?" Engleson closed his eyes and prayed for an affirmative response.

"For a D and C? No, thank you, Doctor. It is a one-man procedure, and I am one man. I shall be in by twelve o'clock. Please put the OR team on notice."

"Fine," Engleson said wearily. He had already scheduled Beverly Vitale for the operating room. He hung up and checked the wall clock over the door of the cluttered resident's office. Only eight minutes. "A record," he announced sardonically to the empty room. "I may have just set a record."

Moments later, he called the operating suite. "Denise, it's Tom Engleson. You know the D and C I scheduled for Dr. Bartholomew? . . . Vitale. That's right. Well, I was wondering if you could switch it to the observation OR. I want to watch. . . . I know you're not supposed to use that room on a weekend. That's why I'm asking in such a groveling tone of voice. . . . Bartholomew doesn't want anyone assisting him, but he can't keep me from watching through the overhead. . . . I owe you one, Denise. Thanks."

Looking down from behind the thick glass observation window into the operating room, Tom Engleson exchanged worried looks with the scrub nurse assisting Dr. Donald K. Bartholomew. The dilatation of Beverly Vitale's cervix and subsequent curettage—scraping—of the inner surface of her uterus was not going well. She had gone to the emergency ward three days before because of vaginal bleeding that started with her period but would not let up. For several years, she had been receiving routine gynecologic care through the Omnicenter—the outpatient facility of the Ashburton Women's Health Service of Metropolitan Hospital. As her Omnicenter physician, D. K. Bartholomew had been called in immediately.

In his admission physical, Bartholomew had noted a number of bruises on the woman's arms and legs, but elected nevertheless to proceed with a D and C—commonly done for excessive bleeding. He did not order blood clotting studies until after his patient's bleeding worsened postoperatively. Now, with the woman loaded with fresh clotting factors, Bartholomew was repeating the curettage.

Beverly Vitale, a thin, delicate young cellist with straight jet hair and fine, artist's hands lay supine on the operating table with her eyes taped shut and her head turned ninety degrees to one side. A polystyrene tube placed through her mouth into her trachea connected her with the anesthesia machine. Her legs, draped in sterile sheets, were held aloft by cloth stirrups hooked beneath each heel. Overhead, in the observation gallery Tom Engleson watched and waited. He was dressed in standard operating room whites, with hair and shoe covers, but no mask.

As he watched the level of suctioned blood rise in the vacuum bottle on the wall, Engleson wondered if D. K. Batholomew was considering removing the woman's uterus altogether. He cursed himself for not throwing protocol to the winds and inviting himself into the OR.

The prospect of the old surgeon moving ahead with a hysterectomy brought a ball of anger to the resident's throat. Much of his reaction, he knew, had to do with Beverly Vitale. Though he had only spoken with her a few times, Engleson had begun fantasizing about her and had become determined to see her when she was released from the hospital. Now his thoughts added, *if* she was released from the hospital. He glanced again at the vacuum bottle and then at Bartholomew. There was a flicker of confusion and uncertainty in the man's eyes.

"Her pressure is dropping a bit."

Engleson heard the anesthesiologist's voice crackle through a barely functional speaker on the wall behind him. "Young lady, get me the freshest unit of blood we have, and see if the blood bank can send us up ten units of platelets."

"Yes, sir," the nurse said. "Dr. Bartholomew, blood loss so far is four hundred and fifty cc's."

Bartholomew did not respond immediately. He stood motionless, staring at the steady flow of crimson from Beverly Vitale's cervix.

"Let's try some pitocin. Maybe her uterus will clamp down," he said finally.

"Dr. Bartholomew," the anesthesiologist said, an even tenseness in his voice, "you've already ordered pitocin. She's been getting it. Maximum doses."

Engleson strained to see the older surgeon's face. If he rushed into the OR and the man did not need assistance, a formal complaint was sure to. . . . Before he could complete the thought, the bellboy hanging from his waistband emitted the abrasive tone signaling a transmission. "Dr. Engleson, call two eight three *stat*. Dr. Engleson, two eight three *stat*, please."

An anxious check of the scene below, and the resident rushed to the nearest phone. It was a rule of the Ashburton Service that all *stat* pages were to be answered within sixty seconds. Telephones had even been installed in the residents' bathrooms for such purposes.

The call concerned a postop patient whose temperature had risen to 103; not a life-or-death situation. By the time Engleson had listened to the nurse's report, given orders for evaluating the patient's fever and returned to the observation window, Bartholomew had begun swabbing antiseptic over Beverly Vitale's lower abdomen.

Engleson switched on the microphone by his right hand. "What's going on?" he asked. Below, no one reacted to his voice. "Can you hear me?" Again no response. Through the door to the scrub area, Engleson saw Carol Nixon, a surgical intern rotating through the Ashburton Service, beginning to scrub. Apparently Bartholomew had called her in to assist, perhaps when Engleson could not be found.

"Over my dead body," Engleson said as he raced down the hall to the stairs. "No way do you open that woman up without my being there." In less than a minute, he had joined Nixon in the scrub room.

"The nurses said Stone Hands was trying to find you," the woman said. "I was just finishing up a case down the hall when Denise grabbed me. Do I have to stay?"

"You might want to learn from the master in there," Engleson responded acidly, cleaning his fingernails with an orange stick. The intern smiled, nodded a thanks-but-no-thanks, and left him to finish his scrub.

"Order a peach and you get a pear," was Bartholomew's comment on the change in assistants. He laughed merrily at his own humor and seemed not to notice the absence of response from around the room.

With Engleson handling sponges and hemostats, Bartholomew used an electric scalpel to make an incision from just below Beverly Vitale's navel to her pubis. The scalpel, buzzing and crackling like hot bacon grease, simultaneously sliced through the skin and cauterized bleeding vessels. Next, with the voltage turned up, he cut through a thin layer of saffron-colored fat to her peritoneum, the opaque membrane covering her abdominal cavity. A few snips with a Metzenbaum scissors, and the peritoneum parted, exposing her bowel, her bladder, and beneath those, her uterus.

In a perfunctory manner, too perfunctory for Engleson's taste, the older surgeon explored the abdominal cavity with one hand. "Everything seems in order," he announced to the room. "I think we can proceed with a hysterectomy."

"No!" Engleson said sharply. The room froze. "I mean, don't you think we should at least consider the possibility of ligating her hypogastric artery?" He wanted to add his feelings about rushing ahead with a hysterectomy in a thirty-year-old woman with no children, but held back. Also unsaid, at least for the moment, was that the hypogastric ligation, while not always successful in stopping hemorrhaging, was certainly accepted practice in a case like this. Bartholomew was still guided by the old school—the school that removed a uterus with the dispatch of a dermatologist removing a wart.

D. K. Bartholomew's pale blue eyes came up slowly and locked on Engleson's. For five seconds, ten, an eerie silence held, impinged upon only by the wheeze of air into the vacuum apparatus. The tall resident held his ground, but he also held his breath. An outburst by the older surgeon now, and there would be a confrontation that could further jeopardize the life of Beverly Vitale. Then, moment by moment, Engleson saw the blaze in Bartholomew's eyes fade.

"Thank you for the suggestion, doctor," the surgeon said distantly. "I think perhaps we should give it a try."

The relieved sighs from those in the room were muffled by their masks.

"You or me?" Engleson asked.

"It . . . it's been a while since I did this procedure," Bartholomew understated.

"Don't worry, we'll do it together."

In minutes, the ligation was complete. Almost instantly, the bleeding from within the woman's uterus began to lessen.

"While we're waiting to see if this works," Engleson said, "would you mind if I got a better look at her tubes and ovaries?"

Bartholomew shrugged and shook his head.

Engleson probed along the fallopian tubes, first to one ovary and then to the other. They did not feel at all right. Carefully, he withdrew the left ovary through the incision. It was half normal size, mottled gray, and quite firm. This time, it was his eyes that flashed. *You said everything was in order.* Bartholomew sagged. There was a bewildered, vacant air about him, as if he had opened his eyes before a mirror and seen a painful truth.

The woman's right ovary was identical to her left.

"I don't think I've ever seen anything quite like this," Engleson said. "Have you?"

"No, well, not exactly."

"Pardon?"

"I said *I* hadn't either." There was an uncertainty, a hesitation, in the older man's words. He reached over and touched the ovary.

"You sure?" Engleson prodded.

"I . . . I may have felt one once. I'm trying to remember. Do you suggest a biopsy?" Engleson nodded. "A wedge section?" Another nod. The man's confidence was obviously shaken.

By the time the wedge biopsy was taken, the bleeding had slowed dramatically. As Engleson prepared to close the abdominal incision over the uterus he had just preserved, he sensed the irony of what was happening tighten in his gut. The uterus was saved, true. A fine piece of surgery. But if the pathology in Beverly Vitale's ovaries was as extensive as it appeared, the woman would never bear children anyhow.

"Denise," he said, "could you find out who's on for surgical path this month; both the resident and the staff person, okay?"

"Right away."

Engleson glanced at the peaceful face and tousled hair of the young cellist. Some women try for years to get pregnant, never knowing whether they can or not, he thought. At least you'll know. Glumly, he began to close.

Twenty minutes later, the two surgeons shuffled into the doctor's locker room.

"Dr. Bartholomew, have you been able to remember where you might have encountered ovarian pathology like this woman's?"

"Oh, yes, well, no. I . . . what I mean is I don't think I've ever seen anything like them."

"You look as if you want to say something more."

"I may have felt something like them once. That's all."

"When? On whom?" There was some excitement in Engleson's voice.

D. K. Bartholomew, MD, Fellow of the American College of Surgeons and Diplomate of the American College of Obstetrics and Gynecology, shook his head. "I . . . I'm afraid I don't remember," he said.

"What are you talking about?"

"It was surgery for something else. Maybe removal of a fibroid tumor. The ovaries felt like this woman's did today, but there was no one around to consult, and I think I had another case or two left to do and . . ."

"So you just ignored them and closed?"

"I felt they were probably a normal variant."

"Yeah, sure. Did you mention them on your operative note?"

"I . . . I don't remember. It might have been years ago."

The wall telephone began ringing. "Dr. Bartholomew," Engleson said, allowing the jangle to continue. "I don't think you should operate anymore." With that he turned and snatched up the receiver.

"Dr. Engleson, it's Denise. I called pathology."

"Yes?"

"I couldn't find out who the resident is on surgicals, but the staff person is Dr. Bennett."

"Good."

"Excuse me?"

"I just said that's good. Thanks, Denise."

"Thank you for what you did in there, Doctor. You made my day."

Kate's back was arched over the pillows beneath her hips as Jared knelt between her legs and used her buttocks to pull himself farther inside her. Again and again he sent jets of pleasure and pain deep into her gut and up into her throat. Her climax grew like the sound of an oncoming train—first a tingle, a vibration, next a hum, then a roar. With Jared helping, her body came off the pillows until only her heels and the back of her head were touching the carpet. Her muscles tightened on him and seemed to draw him in even deeper. He dug his fingers into the small of her back and cried out in a soft, child's voice. Then he came, his erection pulsing in counterpoint to her own contractions.

"I love you," he whispered. "Oh, Katey, I love you so much." Gently, he worked his arms around her waist, and guided her onto her side, trying to stay within her as long as possible. For half an hour they lay on the soft living room carpet, their lover's sweat drying in the warmth from the nearby wood stove. From the kitchen, the aroma of percolating coffee, forgotten for over an hour, worked its way into the sweetness of the birch fire.

A cashmere blanket, one of the plethora of wedding gifts from Jared's father, lay beside them. Kate pulled it over her sleeping husband and then slipped carefully from underneath. For a time, she knelt there studying the face of the man who had, five years before, arranged to have himself and a dozen roses wheeled under a sheet into her autopsy suite in order to convince her to reconsider a rebuffed dinner invitation. Five years. Years filled with so much change—so much growth for both of them. She had been a nervous, overworked junior faculty member then, and he had been the hotshot young attorney assigned by Minton/Samuels to handle beleaguered Metropolitan Hospital. The memory of him in those days—so eager and intense— brought a faint smile.

Kate reached out and touched the fine creases that had, overnight it seemed, materialized at the corners of her husband's eyes.

"A year, Jared?" she asked silently. "Would a year make all that much difference? You understand your own needs so well. Can you understand mine?"

Almost instantly another, far more disturbing question arose in her thoughts. Did she, in fact, understand them herself?

Silently, she rose and walked to the picture window overlooking their wooded backyard. Superimposed on the smooth waves of drifted snow was the reflection of her naked body, kept thin and toned by constant dieting and almost obsessive exercise. On an impulse, she turned sideways and forced her abdomen out as far as it would go. Six months, she guessed, maybe seven. Not too bad looking for an old pregnant lady.

Fifteen minutes later, when the phone rang, Kate was ricocheting around the kitchen preparing brunch. The edge of her terry-cloth robe narrowly missed toppling a pan of sweet sausages as she leapt for the receiver, answering it before the first ring ended. Nevertheless, through the door to the living room, she saw Jared stir from the fetal tuck in which he had been sleeping and begin to stretch.

"Hello," she answered, mentally discarding the exotic plans she had made for awakening her husband.

"Dr. Bennett, it's Tom Engleson. I'm a senior resident on the Ashburton Service at Metro. Do you remember me?"

"Of course, Tom. You saw me at the Omnicenter once. Saved my life when Dr. Zimmermann was away."

"I did?" There was a hint of embarrassment in his voice. "What was the matter?"

"Well, actually, I just needed a refill of my birth control pills. But I remember you just the same. What can I do for you?" Her mental picture of Engleson was of a loose, gangly man, thirty or thirty-one, with angular features and a youthful face, slightly aged by a Teddy Roosevelt moustache.

"Please forgive me for phoning you at home on Sunday."

"Nonsense."

"Thank you. The reason I'm calling is to get your advice on handling a surgical specimen. It's one you'll be seeing tomorrow: a wedge section of a patient's left ovary, taken during a hypogastric artery ligation for menorrhagia."

"How old a woman?" Reflexively, Kate took up a pen to begin scratching data on the back of an envelope. So doing, she noticed that Jared was now huddled by the wood stove with Roscoe, their four-year-old almost-terrier and the marriage's declared neutral love object.

"Thirty," Engleson answered. "No deliveries, no pregnancies, and in fact, no ovaries."

"What?"

"Oh, they're there. But they're unlike any ovaries I've ever seen before. Dr. Bartholomew was with me—the woman is his patient—and he has never seen pathology like this either."

Kate pulled a high stool from beneath the counter and wrapped one foot around its leg. "Explain," she said.

"Well, whatever this is is uniform and symmetrical. We took a slice from the left ovary, but it could just as well have been the right. Shrunken, the consistency of . . . of a squash ball—sort of hard but rubbery. The surface is pockmarked, dimpled."

"What color?" Kate had written down almost every word.

"Gray. Grayish brown, maybe."

"Interesting," she said.

"Does what I've described ring any bells?"

"No. At least not right off. However, there are a number of possibilities. Any idea as to why this woman was having menorrhagia?"

"Two reasons. One is a platelet count of just forty-five thousand, and the other is a fibrinogen level that is fifteen percent of normal."

"An autoimmune phenomenon?" Kate searched her thoughts for a single disease entity characterized by the two blood abnormalities. An autoimmune phenomenon, the body making antibodies against certain of its own tissues, seemed likely.

"So far, that's number one on the list," Engleson said. "The hematology people have started her on steroids."

"Was she on any medications?"

"Hey, Kate." It was Jared calling from the living room. "Do you smell something burning?"

"Nothing but vitamins," Engleson answered.

Kate did not respond. Receiver tucked under her ear, she was at the oven, pulling out a tray of four blackened lumps that had once been shirred eggs—Jared's favorite.

"Shit," she said.

"What?" Both Jared and Tom Engleson said the word simultaneously.

"Oh, sorry. I wasn't talking to you." A miniature cumulonimbus cloud puffed from the oven. "Jared, it's all right," she called out, this time covering the mouthpiece. "It's just . . . our meal. That's all."

"Dr. Bennett, if you'd rather I called back . . ."

"No, Tom, no. Listen, there's a histology technician on call. The lab tech on duty knows who it is. Have whoever it is come in and begin running the specimen through the Technichron. That way it will be ready for examination tomorrow rather than Tuesday. Better still, ask them to come into the lab and call me at home. I'll give the instructions myself. Okay?"

"Sure. Thanks."

"No problem," she said, staring at the lumps. "I'll speak to you later."

"Shirred eggs?" Jared, wrapped in the cashmere blanket, leaned against the doorway. Roscoe peered at her from between his knees.

Kate nodded sheepishly. "I sort of smelled the smoke, but my one-track brain was focused on what this resident from the hospital was saying, and somehow, it dismissed the smoke as coming from the wood stove. I . . . I never was too great at doing more than one thing at once."

"Too bad you couldn't have chosen to let the resident burn to a crisp and save the eggs," he said.

"Next time."

"Good. Any possibilities for replacements?"

"Howard Johnson's?"

"Thanks, but I'll take my chances with some coffee and whatever's in that frying pan. You sure that wasn't Yoda on the phone?"

"Jared . . ."

He held up his hands against her ire. "Just checking, just checking," he said. "Come on, Roscoe. Let's go set the table."

Kate noted the absence of an apology, but decided that two in one day was too much to ask. More difficult to accept, however, was Jared's apparent lack of interest in what the call was about. It was as if by not talking about her career, her life outside of their marriage, he was somehow diminishing its importance. In public, he took special pride in her professionalism and her degree. Privately, he accepted it as long as it didn't burn his eggs. Almost against her will, she felt frustration begin to dilute the warmth and closeness generated by their lovemaking. She walked to where her clothes were piled in the living room and dressed, silently vowing to do whatever she could to avoid another blowup that day.

Minutes later, the crunch of tires on their gravel driveway heralded a test of her resolve. Roscoe heard the arrival first and bounded from his place by the stove to the front door. Jared, now in denims and a flannel work shirt, followed.

"Hey, Kate, it's Sandy," he called out, opening the inside door.

"Sandy?" Dick Sandler, Jared's roommate at Dartmouth, had been best man at their wedding. A TWA pilot, he lived on the South Shore and hadn't been in touch with them for several months. "Is Ellen with him?"

"No. He's alone." Jared opened the storm door. "Hey, flyboy," he called in a thick Spanish accent, "welcome. I have just what you want, señor: a seexteen-year-old American virgin. Only feefty pesetas."

Sandler, a rugged Marlon Brando type, exchanged bear hugs with Jared and platonic kisses with Kate, and then scanned what there was of their brunch. "What, no bloodies?"

Kate winced before images of the two men, emboldened by a few "bloodies," exchanging off-color jokes she seldom thought were funny and singing "I Wanna Go Back to Dartmouth, to Dartmouth on the Hill." Invariably, she would end up having to decide whether to leave the house, try to shut them off, or join in. When Ellen Sandler was around, no such problem existed. A woman a few years older than Kate, and Sandy's wife since his graduation, Ellen was as charming, interesting, and full of life as anyone Kate had ever known. She was a hostess with poise and grace, the mother of three delightful girls, and even a modestly successful businesswoman, having developed an interior design consulting firm that she had run alone for several years from their home and more recently from a small studio cum office in town.

Sandy, with his flamboyance, his stature as a 747 captain, and his versitile wit, was the magnet that drew many fascinating and accomplished people into the Sandlers' social circle. Ellen, Kate believed, was the glue that kept them there.

"So, Sandy," she said, dropping a celery stick into his drink and sliding it across the table, "what brings you north to Boston? How are Ellen and the girls?" It was at that moment that she first appreciated the sadness in his eyes.

"I . . . well actually, I was just driving around and decided to cruise up here. Sort of a whim. I . . . I needed to talk to Jared . . . and to you."

"You and Ellen?" Jared's sense of his friend told him immediately what to ask.

"I . . . I'm leaving her. Moving out." Sandler stared uncomfortably into the center of his drink.

At his words, Kate felt a dreadful sinking in her gut. Ellen had stated on many occasions and in many ways the uncompromising love she bore for the man. How long had they been married, now? Eighteen years? Nineteen, maybe?

"Holy shit," Jared whispered, setting a hand on Sandler's forearm. "What's happened?"

"Nothing. I mean nothing dramatic. Somewhere along the way, we just lost one another."

"Sandy, people who have been married for almost twenty years don't just lose one another," Kate said. "Now what has happened?" There was an irritability in her voice which surprised her. Jared's expression suggested that he, too, was startled by her tone.

Sandler shrugged. "Well, between running the house and entertaining and taking the girls to one lesson or another and scouts and committees at our club and that business of hers, Ellen simply ran out of energy for me. In some areas, meals and such, she still goes through the motions, but without much spark."

"How is Ellen handling all this?" Kate asked, checking Jared's face for a sign that she might be interloping with too many questions. The message she received was noncommittal.

"She doesn't know yet."

"What?" Her exclamation this time drew a *be careful* glare.

"I just decided yesterday. But I've been thinking about it for weeks. Longer. I was hoping you two might have some suggestions as to how I should go about breaking the news to her."

"Have you been to a counsellor or a shrink or something?" Jared asked the question.

"It's too late."

"What do you mean? You just said Ellen doesn't even know what you're planning to do." Jared sounded baffled.

Across the table, Kate closed her eyes. She knew the explanation.

"There's someone else," Sandler said self-consciously. "A flight attendant. I . . . we've been seeing one another for some time."

For Kate the words were like needle stabs. Jared was pressing to get a commitment from her to alter her life along pathways Ellen Sandler could negotiate blindfolded. Yet here was Sandy, like Jared in so many ways, rejecting the woman for not devoting enough energy to him. The image of Ellen sitting there while he announced his intentions made her first queasy and then frightened. The fear, as happened more often than not, mutated into anger before it could be expressed.

263

"Ellen doesn't deserve this," she said, backing away from the table. "'We just lost one another.' Sandy, don't you think that's sort of a sleazy explanation for what's really going on? How old is this woman?"

"Twenty-six. But I don't see what her . . ."

"I know you don't see. You don't see a lot of things."

Jared stood up. "Now just one second, Kate."

"And you don't see a lot of things either, dammit." There were tears streaming down her face. "You two boys work out how you're gonna break the news to Ellen that she did everything she goddamn well could in life—more than both of you put together, probably—but that it just wasn't enough. She's fired. Dismissed. Not flashy enough. Not showy enough. Her services are no longer required. Excuse me, I'm going to the bathroom to get sick. Then I'm going to my hospital. People there are grateful and appreciative for the things I do well. I like that. It helps me to get up in the morning."

Fists clenched, she turned and raced from the room. Roscoe, who had settled himself under the table, padded to the center of the room and after a brief glance at the men, followed.

Ginger Rittenhouse, a first-grade teacher, had just finished her run by the ice-covered Charles River when she began to die. Like the random victim of a crazed sniper, she did not hear the sound or see the muzzle flash of the weapon that killed her. In fact, the weapon was nothing more malevolent than the corner of her bureau drawer; the shot, an accidental bump less than twenty-four hours before to a spot just above her right eye.

"That's one incredible lump!" her new roommate had exclaimed, forcing an icepack against the golfball-sized knot. The woman, a licensed practical nurse, had commented on the large bruise just below her right knee as well. Ginger was too self-conscious to mention the other, similar bruises on her lower back, buttocks, and upper arm.

Her death began with a tic—an annoying electric sensation deep behind her right eye. The wall of her right middle cerebral artery was stretching. Bruised by the shock from the bureau drawer, the vessel, narrow as a piece of twine, had developed a tiny defect along the inner lining. The platelets and fibrinogen necessary to patch the defect were present, but in insufficient amounts to do the job. Blood had begun to work its way between the layers of the vessel wall.

Squinting against the pain, she sat on a bench and looked across the river at the General Electric building in Cambridge. The outline of the building seemed blurred. From the rent in her right middle cerebral artery, blood had begun to ooze, a microdrop at a time, into the space between her skull and brain. Nerve fibers, exquisitely sensitive, detected the intrusion and began screaming their message of warning. Ginger, mindless of the huge lump over her ear, placed her hands on either side of her head and tried to squeeze the pain into submission.

Powered by the beating of her own heart, the bleeding increased. Her thoughts became disconnected snatches. The low skyline of Cambridge began to fade. Behind her, runners jogged by. A pair of lovers passed close enough to read the dial on her watch. Ginger, now paralyzed by pain that was far more than pain, was beyond calling for help.

Suddenly, a brilliant white light replaced the agony. The heat from the light bathed the inside of her eyes. Her random thoughts coalesced about woods and a stream. It was the Dingle, the secret hiding place of her childhood. She knew every tree, every rock. Home and safe at last, Ginger Rittenhouse surrendered to the light, and gently toppled forward onto the sooty snow.

CHAPTER 2
Monday 10 December

FIRST THERE WAS the intense, yellow-white light—the sunlight of another world. Then, subtly, colors began to appear: reds and pinks, purples and blues. Kate felt herself drifting downward, Alice drawn by her own curiosity over the edge and down the rabbit's hole. How many times had she focused her microscope in on a slide? Tens of thousands, perhaps even hundreds of thousands. Still, every journey through the yellow-white light began with the same sense of anticipation as had her first.

The colors darkened and coalesced into a mosaic of cells; the cells of Beverly Vitale's left ovary, chemically fixed to prevent decay, then embedded in a block of paraffin, cut thin as a slick of oil, and finally stained with dyes specific for coloring one or another structure within the cell. Pink for the cytoplasm; mottled violet for the nuclei; red for the cell walls.

With a deep breath calculated at once to relax herself and to heighten her concentration, she focused the lenses and her thoughts on the cells, now magnified a thousand times. Her efforts were less successful than usual. Thoughts of Sandy and Ellen, of Jared and the discussion they had had following her return from the hospital the previous night, continued to intrude.

She had come home late, almost eleven, after meeting with Tom Engleson, interviewing Beverly Vitale, examining the frozen section of her ovary, and finally spending an hour in the hospital library. Her expectations had been to find the former roommates in the den, comatose or nearly so, with the essence of a half a case of Lowenbräu permeating the room. Instead, she had found only a somber and perfectly sober Jared.

"Hi," he said simply.

"Hi, yourself." She kissed him on the forehead and then settled onto the ottoman by his chair. "When did Sandy leave?"

"A couple of hours ago. Did you get done whatever it is you wanted to?"

Kate nodded. His expression was as flat and as drained as his words. No surprise, she realized. First his wife stalks out of the house with no real explanation; then he has to listen to the agonies of the breakup of his best friend's marriage. "I . . . I guess I owe you an apology for the way I acted earlier. Some sort of explanation."

Jared shrugged. "I'll take the apology. The explanation's optional."

"I'm sorry for leaving the way I did."

"I'm sorry you left the way you did, too. I could have used some help—at least some moral support."

"Sorry again." The three feet separating them might as well have been a canyon. "Anything decided?"

"He went home to tell Ellen and to move out, I guess. It got awful quiet here after you left. Neither of us was able to open up very well. We each seemed to be wrapped up in our own bundle of problems."

"Three I'm sorries. That's my limit." She unsnapped her barrette, shook her hair free, and combed it out with her fingers. The gesture was natural enough, but at some level she knew she had done it because it was one Jared liked. "After what happened this morning—in the car, I mean—I couldn't listen to Sandy just brush off Ellen and their marriage the way he did. I mean, here I am, scrambling to do a decent job with my career and to be a reasonably satisfying friend and wife to you, and there's Ellen able to do both of those so easily and raise three beautiful, talented children to boot, and . . ."

"It's not right what you're doing, Kate."

"What's that?"

"You're comparing your insides to Ellen's outsides, that's what. She looks good. I'll give you that. But don't go and cast Sandy as the heavy just because he's the one moving out. There are things that are missing from that relationship. Maybe things too big to overcome. What's that got to do with our discussion this morning, anyway?"

"Jared, you know perfectly well what it has to do. Having children is a major responsibility. As it is, I feel like a one-armed juggler half the

time. Our lives, our jobs, the things we do on our own and together
. . . Toss in a baby at this point, and what guarantee is there I won't
start dropping things?"

"What do you want me to say? I'm almost forty years old. I'm
married. I want to have children. My wife said she wanted to have
children, too. Now, all of a sudden, having children is a threat to our
marriage."

"Christ, Jared, that's not what I mean . . . and you know it. I
didn't say I won't have children. I didn't say it's a threat to our marriage. All I'm trying to say is there's a lot to think about—especially
with the opportunities that have arisen at the hospital. It's not the idea
I'm having trouble with so much as the timing. A mistake here and it's a
bitter, unfulfilled woman, or a neurotic, insecure kid, or . . . or a
twenty-six-year-old stewardess. Can you understand that?"

"I understand that somewhere inside you there are some issues
you're not facing up to. Issues surrounding me or having children or
both."

"And you've got it all together, right?" Kate struggled to stop the
tears that seemed to be welling from deep within her chest.

"I know what I want."

"Well, I don't. Okay? And I'm the one who's going to have to pass
up a chairmanship and go through a pregnancy and change my life so
that I don't make the same horrible mistakes with our child that my
mother made with us. I . . . Jared, I'm frightened." It was, she realized, the first time she had truly recognized it.

"Hi, Frightened. I'm Perplexed. How do you do?"

"You know, you could use a little better sense of timing yourself."

"Okay, folks, here we go. It's time once again to play let's-jump-all-
over-everything-Jared-says. Well, please, before you get rolling, count
me out. I'm going to bed."

"I'll be in in a while."

"Don't wake me."

The section from Beverly Vitale's left ovary was unlike any pathology
Kate had ever encountered. The stroma—cells providing support and,
according to theory, critical feminizing hormones—were perfectly normal in appearance. But the follicles—the pockets of nutrient cells surrounding the ova—were selectively and completely destroyed, replaced
by the spindle-shaped, deep pink cells of sclerosis—scarring. Assuming
the pattern held true throughout both ovaries—and there was no reason to assume otherwise—Beverly Vitale's reproductive potential was
as close to zero as estimate would allow.

For nearly an hour, Kate sat there, scanning section after section,
taking notes on a yellow legal pad. Why couldn't Jared understand what
it all really meant to her? Why couldn't he see what a godsend medi-

cine had been to a life marked by aimlessness and a self-doubt bordering on self-loathing.

"My God, woman, if I didn't know better, I'd swear you were a model the Zeiss Company had hired to plug their latest line of microscopes."

"Aha," Kate said melodramatically, her eyes still fixed on the microscope, "a closet male chauvinist pig. I expected as much all along, Dr. Willoughby." She swung around and, as always, felt a warm jet of affection at the sight of her department head. In his early sixties, Stan Willoughby was egg bald save for a pure white monk's fringe. The pencil-thin moustache partially obscured by his bulbous nose was a similar shade. His eyes sparkled from beneath brows resembling end-stage dandelions. In all, Jared's likening him to the wise imp Yoda was, though inappropriate, not inaccurate.

Willoughby packed his pipe and straddled the stool across the table from Kate. "The young lady on Ashburton Five?" he asked. Kate nodded. "This a good time for me to take a look-see?"

Although Willoughby's primary area of interest was histochemistry, thirty-five years of experience had made him an expert in almost every phase of pathology. Every phase, that is, except how to administer a department. Willoughby was simply too passive, too nice for the dog-maim-dog world of hospital politics, especially the free-for-all for an adequate portion of a limited pool of funds.

"Stan, I swear I've never seen, or even heard of, anything like this."

The chief peered into the student eyepieces on the teaching microscope—a setup enabling two people to view the same specimen at the same time. "All right if I focus?" Kate nodded. Ritualistically, he went from low power magnification to intermediate, to high, and finally to thousand-fold oil-immersion, punctuating each maneuver with a "hmm" or an "uh huh." Through the other set of oculars, Kate followed.

They looked so innocent, those cells, so deceptively innocent, detached from their source and set out for viewing. They were in one sense a work of art, a delicate, geometrically perfect montage that was the antithesis of the huge, cluttered metal sculptures Kate had built and displayed during her troubled Mount Holyoke years. The irony in that thought was immense. Form follows function. The essential law of structural design. Yet here were cells perfect in form, produced by a biologic cataclysm tantamount to a volcano. A virus? A toxin? An antibody suddenly transformed? The art of pathology demanded that the cells and tissues, though fixed and stained, never be viewed as static.

"Did you send sections over to the electron microscopy unit?" Willoughby asked.

"Not yet, but I will."

"And the young woman is bleeding as well?"

"Platelets thirty thousand. Fibrinogen fifteen percent of normal."

"Ouch!"

"Yes, ouch. I spoke with her at some length last night. No significant family history, no serious diseases, nonsmoker, social drinker, no meds. . . ."

"None?"

"Vitamins and iron, but that's all. No operations except an abortion at the Omnicenter about five years ago." The two continued to study the cells as they talked. "She's a cellist with the Pops."

"Travel history?"

"Europe, China, Japan. None to third world spots. I told her how envious I was of people who could play music, and she just smiled this wistful smile and said that every time she picked up her cello, she felt as rich and fulfilled as she could ever want to feel. I only talked to her for half an hour or so, Stan, but I came away feeling like we were . . . I don't know, like we were friends." *Spend a day here sometime, Jared. Come to work with me and see what I do, how I do it.* "The hematology people are talking autoimmune phenomenon. They think the ovarian problem is long-standing, a coincidental finding at this point."

"Never postulate two diseases when one will explain things." Willoughby restated the maxim he had long since engrained upon her. "I suppose they're pouring in steroids."

"Stan, she's in trouble. Real trouble."

"Ah, yes. Forgive me. Sometimes I forget that there's more to this medicine business than just making a correct diagnosis. Thanks for not letting me get away with that kind of talk. Well, Doctor, I think you may really have something here. I have never encountered anything quite like it either."

"Neither had Dr. Bartholomew."

"That fossil? He probably has trouble recognizing his own shoes in the morning. Talk about a menace. All by himself he's an epidemic."

"No comment."

"Good. I have enough comments for both of us. Listen, Kate. Do you mind if I try a couple of my new silver stains on this material? The technique seems perfect for this type of pathology."

"I was about to ask if you would."

Willoughby engaged the intercom on the speaker-phone system— one of the few innovations he had managed to bring into the department. "Sheila, is that you?"

"No, Doctor Willoughby, it's Jane Fonda. Of course it's me. You buzzed my office."

"Could you come into Dr. Bennett's office, please?" There was no response. "Sheila, are you still there?"

"It's not what it sounds like, Dr. Willoughby," she said finally.

"Not what *what* sounds like?"

"Sheila," Kate cut in firmly, "it's me. We're calling because we have a specimen we'd like to try the silver stain on."

For a few moments there was silence. "I . . . I'll be over shortly," the technician said.

Willoughby turned to Kate, his thick brows presaging his question. "Now what was that little ditty all about?"

"Nothing, really."

"Nothing? Kate, that woman has worked for me for fifteen years. Maybe more. She's cynical, impertinent, abrasive, aggressive, and at times as bossy as my wife, but she's also the best and brightest technician I've ever known. If there's trouble between the two of you, perhaps I'd best know about it. Is it that study of the department I commissioned you and your computer friend, Sebastian, to do?"

"It's nothing, Stan. I mean it. Like most people who are very good at what they do, Sheila has a lot of pride. Especially when it comes to her boss of fifteen years. I know it's not my place to decide, but if it's okay, I'd like the chance to work through our differences without involving you. Okay?"

Willoughby hesitated and then shrugged and nodded.

"Thanks," she said. "If I were ever to take over the chairmanship of the department, I'd like to know I had a solid relationship with my chief technician—especially if she were someone as invaluable as Sheila Pierce."

"Invaluable is right. I keep giving her raises and bonuses even though she puts a knot in my ninny just about every time she opens her mouth. Say, did I hear you just give me the green light to submit your name to Reese?"

"I said 'if' and you know it."

Willoughby grinned mischievously. "Your voice said 'if,' but your eyes . . ."

"You rang?" Sheila Pierce saved Kate from a response. Fortyish, with a trim, efficient attractiveness, she had, Kate knew, earned both bachelor's and master's degrees while working in the department. By the time Kate had begun her residence, the one-time laboratory assistant had become chief pathology technician.

"Ah, Sheila," Willoughby said. "Come in."

"Hi, Sheila." Kate hoped there was enough reassurance in her expression and her voice to keep the woman from any further outburst, at least until they had a chance to talk privately.

Their eyes locked for a fraction of a second; then, mercifully, Sheila returned the greeting. The problem between them had, as Stan Willoughby suspected, arisen during Kate's computer-aided study of the pathology department's budget and expenditures, specifically in regard to a six hundred and fifty dollar payment for an educational meeting in Miami that Sheila could not document ever having attended. Kate had decided to drop the matter without involving the department chief, but the technician was clearly unconvinced that she had done so.

"How's my new batch of silver stain coming?" Willoughby asked.

"It's much, much thicker than the old stuff," Sheila said, settling on a high stool, equidistant from the two physicians. "Fourteen hours may be too long to heat it."

"I seem to recall your warning me about that when I suggested fourteen hours in the first place. Is it a total loss?"

"Well, actually I split about half of it off and cooked that part for only seven hours."

"And . . . ?"

"And it looks fine . . . perfect, even."

Willoughby's sigh of relief was pronounced. "Do you know how much that stain costs to make? How much you just saved me by . . . ?"

"Of course I know. Who do you think ordered the material in the first place, the Ghost of Christmas Past?"

Willoughby shot Kate a what-did-I-tell-you glance; then he picked up the slides and paraffin blocks containing tissue from Beverly Vitale's ovary. "Dr. Bennett has an interesting problem here that I think might be well suited to my silver stain. Do you think you could make some sections and try it out?"

"Your command is my command," Pierce said, bowing. "Give me an hour, and your stain will be ready." She turned to Kate. "Dr. Bennett, I think you should have a little review session with our chief here on the basics of hypertension. On his desk, right next to his blood pressure pills, is a half-eaten bag of Doritos. Bye, now."

Sheila Pierce dropped off the paraffin block in histology and then returned to her office. On her desk was the stain Willoughby had referred to as "his." Pierce laughed disdainfully. If it weren't for her, the stain that was soon to be known by his name would be little more than an expensive beaker of shit. There they sat, she thought, Willoughby and that goddamn Bennett, sharing their little physician jokes and performing their physician mental masturbations and issuing orders to a woman with an IQ—a proven IQ—higher than either of theirs could possibly be. One-fifty. That's what her mother said. Genius level. One hundred and fucking fifty. So where was the MD degree that would have put her where she deserved to be?

Pierce glared at the small framed photo of her parents, carefully placed to one side of her desk. Then her expression softened. It wasn't their fault, being poor. Just their fate. They didn't want the stroke or the cancer that had forced their daughter to shelve her dreams and begin a life of taking orders from privileged brats who, more often than not, couldn't come close to her intellectual capacity. One hundred and fifty. What was Kate Bennett? One-ten? One-twenty tops. Yet there she was with the degree and the power and the future.

Listen, Sheila, you're terrific at your job. I don't see that there's any-

thing to gain by bringing this up to Dr. Willoughby, or even by making you reimburse the department. But never again, okay?

"Patronizing bitch."

"Who's a bitch?"

Startled, Sheila whirled. Norton Reese stood propped against the doorjamb, eyeing her curiously.

"Jesus, you scared me."

"Who's a bitch?" Reese checked the corridor in both directions then stepped inside and closed the door behind him.

"Bennett, that's who."

"Ah, yes. What's our little Rebecca of Sunnybrook Farm up to now?"

"Oh, nothing new. It's that damn American Society meeting."

"Miami?"

"Yes. The time you assured me there was no way anyone would ever find out I didn't go."

"She is a resourceful cunt," Reese mumbled. "I'll say that for her."

"What?"

"Didn't she say she was going to do her Girl Scout good deed for the month and let the whole matter drop?"

"That's what she said, but she and Dr. Willoughby are like that." Sheila held up crossed fingers. "Either she's already told him or she's going to hold the thing over my head forever. Either way . . ." She shook her head angrily.

"Easy, baby, easy," Reese said, crossing to her and slipping his hands beneath her lab coat.

Sheila grimaced, but allowed herself to be embraced. Balding, moderately overweight, and wedded to three-piece suits, Reese had never held sex appeal for her in any visceral sense. Still, he was the administrator of the entire hospital complex, and time and experience had taught her that true sex appeal was based not so much on what a man could do *to* her as *for* her.

"You have the most beautiful tits of any woman I've ever known," Reese whispered. "Baby, do you know how long it's been?"

She blocked his move toward her breasts with an outstretched hand. "It's not *my* fault, Norty. I'm divorced. You're the one with all the family commitments. Remember?"

Reese gauged the determination in her eyes and decided against another advance. "So," he said, settling into the chair by her desk, "Wonder Woman has been at it again, huh? Well, believe it or not, she's the reason—one of the reasons—I came down here."

"Oh?"

"Maybe you'd better sit down." Reese motioned her to her chair and then waited until she had complied. "Did you know that old Willoughby has decided to resign?"

"No. No, I didn't, actually." She felt some hurt that Reese had been told of the decision before she was.

"He's giving health as a reason, but I think the old goat just can't cut it anymore. Never could, really."

Sheila shot him a look warning against any further deprecation of the man she had worked under for fifteen years. "That's too bad," she murmured.

"Yeah? Well, baby, hang onto your seat. You don't know what bad is. For his successor, your Willoughby wants to recommend one K. Bennett, MD."

Sheila fought a sudden urge to be sick. For years she had, in effect, run the pathology department, using Willoughby for little more than his signature on purchase orders and personnel decisions. With Bennett as chief, she would be lucky to keep her job, much less her power and influence. "You said *wants* to recommend," she managed.

"Bennett refuses to give him the go-ahead until she's talked it over with her husband."

She picked a tiny Smurf doctor doll off her desk and absently twisted its arm. "How do you feel about it?" she asked.

"After what she did last year, writing what amounted to a letter of complaint about me to the board? How do you *think* I feel?"

"So?" The blue rubber arm snapped off in Sheila's hand.

"I won't have that woman heading a department in my hospital, and that's that."

"What can you do?"

The forcefulness in Reese's voice softened. "There, at least for the moment, is the rub. I've started talking to some of the members of the board of trustees and some of the department heads. It turns out that as things stand, she would have no trouble getting approval. It seems only a few beside me—" he smiled conspiratorially, "and now you— know what an incredible pain in the ass she is."

Sheila flipped the arm and then the body of the doll into the trash. "So we both know," she said.

"Baby, I need something on her. Anything that I can use to influence some people. The prospect of dealing with Bennett's crusades month after month is more than I can take. Keep your eyes and ears open. Dig around. There's got to be something."

"If I do find something," Sheila said, "I'll expect you to be grateful."

"I'll be very grateful."

"Good," Sheila said sweetly. "Then we shall see what we shall see." She rose and kissed him on the forehead, her breasts inches from his eyes. "Very grateful," she whispered. "Now don't you forget that." She backed away at the moment Reese reached for her. "Next time, Norty. Right now I've got work to do."

The Braxton Building was more impressive as an address than it was as a structure. At one time, the twenty-eight story granite obelisk had been the centerpiece of Boston's downtown financial district. Now, surrounded by high-rise glass and steel, the building seemed somehow ill at ease. No uninformed passerby could possibly have predicted from the building's exterior the opulence of the lobby and office suites within, especially the grandeur of the twenty-eighth floor, most elegant of the three floors occupied by the law firm of Minton/Samuels.

J. Winfield Samuels selected a Havana-made panatella from a crystal humidor and offered it to his son. Jared, seated to one side of the huge, inlaid Louis Quatorze desk, groaned. "Dad, it's not even eleven o'clock. Didn't Dr. What's-his-face limit the number you're supposed to smoke in a day?"

"I pay Shrigley to fix me up so I can do whatever the hell I want to do, not to tell me how many cigars I can smoke." He snipped the tip with a bone-handled trimmer and lit it from the smokestack of a sterling silver replica of the QE II. "I swear, if Castro had found a way to keep these little beauties from making it to the States, I would have found a way to cancel the bastard's ticket years ago. Think of it. We'd probably have world peace by now because of a cigar." He took a long, loving draw, blew half of it out, inhaled the rest, and gazed out the floor-to-ceiling window at the harbor and the airport beyond.

Jared sipped at his mug of coffee and risked a glance at his watch. Win Samuels had summoned him and Win Samuels would tell him why when Win Samuels was good and ready to do so. That was the way it had always been between them and, for all Jared knew, that was the way Jared Winfield Samuels, Sr. had related to Win. The notion left a bitter aftertaste. Beyond his grandfather, the family had been traced through a dozen or more generations, three centuries, and three continents. Not that he really cared about such things. His years of rebellion in Vermont had certainly demonstrated that. But now, with the possibility that he represented the end of the line he was . . . more aware.

"So, how's Kate?" The older Samuels was still looking out the window when he spoke.

"She's okay. A little harried at work, but okay." It was unwise, Jared had learned over the years, to offer his father any more information than asked for. At seventy, the man was still as sharp as anyone in the game. What he wanted to know, he would ask.

"And how are the negotiations coming with the union people at Granfield?"

"Fine. Almost over, I think. We're meeting with them this afternoon. If that idiot shop steward can understand the pension package we've put together, the whole mess should get resolved with no more work stoppage."

"I knew you could do it. I told Toby Granfield you could do it."

"Well, like I said, it's not over yet."

"But it will be." The words were an order, not a question.

"Yes," Jared said. "It will be."

"Excellent, excellent. How about a little vacation for you and Kate when everything is signed and sealed. Goodness knows you deserve it. Those union thugs are slow, but they're tough. Bert Hodges says his place in Aruba is available the week after next. Suppose we book it for you."

"I don't . . . what I mean is I'll have to talk with Kate. She's got quite a bit going on at the hospital."

"I know." Win Samuels swung around slowly to face his son. At six feet, he was nearly as tall as Jared and no more than five pounds heavier. His rimless spectacles and discreetly darkened hair neutralized the aging effects of deep crow's feet and a slightly sallow complexion.

"What?"

"I said that I knew she was having a busy time of it at the hospital." Samuels paused, perhaps for dramatic effect. "Norton Reese called me this morning."

"Oh?" The statement was upsetting. For five years, Jared had handled all of Boston Metro's legal affairs. There was no reason for Norton Reese to be dealing directly with his father, even allowing that the two of them had known each other for years.

"He tells me the head of pathology is retiring." Jared nodded that the information was not news. "He also said that this head pathologist, Willoughby, wants Kate to take over for him."

"She mentioned that to me," Jared understated.

"Did she now? Good. I'm glad you two communicate about such minor goings on." The facetiousness in Samuels's voice was hardly subtle.

Kate's independence had been a source of discussion between them on more than one occasion. Somewhere in the drawer of that Louis Quatorze desk was a computer printout showing that while he had received forty-nine percent of the total vote cast in the congressional race, he had garnered only forty-two percent of the women's vote. To Win Samuels, the numbers meant that if Mrs. Jared Samuels had been out stumping for her husband instead of mucking about elbow deep in a bunch of cadavers, Jared would be packing to leave for Washington. Self-serving, contrary, disloyal, thoughtless—the adjectives had, from time to time, flown hot and heavy from the old man, though never in Kate's presence. Toward her, he had always been as cordial and charming as could be.

"Look, Dad," Jared said, "I've still got some preparation to do for that session at Granfield. Do you think . . ."

"Donna," Samuels said through the intercom, "could you bring in another tea for me and another coffee for my son, please?"

Jared sank back in his seat and stared helplessly at the far wall, a wall covered with photographs of politicians, athletes and other celebrities, arm in arm or hand in hand with his father. A few of them were similar shots featuring his grandfather, and one of them was an eight by ten of Jared and the President, taken at a three-minute meeting arranged by his father for just that purpose.

With a discreet knock, Samuels's sensuous receptionist entered and set their beverages and a basket of croissants on a mahogany stand near the desk. Her smile in response to Jared's "Thank you" was vacant—a subtle message that her allegiance was to the man on the power side of the Louis Quatorze.

"So," Samuels said, settling down with a mug of tea in one hand and his Havana in the other, "what do you think of this business at Metro?"

"I haven't given it much thought," Jared lied. "As far as I know, nothing formal has been done yet."

"Well, I'd suggest you start thinking about it."

"What?"

"Norton Reese doesn't want Kate to have that position and, frankly, neither do I. He thinks she's too young and too inexperienced. He tells me that if she gets the appointment, which incidentally is doubtful anyhow, she'll run herself ragged, burn out, and finally get chewed to ribbons by the politicians and the other department heads. According to him, Kate just doesn't understand the way the game is played—that there are some toes that are simply not to be stepped on."

"Like his," Jared snapped.

"Jared, you told me that the two of you were planning on starting your family. Does Kate think she can do that and run a department, too? What about her obligation to you and your career? It's bad enough she's married to you and doesn't even have your name. Christ, her looks alone would be worth thousands of votes to you if she'd just plunk her face in front of a camera a few times. Add a little baby to that, and I swear you could make a run for the Senate and win."

"Kate's business is Kate's business," Jared said with neither enthusiasm nor conviction.

"Take her to the Caribbean. Have a talk with her," Samuels reasoned calmly. "Help her see that marriage is a series of . . . compromises. Give and take."

"Okay, I'll try."

"Good. Kate should see where her obligations and her loyalties lie. Ross Mattingly may be on a downhill slide, but he still managed to hang on and win the election. Don't think he's going to roll over and play dead next time. The fewer liabilities we have the better. And frankly, the way things stand, Kate is a minus. Have I made my thoughts clear?"

"Clear." Jared felt totally depleted.

"Fine. Let me know when the Granfield business is done, and also let me know the date you two decide on, so I can tell Bert Hodges." With a nod, Winfield Samuels signaled the meeting over.

In his sea-green scrub suit and knee-length white coat, Tom Engleson might have been the earnest young resident on a daytime soap opera, loving his way through the nurses one moment, stamping out disease the next. But his eyes gave him away. Kate saw the immense fatigue in them the moment she entered the resident's office on the fourth floor of the building renovated by the Ashburton Foundation and renamed in memory of Sylvia Ashburton. It was a fatigue that went deeper than the circles of gray enveloping them, deeper than the fine streaks of red throughout their sclerae.

"Been to sleep at all?" Kate asked, glancing at the clock as she set two tinfoil pans of salad on the coffee table. It was twenty minutes of two.

Engleson merely shook his head and began to work off the plastic cover of his salad with a dexterity that was obviously far from what it had been when he had started his shift thirty and a half hours before. Studying the man's face, Kate wondered how residency programs could justify the ridiculous hours they required, especially of surgical trainees. It was as if one generation of doctors was saying to the next, "We had to do it this way and we came out all right, didn't we?" Meanwhile, year after year, a cardiogram was misread here, an operation fumbled there; never a rash of problems, just isolated incidents at one hospital then another, one program then another—incidents of no lasting consequence, except, of course, to the patients and families involved.

"I hope you like blue cheese," Kate said. "Gianetti's has great vinaigrette, too. I just guessed."

"It's fine, perfect, Dr. Samuels," Engleson said between bites. "I've missed a meal or two since this Vitale thing started yesterday morning."

"Eat away. You can have some of mine if you want. I'm not too hungry. And it's 'Kate.' We pathologists have a little trouble with formality."

Engleson, his mouth engaged with another forkful of salad, nodded his acknowledgment.

"Sorry I missed you when I was here last evening. The nurse said you were in the delivery room."

"A set of twins."

"How's Beverly Vitale?"

"Her blood count's down this morning. Twenty-five. She's due for a recheck in an hour or two. Any further drop, and we'll give her more blood."

"Her GI tract?" Kate asked, speculating on the site of blood loss.

"Probably. There's been some blood in every stool we've checked. She's on steroids, you know."

"I do know. Withhold steroids, and her antibodies run wild, destroying her own clotting factors; use them, and she risks developing bleeding ulcers. It's one of those situations that makes me grateful I decided on pathology. Stan Willoughby and I reviewed the ovary sections this morning. His impression is that the findings are unique. He's doing some special stains now and has sent slides to a colleague of his at Johns Hopkins, whom he says is as good as anyone in the business at diagnosing ovarian disorders. He also is calling around town to see if anything like this has turned up in another department."

"Etiology?"

"No clues, Tom. Virus, toxin, med reaction. All of the above, none of the above, A and B but not C. She told you she wasn't on any meds, right?"

"None except vitamins. The multivitamin plus iron we dispense through the Omnicenter."

"Well I'm living proof those don't cause any problems. I've taken them for a couple of years. Make frail pathologist strong like bull." Kate flexed her biceps.

"Make pathologist excellent teacher, too."

"Why, thank you." Kate's green eyes sparkled. "Thank you very much, Tom." For a moment, she saw him blush. "How about we go say hello to Beverly. I'd like to make extra sure about one or two aspects of her history. Here, you can stick this salad in that refrigerator for later."

"Provided the bacteria who call that icebox home don't eat it first," Tom said.

The two were heading down the hall toward the stairway when the overhead page snapped to life. "Code ninety-nine, Ashburton five-oh-two; code ninety-nine, Ashburton five-oh-two."

"Oh, Jesus." Tom was already racing toward the exit as he spoke. Kate was slower to react. She was almost to the stairway door before she realized that Ashburton 502 was Beverly Vitale's room.

It had been a year, perhaps two, since Kate had last observed a cardiac arrest and resuscitation attempt. She was certified in advanced cardiac life support, but training and testing then had been on Resusci-Annie, a mannequin. Her practical experience had ended years ago, along with her internship. At the moment, however, none of those considerations mattered. What mattered was the life of a young woman who loved to make music. With an athlete's quickness, Kate bolted after Tom Engleson up the stairs from Ashburton Four to Ashburton Five.

There were more than enough participants in the code. Residents, nurses, medical students, and technicians filled room 502 and overflowed into the hall. Kate worked her way to a spot by the door, from which she watched the nightmare of Beverly Vitale's final minutes of life.

It was a gastric hemorrhage, almost certainly from an ulcer eroding into an artery. The woman's relentless exsanguination was being complicated by the aspiration of vomited blood. Cloaked in abysmal helplessness, Kate witnessed Tom Engleson, desperation etched on his face, issuing orders in a deceptively composed tone; the organized chaos of the white-clad code team, pumping, injecting, monitoring, reporting, respirating, suctioning; and through the milling bodies, the expressionless, blood-smeared face of Beverly Vitale.

For nearly an hour the struggle continued, though there was never a pulse or even an encouraging electrocardiographic pattern. In the end, there was nothing but another lesson in the relative impotence of people and medicine when matched against the capriciousness of illness and death. Tom Engleson, his eyes dark and sunken, shook his head in utter futility.

"It's over," he said softly. "Thank you all. It's over."

CHAPTER 3
Tuesday 11 December

SIMULTANEOUSLY WITH hearing the report from the WEEI traffic helicopter of a monumental backup stemming from the Mystic/Tobin Bridge, Kate became part of it. Commuting to the city from the North Shore was an experience that she suspected ranked in pleasantness somewhere between an IRS audit and root canal work. Although Tuesday was normally a low-volume day, this morning she had encountered rain, sleet, snow, and even a bizarre stretch of sunlight during her thirty-mile drive, far too much weather for even Boston drivers to attack. With a groan, she resigned herself to being half an hour late, perhaps more, for the appointment Stan Willoughby had arranged for her at White Memorial Hospital.

The pathology chief's call had punctuated another confusing, bittersweet morning with Jared. It seemed as if the intensity and caring in their relationship was waxing and waning not only from day to day but from hour to hour or even from minute to minute. In one sentence the man was Jared Samuels, the funny, sensitive, often ingenuous fellow she had married and still loved deeply; in the next he was calculating and distant, a miniature of his father, intransigent on points they should have been working through as husband and wife. At last, after an awkward hour of lighting brush fires of dissension and then scurrying to stamp them out, Jared had suggested a week or ten days together in Aruba, away from the pressures and demands of their careers.

"What do you say, Boots?" he had asked, calling on the pet name she favored most of the four or five he used. "Aruba you all over." The expression in his eyes—urgency? fear?—belied his levity.

"Aruba you too, Jared," she had said finally.

"Then we go?"

"If Stan can give me the time off, and if you can stand the thought of trying to hang onto a woman swathed in Coppertone, we go."

At that moment, Jared looked reborn.

"Grumper-to-grumper, stall-and-crawl traffic headed in a snail trail toward the bridge, thanks to a fender bender in the left-hand lane." The Eye-in-the-Sky was sparing none of his clichés in describing the mess on Route 1 south. Kate inched her Volvo between cars, but gained little ground. Finally, resigned to the situation, she settled back, turned up the volume on the all-news station, and concentrated on ignoring the would-be Lothario who was winking and waving at her from the Trans-Am in the next lane.

The news, like Stan Willoughby's call, dealt with the sudden death of Red Sox hero Bobby Geary, a homegrown boy who had played his sandlot ball in South Boston, not a mile from the luxurious condominium where he was found by his mother following an apparent heart attack. Stan's name was mentioned several times as the medical examiner assigned to autopsy the man who had given away thousands of free tickets and had added an entire floor to Children's and Infants' Hospital in the name of "the kids of Boston."

"Kate," Willoughby had begun, "I hope I'm not interrupting anything."

"No, no. Just getting ready for work," she had said, smiling at Jared, who was nude by the bathroom door dancing a coarse hula and beckoning her to the shower with a long-handled scrub brush.

"Well, I don't want you to come to work."

"What?"

"I want you to go to White Memorial. You have an appointment in the pathology department there at eight-thirty. Leon Olesky will be waiting for you. Do you know him?"

"Only by name."

"Well, I called around town trying to see if anyone had seen a case similar to our Miss Vitale's. Initially there was nothing, but late last night Leon called me at home. From what he described, the two cases —his and ours—sound identical. I told him you'd be over to study his material."

"How old was the woman?" Kate had asked excitedly.

"I don't remember what he said. Twenty-eight, I think."

"Cause of death?"

"Ah ha! I thought you'd never ask. Cerebral hemorrhage, second-ary to minor head trauma."

"Platelets? Fibrinogen?" Her hand was white around the receiver.

"Leon didn't know. The case was handled by one of his underlings. He said he'd try to find out by the time you got there."

"Can't you come?"

"Hell, no. Haven't you heard the news about Bobby Geary?"

"The ball player?"

"Heart attack late last night. Found dead in bed. I'm posting him at ten-thirty. In fact, I'd like you back here before I finish, just in case I need your help."

"You've got it. You know, you are a pretty terrific chief, Stanley. Are you sure you want to retire?"

"Yesterday, if I could arrange it, Katey-girl. You hurry on back to Metro after you see Olesky, now. No telling what this shriveled brain of mine might miss."

White Memorial Hospital, an architectural polyglot of more than a score of buildings, was the flagship of the fleet of Harvard Medical School affiliated hospitals. Overlooking the Charles River near the North End, WMH had more research facilities, professors, grants, and administrative expertise than any hospital in the area, if not the world. Metropolitan Hospital had once held sway, reportedly supplying ninety percent of all the professors of medicine at all the medical schools in the country, but that time had long since been buried beneath an avalanche of incompetent administrators, unfavorable publicity, and corrupt city politicians. Although Metro had made a resurgence of sorts under the guidance of Norton Reese, there was little likelihood of its ever recapturing the prestige, endowments, and fierce patient loyalty of the glory days, when at least one man was known to have had "Take Me To Metro" tattooed across his chest.

It had been some time since Kate had had reason to visit the pathology unit at White Memorial, and she was uncomfortably impressed with the improvements and expansion that had occurred. Equipment her department congratulated itself on acquiring, this unit possessed in duplicate or triplicate. Corridors and offices were brightly lit, with plants, paintings, and other touches that made the work environment less tedious and oppressive. Almost subconsciously, Kate found herself making mental lists of things she would press to accomplish as chief of pathology at Metro.

Leon Olesky, a mild, Lincolnesque man, brushed off her apologies for her tardiness and after exchanging compliments about Stan Wil-loughby, left her alone in his office with the material from the autopsy of Ginger Rittenhouse. On a pink piece of paper by his elegant microscope were the data on the woman's blood studies. Only two of many parameters measured were abnormal: fibrinogen and platelets. The levels of each were depressed enough to have been life threatening. Her hands trembling with anticipation, Kate took the first of the ovarian sections and slid it onto the stage of the microscope. A moment to flex tension from the muscles in her neck, and she leaned forward to begin another journey through the yellow-white light.

Forty-five minutes later, the one had become three. Leon Olesky hunched over one set of oculars of the teaching microscope, controlling the focus with his right hand and moving the slide with his left. Across from him, in the seat Kate had occupied, was Tom Engleson.

"You know," Olesky said, "if Stan hadn't called me about your case, the findings on our young woman would have slipped right past us. I mentioned the matter last night at our weekly department conference, but no one responded. An hour later, Dr. Hickman came to my office. Young Bruce is, perhaps, the brightest of our residents, but at times, I'm afraid, a bit too quick for his own good."

Kate sighed. Olesky's observations described many of the so-called hotshot residents she had worked with over the years. "I'll take methodical over genius any day of the week," she said.

"Both is best," Olesky responded, "but that's a rare combination, indeed. I might mention, though, that it is a combination your mentor feels he is lucky to have found in you."

"Methodical, yes," Kate allowed, "but I've yet to receive a single membership application from Mensa."

"She's only the best in the hospital," Tom interjected somewhat impetuously.

"Finish telling us about your resident." Kate withheld reaction to Engleson's enthusiasm, sensing that what she felt was, in equal parts, flattered and embarrassed.

"Well, it seems our Dr. Hickman was uncertain about the pathology he was seeing in this woman's ovaries. However, rather than think that the finding might be unique, he assumed, although he won't say so in as many words, that the condition was one he should have known about, and hence one he would look foolish asking for help with. Since the cause of death was unrelated to the ovaries, he chose to describe his findings in the autopsy report and leave it at that."

"No harm done," Kate said.

"Quite the contrary, in fact. This event may be the pinprick Hickman's ego needs so he can reach his full potential as a physician. It will make even more of an impression if, as Dr. Willoughby and now yours truly, suspect, this pathology turns out to be one never before described."

Kate and Tom exchanged excited glances. "How would you explain its showing up in two women in the same city at about the same time?" she asked.

The professor's eyes, dark and deeply serious, met first Engleson's and then Kate's. "Considering the outcome of the illness in both individuals, I would suggest that we work diligently to find an answer to that question. At the moment, I have none."

"There must be a connection," Engleson said.

"I hope there is, young man." Olesky rose from his stool. "And I hope the two of you will be able to find it. I have a class to teach right now at the medical school. This evening, I leave for meetings in San Diego, and from there, I go to the wedding of my son in New Mexico. My office and our department are at your disposal."

"Thank you," they said.

Olesky replaced his lab coat with a well-worn mackintosh. He shook hands first with Engleson and then with Kate. A final check of his desk and he shambled from the office.

Kate waited for the door to click shut. "I'm glad you were able to get here so quickly," she said. "Did you have any trouble getting the records people to let you take Beverly's chart out of the hospital?"

"None. I just followed Engleson's first law of chutzpah. The more one looks like he should be doing what he's doing, the less anyone realizes that he shouldn't. I'll have to admit that the crooks with moving vans and uniforms who pick entire houses clean thought of the law before I did, but I was the first one I know to put it in words. Are you okay? I went to find you after the code was over yesterday, but you were gone. Before I could call, I was rushed to the OR to do an emergency C-section."

"I was okay." She paused. "Actually, I wasn't. It hurt like hell to see her lying there like that. I can't remember the last time I felt so helpless." At the thought, the mention of the word, Arthur Everett's grotesque face flashed in her mind, his reddened eyes bulging with the effort of forcing himself inside her. Yes, I do, she thought. I do remember when. "How about you?" she asked.

Engleson shrugged. "I think I'm still numb. It's like I'm afraid that if I let down and acknowledge my feelings about her and what happened, I'll never set foot in a hospital again."

Kate nodded her understanding. "You know, Tom, contrary to popular belief, being human doesn't disqualify you from being a doctor. Are you married?" Engleson shook his head. "I think it's hard to face some of the things we have to face and then have no one to talk them out with, to cry on, if necessary, when we get home." She thought about the difficult morning with Jared and smiled inwardly at the irony of her words. "Had you known Beverly outside the hospital?"

"No. I met her when she came into Metro. But I thought about trying to start up a relationship as soon as she . . ." His voice grew husky. He cleared his throat.

"I understand," Kate said. "Look, maybe we can talk about our work and our lives in medicine some day soon. Right now, we've got to

283

start looking for some common threads between these women. I'm due back at Metro in," she checked her watch, "—shoot, I've only got about twenty minutes."

Tom was thumbing through the thin sheaf of papers dealing with Ginger Rittenhouse. "It shouldn't take long to check. They have next to no information here. Ginger Louise Rittenhouse, twenty-eight, elementary school teacher, lived and worked in Cambridge, but she was running along the Boston side of the river when she collapsed. Apparently she lived long enough to get an emergency CAT scan, but not long enough to get to the OR."

"Married?" Kate asked.

"No. Single. That's the second time you've asked that question about someone in the last two minutes." He narrowed one eye and fingered his moustache. "You have, perhaps, a marriage fixation?"

Kate smiled. "Let's leave my fixations out of this. At least for the time being, okay? What about family? Place of birth? Next of kin? Did they document any prior medical history?"

"Hey, slow down. We obstetricians are hardly famous for our swift reading ability. No known medical history. Next of kin is a brother in Seattle. Here's his address. You know, world's greatest hospital or not, they take a pretty skimpy history."

"It doesn't look like they had time for much more," Kate said solemnly. There had to be a connection, she was thinking. The two cases were at once too remarkable and too similar. Somewhere, the lives of a teacher from Cambridge and a cellist from a suburb on the far side of Boston had crossed.

"Wait," Engleson said. "She had a roommate. It says here on the accident floor sheet. Sandra Tucker. That must be how they found out about her family."

Kate again checked her watch. "Tom, I've got to go. I promised Dr. Willoughby I'd help out with the post on Bobby Geary. Do you think you could try and get a hold of this Sandra Tucker? See if our woman has seen a doctor recently or had a blood test. Don't teachers need yearly physicals or something?"

"Not the ones I had. I think their average age was deceased."

"Are you going to call from here?" Engleson thought for a moment and then nodded. "Fine, give me a ring when you get back to Metro. And Tom? Thanks for the compliment you paid me before." She reached out and shook his hand, firmly and in a businesslike manner. Then she left.

With the pistol-shot crack of bat against ball, thirty thousand heads snapped in horror toward the fence in right center field.

"Jesus, Katey, it's gone," was all Jared could say.

The ball, a white star, arced into the blue-black summer night sky.

On the base paths, four runners dashed around toward home. There were two out in the inning, the ninth inning. The scoreboard at the base of the leftfield wall in Fenway Park said that the Red Sox were ahead of the Yankees by three runs, but that lead, it appeared, had only seconds more to be.

Kate, enthralled by the lights and the colors and the precision of her first live baseball game, stood frozen with the rest, her eyes fixed on the ball, now in a lazy descent toward a spot beyond the fence. Then into the corner of her field of vision he came, running with an antelope grace that made his movements seem almost slow motion. He left the ground an improbable distance from the fence, his gloved left hand reaching, it seemed, beyond its limits, up to the top of the barrier and over it. For an instant, ball and glove disappeared beyond the fence. In the next instant, they were together, clutched to the chest of Bobby Geary as he tumbled down onto the dirt warning track to the roar of thirty thousand voices. It was a moment Kate would remember for the rest of her life.

This, too, was such a moment.

The body that had once held the spirit and abilities of Bobby Geary lay on the steel table before her, stripped of the indefinable force that had allowed it to sense and react so remarkably. To one side, in a shallow metal pan, was the athlete's heart, carefully sliced along several planes to expose the muscle of the two ventricles—the pumping chambers—and the three main coronary arteries—left, right, and circumflex. Images of that night at Fenway more than four years ago intruded on Kate's objectivity and brought with them a wistfulness that she knew had no place in this facet of her work.

"Nothing in the heart at all?" she asked for the second time.

Stan Willoughby, leprechaunish in green scrubs and a black rubber apron, shook his head. "Must a' bin somethin' he et," he said, by way of admitting that, anatomically at least, he had uncovered no explanation for the pulmonary edema, fluid that had filled Bobby Geary's lungs and, essentially, drowned him from within.

Kate, clad identically to her chief, examined the heart under a high-intensity light. "Teenage heart in a thirty-six-year-old man. I remember reading somewhere that he intended to keep playing until he was fifty. This heart says he might have made it."

"This edema says 'no way,' " Willoughby corrected. "I'm inclined to think dysrhythmia and cardiac arrest on that basis. Preliminary blood tests are all normal, so I think it possible we may never know the specific cause." There was disappointment in his voice.

"Sometimes we just don't," Kate said. The words were Willoughby's, a lesson he had repeated many times to her over the years.

Willoughby glared at her for a moment; then he laughed out loud. "You are a saucy pup, flipping my words back at me like that. Suppose you tell me what to say to the police lieutenant drinking coffee and dropping donut crumbs right now in my office, or to the gaggle of reporters in the lobby waiting for the ultimate word. Ladies and gentlemen, the ultimate word from the crack pathology department you help support with your taxes is that we are absolutely certain we have no idea why Bobby Geary went into a pulmonary edema and died."

Kate did not answer. She had grabbed a magnifying glass and was intently examining Geary's feet, especially between his toes and along the inside of his ankles. "Stan, look," she said. "All along here. Tiny puncture marks, almost invisible. There must be a dozen of them. No, wait, there are more."

Willoughby adjusted the light and took the magnifier from her. "Holy potato," he said softly. "Bobby Geary an addict?" He stepped back from the table and looked at Kate, who could only shrug. "If he was, he was a bloomin' artist with a needle."

"A twenty-seven or twenty-nine gauge would make punctures about that size."

"And a narcotics or amphetamine overdose would explain the pulmonary edema." Kate nodded. "Holy potato," Willoughby said again. "If it's true, there must be evidence somewhere in his house."

"Unless it happened with other people around and they brought him home and put him to bed. Why don't we send some blood for a drug screen and do levels on any substance we pick up?"

Willoughby glanced around the autopsy suite. The single technician on duty was too far away to have heard any of their conversation. "What do you say we label the tube 'Smith' or 'Schultz' or something. I'm no sports fan, but I know enough to see what's at stake here. The man was a hero."

"What about the policeman?"

"His name's Detective Finn, and he *is* a fan. I think he'd prefer some kind of story about a heart attack, even if the blood test is positive."

"Schultz sounds like as good a name as any," Kate said. "Are these the tubes? Good. I'll have new labels made up."

"I'll send Finn over to the boy's place, and then I'll tell the newsnoses they will just have to wait until the microscopics are processed. Now, when can you give me a report on the goings on at the WMH?"

"Well, beyond what I've already told you, there's not much to report. We've got some sort of ovarian microsclerosis in two women with profound deficiencies of both platelets and fibrinogen. At this point, we have no connections between the two, nothing even to tell us for sure that the ovarian and blood problems are related."

"So what's next?"

"Next? Well, Tom Engleson, the resident who was involved with Beverly Vitale, is trying to get some information from the roommate of the WMH woman."

"And thou?"

Kate held her hands to either side, palms up. "No plan. I'm on surgicals this month, so I've got a few of those to read along with a frozen or two from the OR. After that I thought I'd talk to my friend Marco Sebastian and see if that computer of his can locate data on a woman named Ginger Rittenhouse."

"Sounds good," Willoughby said. "Keep me posted." He seemed reluctant to leave.

"Is there anything else?" Kate asked finally.

"Well, actually there is one small matter."

"All right, let me have it." Kate knew what was coming.

"I . . . um . . . have a meeting scheduled with Norton Reese this afternoon. Several members of the search committee are supposed to be there and well . . . I sort of wondered if you'd had time to . . ." Willoughby allowed the rest of the thought to remain unspoken.

Kate's eyes narrowed. He had promised her a week, and it had been only a few days. She wasn't at all ready to answer. There were other factors to consider besides merely "want to" or "don't want to." Willoughby had to understand that. "I've decided that if you really think I can do it, and you can get all those who have to agree to do so, then I'll take the position," she heard her voice say.

The girl's name was Robyn Smithers. She was a high school junior, assigned by Roxbury Vocational to spend four hours each week working as an extern in the pathology department of Metropolitan Hospital. Her role was simply defined: do what she was told, and ask questions only when it was absolutely clear that she was interrupting no one. She was one of twelve such students negotiated for by Norton Reese and paid for by the Boston School Department. That these students learned little except how to run errands was of no concern to Reese, who had already purchased a new word processor for his office with the receipts from having them.

Robyn had made several passes by Sheila Pierce's open door before she stopped and knocked.

"Yes, Robyn, what can I do for you?"

"Miss Pierce, I'm sorry for botherin' you. Really I am."

"It's fine, Robyn. I was beginning to wonder what you were up to walking back and forth out there."

"Well, ma'am, it's this blood. Doctor Bennett, you know, the lady doctor?"

"Yes, I know. What about her?"

"Well, Dr. Bennett gave me this here blood to take to . . ." she consulted a scrap of paper, "Special Chemistries, only I can't find where that is. I'm sorry to bother you while you're working and all."

"Nonsense, child. Here, let me see what you've got."

Casually, Sheila glanced at the pale blue requisition form. The patient's name, John Schultz, meant nothing to her. That in itself was unusual. She made it her business to know the names of all those being autopsied in her department. However, she acknowledged, occasionally one was scheduled without her being notified. In the space marked "Patient's Hospital Number" the department's billing number was written. The request was for a screen for drugs of abuse. Penned along the margin of the requisition was the order, "STAT: Phone results to Dr. K. Bennett ASAP."

"Curiouser and curiouser," Sheila muttered.

"Pardon, ma'am?"

"Oh, nothing, dear. Listen, you've been turning the wrong way at that corridor back there. Come, I'll show you." She handed back the vials and the requisition and then guided the girl to the door of her office. "There," she said sweetly. "Just turn right there and go all the way down until you see a cloudy-glass door like mine with Special Chemistries written on it. Okay?"

"Yes. Thank you, ma'am." Robyn Smithers raced down the corridor.

"Glad to help . . . you dumb little shit."

Sheila listened until she heard the door to Special Chemistries open and close; then she went to her phone and dialed the cubicle of Marvin Grimes. Grimes was the department's deiner, the preparer of bodies for autopsy. It was a position he had held for as long as anyone could remember.

"Marvin," Sheila asked, "could you tell me the names of the cases we autopsied today?"

"Jes' two, Ms. Pierce. The old lady Partridge 'n' the ball player."

"No one named Schultz?" Sheila pictured the bottle of Wild Irish Rose Grimes kept in the lower right-hand drawer of his desk; she wondered if by the end of the day the old man would even remember talking to her.

"No siree. No Schultz today."

"Yesterday?"

"Wait, now. Let me check. Nope, only McDonald, Lacey, Briggs, and Ca . . . Capez . . . Capezio. No one named . . . what did you say the name was?"

"Never mind, Marvin. Don't worry about it."

As she replaced the receiver, Sheila tried to estimate the time it would take the technicians in Special Chemistries to complete a stat screen for drugs of abuse.

"Curiouser and curiouser and curiouser," she said.

The dozen or so buildings at Metropolitan Hospital were connected by a series of tunnels, so tortuous and poorly lit that the hospital had recommended that its employees avoid them if walking alone. Several assaults and the crash of a laundry train into a patient's stretcher only enhanced the grisly reputation of the tunnel, as did the now classic Harvard Medical School senior show, *Rats*. Kate, unmindful of the legends and tales, had used the tunnels freely since her medical student days, and except for once coming upon the hours-old corpse of a drunk, nestled peacefully in a small concrete alcove by his half-empty bottle of Thunderbird, she had encountered little to add to the lore. The single greatest threat she faced each time she traveled underground from one building to another was that of getting lost by forgetting a twist or a turn or by missing the crack shaped like Italy that signaled to her the turnoff to the administration building. At various times over the years, she had headed for the surgical building and ended up in the massive boiler room, or headed for a conference in the amphitheater, only to dead end at the huge steam pressers of the laundry building.

Concentrating on not overlooking the landmarks and grime-dimmed signs, Kate made her way through the beige-painted maze toward the computer suite and Marco Sebastian. Nurses in twos and threes passed by in each direction, heralding the approach of the three o'clock change in shift. Kate wondered how many thousands of nurses had over the years walked these tunnels on the way to their charges. The Metro tradition: nurses, professors of surgery, medical school deans, country practitioners, even Nobel laureates. Now, in her own way and through her own abilities, she was becoming part of that tradition. Jared had to know how important that was to her. She had shared with him the ugly secrets of her prior marriage and stifling, often futile life. Surely he knew what all this meant.

In typically efficient Metro fashion, the computer facilities were situated on the top floor of the pediatrics building, as far as possible from the administrative offices that used them the most. Kate paused by the elevator and thought about tackling the six flights of stairs instead. The day, not yet nearly over, had her feeling at once exhausted and exhilarated. Three difficult surgical cases had followed the Geary autopsy. Just as she was completing the last of them, a Special Chemistries technician had dropped off the results of Geary's blood test. The amphetamine level in his body was enormous, quite enough to have thrown him into pulmonary edema. Before she could call Stan Willoughby with the results, she was summoned to his office. The meeting there, with Willoughby and the detective, Martin Finn, had been brief. Evidence found on a careful search of Bobby Geary's condominium had yielded strong evidence that the man was a heavy amphetamine user. It was information known only to the three of them. Finn was adamant—barring any findings suggesting that Geary's death was not an accidental overdose, there seemed little to be gained and much to be lost by making the revelation public. The official story would be of a heart attack, secondary to an anomaly of one coronary artery.

The elevator arrived at the moment Kate had decided on the stairs.

She changed her mind in time to slip between the closing doors. Marco Sebastian, expansive in his white lab coat and as jovial as ever, met her with a bear hug. She had been a favorite of his since their first meeting, nearly seven years before. In fact, he and his wife had once made a concerted effort to fix her up with his brother-in-law, a caterer from East Boston. After a rapid-fire series of questions to bring himself up to date on Jared, the job, Willoughby, and the results of their collaborative study, the engineer led her into his office and sat her down next to him, facing the terminal display screen on his desk.

"Now then, Dr. Bennett," he said in a voice with the deep smoothness of an operatic baritone, "what tidbits can I resurrect for you this time from the depths of our electronic jungle? Do you wish the hat size of our first chief of medicine? We have it. The number of syringes syringed in the last calendar year? Can do. The number of warts on the derriere of our esteemed administrator? You have merely to ask."

"Actually, Marco, I wasn't after anything nearly so exotic. Just a name."

"The first baby born here was . . ." He punched a set of keys and then another. ". . . Jessica Peerless, February eighteenth, eighteen forty-three."

"Marco, that wasn't the name I had in mind."

"How about the two hundredth appendectomy?"

"Nope."

"The twenty-eight past directors of nursing?"

"Uh-uh. I'm sorry, Marco."

"All this data, and nobody wants any of it." The man was genuinely crestfallen. "I keep telling our beloved administrator that we are being underused, but I don't think he has the imagination to know what questions to ask. Periodically, I send him tables showing that the cafeteria is overspending on pasta or that ten percent of our patients have ninety percent of our serious diseases, just to pique his interest, remind him that we're still here."

"My name?"

"Oh, yes. I'm sorry. It's been a little slow here. I guess you can tell that."

"It's Rittenhouse, Ginger Rittenhouse. Here's her address, birthplace, and birthdate. That's all I have. I need to know if she's ever been a patient of this hospital, in or out."

"Keep your eyes on the screen," Sebastian said dramatically. Thirty seconds later, he shook his head. "Nada. A Shirley Rittenhouse in nineteen fifty-six, but no others."

"Are you sure?"

Sebastian gave her a look that might have been anticipated from a judge who had been asked, "Do you really think your decision is fair?"

"Sorry," she said.

"Of course, she still could have been a patient of the Omnicenter."

Kate stiffened. "What do you mean?"

"Well, the Omnicenter is sort of a separate entity from the rest of Metro. This system here handles records and billing for the Ashburton inpatient service, but the Omnicenter is totally self-contained. Has been since the day they put the units in—what is it?—nine, ten years ago."

"Isn't that strange?"

"Strange is normal around this place," Sebastian said.

"Can't you even plug this system into the one over there?"

"Nope. Don't know the access codes. Carl Horner, the engineer who runs the electronics there, plays things pretty close to the vest. You know Horner?"

"No, I don't think so." Kate tried to remember if, during any of her visits to the Omnicenter as a patient, she had even seen the man. "Why do you suppose they're so secretive?"

"Not secretive so much as careful. I play around with numbers here; Horner and the Omnicenter people live and die by them. Every bit of that place is computerized: records, appointments, billing, even the prescriptions."

"I know. I go there for my own care."

"Then you can imagine what would happen if even a small fly got dropped into their ointment. Horner is a genius, let me tell you, but he is a bit eccentric. He was writing advanced programs when the rest of us were still trying to spell IBM. From what I've heard, complete independence from the rest of the system is one of the conditions he insisted upon before taking the Omnicenter job in the first place."

"So how do I find out if Ginger Rittenhouse has ever been a patient there? It's important, Marco. Maybe very important."

"Well, Paleolithic as it may sound, we call and ask."

"The phone?"

Marco Sebastian shrugged sheepishly and nodded.

DEAD END. Alone in her office, Kate doodled the words on a yellow legal pad, first in block print, then in script, and finally in a variety of calligraphies, learned through one of several "self-enrichment" courses she had taken during her two years with Art. According to Carl Horner, Marco Sebastian's counterpart at the Omnicenter, Ginger Rittenhouse had never been a patient there. Tom Engleson had succeeded in contacting the woman's roommate, but her acquaintance and living arrangement with Ginger were recent ones. Aside from a prior address, Engleson had gleaned no new information. Connections thus far between the woman and Beverly Vitale: zero.

Outside, the daylong dusting of snow had given way to thick, wet flakes that were beginning to cover. The homeward commute was going to be a bear. Kate tried to ignore the prospect and reflect instead on what her next move might be in evaluating the microsclerosis cases—

perhaps an attempt to find a friend or family member who knew Ginger Rittenhouse better than her new roommate. She might present the two women's pathologies at a regional conference of some sort, hoping to luck into yet a third case. She looked at the uncompleted work on her desk. Face it, she realized, with the amount of spare time she had to run around playing epidemiologist, the mystery of the ovarian microsclerosis seemed destined to remain just that.

For a time, her dread of the drive home did battle with the need to get there in order to grocery shop and set out some sort of dinner for the two of them. Originally, they had tried to eschew traditional roles in setting up and maintaining their household, but both rapidly realized that their traditional upbringings made that arrangement impractical if not impossible. The shopping and food preparation had reverted to her, the maintenance of their physical plant to Jared. Day-to-day finances, they agreed, were beyond either of their abilities and therefore to be shared. Again she checked out the window. Then after a final hesitation, a final thought about calling home and leaving a message on their machine that she was going to work late, she pushed herself away from the desk.

As she stood up, she decided: if it was going to be dinner, then dammit, it was going to be a special dinner. In medical school and residency, she had always been able to find an extra gear, a reserve jet of energy, when she needed it. Perhaps tonight her marriage could use a romantic, gourmet dinner more than it could her moaning about the exhausting day she had endured. Spinach salad, shrimp curry, candles, Grgich Hills Chardonnay, maybe even a chocolate soufflé. She ticked off a mental shopping list as she slipped a few scientific reprints into her briefcase, bundled herself against the rush-hour snow, and hurried from her office, pleased to sense the beginnings of a surge. It was good to know she still had one.

In the quiet of his windowless office, Carl Horner spoke through his fingertips to the information storage and retrieval system in the next room. He had implicit faith in his machines, in their perfection. If there was a problem, as it now seemed there was, the source, he felt certain, was human—either himself or someone at the company. Again and again his fingers asked. Again and again the answers were the same. Finally, he turned from his console to one of two black phones on his desk. A series of seven numbers opened a connection in Buffalo, New York; four numbers more activated the line to a "dead box" in Atlanta; and a final three completed an untraceable connection to Darlington, Kentucky.

Cyrus Redding answered on the first ring.

"Carl?"

"Orange red, Cyrus." Had the colors been reversed, Redding would have been warned either that someone was monitoring Horner's call or that the possibility of a tap existed.

"I can talk," Redding said.

"Cyrus, a woman named Kate Bennett, a pathologist at Metro, just called asking for information on two women who died from the same unusual bleeding disorder."

"Patients of ours?"

"That is affirmative, although Dr. Bennett is only aware that one of them is. Both women had autopsies that showed, in addition to the blood problems, a rare condition of their ovaries."

"Have you asked the Monkeys about them?"

"Affirmative. The Monkeys say there is no connection here."

"Does that make sense to you, Carl?"

"Negative."

"Keep looking into matters. I want a sheet about this Doctor Bennett."

"I'll learn what I can and teletype it tomorrow."

"Tonight."

"Tonight, then."

"Be well, old friend."

"And you, Cyrus. You'll hear from me later."

CHAPTER 4
Wednesday 12 December

"CORONARY STRIKES OUT BOBBY." Kate cringed at the *Boston Herald* headline on her office desk. The story was one of the rare events that managed to make the front page in both that paper and the *Boston Globe*. Though the *Globe*'s treatment was more detailed, the lead and side articles said essentially the same thing in the two papers. Bobby Geary, beloved son of Albert and Maureen Geary, son of the city itself, had been taken without warning by a clot as thin as the stitching on a baseball. The stories, many of them by sportswriters, were the heart-rending stuff of which Pulitzers are made, the only problem being that they weren't true.

The storm, which had begun the evening before, had dumped a

quick eight inches of snow on the city before skulking off over the North Atlantic. However, neither the columns of journalistic half-truths nor the painful drive into the city could dampen the warmth left by the talking and the sharing that had followed the candlelight meal Kate had prepared for her husband. For the first time in years, Jared had talked about his disastrous first marriage and the daughter he would, in all likelihood, never see again. "Gone to find something better" was all the note from his wife had said. The trail of the woman and her daughter had grown cold in New York and finally vanished in a morass of evanescent religious cults throughout southern and central California. "Gone to find something better."

Jared had cried as he spoke of the Vermont years, of his need then to break clear of his father's expectations and build a life for himself. Kate had dried his tears with her lips and listened to the confusion and pain of a marriage that was far more an act of rebellion than one of love.

Kate was finishing the last of the *Globe* stories when, with a soft knock, a ponderous woman entered carrying a paper bag. The woman's overcoat was unbuttoned, exposing a nurse's uniform, pin, and name tag. Kate read the name as the woman spoke it.

"Dr. Bennett, I'm Sandra Tucker. Ginger Rittenhouse was my roommate."

"Of course. Please sit down. Coffee?"

"No, thank you. I'm doing private-duty work, and I'm expected at my patient's house in Weston in half an hour. Dr. Engleson said that if I remembered anything or found anything that might help you understand Ginger's death I could bring it to you."

"Yes, that's true. I'm sorry about Ginger."

"Did you know her?"

"No. No, I didn't."

"We had shared the house only for a few months."

"I know."

"A week after she moved in, Ginger baked a cake and cooked up a lasagna for my birthday."

"That was very nice," Kate said, wishing she had thought twice about engaging the woman in small talk. There was a sad aura about her—a loneliness that made Kate suspect she would talk on indefinitely if given the chance, patient or no patient.

"We went to the movies together twice, and to the Pops, but we were only just getting to be friends and . . ."

"It's good of you to come all the way down here in the snow," Kate said in as gentle an interruption as she could manage.

"Oh, well, it's the least I could do. Ginger was a very nice person. Very quiet and very nice. She was thinking about trying for the marathon next spring."

"What do you have in the bag? Is that something of hers?" A frontal assault seemed the only way.

"Bag? Oh, yes. I'm sorry. Dr. Engleson, what a nice man he is, asked me to go through her things looking for medicines or letters or doctors' appointments or anything that might give you a clue about why she . . . why she . . ."

"I know it was a hard thing for you to do, Miss Tucker, and I'm grateful for any help."

"It's Mrs. Tucker. I'm divorced."

Kate nodded. "The bag?"

"My God, I apologize again." She passed her parcel across the desk. "Sometimes I talk too much, I'm afraid."

"Sometimes I do, too." Kate's voice trailed away as she stared at the contents of the bag.

"I found them in the top of Ginger's bureau. It's the strangest way to package pills I've ever seen. On that one sheet are nearly two months worth of them, packaged individually and labeled by day and date when to take each one. Looks sort of like it was put together by a computer."

"It was," Kate said, her thoughts swirling.

"Pardon?"

"I said it *was* put together by a computer." Her eyes came up slowly and turned toward the window. Across the street, its glass and steel facade jewellike, was the pride of Metropolitan Hospital of Boston. "The pharmacy-dispensing computer of the Omnicenter. The Omnicenter where Ginger Rittenhouse never went."

"I don't understand."

Kate rose. "Mrs. Tucker, you've been a tremendous help. I'll call if we need any further information or if we learn something that might help explain your friend's death. If you'll excuse me, there are some phone calls I must make."

The woman took Kate's hand. "Think nothing of it," she said. "Oh, I felt uncomfortable at first, rifling through her drawers, but then I said to myself, 'If you're not going to do it, then . . .' "

"Mrs. Tucker, thank you very much." One hand still locked in Sandra Tucker's, Kate used her other to take the woman by the elbow and guide her out the door.

The tablets were a medium-strength estrogen-progesterone combination, a generic birth control pill. Kate wondered if Ginger Rittenhouse had been too shy to mention to her roommate that she took them. Computer printed along the top margin of the sheet were Ginger's name, the date six weeks before when the prescription had been filled, and instructions to take one tablet daily. Also printed was advice on what to do if one dose was missed, as well as if two doses were missed. Common side effects were listed, with an asterisk beside those that should be reported immediately to Ginger's Omnicenter physician. Perforations, vertical and horizontal, enabled the patient to tear off as many pills as might be needed for time away. The setup, like everything at the Omnicenter, was slick—thoughtfully designed, and practical—

further showing why there was a long list of women from every economic level waiting to become patients of the facility.

Kate ran through half a dozen possible explanations of why she had been told Ginger Rittenhouse was not a patient at the Omnicenter; then she accepted that there was only one way to find out. She answered, "Doctor Bennett," when the Omnicenter operator asked who was calling, emphasizing ever so slightly her title. Immediately, she was patched through to Dr. William Zimmermann, the director.

"Kate, this is a coincidence. I was just about to call you. How are you?" It was typical of the man, a dynamo sometimes called Rocket Bill, to forgo the redundancy of saying hello.

"I'm fine, Bill, thanks. What do you mean 'coincidence'?"

"Well, I've got a note here from our statistician, Carl Horner, along with a file on someone named Rittenhouse. Carl says he originally sent word to you that we had no such patient."

"That's right."

"Well, we do. Apparently there was a coding mistake or spelling mistake or something."

"Did he tell you why I wanted to know?"

"Only that this woman had died."

"That's right. Does your Carl Horner make mistakes often?" The idea of an error didn't jibe with Marco Sebastian's description of the man.

"Once every century or so as far as I can tell. I've been here four years now, and this is the first time I've encountered any screwup by his machines. Do you want me to send this chart over to you?"

"Can I pick it up in person, Bill? There are some other things I want to talk with you about."

"One o'clock okay with you?"

"Fine. And Bill, could you order a printout of the record of a Beverly Vitale."

"The woman who bled out on the inpatient service?"

"Yes."

"I've already reviewed it. A copy's right here on my desk."

"Excellent. One last thing."

"Yes?"

"I'd like to meet Carl Horner. Is that possible?"

"Old Carl's a bit cantankerous, but I suspect it would be okay."

"One o'clock, then?"

"One o'clock."

Ellen Sandler clutched her housecoat about her and sat on the edge of her bed staring blankly at a disheveled blackbird foraging for a bit of food on the frozen snow beyond her window. She was expected at the office in less than an hour. The house was woefully low on staples.

Betsy's math teacher had set up a noontime conference to investigate her falling interest and grade in the subject. Eve needed help shopping for a dress for her piano recital. Darcy had come home an hour after weekday curfew, her clothes tinged with a musty odor that Ellen suspected was marijuana. So much to do. So much had changed, yet so little.

The silence in the house was stifling. Gradually, she focused on a few ongoing sounds: the hum of the refrigerator, the drone of the blower on the heating and air conditioning system Sandy had installed to celebrate their last anniversary, the sigh that was her own breathing.

"Get up," she told herself. "Goddamn it, get up and do what you have to do." Still, she did not move. The hurt, the oppressive, constricting ache in her chest seemed to make movement impossible. It wasn't the loneliness that pained so, although certainly that was torture. It wasn't the empty bed or the silent telephone or the lifeless eyes that stared at her from the mirror. It wasn't even the other woman, whoever she was. It was the lies—the dozens upon dozens of lies from the one person in the world she needed to trust. It was the realization that while the anguish and hurt of the broken marriage might, in time, subside, the inability to trust would likely remain part of her forever.

"Get up, dammit. Get up, get dressed, and get going."

With what seemed a major effort, she broke through the inertia of her spirit and the aching stiffness in her limbs, and stood up. The room, the house, the job, the girls—so much had changed, yet so little. She walked to the closet, wondering if perhaps something silkier and more feminine than what she usually wore to the office would buoy her. The burgundy dress she had bought for London caught her eye. Two men had made advances toward her the first day she wore it, and there had been any number of compliments on it since.

As she crossed the room, Ellen felt the morning discomforts in her joints diminish—all, that is, except a throbbing in her left thigh that seemed to worsen with each step. She slipped off her housecoat, hung it up, and pulled her flannel nightgown off over her head. Covering much of the front of her thigh was the largest bruise she had ever seen. Gingerly, she explored it with her fingers. It was somewhat tender, but not unbearably so. She did not know how she had gotten it. She had sustained no injury that she could remember. It must, she decided, have been the way she slept on it.

She selected a blue, thin wool jumpsuit in place of the dress, which, it seemed, might not cover the bruise in every situation. She dressed, still unable to take her eyes off the grotesque discoloration. Her legs had always been one of her best features. Even after three children, she took pride that there were only a few threadlike veins visible behind her knees. Now this. For a moment, she thought about calling Kate for advice on whether or not to have a doctor check things out, but she decided that a bruise was a bruise. Besides, she had simply too much else to do.

A bit of makeup and some work on her hair, and Ellen felt as ready as she ever would to tackle the day. The face in her mirror, thin and fine featured, would probably turn some heads, but the eyes were still lifeless.

She was leaving the room when she noticed the note tacked to the doorjamb. Each day it happened like this, and each day it was like seeing the note for the first time, despite the fact that she had tacked it there more than a year before.

"Take Vit," was all it said.

Ellen went to the medicine cabinet, took the sheet of multivitamins plus iron from the shelf, punched one out, and swallowed it without water. Half consciously, she noticed that there was only a four-week supply remaining, and she made a mental note to set up an appointment with her physician at the Omnicenter.

Although she was limping slightly as she left the house, Ellen found the tightness in her thigh bearable. In fact, compared to the other agonies in her life at the moment, the sensation was almost pleasant.

The sign, a discreet bronze plate by the electronically controlled glass doors, said, "Metropolitan Hospital of Boston; Ashburton Women's Health Omnicenter, 1975." Kate had been one of the first patients to enroll and had never regretted her decision. Gynecological care, hardly a pleasant experience, had become at least tolerable for her, as it had for the several thousand other women who were accepted before a waiting list was introduced. The inscription above the receptionist's desk said it all. "Complete Patient Care with Complete Caring Patience."

Kate stopped at the small coatroom to one side of the brightly lit foyer, and checked her parka with a blue-smocked volunteer. She could have used the tunnel from the main hospital, but she had been drawn outdoors by the prospect of a few minutes of fresh air and a fluffy western omelet sandwich, *spécialité de la maison* at Maury's Diner.

The receptionist signaled Kate's arrival by telephone and then directed her to Dr. Zimmermann's office on the third floor. The directions were not necessary. Zimmermann had been Kate's Omnicenter physician for four years, since the accidental drowning death of Dr. Harold French, his predecessor and the first head of the Omnicenter. Although she saw Zimmermann infrequently—three times a year was mandatory for women on birth control pills—Kate had developed a comfortable patient-physician relationship with him, as well as an embryonic friendship.

He was waiting by his office door as she stepped from the elevator. Even after four years, the sight of the man triggered the same impressions as had their first meeting. He was dashing. Corny as the word was, Kate could think of no better one to describe him. In his late thirties or early forties Zimmermann had a classic, chiseled handsomeness, along with an urbanity and ease of motion that Kate had originally felt might be a liability to a physician in his medical specialty. Time and the man had proven her concerns groundless. He was polite and totally professional. In a hospital rife with rumors, few had ever been circulated regarding him. Those that had gone around dealt with the usual speculations about an attractive man of his age who was not married. Active on hospital and civic committees, giving of his time to his patients and of his knowledge to his students, William Zimmermann's was a star justifiably on the rise.

"Dr. Kate." Zimmermann took both her hands in his and pumped them warmly. "Come in, come in. I have fresh coffee and . . . Have you had lunch? I could send out for something."

"I stopped at Maury's on the way over. I'm sorry for being so thoughtless. I should have brought *you* something."

"Nonsense. I only asked about lunch for your benefit. I have been skipping the meal altogether—part of a weight loss bet with my secretary."

Even if the bet were concocted on the spot, and considering the man's trim frame that was quite possible, his words were the perfect breeze to dispel Kate's embarrassment.

Zimmermann's office was the den of a scholar. Texts and bound journals filled three walls of floor-to-ceiling bookcases, and opened or marked volumes covered much of a reading table at one end of the room. On the wall behind his desk, framed photographs of European castles were interspersed with elegantly matted sayings, quotations, and homilies. "The downfall of any magician is belief in his own magic." "There are two tragedies in life: One is not to get your heart's desire; the other is to get it." And of course, "The Omnicenter: Complete patient care with complete caring patience." There were several others, most of which Kate had heard or read before. One, however, she could not recall having seen. Done in black Benedictine calligraphy, with a wonderfully ornate arabesque border, it said, "Monkey Work for the Monkeys."

Zimmermann followed her line of sight to the saying. "A gift from Carl," he explained. "His belief is that the energy of physicians and nurses should be directed as much as possible to areas utilizing their five senses and those properties unique to human beings—empathy, caring, and intuitiveness. The mechanics of our job, the paperwork, setting up of appointments, filling of prescriptions, and such, he calls 'monkey work.' His machines can do those jobs faster and more accurately than any of us ever could, and it seems Carl teaches them more almost every day."

"So," said Kate, "he's named his computers . . . the Monkeys."

Zimmermann said the last two words in unison with her. Kate sensed a letup in the uneasiness she had developed toward Carl Horner and began looking forward to meeting the man.

"Now," Zimmermann asked, "can you brief me on what you have found in these two patients of ours? I have reviewed their records and found little that might be of help to you."

In the concise, stylized method of case presentation ingrained in physicians from their earliest days in medical school, Kate gave a one-minute capsule of each woman's history, physical exam, laboratory data, and hospital course. "I've brought sections from the ovaries of both patients. I think there's a decent microscope in the lab downstairs," she concluded.

Zimmermann whistled softly. "And the only link to this point is that both were patients here?" Kate nodded. "Well, I can't add much. Miss Rittenhouse had been an Omnicenter patient since nineteen seventy-nine. Nothing but routine checkups since then, except that she was within one missed appointment of being asked to go elsewhere for her gynecologic care. The contract we have our patients sign gives us that option."

"I know. I signed one," Kate said. The contract was another example of the patient-oriented philosophy of the Omnicenter. Fees were on a yearly basis, adjusted to a patient's income. There was no profit to be made from insisting on compliance with periodic routine visits, yet insist they did. "What about Beverly Vitale?"

Zimmermann shrugged. "Six years a patient. Abortion here five years ago by suction. Had a diaphragm. Never on birth control pills or hormones of any kind. Always somewhat anemic, hematocrits in the thirty-four to thirty-six range."

"She was on iron."

"Yes. Dr. Bartholomew has had her on daily supplements since the day of her first exam."

"Who was Ginger Rittenhouse's doctor?" Kate was grasping for any connection, however remote.

"Actually, she was cared for by the residents, with the help of a faculty advisor. In this woman's case, it was me. However, there was never any need for me to be consulted. She became a patient just after I arrived. I saw her once, and she has had no trouble since." He grimaced at what he considered an inappropriate remark. "Excluding the obvious," he added.

DEAD END. Kate's mind's eye saw the words as she had written them. She glanced at her watch. There would be a surgical specimen processed as a frozen section in half an hour. Her reading would determine whether the patient underwent a limited or extensive procedure. Still, she felt reluctant to let go of the one common factor she had found. "I'm due back for a frozen in a short while, Bill. Do you think you could take me by to meet Carl Horner and his trained Monkeys?"

"Certainly," Zimmermann said. "He's expecting us. By the way, I understand congratulations are in order."

"For what?"

"Well, word has it that you are to be the next chief of pathology."

Kate laughed ruefully. "Welcome to the new game show, *I've Got No Secrets*. Actually, I don't even think my name has formally been presented for consideration yet, so you can hold the congratulations. Besides, with the financial mess the department is in, I'm not sure condolences wouldn't be a better response. You don't suppose that Ashburton Foundation of yours has a few extra hundred thousand lying around, do you?"

"I have no idea, Kate. Norton Reese handles that end of things. I am just one of the barge toters and bale lifters. You might talk to him, though. The foundation certainly has taken good care of us."

Kate stepped into the carpeted, brightly lit corridor. "I'll say they have," she said. The chance that Norton Reese would put himself out on behalf of her department was less than none.

"Monkey Work for the Monkeys." The message was displayed throughout Carl Horner's computer facility, which occupied an area at the rear of the first floor several times the size of Marco Sebastian's unit. Ensconced in the midst of millions of dollars in sophisticated electronics, Carl Horner looked to be something of an anachronism. Beneath his knee-length lab coat, he was wearing a plaid work shirt and a pair of farmer's overalls. His battered work boots might just as well have received their breaking in on a rock pile as in the climate-controlled, ultramodern suite.

Horner greeted Kate with an energetic handshake, though she could feel the bulbous changes of arthritis in every joint. Still the man, stoop shouldered and silver haired, had an ageless quality about him. It emanated, she decided, not only from his dress, but also from his eyes, which were a remarkably luminescent blue.

"Dr. Bennett, I owe you my deepest apology. The error regarding the Rittenhouse file was nothing more—nor less—than a spelling mistake on my part."

Kate smiled. "Apology accepted. Incident forgotten."

"Have you found the explanations you were looking for?"

"No. No, we haven't. Mr. Horner, could you show me around a bit? I'm especially interested in how the machines work in the pharmacy."

"Carl," Zimmermann said, "if you and Dr. Bennett don't mind, I'm going to get back to work. Kate, I plan to review those slides later tonight and to do some reading. Together, I promise that we shall get to the bottom of all this. Meanwhile, enjoy your tour. We're certainly proud of Carl and his Monkeys."

Patiently, the old man took Kate through the filling of a prescription.

"These cards are preprinted with the patient's name and code number and included with the patient's chart when she has her appointment. The doctors tear 'em up if they're not needed. As you can see, there are twenty-five separate medications already listed here, along with the codes for dosage, amount, and instructions. The machines dispense only these medications, and then only in the form of a generic—as good as any brand-name pharmaceutical, but only a fraction of the cost. The machines automatically review the patient's record for allergies to the medication prescribed, as well as any interaction with medications she might already be taking." Horner's presentation had all the pride of a grandmother holding court at a bridge party. "If there's any problem at all, the prescription is not filled and the patient is referred to our pharmacist, who handles the matter personally."

"What if the physician wants to prescribe a medication other than the twenty-five on the card?" Kate asked.

"Our pharmacy is fully stocked. However, because of the Monkeys, we need only one pharmacist on duty, and he or she has more time to deal with problems such as drug interaction and side effects."

"Amazing," Kate said softly. "Have the Monkeys ever made an error?"

Horner's smile was for the first time somewhat patronizing. "Computers cannot make errors. There are programs backing up programs to guarantee that. Of course, human beings are a different story."

"So I've learned." Kate's cattiness was reflex. There was something about Horner's limitless confidence in the wires, chips, discs, and other paraphernalia surrounding them that she found disquieting. "Tell me, where do the generics come from that the machines dispense?"

"One of the drug houses. We hold a closed-bid auction each year, and the lowest bidder gets the contract."

"Which one has it now?" Horner's answer had been somewhat evasive, hardly in character with the man. She watched his eyes. Was there a flicker of heightened emotion in them? She couldn't tell.

"Now? Redding has it. Redding Pharmaceuticals."

"Ah, the best and the brightest." Kate was not being facetious. In an industry with a checkered past that included thalidomide and many other destroyers of human life, Redding stood alone in its reputation for product safety and the development of orphan drugs for conditions too rare for the drugs to be profitable. "Well, Mr. Horner, I thank you. Your Monkeys are truly incredible."

"My pleasure. If there's anything else I can do, let me know."

Kate turned to go, but then turned back. "Do you have a list of the companies that have held the contract in years past?"

"Since the Omnicenter opened?"

"Yes." For the second time, Kate sensed a change in the man's eyes.

"Well, it won't be much of a list. Redding's the only one."

"Eight auctions and eight Reddings, huh?"

"No bids have even been close to theirs."

"Well, thanks for your help."

"No problem."

Horner's parting handshake and smile seemed somehow more forced than had his greeting. Kate watched as he ambled off, feeling vaguely uneasy about the man, but uncertain why. She glanced at her watch. The frozen section was due in ten minutes, and the patient would be kept under anesthesia until her diagnosis was made. Aside from alerting Bill Zimmermann as to what was going on, her Omnicenter visit had accomplished essentially nothing. Still, the clinic remained the only factor common to two dead women. As she walked through the lobby to retrieve her coat, Kate ran through the possible routes by which the ovarian and blood disorders might have been acquired. Finally, with time running short, she stopped at the reception desk, and wrote a note to Zimmermann.

Dear Bill—

Thanks for the talk and the tour. No answers, but perhaps together we can find some. Meanwhile, I'm sending over some microbiology people to take cultures, viral and bacterial, if that's okay with you. They will also check on techniques of instrument sterilization—perhaps a toxin has been introduced that way.

Let me know if you come up with anything. Also, check your calendar for a night you could come north and have dinner with my husband and me. I'd enjoy the chance to know you better.

Kate

She sealed the note in an envelope and passed it over to the receptionist. "Could you see to it that Dr. Zimmermann gets this?" The woman smiled and nodded. Kate was halfway to the tunnel entrance when she stopped, hesitated, and then returned. She reclaimed the note, tore the envelope open, and added a PS.

And Bill . . . could you please get me ten tablets of each of the medications dispensed by the Monkeys. Thanx.

K.

"Well, what do you say, Clyde. Can I count on you or not?"

Norton Reese set aside the paper clip he was mangling and stared across his desk at the chief of cardiac surgery. Clyde Breslow was the fourth department head he had met with that day. The previous three had made no promises to help block Kate Bennett's appointment, despite delicately presented guarantees that their departments would receive much-needed new equipment as soon as her nomination was defeated. In fact, two of the men, Milner in internal medicine and Hoyt, the pediatrician, had said in as many words that they were pleased with the prospect of having her on the executive committee. "Bright new blood," Milner had called her.

Breslow, Napoleonic in size and temper, watched Reese's discomfort with some amusement. "Now jes' what is it about that little lady that bothers you so, Norton?" he asked in a thick drawl that often disappeared when he was screaming at the nurses and throwing instruments about the operating room or screaming at the medical students and throwing instruments about the dog lab. "She refuse to spread those cute little buns of hers for ya or what?"

"The bitch made me look bad in front of the board of trustees, Clyde. You should remember that. It was your fucking operating microscope that caused all the trouble. I'll be damned if I'm going to have her on my executive committee."

"Whoa, there, Norton. *Your* executive committee? Now ain't you gettin' just the slightest bit possessive about a group you don't even have a vote in?"

"Look, Clyde, I've had a bad day. Do you back me on this and talk to the surgical boys or don't you?"

"Now that jes' depends, don't it?"

"The extra resident's slot? Clyde, I can't do it. I told you that."

"Then maybe you jes' better get used to seeing that pretty little face of Katey B.'s at the meetin's every other Tuesday."

Reese snapped a pencil in half. "All right. I'll try," he said, silently cursing Kate Bennett for putting him in a position to be manipulated by a man like Breslow."

"You do that. Know what I think, Norton? I think you're scared of that woman. That's what I think. A looker with smarts is more than you kin handle."

Without warning, Reese exploded. "Look, Clyde," he said, slamming his desk chair against the wall as he stood, "you have enough fucking trouble remembering that the heart is above the belly button without taking up playing amateur shrink. Now get the hell out of here and get me some support in this thing. I'll do what I can about your goddamn resident."

With a plastic smile, Clyde Breslow backed out of the office. Reese sank into his chair. Frightened of Kate Bennett? The hell he was. He just couldn't stand a snotty, do-gooder kid going around trying to act grown up. She ought to be home keeping house and screwing that lawyer husband of hers.

"Mr. Reese, there's a call for you on two." The secretary's voice startled him, and lunging for the intercom, he spilled the dregs of a cup of coffee on his desk.

"Dammit, Betty, I told you no calls."

"I know you did, sir. I'm sorry. It's Mr. Horner from the Omnicenter. He says it's very important."

Reese sighed. "All right. Tell him to call me on three seven four four." He blotted up the coffee and waited for his private line to ring. It was unusual for Carl Horner to call at all. Omnicenter business was usually handled by Arlen Paquette, Redding's director of product safety. In the few moments before 3744 rang, he speculated on the nature of a problem that might be of such concern that Horner would call. None of his speculations prepared him for the reality.

"Mr. Reese," Horner said, "I'm calling on behalf of a mutual friend of ours." Cyrus Redding's name was one Horner would never say over the phone, but Reese had no doubt whom he meant.

"How is our friend?"

"A bit upset, Mr. Reese. One of your staff physicians has been nosing about the Omnicenter, asking questions about our pharmacy and requesting Dr. Zimmermann to send her samples of the medications we dispense."

The word "her" brought Reese a bone-deep chill. "Who is it?" he asked, already knowing the answer.

"It's the pathologist, Dr. Bennett. She's investigating the deaths of two women who were patients of ours."

"Damn her," Reese said too softly to be heard. "Horner, are you . . . I mean, is the Omnicenter responsible for the deaths?"

"That appears to be negative."

"What do you mean appears to be? Do you know what's at stake? Paquette promised me nothing like this would happen." Reese began feeling a tightness in his chest and dropped a nitroglycerine tablet under his tongue, vowing that if this discomfort was the start of the big one, his last act on earth would be to shoot Kate Bennett between the eyes.

"Our friend says for you to remain cool and not to worry. However, he would like you to find some effective way of . . . diverting Dr. Bennett's interest away from the Omnicenter until we can fix up a few things and do a little more investigating into the two deaths in question."

"What am I supposed to do?"

"That, Mr. Reese, I do not know. Our friend suggests firing the woman."

"I can't do that. I don't hire and fire doctors, for Christ's sake."

"Our friend would like something done as soon as possible. He has asked me to remind you that certain contracts are up for renewal in less than a month."

"Fuck him."

"Pardon?"

"I said, all right. I'll think of something." Suddenly, he brightened.

"In fact," he said, reaching into his desk drawer, "I think I already have."

"Fine," Carl Horner said. "All of us involved appreciate your efforts. I'm sure our friend will be extremely beholden when you succeed."

Reese noted the use of 'when' instead of 'if,' but it no longer mattered. "I'll be in touch," he said. Replacing the receiver, he extracted a folder marked "Schultz/Geary." Inside were a number of newspaper articles; the official autopsy report, signed by Stanley Willoughby and Kathryn Bennett, MDs; and an explanatory note from Sheila Pierce. Also in the folder were a number of laboratory tests on a man named John Schultz—a patient who, as far as he or Sheila could tell, never existed in Metropolitan Hospital. While the chances of some kind of coverup weren't a hundred percent, they certainly seemed close to that.

Sheila, he thought as he readied a piece of paper in his typewriter, if this works out, I'm going to see to it that you get at least an extra night or two each month. "To Charles C. Estep, Editor, *The Boston Globe*." Reese whispered the words as he typed them. He paused and checked the hour. By the time he was done with a rough draft, the pathology unit would be empty. A sheet of Kate Bennett's stationery and a sample of her signature would then be all he needed to solve any number of problems. The woman would be out of his hair, perhaps permanently, and Cyrus Redding would be—how had Horner put it?—extremely beholden.

"Dear Mr. Estep . . ."

As Norton Reese typed, he began humming "There Is Nothing Like a Dame."

⋀ CHAPTER 5

Thursday 13 December

"DO YOU THINK GOD is a man or a woman, Daddy?"

Suzy Paquette sat cross-legged on the passenger seat of her father's new Mercedes 450 SL, parked by the pump at Bowen's Texaco.

Behind the wheel, Arlen Paquette watched the mid-morning traffic glide by along Main Street, his thoughts neither on the traffic nor on the question he had just been asked.

"Well, Daddy?"

"Well what, sugar?" The attendant rapped twice on the trunk that he was done. "Company account, Harley," Paquette called out as he pulled away.

"Which is it, man or woman?"

"Which is what, darlin'?"

"God! Daddy, you're not even listening to me at all." She was seven years old with sorrel hair pulled back in two ponytails and a China doll face that was, at that moment, trying to pout.

Paquette swung into a space in front of Darlington Army/Navy and stopped. Never totally calm, he was, he knew, unusually tense and distracted this morning. Still, it was Second Thursday and that gave him the right to be inattentive or cross, as he had been earlier with his wife. He turned to his daughter. She had mastered the expression she wanted and now sat pressed against the car door displaying it, her arms folded tightly across her chest. In that instant, Paquette knew that she was the most beautiful child on earth. He reached across and took her in his arms. The girl stiffened momentarily, then relaxed and returned the embrace.

"I'm sorry, sugar," Paquette said. "I wasn't listening. I'm sorry and I love you and I think God is a woman if you're a woman and a man to someone who's a man and probably a puppy dog to the puppy dogs."

"I love you too, Daddy. And I still don't know why I should have to pray to Our Father when God might be Our Mother."

"You know, you're right. I think that from now on we should say . . . 'Our Buddy who art in Heaven.' "

"Oh, Daddy."

Paquette checked the time. "Listen, sugar, my meeting is in half an hour. I've got to get going. You be brave, now."

She flashed a heart-melting smile. "I don't have to be brave, Daddy. It's only a cleaning."

"Well then, you be . . . clean. Mommy will be by in just a little while. You wait if she's not here by the time you're done." He watched as she ran up the stairs next to the Army/Navy and waited until she waved to him from behind the picture window painted *Dr. Richard Philips,* DDS. Then he eased the Mercedes away from the curb, and headed toward the south end of town and his eleven o'clock Second Thursday meeting with Cyrus Redding, president and chairman of the board of perhaps the largest pharmaceutical house in the world. The meeting would start at exactly eleven and end at precisely ten minutes to noon. For seven years, as long as Paquette had been with the company, it had been like that, and like that it would remain as long as Cyrus Redding was alive and in charge. Nine o'clock, labor relations; ten o'clock, public relations; eleven, product safety; an hour and ten minutes for lunch, then research and development, sales and production, and finally from three to three-fifty, legislative liaison: department heads meeting with Cyrus Redding, one on one, the second Thursday of each month. The times and the order of Second Thursday were immutable. Vacations were to be worked around the day, illnesses to be treated and tolerated unless hospitalization was necessary. Even then, on more than one occasion, Redding had moved the meeting to a hospital room. Second Thursday: raises, new projects, criticisms, termination—all, whenever possible, on that day.

The factory covered most of a thirty-acre site bordered to the south and west by pine-covered hills and to the east by Pinkham's Creek. Double fences, nine feet high with barbed wire outcroppings at the top, encircled the entire facility. The inner of the two barriers was electrified —stunning voltage during the day, lethal voltage at night and on weekends. The only approach, paralleling the new railbed from the north, was tree lined and immaculately maintained. Two hundred yards from the outer fence, a V in the roadway directed employees and shippers to the right and all others to the left. A rainbow sign, spanning the approach at that point announced:

REDDING PHARMACEUTICALS, INCORPORATED

DARLINGTON, KENTUCKY

1899

"The Most Good for the Most People at the Least Cost"

Paquette bore to the right beneath the sign and stopped by a brightly painted guardhouse, the first of a series of security measures. He found himself wondering, as he did on almost every Second Thursday, if knowing what he knew now, he would have left his university research position in Connecticut to become director of product safety. The question was a purely hypothetical one. He had taken the job. He had agreed to play Cyrus Redding's game by Cyrus Redding's rules. Now, like it or not, he was Cyrus Redding's man. Of course an annual salary that, with benefits, exceeded four hundred thousand dollars went far toward easing pangs of conscience. Suzy was the youngest of three children, all of whom would one day be in college at the same time. He stopped at the final pass gate, handed the trunk key to the guard, and drummed nervously on the wheel while the man completed his inspection. It hardly paid to be late for a Second Thursday appointment.

Over the hundred and eighty years since Gault Darling led a band of renegades, moonshiners, and other social outcasts to a verdant spot in the foothills of the Cumberlands, and then killed two men for the right to have the new town named after himself, Darlington, Kentucky, had undergone any number of near deaths and subsequent resurgences.

Disease, soldiers, Cherokees, floods, fires, and even a tornado had at one time or another brought the town to its knees. Always, though, a vestige survived, and always Darlington regrew.

In 1858, the Lexington-Knoxville Railway passed close enough to Darlington to send off a spur, the primary purpose of which was the transport of coal from the rich Juniper mines. By the end of the century, however, output from the Junipers had fallen to a trickle, and the railbed was left to rot. Darlington was once again in danger of becoming a ghost town. Shops closed. The schoolhouse and Baptist church burned down and were not rebuilt. Town government dwindled and then disappeared. In the end, where once there had been well over a thousand, only a handful remained. Fortunately for the town, one of those was Elton Darling, self-proclaimed descendant of Gault.

In 1897, Darling engineered a massive hoax utilizing three pouches of low-grade gold ore, two confederates, and a remarkable ability to seem totally inebriated when stone sober. Rumors of the "Darlington Lode" spread quicky through cities from Chicago to Atlanta, and Darlington acquired an instant citizenry, many of whom stayed on, either out of love for the beauty of the area or out of lack of resources to move elsewhere.

Having single-handedly repopulated his town, Elton Darling set about giving it an industry, making use of the area's only readily available resource, the sulfur-rich water of Pinkham's Creek, a tributary of the Cumberland River. In less than a year, with some food coloring, smoky-glassed bottles, an attractive label, and an aggressive sales force, the vile water of Pinkham's Creek, uninhabitable by even the hardiest fish, had become Darling's Astounding Rejuvenator and Purgator, an elixir alleged effective against conditions ranging from dropsy to baldness.

Over the years before his death in 1939, Elton Darling made such changes in his product as the market and times demanded. He also made a modest fortune. By the time his son, Tyrone, took control of the family enterprises, the rejuvenator had been replaced by a variety of vitamin and mineral supplements, and Darlington Pharmaceuticals was being traded, though lightly, on the American Stock Exchange.

Far from being the visionary and businessman his father was, Tyrone Darling spent much of his time, and most of his money, on a string of unsuccessful thoroughbreds and a succession of city women, each of whom was more adept at consuming money than he was at making it. Darling's solution to his diminishing cash reserves was simple: issue more stock and sell off some of his own. In the fall of 1947, at the annual Darlington stockholders meeting, the ax fell. Intermediaries for a man spoken of only as Mr. Redding produced proof of ownership of more than fifty-three percent of Darlington Pharmaceuticals and in a matter of less than a day, took over the company on behalf of Mr. Cyrus Redding of New York, New York. Stripped of influence, as well as of a source of income, Darling tried to negotiate. To the best of anyone's knowledge, he had not succeeded even in meeting with the man who had replaced him when, on the following New Year's Eve, he and a woman named Densmore were shot to death by the woman's husband.

Thus it was that the fortunes of Darlington, Kentucky became tied to a reclusive genius named Cyrus Redding and to the pharmaceutical house that now bore his name. In the years to follow, there were a number of minor successes: Terranyd, a concentrated tetracycline; Rebac, an over-the-counter antacid: and several cold preparations. Redding Pharmaceuticals doubled in size, and the population of Darlington grew proportionally. Then, in the early 1960s, Redding obtained exclusive U.S. patents to several successful European products, including the tranquilizer that was, following a blitzkrieg promotional campaign, to become one of the most prescribed pharmaceuticals in the world. A year after release of the drug, Darlington was selected an All-American City, and shortly after that, the Darlington Dukes minor league baseball franchise was established.

Marilyn Wyman sipped at a cup of tea and risked a minute glance at her gold Rolex. Ten minutes to go and another Second Thursday would be over for Redding's director of public relations. From across his enormous desk, Cyrus Redding appraised her through his Coke-bottle spectacles.

"There are exactly eight minutes and thirty seconds to go, Marilyn," he said. "Does that help?"

"I'm sorry, sir." Wyman, in her midfifties, had been with the company longer than had any other department head. Still, no one had ever heard her refer to her employer as anything other than Mr. Redding or, to his face, sir. She had close-cut gray-brown hair and a sophisticated sensuality that she used with consummate skill in dealing with media representatives of both sexes.

"We have one final piece of business. No small piece, either. It's Arthgard."

"I thought it had been taken off the market."

"In England it has, but not yet here. It has been only eight weeks since we released it and already it is in the top forty in volume and the top twenty-five in actual dollar return."

"That's a shame. The feedback I've gotten from pharmacists and patients has been excellent, too. Still, the British have proven it responsible for how many deaths so far, sixty?"

"Eighty-five, actually."

"Eighty-five." Reflexively, Wyman shuddered. Arthgard had been released to the American market almost immediately after the patent had been acquired by Redding. Though she had no way of knowing how it had been accomplished, the FDA-required testing periods, both laboratory and clinical, seemed to have been circumvented. It was not her place to ask about such things. Testing was the provinoe of Arlen Paquette, and the exchange of information between department heads was not only frowned upon by Redding but, in most cases, forbidden. "Well, we still have Lapsol and Carmalon," she said. "The figures I looked at yesterday showed them both in the top ten of antiarthritic preparations. I'll write a press release announcing the suspension of our Arthgard production and then see what I can do to remind the public about both of those other products."

"You will do no such thing, Marilyn."

"Pardon?"

Redding pulled a computer printout from a file on his desk. "Do you have any idea how many millions it cost us to buy the Arthgard patent, test the product, go into production, advertise, get samples out to physicians, and finally distribute the product to pharmacies and hospitals? Correction, Miss Wyman. Not how many millions—how many tens of millions?" Marilyn Wyman shook her head. Redding continued. "The projections I have here say that, at our present rate of increase in sales, the product would have to stay on the market for another ten weeks just for us to break even. That is where you will be concentrating your efforts."

"But. . . ." Redding's icy look made it clear that there was to be no dialogue on the matter. She stared down at thc toes of her two-hundred-dollar Ferragamo pumps. "Yes, sir."

"I've got some preliminary data from that survey firm you contracted with showing that less than forty percent of physicians and less than ten percent of consumers are even aware of what's going on in England. I want those numbers to stay in that ball park for the next ten weeks."

"But. . . ."

"Dammit, I am not looking for buts. I am looking for ten weeks of sales so that we can get our ass out of this product without having it burned off. Our legislative liaison will do his job with the FDA. Now if you want to give me 'buts,' I'll find a PR person who does her job. And need I remind you that her first job will be to do something creative with that M. Wyman file I have locked away?"

Wyman bit at her lower lip and nodded. It had been several years since Redding had mentioned the collection of photographs, telephone conversations, and recordings from the company hotel suite she had vacationed in at Acapulco. Beneath her expertly applied makeup, she was ashen.

Redding, seeing the capitulation in her eyes, softened. "Marilyn, listen. You do your part. I promise that if there's any trouble on this side of the Atlantic with Arthgard, we'll pull it immediately. Okay? Good. Now tell me, how's that little buggy of yours riding?"

"The Alpha? Fine, thank you. Needs a tune-up. That's all."

"Well, don't bother. Just bring it over to Buddy Michaels at Darlington Sport. He's got a spanking new Lotus just arrived and itching for you to show it the beauty of the Kentucky countryside." He checked the slim digital timepiece built into his desk. "Eight minutes of eleven. It's been a good meeting, Marilyn. As usual, you're doing an excellent job. Why don't you stop by next week and give me a progress report. I also want to hear how that new Lotus of yours handles the downgrade on the back side of Black Mountain." With a smile, a nod, and the smallest gesture of one hand, Marilyn Wyman was dismissed.

Arlen Paquette was drinking coffee in the sumptuous sitting room outside of Redding's office when Wyman emerged. Though they had worked for the same company for years, they seldom met in situations other than Second Thursday. Still, the greeting between them was warm, both sensing that in another place and at another time, they might well have become friends.

At precisely eleven o'clock, Marilyn Wyman exited through the door to the reception area and Paquette crossed to Redding's door, knocked once, and entered. Hour three of Second Thursday had begun.

Redding greeted Paquette with a handshake across his desk. On occasion, usually when their agenda was small, the man would guide his motorized wheelchair to a spot by the coffee table at one end of his huge office and motion Paquette to the maroon Chesterfield sofa opposite him. This day, however, there was no such gesture.

"I've sent for lunch, Arlen. We may run over."

Paquette tensed. In seven years, his eleven o'clock visit had never run over. "I'm all yours," he said, realizing, as he was sure the old man across from him did, that the words were more than a polite figure of speech.

"Have you any problem areas you wish to discuss with me before we start?"

Paquette shook his head. He knew Cyrus Redding abhorred what he called "surprises." If Paquette encountered major problems in the course of his work, a call and immediate discussion with Redding were in order.

"Fine," Redding said, adjusting his tie and then combing his gray crew cut back with his fingers. "I have two situations that we must ponder together. The first concerns Arthgard. Do you have your file handy?"

"I have my files on everything that is current," Paquette said, rummaging through his large, well-worn briefcase.

"Is our testing on Arthgard current?" Redding's tone suggested that he would consider an affirmative response a "surprise."

"Yes and no, sir. The formal testing was completed several months ago. You have my report."

"Yes, I remember."

"However," Paquette continued, "I began reading about the problems in the UK, and decided to continue dispensing the drug to some of the test subjects at the Women's Health Center in Denver."

"Excellent thinking, Arlen. Excellent. Have there been any side effects so far?"

"Minor ones only. Breast engorgement and pain, stomach upsets, diarrhea, hair loss in half a dozen, loss of libido, rashes, and palpitations. Nothing serious or life threatening."

Serious or life threatening. Even after seven years, Paquette's inner feelings were belied by the callousness of his words. Still, he was Redding's man, and Redding was concerned only with those side effects that would be severe enough, consistently enough to cause trouble for the company. Only those were deemed reason to delay or cancel the quick release of a new product into the marketplace. In a business where a week often translated into millions of dollars, and a jump on the competition into tens of millions, Redding had set his priorities.

"How many subjects were involved in the Arthgard testing?"

"Counting those at the Denver facility and at the Omnicenter, in Boston, there were almost a thousand." He checked his notes. "Nine hundred and seventy."

"And no one from the Omnicenter is receiving Arthgard right now?"

"The testing there was stopped months ago. There were too many other products that we had to work into the system."

Paquette knew that the Arthgard recall in Great Britain was going to prove a fiasco, if not a disaster, for Redding Pharmaceuticals, a company that had not suffered a product recall or even an FDA probe since the man in the wheelchair had taken over. Testing of pharmaceuticals in Europe seldom met FDA standards. Still, the UK had a decent safety record, and the Boston and Denver testing facilities served as a double check on all foreign-developed products, as well as on drugs invented in Redding Labs. Problems inherent in various products—at least by Cyrus Redding's definition of problems—had always been identified before any major commitment by the company was undertaken . . . always, until now.

"Tell me, Arlen," Redding said, drawing a cup of coffee from a spigot built into his desk and lacing it with a splash from a small decanter, "what do you think happened? How did this get past us?"

Paquette searched for any tension, any note of condemnation in the man's words. There was none that he could tell. "Well," he said, "basically, it boils down to a matter of numbers." He paused, deciding how scientific to make his explanation. He knew nothing of Cyrus Redding's background, but he was certain from past discussions that there was science in it somewhere. Straightforward and not condescending—that was how he would play it. "The Arthgard side effect—the cardiac toxicity that is being blamed for the deaths in England—seems to be part allergy and part dose related."

"In other words," Redding said, "first the patient has to be sensitive to the drug and then he has to get enough of it."

"Exactly. And statistically, that combination doesn't come up too often. Arthgard has been so effective, though, and so well marketed, that literally millions of prescriptions have been written in the six years since it was first released in the United Kingdom. A death here, a death there. Weeks or months and miles in between. No way to connect them to the drug. Finally, a number of problems show up at just about the same time in just about the same place, and one doc in one hospital in one town in the corner of Sussex puts it all together. A little publicity, and suddenly reports begin pouring in from all over the British world."

"Do you have any idea how many hundreds of thousands of arthritis patients have had their suffering relieved by Arthgard?"

"I can guess. And I understand what you're saying. Risk-benefit ratio. That's all people in our industry, or any health provider for that matter, have to go by."

"I've decided to keep Arthgard on the American market for ten more weeks." Redding dropped the bomb quietly and simply; then he sat back and watched Paquette's reaction. Noticeably, at least, there was none.

"Fine," Paquette said. "Would you like me to continue the Denver testing? We have about an eighteen-month head start on the overall marketplace."

"By all means, Arlen."

Paquette nodded, scratched a note on the Arthgard file, and slid it back in his briefcase, struggling to maintain his composure. There was little to be gained by revealing his true feelings about what Redding was doing, and much—oh, so much—to lose. His involvement in the testing centers alone—involvement of which Redding possessed detailed documentation—was enough to send him to prison. In fact, he suspected that Redding could claim no knowledge of either facility and make that claim stick. Even if no confrontation occurred, the chances were that he would be fired or demoted . . . or worse. Several years before, a department head had been openly critical of Redding and his methods, to the point of discussing his feelings with the editor of the Darlington *Clarion Journal.* Not a week later, the man, a superb horseman, had his neck broken in a riding accident and died within hours of reaching Darlington Regional Hospital.

"Have you the product test reports for this month?"

"Yes, sir. I took them off the computer yesterday evening."

Paquette was rummaging through his briefcase for the progress reports on the fourteen medications currently being investigated when he heard the soft hum of Redding's wheelchair.

"Just leave the reports on my desk, Arlen," Redding said, gliding to the center of the room. "I'll review them later. Could you bring my coffee over to the table, please? I want to apprise you of a potential problem at the Omnicenter, and I could use a break from talking across this desk."

Paquette did as he was asked, keeping his eyes averted from Redding as much as possible, lest the man, a warlock when it came to reading the thoughts of others, realized how distasteful the Arthgard decision was to him. On the day of their first interview, over eight years ago, he had sensed that uncanny ability in the aging invalid. It was as if all the power that would have gone into locomotion had simply been transferred to another function.

"Arlen, the Omnicenter was already operational when you joined us, yes?"

"Sort of, sir." Paquette settled into the Chesterfield and took a long draught of the coffee he had surreptitiously augmented with cognac while Redding was motoring across the room. "The computers were in, our people were in place, and the finances had been worked out, but no formal testing programs had been started."

"Yes, of course. I remember now. You should go easy on that cognac so early in the day, my friend. It's terrible on the digestion. In the course of your dealings in Boston, did you by chance run into a woman pathologist named Bennett, first name Kathryn, or Kate?"

Paquette shook his head. He had set his coffee aside, no longer finding reassurance in the warm, velvety swallows. "Reese keeps me away from as many people as possible." He smiled and whispered, "I think he's ashamed of me."

Redding enjoyed the humor. "Such a reaction would be typical of the man, wouldn't it. He lacks the highly advanced abilities to appreciate and respect. With him, a person is to be either controlled or feared —none of the subtleties in between."

"Exactly." Paquette was impressed, but not surprised, by the insight. As far as he knew, Redding had had but one direct contact with the Metropolitan Hospital administrator, but for the Warlock, one was usually enough. "What about this Dr. Bennett?"

"She has begun investigating the Omnicenter in connection with two unusual deaths she has autopsied. The women in question had similar blood and reproductive organ disease, and both were Omnicenter patients."

"So are a fair percentage of all the women in Boston," Paquette said. "Have you talked to our people?"

"Carl called me. Both women have participated at various times in our work, but never with the same product. The Omnicenter connection appears to be a red herring."

"Unfortunately, we have other herrings in that building which are not so red."

"That is precisely my concern," Redding said, "and now yours. I have sent instructions to Reese that he is to find a way to divert young Dr. Bennett's interest away from our facility. He seems to think he can do so. However, I have had my sources do some checking on this woman, and I tell you, Norton Reese is no match for her, intellectually or in strength of character."

"He would be the last to admit that."

"I agree." Redding opened a manila folder he had apparently placed on the coffee table prior to Paquette's arrival. "Here are copies for you of all the information we have obtained thus far on the woman. I want you to go to Boston and keep tabs on things. Do not show yourself in any way without checking with me first. Meet with our Omnicenter people only if absolutely necessary."

"Yes, sir."

"There is a small item in that report which may be of some help to us. Bennett's father-in-law heads the law firm that handles the Metropolitan Hospital account, as well as some of the Northeast business of the Tiny Tummies line of breakfast cereals. Although the connection is not generally known, Tiny Foods is a subsidiary of ours. The man's name is Winfield Samuels. From all I can tell, he's a businessman."

Paquette nodded. Coming from Cyrus Redding, the appellation "businessman" was the highest praise. It meant the man was, like Redding himself, a pragmatist who would not allow emotions to cloud his handling of an issue. "Do you have any idea of what Reese has in mind to deal with the doctor?"

"No, except that Carl Horner says he seems quite sure of himself."

"If that's the case," Paquette said, "I should be back in just a few days."

Redding smiled benignly. "I told you how I perceive the Bennett-Reese matchup, Arlen," he said. "I've had reservations made for you at the Ritz. Open-ended reservations."

METRO DOC LABELS BOBBY JUNKIE.

The layout editor of the *Herald* had, it seemed, dusted off type that had not been used since D-Day. The paper lay on the living room floor, along with the *Globe* and Roscoe, who was keeping an equal distance between himself and both his masters. It was still afternoon, but the mood and the dense overcast outside made the hour feel much later.

The calls had begun at two that morning and had continued until Jared unplugged their phones at four-thirty. Letters, typed on Kathryn Bennett's stationery and signed by her, had been dropped off at both Boston dailies and all three major television stations sometime during the previous night. The gist of the letters was that, driven by conscience and a sense of duty to the people of Boston, Kate had decided to tell the truth about Bobby Geary. Stan Willoughby, who was mentioned in the letter, and Norton Reese, as Metro administrator, were called immediately by reporters. The pathology chief, not as sharp as he might have been had he not been woken from a sound sleep, confirmed the story, adding that Kate was an honest and highly competent pathologist whom, he was sure, had good reason for doing what she had done. It was not until an hour after speaking with the first newsman that he thought to call her. By then, Kate's line was so busy that it took him almost another hour to get through. Meanwhile, Norton Reese, aided by Marco Sebastian and an emergency session with the hospital computers, had confirmed that there was, in fact, no patient named John Schultz ever treated or tested at Metropolitan Hospital. Reese was careful to add that he knew absolutely nothing of the allegations lodged by Dr. Bennett, whom he described as a brilliant woman with a tendency at times to rebel against traditional modes of conduct. Questioned for details, he refused further comment.

The house was like a mausoleum. Both Kate and Jared had attempted to go to work for business as usual, but both had been forced by harassing reporters to return home. Over the hours that followed, they sat, drapes closed, ignoring the periodic ring of the front doorbell. The telephones remained disconnected. There was a silence between them chilly enough to offset even the warmth from the wood stove.

"Jared, do you want a cup of coffee?"

"Thanks, but no. Three in an hour and a half is a little over my limit." He leaned forward from his easy chair and plucked the *Herald* from beside Roscoe's nose. Beneath the headline were insert photos of Bobby Geary's parents, along with a quotation from each about Kate, neither the least bit complimentary. "Goddamn tabloid really knows how to slobber it on," he said, unable to mask the irritation in his voice.

"Honey, you do believe what I said about not knowing anything about those letters, don't you?"

"Of course I believe you. Why would you think otherwise?"

"No reason, I guess." The anger she had felt earlier in the day had been greatly muted by frustration and the growing realization that beyond a simple denial and the call for a handwriting analysis of her signature, she had absolutely no cards to play. Even the signature was of doubtful assistance to her claims of innocence. No one had yet come forward with the original letter, and on the photostat she had seen, the signature appeared quite accurate.

"Why would somebody do this? Why?" Jared seemed to be talking as much to himself as to her, but it was clear that in his mind, confusion and doubt remained. "You say that Yoda and this Detective Finn were the only two besides you who knew about the amphetamines?"

"I said as far as I knew they were. Reese has it in for me, and he has his finger in just about every pie in Metro. He could have found out somehow, and. . . ." She shrugged and shook her head. "I don't think much of the man, but I can't imagine him doing a thing like this."

317

"You know, Kate, you could have told me you were going to fake Geary's autopsy report. I mean, I am your husband."

Kate glared at him. "Jared, the three of us decided that nobody else should know. Call Mrs. Willoughby or Mrs. Finn and ask if their husbands told them. Do you share all the inner secrets of your work with me?"

"You never ask."

"Give me a break, will you? Listen, I know you're upset. You are a public figure, and directly or indirectly, you're getting negative press. But don't go blaming me, Jared. I didn't do anything."

Jared rose, shuffled to the stove, and began stoking embers that were already burning quite nicely. "I spoke with my father this morning," he said over his shoulder.

"My God, Winfield must be absolutely fried over all this. Do you think it would help matters if I called him?"

"He thinks you should call a press conference and admit that you sent the letters."

"What?"

"It's his feeling that as things stand, it looks like you performed an act of conscience, and then I talked you out of owning up to it."

"So my father-in-law wants me to lie in public to keep his protegé from losing any votes."

Jared slammed the poker against the stove door. "Dammit, you already did lie. That's what caused all this trouble in the first place."

Kate felt herself about to cry. "I did what I thought was the kindest and fairest thing I could do for that boy and his family."

"Well, now you're going to have to think about what's kind and fair to *this* boy and *his* family."

"So you think that's what I should do, too?"

A loud pounding on the front door precluded Jared's response.

"Police. Open up."

Kate opened the door a slit and peered out, expecting to see another overly resourceful reporter. Instead, she saw Detective Lieutenant Martin Finn. Any lingering doubt they might have had about whether or not the policeman was responsible for the letters evaporated with the man's first words.

"You really fucked me, Dr. Bennett. Do you know that?"

"I'm sorry, but I didn't send those letters," she said with exaggerated calm. "Would you like to sit down? Can I get you some coffee?"

Finn ignored her questions, and instead, remained in the center of the room, pacing out a miniature circle on the rug. "I went along with this because I'm Irish and a fan, and look what it gets me. I was up for a promotion. Maybe captain. Now, thanks to you and your fucking grandstand play, I'm going to be lucky I don't get busted to dogcatcher."

"Went along with it?" Kate was incredulous. "Lieutenant Finn, it was your suggestion in the first place. For the kids of Boston. Don't you remember saying all that?" Her voice cracked. The day had been punishing enough without this.

Suddenly, Jared pushed past her and confronted the man. Though he was taller than Finn, the policeman was far stockier. "Finn, if you've said what you came to say, I want you and your foul mouth out of here. If not, say it. Then leave."

"I'll leave when I'm fucking ready."

"Get out."

Jared stepped forward, his fists clenched in front of him. It was only then that Kate sensed how heavily Finn had been drinking. She moved toward them, but not quickly enough. With no warning or windup, Finn sank a vicious uppercut into Jared's solar plexus. A guttural grunt accompanied the explosion of air from his lungs, as he doubled over and dropped to his knees.

Kate knelt beside her husband. "You damn animal," she screamed at Finn.

"I wish it had been you, lady," Finn said as he turned and walked clumsily from the house. The antique vase Kate threw shattered against the door as it closed behind him.

Jared remained doubled over, but his breathing was deepening. "You okay?" she said softly.

"Never laid a glove on me," he responded with no little effort. "Could you bring over the wastebasket, please? Just in case."

"You poor darling. Can I do anything else? Get you anything?"

Slowly, Jared sat back and straightened up. His eyes were glazed. "Just remind me again what I told that minister."

"For better or for worse. That's what you told him. Jared, I don't want to sound corny, but that was a pretty wonderful thing you did standing up to that animal."

"For better or for worse? You sure that was it?"

"Uh-huh."

"Katey, I don't know how to tell you this, but in some perverse way getting hit the way I just did felt good."

"I don't understand."

"Right before Finn came in I was ready to tell you that I agreed with my father in thinking everything would be simpler and look better for all of us if you would just admit to writing the letter. Then that asshole started in. All of a sudden, I realized how wrong I was . . . and I'm sorry. I couldn't stand hearing him talk to you that way. Katey, please just try to remember that there's a lot going on that's confusing to me. Sometimes I feel that living with you is like trying to ride a cyclone. Sometimes I feel like a slab of luncheon meat between one slice of Winfield and one slice of Kate. Sometimes I . . . ." He whirled to the wastebasket and threw up.

◆

Sheila Pierce stared past Norton Reese's sweat-dampened pate at the stucco ceiling of their room in the Mid City Motel and reminded herself to continue the groans that the man found so exciting.

Careful not to disrupt his rhythm, she reached up and reassured herself that her new diamond studs hadn't come dislodged.

"Oh, baby," she murmured. "Oh, baby, you're so good. So good."

She wished she could have seen Kate Bennett's face when the reporters started calling. Reese was hardly a Valentino for her, but she had to give credit where credit was due, and Reese deserved what she was giving him for what he had given Bennett.

"Oh, baby, come to me. Come to me," she moaned.

It had been a thrill just to watch: Kathryn Bennett, MD, Miss Perfect, confused and irritable, suddenly not in control of every little thing. How good at last to be the one pulling the strings. Too bad there was no way for Bennett ever to know.

"Don't stop, Norty. Oh, yes, baby, yes. Don't stop."

⋀ CHAPTER 6
Friday 14 December

COMPARED WITH THE conference rooms of other departments in Metropolitan Hospital of Boston, the one belonging to the pathology unit was spartan. French Impressionist prints mounted on poster board hung on stark, beige walls. Below them, metal, government-surplus bookcases were half filled with worn, dog-eared texts and journals. The meager decor, plus a large, gouged oak table and two dozen variegated folding chairs did little to obscure the fact that prior to a modest departmentwide renovation in 1965, the room had been the hospital morgue. Some among the twenty-nine assembled for the hastily called meeting still sensed the auras of the thousands of bodies that had temporarily rested there.

Kate, Stan Willoughby seated to her right, stood at one end of the table and surveyed the room. There were six pathologists besides the two of them, some residents, and a number of lab technicians. It bothered her terribly to think that one—or more—of them might be capable of an act as malicious as the Bobby Geary letter. Those in the room were, in a sense, her family—people she spent as many waking hours with each week as she did with her husband. It had always been her way to deal with them in a straightforward manner, respectfully, and with no hidden agendas. There were only two characteristics that they knew she would not tolerate—laziness and dishonesty. However, to the best of her knowledge, none in the room could be accused of either.

The closest had been the business of Sheila Pierce's claiming she had misplaced the required vouchers and certification for her Miami trip, and even then, Kate had no proof of her suspicions. Besides, the matter had been settled between them with little disagreement.

John Gilson, the unit's electron microscopist; Liu Huang, a meticulous pathologist, whom Kate tutored in English; Marvin Grimes, the always pleasantly inebriated deiner; Sheila, herself, so very bright, so dedicated to the department; momentarily, Kate's eyes met each of theirs.

"I want to thank you all for taking the time out of your schedules to hear me out," she began. "I know the last day and a half have been . . . how should I say, a bit disrupted around here." There was a murmur of laughter at the understatement. "Well, I'm here to tell you that compared to what you all have been through, my life has been absolutely nuked. At three o'clock this morning, my husband and I caught a reporter trying to sneak out of our bedroom in time to make the morning edition. He had disguised himself as our antique brass coatrack." Laughter this time was more spontaneous and animated. Kate smiled thinly. "Norton Reese has set up a news conference for me in about an hour. He wants me to state my position on the Bobby Geary business once and for all. Well, before I tell those vultures, I wanted to tell you.

"What the press has been saying about Bobby Geary is true. From all we were able to tell at post, he had been a longtime user of intravenous amphetamines. How he could do what he did to his body and still play ball the way he did is a mystery to me, but the chronic scarring we found along certain veins makes the truth clear. Sad for Bobby's family, sad for the baseball fans and the kids, and, I'm sure, a nightmare for Bobby. The decision to withhold our findings from the press was as much mine as Dr. Willoughby's or Detective Finn's." A jet of acid singed her throat at the mention of the man. "I have trouble with deceit in any form, but every sense I have of what is decent says that our decision was the right one. Now someone is doing his best to make me pay for that decision. I did not write the letter, and I have no idea who did, why they did it, how they got the information on Bobby Geary's post, or how they obtained my stationery. The possibility exists that it was someone from this department. I very much hope not—all of you are very important to me. I feel like we're a team, and that helps me show up every day ready to try and practice decent pathology in this dinosaur of a hospital.

"But what's done is done. I've agonized as much as I'm going to,

321

and after the little Q-and-A session in Reese's office, I intend to begin stuffing this whole business into the barrel I use to dispose of the garbage in my life. If any of you have any questions, I'll be happy to answer them as best I can."

Stan Willoughby rose and put his arm around her shoulders. "No questions from me, Kate. Just a statement for everybody. I have submitted this woman's name to the search committee as my personal recommendation to succeed me as department chief. It's possible this whole business is someone's way of trying to sabotage that appointment. I want you all to know that I am more committed than ever to seeing that she gets it."

For a moment there was silence. Then diminutive Liu Huang stood and began applauding. Another joined in and then another. Soon all but one were demonstrating their support.

"We're behind you, Doc," a technician called out.

The reaction was as enthusiastic and sustained as it was spontaneous. In the back of the room, the lone holdout smiled around clenched teeth and then stiffly joined in the applause.

"That was pretty special, wasn't it," Willoughby said to Kate as the room emptied out. "Little Looie Huang standing there in his formal, inscrutable way, leading the cheers. I just love 'im. Are you all right?"

"If you mean am I about to come apart and start bawling like a baby, the answer is yes."

"So bawl," Willoughby said, taking her by the arm as they followed the last of the meeting-goers from the room.

"You know, Stan, I don't understand it. I don't think I ever will."

"What's that?" Willoughby bent over the bubbler he had tried for years to get replaced, and sucked vigorously for a sip of tepid water.

"People, I guess." She shrugged. "You know, you wake up in the morning, you get dressed, you march off for another encounter in the battle of life—all you want to do is grow a little, try your best, and grab some little morsel of peace and contentment along the way. No big deal. Every day you do that, and every day you think that everyone else is doing the same thing, trying for that same smidgen of happiness. It makes so much sense that way."

"Ah, yes, my child, but therein lies the rub. You see, what makes sense and what is are seldom the same thing. The stew you propose cooking up would taste just fine, but it's a bit short on the condiments of reality—greed, envy, bigotry, insecurity, to say nothing of that ol' standby, just plain craziness. No matter who you are, no matter how hard you try to tend your own little garden, no matter how kind you try to be to your fellow man, there's always gonna be someone, somewhere tryin' to stick it to you. You can count on it."

"Terrific."

"It all boils down to priorities."

"What do you mean?"

"Well, I know I have the reputation around here for being too passive. My door is always open. Bring in your troubles and problems whenever you want . . . as long as you bring in the solutions to them at the same time. I wasn't always like that, Kate. There was a time when I would have gone to the mat with the toughest of them. And I did. Many times in the early days before you came on board. Then I started getting the pains beneath the ol' sternum, and I started visiting all those eager young cardiologists. Gradually, my priorities began to shift away from playing with the stick-it-to-you fanatics. I went back to basics. My wife, my children, my grandchildren, my health—physical and mental. I couldn't see how a new microscope or an extra technician or a refurnished room could measure up against any of them."

"But Stan, your work is important. It's your job to fight for the department. Don't you agree?"

"Yes."

"Well then, how do you resolve that fact with what you just said?"

Stanley Willoughby leaned over and kissed her gently on the forehead. "I can't, Kate. Don't you see? That's why I'm stepping down. See you at the conference." With a smile that held more wistfulness and sadness than mirth, he turned and entered the office that, if he had his way, Kate would occupy within a few months.

Kate's office, half the size of her chief's, was on a side corridor next to the autopsy suite. There was room only for a desk and chair, a file cabinet, a small microscope bench, and two high stools. On one of the stools sat Jared.

"Well, hi," she said, crossing to kiss him.

"Hi, yourself."

His response was chilly, perfunctory.

"How's your belly?"

"As long as I don't try to sit down, get up, or walk, it's only painful as hell," he said. "But not nearly as painful as this." He slid a handbill across to her. "Copies of this have been circulating all over South Boston and are beginning to work their way up into the city."

"Damn," she whispered, staring at the paper in disbelief. "Jared, I'm sorry. I really am." The flyer, printed on an orange stock bright enough to offend even the least political Irish Catholic, was headlined PARTNERS IN COMPASSION. Beneath the words were Kate and Jared arm in arm in a photograph she could not remember ever having posed for. It was labeled "Atty. J. Samuels and Dr. K. Bennett." At the bottom of the page was a photograph of Bobby Geary in the midst of his picture-perfect swing. It was captioned simply "Bobby, R.I.P."

"Finn?" she ventured.

"Maybe. Maybe not. He's hardly the only Irish Catholic around who'd like to firebomb us. The name Bobby Geary seems set to take its place right next to Chappaquiddick and Watergate in the list of political death knells. For all I know, Mattingly or his sleazy campaign manager decided to make sure I was no problem for them in the next election."

"I'm sorry."

"You already said that."

Kate sighed and sank down on her desk chair. "Jared, things aren't really going very well for me right now. Do you have to make them worse?"

"Things aren't going well for *you*? Is that all you can think of?"

"Please, honey. I've got this damn news conference in half an hour; I've got a biopsy due from the OR. Don't you remember saying yesterday how you were going to try to be more understanding?" She clenched her teeth against any further outburst.

"I remember getting laid out by a policeman I'd never seen before that moment. That's what I remember. My father tells me that Martin Finn is *numero uno* in power and influence in certain quarters of the BPD. With him for an enemy, it's possible that I might end up having my car towed while it's stopped for a red light."

Kate's eyes narrowed. Suddenly, Jared's appearance in her office made sense. Win Samuels. One of the man's countless sensors, scattered about the city and throughout the media, must have reported that his daughter-in-law was scheduled to meet the press. "Jared, did your father tell you to come here this morning to make sure I didn't disgrace anyone at the news conference?"

"We're just trying to avoid any more of this stuff." He held up the orange handbill.

Kate glared at her husband for a moment; then her expression softened. "You know, when you are yourself, you are the funniest, nicest, gentlest, handsomest man I have ever known. I swear you are. Given a build-it-myself husband erector set, I don't think I could have done any better. But when you start operating with that man in the Braxton Building, I swear. . . ."

"Look, let's leave my father out of this, shall we? I'm the one who's watching a political career go down the toilet, not him."

"I'm not so sure."

"What?"

"Nothing, Jared. Look, I've got some work to finish, and any moment I have to diagnose the biopsy of a woman's thyroid gland that one of the other pathologists is having trouble with. I can't talk about this any more right now."

"How about you just . . ."

His outburst was cut short by the arrival of a technician carrying a stainless steel specimen tray and cardboard slide holder, which she set on the microscope bench.

"Please tell Dr. Huang I'll call him in a few minutes with my diagnosis," Kate said.

Jared watched the young woman leave and then checked his watch.

"Look," he said coolly, "I've got to go. I have an appointment with Norton Reese in two minutes."

"What for?"

"Apparently he's been contacted by a lawyer friend of the Gearys. They're thinking of some kind of action against the hospital based on invasion of privacy."

"Jesus," Kate said, pressing her fingertips against the fatigue burning in her eyes.

Jared stood to go. "Don't forget about the Carlisles' cocktail party tonight." Kate groaned. "I guess you already have, huh?"

"I'm sorry. What time?"

"Seven-thirty."

"Okay, Jared, I. . . ."

"Yes?"

She shook her head. "Never mind." It wasn't, she decided, the moment to tell him that she felt she was losing her mind. Please hold me, Jared, she wanted to say. Come over here and hold me and tell me everything's going to be all right. Instead, she waved weakly and turned to the slide and tissue in the specimen dish.

Before Jared had crossed to the door, the telephone began ringing. Reflexively, he turned back.

"Hello? . . . Oh, hi," Kate said. "How're you holding up? . . . How long? . . . Have you tried pressure? . . . Ice? . . . Ellen, please. Just calm down and get a hold of yourself. Have you ever had any trouble like this before? . . . Any bruising you can't explain? . . . Your whole thigh? . . . Why didn't you call me? . . . Ellen, a few years ago, I helped get you accepted into the Omnicenter. Are you still going there? . . . All right. Now listen carefully. I want you to come up to the emergency ward here, but I don't want you to drive. Can you get someone to bring you? . . . Fine. Pack an overnight bag and ask your sister or someone to cover the girls, just in case. . . . Ellen, relax. Now I mean it. Coming apart will only make things worse. Besides, it raises havoc with your mascara. . . . That's better. Now, maintain pressure as best you can, and come on up here. I'll have the best people waiting to see you. You'll probably be home in a couple of hours. . . . Good. And Ellen, bring your medicines, too. . . . I know they're only vitamins. Bring them anyway."

"Ellen Sandler?" Jared asked as she hung up.

Kate nodded, her face ashen. "Her nose has been bleeding steadily for over two hours. Do you know where Sandy is, by any chance?"

"Europe, I think."

Kate stared down at the specimen tray and thought about the woman on the operating table, waiting word on whether the lump in her neck was cancerous or not. Chances were that the initial biopsy had been done under local, so the woman would be fully awake, frightened. "Jared, there is something you can tell Norton Reese for me. Tell him

325

that I won't be able to make his news conference. Tell him that I didn't do anything and didn't write anything, so I really don't have anything to say anyway."

"But . . ."

"Tell him that as my husband for almost five years, you know that whatever I say is the truth, and that if anyone wants to get at me, they'll have to go through you. Just like last evening. Okay?" She placed a slide under her microscope, and prepared for an encounter with the yellow-white light.

Jared moved to respond, but then stopped himself, walked to the door, and finally turned back. "I hope Ellen's all right," he said softly.

Kate looked up. Every muscle in her body seemed to have tensed at the prospect of what the blood studies on her friend might reveal. "So do I, Jared," she said. "So do I."

Relax. Concentrate. Focus in. Center your mind. Center it. It took a minute or two longer than usual, but in the end, the process worked. It always did. Extraneous thoughts and worries lifted from her like a fog until finally all that remained in her world were the cells.

Arlen Paquette sat by the window of his suite in the Ritz, watching the slow passage of pedestrians along the snow-covered walks of the Public Gardens. His schooling had been at Harvard and MIT, and no matter how long he lived in Kentucky, coming to Boston always felt like coming home. Watching the students and lovers, the vagrants and executives, Paquette found himself longing for the more sheltered, if much more improverished, life in a university. Over the seven years with Redding, he had gained much. The land, the house, the tennis court and pool, to say nothing of the opportunities for his children and lifetime security for himself and his wife. Only now was he beginning to appreciate fully the price he had paid. More and more, especially since the Arthgard recall, he avoided looking at himself in mirrors. More and more, as his self-respect dwindled, his effectiveness as a lover also declined. And now, a thousand miles from his exquisitely manicured lawn and the country club he was about to direct, two women had bled to death. As he looked out on the gray New England afternoon, Paquette prayed that the connection of the dead women to the Omnicenter was mere coincidence.

At precisely three o'clock, a messenger arrived with the large manila envelope he had been expecting. Paquette tipped the man and then spread the contents on the coffee table next to the dossier he had brought with him from Darlington. The thoroughness with which Cyrus Redding approached a potential adversary surprised him not in the least. The Warlock kept his edge, honed his remarkable intuitiveness, through facts—countless snatches of data that taken individually might seem irrelevant, but which, like single jigsaw-puzzle pieces, helped construct the truth; in this case, the truth that was Kathryn Bennett Samuels, MD.

Paquette found the volume of information amassed over just a few days both impressive and frightening. Biographical data, academic publications, medical history from a life insurance application, even grades and a yearbook picture from Mount Holyoke. There were, in addition to the photostats and computer printouts, a dozen black-and-white photographs—five-by-seven blowups of shots obviously taken with a telephoto lens. Instinctively, the chemist glanced out the window of his eighth-floor suite, wondering if there were a spot from which someone might be taking photographs of him.

One at a time, Paquette studied the carefully labeled photographs. "K.B. and husband, Jared Samuels." "K.B. and pathologist Stanley Willoughby. (See p. 4B.)" "Samuels/Bennett residence, Salt Marsh Road, Essex." "K.B. jogging near home." The woman had a remarkable face, vibrant and expressive, with the well-defined features that translated into photogenicity. Her beauty was at once unobtrusive and unquestionable, and as he scanned the photos, Arlen Paquette felt the beginning pangs of loneliness for his wife.

"Pay special attention to Dr. Stein's report," Redding had instructed him. "The man has done this sort of thing for me before, on even shorter notice and with even less data than he has had to work with here. If you have questions, let me know and I'll have Stein get in touch with you."

The report was typed on stationery embossed "Stephen Stein, PhD; Clinical Psychologist." There was no address or telephone number. Paquette mixed himself a weak Dewar's and water and settled onto the brocaded sofa with the three, single-spaced pages.

Much of the report was a condensation of the data from the rest of the dossier. Paquette read through that portion, underlining the few facts he hadn't encountered before. Actually, he was familiar with Stein's work. Nearly seven years before, he had studied a similar document dealing with Norton Reese. He had wondered then, as he did again this day, if somewhere in the hundreds of manila folders locked in Cyrus Redding's files was one containing a Stein study of Arlen Paquette.

Two older brothers . . . high-school cheerleader . . . ribbon-winning equestrian . . . art department award for sculpture, Mt. Holyoke College . . . one piece, *Search #3,* still on display on campus grounds . . . fourteen-day hospitalization for depression, junior year. . . . Paquette added the information to what he already knew of the woman.

"In conclusion," Stein wrote, "it would appear that in Dr. Bennett we have a woman of some discipline and uncommon tenacity who would make a valuable ally or a dangerous foe under any circumstances. Her principles appear solidly grounded, and I would doubt seriously that she can be bought off a cause in which she believes.

Intellectually, I have no reason to believe her abilities have declined from the days when she scored very high marks in the Medical College Admission Test (see p. 1C) and National Medical Boards (also 1C). Her friends, as far as we have been able to determine, are loyal to her and trusting in her loyalty to them. (Statements summarized pp. 2C and 3C.)

"She does, however, have some problem areas that we shall continue to explore and that might yield avenues for controlling her actions. She likely has a deep-seated insecurity and confusion regarding her roles as a wife and a professional. A threat against her husband may prove more effective in directing her actions than a threat against herself. Faced with a challenge, it is likely that she would fight rather than back away or seek assistance.

"The possibility of influence through blackmail (areas for this being investigated) or extortion seems remote at this time.

"Follow-up report in one week or as significant information is obtained.

"Estimate of potential for control on Redding index is two or three."

Paquette set the report aside and tried to remember what Norton Reese had been graded on Redding's scale. An eight? And what about himself?

"A ten," he muttered. "Move over Bo Derek. Here comes Arlen Paquette, an absolute ten." He poured a second drink, this one pure Dewar's, and buried it.

In minutes, the amber softness had calmed him enough for him to begin some assessment of the situation. Bennett had sent specialists to the Omnicenter to take cultures. No problem. If they were negative, as he suspected they would be, the clinic had gotten a free, comprehensive microbiology check. If they were positive, investigation would move away from the pharmacy anyhow. She had asked for, and received, samples of the pharmaceuticals dispensed by Horner's Monkeys. No problem. The samples would prove to be clean. Horner had seen to that.

Would she press her investigation further? Stein's report and what he knew of the woman said yes. However, that was before she had become mired down in the baseball player mess. The more he thought about the situation, the more convinced Paquette became that there was no avenue through which Kate Bennett could penetrate the secret of the Omnicenter, especially since all product testing had been suspended. Tenacity or no tenacity, the woman could not keep him away from home for more than a few days.

As he mixed another drink, Paquette realized that there was, in fact, a way. It was a twisting, rocky footpath rather than an avenue, but it was a way nonetheless. After a moment of hesitation, he placed a call to the 202 area.

"Good afternoon. Ashburton Foundation."

"Estelle?"

"Yes."

"It's Dr. Thompson."

"Oh. Hi, Doctor. Long time no hear."

"Only a week, Estelle. Everything okay?"

"Fine."

"Any calls?"

"Just this one. I almost jumped out of my skin when the phone rang. I mean days of doing nothing but my nails, I . . ."

"Any mail?"

"Just the two pieces from Denver I forwarded to you a while ago."

"I got them. Listen, if any calls come in, I don't want you to wait until I check in. Call me through the numbers on the sheet in the desk. The message will get to me, and I'll call you immediately."

"Okay, but . . ."

"Thank you, Estelle. Have a good day."

"Good-bye, Dr. Thompson."

To Kate Bennett the scene in Room 6 of the Metropolitan Hospital emergency ward was surreal. Off to one side, two earnest hematology fellows were making blood smears and chatting in inappropriately loud tones. To the other side, Tom Engleson leaned against the wall in grim silence, flanked by a nurse and a junior resident. Kate stood alone by the doorway, alternating her gaze from the crimson-spattered suction bottle on the wall to the activity beneath the bright overhead light in the center of the room.

Pete Colangelo, chief of otorhinolaryngology, hunched in front of Ellen Sandler, peering through the center hole of his head mirror at a hyperilluminated spot far within her left nostril.

"It's high. Oh, yes, it's high," he murmured to himself as he strove to cauterize the hemorrhaging vessel that because of its location, was dripping blood out of Ellen's nose and down the back of her throat.

Kate looked at her friend's sheet-covered legs and thought about the bruise, the enormous bruise, which had been a harbinger of troubles to come. *Don't let it be serious. Please, if you are anything like a God, please don't let her tests come back abnormal.*

In the special operating chair, Ellen sat motionless as marble, but her hands, Kate observed, were whitened from her grip on the armrest. *Please . . .*

"Could you check her pressure?" Colangelo asked. He was a thin, minute man, but his hands were remarkable, especially in the fine, plastic work from which surgical legends were born. Kate was grateful beyond words that she had found him available. Still, she knew that the real danger lay not so much in what was happening as in why. Gruesome images of Beverly Vitale and Ginger Rittenhouse churned in her thoughts. At that moment, in the hematology lab, machines and technicians were measuring the clotting factors in a woman who was no more than a name and hospital number to them. *Please* . . .

Colangelo's assistant reported Ellen's pressure at one-forty over sixty. No danger there. The jets of blood into the suction bottle seemed to be lessening, and for the first time Kate sensed a slight letup in the tension around the room.

"Come to papa," Colangelo cooed to the bleeding arteriole. "That's the little fellow. Come to papa, now."

"What do you think?"

Kate spun to her left.

Tom Engleson had moved next to her. "Sorry," he whispered. "I didn't mean to startle you." The concern she was feeling was mirrored in his face. His brown eyes, dulled somewhat by the continued pressures of his job, were nonetheless wonderfully expressive.

"I think Pete is winning," she said, "if that's what you're asking."

"It isn't."

"In that case, I don't have an answer. At least not yet. Not until the hematology report comes back." She continued speaking, but turned her gaze back to the center of the room. "If her counts are normal, and you have the time, we can celebrate. I'll buy you a coffee. If they're low, I'd like to—wait, make that need to—talk with you anyhow. Besides Stan Willoughby, you are the only one who knows as much as I do, and I think these past two days Stan has been battered enough by his association with me."

"I'm free for the rest of the day," Tom said. "If you like, maybe we could have dinner together." The moment the words were out, he regretted saying them. Impetuous, inappropriate, tactless, dumb.

Kate responded with a fractional look—far too little for him to get a fix on. "I think Pete's done it," she said, making no reference to his invitation.

Moments later, Colangelo confirmed her impression. "We've got it, Mrs. Sandler. You just stay relaxed the way you have been, and we should be in good shape. You are a wonderful patient, believe me you are. I love caring for people who help me to do my best work." He took a step back and waited, the reflected light from his head mirror illuminating the blood-smeared lower half of Ellen's face. Then he turned to Kate, his lips parted in a hopeful half-smile.

"Good job, Pete," she whispered. "Damn good."

Colangelo nodded and then turned back to his patient. "Mrs. Sandler, I think it best for you to stay overnight here. There are some lab studies that haven't come back yet, and I would also like to be sure that vessel stays cauterized."

"No," Ellen said. "I mean, I can't. I mean I don't want to if I don't have to. Kate, tell Dr. Colangelo all the things I have to do, and how responsible I am, and how I'll do exactly what he tells me to do if I can go home. Please, Kate. No offense, but I hate hospitals. Hate them. I almost had Betsy in a roadside park because I wanted to wait until the last minute."

Kate crossed to her friend and wiped the dried blood from her face with damp gauze. "Let's see," she said finally. "As I see it, you want me to arbitrate a disagreement in medical philosophy between the chief of ENT surgery, who also happens to be a professor at Harvard, and the chief of E. Sandler Interior Designs, Inc. . . ."

"Kate, please."

Ellen's grip on Kate's hand and the quaver in her voice reflected a fear far more primal than Kate had realized. Kate turned to the surgeon. "Pete?"

Colangelo shrugged. "I get paid to do surgery and give advice," he said. "If you're asking me whether I think admission is one hundred percent necessary, the answer is no. However, as I said, I get paid to give advice, and observation in the hospital is my advice."

Before Kate could respond, a white-coated technician from the hematology service entered and handed her three lab slips, two pink and one pale green. She studied the numbers and felt a grinding fear and anger rise in her throat. "Lady," she said, struggling to mask the tension in her voice, "I'm going to cast in with Dr. Colangelo. I think you ought to stay."

Ellen's grip tightened. "Kate, what do the tests show? Is it bad?"

"No, El. A couple of the numbers are off a bit and should be rechecked, but it's not bad or dangerous at this point." Silently, she prayed that her judgment of the woman's strength was correct, and that she had done the right thing in not lying. Ellen studied her eyes.

"Not bad or dangerous *at this point*, but it could be. Is that what you're saying?" Kate hesitated and then nodded. Ellen sighed. "Then I guess I stay," she said.

"You shouldn't be here long, and you'll have the very best people taking care of you. I'll help you make arrangements for the girls, and I'll also let them know what's going on."

"Thank you."

"I know it sounds foolish to say don't worry, but try your best not to. We'll keep an eye on your nose and recheck the blood tests in the morning. Most likely you'll be home by the end of the weekend." Kate fought to maintain an even eye contact, but somewhere inside she knew that her friend didn't believe the hopeful statement any more than she did.

"It's the Omnicenter. Somehow I just know it is."

Kate grimaced at the coffee she had just brewed, and lightened it with half-and-half ferreted out from among the chemicals in her office refrigerator.

"The Omnicenter is just that pile of glass and stone across the street. Every one of these reports is negative. Bacteriology, chemistry, epidemiology. All negative. Where's the connection?" Tom Engleson flipped through a sheaf of reports from the studies Kate had ordered. There was nothing in any of them so far to implicate the outpatient center.

"I don't know," Kate responded, settling in across the work bench from him. He was dressed in jeans and a bulky, ivory fisherman's sweater. It was the first time she had seen the man wearing anything but resident's whites. The change was a positive one. The marvelous Irish knit added a rugged edge to his asthenic good looks. "I think it's a virus or some sort of toxin . . . or a contaminant in the pharmacy. Whatever it is is in there." She jabbed a thumb in the general direction of the Omnicenter.

"The pharmacy? These reports say that the analyses of Ginger Rittenhouse's medications and of the ones Zimmermann sent you were all perfectly normal. Not a bad apple in the bunch."

"I know."

"So . . .?"

"So, I don't know. Look, my friend has whatever this thing is that has killed two women. Platelets seventy thousand, fibrinogen seventy-five percent of normal. You saw the report. Not as bad as either of the other two, at least not yet, but sure headed in the wrong direction." Her words came faster and her voice grew more strident. "I don't really need you to come down here and point out the obvious. For that I can go get Gus from the newsstand outside. I need some thoughts on what *might* be the explanation, not on what *can't* be." Suddenly she stopped. "Jesus, I'm sorry, Tom. I really am. Between political nonsense here at the hospital, the mess with Bobby Geary and his damn amphetamine addiction, two young women dying like ours did, the everyday tensions of just trying to do this job right, and now Ellen, I'm feeling like someone has plunked me inside a blender and thrown the switch. You don't deserve this."

"It's okay. I'm sorry for not being more helpful." He was unable to completely expunge the hurt from his voice, and Kate reminded herself that while the five or so years difference in their ages meant little in most areas, hypersensitivity might not be one of them. "If you think it's the pharmacy," he said, "maybe you should call the FDA."

"One jot of evidence, and I would. I'm the one who talked her into going to the Omnicenter in the first place." Absently, she slipped her hands into her lab coat pockets. In the right one, folded back and again on itself, was the cardboard and plastic card containing what remained of Ellen's Omnicenter vitamins plus iron. She set them on the bench. "No luck finding any of Beverly Vitale's vitamins?" she asked.

"None."

Kate crossed to her desk, returned with a medication card similar to Ellen's, and slapped it down next to the other. "I think we should try one last time with our friends at the toxicology lab and their magic spectrophotometer. Ellen's vitamins and these. If the reports come back negative, I shall put all my suspicions in the witchhunt file and turn my attention to other pursuits—like trying to regain some of the respect that was snatched away in the Bobby Geary disaster."

"Don't worry," Tom said, "you still have respect, admiration, and caring in a lot of places . . . especially right here." He tapped himself on the breastbone with one finger.

"Thank you for saying that."

"Whose pills are those other ones?" he asked.

"Huh?"

"The other card of pills, whose are they?"

"Oh. They're mine."

$\wedge$ CHAPTER 7

Friday 14 December

THERE WAS AN AIR of excitement and anticipation throughout the usually staid medical suite of Vernon Drexler, MD. The matronly receptionist bustled about the empty waiting room, straightening the magazines and taking pains to see that the six-month-old issue of *Practical Medical Science* with Drexler's picture on the cover was displayed prominently enough to be impossible for Cyrus Redding to miss, even if he were ushered directly into the doctor's office.

In the small laboratory, the young technician replaced the spool of paper in the cardiograph machine and realigned the tubes, needle, and plastic sleeve she would use to draw blood from the arm of the man Drexler had described as one of the most influential if not one of the wealthiest in the country.

Behind her desk, Lurleen Fiske, the intense, severe office manager, phoned the last of their patients and rescheduled him for another day. She had been with Drexler in 1967, when Cyrus Redding had made his first trip up from Kentucky. *Nineteen sixty-seven.* Fiske smiled wistfully. Their office in the Back Bay section of Boston had been little more than two large closets then, one for the doctor and one for herself. Now, Drexler owned the entire building.

It was twelve-thirty. Redding's private 727 had probably touched down at Logan already. In precisely an hour, the woman knew, his limousine would glide to a stop in front of their brownstone. Redding, on foot if he could manage it, in his wheelchair if he could not, would be helped up the walk and before entering the building, would squint up at their office window, smile, and wave. His aide, for the last five or six years a silent, hard-looking man named Nunes, would be carrying a leather tote bag containing Redding's medicines and, invariably, a special, personal gift for each of those working in the office. On Redding's last visit, nearly a year before, his gift to her had been the diamond pendant—almost half a carat—now resting proudly on her chest. Of course, she realized, this day could prove an exception. Some sort of pressing situation had arisen requiring Redding to fly to Boston. He had called the office late on the previous afternoon inquiring as to whether, as long as he had to be in the city, he might be able to work in his annual checkup.

"Mrs. Fiske," Drexler called from his office, "I can't remember. Did you say Dr. Ferguson would be coming in with Mr. Redding, or did you say he wouldn't be?"

"I said 'might,' Doctor. Mr. Redding wasn't sure." The woman smiled lovingly and shook her head. Vernon Drexler may have been a renowned endocrinologist, and a leading expert on the neuromuscular disease myasthenia gravis, but for matters other than medicine, his mind was a sieve. She and his wife had spent many amusing evenings over the years imagining the Keystone Comedy that would result were they not available to orchestrate his movements from appointment to appointment, lecture to lecture.

The thought of Dr. Ferguson sent the office manager hurrying to the small, fire-resistant room housing their medical records; she returned to her desk with the man's file. John Ferguson, MD, afflicted, as was Cyrus Redding, with myasthenia, was a close friend of the tycoon. The two men usually arranged to have their checkups on the same day, and then for an hour or so they would meet with Dr. Drexler. Lurleen Fiske suspected, though Drexler had never made her party to their business, that the two men were in some way supporting his myasthenia research laboratory at the medical school.

"Mrs. Fiske," Drexler called out again, "perhaps you'd better get Dr. Ferguson's chart just in case."

"Yes, Doctor, I'll get it right away," she said, already flipping through the lengthy record to ensure that the laboratory reports and notes from his last visit were in place. Drexler was nervous. She could tell from his voice. He was conducting himself with proper decorum and professional detachment, but she could tell nonetheless. Once, years before, he had been ferried by helicopter to Onassis's yatch for a consultation on the man's already lost battle against myasthenia. That morning, he had calmly bid the office staff good day and then had strode out minus his medical bag, journal articles, and sport coat.

Redding's limousine, slowed by the snow-covered streets, arrived five minutes late. Lurleen Fiske joined the two other employees at the window. Across the room, Drexler, a tall, gaunt man in his midfifties, watched his staff pridefully.

"Look, look. There he is," the receptionist twittered.

"Is he walking?" Drexler wanted to see for himself, but was reluctant to disrupt the ritual that had developed over the years.

Lurleen Fiske craned her neck. "His wheelchair is out," she said, "but yes . . . yes, he's taking a few steps on his own. Another year, Dr. Drexler. You've done it again." There was no mistaking the reverence in her voice.

In spite of himself, Drexler, too, was impressed. In sixty-seven he had predicted three years for Redding, four at the most. Now, after more than fifteen, the man was as strong as he had been at the start, if not stronger. *You've done it again.* Mrs. Fiske's praise echoed painfully in his thoughts. Myasthenia gravis, a progressive deterioration of the neuromuscular system. Cause: unknown. Prognosis: progressive weakness—especially with exertion—fatigue, difficulty in chewing, difficulty in breathing, and eventually, death from infection or respiratory failure. Treatment: stopgap even at its most sophisticated. Yet here were two men, Redding and John Ferguson, who had, in essence, arrested or at least markedly slowed the progress of their disease. And they had performed the minor miracles on their own. Though his staff thought otherwise, and neither patient would ever suggest so, they had received only peripheral, supportive help from him. They were certainly a pair of triumphs, but triumphs that continually underscored the futility of his own life's work.

From the hallway, Drexler heard the elevator clank open. For years, his two prize patients had been treating themselves with upwards of a dozen medications at once, most of them still untested outside the laboratory. For years he had dedicated his work to trying to ascertain which drug or combination of drugs was responsible for their remarkable results. The answer would likely provide a breakthrough of historic proportions. Perhaps this would be his year.

Redding, seated in an unmotorized wheelchair, waved his aide on ahead and then wheeled himself to the doorway. Using the man's arm for some support, he pulled himself upright and took several rickety steps into the office.

"Thank you for seeing me on such short notice, Vernon," he said, extending his hand to give Drexler's a single, vigorous pump. "Mr. Nunes?" The aide, a sullen, swarthy man with the physique of an

Olympic oarsman, slid the wheelchair into place for Redding to sit back down. Across the waiting room, Lurleen Fiske and the two other women beamed like proud grandmothers.

"You look wonderful, Cyrus," Drexler said. "Absolutely wonderful. Come on into my office."

"In a moment. First, I should like to wish your staff an early Merry Christmas. Mr. Nunes?"

The expressionless Nunes produced three gifts of varying sizes from the leather bag slung over his shoulder, and Redding presented them, one at a time, to the women, who shook his hand self-consciously. Lurleen Fiske squeezed his shoulders and kissed him on the cheek.

"My limousine will go for Dr. Ferguson," Redding said, as he was wheeled into Drexler's office. "He will be here to share notes with the two of us, but not to be examined. He would rather keep the appointment he has for next month, if that is agreeable to you."

"Fine, fine," Drexler said.

The two men, Ferguson and Redding, had met perhaps a dozen years before in his waiting room and had developed an instant rapport. By their next appointment, Redding had asked that a half day be set aside for just the two of them. The request, supported as it was by the promise of substantial research funds, was, of course, granted.

Redding's bodyguard wheeled him into Drexler's office, set the bag of medications on the desk, and left to accompany the limousine to John Ferguson's house. Carefully, Redding arranged the vials and plastic containers on the blotter before Drexler. There were, all told, thirteen different preparations.

"Well, Doctor," he said, "here they are. Most of them you already know we have been taking. A couple of them you don't."

"Dr. Ferguson continues to follow exactly the same regimen as you?"

"As far as I know."

The endocrinologist made notes concerning each medication. There were two highly experimental drugs—still far from human testing —that he himself had only learned of in the past six or seven months. He bit back the urge, once again, to warn against the dangers of taking pharmaceuticals before they could be properly investigated, and simply recorded the chemical names and dosages. Somehow, the two men were screening the drugs for side effects. They had let him know that much and no more. As far as Vernon Drexler, MD, was concerned, with a goodly proportion of his own research at stake, there was no point in pushing the matter.

"This one?" Drexler held up a half-filled bottle of clear, powder-filled gelatin capsules.

"From Podgorny, at the Institute for Metabolic Research, in Leningrad," Redding said simply. "He believes the theory behind the compound to be quite sound."

"Amazing," Drexler muttered. "Absolutely amazing." Rudy Podgorny was a giant in the field, but so inaccessible that it had been two years since he had met with him face to face. Redding's resourcefulness, the power of his money, was mind-boggling. "Well," he said when he had finished his tabulations, "these two preparations have finally had clinical evaluations. Both of them have been shown to be without significant effect. We can discuss my thoughts when Dr. Ferguson arrives, but I feel the data now are strong enough to recommend stopping them."

Redding fingered the bottles. "One of these was your baby, yes?"

The physician shrugged helplessly and nodded. "Yes," he said, "I am afraid I have hitched my wagon to a falling star." He failed in his attempt to keep an optimistic tone in his voice. Four years of work had, in essence, gone down the drain.

"Then you must strike out in other directions, eh?"

Just tell me, Drexler thought, *tell me how in the hell you know the medications you are taking won't just kill you on the spot?*

"Yes," he said, through a tight smile, "I suppose I must."

The sleek, stretch limousine moved like a serpent through the light midafternoon traffic on the Southeast Expressway. In the front seat, Redding's portly driver chattered at the taciturn Nunes, whose contribution to the conversation was an occasional nod or monosyllable. In the rear, seated across from one another, surrounded on all sides by smoked glass, Redding and John Ferguson sipped brandy and reviewed the session they had just completed with Vernon Drexler.

"I am sorry things have not been going well with you, John," Redding said. "Perhaps we should have stayed and let Drexler examine you."

"Nonsense. I have an appointment next month, and that will be quite time enough."

"Yes, I suppose so." There was little question in Redding's mind that Ferguson, perhaps eight years his senior, was failing. The man, never robust, had lost strength and weight. He could shuffle only a few dozen steps without exhaustion. His face was drawn and sallow, dominated by a mouth of full, perfect teeth that gave his every expression a cadaverous cast. Only his eyes, sparkling from within deep hollows like chips of aquamarine, reflected the immense drive and intellectual power that had marked the man's life.

Their collaboration, for that is what it quickly became, had begun on the day of their first meeting in Drexler's office. Ferguson, though still ambulatory with a cane, had the more advanced disease of the two. He was employed at the time as medical director of a state hospital outside of the city and was already taking two experimental drugs after testing them for a time on the patients of his facility.

Within a year, Redding had begun locating new preparations, while Ferguson expanded his testing program to include them. Quickly, though, both men came to appreciate the need for a larger number of test subjects than could be supplied by Ferguson's hospital. Establishment of the Total Care Women's Health Center in Denver and, soon after, the Omnicenter in Boston, was the upshot of that need. Vernon Drexler continued as their physician, monitoring their progress and watching over their general states of health.

Redding's driver, still prattling cheerfully at Nunes, swung onto 95 North. Although they would eventually end up at John Ferguson's Newton home, his only other instruction had been for a steady one-hour drive.

"John," Redding said, setting his half-filled snifter in its holder on the bar, "how long has it been since you were at the Omnicenter?"

Ferguson laughed ruefully. "How long since I've been anyplace would be a better question. Two years, perhaps. Maybe longer. It's just too difficult for me to get around."

"I understand."

"I take it from our conversation yesterday evening that there's been some kind of problem. Zimmermann?"

This time it was Redding who laughed. "No, no," he said. "From all I can tell, Zimmermann was the perfect choice for the job. You were absolutely right in recommending him. A harmless fop with the intelligence to implement and monitor our testing program without getting in the way. No, not Zimmermann."

"Well, then?"

"Actually, there may not even be a problem. When you were working with Dr. French to set up the Omnicenter, did you ever run into a Dr. Kathryn Bennett?" Ferguson thought for a moment and then shook his head. "I suspected you wouldn't have," Redding said.

It took only a few minutes for Redding to review the events leading to Kate Bennett's inspection of the Omnicenter.

Ferguson listened with the dispassion of a scientist, his silence punctuated only by occasional gestures that he was following the account.

"Carl Horner assures me," Redding concluded, "that none of the pharmaceuticals we are studying could have been responsible for the problems young Dr. Bennett is investigating."

"But you are not so sure."

"John, you've worked with Carl. You know that being wrong is not something he does very often. The man's mind is as much a computer as any of his machines."

"But you think two such distinctive cases, and now possibly a third, are too many to explain by coincidence?"

Redding stared out the window; he removed his glasses and cleaned them with a towel from the bar. "To tell you the truth, John, I don't know what to think. The facts say one thing, my instincts another. You know the Omnicenter better than I do. Could anyone be fooling around with some drug or other kind of agent behind our backs?"

"I hope not."

"John, mull over what I've told you. See if you can come up with any theories that might explain why all three women with this bleeding problem, and two of them with the same ovary problem, were all patients of the Omnicenter." He flipped the intercom switch. "Mr. Crosscup, you may drive us to Dr. Ferguson's house," he said.

"I will think it over," Ferguson said, "but my impression is that this once at least, your instincts should yield to the facts."

"A week."

"Excuse me?"

"A week, John," Redding said. "I should like to hear something from you about this matter in a week."

Ferguson probed the younger man's eyes. "You seem to be implying that I am holding something back."

"I imply nothing of the kind." He smiled enigmatically. "I am only asking for your help."

The limousine pulled into the snow-banked drive of John Ferguson's house, a trim white colonial on perhaps an acre of land. Redding engaged the intercom. "Mr. Nunes," he said, "our business has been concluded. Kindly assist our guest to his home."

The men shook hands and Redding watched as Nunes aided an obviously exhausted John Ferguson up the walk to the front door. The old man was many things, Redding acknowledged, a brilliant physician and administrator, an exceptional judge of human nature and predictor of human behavior, a gifted philosopher. What he was not, Redding had known since the early days of their association, was John Ferguson. Redding's investigators had been able to learn that much, but no more. There had been a John Ferguson with an educational background identical to this man's, but that John Ferguson had died in the bombing of a field hospital in Bataan. Originally, Redding's instincts had argued against a confrontation with his new associate over what, exactly, the man was hiding from. That decision had proved prudent—at least until now.

Ferguson bid a final good-bye with a weak wave and entered his home.

Behind the smoked glass of the limousine, Cyrus Redding was placing a phone call through the mobile operator. "Dr. Stein, please," Redding said. "Hello, Doctor, this is your friend from Darlington. The man, John Ferguson, of whom I spoke last night: I should like the reinvestigation and close observation instituted at once. Keep me informed personally of your progress. He seems to have materialized shortly after World War Two, so perhaps that is a period to reinvestigate first. Thank you."

All right, my friend, he thought. For fifteen years, I have allowed you your deception. Let us hope that courtesy was not misplaced.

Kate Bennett set her dictaphone headpiece in its cradle and stared across the street at the darkened Omnicenter. Reflections from the headlights of passing cars sparkling off its six-foot windows lent an eerie animation to the structure, which stood out against its dark brick surroundings like a spaceship. Kate knew it was her never-timid imagination at work, knew it was the phone call she was expecting, but she still could not rationalize away her sense of the building as something ominous, something virulent.

The message had been on her desk when she returned from the Friday meeting of the hospital Infection Control Committee, which she had chaired for almost a year.

"Ian Toole at State Toxicology Lab called," the department secretary's note said. "One spec you sent normal, one spec contaminated. Please await phone call with details between six and seven tonight."

Contaminated.

"It's you. I know it is." Her mind spoke the words to the gleaming five stories. "Something inside you, inside your precious Monkeys, has gone haywire. Something inside you is killing people, and you don't even know it."

The ringing of the telephone startled her. "Kate Bennett," she answered excitedly.

"Kate Bennett's husband," Jared said flatly.

"Oh, hi. You surprised me. I was expecting a call from Ian Toole in the toxicology lab and . . . never mind that. Where are you? Is everything all right?"

"At home, where you're supposed to be, and no."

Kate glanced at the clock on her desk and groaned. "Oh, damn. Jared, I forgot about the Carlisles. I'm sorry."

"Apology not accepted," he said with no hint of humor.

Kate sank in her chair, resigned to the outburst she knew was about to ensue, and knowing that it was justified. "I'm sorry anyhow," she said softly.

"You're always sorry, aren't you?" Jared said. "You're so wrapped up in Kate's job and Kate's world and Kate's problems that you seem to forget that there are any other jobs or worlds or problems around. My father and several big-money people are going to be at that party tonight. What kind of an impression is it going to make when I show up without my wife?"

"Jared, you don't understand. Something is going on here. People are dying."

"People like Bobby Geary?"

Kate glanced at the clock. It was five minutes to seven. "Look," she said, "I'm waiting for a call that could help solve this mystery. I can call you back or I can get home as soon as possible, change, and make it over to the Carlisles by eight-thirty or nine."

"Don't bother."

"Jared, what do you want me to do?"

Jared's sigh was audible over the phone. "I want you to do whatever it is you feel you have to do," he said. "I'll go to the Carlisles and make do. We can talk later tonight or tomorrow. Okay?"

"All right," she said, taken somewhat aback by his reasonableness. "How's Ellen?"

"Pardon?" It was one minute to seven.

"Ellen. You remember, our friend Ellen. How is she?"

"She's in the hospital, Jared. Listen, I really am sorry, and I really am in the middle, or at least on the fringes of something strange. Ellen's life may be at stake in what I'm doing."

"Sounds pretty melodramatic to me," Jared said, "but then again, I'm just a poor ol' country lawyer. We'll talk later."

"Thank you, Jared. I love you."

"See you later, Kate."

Ian Toole's call came at precisely seven-fifteen.

"These are some little pills you sent me here, Dr. Bennett," he said. "My assistant, Millicent, and I have been running them most of the afternoon, and we still don't have a final word for you."

"But you said Ellen's pills were contaminated."

"Ellen Sandler's? Hardly. I think your secretary mixed up my message. Probably went to the same school as ours."

"What do you mean?"

"Ellen Sandler's vitamins are a pretty run-of-the-mill, low-potency preparation. B complex, a little C, a little iron, a splash of zinc. It's yours that are weird."

"Mine?" Kate's throat grew dry and tight.

"Uh-huh. You're not only taking the same vitamins as Ellen Sandler, but you're also taking a fairly sizable jolt every day of some kind of anthranilic acid."

"Anthranilic acid?"

"Millicent and I are trying to work out the side chains, but that's the basic molecule."

Kate felt sick. "Mr. Toole, what is it?"

"I'm a chemist, not a doctor, but as far as I've been able to determine, you're taking a painkiller of some sort. Nonnarcotic. Some kind of nonsteroidal anti-inflammatory drug. The basic molecule is listed in our manuals, but I don't think we're going to find the exact side chains. Whatever it is, it's not a commercially available drug in this country. If it were, we'd have it in the book. I'll check out the European manuals as soon as we know the full structure."

"Let me know?" Kate had written out the word "anthranilic" and begun a calligraphic version.

"Of course. Probably won't be until next week, though. I had to promise Millicent a bottle of wine to get her to put off her date with her boyfriend even this long."

"Mr. Toole, is it dangerous?"

"What?"

"Anthranilic acid."

"Like I said, I'm not a doctor. It's not poisonous, if that's what you mean, but it's not vitamins either. Any drug can do you dirt if you're unusually sensitive or allergic to it."

"Thanks," Kate said numbly. "And thanks to Millicent, too."

"No problem," Ian Toole said.

It was a hot, sultry day at Fenway Park when Kate, seated in a box next to Jared, began to bleed to death. Silently, painlessly, thick drops of crimson fell from her nose, landing like tiny artillery bursts on the surface of the beer she was holding, turning the gold to pink.

She squeezed her nose with a napkin, but almost instantly tasted the sticky sweetness flowing down the back of her throat. Jared, unaware of what was happening, sipped at his beer, his attention riveted on the field. Help me. Please, Jared, help me, I'm dying. The words were in her mind, but somehow inaccessible to her voice. Help me, please. Suddenly she felt a warm moistness inside her jeans, and knew that she was bleeding there as well. Help me.

In the box to her right, Winfield Samuels looked her way, smiled emptily as if she weren't even there, and then turned back to the field and genteelly applauded a good play by the shortstop.

The players and the grass, the spectators and the huge green left-field wall—all had a reddish cast. Kate rubbed a hand across one eye and realized she was also bleeding from there.

Giddy with fear, she stood and turned to run. Sitting in the row behind her chatting amiably and smiling as blandly as Jared's father had, were Norton Reese and a man with the overalls and gray hair of Carl Horner but the grotesque face of a monkey.

"I see you're bleeding to death," Reese said pleasantly. "I'm so sorry. Carl, aren't you sorry?"

Jared, please help me. Help me. Help me.

The words faded like an echo into eternity. Kate became aware of a gentle hand on her shoulder.

"Dr. Bennett, are you all right?"

Kate lifted her head and blearily met the eyes of night watchman Walter MacFarlane. She was at a table, alone in the hospital library, surrounded by dozens of books and journals dealing with bleeding disorders, ovarian disease, and pharmacology.

"Oh, yes, Walter," she said, "I'm fine, thank you. Really." Her blouse was uncomfortably damp, and the taste in her mouth most unpleasant.

"Just checking," the man said. "It's getting pretty late. Or should I say early." He tapped a finger on the face of his large gold pocket watch and held it around for her to see.

Twenty after two.

Kate smiled weakly and began gathering her notes together.

"I'll see you to your car if you want, Doctor."

"Thanks, Walter, I'll meet you by the main entrance in five minutes."

She watched as the man shuffled from the library. Then she discarded the notion of calling Jared, knowing that she would just be adding insult to injury by waking him up, and finished packing her briefcase. As she neared the doorway, she glanced out the window. Across the street, the winter night reflected obscenely in its dark glass, stood the Omnicenter.

CHAPTER 8
Sunday 16 December

THE NIGHT WAS heavy and raw. Crunching through slush that had begun to gel and shielding her face from blowgun darts of sleet, Kate crossed Commercial Street and plowed along Hanover into the North End. Traffic and the weather had made her twenty minutes late, but Bill Zimmermann was not the irritable, impatient type, and she anticipated a quick absolution. Demarsco's, the restaurant they had agreed upon, was a small, family-owned operation where parking was as difficult to find as an unexceptional item on the menu.

Initially, when Kate had called and asked to meet with him, Zimmermann had proposed his office at the Omnicenter. It was, perhaps, among the last structures on earth she felt like entering on that night. Unfortunately if there were a list of such things, Demarsco's, his other suggestion, might also have been on it. Demarsco's was one of her and Jared's favorite spots.

And now Jared was gone.

"A sort of separation, but not a separation," he had called it in the note she had found waiting for her at three o'clock on Saturday morning. He had taken some things and gone to his father's, where he would stay until leaving for business in San Diego on Monday.

"A sort of separation, but not a separation."

There was no lengthy explanation. No apology. Not even any anger. But the hurt and confusion were there in every word. It was as if he had just discovered that his wife was having an affair—an up-and-down, intense, emotionally draining affair—not with another man, but with her job, her career. "Space for both of us to sort out the tensions and pressures on our lives without adding new ones," he had written. "Space for each of us to take a hard look at our priorities."

Kate wondered if, standing in the center of his fine, paneled study, his elegant mistress awaiting him on his black satin sheets, Winfield Samuels, Jr., had raised a glass to toast his victory over Kate and the return of his son and to plan how to make a temporary situation permanent. It was a distressing picture and probably not that far from reality.

However, as distressing to her as the image of a gloating Win Samuels, was the realization that her incongruous emotion, at least at that moment and over the hour or so that followed before sleep took her, was relief. Relief at being spared a confrontation. Relief at being alone to think.

Someone was trying to sabotage her reputation and perhaps her career. Her close friend was lying in a hospital bed bleeding from a disorder that had killed at least two other women—a disorder that had no definite cause, let alone a cure. And now, there was the discovery that she herself had been exposed to contaminated vitamins, that her own body might be a time bomb, waiting to go off—perhaps to bleed, perhaps to die.

Priorities. Why couldn't Jared see their marriage as a blanket on which all the other priorities in their lives could be laid out and dealt with together? Why couldn't he see that their relationship needn't be an endless series of either-ors? Why couldn't he see that she could love him and still have a life of her own?

Demarsco's was on the first floor of a narrow brownstone. There were a dozen tables covered with red-and-white checkered tablecloths and adorned with candle-dripped Chianti bottles—a decor that might have been tacky, but in Demarsco's simply wasn't. Bill Zimmermann, seated at a small table to the rear, rose and waved as she entered. He wore a dark sport jacket over a gray turtleneck and looked to her like a mix of the best of Gary Cooper and Montgomery Clift. A maternal waitress, perhaps the matriarch of the Demarsco clan, took her coat and ushered her to Zimmermann with a look that said she approved of the woman for whom the tall dashing man at the rear table had been waiting.

"They have a wonderful soave," Kate answered, settling into her seat, "but you'll have to drink most of it. I haven't been getting much sleep lately, and when I'm tired, more than one glass of wine is usually enough to cross my eyes."

"I have no such problem, unfortunately," he said, nodding that the ample waitress could fill his earlier order. "Sometimes, I fear that my liver will desert me before my brain even knows I have been drinking. It is one of the curses of being European. I stopped by the hospital earlier to see your friend Mrs. Sandler."

"I know. I was with her just before I came here. She was grateful for your visit. Whatever you said had a markedly reassuring effect." Kate smiled inwardly, remembering the girlish exchange she and Ellen had had regarding the Omnicenter director's uncommon good looks and marital status.

"Maybe I could rent him for a night," Ellen had said, "just to parade past Sandy a time or two."

Zimmermann tapped his fingertips together. "The lab reports show very little change."

"I know," Kate said. "If anything, they're worse. Unless there are several days in a row of improvement, or at least stability, I don't think her hematologist will send her home." She felt a heaviness in her chest as her mind replayed the gruesome scene on Ashburton Five during Beverly Vitale's last minutes. Ellen's counts were not yet down to critical levels, but there were so many unknowns. A sudden, precipitous fall seemed quite possible. The stream of thoughts flowed into the question of whether with Ian Toole's findings, Kate herself should have some clotting measurements done. She discarded the notion almost as quickly as she recognized it.

"I hope as you do that there will be improvement," Zimmermann said. He paused and then scanned the menu. "What will it be for you?" he asked finally.

"I'm not too hungry. How about an antipasto, some garlic bread . . . and a side order of peace of mind?"

Zimmermann's blue-gray eyes, still fixed on the leather-enclosed menu, narrowed a fraction. "That bad?"

Kate chewed at her lower lip and nodded, suddenly very glad she had gone the route of calling him. If, as seemed possible, a confrontation with Redding Pharmaceuticals was to happen, it would be good to have an ally with Bill Zimmermann's composure and assuredness, especially considering the fragility of her own self-confidence.

"In that case, perhaps I had best eat light also." Zimmermann called the waitress over with a microscopic nod and ordered identical meals.

"I want to thank you for coming out on such a grisly night," Kate began. "There have been some new developments in my efforts to make sense out of the three bleeding cases, and I wanted to share them with you."

"Oh?" Zimmermann's expression grew more attentive.

"You know I've had sample after sample of medications from the Omnicenter analyzed at the State Toxicology Lab."

"Yes, of course. But I thought the results had all been unremarkable."

"They were . . . until late Friday afternoon. One of the vitamin samples I had analyzed contained a painkiller called anthranilic acid. The basic chemical structure of the drug is contained in several commerical products—Bymid, from Sampson Pharmaceuticals, and Levonide, from Freeman-Gannett, to name two. However, the form contaminating the vitamins is something new—at least in this country. Ian Toole at the state lab is going to check the European manuals and call me tomorrow."

"Is he sure of the results?"

"He seemed to be. I don't know the man personally, but he has a reputation for thoroughness."

"What do you think happened?"

"Contamination." Kate shrugged that there was no other explanation that made any sense. "Either at Redding Pharmaceuticals or perhaps at one of the suppliers of the vitamin components, although I would suspect that a company as large as Redding can do all the manufacturing themselves."

"Yes. I agree. Do you think this anthranilic acid has caused the bleeding disorders in our three women?"

"Bleeding *and* ovarian disorders," Kate added, "at least ovarian in two of the women. We don't know about Ellen. The answer to your question is I don't know and I certainly hope not."

"Why?"

"Because, Bill, the vitamins that were finally positive for something were mine. Ones you prescribed for me."

Zimmermann paled. The waitress arrived with their antipasto, but he did not so much as glance up at her. "Jesus," he said softly. It was the first time Kate had ever heard him use invective of any kind. "Are you sure this Toole couldn't have made a mistake? You said yourself there were any number of samples that were negative."

"Anything's possible," she said. "I suppose Ian Toole and his spectrophotometer are no more exempt from error than . . . Redding Pharmaceuticals."

"Do you have more of a sample? Can we have the findings rechecked at another lab?"

Kate shook her head. "It was an old prescription. There were only half a dozen left. I think he used them all."

Zimmermann tried picking at his meal but quickly gave up. "I don't

346

mean to sound doubtful about what you are saying, Kate. But you see what's at stake here, don't you?"

"Of course I do. And I understand your skepticism. If I were in your position and the Omnicenter were my baby, I'd want to be sure, too. But Bill, the situation is desperate. Two women have died. My friend is lying up there bleeding, and I have been unknowingly taking a medication that was never prescribed for me. Someone in or around Redding's generic drug department has made an error, and I think we should file a report with the FDA as quickly as possible. I spoke to the head pharmacist at Metro about how one goes about reporting problems with a drug."

"Did you mention the Omnicenter specifically?" Zimmermann asked.

"I may be nervous and frightened about all this, Bill, but I'm neither dumb nor insensitive. No. Everything I asked him was hypothetical."

"Thank you."

"Nonsense. Grandstand plays aren't my style." She smiled. "Despite what the papers and all those angry Red Sox fans think. Any decisions concerning the Omnicenter we make together." Kate nibbled on the edge of a piece of garlic bread and suddenly realized that for the first time since returning home to Jared's note, she had an appetite. Perhaps, after the incredible frustrations of the week past, she was feeling the effects of finally doing something. She passed the basket across to Zimmermann. "Here," she offered, "have a piece of this before it gets cold."

Zimmermann accepted the offering, but deep concern continued to darken his face. "What did the pharmacist tell you?"

"There's an agency called the U.S. Pharmacopia, independent of both the FDA and the drug industry, but in close touch with both. They run a drug-problem reporting program. Fill out a form and send it to them, and they send a copy to the FDA and to the company involved."

"Do you know what happens then?"

"Not really. I assume an investigator from the FDA is assigned to look into matters."

"And the great bureaucratic dragon rears its ugly head."

"What?"

"Have you had many dealings with the FDA? Speed and efficiency are hardly their most important products. No one's fault, really. The FDA has some pretty sharp people—only not nearly enough of them."

"What else can we do?" Absently, Kate rolled a black olive off its lettuce hillock and ate it along with several thin strips of prosciutto. "I need help. As it is, I'm spending every spare moment in the library. I've even asked the National Institutes of Health library to run a computer cross on blood and ovarian disorders. They should be sending me a bibliography tomorrow. I've sent our slides to four other pathologists to see if anyone can make a connection. The FDA seems like the only remaining move."

"The FDA may be a necessary move, but it is hardly our only one. First of all I want to speak with Carl Horner and our pharmacist and see to it that the use of any Redding products by our facility will be suspended until we have some answers."

"Excellent. Will you have to bring in extra pharmacists?"

"Yes, but we've had contingency plans in place in case of some kind of computer failure since . . . well, since even before I took over as director. We'll manage as long as necessary."

"Let's hope it won't be too long," Kate said, again thinking of Beverly Vitale's lifeless, blood-smeared face.

"If we go right to the FDA it might be."

"Pardon?"

"Kate, I think our first move should be to contact Redding Pharmaceuticals directly. I think the company deserves that kind of consideration for the way they've stood up for orphan drugs and for all the other things they've done to help the medical community and society as a whole. Besides, in any contest between the bureaucratic dragon and private industry, my money is on industry every time. I think it's only fair to the Omnicenter and our patients to get to the bottom of matters as quickly as possible."

Kate sipped pensively at her wine. "I see what you mean . . . sort of," she said. "Couldn't we do both? I mean contact Redding and notify the FDA?"

"We could, but then we lose our stick, our prod, if you will. The folks at Redding will probably bend over backward to avoid the black eye of an FDA probe. I know they will. I've had experience with other pharmaceutical houses—ones not as responsive and responsible as Redding. They would go to almost any length to identify and correct problems within their company without outside intervention."

"That makes sense, I guess," she said.

"You sound uncertain, Kate. Listen, whatever we do, we should do together. You said that yourself. I've given you reasons for my point of view, but I'm by no means inflexible." Zimmermann drained the last half of his glass and refilled it.

Kate hesitated and then said, "I have this thing about the pharmaceutical industry. It's a problem in trust. They spend millions and millions of dollars on giveaways to medical students and physicians. They support dozens upon dozens of throwaway journals and magazines with their ads. I get fifty publications a month I never ordered. And I don't even write prescriptions. I can imagine how many you get." Zimmermann nodded that he understood. "In addition, I have serious questions about their priorities—you know, who comes first in any conflict between profit and people."

"What do you mean?"

"Well, look at Valium. Roche introduces the drug and markets it well, and the public literally eats it up. It's a tranquilizer, a downer, yet in no time at all it becomes the most prescribed and taken drug in the country. Unfortunately, it turns out to be more addicting than most physicians appreciated at first, and lives begin to get ruined. Meanwhile, a dozen or so other drug houses put out a dozen or so versions of Valium, each with its own name and its own claim. Slower acting. Faster acting. Lasts all night. Removed more rapidly. Some busy physicians get so lost in the advertising and promises that they actually end up prescribing two of these variants to the same patient at the same time. Others think they're doing their patients a big favor by switching. Some favor."

"Pardon me for saying it, Kate, but you sound a little less than objective."

"I'm afraid you hear right," she said. "I had some emotional stresses back in college, and the old country doctor who served the school put me on Valium. It took a whole team of specialists to realize how much my life came to revolve around those little yellow discs. Finally, I had to be hospitalized and detoxed. So I just have this nagging feeling that the drug companies can't be trusted. That's all."

Zimmermann leaned back, rubbed his chin, and sighed. "I don't know what to say. If speed is essential in solving this problem, as we both think it is, then the route to go is the company. I'm sure of that." He paused. "Tell you what. Let's give them this coming week to straighten out matters to our satisfaction. If they haven't done so by Friday, we call in the FDA. Sound fair?"

Kate hesitated, but then nodded. "Yes," she said finally. "It sounds fair and it sounds right. Do you want to call them?"

Zimmermann shrugged. "Sure," he said, "I'll do it first thing tomorrow. They'll probably be contacting you by the end of the day."

"The sooner the better. Meanwhile, do you think you could talk to some of your Omnicenter patients and get me a list of women who would be willing to be contacted by me about having their medications analyzed?"

"I certainly can try."

"Excellent. It's about time things started moving in a positive direction. You know, there's not much good I can say about all that's been happening, except that I'm glad our relationship has moved out of the doctor-patient and doctor-doctor cubbyholes into the person-person. Right now I'm the one who needs the help, but please know that if it's ever you, you've got a friend you can count on."

Zimmermann smiled a Cary Grant smile. "That kind of friend is hard to come by," he said. "Thank you."

"Thank you. Except for Tom Engleson, I've felt pretty much alone in all this. Now we're a team." She motioned the waitress over.

"Coffee?" the woman asked.

"None for me, thanks. Bill?" Zimmermann shook his head. "In that case could I have the check, please?"

"Nonsense," Zimmermann said, "I won't . . ."—the reproving look in Kate's eyes stopped him in midsentence—". . . allow you to do this too many times without reciprocating."

Kate beamed at the man's insight. "Deal," she said, smiling broadly.

"Deal," Zimmermann echoed.

The two shook hands warmly and, after Kate had settled their bill, walked together into the winter night.

Numb with exhaustion, John Ferguson squinted at the luminescent green print on the screen of his word processor. His back ached from hunching over the keyboard for the better part of two full days. His hands, feeling the effects of his disease more acutely than at any time in months, groped for words one careful letter at a time. It had been an agonizing effort, condensing forty years of complex research into thirty pages or so of scholarly dissertation, but a sentence at a time, a word at a time, he was making progress.

To one side of his desk were a dozen internationally read medical journals. Ferguson had given thought to submitting his completed manuscript to all of them, but then had reconsidered. The honor of publishing his work would go only to *The New England Journal of Medicine,* most prestigious and widely read of them all.

The New England Journal of Medicine. Ferguson tapped out a recall code, and in seconds, the title page of his article was displayed on the screen.

STUDIES IN ESTRONATE 250
A Synthetic Estrogen Congener and
Antifertility Hormone
John N. Ferguson, MD

It would almost certainly be the first time in the long, distinguished publication of the journal that an entire issue would be devoted to a single article. But they would agree to do that or find the historic studies and comment in *Lancet* or *The American Journal of Medicine.* Ferguson smiled. Once *The New England Journal's* editors had reviewed his data and his slides, he doubted there would be much resistance to honoring his request. For a time he studied the page. Then, electronically, he erased the name of the author. There might be trouble for him down the road for what he was about to do, but he suspected not. He was too old and too sick even for the fanatic Simon Weisenthal to bother with.

With a deliberateness that helped him savor the act, he typed

Wilhelm W. Becker, MD, PhD where Ferguson's name had been. Perhaps, he thought with a smile, some sort of brief funeral was in order for Ferguson. He had, after all, died twice—once in Bataan, forty years ago, and a second time this night.

With the consummate discipline that had marked his life, Willi Becker cut short the pleasurable interlude and advanced the text to the spot at which he had left off. Because of a pathologist named Bennett, Cyrus Redding had picked up the scent of his work at the Omnicenter. Knowing the man as well as Becker did, he felt certain the tycoon would now track the matter relentlessly. There was still time to put the work on paper and mail it off, but no way of knowing how much. He had to push. He had to fight the fatigue and the aching in his muscles and push, at least for another hour or two. The onset of his scientific immortality was at hand.

Furtively, he glanced at the small bottle of amphetamines on the table. It had been only three hours. Much too soon, especially with the irregular heartbeats he had been having. Still, he needed to push. It would only be a few more days, perhaps less. Barely able to grip the top of the small vial, Becker set one of the black, coated tablets on his tongue, and swallowed it without water. In minutes, the warm rush would begin, and he would have the drive, however artifical and short lived, to overcome the inertia of his myasthenia.

"You really shouldn't take those, you know, father. Especially with your cardiac history."

Becker spun around to face his son, cursing the diminution in his hearing that enabled such surprises. "I take them because I need them," he said sharply. "What are you doing sneaking up on me like that? What do you think doorbells are for?"

"Such a greeting. And here I have driven out of my way to stop by and be certain you are all right."

Three blocks, Becker thought. Some hardship. "You startled me. That's all. I'm sorry for reacting the way I did."

"In that case, father, it is I who should be sorry."

Was there sarcasm in his son's voice? It bothered Becker that he had never been able to read the man. Theirs was a relationship based on filial obligation and respect, but little if any love. For the greater portion of his son's years, they had lived apart: Becker in a small cottage on the hospital grounds where he worked, and his wife and son in an apartment twenty miles away. It was as necessary an arrangement as it was painful. Becker and his wife had tried for years to make their son understand that. There were those, they tried to explain, who would arrest Becker in a moment on a series of unjust charges, put him in prison, and possibly even put him to death. In the hysteria following the war, he had been marked simply because he was German, nothing more than that. For their own safety, it was necessary for the boy and his mother to keep their address and even their name separate from his.

Although Becker would provide for them and would visit as much as he could, no one would ever know his true relationship to the woman, Anna Zimmermann, and the boy, William.

"So," Becker said. "Now that we have apologized profusely to one another, come in, sit down, pour yourself a drink."

William Zimmermann nodded his thanks, poured an inch of Wild Turkey into a heavy glass, and settled into an easy chair opposite his father.

"I see you've started putting your data together," he said. "Why now?"

"Well, I . . . no special reason, really. It would seem that the modifications I made have greatly, if not completely, eliminated the bleeding problems we were experiencing with the Estronate. So what else is there to wait for?"

"Which journal will you approach?"

"I think *The New England Journal of Medicine.* I plan to submit the data and discussion but to withhold several key steps in the synthesis until a commission of the journal's choosing can take charge of my formulas and decide how society can best benefit from them."

"Sounds fine to me," Zimmermann said. "With all that's been happening this last week, the sooner I see the last of Estronate Two-fifty, the better."

"Have any further bleeding cases turned up?"

Zimmermann shook his head. "Just the Sandler woman I told you about. The one who's the friend of Dr. Bennett's. She was treated over eighteen months ago, in the July/August group, the last group to receive the unmodified Estronate."

"How is she doing?"

"I think she is going to end up like the other two."

"Couldn't you find some way of suggesting that they try a course of massive doses of delta amino caproic acid and nicotinic acid on her?"

"Not without risking a lot of questions I'd rather not answer. I mean I am a gynecologist, not a hematologist. Besides, you told me that that therapy was only sixty percent effective in such advanced states."

Becker shrugged. "Sixty percent is sixty percent."

"And my career is my career. No, father, I have far too much to lose. I am afraid Mrs. Sandler will just have to make it on her own."

"Perhaps you are right," Becker said.

The men shook hands formally, and William Zimmermann let himself out. Twelve miles away, on the fourth floor of the Berenson Building of Metropolitan Hospital of Boston, in Room 421, Ellen Sandler's nose had again begun to bleed.

CHAPTER 9
Monday 17 December

"Now, Suzy, promise Daddy that you will mind what Mommy tells you and that you will never, never do that to the cat again. . . . Good. . . . I have to go now, sugar. You better get ready for your piano lesson. . . . I know what I said, but my work here isn't done yet, and I have to stay until it's finished. . . . I don't know. Two, maybe three more days. . . . Suzy, stop that. You're not a baby. I love you very much and I'll see you very soon. Now, tell Daddy you love him and go practice that new piece of yours. . . . Suzy? . . ."

"Damn." Arlen Paquette slammed the receiver down. He had protested to Redding the futility of remaining in Boston over the weekend, but the man had insisted he stay close to the situation and the Omnicenter. As usual, events had proven Redding right. Paquette stuffed some notes in his briefcase and pulled on his suitcoat. Right for Redding Pharmaceuticals, but not for Suzy Paquette, who was justifiably smarting over her father's absence from her school track meet earlier in the day. How could he explain to a seven-year-old that the very thing that was keeping him away from home was also the sole reason she could attend a school like Hightower Academy? He straightened his tie and combed his thinning hair with his fingers. How could he explain it to her when he was having trouble justifying it to himself? Still, for what he and his family were gaining from his association with Redding, the dues were not excessive. He glanced down at the photographs of Kate Bennett piled on the coffee table. At least, he thought, not yet.

The cab ride from the Ritz to Metropolitan Hospital took fifteen minutes. Paquette entered the main lobby through newly installed gliding electronic doors and headed directly for Norton Reese's office, half expecting to have the woman whose life and face he had studied in such detail stroll out from a side corridor and bump into him.

"Arlen, it's good to see you. You're looking well." Norton Reese maneuvered free of his desk chair and met Paquette halfway with an ill-defined handshake. Theirs was more an unspoken truce than a relationship, and no amount of time would compensate for the lack of trust and respect each bore the other. However, Paquette was the envoy of Cyrus Redding and the several millions of Redding dollars that had sparked Reese's rise to prominence. Although it was Reese's court, it was the younger man's ball.

"You're looking fit yourself, Norton," Paquette replied. "Our mutual friend sends his respects and regards."

"Did you tell him about our speed freak outfielder and the letters to the press and TV?"

"I did. I even sent a packet of the articles and editorials to him by messenger. He commends your ingenuity. So, incidentally, do I." Try as he might, he could put no emotion behind the compliment.

Still, Reese's moon face bunched in a grin. "It's been beautiful, Arlen," he gushed. "Just beautiful. I tell you, ever since that story broke, Kathryn Bennett, MD, has been racing all over trying to stick her fingers in the holes that are popping open in her reputation. By now I doubt if she would know whether she had lost a horse or found a rope."

"You did fine, Norton. Just fine. Only, for our purposes, not enough."

"What?" Reese began to shift uneasily. "A diversion. That's what Horner asked me for, and by God, that's what I laid on that woman. A goddamn avalanche of diversion."

"You did fine, Norton. I just told you that."

"Why, she's had so much negative publicity it's a wonder she hasn't quit or been fired by the medical school." Reese chattered on as if he hadn't heard a word. "In fact, I hear the Medical School Ethics Committee is planning some kind of an inquiry."

Paquette silenced him with raised hands. "Easy, Norton, please," he said evenly. "I'm going to say it one more time. What you did, the letter and all, was exactly what we asked of you. Our mutual friend is pleased. He asked that I convey to you the Ashburton Foundation's intention to endow the cardiac surgical residency you wrote him about."

"Well, then, why was what I did not enough?" Reese realized that in his haste to defend himself, he had forgotten to acknowledge Redding's generosity. Before he could remedy the oversight, Paquette spoke.

"I'll convey your thanks when I return to Darlington," he said, a note of irritation in his words. "Norton, do you know what has been going on here?"

"Not . . . not exactly," he said, nonplussed.

Paquette nodded indulgently. "Dr. Bennett, in her search to identify the cause of an unusual bleeding problem in several women, has zeroed in on the Omnicenter. Although the women were Omnicenter patients, we see no other connection among them."

"The . . . the work you're doing . . . I mean none of the women got . . . ." After years of scrupulously avoiding the Omnicenter and the people involved in its operation, Reese was uncertain of how, even, to discuss the place.

Paquette spared him further stammering. "From time to time, each of the women was involved in the evaluation of one or more products," he said. "However, Carl Horner assures me that there have been no products common to the three of them. Whatever the cause of their problem, it is not the Omnicenter."

"That's a relief," Reese said.

"Not really," Paquette said, his expression belying his impatience. "You see, our Dr. Bennett has been most persistent, despite the pressures brought about by your letter."

"She's a royal pain in the ass. I'll grant you that," Reese interjected.

"She has tested several Omnicenter products at the State Toxicology Lab, charging the analyses, I might add, to your hospital."

"Damn her. She didn't find anything, did she? Horner assured me that there was nothing to worry about."

Paquette's patience continued to fray. "Of course she found something, Norton. That's why I'm here. She even had Dr. Zimmermann phone the company to tell us about it."

"Oh. Sorry."

"Our friend in Kentucky has asked that we step up our efforts to discredit Dr. Bennett and to add, what was the word you used? distraction? . . . no, diversion, that was it—diversion to her life. We have taken steps to obscure, if not neutralize, her findings to date, but there is evidence in dozens of medicine cabinets out there of what we have been doing. If Dr. Bennett is persistent enough, she will find it. I am completely convinced of that, and so is our friend. Dr. Bennett has given us one week to determine how a certain experimental painkiller came to be in a set of vitamins dispensed at the Omnicenter. If we do not furnish her with a satisfactory explanation by that time, she intends to file a report with the US Pharmacopia and the FDA."

"Damn her," Norton Reese said again. "What are we going to do?"

"Not we, you. Dr. Bennett's credibility must be reduced to the point where no amount of evidence will be enough for authorities to take her word over ours. The letter you wrote was a start, but, as I said, not enough."

Once again, Reese began to feel ill at ease. Paquette was not making a request, he was giving an order—an order from the man who, Reese knew, could squash him with nothing more than the eraser on his pencil. He unbuttoned his vest against the uncomfortable moistness between the folds of his skin.

"Look," he pleaded, "I really don't know what I can do. I'll try, but I don't know. You've got to understand, Arlen; you've got to make him understand. Bennett works in my hospital, but she doesn't work for me." There was understanding in Paquette's face, but not sympathy. Reese continued his increasingly nervous rambling. "Besides, the woman's got friends around here. I don't know why, but she does. Even after that letter, she's got supporters. Shit, I'd kill to make sure she didn't. . . ." His voice trailed away. His eyes narrowed.

Paquette followed the man's train of thought. "The answer is no, Norton," he said. "Absolutely not. We wish her discredited, not eliminated, for God's sake. We want people to lose interest in her, not to canonize her. She has already involved Dr. Zimmermann, a chemist at the state lab, and a resident here named Engleson. There may be others, but as far as we can tell, the situation is not yet out of control. We are doing what we can do to ensure it remains that way. Dr. Bennett's father-in-law does some business with our company. I believe our friend has already called him and enlisted his aid. There are other steps being taken as well." He rose and reached across the desk to shake Reese's hand. "I know we can count on you. If you need advice or a sounding board, you can reach me at the Ritz."

"Thank you," Reese said numbly. His bulk seemed melted into his chair.

Paquette walked slowly to the door, then turned. "Our friend has suggested Thursday as a time by which he wants something to have been done."

"Thursday?" Reese croaked.

Paquette nodded, smiled blankly, and was gone.

Half an hour later, his shirt changed and his composure nearly regained, Reese sat opposite Sheila Pierce, straightening one paper clip after another and thinking much more than he wanted to at that particular moment of the chief technician's breasts.

"How're things going down there in pathology?" he asked, wondering if she would take off her lab coat and then reminding himself to concentrate on business. The woman was going to require delicate handling if she was going to put her neck on the line to save his ass.

"You mean with Bennett?" Sheila shrugged. "She's getting some letters and a few crank phone calls every day, but otherwise things seem pretty much back to normal. It's been . . . amusing."

"Well," Reese said, "I know for a fact that the Bobby Geary business is hardly a dead issue."

"Oh?"

"I've heard the matter's going to the Medical School Ethics Committee."

"Good," Sheila said. "That will serve her right, going to the newspapers about that poor boy the way she did." They laughed. "Do you think," she went on, "that it will be enough to keep her from becoming chief of our department?"

Inwardly, Reese smiled. The question was just the opening he needed. "Doubtful," he said grimly. "Very doubtful."

"Too bad."

"You don't know the half of it."

"What do you mean?"

"Well . . ." He tapped a pencil eraser on his desk. He closed his eyes and massaged the bridge of his nose. He chewed at his lower lip. "I got a call this morning from Dr. Willoughby. He requested a meeting with the finance and budget committee of the board, at which time he and Kate Bennett are going to present the results of a computer study she's just completed. They plan to ask for six months worth of emergency funding until a sweeping departmental reorganization can be completed."

Sheila Pierce paled. "Sweeping departmental reorganization?"

"That's what the man said."

"Did he say anything about . . . you know."

Reese sighed. "As a matter of fact, baby, he did. He said that by the time of the meeting next week, Bennett will have presented him with a complete list of lost revenues, including the misappropriation of funds by several department members."

"But she promised."

"I guess a few brownie points with the boss and the board of trustees outweigh her promise to a plain old technician."

"*Chief* technician," she corrected. "Damn her. Did it seem as if she had already said something about me to Willoughby?"

The bait taken, Reese set the hook. "Definitely not. I probed as much as I could about you without making Willoughby suspicious. She hasn't told him anything specific . . . yet."

"Norty, we've got to stop her. I can't afford to lose my job. Dammit, I've been here longer than she has. Much longer." Her hands were clenched white, her jaw set in anger and frustration.

"Well," Reese said with exaggerated reason, "we've got two days, three at the most. Any ideas?"

"Ideas?"

"I don't work with the woman, baby, you do. Doesn't she ever fuck up? Blow a case? Christ, the rest of the MD's in this place do it all the time."

"She's a pathologist, Norty. Her cases are all dead to begin with. There's nothing for her to blow except . . ." She stopped in mid-sentence and pulled a typed sheet from her lab coat pocket.

"What is it?"

"It's the surgical path schedule for tomorrow. Bennett and Dr. Huang are doing frozen sections this month." She scanned the entries.

"Well?"

Sheila hesitated, uncertainty darkening her eyes. "Are you sure she's going to report me to Willoughby?"

"Baby, all I can say is that Dr. Willoughby asked me for a copy of the union contract, expressly for the part dealing with justifiable causes for termination."

"She has no right to do that to me after she promised not to."

"You know about people with MD degrees, Sheila. They think they're better and smarter than the rest of us. They think they can just walk all over people." Sheila's eyes told him that the battle—this phase of it at any rate—was won.

"We'll see who's smarter," she muttered, tapping the schedule thoughtfully. "Maybe it's time Bennett found out that there are a few people with brains around who couldn't go to medical school."

"Make it good, baby," Reese urged, "because if she's in, you're out."

"No way," she said. "There's no way I'm going to let that happen. Here, look at this."

"What?"

"Well, you can see it's a pretty busy schedule. There's a lung biopsy, a thyroid biopsy, a colon, and two breast biopsies. Bennett will be working almost all day in the small cryostat lab next to the operating rooms. Usually, she goes into the OR, picks up a specimen, freezes it in the cryostat, sections it, stains it, and reads it, all without leaving the surgical suite."

"And?"

"Well, there are a lot of ifs," Sheila said in an even, almost singsong voice. "But if we could disable the surgical cryostat and force Bennett to use the backup unit down in the histology lab, I might be able somehow to switch a specimen. All I would need is about three or four minutes."

"What would that do?"

Sheila smiled the smile of a child. "Well, with any luck, depending on the actual pathology, we can have the great Dr. Bennett read a benign condition as a malignancy. Then, when the whole specimen is taken and examined the next day, her mistake will become apparent."

"Would a pathologist make a mistake like that?" Reese asked.

Again Sheila smiled. "Only once," she said serenely. "Only once."

Louisburg Square, a score of tall, brick townhouses surrounding a raggedy, wrought-iron-fenced green on the west side of Beacon Hill, had been *the* address in Boston for generations. Levi Morton lived there after his four years as vice president under Benjamin Harrison. Jennie Lind was married there in 1852. Cabots and Saltonstalls, Lodges and Alcotts—all had drawn from and given to the mystique of Louisburg Square.

Kate had the cab drop her off at the foot of Mount Vernon Street; she used the steep two-block walk to Louisburg Square to stretch her legs and clear her thoughts of what had been a long and trying day at the hospital. Two committee meetings, several surgical specimens, and a lecture at the medical school, combined with half a dozen malicious phone calls and an equal number of hate letters, all relating to her callous treatment of Bobby Geary and his family.

Ellen's nose had begun bleeding again—just a slow trickle from one nostril, but enough to require Pete Colangelo to recauterize it. Her clotting parameters were continuing to take a significant drop each day, and the unencouraging news was beginning to take a toll on her spirit. Late that afternoon, the National Institutes of Health library computer search had arrived. There were many articles listed in the bibliography dealing with sclerosing diseases of the ovaries, and a goodly number on clotting disorders similar to the Boston cases. There were none, however, describing their coexistence in a single patient. Expecting little, Kate had begun the tedious process of locating each article, photocopying it, and finally studying it. The project would take days to complete, if not longer, but there was a chance at least that something, anything, might turn up that could help Ellen.

At the turnoff from Mount Vernon Street, Kate propped herself against a gaslight lamp post and through the mist of her own breath, reflected on the marvelous Christmas card that was Louisburg Square. Single, orange-bulbed candles glowed from nearly every townhouse window. Tasteful wreaths marked each door. Christmas trees had been carefully placed to augment the scene without intruding on it.

Having, season after season, observed the stolid elegance of Louisburg Square, Kate had no difficulty understanding why, shortly after the death of his agrarian wife, Winfield Samuels had sold their gentleman's farm and stables in Sudbury and had bought there. The two—the address and the man—were made for one another. Somewhat reluctantly, she mounted the granite steps of her father-in-law's home, eschewed the enormous brass knocker, and pressed the bell.

In seconds, the door was opened by a trim, extremely attractive brunette, no more than two or three years Kate's senior. Dressed in a gold blouse and dark straight skirt, she looked every bit the part of the executive secretary, which, in fact, she had at one time been.

"Kate, welcome," she said warmly. "Come in. Let me take your coat."

"I've got it, thanks. You look terrific, Jocelyn. Is that a new hairstyle?"

"A few months old. Thanks for noticing. You're looking well yourself."

Kate wondered if perhaps she and Jocelyn Trent could collaborate on a chapter for Amy Vanderbilt or Emily Post: "Proper Conversation Between a Daughter-in-law and her Father-in-law's Mistress When the Father-in-law in Question Refuses to Acknowledge the Woman as Anything Other Than a Housekeeper."

"Mr. Samuels will be down in a few minutes," Jocelyn said.

"There's a nice fire going in the study. He'll meet you there. Dinner will be in half an hour. Can I fix you a drink?"

Mr. Samuels. The inappropriate formality made Kate queasy. At seven o'clock, the woman would serve to Mr. Samuels and his guest the gourmet dinner she had prepared; then she would go and eat in the kitchen. At eleven or twelve o'clock, after the house was quiet and dark, she would slip into his room and stay as long as she was asked, always careful to return to her own quarters before any houseguest awoke. Mr. Samuels, indeed.

"Sure," said Kate, following the woman to the study. "Better make it something stiff. As you can tell from your houseguest the last few days, things have not been going too well in my world."

Jocelyn smiled understandingly. "For what it's worth," she said, "I don't think Jared is very pleased with the arrangement either."

"I appreciate hearing that, Jocelyn. Thank you. I'll tell you, on any given Sunday in any given ballpark, marriage can trounce any team in the league." When she could detach the woman from her position, Kate liked her very much and enjoyed the occasional one-to-one conversations they were able to share.

"I know," Jocelyn said. "I tried it once, myself. For me it was all of the responsibility, none of the pleasure."

The words were said lightly, but Kate heard in them perhaps an explanation of sorts, a plea for understanding and acceptance. Better to be owned than to be used.

Kate took the bourbon and water and watched as Jocelyn Trent returned to the kitchen. The woman had, she knew, a wardrobe several times the size of her own, a remarkable silver fox coat, and a stylish Alfa coupé. If this be slavery, she thought with a smile, then give me slavery.

It was, as promised, several minutes before Winfield Samuels made his entrance. Kate waited by the deep, well-used fireplace, rearranging the fringe on the Persian rug with the toe of her shoe and trying to avoid eye contact with any of the big-game heads mounted on the wall. Samuels had sent Jared away on business—purposely, he made it sound —so that he and Kate could spend some time alone together talking over "issues of mutual concern." Before her marriage, they had met on several occasions for such talks, but since, their time together had always included Jared. Samuels had given no hint over the phone as to what the "issues" this time might be, but the separation—causes and cures—was sure to be high on the list. Kate was reading a citation of commendation and gratitude from the governor when the recipient entered the room.

"Kate, welcome," Win Samuels said. "I'm so glad you could make it on such short notice." They embraced with hands on shoulders and exchanged air kisses. "Sit down, please. We have," he consulted his watch, "twenty-three minutes before dinner."

Twenty-three minutes. Kate had to hand it to the man. Dinner at seven did not mean dinner at seven-oh-three. It was expected that the stunning cook cum housekeeper cum mistress would be right on time. "Thank you," she said. "It's good to see you again. You look great." The compliment was not exaggeration. In his twill smoking jacket and white silk scarf, Samuels looked like most men nearing seventy could only dream of looking.

"Rejuvenate that drink?" Samuels asked, motioning her to one of a pair of matched leather easy chairs by the hearth.

"Only if you're prepared to resuscitate me."

Samuels laughed and drew himself a bourbon and soda. "You're quite a woman, Kate," he said, settling in across from her. "Jared is lucky to have nabbed you."

"Actually, I did most of the nabbing."

"This . . . this little disagreement you two are having. It will blow over before you know it. Probably has already."

"The empty half of my bed wouldn't attest to that," Kate said.

Samuels slid a cigar from a humidor by his chair, considered it for a moment, and then returned it. "Bad for the taste buds this close to dinner, particularly with Jocelyn's duck à l'orange on the menu."

"She's a very nice woman," Kate ventured.

Samuels nodded. "Does a good job around here," he said in an absurdly businesslike tone. "Damn good job." He paused. "I'm a direct man, Kate. Some people say too direct, but I don't give a tinker's damn about them. Suppose I get right to the business at hand."

"You mean this wasn't just a social invitation?"

Samuels was leaping to equivocate when he saw the smile in her eyes and at the corners of her mouth. "Do you zing Jared like this, too?" he asked. Kate smiled proudly and nodded.

They laughed, but Kate felt no letup in the tension between them.

"Kate," he continued, "I've accomplished the things I've accomplished, gained the things I've gained, because I was brought up to believe that we are never given a wish or a dream without also being given the wherewithal to make that dream, that wish, a reality. Do you share that belief?"

Kate shrugged. "I believe there are times when it's okay to wish and try and fail."

"Perhaps," he said thoughtfully. "Perhaps there are. Anyhow, at this stage in my life, I have two overriding dreams. Both of them involve my son and, therefore, by extension, you."

"Go on."

"Kate, I want a grandchild, hopefully more than one, and I want my son to serve in the United States Congress. Those are my dreams, and I am willing to do anything within my power to help them come to pass."

"Why?" Kate asked.

"Why?"

"Yes. I understand the grandchild wish. Continuation of the family, stability for Jared's home life, new blood and new energy, that sort of thing, but why the other one?"

"Because I feel Jared would be a credit to himself, to the state, and to the country."

"So do I."

"And I think it would be a fulfilling experience for him."

"Perhaps."

Samuels hesitated before adding, "And, finally, it is a goal I held for myself and never could achieve. Do you think me horrid for wanting my son to have what I could not?"

"No," Kate responded. "Provided it is something Jared wants, too, for reasons independent of yours."

"The time in life when a father no longer knows what is best for his son is certainly moot, isn't it?"

"Win, what you want for Jared, what you want for me, too, will always matter. But the hardest part about loving someone is letting him figure out what's best for himself, especially when you already know— or at least think you know."

"And you think I'm forcing my will on Jared?"

"You have a tremendous amount of influence on him," she replied. "I don't think I'm giving away any great secrets by saying that."

Samuels nodded thoughtfully. "Kate," he said finally, "humor this old man and let me change the subject a bit, okay?"

Old man. Give me a break, counselor, she wanted to snap. Instead she sat forward, smiled, and simply said, "Sure."

"Why do you want to be the chief of pathology at Metro?"

Kate met his gaze levelly and said silent thanks for the hours she had spent answering that question for herself. "Because it would be a fascinating experience. Because I think I could do a credible job. Because my work—and my department—mean a great deal to me. Because I feel a person either grows or dies."

"Jared tells me you feel accepting the position will delay your being able to start your family for at least two years."

"Actually, I said one or two years, but two seems a reasonable guess."

Samuels rose slowly and walked to the window and then back to the fire. If he was preparing to say something dramatic, she acknowledged, he was doing a laudable job of setting it up.

"Kate," he said, still staring at the fire, "when I phoned, I invited you to stay the night if you could. Are you going to be able to do that?"

"I had planned on it, yes." Actually, the invitation had been worded in a way that would have made it nearly impossible for her to refuse.

"Good. I'd like to take you for a ride after dinner. A ride and a visit. I . . . I know I sound mysterious, but for the moment you'll have to indulge me. This is something I never thought I would be doing."

There was a huskiness, an emotion to the man's voice that Kate had never heard before. Was he near crying? For half a minute there was silence, save for the low hiss of the fire. But when her father-in-law turned to her, his composure had returned.

"Kate," he said, as if the moment by the fire had never happened, "do you think that you are ready to handle the responsibilities of a whole department?"

She thought for a moment. "This may sound funny, but in a way it doesn't matter what I think. You see, Dr. Willoughby, the only person who knows both me and the job, thinks I can handle it. It's like becoming a doctor—or, for that matter, a lawyer. You only decide you *want* to do it. They—the bar or the medical examiners—decide whether or not you can and should. From then on, your only obligation is to do your best." She paused. "Does that sound smug?"

"Not really."

"I hope not, Win. Because actually I'm scared stiff about a lot of things. I'm frightened of taking the job and I'm frightened of not taking it. I'm frightened of having children and I'm frightened of not having them. And most of all, I am frightened of having to face the dilemma of either losing my husband or losing myself."

"There *are* other possibilities," Samuels said.

"I know that, but I'm not sure Jared does, and to be perfectly honest, until this moment, I wasn't sure you did, either."

"There are *always* other possibilities," he said with a tone that suggested he had voiced that belief before. "Kate, you know hospital politics are no different from any other kind of politics. There's power involved and there's money involved, and that means there are things like this handbill involved."

He took the garish orange flyer from his desk drawer and held it up for her to see. Kate shuddered at the sight of it. "Do you think that brilliant effort was aimed at me or at Jared?" she asked.

"The truth is it makes no difference. Politics is politics. The minute you start playing the game you have enemies. If they happen to be better at the game than you are, you get buried. It's that simple." He held up the flyer again. "My sense of this whole business—assuming, of course, that you didn't send Bobby Geary's autopsy report to the papers —is that someone is determined to keep you from becoming head of your department. If they have any kind of power, or access to power, your department could suffer dearly."

"My department?"

"Certainly. Your people end up overworked because of staffing cutbacks and outmoded equipment. Turnover is high, morale low. Quality of work drops. Sooner or later there's a mistake. You may be the best pathologist in the world, Kate, and the best-intentioned administrator, but unless you play the politics game and get past the competition to people like the Ashburton Foundation, you will end up an unhappy, harried, unfulfilled failure. And take it from me, winning that game means plenty of sacrifice. It means that if you know the competition is getting up at six, you damn well better be up at five-thirty."

"I appreciate your thoughts," she said. "I really do. All I can say is that the final decision hasn't been made yet, and that I was hoping to work the whole thing out with Jared."

"But you have okayed submission of your name."

"Yes," she said, averting her gaze for the first time. "Yes, I have." Samuels turned and walked again toward the window. For a time, there was only the fire. "Say, Win," she said, hoping to lead them in other directions, "how much do you know about the Ashburton Foundation?"

He turned back to her. "I really don't know anything. In the early days of their involvement here, my firm handled some of their correspondence with the hospital. But I haven't dealt with them in years. Why?"

"Just some research I've been doing at work. Nothing, really. Do you by any chance have their address?"

"I don't know," Samuels said, somewhat distractedly. "In the Rolodex over there on my desk, perhaps. I really don't know. Kate, you know it is my way to reason, not to beg. But for the sake of my son and myself, if not for yourself, I'm begging you to put the chairmanship on the back burner and devote yourself for a few years to your family and to helping Jared get his foot in the political door."

At that instant, a chime sounded from the kitchen. Kate glanced instinctively at her watch, but she knew that it was exactly seven o'clock. She rose. "When is Jared due back?" she asked.

"Wednesday or Thursday, I suspect."

"Win, I have no response to what you just asked. You know that, don't you?"

"Perhaps before too much longer you might. Let us eat. After our meal, there is a trip we must take."

With a faint smile, Samuels nodded Kate toward the dining room and then took her elbow and guided her through the door.

The IV nurse, a square-shouldered woman overweight by at least thirty pounds, rubbed alcohol on the back of Ellen Sandler's left hand, slapped the area a dozen times, and then swabbed it again.

"Now, Ellen," she said in the patronizing, demeaning tone Ellen had come to label *hospitalese,* "you've got to relax. Your veins are in spasm. If you don't relax, it will take all night for me to get this IV in."

Relax? Ellen glared at the woman, who was hunched over her hand. *Can't you tell I'm frightened? Can't you see I'm scared out of my wits by all that's happening to me? Take a minute, just a minute, and talk to me. Ask me, and I'll try to explain. I'll tell you how it feels to be seven years old and to learn that your father, who entered the hospital for a "little opera-tion," has been taken to a funeral home in a long box with handles. Relax? Why not ask me to float off this bed? Or better still, just demand that I make the blood in my body start clotting, so you'll be spared the inconve-nience of having to plunge that needle into the back of my hand. Relax?*

"I . . . I'm trying," she said meekly.

"Good. Now you're going to feel a little stick."

Ellen grabbed the bedrail with her free hand as electric pain from the "little stick" shot up her arm.

"Got it," the nurse said excitedly. "Now don't move. Don't move until I get it taped down, okay? You know," she continued as she taped the plastic catheter in place, "you've got the toughest veins I've seen in a long time."

Ellen didn't answer. Instead, she stared at the ceiling, tasting the salt of the tears running over her cheeks and into the corners of her mouth, and wondering where it was all going to end. Apparently, blood had begun appearing in her bowel movements. The intravenous line was, according to the resident who announced she was going to have it, merely a precaution. He had neglected to tell her what it was a precau-tion against.

"Okay, Ellen, we're all set," the nurse announced, stepping back to admire her handiwork. "Just don't use that hand too much. All right?"

Ellen pushed the tears off her cheeks with the back of her right hand. "Sure," she said.

The woman managed an uncomfortable smile and backed from the room.

It isn't fair. With no little disgust, Ellen examined the IV dripping saline into her hand. Then she shut off the overhead light and lay in the semidarkness, listening to the sighs of her own breathing and the still alien sounds of the hospital at night. *It isn't fair.* Over and over her mind repeated the impotent protest until she was forced to laugh at it in spite of herself.

Betsy, Eve, Darcy, Sandy, the business, her health. Why had she never appreciated how fragile it all was? Had she taken too much for granted? asked too few questions? Dammit, there were no answers, anyhow. What else could she do? What else could anyone do? Here she was, almost forty, lying in a hospital bed, possibly bleeding to death, with no real sense of why she had been alive, let alone why she should have been singled out to die. It just wasn't fair.

A soft tap from the doorway intruded on her painful reverie. Stand-ing there, silhouetted by the light from the hall, was Sandy. He was holding his uniform hat in one hand and a huge bouquet in the other.

"Permission to come aboard," he said.

Ellen could feel, more than see or hear, his discomfiture. "Come on in," she said.

"Want the light on?"

"I don't think so. On second thought, I'd like to see the flowers."

Sandy flipped on the light and brought them to her. Then he bent over and kissed her on the forehead. Ellen stiffened for an instant and then relaxed to his gentle hug.

"How're you doing?" he asked.

"On which level?"

"Any."

"The flowers are beautiful. Thank you. If you set them over by the sink, I'll have the nurse get a vase for them later on."

"Not so great, huh." He did as she asked with the bouquet, then pulled a green vinyl chair to the bedside and sat down.

Ellen switched off the overhead light. "You look nice in your uniform. Have you been home yet?"

"Just long enough to drop off my things and look in on the girls."

"How do they seem to you?"

"Concerned, confused, a little frightened maybe, but they're okay. I think it helped when your sister brought them up to see you yesterday. I've moved back into the house until you're better."

"You may be there a long time."

"That bad?"

"Kate says no, but her eyes, and now this"—she held up her left hand—"say something else."

"But they don't really know, do they?"

"No. No, I guess not."

"Well, then, you just gotta hang in there a day or an hour or if necessary a minute at a time and believe that everything's going to be all right. I've taken an LOA from the air line to be with the girls, so you don't have anything to worry about on that account. I'll see to it that they get up here every day."

"Thanks. I . . . I'm grateful you're here."

"Nonsense. We've been through a lot these nineteen years. We'll make it through this."

Softly, Ellen began to cry. "Sandy, I feel like such a . . . a clod, an oaf. I know it's dumb, but that's how I feel. Not angry, not even sick, just helpless and clumsy."

"Well, you're neither, and no one knows that better than I do. Hey, that's the second time you've yawned since I got here. Are you tired, or just bored?"

She smiled weakly. "Not bored. A little tired, I guess. It turns out that lying in bed all day doing nothing is exhausting."

"Then how about you don't pay any attention to me and just go to sleep. If it's okay with you, I'll sit here for a while."

"Thanks, Sandy."

"It's going to be okay, you know."

"I know."

He took her hand. "Kate's watching out for you, right?"

"She's in twice a day, and she's doing everything she can to find out why I'm bleeding." Her voice drifted off. Her eyes closed. "Don't be afraid."

"I'm not," he said. "I'm not afraid. . . . It's going to be okay."

The ride in Win Samuels's gray Seville took most of an hour along a network of dark country roads heading south and east from the city. They rode largely in silence, Samuels seeming to need total concentration to negotiate the narrow turns, and Kate staring out her window at dark pastures and even darker woods, at times wondering about the purpose of their journey and at times allowing disconnected thoughts to career through her mind. Jared . . . Stan Willoughby . . . Bobby Geary . . . Roscoe . . . Ellen . . . Tom . . . even Rosa Beekes, her elementary school principal—each made an appearance and then quickly faded and was replaced by the image of another.

"We're here," Samuels said at last, turning onto a gravel drive.

"Stonefield School." Kate read the name from a discreet sign illuminated only by the headlights of their car. "What town is this?"

"No town, really. We're either in southernmost Massachusetts or northwestern Rhode Island, depending on whose survey you use. The school has been here for nearly fifty years, but it was rebuilt about twenty-five years ago, primarily with money from a fund my firm established."

The school was a low, plain brick structure with a small, well-kept lawn and a fenced-in play area to one side. To the other side, a wing of unadorned red brick stretched towards the woods. They entered the sparsely furnished lobby and were immediately met by a stout, matronly woman wearing a navy skirt, dull cardigan, and an excessive number of gold bracelets and rings.

"Mr. Samuels," she said, "it's good to see you again. Thank you for calling ahead." She turned to Kate. "Dr. Bennett, I'm Sally Bicknell, supervisor for the evening shift. Welcome to Stonefield."

"Thank you," Kate said uncertainly. "I'm not exactly sure where I am or why we're here, but thank you, anyway."

Sally Bicknell smiled knowingly, took Kate by the arm, and led her down the hall to a large, blue velvet curtain. "This is our playroom," she said, drawing the curtain with some flair to reveal the smoky glass of a one-way mirror. The room beyond was large, well lit, and carpeted. There were two tumbling mats, a number of inflatable vinyl punching dummies, and a stack of large building blocks. To one corner, her back toward them, a chunky girl with close-cropped sandy hair hunched over a row of large cloth dolls.

"She's never in bed much before two or three in the morning," Sally Bicknell explained.

"Kate," Samuels said. "I brought you here because I thought that seeing this might help you understand some of my urgency as regards your moving forward with starting your family. Mrs. Bicknell."

The evening shift supervisor rapped loudly on the glass three times, then three times again. The girl in the playroom cocked her head to one side and then slowly turned around.

"Kate, meet your sister-in-law, Lindsey."

The girl was, physically, a monster. Her eyes were lowset and narrow, her facial features thick and coarse, with heavy lips and twisted yellow teeth. What little there was of her neck forced her head to the right at an unnatural angle. Her barrel chest merged with her abdomen, and her legs were piteously bowed.

"That can't be," Kate said softly, her attention transfixed by the grotesquery. "Jared's sister Lindsey . . ."

"Died when she was a child," Samuels finished the sentence for her. "I'm afraid his mother and I chose not to tell him the truth. It seemed like the best idea at the time, considering that we were assured Lindsey would live only a few years. She has Hunter's Syndrome. You are familiar with that, yes?" Kate nodded. "Severe mental retardation and any number of other defects. Her mother, my wife, was nearly forty when she gave birth."

Kate continued staring through the glass as the gargoylelike child—no, woman, for she had to be in her thirties—lumbered aimlessly about the playroom. Reflected in the window, Kate saw the faces of Sally Bicknell and her father-in-law, watching for her reaction. You are the monster, Win Samuels, not that poor thing, her thoughts screamed. What do you think I am, a piece worker in a factory? Did you think this . . . this demonstration would frighten me? Do you think I know nothing of amniocentesis and prenatal diagnosis and counseling? Did you think I would just brush off the enormous lie you have been telling my husband for the past thirty years? Why? Why have you brought me here? Why haven't you included Jared?

"Take me home," she ordered softly. "Take me home now."

The antique clock on Win Samuels's huge desk said two-fifty. It had been nearly two hours since Kate had abandoned her efforts to sleep and wandered into the study searching for reading matter distracting enough to close her mind to the events of the evening. Something was wrong. Something did not sit right in the bizarre scenario to which her father-in-law had treated her. But what?

On the ride home from Stonefield, Samuels had quietly assailed her with statistics relating maternal age to infertility, fetal death, chromosome abnormalities, genetic mutation, spontaneous abortions, and mental retardation. He had, over many years apparently, done his homework well. The few arguments she had managed to give him on the accuracy of intrauterine diagnosis were countered with more facts and more statistics. Still, nothing the man said could dispel her gut feeling that something was not right. At one time during his presentation—for that is what it was—she came close to crying out that their whole discussion was quite possibly a futile exercise, because a production error at Redding Pharmaceuticals might have already cost her any chance of seeing her forties, let alone conceiving in them.

From the direction of Samuels's room on the second floor, she heard a door open and then close softly. Seconds later, the sound was repeated further down the hall. Jocelyn Trent had returned to her room.

The study, now divested of its fire, was chilly and damp. Kate shuddered and tightened the robe Jocelyn had given her. It was only around midnight in San Diego. Jared wouldn't mind a call, she thought, before realizing that she had forgotten to ask Win at which hotel he was staying. As she reached for a pad and pen to write herself a reminder, she noticed Samuels's Rolodex file. She spun it to "A." The man was right about having a card for the Ashburton Foundation. On it were an address and a number that had been crossed out. A second, apparently newer, address and number were written in below.

Kate copied the new address and added a note to check in the morning on Jared's hotel. She glanced at the clock. Three-fifteen. How many surgicals were scheduled for the day? Five? Six? Too many. Desperate for sleep, she took her note and an anthology of Emily Dickinson and padded up two flights of stairs to her room.

Forty-five minutes of reading were necessary before Kate trusted the heaviness in her eyes and the impotence in her concentration enough to flip off the light. The realization that her drowsiness was continuing to deepen brought a relieved, contented smile. Then, in her final moments of consciousness, she sensed a troublesome notion. It appeared, then vanished, then appeared again like a faint neon sign. It was not the trip or the school or even the girl. No, it was the address— the address of the Ashburton Foundation; not the newer Washington, DC, address, but the one that was crossed out. With each flash, the neon grew dimmer, the thoughts less distinct. There was something, she thought at the moment of darkness, something special about Darlington, Kentucky. Something.

CHAPTER 10

Tuesday 18 December

SOUNDLESSLY, KATE unlocked the heavy oak door and slipped out of her father-in-law's home into the gray glare of morning. The deserted streets, sidewalks, and stone steps were covered with an immaculate dusting of white. Over the three days past, a blizzard had crushed the midwest and moved, unabated, into the mid-Atlantic states. Stepping gingerly down Beacon Hill toward Charles Street, Kate wondered if the feathery snow was, perhaps, the harbinger of that storm.

She had slept far too little. Her eyes were dry and irritated, her temples constricted by the ache of exhaustion—an ache she had not experienced so acutely since her days as a medical student and intern. She thought about the surgicals scheduled to begin at ten o'clock and run through most of the rest of the day. With tensions thrusting at her life from one direction after another like the spears in some medieval torture, she debated asking one of the others to take over for her. No way, she decided quickly. As it was, the members of her department were stretched beyond their limits. Stan Willoughby's repeated requests for an additional pathologist had been laughed at. No, she was expected to do her part, and she would find whatever concentration it took to do it right.

As she made her way toward the cab stand near White Memorial, Kate began her morning ritual of mentally ticking off the events and responsibilities of her day. The cab was halfway to Metro when she ended the ritual, as she inevitably did, by scrambling through her purse for her daily calendar, certain that she had forgotten something crucial. Her schedule was abbreviated, due largely to a block of time marked simply "surgicals." Penciled in at the bottom was the one item she had forgotten, "Drinks with Tom." The three words triggered a surprising rush of feelings, beginning with the reflex notion to call and cancel, and ending with the sense of what her return home to an empty house would be like. Scattered in between were any number of images of the intense, gangly resident who had been her staunchest supporter during the difficult days that had followed the biopsy of Beverly Vitale. Tom Engleson was a man and a youth, enthusiastic at times even to exuberance, yet sensitive about people, about medicine, and especially about what her career involved and meant to her. The prospect of an hour or two together in the corner of some dark, leather and wood lounge might be just the carrot to get her through the day.

"Dammit, Jared," she muttered as the cab rolled to a stop in front of her hospital. "I need you."

She began her day as she had each of the last several working days, with a visit to Room 421 of the Berenson Building.

Ellen was lying on her back, staring at the wall. Her breakfast was untouched on the formica stand by her bed. Suspended from a ceiling hook, a plastic bag drained saline into her arm.

"Hi," Kate said.

"Hi, yourself." Ellen's eyes were shadowed. Her skin seemed lacking in color and turgor. Bruises, large and small, lined both arms. There was packing in one side of her nose.

Kate set the *Cosmopolitan* and morning *Globe* she had brought on the stand next to the breakfast tray. "Something new's been added, huh?" She nodded toward the IV.

"Last night. A little while after you left."

Kate raised Ellen to a sitting position and then settled onto the bed by her knee. "They say why?"

"All they'll tell me is that it's a precautionary measure."

"Have you had some new bleeding?"

"In my bowel movements, and I guess in my urine, too." She took a glass of orange juice from her tray and sipped at it absently.

"That's probably why the IV," Kate said. "In case they have to inject any X-ray dye or give you any blood." *How much do you want to hear, El? Give me a sign. Do you want to know about sudden massive hemorrhage? About circulatory collapse sudden and severe enough to make emergency insertion of an intravenous line extremely difficult? Do you want to know about Beverly Vitale?*

"Listen, Kate. As long as you're on top of what's going on, I'm satisfied."

"Good." *Thank you, my friend. Thank you for making it a little easier.*

"Sandy's back. He flew in late last night and then moved into the house to look after the girls."

Kate motioned to a vase of flowers by the window. "From him?"

"Uh-huh."

"So?"

Ellen shrugged. "No significance. He's still on his way out, I think."

"I hope not."

"Am I?"

"Are you what?"

"On my way out."

"Jesus, Sandler, of course not."

Ellen took her hand. "Don't let me die, Katey, okay?"

"Count on it," Kate said, having to work to keep from breaking down in front of her friend. Silently, she vowed to place her efforts on Ellen's behalf ahead of every other task, every other pressure in her life. Somewhere, there was an answer, and somehow she would find it. "Listen, I've got to go and get ready for some biopsies. I'll check on your lab tests and speak with you later this afternoon. Okay?"

"Okay." The word was spiritless.

"Anything I can bring you?"

"A cure?"

Kate smiled weakly. "Coming right up," she said.

The flowers, in a metallic gray box with a red bow, were on her desk when Kate returned from the Berenson Building. First a huge bouquet for Ellen from Sandy and now flowers from Jared. The former Dartmouth roommates had come through in the clutch.

"I knew you guys must have learned something at that school besides how to tap a keg," she said, excitedly opening the box.

They were long-stem roses, eleven red and one yellow—the red for love and the yellow for friendship, she had once been told. She scurried about her office, opening and closing doors and drawers until she found a heavy, green-glass vase. It was not until the roses were arranged to her satisfaction and set on the corner of her desk that she remembered the card taped to the box. It would say something at once both witty and tender. That was Jared's style—his way.

"To a not so unexceptional pathologist, from a not so secret admirer. Tom."

Kate groaned and sank to her desk chair, feeling angry and a little foolish. Try as she might, she could not dispel the irrational reaction that Jared had somehow let her down.

Call Tom. She wrote the reminder on a scrap of paper and taped it in a high-visibility spot on the shade of her desk lamp. Still, she knew from experience that even a location only inches from her eyes gave her at best only a fifty-fifty chance of remembering. Perhaps now was the time to call. It was almost nine. If Tom wasn't in the OR, a page would reach him. Things were beginning to get out of hand, and at this point, meeting Tom for a drink hardly seemed fair.

Kate was reaching for the phone when it rang.

"Hello. Kate Bennett," she said.

"Dr. Bennett, how do you do? My name is Arlen Paquette, *Doctor* Arlen Paquette, if you count a PhD in chemistry. I'm the director of product safety for Redding Pharmaceuticals. If this is an inopportune time for you, please tell me. If it is not, I would like to speak with you for a few minutes about the report Dr. William Zimmermann phoned in to us yesterday."

"I have a few minutes," Kate said, retaping the Tom note to her lampshade.

"Fine. Thank you. Dr. Bennett, I spent a fair amount of time taking information from Dr. Zimmermann. However, since you seem to have done most of the legwork, as it were, I had hoped you might go over exactly what it was that led you to the conclusion there was a problem with one of our Redding generics."

"I'd be happy to, Dr. Paquette."

It was obvious from the few questions Paquette asked during her three-minute summary that Zimmermann's account to him had been a complete one and, further, that the director of product safety had studied the data well.

"So," the caller said when she had finished, "as I see it, your initial suspicions of trouble at the Omnicenter were based on a coincidence of symptoms in three patients of the thousands treated there. Correct?"

"Not exactly," Kate said, suddenly perturbed by the tone of the man's voice.

"Please," he said, "bear with me a moment longer. You then decided to focus your investigation on the pharmaceuticals provided for the Omnicenter by my company, and . . ."

"Dr. Paquette, I don't think it's at all fair to suggest that I jumped to the conclusion that the drugs were at fault. Even now I am not at all sure that is the case. However, of all the factors I checked—sterilization techniques, microbiology, and all others common to my three patients —the contaminated vitamins were the only finding out of the ordinary."

"Ah, yes," Paquette said. "The vitamins. Several dozen samples analyzed, yet only one containing a painkiller. Correct?"

"Dr. Paquette," Kate said somewhat angrily, "I have a busy schedule today, and I've told you about all there is to tell. You are sounding more and more like a lawyer and less and less like a man concerned with correcting a problem in his company's product. Now, I don't know whether Dr. Zimmermann told you or not, but I feel that the need to get to the bottom of all this is urgent, critical. A woman who happens to be a dear friend of mine is in the hospital right now, with her life quite possibly at stake, and for all I know, there may be others. I shall give you two more days to come up with a satisfactory explanation. If you don't have one, I am going to get the chemist from the state toxicology lab, and together we will march straight down to the FDA."

"By chemist, I assume you mean Mr. Ian Toole?"

"Yes, that's exactly who I mean."

"Well, Doctor, I'm a little confused. You see, I have in front of me a notarized letter, copies of which I have just put in the mail to you and Dr. Zimmermann. It is a letter from Mr. Ian Toole stating categorically that in none of his investigations on your behalf did he find *any* contamination in *any* product dispensed at the Omnicenter."

"What?" Kate's incredulity was almost instantly replaced by a numbing fear. "That's not true," she said weakly.

"Shall I read you the letter?"

"You bought him off."

"I beg your pardon."

"I gave you the courtesy of reporting this to your comapny instead of going to the FDA, and you bought off my chemist."

"Dr. Bennett, I would caution you against carelessly tossing accusations about," Paquette said. "The statement in front of me is, as I have said, notarized."

"We'll see about that," she said with little force. The vitamins she had sent to Toole were all she had. In a corner of her mind, she wondered if Arlen Paquette knew that.

"I would like to confirm my company's sincere desire to correct any shortcomings in its products, and to thank you for allowing us to investigate the situation at your hospital." Paquette sounded as if he was reading the statement from a card.

"You may think this is the end of things, Dr. Paquette," Kate said, "but you don't know me. Please be prepared to hear from the FDA."

"We each must do what we must do, Doctor."

Kate had begun to seethe. "Furthermore, you had better hope that whatever you paid Ian Toole was enough, because that man is going to be made to visit a certain hospital bed to see first hand the woman he may be helping to kill." She slammed the receiver to its cradle.

Seated in his suite at the Ritz, Arlen Paquette hung up gently. He was shaking.

You don't know me.

Paquette snorted at the irony of Kate Bennett's words, splashed some scotch over two ice cubes, drank it before it had begun to chill, and then set the glass down on the photographs of the woman he had just helped nail to a cross of incompetence, mental imbalance, and dishonesty. Cyrus Redding had decreed that she be discredited, and discredited she would be. Kate Bennett had only herself and a few shaky allies. Cyrus Redding had an unlimited supply of Norton Reeses, Winfield Samuelses, Ian Tooles, and, yes, Arlen Paquettes.

He glanced down at the pad where he had written the words he had rehearsed and then used when talking to the woman, and he wondered if he could have come off so self-assured in a face-to-face confrontation. Doubtful, he acknowledged. Extremely doubtful. Their conversation had lasted just a few minutes, with all of the surprises coming from his end. Yet here he was, soaked with sweat and still trembling. He'd take a dozen in-person encounters with Norton Reese over the one phone call he had just finished. Water. That was it, he needed some water. No more goddamn scotch.

He snatched his empty glass from the coffee table. Beneath it was one of the five-by-seven blowups of Kate Bennett, this one of her bundled in a sweatsuit, scarf, and watch cap, jogging with her dog along a snowbanked road. Paquette turned and unsteadily made his way to the bathroom.

"You bastard," he said to the thin, drawn face staring at him from the mirror. "You weak little fucking bastard."

He hurled the glass with all his strength, shattering it and the mirror. Then he dropped to his knees amidst the shards and, clutching the ornate toilet, retched until he felt his insides were tearing in two.

"Don't you see, Bill? Someone at Redding Pharmaceuticals, maybe this . . . this Paquette, bought off Ian Toole. Damn, I knew I was right not to trust them. I knew it. I knew it." Kate, still breathless from her run across the snowy street and up three flights of stairs, screamed at herself to calm down.

William Zimmermann, as relaxed as Kate was intense, rose from behind his desk and crossed to the automatic coffee maker on a low table by his office door. His knee-length clinic coat was perfectly creased and spotless, his demeanor as immaculate as his dress. "How about a few deep breaths and a cup of coffee?"

"Coffee's about the last thing I need in my state, thanks, but I will try the deep breaths. Vacation. Can you believe it? One day the man is at his little spectrophotometer running tests, and the next he's off on vacation and nobody knows when he'll be back. Now if that isn't a payoff, I don't know what is. Next thing you know, Ian Toole's name will be on a lab door somewhere in Redding Pharmaceuticals."

"The deep breaths?" Zimmermann asked, returning to his desk.

"Oh, yes. I'm sorry, Bill. But you don't blame me, do you?"

"No, I don't blame you." He paused, obviously searching for words. "Kate," he said finally, "I want to be as tactful as possible in what I have to ask, and if I'm not, please excuse me, but . . ."

"Go on."

"Well, since you brought the subject up at our dinner the other night, I feel I must ask. Just how badly do you have it in for the pharmaceutical industry?"

The question startled her. Then she understood. "What you're saying is that without Ian Toole, it becomes a matter of my word against theirs. Is that it?"

"If I'm out of line, Kate, I'm sorry. But remember, there is a lot at stake here—for me and my clinic, and as far as I know, this whole matter was between you and your Mr. Toole. I mean I called in the report because it was our facility, but the hard data are strictly . . ."

"Wait," Kate interrupted excitedly. "There is someone else. I just remembered."

"Who?"

"Her name's Millicent. She's Toole's assistant, and I remember him telling me she was put out about having to work late on the stuff I sent him."

"Do you have a last name?"

"No, but how many Millicents can there be at the State Toxicology Lab?" She was already reaching for the phone and her address book. "You don't know me, Dr. Paquette," she murmured as she dialed. "Oh, no, you don't know me at all."

The call lasted less than a minute.

"Millicent Hall is no longer in the employ of the state lab," Kate said as she hung up, her expression and tone an equal mix of embarrassment, dejection, and anger. "They wouldn't give out any further information."

This time it was Zimmermann who took a deep breath. "First the baseball player and now this," he said. "You certainly aren't having a very easy time of it."

Kate's eyes narrowed. An emptiness began to build inside her. "You're having trouble believing me, aren't you?"

Zimmermann met her gaze and held it. "Kate, what I can say in all honesty is that at this moment I believe that you believe." He saw her about to protest, and held up his hands. "And at this moment," he added reassuringly, "that is enough. There is too much at stake for me to make any hasty moves. I shall await Redding's formal response to my report, meanwhile keeping our pharmacy on backup. No Redding generics until then. However, if there have been no further cases or further developments in, say, a week, I plan to reinstate our automated system."

"With Redding products?"

"We have a contract."

"But they . . ."

"Facts, Kate. We need substantiated facts."

Kate sighed and sank back in her seat, deflated. It was nearly ten and she had done nothing to prepare for the day's surgicals. "Have you started working on that list of patients who might be willing to allow me to have their medications analyzed?"

Zimmermann smiled patiently. "You can see how that might be a bit tricky to explain to a patient, can't you?" He handed her a brief list and five Omnicenter medication cards. "These belong to long-term patients of mine, who agreed to exchange them as part of what I said was a routine quality-control check."

"It is," Kate said. "Thanks, Bill. I know this isn't easy for you and I'm grateful."

"I'll try and get you some more today."

"Thanks. You're being more than fair. I know I'm right, and sooner or later I'm going to prove it." She stood to go.

"You know," Zimmermann said, "even if you find there was a manufacturing error at Redding, you have no way of tying it in with the cases you are following."

The faces of three women—two dead and one her friend—flashed in her thoughts. "I know," she said grimly. "But it's all I . . . it's all *we* have. Say, before I forget. Have you got the purchase invoices for the Redding generics that I asked you about?"

Zimmermann opened his file cabinet. "Carl Horner does the ordering. He gave me these and asked that I convey his desire to cooperate with you as fully as possible. He also asked that you return these as soon as you're done."

"Of course," Kate said, glancing at the pile of yellow invoice carbons. Redding Pharmaceuticals, Inc.; Darlington, Kentucky. The words sputtered and sparked in her mind. Then they exploded.

"Kate, are you all right?" Zimmermann asked.

"Huh? Oh, yes, I'm fine. Bill, something very strange is going on here. I mean *very strange.*" Zimmermann looked at her quizzically. "I don't know how long ago they moved, but at one time, the Ashburton Foundation was located in Darlington, Kentucky."

"How do you know?"

"I found their old address in my father-in-law's Rolodex."

"So?"

Kate held up an invoice for him to see. "Darlington. That's where Redding Pharmaceuticals is headquartered."

For the first time, William Zimmermann seemed perturbed. "I still don't see what point you're trying to make."

Kate heard the irritation in the man's voice and, recalling his oblique reference to the Bobby Geary letter, cautioned herself to tread gently. Her supporters, even skeptical ones, were few and far between. "I . . . I guess I overreacted a little," she said with a sheepishness she was not really feeling. "Ellen's being in the middle of all this has me grasping at straws, I guess." She glanced at her watch. "Look, I've got to get over to the OR. Thanks for these. If I come up with any facts," she corrected herself with a raised finger, "make that substantiated facts, I'll give you a call."

"Fine," Zimmermann said. "Let me know if there's any further way I can help."

Kate hurried outside and across the street, mindless of the wind and snow. Ashburton and Redding—once both in Darlington, and now both at the Omnicenter. A coincidence? Not likely, she thought. No, not likely at all. The lobby clock read two minutes to ten as she sped toward the surgical suite and the small frozen-section lab. The room was dark. Taped to the door was a carefully printed note.

OR CRYOSTAT INOPERATIVE. BRING
BIOPSY SPECS
TO PATH DEPARTMENT CRYOSTAT FOR
PROCESSING

"Ten seconds to ignition. Nine. Eight. Seven. Six. Five. Four. Three. Two. One. Ignition." Tom Engleson struck the wooden match against the edge of an iron trivet and touched the brandy-soaked mound of French vanilla ice cream. "Voilà!" he cried.

"Bravo!" Kate cheered.

Tom filled two shallow dishes and set Kate's in front of her with a flourish.

The evening had been a low-key delight: drinks at the Hole in the Wall Pub, dinner at the Moon Villa, in Chinatown, and finally dessert in Tom's apartment, twenty stories above Boston Harbor. She had forgotten to break their date, and for once her poor memory had proven an asset. Twenty minutes into their conversation at the Hole in the Wall, Kate had given up trying to sort out what she wanted from the evening and the man and had begun to relax and enjoy both. Still, she knew, thoughts of Jared were never far from the surface; nor were thoughts of Redding Pharmaceuticals and the Ashburton Foundation.

"Okay," Tom said as he poured two cups of coffee and settled into the chair next to her, "now that my brain is through crying for food and drink and such, it's ready to try again to understand. There is no Ashburton Foundation?"

"No, there's something *called* the Ashburton Foundation, but I'm not at all certain it's anything other than a laundry for money."

"Pharmaceutical company money."

"Right. I called the number I got from my father-in-law's Rolodex and got a receptionist of some sort. She referred every question, even what street they were located on in DC, to someone named Dr. Thompson, apparently the director of the so-called foundation."

"But Dr. Thompson was out of the office and never called you back."

"Exactly. I tried calling the receptionist again, and this time she said that Thompson was gone for the day and would contact me in the morning. It was weird, I tell you, weird. The woman, supposedly working for this big foundation, didn't have the vaguest idea of how to handle my call."

"Did you ask Reese about all this?"

"He was gone for the day by the time I called, but tommorrow after I see Ellen, I intend to camp out on his doorstep."

"But why? What does Redding Pharmaceuticals get out of funneling all this money into our hospital?"

Kate shrugged. "That, Thomas, is the sixty-four dollar question. At the moment, every shred of woman's intuition in my body is screaming that the tie-in has something to do with the contaminated vitamins our friend Dr. Paquette has gone to such lengths to cover up."

"Incredible."

"Incredible, maybe. Impossible?" She took a folded copy of an article from her purse and passed it over. "I came across this yesterday during one of my sessions in the library. It's part of a whole book about a drug called MER/29, originally developed and marketed by Merrell Pharmaceuticals."

"That's a big company," Tom said, flipping through the pages.

"Not as big as Redding, but big enough. This MER/29 was supposed to lower cholesterol and thereby prevent heart disease. Only trouble was that other companies were racing to complete work on other products designed to do the same thing. The good folks at Merrell estimated a potential yearly profit in the billions at just one twenty-cent capsule a day for each person over thirty-five. However, they also knew that the lion's share of that profit would go to the first company whose product could get cleared by the FDA and launched into the marketplace."

"I'm not going to want to hear the rest of this, am I," Tom said.

"Not if you have much trust in the pharmaceutical industry. Remember, the FDA doesn't evaluate products; the pharmaceutical companies do. The FDA only evaluates the evaluations. In its haste to get MER/29 into the bodies of the pharmaceutical-buying public, Merrell cut corner after corner in their laboratory and clinical testing. But since none of the shortcuts was evident in the massive reports they submitted to the FDA, in 1961, MER/29 was approved by the FDA and launched by Merrell. Two years later, almost by accident, the FDA discovered what the company had done and ordered the drug removed. By that time, a large number of people had gone blind or developed hideous, irreversible skin conditions or lost all their hair."

Tom whistled.

"Kids with no arms because their mothers took a sleeping pill called thalidomide. Kids with irreparably yellow teeth because tetracycline was rushed into the marketplace before all its side effects were known. The list goes on and on."

"You sound a little angry," Tom said, taking her hand and guiding her to the couch across the room.

"They paid off my chemist, Tom," she said. "They've made me look like a fool, or worse, a liar. You're damn right I'm angry." She sighed and leaned back, still holding his hand. "Forgive me for popping off like that, but I guess I needed to."

Tom slipped his free arm around her shoulders and drew her close. Together they sat, watching fat, wind-whipped flakes of snow tumble about over the harbor and melt against the huge picture window.

"Thank you," she whispered. "Thank you for understanding."

Again and again they kissed. First her blouse, then her bra, then Tom's shirt dropped to the carpet, as he bore her gently down on the couch. His lips, brushing across the hollow of her neck and over the rise of her breasts, felt wonderful. His hand, caressing the smooth inside of her thigh was warm and knowing and patient. She felt as excited, as frightened, as she had during her earliest teenage encounters. But even as she sensed her body respond to his hunger, even as her nipples grew hard against his darting tongue, she sensed her mind begin to pull back.

"Kate. Oh, Kate," Tom whispered, the words vibrating gently against the skin of her breast.

"Tom?" The word was a soft plea, almost a whimper.

"Hold me, Kate. Please don't stop."

She took his face in her hands. "Tom," she said huskily. "I . . . just can't."

Her emotions swirling like the snow on the interstate, Kate took most of an hour and a half to make the drive from Boston to Essex. Tom had been hurt and frustrated by her sudden change in attitude, but in the end he had done his best to understand and accept.

"I only hope Jared knows how goddamn lucky he is," he had snapped as she was dressing. Later, he had insisted on driving her back to Metro and her car, where they had shared a quasi-platonic good-bye kiss.

The phone was ringing as she opened the door from the garage to her house. Roscoe, who had spent most of the past two days at a sleep-over with neighbors and their golden retriever, bounded down the hall, accepted a quick greeting, and then followed her to the den.

It was Jared. "Hi," he said. "I called the house at three A.M. and no one was home. Are you okay?"

"I'm fine, Jared. I spent the night at your father's. Didn't he tell you he had invited me?"

"No." There was no mistaking the curiosity in Jared's voice. "Did you get my letter?"

Kate thumbed through the pile of bills and throwaway journals she had carried in with her. Jared's letter was sandwiched between the magazines *Aches and Pains* and *Pathologist on the Go.*

"I just brought it in," she said. "If you want to wait, I'll read it right now."

"No need, Kate. I've got it memorized." Kate opened the letter and read along as he said the words. "It says 'I love you, I miss you, and I don't want to not live with you anymore. Jared.' "

Kate's heart was pounding so much she could barely respond. "I love you too, Jared. Very, very much. When are you coming home?"

"Day after tomorrow, unless you want me to hitch home now."

"Thursday's fine, honey. Just fine. I'll pick you up at the airport."

"Seven P.M. United."

"Perfect. I have a lot to tell you about. Maybe we'll take a ride in the country. There's someone you should visit."

"Who?"

"You'll see. Let me leave it at that until Thursday. Okay?"

"Okay, but . . ."

"I love you."

"I love you, Boots. Sometimes I don't know who the heck you are or where Jared Samuels is on your list of priorities, but I love you and I want to ride it all out with you as long as I can hang on."

"We'll do just fine, honey. Everything is going to be all right."

As she hung up, Kate realized that for the first time in weeks she believed that.

CHAPTER 11
Wednesday 19 December

ARLEN PAQUETTE, stiff and sore from lack of sleep, cruised along the tree-lined drive toward Redding Pharmaceuticals. Paralleling the icy roadway were the vestiges of the first December snow in Darlington in eleven years. His homecoming the evening before had been a fiasco, marked by several fights with the children, too much to drink before, during and after dinner, and finally, impotence and discord in bed—problems he and his wife had never encountered before.

He adjusted the rearview mirror to examine his face and plucked off the half dozen tissue-paper patches on the shaving nicks caused by his unsteady hand. Even without the patches he looked like hell. It was the job, the job he couldn't quit. Bribery, payoffs, deceptions, threats, ruined lives. Suddenly he was no longer a chemist. Suddenly he was no longer even an administrator. He was a lieutenant, a platoon leader in Cyrus Redding's army. It was an army of specialists, held together by coercion, blackmail, and enormous amounts of money—poised to strike at anything or anyone who threatened Cyrus Redding or the corporation he had built.

The guard greeted him warmly and performed a perfunctory search of the Mercedes. Paquette had once asked the man exactly what it was he was checking for. His polite, but quite disconcerting, reply was, "Anything Mr. Redding doesn't want to be there."

The executive offices, including Cyrus Redding's, were at the hub of the wagon wheel of six long, low structures that made up the manufacturing and packaging plants. Research and other laboratory facilities occupied an underground annex, joined to the main structure by tunnels, escalators, and moving walkways. Paquette parked in the space marked with his name, stopped at his office to leave his coat, and then headed directly for Redding's suite. He was ushered in immediately.

"Arlen, Arlen," Redding said warmly, "welcome home." He was in his wheelchair behind his desk and was dressed in the only outfit Paquette could remember him wearing at work, a lightweight blue-gray suit, white shirt, and string tie, fastened with a turquoise thunderbird ring.

"So," Redding said, when they had moved to the sitting area with coffee and a sugary pastry, "you look a bit drawn. This Boston business has not been so easy, has it?"

"You told me it might not be," Paquette said. "Do you remember when we decided to move the mailing address of the Ashburton Foundation?"

"Of course. A few months after you started working here. Six, no, seven years ago, right?" Paquette nodded. "It was an excellent suggestion and the first time I fully appreciated what a winning decision it was to hire you."

Paquette smiled a weak thank you. "Well," he said, "it was my feeling at that time that with the foundation registered as a tax-exempt philanthropic organization and located in DC, there was no way Redding Pharmaceuticals could ever be connected to it."

"And yet our tenacious friend Dr. Bennett has done so."

"Yes, although as I told you last night, I'm not certain she has put it all together."

"But she will," the Warlock said with certainty.

"She called twice yesterday trying to reach me—that is, trying to reach Dr. Thompson, the foundation director. I couldn't even call her back for fear of having her recognize my voice."

"It was a wise decision not to."

"She's got to hear from someone today."

"She will," Redding said. He glanced at his watch. "At this moment, our persuasive legislative liaison, Charlie Wilson, is on his way to the foundation office to become Dr. James Thompson."

"Office?"

"Of course. We wouldn't want Dr. Bennett to try and locate the Ashburton Foundation only to find a desk, phone and secretary, would we?" Paquette shook his head. The man was absolutely incredible, and efficient in a way that he found quite frightening. "By eleven o'clock this morning, the office, its staff, photographic essays describing its good works, testimonial letters, and a decade or so of documented service will be in place, along with Charlie Wilson, who is, I think you'll agree, as smooth and self-confident as they come."

"Amazing," Paquette said.

"Are you feeling a bit more relaxed about things now?"

"Yes, Mr. Redding. Yes, I am."

"Good. You'll be pleased to know that the company will be taking care of that mirror at the Ritz."

Paquette froze. He had gone to great pains to pay for the damage himself and to insure that in no way would Redding find out about what had happened. Instability under fire was hardly the sort of trait the man rewarded in his platoon leaders. "I . . . I'm sorry about that, sir. I really am."

Redding gestured to the coffee table before them. Sealed under thick glass was the emblem of Redding Pharmaceuticals: a sky-blue background with white hands opening to release a pure, white dove. Below the dove was the name of the company; above it, in a rainbow arc, the motto: *The Greatest Good for the Most People at the Least Cost.* "Arlen, ever since the day I took over this company, I have tried to chart a course that would lead to exactly what this motto says. In this business—in any business—there are always choices to be made, always decisions that cannot be avoided. In the thirty-five years since I first came to Darlington, I've made more gut-wrenching decisions and smashed more glasses and more mirrors in anguish than I care to count. But always, when I needed direction, when I needed advice or council, it was right in front of me." He tapped the motto with his finger. "The legislators, state and federal, the competition, and especially the god-damn FDA are all doing their best to cloud the issue, but in the end it always boils down to this." Again, he tapped the glass.

If the pep talk was meant to buoy Paquette's flagging morale, it failed miserably. The greatest good for the most people at the highest profit was all he could think of. The shortcuts and the human testing, the clinics in Denver and Boston, the bribery and extortion involving FDA officials—all had been tolerable for him because all were abstractions. Kate Bennett was flesh and blood, a voice, a face, a reality; and worse than that, a reality he was growing to admire. Paquette snapped out of his reverie, wondering how long it had lasted. A second? A minute? Then he realized that Redding's eyes were fixed on him.

"I understand, sir," he said, clearing away the phlegm in his throat, "and I assure you, you have nothing to worry about." How did the man know about the stinking mirror? Spies in Boston? A bug in the room? Damn him, Paquette thought viciously. Damn him to hell.

"Fine, Arlen," Redding said. "Now, you have a flight back to Boston this afternoon?"

"Two o'clock."

"I suspect that our meddlesome pathologist is on the ropes. However, her father-in-law assures me that she is far from out on her feet. Her discovery regarding the Ashburton Foundation suggests that he is quite correct."

"I believe Norton Reese is arranging a surprise for her that may help," Paquette said, vividly recalling the glee in Reese's voice as he announced that something was set to fall heavily on Kate Bennett.

"Excellent," Redding said. "Her father-in-law has promised to do what he can to help us as well. One final thing."

"Yes?"

"Has anything further surfaced on the cause of the ovary and blood problems in those three women?" Paquette shook his head. "Strange," Redding said, more to himself than to the other man. "Very strange . . ." For several seconds, he remained lost in thought, his eyes closed, his head turning from side to side as if he were internally speed-reading a page. "Well, Arlen," he said suddenly, opening his eyes, "thank you for the excellent job you are doing. I know at times your duties are not easy for you, but continue to carry them out the way you have, and your rewards will be great."

"Yes, sir," Paquette said. He sat for nearly half a minute before realizing that the Warlock had said all he was going to. Sheepishly, he rose and hurried from the room.

Cyrus Redding studied the man as he left. The Boston business seemed to be having some untoward effects on him, particularly in the area of his drinking. As he motored from the sitting area to his desk, Redding made a mental note to arrange a vacation of some sort for Paquette and his wife as soon as Boston was over. That done, he put the issue and the man out of his head. There was more important business needing attention.

Stephen Stein, the enigmatic, remarkably resourceful investigator, had made a discovery that he suspected would unlock the mystery of John Ferguson.

"Mr. Nunes," Redding said through the intercom of his desk, "would you bring that package to me now."

At the far end of the office, a perfectly camouflaged panel and one-way mirror slid open. The man Nunes emerged from the small, sound-proof room from which he kept vigil, revolver at hand, whenever Redding was not alone in his office. The package, containing a book, several typewritten pages, and an explanatory letter from Stein, had arrived by messenger only minutes before Arlen Paquette.

"If you have errands to run, Mr. Nunes, this would be a good time. When you return in, say, an hour, we could well have a new slant on our friend, Dr. Ferguson." He smiled, nearly beside himself at the prospect. "I think this occasion might call for a pint of that mint chip ice cream I have forbidden you to let me talk you into buying."

The taciturn bodyguard nodded. "I can't let you talk me into it," he said, "but perhaps I could purchase some on my own."

Redding waited until his office door had clicked shut; then he locked it electronically and spread the contents of the package on his desk.

"My apologies," Stein wrote, "for missing this volume during the course of earlier efforts to tie our mysterious Dr. Ferguson's background in with the war. I borrowed it from the Holocaust Library at the university here with assurances of its return, along with some token of our gratitude. Its title, according to the German professor who did the enclosed translation for us, is *Doctors of the Reich; The Story of Hitler's Monster Kings.* The work is the product of painstaking research and countless interviews by a Jewish journalist named Sachs, himself a death camp survivor, and is believed by my source to be accurate within the limits of the author's prejudices. Only the chapters dealing with the experiments at the Ravensbrück concentration camp for women have been translated. The photographs on pages three sixty-seven and three sixty-eight will, I believe, be of special interest to you."

For most of the next hour, Cyrus Redding sat transfixed, moving only to turn the pages of the translation or to refer to specific photographs in the worn, yellowed text. John Ferguson was a physician and scientist named Dr. Wilhelm Becker. The photographs, though slightly blurred and taken nearly forty years before, left no doubt whatsoever.

"Amazing," Redding murmured as he read and reread the biography of his associate. "Absolutely amazing."

There were two snapshots of Wilhelm Becker, one a full-face identification photo and one a group shot with other physicians at the Ravensbrück Camp. There was also a shot of what remained of the laboratory in which Becker was purported to have died, with the bodies of the man and his staff sergeant still curled amidst the debris on the floor. Redding withdrew a large, ivory-handled magnifying glass from his desk and for several minutes studied the detail of the scene. The body identified as Willi Becker was little more than an ill-defined, charred lump.

"Nicely done, my friend," Redding said softly. "Nicely done."

Familiar now with the man and with his spurious death, Redding turned to the page and a half dealing with Becker's research, specifically, with his research on a substance called Estronate 250. Much of the information presented was gleaned from transcripts of the war-crimes trial of a physician named Müller and another named Rendl, both of whom were sentenced to Nuremberg Prison in large measure because of their association with the supposedly late Wilhelm Becker. Redding found the men in the Ravensbrück group photo. Müller had served five years at hard labor before certain Ravensbrück survivors were able to document his acts of heroism on their behalf and get his sentence commuted. For Rendl, the revelations of his humanitarianism came too late. Three years after his incarceration, he hanged himself in his cell.

Redding read the Estronate material word by word, taking careful notes. By the time he had finished, he was absolutely certain that neither Wilhelm Becker nor the notebook containing his work on the hormone had perished in the Ravensbrück fire.

A substance, harmless in every other way, that could render a woman sterile without her knowledge. Redding was staggered by the potential of such a drug. China, India, the African nations, the Arabs. What would governments be willing to pay for a secret that might selectively thin their populations and thereby solve so many of their economic and political woes? What would certain governments pay for a weapon which, if delivered properly, could decimate their enemies in a single generation without the violent loss of one life?

Redding's thoughts were soaring through the possibilities of Estronate 250 when, with a soft knock, Nunes entered the office, set a package on the desk, and retired to his observation room. For another hour, Redding sat alone, savoring his mint chip ice cream and deciding how he might best break the news to Dr. John Ferguson that their fifteen-year-old collaboration was about to take on a new dimension.

"I love you, I miss you, and I don't want to not live with you anymore."

Kate read Jared's note again and then again, drawing strength and confidence from it each time. She had returned to her office following two distressing and frightening visits. One was to Ellen, who was, for the first time, receiving a transfusion of packed red blood cells. The second was to Norton Reese. If the connection between Metropolitan Hospital of Boston, the Ashburton Foundation, and Redding Pharmaceuticals was as intimate as Reese's clumsy evasions were leading her to believe, she would need all the strength and confidence she could muster. Thank you, Jared, she thought. Thank you for pulling me out from under the biggest pressure of all.

Her meeting with Reese had started off cordially enough. In fact, the man had seemed at times to be inappropriately jovial and at ease. Ever since their confrontation before the board of trustees over his diversion of budgeted pathology department funds to the cardiac surgical program, Reese had dealt with her with the gingerliness of an apprentice handling high explosives. Now, suddenly, he was all smiles. His congeniality lasted through several minutes of conversation about her department and Stan Willoughby's recommendation that she succeed him as chief, and ended abruptly with mention of the Ashburton Foundation. Whatever fortes the man might have, Kate mused at that moment, they certainly did not include poker faces. His eyes narrowed fractionally, but enough to deepen the fleshy crow's feet at their corners. His lips whitened, as did the tips of his fingers where they were touching one another.

"I'm afraid I'm not at liberty to open the Ashburton Foundation files to you," he had said, his eyes struggling to maintain contact with hers and failing. "However, I shall be happy to answer what questions I can."

"Okay," Kate said, shrugging. "My first question is why aren't you at liberty to open the Ashburton Foundation files to me?"

"It's . . . it's part of the agreement we signed when we accepted a grant from them." It was bizarre. In a very literal sense, the man was squirming in his seat.

"Well, suppose I wanted to apply for a grant for my department. How would I go about contacting them?"

"I'll have Gina give you the address on your way out. You can write them yourself."

"I already have a post office box number in Washington, DC. Is that it?"

"Yes. I mean, probably."

"Well, suppose I wanted to visit their offices in person. Could you ask Gina to give me a street address as well?"

Reese continued to fidget. "Look," he said, "I'll give you their mailing address and phone number. I'm sorry, but that's all I can do. Why do you want to know about the Ashburton Foundation anyway?" he managed.

"Mr. Reese," Kate said calmly, "If I answer that question, will you open their files to me?"

"Not without written permission from the Ashburton Foundation."

"Well then, it appears we've got a Mexican standoff, doesn't it? I'll tell you this much," her voice grew cold. "Two women have died and a third may be dying. If I find out the Ashburton Foundation is connected in any way with what has happened to them, and you have kept significant information from me, I promise that I won't rest until everyone who matters knows what you have done. Is that clear?" Her uncharacteristic anger had, she knew, been prodded by the sight of Ellen Sandler mutely watching the plastic bag dripping blood into her arm and by the knowledge that this was, in all likelihood, just the first of many transfusions to come.

Reese checked his watch in a manner that was as inappropriate as it was unsubtle. It was as if he had left a message to be called at precisely nine-twelve and was wondering why the phone hadn't rung.

"Mr. Reese?"

The administrator shifted his gaze back to her. His face was pinched and gray with anger—no, she realized, it was something deeper than anger. Hatred? Did the poor man actually hate her?

"You really think you're something, don't you," he rasped in a strained, muddy voice.

"I beg your pardon?"

"Who made you the crusader? Do you think that just because you have an MD degree and all that old family money you can ride all over people?"

"What? Mr. Reese, I nev—"

"Well, let me tell you something. You don't intimidate me like you do some around here. No, sir, not one bit. So you just ride off on that high horse of yours and let me and the department heads—the *official* department heads—worry about grants and foundations and such."

Kate watched as the man sat there, panting from the exertion of his outburst. For five seconds, ten, her green eyes fixed on him. Then she rose from her chair and left, unwilling to dignify Reese's eruption with a response.

Now, alone in her office, Kate sat, trying to crystallize her thoughts and doodling a calligraphic montage of the words "Reese" and "Asshole." After finishing four versions of each, she began adding "Ashburton" and "Paquette." First there was the bribery of Ian Toole, an act which seemed to her equivalent to shooting a chipmunk with an elephant gun. She would have been quite satisfied with an admission by Redding Pharmaceuticals that they had somehow allowed a batch of their generic vitamins to become contaminated and would gladly recall and replace them. Their illogically excessive response had to have been born out of either arrogance or fear. But fear of what? "Omnicenter" made its first appearance in the montage.

The Ashburton Foundation had endowed an entire ob-gyn department and subsidized a massive, modern women's health center. Philanthropic acts? Perhaps, she thought. But both of her calls to the foundation had gone unanswered by Dr. Thompson, the director, and her efforts, though modest, had failed to come up with an address for the place. Then there was Reese's refusal to discuss the organization that had been, at least in part, responsible for the resurgence of his hospital. At that moment, almost subconsciously, she began adding another name to the paper. Again and again she wrote it, first in the calligraphic forms she knew, then in several she made up on the spot. "Horner." Somehow the cantankerous, eccentric computer genius was involved in what was going on. The notion fit too well, made too much sense. But how? There really was only one person who could help her find out. Another minute of speculation, and she called William Zimmermann.

Fifteen minutes later, she was on her way through the tunnel to the Omnicenter when Tom Engleson entered from the cutoff to the surgical building.

"Hi," she said, searching his face for a clue as to how he was handling the abortive end to their evening together.

"H'lo," his voice was flat.

She slowed, but continued walking. "Going to the Omnicenter?"

Tom nodded. "I have a clinic in twenty minutes."

"You all right?"

"Yeah, sure. Great."

"Tom, I—"

"Look, Kate, it's my problem, not yours."

"Dr. Engleson, you weren't exactly alone on the couch last night," she whispered, glancing about to ensure that none of the tunnel traffic was too close. "I feel awful about giving out such mixed messages. But you are an incredibly comfortable and understanding man. With all the trouble at the hospital I'm afraid I just allowed myself to hide out in your arms. It was wrong and unfair—more so because I really care very much for you. I'm sorry, Tom."

They reached the stairwell leading up to the Omnicenter.

"Wait," Tom said. "Please." He guided her to a small alcove opposite the staircase.

"You know, considering the nature of the Metro grapevine, we'll probably be an item by . . ." Two nurses chattered past them and up the stairs. "Hell," she said, following them with her eyes, "we most likely are already."

"Do you really mean that, about caring for me?"

"Tom, I love my husband very much. We've had some trouble getting our lives back in sync since the election, but my feelings for him haven't changed. Still, you're very special to me. Believe me, if my home situation, my marriage, were any different, we would have been lovers last night."

"Yeah?" The muscles in his face relaxed, and some measure of energy returned to his voice.

"Yes," she said. Tom Engleson might have been nine years Jared's junior, but they still had much in common, including, it now appeared, the need for strong reassurance about such things.

"I said it last night, and I'll say it again. Jared is a very lucky man." Acceptance had replaced the strain in Tom's voice.

"I know," Kate said. "Tom, seriously, thank you for not making it any harder for me. Between the wretched business with Bobby Geary, the disappearance of my chemist, and some incredible crap from Norton Reese, I feel like I need all the friends—all the help—I can get." She glanced at her watch. "Say, do you have a few minutes?"

"Sure, why?"

"I'm going to see Bill Zimmermann to discuss the Ashburton Foundation. I'd love to have you come along if you can."

"Rocket Bill? I do have a little time if you think he wouldn't mind."

"Hardly," Kate said. "He knows how much help you've been to me through all this. Okay?"

During the four-flight climb, Tom reviewed for her the protocols for patient care in the Omnicenter. On arrival, both new and returning patients met with a specially trained female intake worker, who blackened in the appropriate spaces in a detailed computer-readable history sheet. Medications, menstrual history, new complaints, and side effects of any treatment were carefully recorded. The worker then slid the history sheet into a computer terminal on her desk, and in thirty seconds or less, instructions as to where the patient was to go next would appear on the screen along with, if necessary, what laboratory tests were to be ordered.

"Do you feel the system is a bit impersonal?" Kate asked.

"You're a patient here. Do you?"

"No, not really, I guess," she said. "I can remember when a visit to the gynecologist consisted of sitting for an hour in a ten-foot-square waiting room with a dozen other women, having my name called out, stripping in a tiny examining room, and finally having the doctor rush in, thumbing through my chart for my name, and then as often as not telling me to put my heels in the stirrups before he even asked why I was there."

"See," Tom laughed, "no system is perfect. But seriously, the one here is damn good. It frees me up to do a careful exam and to answer as many questions as my patients have."

The system might be great, Kate thought, but something, somewhere inside it, was rotten. Something was killing people.

Large, colored numbers marked each floor. The 3, filling half a wall at the third-floor landing, was an iridescent orange. Kate reached for the handle of the door to the corridor, but then stopped, turned to Tom, and kissed him gently on the cheek.

"Thank you for last night, my friend," she said.

Tom accepted the kiss and then squeezed her hand and smiled. "If you need anything at all, and I can do it or get it, you've got it," he said.

William Zimmermann greeted Kate warmly and Tom with some surprise. It was clear from his expression and manner that he was concerned about anything that might affect the reputation of the Omnicenter, including involvement of one of the Ashburton Service senior residents.

Kate sought immediately to reassure him. "Bill, as you know, Dr. Engleson's been an enormous help to me in sorting all this out. He knows, as do I, the importance of absolute discretion in discussing these matters with anyone."

"You've spoken to no one at all about this?" Zimmermann asked Tom.

"No, sir. Only K . . . only Dr. Bennett."

"Good. Well, sit down, sit down both of you."

"I'll try not to take up too much of your time," Kate began, "but I want to keep you abreast of what has been happening since we talked yesterday."

"You were concerned about the Ashburton Foundation."

"Exactly. You know how upset I was with Redding Pharmaceuticals after they bribed my chemist. Well—"

Zimmermann stopped her with a raised hand. "Kate, please," he said, with an edge of irritation she had never heard before. "I told you how I felt about the situation with the chemist. I believe that you believe, but no more than that." He turned to Tom. "Do you have any personal knowledge of this chemist, Toole?"

Tom thought for a moment and then shook his head. "No, not really."

"All right, then," Zimmermann said. "Substantiated facts."

Kate took a breath, nodded, and settled herself down by smoothing out a pleat in her charcoal gray skirt. "Sorry, Bill. Okay, here's a substantiated fact." She passed a telephone number across to him. "It's the number of the Ashburton Foundation in Washington, DC. At one time, maybe seven or eight years ago, the foundation was located in Darlington, Kentucky, the same town as Redding Pharmaceuticals. I tried calling them yesterday, several times, but all I got was a stammering receptionist who promised I would hear from a Dr. James Thompson, the director, as soon as he returned to the office. I never heard. Then this morning, I went to see Norton Reese and asked to see the Ashburton Foundation files. You would have thought I asked to read his diary. He refused and then exploded at me."

"Did he give any reason for refusing?" Tom asked.

Kate shook her head. "Not really. He seemed frightened of me. Scared stiff."

"Kate," Zimmermann asked, fingering the paper she had given him, "just what is it you're driving at?" The edge was still in his voice.

Even before she spoke, she sensed her theory would not sit well with the Omnicenter director. Still, there was no way to back off. "Well, I think Redding Pharmaceuticals may be investing money in hospitals— or at least this hospital—and using the Ashburton Foundation as some kind of front, sort of a middle man."

Zimmermann's pale eyes widened. "That's absurd," he said, "absolutely absurd. What would they have to gain?"

"I'm not certain. I have an idea, but I'm not certain. Furthermore, I think Norton Reese knows the truth."

"Well?"

Substantiated facts. Suddenly, Kate wished she had taken more time, prepared herself more thoughtfully. Then she remembered Ellen. Time was, she felt certain, running out for her friend. With that reality, nothing else really mattered. She girded herself for whatever Zimmermann's response was to be and pushed on.

"I don't think the anthranilic acid in my vitamins was an accidental contaminant," she said, forcing a levelness into her voice though she was shaking inside. "I think it was being tested on me, and probably on others as well; not tested to see whether or not it worked, because I didn't have any symptoms, but rather for adverse reactions, for side effects, if you will."

Zimmermann was incredulous. "Dr. Bennett, if such a thing were going on in the Omnicenter, in *my* facility, don't you think I would know about it?"

"Not really," Kate said. "It was starting to come together for me, but Tom's description of how the intake process works made it all fit. It's Carl Horner, downstairs. Horner and his Monkeys. You and the other docs here just go on prescribing his medications and then recording his data for him. There's no reason you have to know anything, as long as the computers know."

"And you think the Ashburton Foundation is bankrolling his work?" Kate nodded. "This is getting out of control." He turned to Tom. "Do you follow what she is saying?" Reluctantly, Tom nodded. "And do you believe it?"

"I . . . I don't know what to believe."

"Well, I think it's time I checked on some of these things for myself," Zimmermann said, snatching up the telephone and setting the Ashburton number on his desk. "Dr. William Zimmermann, access number three-oh-eight-three," he told the operator, as Kate looked on excitedly, "I'd like a Watts line, please."

Only a few more minutes, Kate told herself. Only a few more minutes, a few words from the confused, stammering receptionist, and Zimmermann would at least realize that something was not right at the Ashburton Foundation. For the moment, that would be enough. Measured against the fiascoes surrounding Bobby Geary and Ian Toole, the planting of even a small seed of doubt in the man's mind would be a major victory.

"Yes, good morning," she heard Zimmermann say. "I am Dr. William Zimmermann, from Boston. I should like to speak with the director. . . . Yes, exactly. Dr. Thompson." Kate turned to Tom and gave him a conspiratorial smile. Suddenly, she realized that Zimmermann was waving to get her attention and pointing to the extension phone on the conference table. She came on the line just as did Dr. James Thompson.

"This is Dr. Thompson," the man said.

"Dr. Thompson, I'm sorry to disturb you. My name is Zimmermann. I'm the director of the Omnicenter here in Boston."

"Oh, yes, Dr. Zimmermann, I know of you," Thompson said. "You took over for poor Dr. French, what was it, four years ago?"

"Five."

"Tragic accident, tragic, as I recall."

"Yes, he drowned," Zimmermann said, now looking directly at Kate, who was beginning to feel sick.

"What can I do for you, sir?" Thompson had a deep, genteel voice.

"I'm here with Dr. Kate Bennett, one of our physicians."

"Ah, yes. Her name is right in front of me here on my desk. Twice, in fact. She phoned here yesterday and was told I would return her call.

However, my secretary had no way of knowing that my son, Craig, had fallen at school and broken his wrist and that I was going to be tied up in the emergency room for hours."

"He's all right, I hope?"

Thompson laughed. "Never better. That plaster makes him the center of attention. Now, what can I do for you and Dr. Bennett?"

"Nothing for me, actually, but Dr. Bennett has a question or two for you. One moment."

"Certainly."

Zimmermann, his expression saying, "Well, you asked for it, now here it is," motioned for her to go ahead.

Kate felt as if she were being bludgeoned. She had been sure, so sure, and now. . . . "Dr. Thompson," she managed, "my apologies for not being more patient." She glanced over at Tom, who shrugged helplessly. "I . . . I was calling to find out if there was any connection between the Ashburton Foundation and Redding Pharmaceuticals." There was no sense in trying anything other than a direct approach. She was beaten, humiliated again, and she knew it.

"Connection?"

"Yes, sir. Isn't it true that the foundation was once located in Darlington, Kentucky, the same town as Redding?"

"As a matter of fact, it was. John and Sylvia Ashburton, whose estate established the foundation, were from Lexington. Their son, John, Jr., ran one of their horse farms, Darlington Stables. For two years after his parents died, John stayed at the farm, tidying up affairs and setting up the mechanics of the foundation. I was hired in, let me see, seventy-nine, but by then, the center of operations had already been moved to Washington. I'm afraid that as far as Redding Pharmaceuticals goes, the geographical connection was pure coincidence."

"Thank you," Kate said meekly. "That certainly helps clear up my confusion." Another glance at Tom, and she grasped at one final straw. "Dr. Thompson, I was trying to find out the street address of your office, but there's no Ashburton Foundation listed in the DC directory."

"By design, Dr. Bennett, quite by design. You see, where there is grant money involved, there are bound to be, how should I say it, somewhat less than fully qualified applicants contacting us. We prefer to do our own preliminary research and then to encourage only appropriate institutions and agencies to apply. Our offices are at 238 K Street, Northwest, on the seventh floor. Please feel free to visit any time you are in Washington. Perhaps your pathology department would be interested in applying for a capital equipment grant."

"Perhaps," Kate said distractedly.

William Zimmermann had heard enough. "Dr. Thompson," he said, "I want to thank you for helping to clear up the confusion here, and also for the wonderful support your agency has given my Omnicenter."

"Our pleasure, sir," Dr. James Thompson said.

"Well?" Zimmermann asked after he had hung up.

"Something's not right," she said.

"What?"

"He mentioned my pathology department. How did he know I was a pathologist?"

"I told him you were at the very start of the call."

"I'm not trying to be difficult, Bill—really, I'm not—but you referred to me as a physician, not a pathologist. You remember, Tom, don't you?" A look at the uncertainty in Tom's eyes, and she began having doubts herself. "Well?"

"I . . . I'm not sure," was all the resident could say.

Kate stood to go. "Bill, I may seem pigheaded to you, or even confused, but I tell you, something still doesn't feel right to me. I just have a sense that Dr. Thompson knew exactly who I was and what I wanted before you ever called."

"You must admit, Kate," Zimmermann said clinically, "that when one looks first at the business with the baseball player, then at the conflict over whether or not a chemist actually performed tests he swears he never ran, and now at what seem to be groundless concerns on your part regarding the Ashburton Foundation and my long-standing computer engineer, it becomes somewhat difficult to get overly enthusiastic about your hunches and senses and theories. Now, if you've nothing further, I must get back to work."

"No," Kate said, smarting from the outburst by the usually cordial man. "Nothing, really, except the promise that no matter how long it takes, I will find out who, or what, is responsible for Ellen's bleeding disorder. Thanks for coming, Tom. I'm sorry it worked out this way." With a nod to both men, she left, fingers of self-doubt tightening their grip in her gut.

She bundled her clinic coat against the wind and snow and pushed head down out of the Omnicenter and onto the street. What if she were wrong, totally wrong about Redding and Horner, about the Omnicenter and Ellen's bleeding, about Reese? Perhaps, despite the critical situation in Berenson 421, despite the nagging fears about her own body, she should back off and let things simmer down. Perhaps she should listen to the advice of her father-in-law and reorder her priorities away from Metropolitan Hospital.

They were waiting for her in her office: Stan Willoughby, Liu Huang, and Rod Green, the flamboyant, black general surgeon who was, it was rumored, being groomed for a Harvard professorship.

"Kate," Willoughby said. "I was just writing you a note." He held the paper up for her to see.

Kate greeted the other two men and then turned back to Willoughby. He was tight. His stance and the strain in his smile said so. "Well?" she asked.

"Pardon?"

"The note, Stan. What would it have said?"

"Oh, I'm sorry. My mind is racing." He cleared his throat. "Kate, we need to talk with you."

"Well, sit down then, please." She felt her heart respond to her sudden apprehension. "A problem?"

Willoughby was totally ill at ease. "I . . . um . . . Kate, yesterday you did a frozen section of a needle biopsy on one of Dr. Green's patients."

"Yes, a breast. It was an intraductal adenocarcinoma. I reported the results to Dr. Green myself." Her pulse quickened another notch.

"Was there, um . . . any question in your mind of the—"

"What Dr. Willoughby is trying to say," Rod Green cut in, "is that I did a masectomy on a woman who, it appears, has benign breast disease." The man's dark eyes flashed.

"That's impossible." Kate looked first to Willoughby and then to Liu Huang for support, but saw only the tightlipped confirmation of the surgeon's allegation. "Liu?"

"I have examined specimen in great detail," the little man said carefully. "Track of biopsy needle enters benign adenoma. No cancer there or in any part of breast."

"Are . . . are you sure?" She could barely speak.

"Kate," Willoughby said, "I reviewed the slides myself. There's no cancer."

"But, there was. I swear there was."

"There was no cancer in my patient," Green said. "None." His fury at her was clearly under the most marginal control. "You have made a mistake. A terrible, terrible mistake."

Kate stared wide-eyed at the three men. It was a dream, a grotesque nightmare from which she would awake at any moment. Their stone faces blurred in and out of focus as her mind struggled to remember the cells. There were three breast biopsies, no, two, there were two. Green's patient was the first. The pathology was a bit tricky, but it was nothing she would ever miss in even one case out of a thousand, unless. . . . She remembered the fatigue and the strain of the previous morning, the stress of Jared's being away, the crank phone calls, and the disappearance of Ian Toole. No, her thoughts screamed, she couldn't have made such a mistake. It wasn't as if they were saying she had missed something, although even that kind of error would have been hard to believe, they were claiming she had read a condition that wasn't there. It was . . . impossible. There was just no other word.

"Did you check the slides from yesterday?" she managed. "The frozens?"

Willoughby nodded grimly. "Benign adenoma. The exact same pathology as in the main specimen." He handed her a plastic box of slides.

Green stood up, fists clenched. "I have heard enough. Dr. Bennett, thanks to you, a woman who came to me in trust has had her breast removed unnecessarily. When she sues, even though I will in all likelihood be one of the defendants, I shall also be her best witness." He started to leave and then turned back to her. "You know," he said, "that letter you sent to the papers about Bobby Geary was a pretty rotten thing to do." He slammed the door hard enough to shake the vase of roses on the corner of her desk.

Kate could barely hold the slide as she set it on the stage of her microscope. This time, the yellow-white light held no excitement, no adventure for her. She knew, even before she had completed focusing down, that the specimen was benign. It was that clear-cut. Her mistaking the pattern for a cancer would have been as likely as an Olympic diver springing off the wrong end of the board.

"Something's wrong," she said, her eye still fixed on the cells. The words reverberated in her mind. Something's wrong. She had said that to Bill Zimmermann not half an hour ago.

"Kate," Willoughby said gently, "I'm sorry."

Only after she looked up from the microscope did she realize she was crying. "Stan, I swear this is not the slide I read yesterday. It can't be." But even as she said the words, she admitted to herself that, as in the situation with Bobby Geary, her only defense was a protestation of innocence.

"You've been under a great deal of stress lately, Kate. Do you suppose that—"

"No!" She forced herself to lower her voice. "I remember the biopsy I saw yesterday. It was cancer. I didn't make a mistake."

"Look," Willoughby said, "I want you to take a few days off. Rest. After this coming weekend we can talk."

"But—"

"Kate, I'm taking you off the schedule for a while. Now I don't want you coming back into work until after we've had a chance to discuss things next week. Okay?" There was uncharacteristic firmness in the man's voice.

Meekly, she nodded. "Okay, but—"

"No buts. Kate, it's for your own good. I'll call you at home and check on how you're doing. Now off you go."

Kate watched her colleagues leave: Stan Willoughby, head down, shuffling a few feet ahead of Liu Huang, who turned for a moment and gave her a timid, but hopeful, thumbs-up sign. Then they were gone.

For a time she sat, uncertainly, isolation and self-doubt constricting every muscle in her body, making it difficult to move or even to breathe. With great effort, she pulled the telephone over and lifted the receiver. "I want to place a long-distance call, please," she heard her voice say. "It's personal, so charge it to my home phone. . . . I'm calling San Diego."

CHAPTER 12
Thursday 20 December

IT HAD TAKEN narcotic painkillers and amphetamines along with his usual pharmacopoeia, but in the end, Becker had prevailed. Now he ached for sleep. He could not remember his last meal. Catnaps at his desk, cool showers every six or seven hours, bars of chocolate, cups of thick coffee for four days, or was it five? These had been his only succor.

Still, he had endured. In the morning, a messenger would hand deliver his manuscript and box of slides to the editor in chief of *The New England Journal of Medicine.* The letter accompanying the manuscript would give the man ten days to agree to publish the Estronate studies in their entirety within four months and to oversee the appointment of an international commission to assume responsibility for the initiation of Beckerian population control.

The study was in a shambles, with reference books, scrap paper, coffee cups, discarded drafts, candy-bar wrappers, and dirty glasses covering the furniture and much of the floor. Like a prizefighter at the moment of triumph, Willi Becker, more skeleton than man, stood in the midst of the debris and pumped his fists in the air. After forty years and through hardship almost unimaginable, he had finished. Now there was only the matter of gaining acceptance.

It was ironic, he acknowledged, that decades of the most meticulous research had come down to a few frenetic days, but that was the way it had to be. With the pathologist Bennett snooping about the Omnicenter and Cyrus Redding's antennae up, time had become a luxury he could no longer afford.

Studies in Estronate 250. Becker cleared off his easy chair, settled down, and indulged in thoughts of the accolades, honors, and other tributes to his genius and dedication certain to result from the publication and implementation of his work. He was nearing receipt of a Nobel

Prize when the phone began ringing. It took half a dozen rings to break through his reverie and another four to locate the phone beneath a pile of journals.

"Hello?"

"John? Redding here."

The voice brought a painful emptiness to Becker's chest. For several seconds, he could not speak.

"John?"

Becker cleared his throat. "Yes, yes, Cyrus. I'm here."

"Good. Fine. Well, I hope I'm not disturbing anything important for you."

"Not at all. I was just . . . doing a little reading before bed." Did his voice sound as strained, as strangled, as it felt? "What can I do for you?" Please, he thought, let it be some problem related to their myasthenia. Let it be anything but . . .

"Well, John, I wanted to speak with you a bit about that business at the Omnicenter." Becker's heart sank. "You know," Redding continued, "the situation with these women having severe scarring of their ovaries and then bleeding to death."

"Yes, what about it?"

"Have you learned anything new about the situation since we spoke last?"

"No. Not really." Becker sensed that he was being toyed with.

"Well, John, you know that the whole matter has piqued my curiosity, as well as my concern for the safety of our testing programs. Too many coincidences. Too much smoke for there not to be a fire someplace."

"Perhaps," Becker said, hanging onto the thread of hope that the man, a master at such maneuvers, was shooting in the dark. For a time, there was silence from Redding's end. Becker shifted nervously in his chair. "Cyrus?" he asked finally.

"I'm here."

"Was there . . . anything else?"

"John, I won't bandy words with you. We've been through too much together, accomplished too many remarkable things for me to try and humiliate you by letting you trip over one after another of your own lies."

"I . . . I don't understand."

"Of course you understand, John." He paused. "I know who you are. That is the gist of what I am calling to say. I know about Wilhelm Becker, and even more importantly, I know about Estronate Two-fifty."

Becker glanced over at his manuscript, stacked neatly atop the printer of his word processor, and forced himself to calm down. There was little he could think of that Redding could do to hurt him at this stage of the game. Still, Cyrus Redding was Cyrus Redding, and no

amount of caution was too much. *Stay calm but don't underestimate.*
"Your resourcefulness is quite impressive," he said.

"John, tell me truly, it was Estronate Two-fifty that caused the problems at the Omnicenter, wasn't it?"

"It was."

"The hemorrhaging is an undesirable side effect?"

Becker was about to explain that the problem had been overcome and that his hormone was, to all intents, perfected. He stopped himself at the last moment. "Yes," he said. "A most unfortunate bug that I have not been able to get out of the system."

"You should have told me, John," Redding said. "You should have trusted me."

"What do you want?"

"John, come now. It is bad enough you didn't respect me enough to take me into your confidence. It is bad enough your uncondoned experiments have put my entire company in jeopardy. Do not try to demean my intelligence. I want to extend our partnership to include that remarkable hormone of yours. After all, it was tested at a facility that I fund."

"Work is not complete. There are problems. Serious problems."

"Then we shall overcome them. You know the potential of this Estronate of yours as well as I do. I am prepared to make you an on-the-spot offer of, say, half a million dollars now and a similar amount when your work is completed to the satisfaction of my biochemists. And of course, there would be a percentage of all sales."

Sales. Becker realized that his worst possible scenario was being enacted. Redding understood not only the chemical nature of Estronate, but also its limitless value to certain governments. How? How in hell's name had the man learned so much so quickly? "I . . . I was planning eventually on submitting my work for publication," he offered.

Redding laughed. "That would be bad business, John. Very bad business. The value of our product would surely plummet if its existence and unique properties became general knowledge. Suppose you oversee the scientific end and let me deal with the proprietary."

"If I refuse," Becker said, "will you kill me?"

Again Redding laughed. "Perhaps. Perhaps I will. However, there are those, I am sure, who would pay dearly for information on the physician whom the Ravensbrück prisoners called the Serpent."

For a time there was silence. "How did you learn of all this?" Becker asked finally.

"Why don't we save explanations, Dr. Becker, for a time after our new business arrangement has been consummated."

"I need time to think."

"Take it. Take as much as you need up to, say, twenty-four hours."

"The intrinsic problems of the hormone may be insurmountable."

"A chance I will take. You owe me this. For the troubles you have caused at our testing facility, you owe me. In fact, there is something else you owe me as well."

"Oh?"

"I wish to know the individual at the Omnicenter who has been helping you with your work."

Becker started to protest that there was no such person, but decided against testing the man's patience. In less than twelve hours a messenger would deliver the Estronate paper and slides to *The New England Journal of Medicine,* making the hormone, in essence, public domain. He had already decided that exposure of his true identity and the risk of spending what little was left of his life in prison was a small price to pay for immortality. "Forty-eight hours," he said.

Redding hesitated. "Very well, then," he said finally. "Forty-eight hours it will be. You have the number. I shall expect to hear from you within two days. The Estronate work and the name of your associate. Good-bye." He hung up.

"Good-bye," Becker said to the dial tone. As he drew the receiver from his ear, he heard a faint but definite click. The sound sent fear stabbing beneath his breastbone. Someone, almost certainly William, was on the downstairs extension. How long? How long had he been there?

In the cluttered semidarkness of his study, Willi Becker strained his compromised hearing. For a time, there was only silence. Perhaps, he thought, there hadn't been a click at all. Then he heard the unmistakable tread of footsteps on the stairs.

"William?" Again there was silence. "William?"

"Yes, Father, it is." Zimmermann appeared suddenly in the doorway and stood, arms folded, looking placidly across at him.

"You . . . ah . . . you surprised me. How long have you been in the house?"

"Long enough." Zimmermann strode to the bookcase and poured himself a drink. He was, as usual, immaculately dressed. Light from the gooseneck reading lamp sparked off the heavy diamond ring on the small finger of his left hand and highlighted the sheen on his black Italian-cut loafers.

"You were listening in on my conversation, weren't you?"

"Oh, perhaps." Zimmermann snapped a wooden swizzle stick in two and used one edge to clean beneath his nails.

"Listening was a rude thing to do."

"Me, rude? Why, Father . . ."

"Well, if you heard, you heard. It really makes no difference."

"Oh?"

"Just how long *were* you listening in?"

Zimmermann didn't answer. Instead, he walked to the printer, picked up the Estronate manuscript, and turned it from one side to the other, appraisingly. "A half million dollars and then some. It would seem there is some truth about good things coming in small packages."

"Give me that." Becker was too weak, too depleted by the drugs, even to rise.

Zimmermann ignored him. "Wilhelm W. Becker, MD, PhD," he read. "So that's who my father is."

"Please, William."

"How good it is to learn that the man John Ferguson, who so ignored and abused my mother all those years, was not my father. The Serpent of Ravensbrück. That's my real father."

"I never abused her. I did what I had to do."

"Father, please. She knew that you could have come home much more often and didn't. She knew about your women, your countless women. She knew that neither of us would ever mean anything to you compared to your precious research."

Becker stared at his son with wide, bloodshot eyes. "You hate me, don't you?" There was incredulity in his voice.

"Not really. The truth is, I don't feel much for you one way or the other."

"But I was behind you all the way. My money sent you through school. Your position at the Omnicenter, how do you think that came about? Do you think Harold French just happened to drown accidentally at the moment you were experienced enough to take over for him? It was me!" Becker's hoarse, muddy voice had become barely audible. "If you care so little about me, William, then why have you helped me in my work all these years? Why?"

Zimmermann gazed blandly at his father. "Because of your connections, of course. Your friend Redding triples what the hospital pays me. You suggested my name, and he arranged for me to get my professorship. I know he did."

"He got you the position on my say-so, and he can have it taken from you the same way."

"Can he, now." Zimmermann held up the Estronate manuscript. "You lied to him. You told him there were still flaws in the work. Why? Are you thinking that once he finds out you have sent this off for publication, he will just walk away and leave us alone? Do you think he won't find out who I am? What I have been helping you do behind his back? Do you?" He was screaming. "Well, I tell you right here and now, Father, this is mine. I have paid for it over the years with countless humiliations. Cyrus Redding will have his Estronate, and I shall have my proper legacy."

"No!" Even as he shouted the word, Willi Becker felt the tearing pain in his left chest. His heart, weakened by disease, and sorely compromised by amphetamines, pounded mercilessly and irregularly. "My oxygen," he rasped. "In the bedroom. Oxygen and nitroglycerine." The study was beginning a nauseating spin.

For the first time, William Zimmermann smiled. "I'm afraid I can't hear you, Father," he said, benevolently. "Could you please speak up a bit?"

"Will . . . iam . . . please . . ." Becker's final words were muffled by the gurgle of fluid bubbling up from his lungs, and vomitus welling from his stomach. He clawed impotently in the direction of his son and then toppled over onto the rug, his face awash in the products of his own death.

Stepping carefully around his father's corpse, Zimmermann slipped the Estronate paper into a large envelope; then he removed the disc from the word processor and dropped it in as well. Next he copied a number from the leather-bound address book buried under some papers on one corner of the desk. Finally, he stacked the three worn looseleaf notebooks containing the Estronate data and tucked them under his arm. He would phone Cyrus Redding from the extension downstairs.

The pharmaceutical magnate evinced little surprise at Zimmermann's call or at the rapid turn of events in Newton. Instead, he listened patiently to the details of Willi Becker's life as the man's son knew them.

"Dr. Zimmermann," he said finally, "let us stop here to be certain I fully understand. Your father, when he was supervising construction of the Omnicenter, secretly had a laboratory built for himself in the subbasement?"

"Correct," Zimmermann said. "On the blueprints it is drawn as some sort of dead storage area, I think."

"And the only way to get into the laboratory is through an electronic security system?"

"The lock is hidden and coded electronically. The door is concealed behind a set of shelves."

"Does anyone besides you have the combination?"

"No. At least not as far as I know."

"Remarkable. Dr. Zimmermann, your father was a most brilliant man."

"My father is dead," Zimmermann said coolly.

"Yes," Redding said. "Yes, he is. Tell me, this bleeding problem, it *has* been eliminated?"

"Father modified his synthesis over a year ago. It was taking from six to eighteen months after treatment for the bleeding problem to develop. The three patients you know about were all treated a year ago last July. There have, to our knowledge, been no new cases since. Keep in mind, too, that there weren't that many to begin with. And most of those were mild."

"Yes, I understand. It is remarkable to me that you were able to insert your testing program into Carl Horner's computer system without his ever knowing."

"As you said, Mr. Redding, my father was a brilliant man."

"Yes. Well, then, I suppose we two should explore the possibility of a new partnership."

"The terms you laid out for my father are quite acceptable to me. I have the manuscript and the notebooks. Since the work is already completed, I would be willing to turn them over to you, no further questions asked, for the amount you promised him."

"That is a lot of money, Doctor."

"The amazing thing is that until I overheard your conversation with my father, I had not fully appreciated the valuable potential of the hormone." Zimmermann could barely keep from laughing out loud at his good fortune.

"Are you a biochemist, Doctor?"

"No. Not really."

"In that case, I should like to reserve my final offer until my own biochemist has had the chance to review the material, to see the laboratory, and to take himself through the process of synthesizing the hormone."

"When?"

"Why not tomorrow? Dr. Paquette, whom you know, will meet you at your office at, say, seven o'clock tomorrow night. My man Nunes will accompany him and will have the authority and the money to consummate our agreement if Dr. Paquette is totally satisfied with what he sees."

"Sounds fine. I'll make certain the side door to the Omnicenter is left open."

"That won't be necessary, Dr. Zimmermann. Paquette has keys."

"All right, then, seven o'clock. . . . Was there something else?"

"As a matter of fact, Dr. Zimmermann, there is. It's this whole business with the Omnicenter and that pathologist."

"You mean Bennett?"

"She has proven a very resilient young woman. Do you believe she was convinced by her conversation with our man at the Ashburton Foundation?"

"No. Not completely. She said she was going to continue investigating. The woman currently hospitalized here with complications from Estronate treatment is a close friend of hers."

"I see. You know, Doctor, none of this would have happened if you and your father hadn't conducted your work so recklessly and independently." His voice had a chilling edge. "Don't you feel a responsibility to this company for what you have done?"

"Responsibility?"

"If we are to have a partnership, I should like to know that the

403

millions I have spent on the Omnicenter will not be lost because we were unable to neutralize one woman."

"But she has been neutralized. A serious mistake on a pathology specimen. She's been put on leave by her department head. Isn't that enough to discredit her?"

"I am no longer speaking of discrediting her, my friend. I am speaking of stopping her. You heard my conversation with your father. You know the importance of keeping Estronate a secret. It has been bad enough that Dr. Bennett is threatening, by her doggedness, to bring the Omnicenter tumbling down about our ears. If she uncovers Estronate, we stand to lose much, much more."

"I'll see to it that won't happen."

"Excellent. But remember, I don't handle disappointment well. Until tomorrow, then, Doctor."

"Yes, tomorrow."

William Zimmermann made a final inspection of the house, taking pains to wipe off anything he had touched. The precaution was, in all likelihood, unnecessary. The houseboy was due in at eight in the morning, and the death he would discover upstairs would certainly appear due to natural causes.

As he slipped out the back door of his father's house, a fortune in notebooks and computer printouts under his arm, Zimmermann was thinking about Kate Bennett.

The nightmare was a juggernaut, more pervasive, more oppressive it seemed with each passing hour. Its setting had changed from the clutter of her office to the deep-piled, fire-warmed opulence of Win Samuels's study, but for Kate Bennett, the change meant only more confusion, more humiliation, more doubt.

I know what it looks like, I know what it sounds like. But it isn't true. . . . I don't know who did it. . . . I don't know. . . . Dammit all, I just don't know.

Jared's return earlier in the evening had started on a positive note —an emotional hug and their first kiss in nearly a week. For a time, as they weaved their way through the crowds to the baggage area, he seemed unable to keep his hands or his lips off her. It seemed he was reveling in the freedom of at last truly acknowledging his love for her. *I accept you, regardless of what you are involved in, regardless of what the impact might be on me. I accept you because I believe in you. I accept you because I love you.*

But as she shared her nightmare with him, she could feel him pulling back, sense his enthusiasm erode. It showed first in his eyes, then in his voice, and finally in his touch. He was trying, Kate knew, perhaps even trying his best. But she also knew that confusion and doubt were taking their toll. Why would a company as large as Redding Pharmaceuticals do the things of which she was accusing them? The Ashburton Foundation had an impeccable reputation. What evidence was there that they were frauds? Why would anyone do something as horrible as switching biopsies? How did they do it? Weren't there any records of the tests she had run at the state lab? How did the letter about Bobby Geary fit in with all this?

I know what it looks like. I know what it sounds like. But it isn't true.

With each *why*, with each *I don't know*, Kate felt Jared drifting further and further into her nightmare. By the time the subject of his father and sister came up, she was feeling isolated, as stifled as before, perhaps more so. They were nearly halfway home to Essex.

"That is absolutely incredible," Jared had said, swinging sharply into the breakdown lane and jamming to a stop. "I . . . I don't believe it." It was the first time since his return that he had said those words. "After all these years, why wouldn't he tell me my sister was alive?"

"I don't know." The phrase reverberated in her mind. "Perhaps he was trying to spare you the ugliness."

"That makes no sense. You say he took you to this insititution to convince you to turn down the position at Metro and concentrate on having babies?"

"That's what he said."

Jared shook his head. "Let me be sure I have this straight. My father, who has never communicated all that well with my wife to begin with, sends me out of town so that he can take her to an institution in the middle of nowhere and introduce her to the sister he had led me to believe died thirty-odd years ago. Does that make sense to you?"

"Jared," she said, her voice beginning to quaver, "nothing has made sense to me for days. All I can do is tell the truth."

"Well, if that's the case," he said finally, "I think I'd like to find out first hand why my father has been holding out on me."

"Couldn't we at least wait until—"

"No! I can't think of a damn thing to do about Bobby Geary or the Omnicenter or the Ashburton Foundation or the runaway technician or the goddamn breast biopsies, but I sure as hell can do something about my father."

Without waiting for a reply, he had swung off and under the highway and had screeched back onto the southbound lane, headed for Boston.

Now, in the uncomfortably warm study, Kate sat by a hundred-and-thirty-year-old leaded glass window, watching the fairyland Christmas lights of Louisburg Square and listening to her husband and her father-in-law argue over whether she was a liar, a woman in desperate need of professional help, or some combination of the two. Jared, in all fairness, was doing his best to give her the benefit of the doubt, but it had, purely and simply, come down to her word against his father's. When taken with the other issues, the other confusions she had regaled him with since his landing at Logan, it was not hard to understand why he was having difficulty taking her side.

"Once again, Jared," Win Samuels said with authoritative calm, "we dined together—Jocelyn's special duck. After dinner we talked. Then we went for a long drive in the country. I hadn't been out of the house all day and was getting a severe case of cabin fever. We did stop at the Stonefield School; I'm on the board of trustees there. But I assure you, Son, our visit was quite spur of the moment. We were only a few miles from the school when I remembered a set of papers in the back seat that I was planning on mailing off tomorrow to Gus Leggatt, the school administrator. While we were there, we did look in on some of the children. Largely because of our visit, on the way home I was able to share my fears with Kate about what happens to the rate of birth defects in children of older mothers. Kate explained the advances in amniocentesis to me; facts, I might add, that I found quite reassuring. I mentioned your sister, certainly, but I never implied she was alive. I'm sorry, Jared. And I am sorry for you, too, Kate." He looked at her levelly. "You've been under a great deal of pressure. Perhaps . . . a rest, some time off."

Time off. Kate sighed. Winfield had no way of knowing Stan Willoughby had already seen to that. She rose slowly, and crossed to Jared. "Stonefield School is listed in information," she said wearily. "Broderick, Massachusetts. If the snow doesn't get any worse, I can drive us there in forty-five minutes to an hour. That should settle this once and for all."

"Do you want to come with us, Dad?" Jared asked.

"There is no reason to go *anyplace*," Win Samuels said simply. "Kate, Jared's sister had severe birth defects and died exactly when he thinks she did, thirty years ago. Perhaps you had a dream of some sort. Strands of fantasy woven into reality. It happens, especially when one has been under an inordinate amount of stress such as you—"

"It is not stress! It is not stress, it is not a dream, it is not the desperate lie of a desperate woman, it is not . . . insanity." She confronted him, her eyes locked on his. Samuels held his ground, his face an expressionless mask. "It is the truth. The truth! I don't know why you are doing this, I don't know what you hope to accomplish. But I do know one thing. I'm not going to break. You manipulate the people in your life like they were pieces on some some enormous game board. Jocelyn to king's knight four, Jared to queen three. Not your turn? Well you'll just throw in a few thousand dollars and make it your turn."

Samuels moved to speak, but Kate stopped him with raised hands. "I'm not through. I want to tell you something, Win. You've underestimated me. Badly. I've made it through a childhood of total loneliness, an education of total aimlessness, and a marriage to an alcoholic madman who insisted on picking out my pantyhose for me. I've survived and grown in a profession where I am patronized, and discriminated against. I've dealt with men who couldn't bring their eyes, let along their minds, above my breasts. I've dealt with them and I've succeeded.

"It's been hard. At times, it's been downright horrible. But for the last five years, I've had a secret weapon. He's right there, Win. Right over there." She nodded toward Jared. "When I forget that I'm okay, he reminds me. When I have to face the Norton Reeses and the Arlen Paquettes and, yes, the Winfield Samuelses of this world, he gives me strength. I love him and I have faith in him. Sooner or later, he's going to see the way you toy with the lives of those around you. Sooner or later, you'll go to move him, and he won't be there."

"Are you done?" Samuels said.

"Yes, I'm done. And I don't want to hear any more from you unless it's an apology and the truth about the other night. How could you think I wouldn't tell Jared? How could you think I wouldn't remember where we went, what we did? Please, Jared, let's get going. It's late, and we have quite a drive ahead of us."

At that moment, there was a noise, the clearing of a throat, from the doorway. The three of them turned to the sound. Jocelyn Trent stood holding a silver tray with coffee and tea.

"How long have you been there?" Samuels demanded. The woman did not answer. "Well?"

She hesitated; then she set the tray on the nearest table and ran from the room.

"Stonefield School," Kate said. "See, I told you I could find it. Only two wrong turns." She swung into the driveway, past the small sign, and up to the front door. "This is almost the exact hour we were here the other night. With any luck, the nurse who was on duty then will be on again. Her name was Bicknell, Sally Bicknell; something like that. I'll recognize her. She wore about eighty gold bracelets and had rings on three or four fingers of each hand. What a character!"

Her chatter was, she knew, somewhat nervous. Jared had said little during their drive. His pensiveness was certainly understandable, but she found herself wishing he could recapture at least some of the emotion he had shown at the airport. No matter, she consoled herself. Two minutes at Stonehill, and he would know that, in this arena, at least, she was telling the truth. How foolish of Win to think things would not develop the way they had. How unlike the man to miss predicting a person's actions as badly as he had missed hers.

The nurse, Bicknell, was working at her desk in a small office just off the lobby. Her hair was pulled back in a tight bun, and she was wearing only a single gold chain on one wrist. Hardly the flamboyant eccentric Kate had depicted. It was an observation, Kate noted uneasily, that was not overlooked by her husband.

"Are you sure it's the same woman?" he whispered, as they crossed the lobby.

"It's her. Hi, Miss Bicknell. Remember me?"

The woman took only a second. "Of course. You were with Mr. Samuels four—no, no,—three nights ago. Right?"

"Exactly. You have an excellent memory."

"An elephant," Sally Bicknell said, tapping one finger against her temple.

"This is my husband, Jared, Miss Bicknell. Mr. Samuels's son."

"Pleased to meet you." The woman took the hand Jared offered. "We don't get too many evening visitors here at Stonefield. In fact, we don't get too many visitors at other times, either." She looked around. "Sort of a forgotten land, I guess."

"Miss Bicknell, we came to see my husband's sister."

The woman's expression clouded. "I . . . I'm afraid I don't understand."

Kate felt an ugly apprehension set in. "Lindsey Samuels," she said, a note of irritation—or was it panic?—in her voice, "the girl we saw Monday night right over there." She pointed to the blue velvet curtain.

Sally Bicknell looked at her queerly and then ushered them over and drew back the curtain. "Her?" The girl was there, lumbering about exactly as she had been before.

"Yes, exactly," Kate said. "That's her, Jared. That's Lindsey."

"I'm sorry, Mrs. Samuels, but you're mistaken. That girl's name is Rochelle Coombs. She is sixteen years old and has a genetic disease called Hunter's Syndrome."

Kate stopped herself at the last possible moment from calling the woman a liar. "Could I see her medical records, please?"

The nurse snapped the curtain shut. "Her medical records are confidential. But I assure you, her name is Rochelle Coombs, not—what did you say?"

"Lindsey," Jared said, "Lindsey Samuels." It was, Kate realized, the first time he had spoken since just after their arrival.

"It is not Lindsey Samuels." Sally Bicknell completed her sentence.

In that moment, Kate realized what had bothered her so about the girl the first time she had observed her. She was too young to have been Jared's sister. Far too young. Her thick features and other physical distortions added some years, but not twenty of them. The girl's grotesqueness had made her too uncomfortable to look very closely. Had Win Samuels counted on that? Silently, she cursed her own stupidity. Helpless and beaten, she could only shrug and shake her head.

"Will there be anything else?" Bicknell asked.

Kate looked over at Jared, who shook his head. "No," she said huskily. "We're . . . we're sorry for the intrusion."

"In that case," the woman said, "I have rounds to make." She turned and, without showing them out, walked away.

Kate felt far more ill than angry. As they approached the car, she handed Jared the keys. "You drive, please. I'm not up to it. Your father told me it was Lindsey, Jared. I swear he did. And that woman was right there when he said it."

There was, she realized, no sense in discussing the matter further. Win Samuels had set up a no-lose situation for himself. Either she would be impressed by his demonstration, in which case she might have agreed to back off at the hospital and, as he wished, turn her attention to domestic issues; or she would be angered enough to do exactly what she had done. His son, already in doubt about her, would be drawn further away from their marriage and toward a political future, unencumbered by a wife whose priorities and mental state were so disordered. All that for only the price of a tankful of gas and whatever it cost to buy off Sally Bicknell. Nice going, Win, she thought. Nice goddamn going. She sank into her seat and stared sightlessly into the night.

CHAPTER 13
Friday 21 December

"SHE'S OUT, SUSPENDED, finished. I did it," Norton Reese boasted exultantly. "Yesterday afternoon. I tried to call you then, but there was no answer."

Still in his bed at the Ritz, Arlen Paquette squinted at his watch, trying to get the numbers in focus. Seven-thirty? Was that right? Was goddamn Reese waking him up at seven-thirty in the morning? He fumbled for the bedside lamp, wincing at the shellburst in his temples. Somewhere in the past four hours, he had passed from being drunk to being hung over. His mouth tasted like sewage, and his muscles felt as if he had lost a gang fight.

"Norton, just a second here while I wake up a little bit." He worked a cigarette from a wrinkled packet and lit it on the third try. Over the past week, his smoking had gone from his usual four or five cigarettes a day to three packs. For a moment, he eyed the half-empty quart of Dewar's on the bureau. "No, goddamn it," he muttered, "At least not yet." It took two hands to hold the phone steady against his ear. "Now, sir, just how did you go about accomplishing this remarkable feat of yours?"

Paquette listened to Reese's excited recap of the events leading to the unofficial suspension of Kate Bennett by her chief, Stan Willoughby. By the time the administrator had finished, Paquette had made his way across to the scotch and buried half a water glass full. The story was disgusting. A woman had lost her breast unnecessarily, and another had been professionally destroyed, and he, as much as the idiot on the other end of the phone, was responsible. As he listened to Reese's crowing, a resolve began to grow within him. He picked up a picture of Kate Bennett from the floor by his bed, wondering briefly how it had gotten there.

"Norton," he said cheerfully, "you've done one hell of a job there. Our friend's gonna be pleased when I tell him. Real pleased. Say, listen. Are you going to be at your office for a while . . . Good. I'd like to stop by and get some of the details in person. Probably be nine-thirty or so . . . Great. See you then."

He hung up and studied the picture in his hand. The scotch had stilled the shakes and begun to alleviate the pounding in his head. "I think you've taken enough shit from us, Dr. Bennett," he said. "It's time someone helped you fight back."

A glance at his watch, and he called Darlington. His wife answered on the second ring. "Honey, have the kids left for school yet? . . . Good. They're not going. I want you to pack them up and drive to your mother's house. . . . Honey, I know where your mother lives. If you step on it, you can be there by dinner time. There've been some problems here with old Cyrus, and I just want to be sure you and the kids are safe. . . . Maybe a few days, maybe a week. I don't know. Please, honey. Trust me on this one for a little while. I'll explain everything. And listen, I love you. I'm sorry about the other night and I love you. Not a word to anyone, now. Just get out and go to your mother's."

Paquette showered and then shaved, taking greater pains than usual not to nick himself. He dressed in a suit he had just bought, eschewing the vest in favor of a light brown cashmere sweater. Some Visine, another shot of scotch, some breath mints, and he was ready. On his way to the hospital, he would attend to one final item of business, stopping at an electronics store to purchase a miniature tape recorder.

"Okay, Doctor," he said to Kate's picture, "let's go get us some evidence." He glanced at the mirror. For the first time in nearly two weeks he liked what he saw.

Nothing to do. Nowhere to go. No one to hold. The thoughts, the futility, kept intruding on Kate's efforts to wring another hour, even another half hour, of sleep from the morning. They had spent the night—what was left of it after their return from Stonehill—in separate beds. Or perhaps Jared hadn't slept at all. She had offered him food, then company, and then sex, but his only request had been to be left alone. After an hour or so of staring at the darkened ceiling over their bed, she had tiptoed down the hall and peeked into the living room. He was right where she had left him, on the couch, chewing on his lower lip, and studying the creases in his palm. Her immediate impulse was to go to him, to beg him to believe her, to plead for his faith. The feeling disappeared as quickly as it had arisen. If their marriage had come down to begging, she was beaten. Aching with thoughts of what he was going through, at the choices he was trying to make, she had crept quietly back to bed, hoping that before long, she would feel him nudging his way under the covers.

Nothing to do. Nowhere to go. No one to hold. The ringing of the phone interrupted the litany. Kate glanced at the clock. Eight-thirty. Not too bad. The last time she had looked it was only six.

"Hello?"

"Kate?" It was Ellen.

"Hi. How're you feeling?"

"I got concerned when you didn't stop by this morning, and I called your office." Her voice was quite hoarse, her speech distorted. "When you didn't answer I rang the department secretary. Kate, what's the matter? Are you sick?"

"Hey, wait a minute, now. Let us not forget who is the patient here, and who is the doctor, okay?"

"Kate, be serious. She said she didn't know what day you'd be back. I . . . I got frightened. They're giving me more blood, and now I have a tube down my nose. I think the inside of my stomach has started bleeding."

"Shit," Kate said softly.

"What?"

"I said 'shit.' "

"Oh. Well, *are* you all right?"

Kate pulled a lie back at the last possible instant. "Actually, no," she said. "Physically I'm fine, but there's been trouble at work and here at home. I've been asked to take some time off while my department head sorts through some problems with a biopsy."

"Oh, Kate. And here I am all wrapped up in my own problems. I'm sorry. I know it sounds foolish coming from where I'm lying, but is there anything I can do?"

"No, El, just be strong and get well, that's all."

"Don't talk to *me*, Katey. Talk to these little platelets or whatever they're called. They're the ones who are screwing up. You said trouble at home, too. Jared?"

Stop asking about me, dammit. You're bleeding to death! "I'm afraid Jared's wife and his father in all their infinite wisdom have put him in a position where he's going to have to choose between them." At that moment, she began wondering where he was. Upstairs in the guest-room, perhaps? Maybe still on the couch. She listened for a telltale sound, but there was only heavy silence.

"You versus Win?" Ellen said. "No contest. Thank goodness. I thought it was something serious." Her cheer was undermined by the weakness in her voice.

"Listen, my friend," Kate said. "I'll see you later today. I may be shut out of the pathology department, but I'm not shut out of the library. There are two Australian journals I'm expecting in from the NIH. Together, we're going to beat this. I promise you."

"I believe you," Ellen said. "I really do. See you later, Doc."

Kate set the receiver down gently, then slipped into a blue flannel nightshirt, a gift from Jared, and walked to the living room. Roscoe, who had materialized from under the bed, padded along beside her. She glanced through the doorway and then systematically checked the rest of the house. She had, as she feared, read the silence well. Jared had left.

"Well, old shoe," she said, scratching her dog behind one ear, "it looks like you and me. How about a run together and then some shirred eggs for breakfast. Later, maybe we'll make love."

The letter, in Jared's careful printing, was on the kitchen table. He had taken their wedding picture from the mantel, and used it as a weight to keep the single sheet in place. Kate moved the photograph enough to read his words, but left it touching the page.

It sounds so easy, so obvious, that I'm not sure I even listened when the minister said the words. "For better or for worse." It all sounds so easy until one day you stop and ask yourself, For whose better? For whose worse? What do I do when her better seems like my worse? Dammit, Kate, I'm forty years old and I feel like such a child. Do you know that in all the time she was alive, I never once heard my mother say no to my father? Some role model, huh? Next came Lisa—bright, beautiful, and imbued with absolutely no ambition or direction. I thought she would make a perfect wife. She cooked the soup and pinched back the coleus, and I kept her pipe filled with good dope and decided when we could afford to do what, and that was that. I still don't know why she ran off the way she did, and if another Lisa had come along, I probably would have married her in a snap. But another Lisa didn't. You did.

Almost before I knew it, I had fallen in love with and married a woman who had as rich and interesting and complicated a life outside of our marriage as I did. Probably, more so. After first mother and then Lisa, it was like moving to a foreign country for me. New customs. New mores. What do you mean I was wrong to assume we'd have the same last name? What do you mean I was wrong to assume that you would be free to attend three rallies and a campaign dinner with me? What do you mean I should have asked first? What do you mean you've been involved in trouble at your job that might affect my career? I could go on all night listing my misguided assumptions in this marriage. It's as though I don't have the programming to adapt.

Well, I may not have the programming, but I do have the desire. It's taken most of the night sitting here to feel sure of that. If what you've said is all true, I want to do whatever I can to help straighten it out. If what you've told me is not true, then I also want to face that issue and my commitment to you, and we'll get whatever kind of help is necessary. If we don't make it, it won't be because I ran away.

I've gone to speak to my father and then, who knows, perhaps a chat with Norton Reese. Bear with me, Kate. It may say five years on the calendar, but this marriage business is still new stuff for me. I love you. I really do.

Jared

Kate reread the letter, laughing and crying at once. Jared's words, she knew, meant no more than a temporary reprieve, a respite from the nightmare. Still, he had given her the one thing she needed most next to answers: time. Time to work through the events that were steamrolling her life.

"We're going to find out, Rosc," she said grimly. "We're going to find out who, and we're going to find out why."

A sharp bark sounded from the living room, and Kate realized that she had been talking to herself. Through the doorway, she could see Roscoe prancing uncomfortably by the door to the rear deck.

"Oh, poor baby," she laughed. "I'm sorry." Focused on letting the dog out, she missed the slight movement outside the kitchen window and failed to sense the eyes watching her. She pulled open the slider, and Roscoe dashed out into a most incredible morning. The temperature, according to the thermometer by the door, was exactly freezing. Fat, lazy flakes, falling from a glaring, silver-white sky vanished into a ground fog that was as dense as any Kate could remember. Roscoe dashed across the deck, and completely disappeared into the shroud halfway down the steps to the yard.

Kate estimated the height of the fog at three or four feet. Much of it, she guessed, was arising off the surface of nearby Green Pond, a small lake that because of warm underground feeders, was always late to freeze and early to thaw. Winter fog was not uncommon on the North Shore, especially around Essex, but this was spectacular. It was a morning just begging to be run through.

She dressed and then stretched, sorting out the route they would run, mixing low spots and high hills and straight-aways along five miles of back roads. Wearing a gold watch cap and a high-visibility red sweatsuit, she trotted out the front door and whistled for Rosco. He was almost at her side before she could see him.

"A fiver this morning, dog," she said, as they moved up the sloping driveway and out of the fog. "Think you're mutt enough to handle it?"

At the end of the drive, she turned right. Had she mapped their route to the left, she might have wondered about the BMW, parked not particularly near anyone's house, and perhaps even noticed the blue Metropolitan Hospital parking sticker on the rear window.

It was near perfect air for running, cold and still. To either side of the narrow roadway, the fog covered the forest floor like cotton batting.

"Race pace, today, Rosc," she said. "Eight-minute miles or less. And I'm not waiting for you, so keep up." In reality, she knew Roscoe could maintain her pace all day, and still stop from time to time to sniff out a shrub or two. After a quarter of a mile, they left the pavement and turned onto a plowed dirt road meandering along an active stream named on the maps as Martha's Brook. Kate loved crossing the picturesque, low-walled fieldstone bridges that spanned the water; in part, she had chosen this route because of them.

By the end of the first mile, her thoughts had begun to separate themselves from the run. For the next two or three miles, she knew, her ideas would flow more freely, her imagination more clearly, than in any other situation. Following a kaleidoscope of notions, a kind of sorting-out process, her mind settled on the breast biopsy. Perhaps under the stress of exhaustion, Ellen's deteriorating condition, and the rest of the chaos in her life, she actually *had* made a mistake. For a time, the grisly thought held sway, bringing with it a most unpleasant tightness in her gut. Gradually, though, the truth reappeared, emerging like a phoenix from the ashes of her self-doubt. The cells she had read had been, she was certain, cancerous. But if they had been, then somewhere a switch had been made and later reversed. But how? who? The broken cryostat was, she decided, part of the puzzle. Sheila? Possible. But why? The images led into those of other tissues, other cells—the ovaries of Beverly Vitale and Ginger Rittenhouse. Ever since the discovery of anthranilic acid in her own vitamins, Kate had, several times a day, been checking herself for bruises and wondering if pockets of scar tissue in her ovaries had already made a mockery of their discussions about having children. She had to find out. The answer, almost certainly, lay in the Omnicenter, and more specifically, in the data banks of Carl Horner's Monkeys.

Kate was heading down a steep grade toward the first of the fieldstone overpasses when the blue BMW crested the hill behind her and accelerated. Immersed in the run and her thoughts, she lost several precious seconds after hearing the engine before she turned to it. The speeding automobile made a sharp, unmistakably deliberate swing to the right and headed straight for her. There was no time to think.

There was only time to react. The waist-high wall of the bridge was only a few feet away. A single step, and she dove for the top of it. She was in midair when the BMW hit her just below her right knee. The impact spun her in a horizontal pinwheel. She struck the edge of the wall midthigh and then tumbled over it. As she fell, she heard the crunch of metal against stone and the agonizing cry of her dog.

The fall, twelve feet from the top of the wall, was over before she could make any physical adjustment whatsoever. She landed on her back in a drift of half-frozen snow; air exploded from her lungs, and a branch from a rotting log tore through her sweatshirt and her right side, just below her ribs. Desperately, she tried to draw in a breath. For five seconds, ten, nothing would move. Finally, she felt a whisper of air, first in the back of her throat and then in her chest. She tried to deepen her effort, but a searing pain from her side cut her short. She touched the pain and then checked the fingertips of her tan woolen gloves. They were soaked with blood.

Frantically, she tried to sort out what had happened. She had been hit. Roscoe had been hit, too. Possibly killed. It had not been an accident. Whoever was driving had tried to run them down. Gingerly, she tested her hands and then her legs. Her right leg throbbed, and her right foot, which was dangling in the icy water of the brook, seemed twisted at an odd angle. *Please, God, don't let it be broken.* There was pain, but, gratefully, there was full movement as well.

At that moment, overhead, a car door opened and closed. She turned toward the noise, but could see nothing. It took several seconds to realize why. She was quite literally buried in the fog. From somewhere above and to her left, a branch snapped; then another. The driver of the car was making his way down the steep embankment, more than likely to check the completeness of his work. Could he see where she was? Possibly not. The fog might well be concealing her, at least from farther away than ten feet or so. Carefully, she slipped off her gold cap and stuffed it into the snow. The burning rent in her side was making it hard to concentrate. Should she try crawling away beneath the fog? Would her battered legs even hold weight? Her back was hurting. Should she test it, roll to one side? Could she?

From farther to her left, she heard still another snap and then a soft splash and a groan. Her pursuer had stepped or slipped into the brook. It was definitely a man, or perhaps there were two. She thought about Roscoe. Was he still alive? Was he helpless? in pain? The images sickened her.

For a time, there was silence. Kate peered into the mist, but could see nothing. The pain in her legs, back, and side sent chilly tears down her cheeks. Then she heard it, a soft crunch, still downstream from where she was lying, but almost certainly moving in her direction. She swept her hand over the snow, searching for a rock or a stick of some sort. Her fingers touched and then curled about a dead branch, perhaps an inch and a half in diameter. She drew it toward her. Was it too long, too unwieldy, to use? She would get one swing, if that, and no more. Again, she jiggled the branch. It seemed unentangled, but she would not know for sure until she made her move.

Suddenly, she saw movement to her left, the legs and gloved hand of a man, not ten feet away. Dangling from his hand, swinging loosely back and forth, was a tire wrench. Kate drew in a breath, held it, and tensed. At any moment she would be seen. The legs were just turning toward her when she lunged, rising painfully to her knees and swinging the branch in the same motion. Her weapon, three feet long with several protruding wooden spikes, came free of the snow and connected with the side of the man's knee. He dropped instantly to the water, as much from the surprise and location of the blow as from its force.

Ignoring the pain in her legs and side, Kate stood up, readying the branch for another swing. It was then she saw her attacker's face.

"Bill!" she cried, staring at the wild-eyed apparition. Her hesitation was costly. Zimmermann lashed out with his feet, sweeping her legs out from under her and sending her down heavily against the rocks and into the shallow, icy water. The wrench lay in the snow, just to his right. Zimmermann grabbed at it and still on his knees in the brook, swung wildly. Sparks showered from a small boulder, inches from Kate's hip. She rolled to her left as he swung again, the blow glancing off her thigh. Another spin and she was free of the water, scrambling for footing on the icy rocks and snow. Zimmermann, still clutching the wrench, crawled from the brook and dove at her ankles. He grabbed the leg of her sweatpants, but she was on her feet with enough leverage to jerk away. Before he could make another lunge, she was off, stumbling along the bank and then under the fieldstone bridge.

The ground fog, once her shield, was now her enemy. Again and again, she slipped on rocks she could not see and tripped over fallen logs. From the grunts and cries behind her, though, she could tell that Zimmermann was encountering similar difficulties. Still, the man was coming. She had been so stupid not to have considered that he might be involved in the evil at the Omnicenter, so foolish to think that he didn't know what was going on.

She glanced over her shoulder. Zimmermann, visible from the chest up, was bobbing along not thirty yards behind her. He was over six feet tall, and the deep snow was, she feared, more difficult for her to negotiate than it was for him. In addition, she was hobbled by the tightness and pain in her leg where the fender of Zimmermann's car had struck. She had only two advantages: her conditioning and her knowledge of the area. If the man caught up with her, she knew neither would matter. She risked another check behind her. He was closer, unquestionably closer. The snow was slowing her down too much. She cut to her left and into the brook. There, at least, Zimmermann's longer legs would be no advantage, possibly even a hindrance. The frigid, ankle-high water sloshed in her running shoes and bathed her lower legs in pain. Could she outrun or at least outlast him? It was possible, but one slip, one misplaced branch, and it would be over for her. She had to get back to the road. Either back to the road or . . . or hide.

She slowed, casting about for familiar landmarks. Somewhere nearby was a culvert, a steel tube, perhaps three feet across, running fifty or so feet through the high embankment on which the road had been built. If she could find it, and if it were not blocked, she could crawl inside, hoping that Zimmermann would not see her or, even if he did, would be too broad across the shoulders to follow.

She glanced downstream just as the man fell. In seconds, however, he was on his feet and, arms flailing for balance, was again beginning to close on her. If she was to do something, anything, it had to be soon. At that moment, she saw what she had been seeking. It was a huge old elm, sheared in two by lightning, its upper half forming a natural bridge across Martha's Brook. Fifty yards beyond it, if her memory hadn't failed her, the stream would bend sharply to the left, and just beyond the bend, at about knee level, would be the culvert that Roscoe had discovered two or three years before.

She ducked beneath the elm and ran low to the water, her eyes barely above the fog. At the bend, she dropped to all fours, and began crawling along the icy embankment. *Please, be there. Be there.* Frozen chunks of snow scraped her face, and rocks tore away the knees of her sweatpants. She felt a fullness in her throat and coughed, spattering the snow beneath her with blood, more than likely, she knew, from a punctured lung.

She crawled ahead, sliding one hand along the slope at the height where she remembered the culvert. Her hopes had begun to fade when she saw it. The diameter was even less than she had thought, nearer two feet than three, but it was still wide enough for her to fit. A fine trickle of water suggested that the small pond on the other side of the embankment was lower than her exit point. From somewhere in the fog, not far back, came a splash. Zimmermann was close. Kate ducked into the dank, rusty pipe; inches at a time, she began to pull herself toward the faint, silver-gray light at the other end.

The culvert, coarse and corroded, was painfully cold. With the exertion of her run now past, Kate was beginning to freeze. Her feet, especially her toes, throbbed, and the sound of her teeth chattering like castanets was resonating through the metal tube. Again she coughed. Again there was the spattering of blood. She was, perhaps, a third of the way along when she heard him, crunching about in the snow behind her. Fearing the noise her movement was making, she stopped, biting down on the collar of her sweatshirt to stop the chattering.

"Kate, I know you're hurt," he called out. "I want to help you. No more violence. We can work things out."

Did he know where she was? Dammit, why couldn't she stop shaking?

"Kate, you want to know about the drugs, about whether or not you are sterile, about how you can stop your friend's bleeding. I can answer all your questions. I can get you someplace warm."

Frightened of the bleeding in her chest and numb in those areas of her body that weren't in merciless pain, Kate found herself actually considering the man's offer. Warm. He had promised she would be warm. Warmth and answers. Maybe she *should* try and reason with him. She forced her mind to focus on the wrench and bit down on her sweatshirt all the harder.

"You know," Zimmermann called out, "even if you make it back, no one is going to believe your story. I have my whereabouts at this moment completely vouched for. You're crazy and a pathological liar. Everyone knows that. You're the talk of the hospital. Half the people think you're on drugs, and the other half think you're just plain sick. I'm the only person who can help you, Kate. I'm the only one who can save your friend. I'm the only one who can get you warm. Now come on over here, and let's talk."

Twenty feet away from where Zimmermann stood, Kate buried her face in the crook of her arm and struggled against the insanity that was telling her the man meant what he was saying about no violence.

"Suit yourself," she heard him say. "It's your funeral. Yours and your friend's."

Steaming coffee. Crackling, golden fire. Sunshine. White beach. Flannel. Down comforter. Fur slippers. Stifling her sobs in the sleeve of her sweatshirt, Kate fought the fear and the pain and the cold with images of anything that was warm. Cocoa. Wood stove. Jacuzzi. Tea. Quartz heater. Electric blanket. Soup. Behind her now, there was only silence. Had he left? She strained to hear the engine of his car. Had he found the culvert and crossed over the road to wait by the far end? Her legs and arms were leadened by the cold. Could she even make it out? *Damn him,* she thought, forcing herself ahead an inch. He knew how to save Ellen. *Damn him.* Another inch. He even knew whether she herself had been sterilized or not. *Damn him. Damn him. Damn him.* The silver-gray hole grew fainter. Her eyes closed. Her other senses clouded. Seconds later, what little consciousness remained slipped away.

It was as if a decade had melted away. Jared faced his father as he had so many times during the confused years of Lisa and Vermont, struggling to remain reasonably calm and maintain eye contact.

"Kate is sick, son. Very sick," Samuels said. "I would suggest we make arrangements for her hospitalization as soon as possible, and as soon as that is done, you should begin to separate your career from her.

She will bring you down. I promise you that. Martha Mitchell did it to her husband, and I assure you, Kate will do it to you—if she hasn't already. I've contacted Sol Creighton at Laurel Hill. He has a bed waiting for her, and he says we have grounds for commitment if necessary. With some time, and perhaps some medication, he assures me that even the worst sociopathic personality can be helped."

"Dad, stop using that word. You have no right to diagnose her."

"Jared, face the facts. Kate is a lovely woman. I care for her very much. But she is a liar, and quite possibly a liar who completely believes her own fabrications. I know she looks perfectly fine and sounds logical, but the hallmark of a sociopath is exactly that physical and verbal glibness. The only way to realize what one is dealing with is to catch her in lie after lie."

"But—"

"Do you really think someone other than Kate sent that letter to the papers about Bobby Geary?"

"I don't know."

"And the chemist, and the Ashburton Foundation, and the nurse at Stonefield. Do you think they were all lying?"

"I don't—"

"And what about the biopsy? You tell me everyone in Kate's department says she made a mistake. The truth is right there in the slides. Yet there is Kate, insisting she did nothing wrong."

Samuels withdrew a cigar from his humidor, tested the aroma along its full length, and then clipped and lit it. He motioned for Jared to have one if he wished.

Jared glanced at his watch, made an expression of distaste, and shook his head. "Christ, Dad, it's only eight-thirty in the morning."

Samuels shrugged. "It's my morning and it's my cigar."

Jared looked across the desk at his father, trim and confident, wearing the trappings of success and power as comfortably as he wore his slippers. Unable to speak, Jared stared down at the gilded feet of his father's desk, resting on the exquisite oriental carpet. A secret weapon, that's what Kate had called him. A source of strength for her. She had spoken the words to his father, but they were really meant for him. With tremendous effort, he brought his eyes up.

"I hear what you are saying, Dad. And I understand what you want."

"And?"

"I can't go along with it. Kate says she's innocent of any lying, and I believe her."

"You what?"

Jared felt himself wither before the man's glare. "I believe her. And I'm going to do what I can to help clear her." There was a strength in his words that surprised him. He stood up. "I'll tell you something else,

Dad. If I find that she's telling the truth, you're going to have a hell of a lot of explaining to do."

Samuels rose, anger sparking from his eyes. "I seem to recall a conversation similar to this. We were in that matchbox office of yours in Vermont. I warned you not to marry that rootless hippie you were living with. I told you there was nothing to her. You stood before me then just as you are now and as much as threw me out of your office. Two years later your wife and daughter were gone, and you were crawling to me for help. Have you forgotten?"

"Dad, that was then. This is—"

"Have you forgotten?"

"No, I haven't."

"Have you forgotten the money and the time I spent trying to find that woman despite my own personal feelings about her?"

"Look, I don't want to fight."

"Get out," Samuels said evenly. "When you come to your senses, when you discover once again that I was right, call me."

"Dad, I—"

"I said get out." Samuels turned his back and stared out the window.

As Jared opened the door, he nearly collided with Jocelyn Trent, who was standing up and backing away at the same time. Quickly, he closed the door behind him.

"What were you doing there?" he asked.

"Jared, please, don't make me explain." She took him by the arm, led him to the hall closet, and began helping him on with his coat. "Meet me in ten minutes," she whispered in his ear. "The little variety store on the corner of Charles and Mount Vernon. I have something important for you, for Kate actually."

The study door opened just as she was letting Jared out. Winfield Samuels stood, arms folded tightly across his chest, and watched him go.

Even dressed down, in pants and a plain wool overcoat, Jocelyn Trent turned heads. Jared stood by the variety store and watched several drivers slow as they passed where she was waiting to cross Charles Street. He left the shelter of the recessed doorway and met her at the corner. Their relationship, while cordial, had never approached a friendship in any sense. His father had taken some pains to keep the interaction between them superficial, and neither had ever been inclined to push matters further.

"Thank you for meeting me like this," she said, guiding him back to the shadow of the doorway. "I don't have much time, so I'll say what I have to say and go."

"Fair enough."

"Jared, I'm leaving your father. I intend to tell him this afternoon."

"I'm sorry," he said. "I know how much he cares for you."

"Does he? I think you know as well as I do that caring isn't one of Win Samuel's strong suits. It's too bad, too, because strange as it might sound, I think I might actually love him."

"Then why—"

"Please, Jared. I really don't have much time, and what I'm doing is very hard for me. Just know that I have my reasons—for leaving him and for giving you this." She handed him a sealed envelope. "Kate's a wonderful woman. She doesn't deserve the treatment he's giving her. I've been completely loyal to your father. That is until now. I know how hard it is to stand up to him. Lord knows I've wanted to enough. I think you did the right thing back there."

"Jocelyn, do you know if my father is lying or not? It's very important."

She smiled. "I'm aware of how important it is. I was listening at the door, remember? The answer is that I don't know, at least not for sure. There's a phone number in that envelope, Jared. Go someplace quiet and dial it. If my suspicions about that number are correct, you should be able to decide for yourself which of the two, Kate or your father, is telling the truth."

"I don't understand," he said. "What is this number? Where did you get it?"

"Please, I don't want to say any more because there's a small chance I might be wrong. Let's just leave it that the number is one your father has called from time to time since I've known him. I handle all of the household bills, including the phone bill, so I know. A year or two ago I accidentally overheard part of a conversation he was having. Some of what I heard disturbed me, so I noted down the exact time of the call. That's how I learned this number. I don't want to say any more. Okay?"

"Okay, but—"

"I wish you well, Jared. Both of you. The things I overheard Kate say last night have really helped me make some decisions I should have made a long time ago. I hope that what I've done will help her." She took his hand, squeezed it for a moment, and was gone.

Jared watched her hurry up Mt. Vernon Street; then he tore open the plain envelope. The phone number, printed on a three-by-five card, was in the 213 area. Los Angeles.

He drove to his office, trying to imagine what the number might be. Once at his desk, he sat for nearly a minute staring at the card before he finally dialed.

A woman, clearly awakened by the call, answered on the third ring. "Hello?" she said.

Jared struggled for a breath and pressed the receiver so tightly against his ear that it hurt.

"Hello?" the woman said again. "Is anybody there?"

Even after so many years he knew. "Lisa?" He could barely say the word.

"Yes. Who is this? Who is this, please?"

Slowly, Jared set the receiver back in its cradle.

CHAPTER 14

Friday 21 December

IT WAS PRESSURE PAIN from the pipe more than cold that tugged Kate free of a sleep that was deeper than sleep. In the twilight moment before she was fully conscious, she imagined herself buried alive, the victim of some twisted, vicious kidnapper. In just a few hours she would suffocate or freeze to death. Jared had that little time to raise her ransom, and the only one he could turn to, she knew, was his father. The sound of Win Samuels's laughter echoed in her tomb, growing louder and louder until with a scream she came fully awake.

She was on her back. Her lips and cheeks were caked with dried and frozen blood. Dim light from the ends of the culvert barely defined the corroding metal, just a foot or so from her face. *Lie still,* she thought. *Just don't move. Sleep until Jared comes. Close your eyes again and sleep.* The thoughts were so comforting, so reassuring, that she had to struggle to remember that they were no more than the cold, lying to her, paralyzing her from within. For a time, all she could think about was sleep, sleep and Zimmermann's taunting warning that even if she survived, no one would believe her story. Sick, crazy, drugged up, that's what they all believed. It was hopeless for her. Zimmermann said it, and he was right. Over and over again, in a voice as soothing as a warm tub, the cold spoke to her of hopelessness and sleep.

Kate flexed her hands and her feet, struggling against the downy comfort of the lies and the inertia. *Remain still and you will die. Surrender to the cold and you will never see Jared again; never get the chance to tell him how much his letter and his decision mean to you.*

She tried pushing herself along with her feet, but could not bend her knees enough to get leverage. She had to see him. She had to tell him that she, too, was ready to make choices. Aroused by the aching in her legs and the far deeper pain in her side, she twisted and wriggled onto her belly. She had been wrong to allow Willoughby to nominate her without trying harder to see things from Jared's perspective. She had been wrong. Now she could only admit that and hope Jared believed it had been he, and not the devastating events, who had helped her see the true order of her priorities.

She was less than halfway from the far end of the pipe. The fog seemed to have lifted. She could now make out the silhouettes of trees against the white sky. A few more feet and there was enough light to read the numbers on her watch. Eleven fifteen. She had been entombed for over an hour. *Was Zimmermann still out there? Could he possibly have stayed around in the snow and the cold for over an hour?*

Driven by the need to see Jared again, to set matters straight, she worked herself arm over arm along the icy metal. A foot from the edge she stopped and listened. Beyond the soft wisp of her own breathing, there was nothing. Had an hour been long enough? Wouldn't Zimmermann have left, concerned about having his car attract attention? Finally, she abandoned her attempts at reasoning through the situation. If he was out there, waiting, there was little she would be able to do. If he wasn't, she would overcome whatever pain and cold she had to and make it home. There were amends to be made.

With a muted cry of pain, she curled her fingers around the edge of the culvert and pulled.

"We're sorry, but we are unavailable to take your call right now. Please wait for the tone, leave your name, number, and the time, and Kate or Jared will get back to you as soon as possible."

"Kate, it's just me again. Ignore the previous two messages. I'm not going to stay at the office, and I'm not going to speak with Reese. I'm coming home. Please don't go anywhere. Thanks. I love you."

Something was wrong. In almost five years of marriage, Jared had never felt so intense a connection to his wife. With that heightened sensitivity and three unanswered calls home had come a foreboding that weighed on his chest like an anvil. The feeling was irrational he told himself over and over again, groundless and foolish. She was at a neighbor's or on a run. With his MG still in the office garage, where it had been all week, he had taken her Volvo; but still, there were plenty of places to which she could have walked.

He left the city and crossed the Mystic River Bridge, the rational part of him struggling to keep the Volvo under seventy. She was fine. There was some perfectly logical explanation why she hadn't answered his calls the past hour and a half. He just hadn't hit on it. Certainly, his concentration and powers of reason were not all they could be. It had been one hell of a morning.

The call to California, the sound of Lisa's voice, had left him at once elated and sickened. His father had lied. He had lied about Lisa and possibly about Stonefield as well. Jared cringed at the thought of how close he had come to siding with the man. Silently, he gave thanks that he had made his decision, set down on paper his commitment to Kate, before he had learned the truth about his father. The man had been paying Lisa off all those years. That conclusion was as inescapable as it was disgusting. They were some pair, his ex-wife and Winfield. One totally vapid, one totally evil. Some goddamn pair.

Then there was Stacy. As he weaved along past Route 1's abysmal stretch of fast-food huts, factory outlets, budget motels, garish restaurants, and raunchy nightclubs, Jared ached with thoughts of her. What did she believe had become of her father? Would there ever be a way he could reenter her life without destroying whatever respect she had for her mother, possibly thereby destroying the girl herself? Kate would have a sense of what was right to do. Together they could decide. Damn, but he had come close, so close, to blowing it all.

The house was deserted. Kate's running gear was gone, and so was Roscoe. It had been several hours since his first call—far too long. He checked the area around the house and yard. Nothing. There were but two choices: wait some more or call the police. The heavy sense of apprehension, so ill-defined while he was in Boston, seemed more acute. There was no sense in waiting.

As he walked to the phone in the kitchen, he glanced out the front window. Three neighborhood children, all around eight, were trudging up the driveway pulling a sled. On the sled was a cardboard carton. The path to the front door, only as wide as a shovel, was too narrow for the sled. Two youngsters stayed behind, kneeling by the box, while the third ran up the walk. Jared met her at the door.

"Mr. Samuels, it's Roscoe," she panted. "We found him in the snow."

Jared, a dreadful emptiness in his gut, raced past the girl to the sled. Roscoe, packed in blankets, looked up and made a weak attempt to rise. His tail wagged free of the cover and slapped excitedly against the cardboard.

"His leg is broke," one of the other children, a boy, said simply.

Jared held the dog down and pulled back the blanket. Roscoe's right leg was fractured, the bone protruding from a gash just above the knee. "Come kids," he said, scooping up the box. "Come inside, please, and we'll take care of Rosc. Do you think you can take me to where you found him?"

"Yes, I know," the little girl said. "We have teacher's conference today, so no school. We were sledding down the hill to the bridge, and there he was, just lying in the snow. My mom gave us the blankets and the box."

"It looks like he's been hit by a car," Jared said. "Kids, this is important. Did any of you see Kate—you know, my wife?" The children shook their heads. He reached down and stroked the dog's forehead. Blood trickled from the corner of his mouth where his teeth had torn through. "Well, let's get some help for Roscoe; then we'll go back to the spot where you found him." He felt consumed by feelings of panic and dread, and struggled to keep a note of calm in his voice. Frightened, confused children would be no asset to him—or to Kate.

Minutes later three of them, Jared and two of the youngsters, were in the car. The third had been left behind to keep the dog still and await the arrival of the veterinarian.

"Okay, kids," Jared said, "you said you were sledding near a bridge. The stone bridge over the little stream?" Both nodded enthusiastically. "Good. I know just where that is."

The short drive over the narrow, snowy road seemed endless. Finally, Jared parked the Volvo at the top of the hill and then half ran, half slid to the indentation in the snow where the children assured him they had found Roscoe. He had thought to take his parka but had not changed his slacks or loafers, and the trek from the spot into the surrounding woods was both awkward and cold. The snow around him was, save for his own footprints, smooth and unbroken. After a scanning search, he made his way back to the road and started down the hill. At his request, the children followed, one on each side of the road, checking to be sure he had not missed anything.

At the stone bridge, he stopped. There was evidence of some sort of collision at the base of the wall. A piece of granite had been sheared off, and a gouge, perhaps two feet long, extended along the wall from that point. He searched the roadway and then looked over the wall. The snow on one side of the shallow brook seemed disrupted. In the very center of the area, he saw a flash of bright yellow, partially buried in the snow.

Ordering the children to remain where they were, he raced down the steep embankment to the water. It was Kate's cap, quite deliberately, it seemed, wedged into the snow. Then, only a few feet from the cap, he saw a swatch of another color. It was blood, almost certainly, dried blood smeared across a small stretch of packed snow. There had been some kind of struggle. The marks around him made that clear. Had Kate been dragged off somewhere? He looked for signs of that, but instead noticed footprints paralleling the stream just beyond the bridge. Slipping in and out of the water, he ran to the spot. There were, he was certain, two sets. He looked overhead. The children, following his progress, had crossed the road and were peering down at him from atop the wall. The girl, he knew, lived just past the end of the road, half a mile, perhaps a bit more, away.

"Crystal," he called out, "is your mommy still home?"

"Yes."

"Can you two make it back home to her?"

"Yes."

"Please do that, then. Tell her Kate is lost and may be hurt. Ask if she can drive out here and help look for her. Okay?"

"Okay."

"And Crystal, you all did a fine job bringing Roscoe in the way you did. Hurry on home, now."

Jared stayed where he was until the crunch of the children's boots had completely vanished. Then he closed his eyes and listened within the silence for a sound, any kind of sign. He heard nothing. Increasingly aware of the cold in his feet and legs, he stepped in the deep tracks, fearing the worst, and expecting, with each stride, to have his fears become reality. A hundred yards from the bridge, the tracks turned sharply to the left and vanished into the stream.

"Kate?" He called her name once and then again. His voice was instantly swallowed by the forest and the snow. "Kate, it's me. It's Jared." There was a heaviness, a fastness, to the place and a silence that was hypnotic. As he trudged along the side of the stream looking for renewed signs, he felt the silence deepen.

Then suddenly, he knew. He felt it as surely as he felt the cold. Kate was somewhere nearby. She was nearby, and she was still. He called to her every few feet, as he ducked under a huge fallen tree and followed the stream bed in a sharp bend to the left. Then he stopped. There was something different about this place. Far to his right, embedded in the steep slope that he guessed led up to the road, was a drainage pipe. At the base of the pipe were footprints.

"Kate?" He closed his eyes and almost immediately felt a strange sense of detachment. She was not far, and she was alive. He felt it clearly. It was as if their lives, their energies, were joined by a thin, silken strand of awareness.

"Jared?" It was a word, but not a word; a sound, but not a sound. His eyes still closed, he exhaled slowly and then listened. "Jared, help me." Her voice, it seemed, was more within him than without. He worked his way along the embankment, calling her name. Then he shouted it several times into the long, empty culvert. Finally, hoping for a better vantage point, he hauled himself up to the road.

She was there, face down, a third of the way down the slope on the far side, still clawing, though feebly, at the snow. Jared leapt over the edge, sliding and tumbling down to her. Gently, he turned her onto his lap. Her hair was matted and frozen, her face spattered with blood. Her warm-up suit, shredded in spots, was stiffened with ice. Her eyes were closed.

"Katey, it's me," he said. "I've got you. You're going to be all right."

He worked her hair free from where it had frozen to her face. Her breathing was shallow, each expiration accompanied by a soft whimper of pain.

"Honey, can you hear me?"

Her eyes opened and then slowly focused on his face. "Oh, Jared . . . please . . . Roscoe . . ."

He kissed her. "He's hurt, but he's okay. Dr. Finnerty's coming to get him. What about you? Have you broken anything?"

"Ribs," she managed in a voice that was half groan, half cough. "Lung . . . may . . . be . . . punctured."

"Jesus. Kate, I'm going to lift you up. I'll try not to hurt you, but we've got to get up to the road."

With strength enhanced by the urgency of the moment, he had no trouble lifting her. Negotiating the steep, icy slope, however, was another matter. Footing was treacherous, and every two or three baby steps upward, he was forced to set her down in order to regain purchase. Inches at a time, they moved ahead. When he finally heaved over the top of the slope onto the roadside, Jared fell to his knees, clutching her to his chest and gasping for air.

Helplessly, he sat there, warming her face with his breath and watching the minute but steady rise and fall of her chest. Then through the silence surrounding their breathing, he heard the soft hum of an approaching car. Moments later, a beige station wagon rounded the bend ahead of them. In the front seat were a woman and two very excited children.

"Way to go, Crystal," Jared whispered. He put his lips by Kate's ear. "Help is here, honey. Just hang in there. Help is here."

Her eyes opened momentarily. Her lips tightened in a grim attempt at a smile. "Zimmermann did this," she said.

Jared paced from the small, well-appointed quiet room out to the hall and back. Mary T. Henderson Hospital was reputed to be among the best community hospitals in the state, but it was still a community hospital, only a fraction of the size of the Boston teaching facilities.

Nearly three hours had passed since the surgeon, Lee Jordan, had taken Kate into the operating room. Jordan was, according to the emergency room physician, the finest surgeon on the hospital staff. Jared had to laugh at his total surprise when the distinguished, gray-templed man his mind had projected as Lee Jordan turned out, in fact, to be a slender, extremely attractive woman in her midforties. Would he ever truly overcome all the years of programming?

Kate's wound was a bad one. The gash, Jordan had explained, required debridement in the operating room, and in all likelihood, an open-chest procedure would be needed to repair the laceration to her lung.

Jared had been allowed to see Kate briefly during the wait for the OR team to arrive, but there had been no real chance to discuss any details of William Zimmermann's attempt on her life. An officer from the Essex Police Department had come, taken what little information was available from him, and left with promises of state police involvement as soon as Kate could assist them with a statement. Meanwhile, it was doubtful that Jared's word would be enough to issue an arrest warrant.

Jared was studying the small plaque proclaiming that the quiet room was the gift of a couple named Berman when Lee Jordan emerged through the glass doors to the surgical suite. Her face, which had been fresh and alert on her arrival in the emergency ward four hours before, was gray and drawn, and for a moment, he feared the worst.

"Your wife's okay," Jordan said as soon as she was close enough to speak without raising her voice. She appraised him. "Are you?"

"I . . . yes, I'm okay." He braced himself against the wall. "It's just that for a moment there I was frightened that . . ."

Jordan patted him on the shoulder. "You married one tough lady, my friend," she said. "There's frostbite on the tips of her toes, ears, and nose, but it looks like she came in from the cold in time to save everything. The tear in her lung wasn't too, too big. I sewed it up and then fixed that gash in her side. She's in for a few pretty achy days, but I hope nothing worse than that. You'll be able to see her in half an hour or so. I've asked the nurses to come and get you."

"Thank you. Thank you very much."

"I'm glad she's all right," Dr. Lee Jordan said.

It was after five by the time Jared arrived home. Medicated and obviously affected by her anesthesia, Kate had managed only to squeeze his hand and acknowledge that she knew he was in her hospital room. Even so, Dr. Jordan had warned him that she would, in all likelihood, remember nothing of the first five or six hours postop.

Roscoe was another story. As soon as Jared arrived at the veterinarian's, the dog was up and hopping about his cage, mindless of his plaster cast and showing no residual effects from the anesthesia that had allowed a metal plate to be screwed in place across the fracture in his leg. After seeing Kate with half a dozen tubes running into and out of her body, the sight of the battered and broken animal was the last straw. Zimmermann would pay. Whatever it took, Jared vowed, the man would pay dearly.

Exhausted from the day and, in fact, from almost thirty-six hours without sleep, Jared brought a bottle of Lowenbräu Dark to the bedroom, finished half of it in two long draughts, and then stripped to his underwear and stretched out on the bed. There was little sense, the nurses had told him, in returning to the hospital before morning. So be it. He would rest and read and say a dozen prayers of thanks for Kate's life and for Roscoe's, and for Jocelyn Trent, and for being allowed to learn the sad truth about his father before it was too late.

He had bunched up two pillows and was looking through the magazines on the bedside table when he noticed their telephone answering machine. It had been on since Kate left for her run, and there were a number of messages. The first three were from Jared himself, another was from Ellen, and still another was from one of the firm's VIP clients, who had apparently been assured that Winfield's son wouldn't mind in the least being called at home. The final message was for Kate from a man named Arlen Paquette.

"Kate Bennett, this is Arlen Paquette from Redding," the man said in a rushed, anxious tone. "I won't be alone for more than a few seconds. I have answers for you. Many answers. Come to the subbasement of the Omnicenter at precisely eight-thirty tonight. Bring help. There may be trouble. Please, trust me. I know what we've done to you, but please trust me. He's coming. I've got to go. Good-bye."

Jared raced for pen and paper; then he played the message over and wrote it down verbatim. Answers. At last someone was promising answers. He scrambled into a pair of jeans, a work shirt, and a sweater. It was already after seven. There would barely be time to get to Metro by eight-thirty, let alone to try and pick up police help on the way. He would have to hurry to the subbasement of the Omnicenter and rely on himself. *The Omnicenter.* He threw on his parka and rushed to Kate's Volvo. That was Zimmermann's place. The man would be there. He felt certain of it.

"I'm coming for you, you fucker," he panted as he skidded out of the drive and down Salt Marsh Road.

CHAPTER 15

Friday 21 December

LIKE SO MANY works of greatness, the formulas derived by William Zimmermann's father were elegant in their simplicity. Even without Zimmermann's help in translating the explanatory notes from the German, Arlen Paquette suspected he would have been able to follow the steps involved in the synthesis of the

429

hormone Estronate 250—especially in the subbasement Omnicenter laboratory, which was specifically equipped for the job.

The message to call Cyrus Redding had been waiting at the front desk when Paquette returned to the Ritz from surreptitiously recording a conversation with Norton Reese during which the gloating administrator had incriminated himself and a technician named Pierce a number of times. The compact recorder still hooked to his belt, Paquette had entered the elevator to his floor.

"I was beginning to think you had run away," a man's voice said from behind.

Startled, the chemist whirled. It was Redding's bodyguard, a wiry, seemingly emotionless man whom Paquette had never heard called any name other than Nunes.

"Why, hello," Paquette said, wishing he had stayed at the tavern on the way back for a third drink. "I just picked up a message from Mr. Redding, but it says to call him at the Darlington number. Is he—?"

"He's there," Nunes said, showing nothing to dispel Paquette's image of a gunman whose loyalty to the pharmaceutical magnate had no limits. "He's waiting for your call."

From that moment on, Paquette had barely been out of Nunes's sight.

Now, in the bright fluorescence of the subbasement laboratory, Paquette glanced first at Zimmermann and then at Nunes and prayed that the forty-five minutes until eight-thirty would pass without incident. A deal had been struck between Redding and Zimmermann—money in exchange for a set of formulas. Redding had let him in on that much. However, the presence of the taciturn thug suggested that Redding anticipated trouble, or perhaps he had no intention of honoring his end of the bargain—quite possibly both.

"Okay, that's seven minutes," Zimmermann said, seconds before the mechanical timer rang out. "There's a shortcut my father used at this juncture, but I never did completely understand it. Dr. Paquette, I suggest you just go on to the next page and continue the steps in order. He performed these next reactions over in that corner, and he checked the purity of the distillate with that spectrophotometer."

Paquette nodded and moved around the slate work-bench to the area Zimmermann had indicated. The Omnicenter director was neither biochemist nor genius, but he had observed his father at work enough to be able to oversee each step of the synthesis. And oversee he had— each maneuver and each microdrop of the way.

The laboratory was quite remarkable. Hidden behind a virtually invisible, electronically controlled door, it had no less than three sophisticated spectrophotometers, each programmed to assess the consistency of the hormone at various stages of its synthesis and, through feedback mechanisms, to adjust automatically the chemical reaction where needed. It was a small area, perhaps fifteen feet by thirty, but its designer had paid meticulous attention to the maximum use of space.

"Did your father design all this?" Paquette asked.

"Be careful, Doctor, your reagent is beginning to overheat," Zimmermann said, ignoring the question as he had most others about his father. "Excuse me, but are you timing a reaction I don't know about?"

"No, why?"

"That's the third time you've looked at your watch in the past ten minutes."

"Oh, that." Paquette hoped his laugh did not sound too nervous. Out of the corner of his eye, he saw Nunes, seated on a tall stool at the end of the lab bench, adjust his position to hear better. "A habit dating back to high school, perhaps beyond, that's all."

He had made up his mind that there was no way he would complete the Estronate synthesis and turn the three notebooks over to Nunes. That act, he suspected, would be his last. He and Zimmermann were not scripted to leave the laboratory alive. The more the evening had worn on, the more certain he had become of that. He glanced at the metal hand plate to the right of the entrance. Though unmarked, it had to be the means of opening the door.

There were less than thirty minutes to go. If Kate Bennett had gotten his message, and if she had taken it seriously, she would be waiting, with help, in the storage area outside the laboratory.

Paquette's plan was simple. At eight thirty-five, allowing five minutes for any delay on Bennett's part, he would announce the need to use the men's room. They had passed one a floor above on their way in. With surprise on their side, whatever muscle Bennett had brought with her should have a decent chance at overpowering Nunes. If there was no one in the storage room when the door slid open, he would have to improvise. There was one thing of which he was sure: once outside the laboratory, he was not going back in. God, but he wished he had a drink.

Traffic into the city was inordinately light for a Friday evening, and it was clear to Jared that barring any monstrous delays, he would make it to Metro with time to spare. Still, he used his horn and high beams to clear his way down Route 1.

Risks. Bring help. There may be trouble. With each mile, Arlen Paquette's warning grew in his thoughts. He had made a mistake in not calling the Boston police before he left Essex. He could see that now. Still, what would he have said? How lengthy an explanation would have been required? His father, he knew, could pick up the phone and with no explanation whatsoever have half a dozen officers waiting for him at the front door to the Omnicenter. Answers. Paquette had promised answers. Perhaps for Kate's sake it was worth swallowing his pride and anger and calling Winfield. Then he realized that the issue went far deeper than pride and anger. The man could not be trusted. Not now, not ever again.

Bring help. Jared pulled off the highway and skidded to a stop by a bank of pay phones. It was seven forty-five. He was twenty minutes, twenty-five at the most, from the Omnicenter. There was still time to do something, but what? With no clear idea of what he was going to say, he called the Boston Police Department.

"I'd—ah—I'd like to speak to Detective Finn, please," he heard his own voice say. "Yes, that's right, Martin Finn. I'm sorry, I don't know what district. Four, maybe."

Finn. The thought, Jared saw now, had been in the back of his mind all along. Tough but fair: that's how his father had described the man. If that was the case, then it would take only the promise of some answers to get him to the Omnicenter.

Finn was not at his desk.

"Has he gone home for the night?" Jared asked of the officer who answered Finn's phone. "Well, does anyone know?" . . . "Samuels. Jared Samuels. I'm a lawyer. Detective Finn knows me. What is your name?" . . . "Well, please Sergeant, this is very urgent and there isn't much time. Could you see if you could get a message to Lieutenant Finn to meet me at eight-fifteen at the front entrance to the Omnicenter at Metropolitan Hospital?" . . . "That's right, in half an hour. And Sergeant, if you can't locate him, could you or some other officer meet me instead?" . . . "I don't know if it's a matter of life or death or not. Listen, I don't have time to explain. Please, just try."

Jared hurried back to the Volvo, wishing he had more of an idea of who Arlen Paquette was or at least of what was awaiting him at the Omnicenter. It was exactly eight o'clock when he sped over the crest of a long upgrade and saw, ahead and to his right, the glittering tiara of Boston at night.

Perhaps it was the tension of the moment, perhaps the six hours since his last drink; whatever the reason, Arlen Paquette felt his hands beginning to shake and his concentration beginning to waver. He pulled a gnarled handkerchief from his back pocket and dabbed at the cold sweat on his forehead and upper lip. It was only ten minutes past the hour. The hormone synthesis, which had proceeded flawlessly, was well over half completed.

"Are you all right?" Zimmermann asked.

"Fine, I'm fine," Paquette said, clutching a beaker of ice water with two hands to keep its contents from sloshing about. "I . . . I'd like to talk with Mr. Nunes for a moment. Privately."

"Why?" Zimmermann asked with a defensiveness in his voice. "There's no problem with the procedure up to now. I assure you of that. You are doing an excellent job of following my father's notes. Just keep going."

"It's not that. Listen, I'll be right back. Nunes," he whispered, his back turned to Zimmermann, "I need a drink."

"No booze until you finish this work. Mr. Redding's orders." As Nunes leaned forward to respond, the coat of his perfectly tailored suit fell away just enough for Paquette to see the holstered revolver beneath his left arm. Any doubt he harbored regarding his fate once the formulas were verified vanished.

"Nunes, have a heart."

The gunman's only response was an impatient nod in the direction of the incomplete experiment.

"Any problem?" Zimmermann called out.

"No problem," Nunes said as Paquette shuffled back. "Say, Dr. Zimmermann, where's the nearest john?"

Paquette slowed and listened. In less than twenty minutes he planned to ask the same question and wait for Nunes to open the door for him. Then an unexpected push from behind, and the man would be in the arms of the police. It was perfect, provided, of course, that Kate Bennett had gotten his message.

William Zimmermann pointed to the wall behind the gunman. "See that recessed handle in the wall right under that shelf? Just twist it and pull."

Nunes did as he was instructed, and a three-foot-wide block of shelves pulled away from the wall, revealing a fairly large bathroom and stall shower.

"Father had this obsession about hidden doorways and the like," Zimmermann said.

His next sentence, if there was to be one, was cut off by the beaker of ice water, which slipped from Paquette's hands and shattered on the tile floor.

Save for the security light in the front lobby, the Omnicenter was completely dark. Jared parked across the street and was beginning a walking inspection of the outside of the building when a blue and white patrol car pulled up. Martin Finn stepped out, looking in the gloom like a large block of granite with a homberg perched on top. Even at a distance, Jared could sense the man's impatience and irritation.

"I got your message," Finn said, with no more greeting than that. "What's going on?" Behind him, a uniformed officer remained at the wheel of the cruiser. The engine was still running.

"Thanks for coming so quickly," Jared said. "I . . . didn't know whom to call."

"Well?"

Jared checked the time. There were thirteen minutes. "My wife is in Henderson Hospital. Someone tried to run her down with a car earlier today while she was jogging." Finn said nothing. "She's had to have surgery, but she's going to be okay." Still nothing. "She couldn't speak much, but she said it was Dr. Zimmermann, the head of the Omnicenter, who tried to run her down and then chased her with a tire wrench."

"William Zimmermann?"

"Yes. Do you know him?"

Finn looked at him icily. "He delivered my daughter."

Inwardly, Jared groaned. "Well, he was involved in something illegal, possibly in connection with one of the big pharmaceutical houses. Kate discovered what was going on, so he tried to kill her."

"But he missed." There was neither warmth nor the slightest hint of belief in the man's voice.

"Yes, he missed." Jared swallowed back his mounting anger. There was far too much at stake and hardly time for an argument. "When I returned home from the hospital a short while ago, there was a message on our answering machine for Kate from a man named Arlen Paquette. I think he works for the drug house. He asked that she meet him here, in the subbasement of this building, and that she bring help. That's why I called you. I suspect that Zimmermann is in the middle of all this and that he's in there right now."

"In there?" Finn gestured at the darkened building.

"He said the *subbasement.*"

"Mr. Samuels, Dr. Zimmermann's office is on the third floor. On the corner, right up there. I've been there several times. Now what on earth would he be doing in the subbasement?"

"I . . . I don't know." There were eleven minutes. "Look, Lieutenant, the man said exactly eight-thirty. There isn't much time."

"So you want me to go busting into a locked hospital building, looking to nail my wife's obstetrician, because you got some mysterious message on your telephone answering machine?"

"If the doors are all locked, we can get in through the tunnels. We don't have to break in. Dammit, Lieutenant, my wife was almost killed today. Do you think she's lying about the broken bones and the punctured lung?"

"No," Finn said. "Only about everything else. Mr. Samuels, I had a chance to do some checking up on your wife. She's in hot water with just about everyone in the city, it seems. Word has it she's just been fired for screwing up here at the hospital, too. Face it, counselor, you've got a sick woman on your hands. You need help, all right, but not the kind I can give."

"Then you won't come with me?" Jared could feel himself losing control.

"Mr. Samuels, because of your wife, I still have enough egg on my face to make a fucking omelet. I'll file a report if you want me to, and even get a warrant if you can give me some hard facts to justify that. But no commando stuff. Now if I were you, I'd just go on home and see about lining up some professional help for your woman."

Before he could even weigh the consequences, Jared hit the man— a roundhouse punch that landed squarely on the side of Finn's face and sent him spinning down into a pile of plowed snow. Instantly, the uniformed officer was out of the cruiser, his hand on the butt of his service revolver. Finn, a trickle of blood forming at the corner of his mouth, waved him off.

"No, Jackie," he said. "It's all right. The counselor, here, felt he had a score to settle with me, and he just settled it." He pushed himself to his feet, still shaking off the effects of the blow. "Now, counselor, you just get the fuck out of my sight. If I hear of any trouble involving you tonight, I'm going to bust your ass from here to Toledo. Clear?"

Jared glared at the detective. "You're wrong, Finn. About my wife, about refusing to help me, about everything. You don't know how goddamn wrong you are."

He glanced at his watch, then turned and raced down the block toward the main entrance to the hospital and the stairway that would lead to the Omnicenter tunnel. There were less than five minutes left.

Visiting hours had ended. The hospital was quiet. Jared crossed the lobby as quickly as he dared without calling attention to himself and hurried down the nearest staircase. Although he used the dreary tunnels infrequently, he distinctly remembered seeing a sign indicating that the Omnicenter had been tacked onto the system. But where?

The tunnel was deserted, and it seemed even less well lighted than usual. A caravan of stretchers lined one wall, interspersed with empty, canvas industrial laundry hampers. On the wall opposite was a wooden sign with arrows indicating the direction to various buildings. The bottom three names, almost certainly including the Omnicenter, were obscured by a mixture of grime and graffiti. Kate had once told him that it took a special kind of character to love working at Metro, intimating that the spirit of the hospital staff and the loyalty of many of its patients were somehow bound to the physical shortcomings of the place. The concept, like so much else about his wife, was something Jared realized he would have to work a little harder at understanding.

His often far from dependable sense of direction urged him toward the right. There was no time to question the impulse. His footsteps echoing off the cement floor and walls, Jared raced that way, instinctively casting about for something he could use as a weapon, and at the same time, cursing his failure to obtain help.

His sense, this time at least, was on the mark. The spur leading to the Omnicenter was fifty yards away.

It was exactly eight-thirty. The darkened passageway was illuminated only by the dim glow from the main tunnel. Sprinting head down, Jared caught a glimpse of the metal security gate only an instant before he hit it. The gate, an expanded version of the sort used to child-proof stairways, was pulled across the tunnel and bolted to the opposite wall. Stunned, he dropped to one knee, pawing at the spot just above his right eye that had absorbed most of the impact. Then he sank to all fours. If timing was as critical as Arlen Paquette's message had made it sound, he was beaten. The gate, with no space below, and less than a foot on top, was solid.

Exhausted and exasperated, Jared hauled himself up, grabbed the metal slats, and like a caged animal, rattled them mercilessly. *I'm sorry, Katey,* was all he could think. *I'm sorry I fucked up everything so badly.*

"Just hold it right there, son, and turn around very slowly." Jared froze, his hands still tight around the gate. "I've got a gun pointed in your general direction, so don't you go getting too rattled or too adventurous."

Jared did as he was told. Thirty or forty feet away, silhouetted by the light from behind him, was a night watchman.

"Who are you? What are you doin' down here?" the man demanded.

"Please, you've got to help me!" Jared took a few steps forward.

"That'll be far enough. Now how can I go about helpin' you, young man, if I don't even know who in the hell you are?"

Jared forced himself to calm down. "My name is Samuels. My wife is a doctor on the staff here. Dr. Bennett. Dr. Kathryn Bennett. Do you know her?"

The night watchman lowered his revolver. "You the lawyer?"

"Yes. Yes, I am. Listen, you've got to help me." He approached the watchman, who this time made no attempt to stop him.

"Do I, now," the man said. His khaki uniform appeared a size, perhaps two, too big for him. A shock of gray hair protruded from beneath his cap. Even with the revolver, he was hardly a menacing figure.

"Please, Mister—"

"MacFarlane. Walter MacFarlane. Known your wife for years— even before you were married to her."

"Well, Mr. MacFarlane, my wife's in a hospital on the North Shore right now. Someone tried to run her down. We know who, but not why. A few hours ago, a man called and promised me answers if I would meet him in the Omnicenter subbasement right now."

"Subbasement?"

"Yes. He said to bring help because there might be trouble, but there just wasn't enough time for me to get any."

"You sure it's the subbasement? That's the level beneath this one. Ain't nothin' down there but a bunch of cartons and spare cylinders of oxygen."

"All I know is what he said. Please. It's already past time."

"That Kate has been gettin' herself into some kinds of trouble lately."

"I know. Please, Mr. Mac—"

"People talk and talk. You know how it is. Well I'll tell you something, mister. They have their thoughts and I have mine. Ten years I've walked that woman to her car when she stayed until late at night. Ten years. She's class, I tell you. Pure class."

"Then you'll help me?"

Walter MacFarlane sorted a key out from the huge ring on his belt and opened the security gate. "If it'll help straighten things out for Dr. Bennett, count me in," he said.

Arlen Paquette was terrified. There was no way out of the laboratory except past the killer, Nunes, and yet to stay, to complete the Estronate synthesis meant, he was convinced, to die. It was twenty-five minutes to nine. As yet there had not been even the faintest sound from beyond the electronically controlled door. Kate Bennett either had not received his message or had disregarded it. Either way, he was on his own.

Desperately, he tried to sort out the situation and his options. There was no way he could buy time by claiming the procedure was inaccurate. Zimmermann was watching his every step. Could he somehow enlist Zimmermann's help in overpowering Nunes? Doubtful. No, worse than doubtful: impossible. Nunes had already shown him the money, packed neatly in a briefcase that now rested on the benchtop. Zimmermann's expression had been that of a starving wolf discovering a trapped hare.

"Anything the matter?" Zimmermann asked, indicating that once again Paquette was dawdling.

"No!" Paquette snapped. "And I want you off my back. It's my responsibility to verify these formulas, and I'll take all the time I need to do the job right."

At the far end of the lab, Nunes adjusted his position to keep a better eye on the two of them. Suddenly he waved to get their attention and placed a silencing finger over his lips. With his other hand, he pointed to the door. Someone was outside. With the sure, fluid movements of a professional, he slid the revolver from its holster and flattened himself against the wall beside the door.

Paquette decided that he had but one option—and not a very appealing one. He had been a wrestler during his freshman and sophomore years in high school, but had never been that good and, in fact, had been grateful when a neck injury forced him to quit. Since that time, he had never had a fight in any physical sense with anyone. Nunes was taller than he by perhaps two inches and certainly more experienced, but he had surprise and desperation on his side.

Separated from the gunman by one of the spectrophotometers and a tangle of sophisticated glass distillation tubing, Paquette eased his way along the slate-topped work bench until he was no more than ten feet from him. For several seconds, all was quiet. Then he heard muffled voices, at least two of them, from the storage room beyond the door. He strained to pick up their conversation, but could make out only small snatches. Nunes, that much closer, was probably hearing more. Paquette wondered if those outside the door had mentioned his name. If so, and if Nunes had heard, it was the final nail in his coffin.

The voices grew less distinct. Had they just moved away, or were they leaving, Paquette wondered. Even if they were to discover the door —and that was most unlikely—there was no way they could locate and activate the coded electronic key.

Carefully, Paquette slid the final few feet to the end of the laboratory bench. Zimmermann was a good twenty-five feet away—far enough to keep him from interfering. Paquette gauged the distance and then focused on his two objectives: Nunes's gun and the electronic plate on the right side of the door. A single step, and he hurled himself at the man, grasping his gun arm at the wrist with both his hands and spinning against the metal plate.

The door slid open, and Paquette caught a glimpse of a uniformed man fumbling for the pistol holstered at his hip. There was a second figure behind the man, whom he recognized as Kate Bennett's husband. In that moment, Nunes freed his hand and whipped Paquette viciously across the face with the barrel of his revolver. Paquette dropped to his knees, clutching at the pain and at the blood spurting from his cheek and temple.

"All right, mister, drop it! Right now, right there!"

Walter MacFarlane stood in the doorway, his heavy service revolver leveled at Nunes, whose own gun was a foot or so out of position. Nunes froze, his head turned, ever so slightly, toward the intruder.

From his position four feet behind and to the left of MacFarlane, Jared could see the gunman's expression clearly. He seemed placid, composed, and totally confident.

Back up! Get away from him! Before Jared could verbalize the warning, the gunman was in action. He flicked his revolver far enough away to draw MacFarlane's eyes and then lunged out of the watchman's line of fire and up beneath his arm. MacFarlane's revolver discharged with a sharp report.

The bullet splintered several glass beakers, ricocheted off a wall, and then impacted with a large can of ether on the shelf behind William Zimmermann. The can exploded, the blast shattering most of the glassware in the room. Jared watched in horror as Zimmermann's hair and the skin on the back of his scalp were instantly seared away, his clothes set ablaze.

"Help!" he shrieked, reeling away from the wall. "Oh, God, someone help me!"

He flailed impotently at the tongues of flame that were darting upward through the crotch of his trousers and igniting his shirt. His struggles sent a shelf of chemicals crashing to the floor. There was a second explosion. Zimmermann's right arm disappeared at the elbow. Still, he stayed on his feet, lurching in purposeless circles, staring at the bloody remains of his upper arm, and screaming again and again. A third blast, from just to his left, sent his body, now more corpse than man, hurtling across the slate tabletop, through what remained of the glassware.

Zimmermann's screeching ended abruptly as he toppled over the edge of the table and onto Arlen Paquette. The chemist, though shielded from the force of the explosion by the counter, was far too dazed from the blow he had absorbed to react.

MacFarlane and Nunes both went down before the blast of heat and flying glass. Jared, still outside the laboratory door, was knocked backward, but managed to keep his feet. He stumbled to the doorway, trying frantically to assess the situation.

Intensely colored flames were breaking out along the benchtops, filling the air with thick, fetid smoke. To his right, Walter MacFarlane and the gunman lay amidst shards of glass. The side of the watchman's face looked as if it had been mauled by a tiger. Both men were moving, though without much purpose. To his left there was also movement. The man he assumed was Arlen Paquette was trying, ineffectually, to extricate himself from beneath the charred body of William Zimmermann.

Crawling to avoid the billows of toxic smoke, Jared made his way to Zimmermann, grabbed the corpse by its belt and the front of its smoldering shirt and heaved it onto its back.

"Paquette?" Jared gasped. "Are you Paquette?"

The man nodded weakly and pawed at the blood—his and Zimmermann's—that was obscuring his vision. "Notebooks," he said. "Get the notebooks."

Jared batted at the few spots on Paquette's clothing that were still burning, pulled him to a sitting position, and leaned him against the wall. The fumes and smoke were worsening around them.

"I've got to get you out of here. Can you understand that?"

Paquette's head lolled back. "Notebooks," he said again.

Jared glanced about. On the floor beneath Zimmermann's heel was a black looseleaf notebook. He tucked the book under his arm and then began dragging Paquette toward the doorway. Several times, glass cut through Jared's pants and into his leg. Once he slipped, slicing a flap of skin off the edge of his hand. The wooden cabinets and shelves had begun to blaze, making the room unbearably hot.

Paquette was making the task of moving him from the room harder by clawing at Jared, at one point getting his hand entangled in Jared's parka pocket.

"For Christ's sake, let go of me, Paquette," Jared shouted. "I'm trying to get you out of here. Can you understand that? I'm trying to get you out."

The smoke was blinding. His eyes tearing and nearly closed, Jared hunched low, breathed through his parka, and with great effort, pulled Paquette's arm over his shoulder, hauling the man to his feet. Together they staggered from the lab. Jared was about to set Paquette down against a wall in order to return for MacFarlane when he remembered the oxygen. There were thirty or forty large green cylinders bunched in the far corner of the storage area. They possessed, he suspected, enough explosive potential to level a good portion of the building.

"Paquette," he hollered, "I'm going to help you up the stairs. Then you've got to get down the tunnel and as far away from here as possible. Do you understand?" Paquette nodded. "Can you support any more of your own weight?"

"I can try." Paquette, his face a mask of blood, forced the words out between coughs.

One arduous step at a time, the two made their way up to the landing on the basement level. Acrid chemical smoke, which had largely filled the storage area below, drifted up the stairway around them.

"Okay, we're here," Jared said loudly. "I've got to go back down there. You head that way, through the tunnel. Understand? Good. Here, take your book with you and just keep going." He shoved the notebook into the man's hands.

At that instant, from below, there was a sharp explosion. Then another. Jared watched as Paquette lurched away from him and then pitched heavily to the floor, blood pouring from a wound on the side of his neck.

Jared dropped to one knee beside the man, surprised and confused by what was happening. "Paquette!"

"Notebook . . . Kate . . ." were all Paquette could manage before a torrent of blood sealed his words and closed his eyes.

It was then Jared realized the man had been shot, that the explosions he had heard were from a gun, not from the lab. He turned at the moment Nunes fired at him from the base of the stairs. The bullet tore through his right thigh and caromed off the floor and wall behind him. The man, blackened by smoke and bleeding from cuts about his face, leveled the revolver for another shot.

Distracted by the burning pain in his leg, Jared barely reacted in time to drop out of the line of fire. Behind him and from the mouth of the tunnel, alarms had begun to wail. Below him, the man had started up the stairs through the billowing smoke.

Notebook . . . Kate . . . Jared plucked the black notebook from beside Arlen Paquette's body, tucked it under his arm like a football, and in a gait that was half hop and half sprint, raced down the tunnel toward the main hospital. Zimmermann, Paquette, and probably Walter MacFarlane as well: all dead, quite possibly because he had gone to the subbasement rendezvous without enough help. The distressing thought took his mind off the pain as he pushed on past the security gate. Paquette had promised answers for Kate, and now he was dead. Silently, Jared cursed himself.

A gunshot echoed through the tunnel. Hunching over to diminish himself as a target, Jared limped on, weaving from side to side across the tunnel, and wondering if the evasive maneuver was worth the ground he was losing. The main tunnel was less than thirty yards away. There would be people there—help—if only he could make it. Another shot rang out, louder than the last. The bullet, fired, Jared realized now, from MacFarlane's heavy service revolver, snapped through the sleeve of his parka and clattered off the cement floor. He stumbled, nearly falling, and slammed into the far wall of the main tunnel.

"Help," he screamed. "Somebody help!" The dim tunnel was deserted.

A moment later he was shot again, the bullet impacting just above his left buttock, spinning him a full three hundred and sixty degrees, and sending white pain lancing down his leg and up toward his shoulder blade. He tumbled to one knee, but just as quickly pulled himself up again, clutching the notebook to his chest and rolling along the wall of the tunnel. Somewhere in the distance he could hear another series of alarms, then sirens, and finally a muffled explosion.

He was, for the moment at least, out of the killer's line of fire, stumbling in the direction away from the main hospital and toward the boiler room and laundry. Despite the pain in his leg and back, he was determined that nothing short of a killing shot was going to bring him down. With Paquette and Zimmermann dead, the black notebook, whatever it was, might well represent Kate's only chance.

The gunman, crouching low and poised to fire, slid around the corner of the Omnicenter tunnel just as Jared reached the spur to the laundry. Jared sensed the man about to shoot, but there was no explosion, no noise. Or was there? As he pushed on into the darkened laundry, he could swear he had heard a sound of some sort. Then he understood. The killer *had* fired. MacFarlane's revolver was out of bullets, tapped dry. Now, even wounded, he had a chance.

The room he had entered was filled with dozens of rolling industrial hampers, some empty, some piled high with linen. Beyond the crowded hamper lot, Jared could just discern the outlines of rows of huge steam pressers. He gave momentary consideration to diving into one of the hampers, but rejected the notion, partly because of the helpless, passive situation in which he would be and partly because his pursuer had already turned into the tunnel and was making his way, though cautiously, toward the laundry.

Ignoring the pain in his back, Jared dropped to all fours and inched his way between two rows of hampers toward the enormous, cluttered hall housing the laundry itself. Pressers, washers, dryers, shelves and stacks of linens, more hampers—if he could make it, there would be dozens of places to hide . . . *if* he could make it.

There were twenty feet separating the last of the canvas hampers from the first of the steam pressers. Twenty open feet. He had to cross them unnoticed. Kneeling in the darkness, he listened. There was not a sound—not a breath, not the shuffle of a footstep, nothing. Where in hell was the man? Was the chance of catching a glimpse of him worth the risk of looking? The aching in his back was in crescendo, dulling his concentration and his judgment. Again he listened. Again there was nothing. Slowly, he brougth his head up and turned.

The killer, moving with the control and feline calm of a professional, was less than five feet away, preparing to hammer him with the butt of MacFarlane's heavy revolver. Jared spun away, but still absorbed a glancing blow just above his left ear. Stunned, he stumbled backward, pulling first one, then another hamper between him and the man, who paused to pick up the notebook and set it on the corner of a hamper before matter-of-factly advancing on him again.

"It's no use, pal," he said, shoving the hampers aside as quickly as Jared could pull them in his way, "but go ahead and make it interesting if you want."

Jared, needing the hampers as much for support as for protection, knew the man was right. Wounded and without a weapon, Jared had no chance against him.

"Who are you?" he asked.

Nunes smiled and shrugged. "Just a man doing a job," he said.

"You work for Redding Pharmaceuticals, don't you."

"I think this little dance of ours has gone on long enough, pal. Don't you?"

In that instant, Jared thought about Kate and all she had been through; he thought about Paquette and the aging watchman, MacFarlane. If he was going to die, then, dammit, it wouldn't be while backing away. With no more plan in mind than that, he grabbed another hamper, feigned pulling it in front of him, and instead drove it forward as hard as he could, catching the surprised gunman just below the waist. Nunes lurched backward, colliding with another hamper and very nearly going down.

Jared moved as quickly as he could, but the advantage he had gained with surprise was lost in the breathtaking pain of trying to push off his left foot. The killer, his expression one of placid amusement, parried the lunge with one hand, and with the other, brought the barrel of the revolver slicing across Jared's head, opening a gash just above his temple. Jared staggered backward a step, then came on again, this time leading with a kick which connected, though not powerfully, with the man's groin.

Again Nunes lashed out with the gun, landing a solid blow to Jared's forearm and then another to the back of his neck. Jared dropped to one knee. As he did, Nunes stepped behind him and locked one arm expertly beneath his chin.

"Sorry, pal," he said, tightening his grip.

Jared flailed with his arms and shoulders and tried to stand, but the man's leverage was far too good. The pressure against his larynx was excruciating. His chest throbbed with the futile effort of trying to breathe. Blood pounded in his head and the killer's grunting breaths grew louder in his ear. Then the sound began to fade. Jared knew he was dying. Every ounce of his strength vanished, and he felt the warmth of his bladder letting go. *I'm sorry, Kate. I'm sorry.* The words tumbled over and over in his mind. *I'm sorry.*

Through closed eyes, he sensed, more than saw, a bright, blue-white light. From far, far away, he heard a muffled explosion. Then another.

Suddenly the pressure against his neck diminished. The killer's forearm shook uncontrollably and then slid away. Jared fell to one side, but looked up in time to see the man totter and then, in grotesque slow motion, topple over into a hamper.

Jared struggled to sort out what was happening. The first thing he saw clearly was that the overhead lights had been turned on; the second thing was the stubbled, slightly jowled face of Martin Finn.

"I was halfway back to the station when I decided there was no way you would have chanced popping me like you did unless the situation was really desperate," Finn said. "How bad are you hurt?"

Jared coughed twice and wasn't sure he was able to speak until he heard his own voice. "I've been shot twice," he rasped, "once just above my butt and once in my thigh. My legs are all cut up from broken glass. That lunatic beat the shit out of me with his gun."

"The emergency people are on their way," Finn said, kneeling down. "It may be a few minutes. As you might guess, there's a lot of commotion going on around here right now. Is Zimmermann dead?"

Jared nodded. Then he remembered MacFarlane. "Finn," he said urgently, "there's a man, MacFarlane, a night watchman. He was—"

"You mean him?" The detective motioned to his left.

Walter MacFarlane, one eye swollen shut and the side of his face a mass of dried and oozing blood, stood braced against a hamper.

"Thank God," Jared whispered.

"We would never have known what direction to go in without him," Finn explained.

At that moment a team of nurses and residents arrived with two stretchers. They helped MacFarlane onto one and then gingerly hoisted Jared onto the other.

"As soon as these people get you fixed up, Counselor, you're going to have a little explaining to do. You know that, don't you?"

443

"I know. I'll tell you as much as I can. And Finn . . . I appreciate your coming back."

"I think I might owe you an apology, but I'll save it until someone explains to me what the fuck has been going on around here."

"Okay," one of the residents announced. "We're all set."

"Wait. Please," Jared said. "Finn, there's a notebook around here somewhere. A black, looseleaf notebook."

The detective searched for a few moments and then brought it over. "Yours?" he asked.

"Actually, no." Jared tucked the notebook beneath his arm. Then he smiled. "It belongs to my wife."

CHAPTER 16

Saturday 22 December

"MR. SAMUELS, I'm here to take you up to your room. Mr. Samuels?"

Jared's eyes opened from a dreamless sleep. He was on a litter, staring at the chipped, flaking ceiling of the emergency ward where a team of surgical residents had worked on his wounds. His last clear memory was of one of the doctors, a baby-faced woman with rheumy eyes behind horn-rimmed glasses, announcing that she was about to give him a "little something" so that his wounds could be explored, cleaned, and repaired.

"I'm Cary Dunleavy, one of the nurses from Berenson Six," the man's voice said from somewhere at the head of the litter.

Jared tried to crane his neck toward the nurse, but was prevented by a thick felt cervical collar and a broad leather restraining belt across his chest. He ached in a dozen different places, and he sensed that he was seeing little or nothing through his left eye.

Dunleavy took several seconds to appreciate his patient's predicament. Then he muttered an apology and moved to a spot by Jared's right hand. "Welcome to the land of the living," he said. His voice was kind, but his eyes were sunken and tired. "You've been out for quite a while. Apparently they overestimated how much analgesia to give you."

Jared brought his left hand up and gingerly touched the area about his left eye.

"It's swollen shut," the nurse announced. "You look like you've been kicked by a mule."

Jared felt his senses begin to focus, and he struggled to reconstruct the hazy events following the explosion in the Omnicenter. His first clear image was of William Zimmermann spinning wildly about, his clothes ablaze, the skin on one side of his face hideously scorched. That one was for you, Katey, he thought savagely. An I'm-sorry-for-not-believing-you present from your husband. "What time is it?" he asked.

"Almost four."

"In the morning?"

The nurse nodded. "According to the report I got from the ER nurses, you've been out for about three hours since they finished working on you. We've been too busy on the floor for anyone to come and get you until now. Sorry."

"I need to get out of here," Jared said, fumbling at the restraining strap with his left hand. His right hand, with an intravenous line taped in place, was secured to the railing of the litter.

"Hey, partner," the nurse said, setting a hand on his shoulder. "Easy does it."

"I've got to see my wife. I've—" Suddenly, he remembered the notebook. "My things. Where are my things?"

"We've got 'em, Mr. Samuels. They're put away safe awaiting the moment when we read a legitimate order from your doctor discharging you. Rounds are usually at seven. Until then, if you go, you go in a Johnny."

Jared glared at the man. *I'm a lawyer,* he wanted to shout. I can sue you and this whole hospital for violating my civil rights, and win. Instead, he assessed his situation. In just three hours or so his physicians would make rounds and he could explain to them his need to leave. Three hours. Almost certainly, Kate would be sleeping through them anyhow, under the effects of her anesthesia. He sank back on the litter. "You win," he said.

The nurse said silent thanks with a skyward look and started maneuvering the litter out of the small examining room.

"Just one thing," Jared said.

The man stopped short and again walked around to make eye contact. "I'll listen, but no promises." His tired voice was less good-natured than he intended.

"I had a notebook. A black, looseleaf notebook. It should be in with my things. Get me that, and I promise to be a model patient."

Cary Dunleavy hesitated, but then withdrew the notebook from the patient's belongings bag, which was stashed on the litter beneath Jared. "I'm taking you at your word, Mr. Samuels. Model patient. I'm nearing the end of a double. That's over sixteen straight hours of nursing on a floor that would fit right in at the Franklin Zoo. It's been one hell of a long night, and my usual overabundance of the milk of human kindness is just about dried up. So don't cross me."

Jared smiled, made a feeble peace sign with his bandaged left hand, and tucked the notebook between his arm and his side.

The exhausted nurse returned to the head of the litter and resumed the slow trek through the tunnels to the Berenson Building.

The doors to one of the Berenson elevators opened as they approached, and a patient was wheeled out by two nurses. Jared saw the two bags of blood draining into two separate IVs, and a woman's tousled black hair, but little else, as Cary Dunleavy stopped and spoke to the nurses.

"What gives?" Dunleavy asked.

"GI bleeding. Getting worse. She's going to the OR for gastroscopy. The team's already up there waiting."

"Good luck. Let me know how it goes."

"Will do," the nurse said. The stretchers glided past one another. "Sorry for the delay, Mrs. Sandler," she continued. "We'll be there in just a minute or two."

Mrs. Sandler. Several seconds passed before the name registered for Jared. "Ellen!" he called out, struggling once again against the leather strap.

Dunleavy stopped. "Hey, what're you doing?"

Jared forced himself to calm down. Ellen was on her way to the operating room, hemorrhaging. The option of waiting for seven o'clock rounds no longer existed. Kate had to see the notebook as quickly as possible. Even if the odds were one in a million against finding an answer for Ellen, she had to see it.

"Dunleavy, I've got to talk to you," he said with exaggerated reason. "Please."

Wearily, the nurse again walked to where he could be seen.

"Dunleavy, you care. I can see it in your face. You're tired and wasted, but you still care."

"So?"

"That woman who just went past here on the litter is Ellen Sandler, a friend of my wife's and mine. Dunleavy, she's bleeding—maybe bleeding to death. There's a chance the answer to her bleeding problem may be in this notebook, but it's written half in German and half in English, and it's technical as hell."

"So?"

"My wife is Kate Bennett, a pathologist here. Do you know her?" Dunleavy's acknowledging expression suggested that he might actually know too much. "Well, she speaks some German, and she knows what's been going on with that woman who just passed us. I've got to get this to her. She's a patient at Henderson Hospital in Essex."

"Mr. Samuels, I can't—"

"Dunleavy, please. There's no time to fuck around. Undo this strap and help me get to a cab. I can move all my extremities, see? I'll be fine."

"I—"

"Dammit, man, look at me! That woman is dying and we might be able to help her. Get me an against-medical-advice paper and I'll sign it. I'll sign whatever the hell you want. But, please, do it now!"

The nurse hesitated.

"That woman needs us, my friend," Jared said. "Right this minute she needs us both."

Dunleavy reached down and undid the restraint. "It's my ass unless you come back and talk to the nursing office. Probably my ass anyway."

"I'll speak to them. I promise. So will my wife."

Dunleavy's eyes narrowed. "Please, Mr. Samuels," he said. "Don't do me any favors."

Even through the analgesic mist of Demerol and the distracting pain in her chest, Kate Bennett could sense the change in her husband. Bandaged, bruised, and needing a crutch to navigate, he had made a wonderful theatrical entrance into her room, sweeping through the doorway past a protesting night supervisor and announcing loudly, "The fucker's dead, Katey. Dead. He won't ever hurt you again." Then he had crossed to the bed, kissed her on the lips, and firmly but politely dismissed the supervisor and the special duty nurse.

Now he sat on a low chair by her left hand, mindless of his own discomfort, watching intently as she opened the black notebook—the sole useful vestige of the fire, pain, and death in the Omnicenter. There was a strength about the man, an assuredness, she had never sensed before. *The fucker's dead, Katey. He won't ever hurt you again.*

The words on the first page landed like hammer blows. *Studies in Estronate 250, Volume III of III.* Kate's heart sank.

"Jared," she said, swallowing at the sandpaper in her mouth and painfully adjusting the plastic tube that was draining bloody fluid from her chest, "have you looked at this?"

"Just to flip through. Why? Too much German? We'll find someone to translate."

"No. Actually, there's not that much. . . . Honey, it says here volume three of three."

"What?" He shifted forward and read the page. "Damn. I never saw any other books. There might have been others, but there was so much smoke. Everything was happening so fast. . . . Paquette could have explained everything if he had made it."

Kate searched her husband's face as he spoke. It was not an excuse, not an apology, but a statement of fact. Paquette had held the key to a deadly mystery. But Paquette was dead. And Jared, battered, bruised, clearly in great pain, was alive. If she could unlock the answers, it would be because he had risked his life for her. "We'll do the best we can with what we have," Kate said, turning to the first page of what appeared to be a series of clinical tests on a substance called Estronate 250. "I'm still foggy as hell from the anesthetic and that last shot, so bear with me."

There were, all told, one hundred and twenty carefully numbered pages. Paquette, or whoever had conducted this research, had been meticulous and precise. Stability studies; dosage modification studies; administration experiments in milk, in water, in solid food; investigation of side effects. Kate plodded through thirty years of terse German and English explanations and lengthy lists of test subjects, first from the state mental hospital at Wickford and in more recent years, from the Omnicenter. *Thirty years.* Arlen Paquette had not sounded that old over the phone, but perhaps he had taken over the Estronate research from someone else.

Ten minutes passed; then twenty. Jared shifted anxiously in his seat, and stared outside at the sterile, gray dawn. "How long does a gastroscopy take?" he asked.

Kate, unwilling to break her fragile concentration, glanced over at him momentarily. "That depends on what they find, and on what they choose to do about it. Jared, I'm close to figuring out some things. I need a few more minutes."

"You look pretty washed out. Stop if you need to."

"I'm okay."

"Here. Here's some water."

She took a sip and then moistened her cracked, bleeding lips; then she returned her attention to the notebook. Another ten minutes passed before she looked up. Despite the pain and the drugs, her eyes were sparkling.

"Jared," she said, "I think I understand. I think I know what Estronate Two-fifty is."

"Well?"

"This is amazing. Assuming he's the one who conducted this research—or at least completed it—the late Dr. Paquette was worth his weight in gold to Redding Pharmaceuticals. Estronate Two-fifty is an oral antifertility drug that causes irreversible sterilization. It can be given to a woman by pill or even secretly in a glass of milk."

"Irreversible?"

Kate nodded vigorously, wincing at the jab of pain from her side. "Exactly. Think of it. No more tubal ligations, fewer vasectomies, help for third-world countries battling overpopulation."

"Then the scarred ovaries weren't a mistake?"

"Hardly. If I'm right, the microsclerosis was the desired result, not a side effect."

"But what about the bleeding? What about Ellen?"

Kate motioned him to wait. She was scanning a column marked *Nebenwirkung*.

"Look, Jared," she said excitedly. "See this word? It means side effects. All these women were apparently given this Estronate and monitored for side effects. Jesus, they're crazy. Paquette, Zimmermann, Horner—all of them. Absolutely insane. They used hundreds of people as guinea pigs."

"E. Sandler," Jared said.

"What?"

"E. Sandler. There it is right at the bottom of the page."

Kate groaned. "I may be even worse off than I think I am. Twice over the page and I missed it completely. Bless you, Jared."

Ellen's name was next to last in a column of perhaps three dozen. Halfway down a similar list on the following page, Kate found the names B. Vitale and G. Rittenhouse. She pointed them out to Jared and then continued a careful line-by-line check of the rest of the column and yet another page of subjects.

"I thought those were all the bleeding problems you know about," he said.

"They are."

"Well, whose name are you looking for?"

She looked up and for a moment held his eyes with hers. "Mine," she said.

She checked the pages once and then again before she felt certain. "I'm not here, Jared. I may be in some notebook marked anthranilic acid, but I'm not here."

"Thank God," he whispered. "At least volume three's given us that much."

Kate did not respond. She was again immersed in the columns of data, turning from one page to another, and then back. From where he sat, Jared studied her face: the intensity in her eyes, the determination that had taken her through twelve years of the most demanding education and training. At that moment, more so than at any other time in their marriage, he felt pride in her—as a physician, as a person, as his wife.

"Jared," she said breathlessly, her attention still focused on the notebook, "I think you did it. I think it's here."

"Show me."

"See these two words: *Thrombocytopenie* and *Hypofibrinogenamie*? Well, they mean low platelets and low fibrinogen. Just what Ellen is bleeding from. There's a notation here referring to Omnicenter Study Four B. Modification of *Thrombocytopenie* and *Hypofibrinogenamie* Using a Combination of Nicotinic Acid and Delta Amino Caproic Acid."

"I've heard of nicotinic acid. Isn't that a vitamin?"

"Exactly—another name for niacin. The other is a variant of a drug called epsilon amino caproic acid, which is used to reverse certain bleeding disorders. See, look here. All together, seven women on these three pages developed problems with their blood. They were picked up early, on routine blood tests in the Omnicenter."

"But Ellen and the other two aren't listed as having problems with their blood. There's nothing written next to their names in the side effects column."

She nodded excitedly. "That's the point, Jared. That's the key. Ellen and the two women who died were never diagnosed. Maybe they just didn't have Omnicenter appointments at the right time."

"The others were treated?"

Kate nodded. "That's what this Study Four B is all about. They got high doses of nicotinic acid and the other drug, and all of them apparently recovered. Their follow-up blood counts are listed right here. I think you did it. I think this is the answer. I just hope it's not too late and that somebody at Metro can get hold of the delta form of this medication. If not, maybe they can try the epsilon."

Jared handed her the receiver of the bedside telephone. "Just tell me what to dial," he said.

Kate's hand was shaking visibly as she set the receiver down. "Ellen's still in the operating room. Nearly three hours now."

"Who was that you were talking to?"

"Tom Engleson. He's a resident on the Ashburton Service. In fact, he's the one who called— Never mind. That's not important. Anyhow, he's been up to the operating room several times to check how it's going. The gastroscopist has found a bleeding ulcer. They've tried a number of different tricks to get it to stop, but so far no dice. They've had to call in a surgical team."

"They're going to operate?"

Kate shook her head. "Not if they can't do something with her clotting disorder."

"And?"

"Tom's gone to round up the hematologist on call and the hospital pharmacist. I'm sure they can come up with the nicotinic acid. It's that delta version of the EACA I'm not sure of. Goddamn Redding Pharmaceuticals. I'm going to nail them, Jared. If it's the last thing I do, I'm going to nail them for what they've done."

"I know a pretty sharp lawyer who's anxious to help," he said.

"I'm afraid even you may not be that sharp, honey."

"What do you mean?"

"Well, we've got this notebook and your word that it belongs to Paquette, but beyond that all we have is me, and I'm afraid my word isn't worth too much right now."

"It will be when they see this."

"Maybe."

"Either way, we're going to try. I mean somebody's going to have to come up with a logical explanation for all this that doesn't involve Redding Pharmaceuticals, and I really don't think that's possible. Do you?"

"I hope not."

"How long do you think it will take before we hear from this resident—what's his name?"

Kate suddenly recalled a gentle, snowy evening high above Boston Harbor and felt herself blush. "Tom. Tom Engleson." Did her voice break as she said his name? "I don't know. It shouldn't be long." It had better not be, she thought.

They waited in silence. Finally, Jared adjusted his cervical collar and rubbed at his open eye with the back of his hand. "Kate, there's something else, something I have to tell you," he said. "It has a good deal to do with what you were saying before about your word not being worth too much."

She looked at him queerly.

He held her hand tightly in his. "Kate, yesterday morning I spoke to Lisa."

Kate sat in the still light of dawn, stroking Jared's forehead and feeling little joy in the realization that, in his eyes at least, she had been vindicated. Nearly fourteen years that he might have shared in some way with his daughter had been stolen. Fourteen years. His hatred of Win Samuels was almost palpable. To her, the man was pitiful—not worth hating.

She had tried her best to make Jared see that and to convince him that whatever the circumstances, no matter how much time had gone by, he had a right to be a father to his daughter. He had listened, but it was clear to her that his pain and anger were too acute for any rational planning. There would be time, she had said, as much to herself as to him. If nothing else, there would be time.

The telephone rang, startling Jared from a near sleep.

Kate had the receiver in her hand well before the first ring was complete. For several minutes, she listened, nodding understanding and speaking only as needed to encourage the caller to continue.

Jared searched her expression for a clue to Ellen's status, but saw only intense concentration.

Finally, she hung up and turned to him. "That was the hematologist," she said. "They've started her on the drugs."

"Both of them?"

Kate nodded. "Reluctantly. They wanted more of a biologic rationale than Tom was able to give them, but in the end, her condition had deteriorated so much that they abandoned the mental gymnastics. They have her on high doses of both."

451

"And?"

She shrugged. "And they'll let us know as soon as there's any change . . . one way or the other. She's still in the OR."

"She's going to make it," Jared murmured, his head sinking again to the spot beside her hand.

Less than ten minutes later, the phone rang again.

"Yes?" Kate answered anxiously. Then, "Jared, it's for you. Someone named Dunleavy. Do you know who that is?"

Bewildered, Jared nodded and took the receiver. "Dunleavy? It's Jared Samuels."

"Mr. Samuels. I'm glad you made it all right."

"Are you in trouble for letting me go?"

"Nothing I can't handle. That's not why I'm calling."

Jared glanced at his watch. Seven-fifty. Dunleavy's sixteen-hour double shift had ended almost an hour before. "Go on."

"I'm at the nurses' station in the OR, Mr. Samuels. They've just started operating on Mrs. Sandler. I think they're going to try and oversew her bleeding ulcer."

Jared put his hand over the mouthpiece. "Kate, this is the nurse who took care of me at Metro. They're operating on Ellen." He released the mouthpiece. "Thank you, Cary. Thank you for staying and calling to tell me that."

"That's only one of the reasons I called. There are two others."

"Oh?"

"I wanted you and Dr. Bennett to know I'm going to stay on and special Mrs. Sandler after she gets out of surgery."

"But you've been up for—"

"Please. I was a corpsman in Nam. I know my limitations. I feel part of all this and . . . well, I just want to stay part of it for a while longer. I'll sign off if it gets too much for me."

"Thank you," Jared said, aware that the words were not adequate.

But Dunleavy had something more to say. "I . . . I also wanted to apologize for that last crack I made about your wife." He went on, "It was uncalled for, especially since I only know what I know second or third hand. I'm sorry."

"Apology accepted," Jared said. "For what it's worth, she didn't do any of the things people are saying she did, and no matter how long it takes, we're going to prove it."

"I hope you do," Cary Dunleavy said.

"That was a curious little exchange," Kate said after Jared had replaced the phone on the bedside table. "At least the half I got to hear."

Jared recounted his conversation with the nurse for her.

"They've gone ahead with the surgery. That's great," she said, deliberately ignoring the reference to her situation. "Ellen's bleeding must have slowed enough to chance it. . . ."

Her words trailed off and Jared knew that she was thinking about her own situation. "Katey," he said. "Listen to me. Zimmermann is dead and Ellen isn't and you're not, and I'm not. And as far as I'm concerned that's cause for celebration. And I meant what I said to Dunleavy. You are innocent—of everything. And we're going to prove it. Together." He leaned over and kissed her gently. Then he straightened and said, "Rest. I'll wait with you until we hear from Metro." Kate settled back on the pillow.

A moment later, as if on cue, the day supervisor and another nurse strode into the room.

"Dr. Bennett," the supervisor said, "Dr. Jordan is in the hospital. She'll be furious if she finds out we haven't even done morning signs on her prize patient, let alone any other nursing care."

"Don't mind me," Jared said. "Nurse away."

The supervisor eyed him sternly. "There are vending machines with coffee and danish just down the hall. Miss Austin will come and get you as soon as we're through."

Jared looked over at Kate, who nodded. "I'll send for you if they call," she said.

"Very well, coffee it is." He rose and swung his parka over his shoulder with a flourish. As he did, something fell from one of its pockets and clattered to the floor by the supervisor's feet.

The woman knelt and came up holding a miniature tape cassette.

"Did that fall from my parka?" Jared asked, examining the cassette, which had no label.

"Absolutely," the supervisor said. "Isn't it yours?"

Jared looked over at Kate, the muscles in his face suddenly drawn and tense. "I've never seen that tape before." His mind was picturing smoke and flames and blood . . . and a hand desperately clawing at the pocket of his parka. "Kate, we've got to play this tape. Now." He turned to the nurses. "I'm sorry. Go do whatever else you need to do. Right now we've got to find a machine and play this."

The supervisor started to protest, but was stopped by the look in Jared's eyes. "I have a machine in my office that will hold that, if it's that important," she said.

Again, Jared saw the hand pulling at him, holding him back. *For Christ's sake, Paquette, let go of me. I'm trying to get you out of here. Let go!* "It just might be," he said. "It just might be."

"So, Norton, first that brilliant letter to the newspapers about the ballplayer and now this biopsy thing. We asked you for something creative to stop Bennett, and you certainly delivered."

The entire tape, a conversation between Arlen Paquette and Norton Reese, lasted less than fifteen minutes. Still, for the battered audience of two in room 201 of Henderson Hospital, it was more than enough.

"It was my pleasure, Doctor. Really. The woman's been a thorn in my side from the day she first got here. She's as impudent as they come. A do-gooder, always on some goddamn crusade or other. Know what I mean?"

For Kate and Jared, the excitement of Reese's disclosures was tempered by an eerie melancholy. Paquette's conscience had surfaced, but too late for him. The man whose smooth, easy voice was playing the Metro administrator like a master angler was dead—beaten, burned, and then most violently murdered.

"You know what amazes me, Norton? What amazes me is how quickly and completely you were able to eliminate her as a factor. We asked, you did. Simple as that. It was as if you were on top of her case all the time."

"In a manner of speaking I was. Actually, I was on top of her chief technician—in every sense of the word, if ya know what I mean."

"Sheila." Kate hissed the word. "You know, I tried to believe she was the one who had set me up, but I just couldn't."

"Easy, boots. If you squeeze my hand any tighter, it's going to fall off."

"Jared, a woman lost her breast. Her breast!"

"You must be some lover, sir, to command that kind of loyalty. Maybe you can give me a few pointers some time."

Maybe I can, Arlen. Actually, it wasn't that tough to get Sheila to switch biopsy specimens. She had a bone of her own to pick with our dear, lamented, soon-to-be-ex pathologist. I just sweetened the pot by letting her pick on my bone for a while beforehand.

Norton Reese's laughter reverberated through the silent hospital room, while Kate pantomimed her visceral reaction to the man.

"I wonder," Jared mused, "how the lovely Ms. Pierce is going to respond when a prosecutor from the DA's office plays this for her and asks for a statement. I bet she'll try to save herself by turning State's evidence."

"She can try anything she wants, but she's still going to lose her license. She'll never work in a hospital again."

"Well, you really stuck it to her, Norton. With that chemist from the state lab in our pocket, Bennett's father-in-law doing what he can to discredit her even more, and now this biopsy coup, I doubt she'll ever be in a position to cause us trouble at the Omnicenter again. Our friend is going to be very impressed."

"And very grateful, I would hope."

"You can't even begin to imagine the things in store for you because of what you've done, Nort. Good show. That's all I can say. Damn good show."

"We aim to please."

The tape ran through a few parting formalities before going dead.

Jared snapped off the machine and sat, looking at his wife in absolute wonder. "I would have broken," he said.

"Pardon?"

"If those things had come down on me like they did on you, I would have cracked—killed someone, maybe killed myself. I don't know what, but I know I would have gone under. It makes me sick just to think of how isolated you were, how totally alone."

"That's where you're wrong. You see, you may have had doubts about me, and justifiably so, but I never had doubts about you; so I wasn't really as alone as you might think."

"Never?"

Kate took her husband's hand and smiled. "What's a doubt or two between friends, anyway?" she asked.

$\wedge$ EPILOGUE

Friday 9 August

THOUGH IT WAS barely eight-thirty in the morning, the humidity was close to saturation and the temperature was in the mideighties. August in DC. It might have been central Africa.

Silently, Kate and Jared crossed the mall toward the Hubert H. Humphrey building and what was likely to be the final session regarding her petition to the FDA for action against Redding Pharmaceuticals.

The hearings had been emotional, draining for all concerned. Terry Moreland, a law-school classmate whom Jared had recruited to represent them, had been doing superb work, overcoming one setback after another against a phalanx of opposition lawyers and a surprisingly unsympathetic three-man panel. One moment their charges against the pharmaceutical giant would seem as irrefutable as they were terrifying, and the next, the same allegations were made to sound vindictive, capricious, and unsubstantiated. Now the end of the hearings was at hand —all that remained were brief closing statements by each side, a recess, and finally a decision.

"Yo, Kate! Jared!" Stan Willoughby, mindless of the sultry morning, trotted toward them carrying his briefcase and wearing a tweed jacket that was precisely six months out of phase with the season. He had attended all the sessions and had testified at some length as to Kate's character and qualifications. "So, this is going to be it, yes?" he said, kissing Kate on the cheek and shaking Jared's hand warmly.

Over the months that had followed the arrest and resignation of Sheila Pierce and Norton Reese, the two men, Willoughby and Jared, had formed a friendship based on more than superficial mutual respect. In fact, it had been Jared who suggested a year or two of cochairpersons for the department of pathology, and who had then cooked the dinner over which Willoughby and Kate had come up with a working arrangement for dividing administrative responsibilities.

"We can't think of anything else that could go wrong—I mean go on—this morning," Jared said.

"You were more correct the first time," said Kate. "Most of this has been pretty brutal. First, all the threads connecting that animal Nunes to Redding Pharmaceuticals evaporate like morning dew. Then, suddenly, Carl Horner gets admitted to Darlington Hospital with chest pains and gets a medical dispensation not to testify. I don't know. I just don't know."

"We still have the notebook and the tape," Jared said.

Kate laughed sardonically. "The notebook, the tape, and—you neglect to add—a dozen earnest barristers asking over and over again where the name Cyrus Redding or Redding Pharmaceuticals is mentioned even once."

"Come, come, child," Willoughby chided. "Where's that Bennett spirit? We've made points. Plenty of them. Trust this old war horse. We may not have nailed them, but we've sure stuck 'em with a bunch of tacks."

"I hope you're right," she said, as they spotted Terry Moreland waiting for them by the steps to the Humphrey building.

The gray under Moreland's eyes and the tense set of his face spoke of the difficult week just past and of the ruling that was perhaps only an hour or two away.

"How're your vibes?" Kate asked after they had exchanged greetings and words of encouragement.

Moreland shook his head. "No way to tell," he said. "Emotionally, what with your testimony and Ellen's account of her ordeal, I think we've beaten the pants off them. Unfortunately, it doesn't seem as if we have a very emotionally oriented panel. When that fat one blew his nose in the middle of the most agonizing part of Ellen's testimony, I swear, I almost hauled off and popped him one. Watching the indifference creep across his face again and again, I couldn't help wondering if he hadn't already made up his mind."

"Or had it made up for him," Jared added.

"Absolutely," Moreland said as they pushed into the air-conditioned comfort of the office building and headed up to the second floor. "That sort of thing doesn't happen too often, I don't think, but it does happen. And all you have to do is look across the room to realize what we're up against. Hell, they could buy off St. Francis of Assisi with a fraction of what those legal fees alone come to."

The hearing room, modern in decor, stark in atmosphere, was largely empty, due in part to the surprisingly scant media coverage of the proceedings. Moreland had called the dearth of press a tribute to the power of Cyrus Redding and the skill of his PR people.

Redding's battery of lawyers was present, as were two stenographers and the counsel for the Bureau of Drugs. The seats for the three hearing officers, behind individual tables on a raised dais, were still empty.

Moreland and Stan Willoughby led the way into the chamber. Kate and Jared paused by the door. Through the windows to the north, they could see the American flag hanging limply over the Senate wing of the Capitol.

"I don't know which is scarier," Kate said, "the pharmaceutical industry controlling itself or the government doing it for them. I doubt Cyrus Redding's tactics would make it very far in the Soviet Union."

"I wouldn't bet on that, Dr. Bennett."

Startled, they turned. Cyrus Redding was less than five feet from them, wheeled in his chair by a blond buck who looked like a weightlifter. The words were the first they had heard the man say since the hearings had begun.

"I have many friends—and many business interests—in the USSR," he continued. "Believe me, businessmen are businessmen the world over."

"That's wonderfully reassuring," Kate said icily. "Perhaps I'd better submit an article to the Russian medical literature on the reversal of the bleeding complications of Estronate Two-fifty."

"I assure you, Doctor, that all I know of such matters, you have taught me at these hearings. If you have a moment, I was wondering if I might speak with you."

Kate looked at Jared, who gestured that he would meet her inside and then entered the hall.

Redding motioned his young bodyguard to a bench by the far wall.

"I suspect our hearing to end this morning," he said.

"Perhaps."

"I just want you to know what high regard I have for you. You are a most remarkable, a most tenacious, young woman."

"Mr. Redding, I hope you don't expect a thank you. I appreciate compliments only from people I respect."

Redding smiled patiently. "You are still quite young and most certainly naive about certain facts."

"Such as?"

"Such as the *fact* that it costs an average of sixty million dollars just to get a new drug on the market; often, quite a bit more."

"Not impressed. Mr. Redding, because of you and your policies, people have suffered and died unnecessarily. Doesn't that weigh on you?"

"Because of me and my policies, dozens of so-called orphan drugs have found their way to those who need them, usually without cost. Because of me and my policies, millions have had the quality of their lives improved and countless more their lives saved altogether. The greatest good for the most people at the least cost."

"I guess if you didn't believe that, you'd have a tough time looking at yourself in the mirror. Maybe you do anyway. I mean, a person's denial mechanism can carry him only so far."

Redding's eyes flashed, but his demeanor remained calm. "Considering the hardship my late employee has put you through, I can understand your anger," he said. "However, soon this hearing will be over, and soon we both must go on with our lives. I would like very much to have you visit me in Darlington, so that we might discuss a mutually beneficial joint endeavor. You are a survivor, Dr. Bennett, a woman who knows better than to subvert her needs in response to petty pressures from others. That makes you a winner. And it makes me interested in doing business with you."

"Mr. Redding," she said incredulously, "you seem to be ignoring the fact that the reason we're here is so that I can put you *out* of business."

Redding's smile was painfully patronizing. "Here's my card. The number on it will always get through to me. If you succeed in putting Redding Pharmaceuticals out of business, you don't have to call."

Kate glared at him. He was too smug, too confident. Was Terry Moreland's fear about some sort of payoff justified? "We're going to win," she said, with too little conviction. She turned and, disregarding the proffered card, entered the hearing room.

"What did Dr. Strangelove want?" Jared asked as she slid in between him and Terry Moreland.

Kate shook her head disparagingly. "The man is absolutely certifiable," she said. "He told me how little understanding I had for the difficulty, trials, and tribulations of being a multimillion-dollar pharmaceutical industry tycoon, and then he offered me a job."

"A job?"

"A mutually beneficial endeavor, I think he called it."

"Lord."

At that moment, without ceremony, the door to the right of the dais opened, and the three hearing officers shuffled into their seats, their expressions suggesting that there were any number of places they would rather have been. Before he sat down, the overweight, disheveled chairman pulled a well-used handkerchief from his pocket and blew his bulbous nose.

Kate and Jared stood by the stairway, apart from the groups of lawyers, reporters, and others who filled the corridor outside the hearing room. The recess was into its second hour, and with each passing minute, the tension had grown.

If over the previous four days the Redding forces had held the upper hand, the brilliant summation and indictment by Terry Moreland had placed the final verdict very much in doubt.

Of all those in the hallway, only Cyrus Redding seemed totally composed and at ease.

"I have this ugly feeling he knows something we don't," Kate said, gesturing toward the man.

"I don't see how the panel can ignore the points Terry made in there, boots. He's even better now than he was in law school, and he was a miniature Clarence Darrow then. But I will admit that Strangelove over there looks pretty relaxed. Say, that reminds me. You never said what your response was to his offer of a job."

Kate smiled. "I thought you were never going to ask. The truth is, I told him I would be unsuitable for employment in his firm because the first thing I'd have to do is take maternity leave."

Jared stared at her. "Slide that past me one more time."

"I was saving the news until after the verdict, but what the heck. We're due in April. Jared, I'm very excited and very happy. . . . Honey, are you all right? You look a little pale."

"This is for real, right?"

Kate nodded. "You sure you're okay? I can see where going from having no children to having a fourteen-year-old daughter and a pregnant wife might be a bit, how should I say, trying."

Jared held her tightly. "I keep thinking I should say something witty, but all that wants to come out is thanks. Thank you for this and for helping me reconnect with Stacy."

"Thanks accepted, but I expect something witty from you as soon as the business in this chamber is over. And please, don't make it sound like I've done something altruistic. I'm as excited about Stacy's visit as you are."

Jared's daughter would be in Boston in just ten days. Her first trip east. It was a journey that would include visits to Cape Cod and Bunker Hill, to Gloucester and the swan boats and the Old North Church. But there would be no visit to Win Samuels. Not now, and if Jared had his way, not ever.

"Hey, you two, they're coming in," Terry Moreland called from the doorway.

"What's the worst thing the panel could do to Redding?" Kate asked, grateful that Jared had chosen not to distract his friend with the news of her pregnancy.

"I guess turning the case over to the Justice Department for further investigation and prosecution would be the biggest victory for us. A hedge might be the referral of the whole matter to administrative channels within the FDA, in order to gather more information prior to a follow-up hearing." They settled into their seats. "Either way," Moreland added, "we'll know in a minute."

Kate slid the black notebook off the table before them, and held it tightly in her lap.

"Ladies and gentleman," the chairman announced, shuffling

through a sheaf of papers and then extracting one sheet to read, "this panel has reached a unanimous decision regarding the charges brought by Dr. Kathryn Bennett against Redding Pharmaceuticals, Incorporated, of Darlington, Kentucky. It is our feeling that the late Dr. Arlen Paquette did, in fact, conduct illegal and dangerous human research on the synthetic hormone Estronate Two-fifty and that he may well have also experimented illegally with other unproven substances. However, all available evidence indicates that the man, though in the employ of Redding Pharmaceuticals, was acting on his own and for his own personal gain. There is insufficient evidence to demonstrate prior knowledge of Dr. Paquette's criminal activities by Mr. Cyrus Redding or any other director of Redding Pharmaceuticals.

"Therefore, it is our recommendation that no further action be taken on this matter, and that all charges against Redding Pharmaceuticals be considered dealt with in a fair and just manner. Thank you all for your cooperation."

Without another word, the panel rose and marched from the chamber.

Kate and the three men with her sat in stunned disbelief, while across the room, lawyers were congratulating one another boisterously.

"I don't believe it," she said. "Not a recommendation for further study, not a reprimand for hiring someone as unprincipled as Arlen Paquette, nothing."

She glanced to one side, and almost immediately her eyes locked with Cyrus Redding's. The man favored her with another of his patronizing grins, and a shrug that said, "You have to expect such things when you play hardball with the big boys, young lady."

Kate glared at him. The battle may be over, Cyrus, she was thinking, but not the war. Somewhere out there is a noose so tight that even you won't be able to wriggle free—and I'm going to find it. Reese, Horner, Sheila Pierce. Somewhere, somehow, someone's going to come forward with proof of what you've done.

Jared took her hand, and together, they walked from the hearing room. "I'm sorry," he said softly.

"Me, too. But mostly, Jared, I'm frightened."

"Frightened? I don't think they'd dare try and hurt you."

She laughed sardonically. "You heard the verdict in there. I'm sure they don't even think I'm worth bothering to hurt."

"Then what?"

"It's the damn drugs, Jared. Starting with Estronate. Think of how many human guinea pigs there are in this one notebook. We contacted as many of the women as we could find, but there are others we just couldn't locate—and, I'm sure, other drugs. How many women out there are just starting to bruise? How many people—men and women —are developing weird tumors from medications they are trusting to make them well or keep them healthy?"

461

Jared gestured helplessly. "Kate, there are injustices all around. You've done what you could do."

"It's not enough. Jared, these drugs are like time bombs—unpredictable little time bombs capable of exploding inside anyone. I've got to keep after Redding. I've got to find some way to turn some heads around here, and if not here, then publicly. Somewhere, there's got to be a way. There's—"

"What is it, Kate?"

"What about an ad?"

"An ad?"

"In *The Globe, The Herald,* all the Boston and suburban papers—a classified ad asking women to search through their medicine cabinets for Omnicenter medications we can analyze. Maybe that's where the rope is to hang that bastard and put the other companies on notice. Right in those medicine cabinets. If enough Redding products were found contaminating enough Omnicenter medications, even the FDA panel wouldn't be able to ignore the company's involvement. I'm going to do it, Jared. As soon as we get back to Boston, I'm going to do it. And if it doesn't work, I'll try something else."

She glanced back down the corridor just as Redding was wheeled into the elevator. That sound you keep hearing in your ears is my footsteps, Cyrus, she was thinking. You had better get used to it.

FLASHBACK

To N.M.S.

ACKNOWLEDGMENTS

Over the three-year birthing of *Flashback* a number of people have given me encouragement, criticism, and support. My agent, Jane Rotrosen Berkey; my publisher, Linda Grey; my editor, Beverly Lewis; my family; and many friends of Bill W. share my deepest gratitude.

M.S.P.
Falmouth, Massachusetts
1988

If I fulfill this oath and do not violate it, may it be granted to me to enjoy life and art, being honored with fame among all men and for all time to come; if I transgress it and swear falsely, may the opposite of all this be my lot.

—Conclusion of The Oath of Hippocrates;
377? B.C.

Saint Peter don't you call me
'cause I can't go.
I owe my soul to
The Company Store.

—Merle Travis

⚡ PROLOGUE

Two . . . three . . . four . . .

Toby Nelms lay on his back and counted the lights as they flashed past overhead. He was eight years old, but small even for that age, with thick red-brown hair, and freckles that ran across the tops of his cheeks and over the bridge of his nose. For a time after his father's job relocation from upstate New York to the T.J. Carter Paper Company of Sterling, New Hampshire, Toby's classmates in the Bouquette Elementary School had called him "dot face," and "shrimp," and had pushed him around in the school cafeteria. But things were better now, much better, since the day he had held his ground and absorbed a beating at the hands of Jimmy Barnes, the school bully.

Five . . . six . . . seven . . .

Toby rubbed at the lump at the top of his leg, next to his peenie, where the pain had started and still persisted. The doctors had said that the shot would take the pain away, but it hadn't.

The music that the nurses had promised would relax him wasn't helping, either. The song was okay, but there weren't any words. His hand shaking, Toby reached up and pulled the padded earphones off his head.

Eight . . . nine . . . The lights turned from white to yellow to pink, and finally to red. *Ten . . . eleven . . .*

Following the fight with Jimmy, the kids had stopped pushing him and had begun asking him to walk home with them after school. They had even elected him to be the class representative to the student council. After months of inventing illnesses to stay home, it felt so good to want to go to school again every day. Now, because of the lump, he would miss a whole week. *It wasn't fair.*

Twelve . . . thirteen . . . The red lights passing overhead grew brighter, more intense. Toby squeezed his eyes as tightly as he could, but the red grew warmer and brighter still. He tried putting his arm across them, but the hot, blood light bore through and began to sting them. Softly, he began to cry.

"Now, now, Toby, there's no need to cry. Doctor's going to fix that little bump, and then you'll be all better. Are you sure you don't want to listen to the music? Most of our patients say they feel much better because of it."

Toby shook his head and then slowly lowered his arm. The lights were gone from overhead. Instead, he saw the face of the nurse, smiling down at him. She was gray-haired and wrinkled and old—as old as Aunt Amelia. Her teeth were yellowed at the tops, and smears of bright red makeup glowed off her cheeks. As he watched, the skin on her face drew tighter, more sunken. Her wrinkles disappeared and the spaces below the red makeup, and above, where her eyes had been, became dark and hollow.

"Now, now, Toby . . . now, now . . . now, now . . ."

Once again, Toby threw his arm across his eyes, and once again, it did no good. The nurse's skin tightened still further, and then began to peel away, until the white of her bones shone through. The red dripped like blood over her skeleton face, and the holes where her eyes had been glowed.

"Now, now . . . now, now . . ."

"Let me up. Please let me up."

Toby screamed the words, but heard only a low growl, like the sound from the stereo when he turned the record with his finger.

"Let me up. Please, let me up."

The sheet was pulled from his body, and he shook from the chilly air.

"I'm cold," he cried wordlessly. "Please cover me. Please let me up. Mommy. I want my mommy."

"Okay, big fella. Up you go."

It was a man's voice, deep and slow. Toby felt hands around his ankles and beneath his arms, lifting him higher and higher off the bed with wheels, higher and higher and higher. That same music was in the room. Now, even without the earphones, he could hear it.

"Easy does it, big fella. Just relax."

Toby opened his eyes. The face above his was blurred. He blinked, then blinked once more. The face, beneath a blue cap, remained blurred. In fact, it wasn't a face at all—just skin where the eyes and nose and mouth should have been.

Again, Toby screamed. Again, there was only silence. He was floating, helpless. *Mommy, please. I want Mommy.*

"Down you go, big fella," the faceless man said.

Toby felt the cold slab beneath his back. He felt the wide strap pulled tightly across his chest. *Just the lump,* his mind whimpered. *Don't hurt my peenie. You promised. Please, don't hurt me.*

"Okay, Toby, you're going to go to sleep now. Just relax, listen to the music, and count back from one hundred like this. One hundred . . . ninety-nine . . . ninety-eight . . ."

"One hundred . . . ninety-nine . . ." Toby heard his own voice say the words, but he knew he wasn't speaking. "Ninety-eight . . . ninety-seven . . ." He felt icy cold water being swabbed over the space between his belly and the top of his leg—first over the lump, and then over his peenie. "Ninety-six . . . ninety-five." *Please stop. You're hurting me. Please.*

"That's it, y'all, he's under. Ready, Jack? Team?" The voice, a man's, was one Toby had heard before. But where? Where? "Okay, Marie, turn up the speakers just a hair. Good, good. Okay, then, let's have at it. Knife, please . . ."

The doctor's voice. Yes, Toby thought. That was who. The doctor who had come to see him in the emergency ward. The doctor with the kind eyes. The doctor who had promised he wouldn't . . .

A knife? What kind of knife? What for?

Then Toby saw it. Light sparked off the blade of a small silver knife as it floated downward, closer and closer to the lump above his leg. He tried to move, to push himself away, but the strap across his chest pinned his arms tightly against his sides.

For a moment, Toby's fear was replaced by confusion and a strange curiosity. He watched the thin blade glide down until it just touched the skin next to his peenie. Then pain, unlike any he had ever known, exploded through his body from the spot.

"I can feel that! I can feel that," he screamed. "Wait! Stop! I can feel that!"

The knife cut deeper, then began to move, over the top of the lump, then back toward the base of his peenie. Blood spurted out from around the blade as it slid through his skin.

Again and again, Toby screamed.

"That's it. Suction now, suction," he heard the doctor say calmly.

"Please, please, you're hurting me. I can feel that," Toby pleaded hysterically.

He kicked his feet and struggled against the wide strap with all his strength. "Mommy, Daddy. Please help me."

"Metzenbaums."

The blade of the shiny knife, now covered with blood, slid free of the gash it had made. In its place, Toby saw the points of a scissors pushing into the cut, first opening, then closing, then opening again, moving closer and closer to the base of his peenie. Each movement brought a pain so intense, it was almost beyond feeling. Almost.

"Don't you understand?" Toby screamed, struggling to speak with the reasoning tone of a grown-up, "I can feel that. It hurts. It hurts me."

The scissors drove deeper, around the base of his peenie.

"No! Don't touch that! Don't touch that!"

"Sponge, I need a sponge right here. Good, that's better. That's better."

The scissors moved further. Toby felt his peenie and his balls come free of his body.

Don't do that . . . don't do that. . . . The words were in his mind, no longer in his voice.

Again, with all his strength, Toby tried to push up against the strap across his chest. Overhead, he saw the doctor—the man whose eyes had been so kind, the man who had promised not to hurt him. He was holding something in his hand—something bloody—and he was showing it to others in the room. Toby struggled to understand what it was that he was showing, what it was that was so interesting. Then, suddenly, he knew. Terrified, he looked down at where the lump had been. It was gone, but so was his peenie . . . and his balls. In their place was nothing but a gaping, bloody hole.

In that instant, the strap across Toby's chest snapped in two. Flailing with his arms and legs, he threw himself off the table, kicking at the doctors, at the nurses, at anything he could. The bright overhead light shattered. Trays of sparkling steel instruments crashed to the floor.

"Get him, get him," he heard the doctor yell.

Toby lashed out with his feet and his fists, knocking over a shelf of bottles. Blood from one of them splattered across his legs. He ran toward the door, away from the hard table . . . away from the strap.

"Stop him! . . . Stop him!"

Strong hands caught him by the arms, but he kicked out with his feet and broke free. Moments later, the hands had him again. Powerful arms squeezed across his chest and under his chin.

"Easy, Toby, easy," the doctor said. "You're all right. You're safe. It's me. It's Daddy."

Toby twisted and squirmed with all his might.

"Toby, please. Stop. Listen to me. You're having a nightmare. It's just a dream. That's all. Just a bad dream."

Toby let up a bit, but continued to struggle. The voice wasn't the doctor's anymore.

"Okay, son, that's it. That's it. Just relax. It's Daddy. No one's going to hurt you. You're safe. No one's going to hurt you."

Toby stopped struggling. The arms across his chest and under his chin relaxed. Slowly, they turned him around. Slowly, Toby opened his eyes. His father's face, dark with concern, was inches from his.

"Toby, can you see me? It's Daddy. Do you know who I am?"

"Toby, it's Mommy. I'm here, too."

Toby Nelms stared first at his father, then at the worried face of his mother. Then, with an empty horror swelling in his chest, he slid his hand across the front of his pajama bottoms. His peenie was there, right where it was supposed to be. His balls, too.

Was this the dream?

Too weak, too confused to cry, Toby sank to the floor. His room was in shambles. Toys and books were everywhere. His bookcase had been pulled over, and the top of his desk swept clean. His radio was smashed. The small bowl, home of Benny, his goldfish, lay shattered on the rug. Benny lay dead amidst the glass.

Bob Nelms reached out to his son, but the boy pulled away.

His eyes still fixed on his parents, Toby pushed himself backward, and then up and onto his bed. Again, he touched himself.

"Toby, are you all right?" his mother asked softly.

The boy did not answer. Instead, he pulled his knees to his chest, rolled over, and stared vacantly at the wall.

∧CHAPTER 1

THE DAY, SUNDAY, June 30, was warm and torpid. On New Hampshire 16, the serpentine roadway from Portsmouth almost to the Canadian border, light traffic wound lazily through waves of heated air. Far to the west, a border of heavy, violet storm clouds rimmed the horizon.

The drive north, especially on afternoons like this, was one Zack Iverson had loved for as long as he could remember. He had made the trip perhaps a hundred times, but each pass through the pastureland to the south, the villages and rolling hills, and finally, the White Mountains themselves, brought new visions, new feelings.

His van, a battered orange VW camper, was packed solid with boxes, clothes, and odd pieces of furniture. Perched on the passenger seat, Cheapdog rested his muzzle on the windowsill, savoring the infrequent opportunity to view the world with his hair blown back from in front of his eyes.

Zack reached across as he drove and scratched the animal behind one ear. With Connie gone from his life, and most of his furniture sold, Cheapdog was a rock—an island in a sea of change and uncertainty.

Change and uncertainty. Zack smiled tensely. For so many years, June the thirtieth and July the first had been synonymous with those words. Summer jobs in high school; four separate years in college, and four more in medical school; internship; eight years of surgical, then neurosurgical, residency—so many changes, so many significant June-the-thirtieths. Now, this day would be the last in that string—a clear slash between the first and second halves of his life.

Next year, the date would, in all likelihood, slip past as just another day.

Highway 16 narrowed and began its roller-coaster passage into the mountains. Zack glanced at his watch. Two-thirty. Frank and the Judge were at their club, probably on the fourth or fifth hole by now. Dinner wasn't until six. There was no need to hurry. He pulled off into a rest area.

Cheapdog, sensing that this was to be a stop of substance, shifted anxiously in his seat.

"That's right, mop-face," Zack said. "You get to escape for a while. But first . . ."

He took a frayed paperback from between the seats and propped it up on the dash. Instantly, the dog's squirming stopped. His head tilted.

"You appreciate, I can see, the price that must be paid for the freedom you are about to enjoy. Yes, dogs and girls, it's time for"—he took the silver dollar from his shirt pocket and read from the page—"a classic palm and transfer, Italian style."

The book, Rufo's *Magic with Coins,* was a 1950s reprint Zack had stumbled upon in a Cambridge secondhand bookstore.

Amaze your friends . . . Amuse your family . . . Impress members of the opposite sex . . . Sharpen your manual dexterity.

The four claims, embossed in faded gold leaf on the cover, each held a certain allure for him. But it was the last one of the group that clinched the sale.

"Don't you see?" he had tried to explain to a neurosurgical colleague, as he was fumbling through the exercises in Chapter One. "We're only in the O.R.—what?—a few hours a day at best. We need something like this to keep our hands agile between cases—to sharpen our manual dexterity. The way things are, we're like athletes who never practice between games, right?"

Unfortunately, although the principle behind that thought was noble enough, the implementation had given rise to a most disconcerting problem. For while Zack's hands were quite remarkable in the operating room, even for a neurosurgeon, he had as yet been unable to master even the most elementary of Rufo's tricks, and had been reduced to practicing before mirrors, animals, and those children who were unaware of his vocation.

"Okay, dog," he said, "get ready. I'm going to omit the patter that goes with this one because I can see you eyeing those birches out there. Now, I place the coin here . . . and snap my wrist like this, and . . . and *voila!* the coin it is gone. . . . Thank you, thank you. Now, I simply pass my other hand over like this, and . . ."

The silver dollar slipped from his palm, bounced off the emergency-brake lever, and clattered beneath the seat.

The dog's head tilted to the other side.

"Shit," Zack muttered. "It was the sun. The sun got in my hands. Well, sorry, dog, but one trick's all you get."

He retrieved the coin and then reached across and opened the passenger door.

Cheapdog bounded out of the camper, and in less than a minute had relieved himself on half a dozen trees, shambled down a steep, grassy slope, and belly flopped into the middle of a mountain stream.

Zack followed at a distance. He was a tall man with fine green eyes and rugged looks that Connie had once described as "pretty damn handsome . . . in a thuggy sort of way."

He wandered along the edge of the slope, working the stiffness of the drive from his bad knee and watching as Cheapdog made a kamikaze lunge at a blue jay and missed.

Do you know, boy? he wondered. *Do you know that the rehearsal's over? That we're not going back to the city again?*

He squinted up at the mountains. The Rockies, the Tetons, the Smokies, the Sierras, the northern Appalachians—an avid rock climber since his teens, he had climbed at one time or another in all of them. There was something special, though, something intimate and personal that he felt in the White Mountains and nowhere else; they seemed to be giving him a message—that the world, his life, were right where they should be.

The demands of surgical training had exacted a toll on every aspect of his existence. But of all those compromises and sacrifices, the unavoidable cutback in his climbing was the one he had accepted the most reluctantly. Now, at almost thirty-six, he was anxious to make up for lost time.

Thin Air . . . Turnabout and Fair Play . . . The Widow-Maker . . . Carson's Cliff . . . Each climb would be like rediscovering a long-lost friend.

Zack closed his eyes and breathed in the mountain air. For months he had wrestled with the choice of a career in academic medicine or one in private, small-town practice. Of all the decisions he had ever made—choosing a college, medical school, a specialty, a training program—this was the one that had proved the most trying.

And even after he had made it—after he had weighed all the pros and cons, gotten Connie's agreement, and opted to return to Sterling—his tenuous decision was challenged. The ink was barely dry on his contract with Ultramed Hospitals Corporation when Connie announced that she had been having serious second thoughts about relocating from the Back Bay to northern New Hampshire, and in fact, that she was developing a similar case of cold feet over being engaged to the sort of man who would even consider such a move.

Not two weeks later, the ring had arrived at his apartment in its original box, strapped to a bottle of Cold Duck.

Zack sighed and combed his dark brown hair back with his fingers. They were striking, expressive fingers—sinewy, and so long, even for the hands of a six-footer, that he had taken to sending to a medical supply house in Milwaukee for specially made gloves. Early on, those fingers had set him apart in the operating room, and even before that, on the rock face.

He gazed to the northwest and swore he had caught a glimpse of Mirror, an almost sheer granite face so studded with mica that summer sun exploded off it like a star going nova.

Lion Head . . . Tuckerman Ravine . . . Wall of Tears . . .

There was so much magic in the mountains, so much to look forward to. True, life in Sterling might prove less stimulating than in the city. But there would be peace and, as long as he could climb, more than enough excitement as well.

And, of course, there would be the practice itself—the challenges of being the first neurosurgeon ever in the area.

In less than twenty-four hours, he would be in his own office in the ultramodern Ultramed Physicians and Surgeons clinic, adjacent to the rejuvenated Ultramed-Davis Regional Hospital.

After three decades of preparation and sacrifice, he was finally set to get on with the business of his life—to show his world, and himself, exactly what he could do. The prospect blew gently across what apprehensions he had, scattering them like dry leaves.

Connie or no Connie, everything was going to work out fine.

Homemade bread and vegetable soup; goose paté on tiny sesame wafers; Waterford crystal wineglasses and goblets; rack of lamb with mint jelly; Royal Doulton china; sweet potatoes and rice pilaf; fresh green beans with shaved almonds; fine Irish linen.

The meal was vintage Cinnie Iverson. Zack was aware of a familiar mixture of awe and discomfort as he watched his mother, wearing an apron she had embroidered herself, flutter between kitchen and dining room, setting one course after another on the huge cherrywood table, clearing dishes away, pausing to slip in and out of conversations, even pouring water; and all the while, skillfully and steadfastly refusing offers of assistance from Lisette and himself.

The table was set for eight, although Cinnie was seldom at her seat. The Judge held sway from his immutable place at the head. His heavy, high-backed chair was not at all unlike the one behind the bench in his county courtroom. Zack had been assigned the place of honor, at the far end of the table, facing his father. Between them sat his older brother, Frank; Frank's wife, Lisette; their four-year-old twins, Lucy and Marthe; and Annie Doucette, the Iversons' housekeeper, now a widow in her late seventies and part of the family since shortly after Frank was born.

In sharp contrast to Cinnie Iverson's bustlings, the atmosphere at the table was, as usual, restrained, with periods of silence punctuating measured exchanges. Zack smiled to himself, picturing the noisy, animated chaos in the Boston Municipal Hospital cafeteria where, for the past seven years, he had eaten most of his meals. He had been raised in this house, this town, and in that respect, he belonged; but in most others, after almost seventeen years, it was as if he had packed up his belongings in Boston and moved to another planet.

Of those at the table, Zack observed, Lisette had changed the most over the years. Once a vibrant, if flighty, beauty, she had cut her hair short, eschewed any but the lightest makeup, and appeared to have settled in quite comfortably as a mother and wife. She was still trim, and certainly attractive, but the spark of adventure in her eyes, once a focus of fantasy for him, was missing. She sat between the twins, across from Frank and Annie, and reserved most of her conversation for the girls, carefully managing their etiquette, and smiling approvingly when one or the other of them entered the conversation without interrupting.

Lisette was a year younger than Zack, and for nearly two years— from the middle of his junior year at Sterling High until her one trip to visit him at Yale—she had been his first true love. The pain and confusion of that homecoming weekend in New Haven, the realization of how far apart just six weeks had taken them, marked a turning point in both their lives.

For a while after Lisette's return to Sterling, there were scattered calls from one to the other, and even a few letters. Finally, though, there was nothing.

Eventually, she moved away to Montreal and made brief stabs first at college, then marriage—to a podiatrist or optometrist, Zack thought. Following the breakup of her marriage, she had returned to Sterling, and within a year was engaged to Frank. Zack had been best man at their wedding and was godfather to the twins.

Like Lisette, Annie kept pretty much to herself, picking at, more than eating, her food, and speaking up only to bemoan, from time to time, the arthritis, or dizzy spells, or swollen ankles which kept her from being more of a help to "Madame Cinnie." It was difficult, and somewhat painful, for Zack to remember the wise, stocky woman of his boyhood, hunkered over a football then hiking it between her legs to Frank as he practiced passing to his little brother in the field behind their house.

One of the curses of being a physician was to see people, all too often, as diagnoses, and each time Zack returned home and saw Annie Doucette, he subconsciously added one or two to her list. Today Annie looked more drawn and haggard than he had ever seen her.

Frank, of all those in the room, had changed the least over the years. Now thirty-eight, he was in his fourth year as the administrator of Ultramed-Davis Hospital. He was also, if anything, slimmer, handsomer, and more confident than ever.

"What are the possibilities," Zack had once asked a genetics professor, "of two brothers sharing none of the same genes?"

The old man had smiled and patiently explained that with millions of maternal and paternal genes segregating randomly into egg and sperm, all siblings, brother or sister, were, in essence, fifty percent the same and fifty percent different.

"You should meet my brother sometime," Zack had said.

"If that's the case," the professor had countered with a wink, "then perhaps I should meet the family milkman, instead."

In the end, science had prevailed, although the notion that he and Frank were fifty percent alike was only slightly less difficult for Zack to accept than the possibility of his mother having had a child by any gene pool other than the Judge's.

It was nearly seven o'clock and the meal was winding down. The twins were getting restless, but were held in place by Lisette's glances and the prospect of Grandmama's apple pie. Although snatches of conversation had dealt with Zack's upcoming practice, most of it had centered around golf. The Judge, blind to anyone else's boredom with the subject, was on the sixteenth green of a hole-by-hole account of his match with Frank.

"Thirty feet," he said, nudging his wineglass, which in seconds was refilled by his wife. "Maybe forty. I swear, Zachary, I have never seen your brother putt like that—Marthe, a young lady does not play with her dress at the dinner table. He steps up to the ball, then looks over at me and, just as calmly as you please, says 'double or nothing.' It was—what, Frank, three dollars. . . ?"

"Five," Frank said, making no attempt to mask his ennui.

"*Mon dieu*, five. Well, I tell you, he just knocked that ball over hill and dale, right into the center of the cup for a three. The nerve. Say, maybe next weekend we can make it a threesome."

"Hey, Judge," Frank said, "leave the man alone. He's an Ultramed surgeon now. It's in his contract: no golfing for the first year." He turned to his brother, his hands raised in mock defense. "Just kidding, Zack-o, just kidding. You play any down in Boston?"

"Only the kind where you shoot it into the whale's mouth and out its tail," Zack said.

Annie laughed out loud and choked briefly on a piece of celery.

"We played that, Uncle Zack," Lucy said excitedly. "Mama took us.

Marthe hit herself in the head with her club. Will you take us again sometime?"

"Of course I will."

"You're not going away like all the other times, are you?"

"No, Lucy. I'm staying here."

"See, Marthe. I told you he wasn't going away this time. Will you take us to McDonald's, too? We never get to go except when you take us."

Zack shrunk in his seat before Lisette's reproving glare. "They get confused sometimes," he said.

"I spoke to Jess Bishop," the Judge went on. "He's membership chairman at the club. You remember him, Zachary? Well, no matter. Jess says that being as your father and brother are members in good standing, you won't even have to go through the application process."

"Thank goodness," Zack said, hoping, even as he heard his own words, that the Judge would miss the facetiousness in his voice. "So, who finally won today?"

"Won? Why, me, of course," the Judge said, shifting his bulk in his chair. His Christian name was Clayton, but even his wife rarely called him anything but Judge. He was, like both his sons, over six feet, but his athlete's body had, years before, yielded to his sedentary job and rich tastes. A civic leader and chairman of the board of Davis Regional Hospital until its sale to Ultramed, the Judge had no less than six plaques tacked up in the den proclaiming him Sterling Man of the Year. He was also, though in his mid-sixties, a ten handicap. "It was close, though, Frank," he went on. "I'll give you that."

"Close," Frank humphed. "Judge, you're the one who pounded it into us that close only counts in hand grenades and horseshoes."

Again, Annie Doucette laughed out loud, and again her laugh was terminated by a fit of coughing. This time, Zack noted, she was massaging her chest after she had regained control, and her color was marginally more pale than it had been.

"You okay, Annie?" he asked.

"Fine, I'm fine," the woman said in the Maurice Chevalier accent she had never shown the least inclination to change. She lowered her hand slightly, but not completely. "Now you just stop eyeing me like you want to take out my liver or something, and go on about your talking. There'll be plenty of time for you to play doctor starting tomorrow. All my friends are busy thinking up brain problems just so they can come in and see you in your office."

Before Zack could respond, Cinnie Iverson reappeared, a pie in each hand, and began her rounds of the table, insisting that everyone take a slice half again larger than he or she desired. Annie flashed him a look that warned, "Now don't you dare say anything that will upset your mother." Still, there was something about her color, about the cast of her face, that made him uneasy.

Dessert conversation was dominated by the twins, who competed with each other to give "Uncle Jacques" the more complete account of what had been happening in their lives. Completely Yankee on one side of their family and completely French-Canadian on the other, the girls were interchangeably bilingual, and as they became more and more animated, increasingly difficult to understand. What fascinated—and disturbed—Zack was the lack of outward interaction between the twins and their father, or, for that matter, between Frank and Lisette.

Perhaps it was the seating arrangement, perhaps Frank's preoccupation with issues at the hospital, in particular the arrival of his younger brother as the new neurosurgeon on the block. Whatever the reason, Zack noted that Frank had spoken scarcely a word to the girls and none, that he could recall, to Lisette. In all other respects, Frank was Frank—full of plans for expanding the scope and services of Ultramed-Davis, and tuned into every potential new real estate development and industrial move in the area.

Watching the man, listening to him expound on the risks and benefits of entering the bond market at this time, or on the possibilities of developing the meadows north of town into a shopping mall, Zack could not help but be impressed. Frank had overcome one of the most difficult obstacles in life: early success. And, Zack knew, it hadn't been easy.

A legend in three sports at Sterling High, voted class president and most likely to succeed, he had gone to Notre Dame amidst a flurry of press clippings touting him as one of the great quarterback prospects in the country. His high school grades and board scores were only average, if that, and his study habits were poor, but the coaching staff and administration at the Indiana school had promised him whatever tutoring help he might need to keep him on the field. And help him they did —at least until his passes began to fall short.

Midway through Frank's sophomore year, the angry, defensive calls and letters home began. There were too many quarterbacks. The coaches weren't paying enough attention to him. Teachers were discriminating against him because he was an athlete. Next came a series of nagging injuries—back spasms, a torn muscle, a twisted ankle. Finally, there was a visit to Cinnie and the Judge from one of the assistant coaches. Although his parents had never made him privilege to that conversation, Zack was able to piece together that Frank had developed an "attitude problem" and had become more adept at hoisting a tankard than at directing an offense.

By the middle of Frank's junior season, he was back in Sterling, working construction, complaining about his ill treatment at Notre Dame, interviewing with the coaches and administration at the University of New Hampshire, and partying. A knee injury midway through his first season at the state school put an end to his athletic career.

And as if those failures weren't enough, Frank had to endure the rising star of his younger brother, whose participation in all sports except climbing had been curtailed by a vicious skiing injury. Following that accident, Zack had suffered through a brief period of depression and rebellion, and then had quietly but steadily built a grade-point average that enabled him to be accepted at Yale—the first Sterling graduate to be so honored.

There was every reason for Frank to fold, to become embittered and jealous, to drop out. But he didn't. It took an extra year, but he got his degree. Then, to the surprise of many, he stayed on in school and earned a masters in business administration.

The walls of expectation erected by the Judge were sheer glass, but bit by bit, in his own way, Frank had scaled them, and now he was a success once again, at least in terms of lifestyle, power, and accomplishments.

Cinnie Iverson had poured the final round of coffee, and the twins had at last been allowed to leave their seats, when Frank stood and raised his half-filled wineglass.

"A toast," he announced. The others raised their glasses, and the twins insisted that theirs be refilled with milk so they could join in. "To my little brother, Zachary, who proved that brains are always better than brawn when it comes to making it in this world. It's good to have you back in Sterling."

"Amen," said the Judge.

"Amen," the twins echoed.

Zack stood and raised his glass toward Frank, wondering if anyone at the table besides himself thought the message in the toast a bit strange. For a moment, his eyes and his brother's met. Almost imperceptibly, Frank nodded. The toast was no accident. For all of his status and accomplishments, Frank still measured himself against the MD degree of his younger brother, and found himself wanting.

"To you all," Zack said finally. "And especially to my new partner in crime. Frank, I'm proud to be working with you."

"Amen," shouted the twins. "Amen."

CHAPTER 2

THE THREE OF THEM, father and sons, sat alone at the table. Outside, the storm clouds had arrived, bringing with them a premature dusk. The women were in the kitchen; Annie in the breakfast nook, Cinnie and Lisette by the sink, loading the dishwasher for the second time, chatting about the upcoming Women's Club bake sale, and keeping watch on the twins, who had taken Cheapdog out back to play in the meadow.

In a manner quite consistent with his belief that business matters and women should be separated whenever possible, the Judge had kept the conversation light until the last of them, Annie, had left the room. Then, after a few sips of coffee, he turned abruptly to Frank.

"Guy Beaulieu came to see me yesterday," he said.

"So?"

"He says Ultramed and that new surgeon, Mainwaring, have just about put him out of business at the hospital."

"Jason Mainwaring's not new, Judge," Frank said patiently. "He's been here almost two years. And no one—not him, not Ultramed, not me, not anyone—is trying to put Beaulieu out of business. Except maybe Beaulieu himself. If he'd be a little more cooperative and a little more civil to people around the hospital, none of this would be happening."

"Guy's a crusty old devil," the Judge said, "I'll grant you that. But he's also been around this town nearly as long as I have, and he's helped a lot of folks."

"What's all this about?" Zack asked. The Judge was hardly a spontaneous man, and Zack could not help but wonder if there was a reason he had postponed this conversation through four hours of golf to have it now.

Frank and the Judge measured one another, silently debating whose version of the story Zack was to hear first. The contest lasted only a few seconds.

"A short while back," the Judge began, obviously unwilling openly to concede Frank's "almost two years," "Ultramed-Davis brought a new surgeon into town: this Jason Mainwaring."

"I met him, I think," Zack said. He turned to Frank. "The tall, blond guy with the southern drawl?" Frank nodded. Zack remembered the man as somewhat distant, but polished, intense, and, during their brief contact, quite knowledgeable—more the type he would have expected to see as a university medical-center professor than as a mountain community-hospital general surgeon.

"Well," the Judge went on, "apparently Guy was already beginning to have some trouble getting a lot of his patients admitted to the hospital."

Frank sighed audibly and bit at his lower lip, making it clear that only courtesy kept him from interrupting to contest the statement.

"More and more, his patients—especially the poor French-Canadian ones—were being shipped to the county hospital in Clarion. Then rumors started floating around town about Guy's competence and all of a sudden, all the surgical cases who could pay—those with insurance, or on Medicaid—were going to this Mainwaring. I've heard some of the rumors myself and, let me tell you, they are vicious. Drinking, doing unnecessary internal exams on women, taking powerful drugs because of a small stroke . . ."

"Is there truth to any of them?" Zack asked.

During the summer between his sophomore and junior years at Yale Med, he had worked as an extern at the then Davis Regional Hospital, and Beaulieu had gone out of his way to bring him into the operating room and to nurture his growing interest in surgery. It was a concern he had never forgotten.

The Judge shook his head. "According to Guy, there have been no specific complaints from anyone. Just rumors. He says that about eighty percent of his work now is charity stuff at Clarion County, and that he hasn't operated on a non-French-Canadian patient at Ultramed for almost a year. He says the whole thing is a conspiracy to get back at him because he was so opposed to the sale of the hospital to Ultramed in the first place."

"That's ridiculous," Frank said. "Mainwaring's getting the cases because he's good and he works like hell. It's as simple as that. You know, Judge, I don't think it's fair for you to take Beaulieu's side in this thing."

Clayton Iverson slammed his hand down on the table. "Don't you ever dare tell me what's fair, young man!" he snapped. "The provisional phase in our contract with Ultramed still has a month to run. I convinced the board of trustees to sell out to them in the first place, and by God, the three weeks until our meeting and vote is more than enough time for me to convince them to exercise our option and buy the damn place back."

He breathed deeply and calmed himself.

Zack glanced over at Frank. Though he was staring at their father impassively, his hands were clenched and his knuckles were bone-white.

"And let me make this clear," the Judge went on, "I haven't taken anyone's side. As a matter of fact, Frank, I resented his implications that you were in any way involved with his problems, and I told him so. He apologized and backed off some, but he's hurt, and he's angry. I promised him I'd speak to you—both of you—about it . . . ask you to keep your eyes and ears open. I feel we owe it to him. You were too young to remember, Frank, but that man all but saved your life when your appendix burst."

Frank's fists relaxed a bit, though Zack could tell that he was still smarting from the Judge's threat. Personality clashes, power plays, and political machinations were, he knew all too well, as omnipresent and as integral a part of hospital life as IVs and bedpans. But he sensed something more to all of this—something virulent.

"Annie!"

Cinnie Iverson's cry was followed instantly by the crash of dishes. With reflexes born of years of crisis, Zack was on his feet and headed toward the kitchen as Frank and the Judge were just beginning to react.

Annie Doucette was on the floor. Her back and neck were arched, and her limbs were flailing uncontrollably in a grand mal seizure.

As Zack knelt beside the woman, he felt *the change* sweep over him. Early on, he had heard about the phenomenon from other, older docs, but did not undergo it himself until midway through his second year of residency, when he witnessed the cardiac arrest of a patient. In that moment, his world suddenly began to move in slow motion. His voice lowered and his words became more measured; he sensed his pulse rate drop and all his senses heighten. It was unlike anything he had ever experienced in similar emergencies. Movements became automatic, observations and orders instinctive. Dozens of facts and variables were processed instantly and simultaneously.

Later, with the patient successfully resuscitated and stabilized, he would learn from the nurses that he had acted quickly, decisively, and calmly. It was only after hearing their account of his performance that he realized fully what he had done.

The change had been part of him ever since.

"Mom, call an ambulance, please," he said as he rolled Annie to one side to prevent her from aspirating her own stomach contents, should she vomit. His fingertips were already at the side of her neck, feeling for a carotid pulse.

As *the change* intensified, all sense of the woman as a friend, a loved one, a patient, yielded to the objectivity of assessment. If it became necessary, in any way, to hurt in order to heal, then hurt he would.

"Frank, my medical bag is in a large carton at the back of the van. Could you get it, please?" *Please. Thank you.* The use of these words during a crisis kept everybody calmer, including, he suspected, himself.

Stroke; heart attack with arrhythmia; epilepsy; sudden internal hemorrhage causing shock; hypoglycemia; simple faint mimicking a grand mal seizure; the most likely diagnostic possibilities flowed through his mind, each accompanied by an algorithm of required observations and reactions.

Annie's color was beginning to mottle. Her back remained arched and her arms and legs continued to spasm. Her jaw was clenched far too tightly to slip any buffer between her teeth. Again and again, Zack's fingertips probed up and down along the side of her windpipe, searching for a pulse. She had had chest pain at the table. Zack felt certain of that now. Heart attack with an irregular, ineffective beat or complete cardiac standstill moved ahead of all other possibilities in his mind.

"Judge, are you okay to come down here and help? Good. I'm going to put her over on her back. If she starts to vomit, please flip her back on her side, regardless of what I'm doing. Lisette, check the time, please, and keep an eye on it."

Zack eased the woman onto her back. Her seizure was continuing, though her movements were becoming less violent. Again he checked for pulses, first at her neck, then in each groin. There were none. He delivered a sharp, two-fisted blow to the center of her chest and began rhythmic cardiac compressions as Frank arrived with his medical bag.

"Judge, please fold something up and put it beneath her neck, then lay that chair over and put her feet up on it if you can. That's it. Frank, there are some syringes with needles already attached in the bottom of the bag. I need two. Also, there's a little leather pouch with vials of medicines in it. I'll need Valium and adrenaline. That one may say 'epinephrine' on it. Mom, did you get the ambulance? Good. How long?"

"Five minutes at the most."

"Frank, can you do CPR?"

"I took the course twice."

"Good. Take over here, please, while I get some medicine into her to stop her seizing. Don't bother trying mouth-to-mouth until she stops. Just pump. You're doing fine. Everyone's doing fine." Zack placed his fingertips over the femoral artery. "A little harder, Frank, please," he said. "Time, Lisette?"

"Just over a minute."

Without bothering with a tourniquet, Zack injected Valium and adrenaline into a vein in the crook of Annie Doucette's arm. In seconds, her seizure stopped. Frank continued pumping as Zack hunched over the woman and administered half a dozen mouth-to-mouth breaths. Moments later, Annie took one on her own.

"Hold it, Frank, please," Zack said as he searched, once again, for a cartoid artery pulse. This time he felt one—slow and faint, but definite. He checked in her groin. Both femoral artery pulses were palpable.

Again, the woman took a breath, then another. *Come on, Annie*, his mind urged. *Do it again. Just one more. Just one more.*

He slipped a blood pressure cuff around her arm and then worked his stethoscope into place with one hand while he returned his other to the side of the woman's neck.

"I hear a pressure," he announced softly. "It ain't much, but for right now, it's enough."

Annie's breathing was still shallow, but much more regular. Softly, but steadily, she began to moan. Her lips were dusky, but the terrible mottling of her skin had lessened. At that moment, they heard the whoop of the ambulance, and seconds later, strobelike golden lights appeared in the living room window.

Zack looked up at his older brother, who knelt across the woman from him. For an instant, he flashed on two young boys kneeling opposite one another in a dusty, vacant lot, shooting marbles.

For ten seconds, twenty, neither man moved or spoke. Then Frank reached over and took his hand.

"Welcome to Sterling," he said.

⚡CHAPTER 3

THE AMBULANCE WAS one of several well-equipped vans owned by Ultramed-Davis and operated by the Sterling Fire Department. Zack sat beside Annie in the back, watching the monitor screen as the vehicle jounced down the narrow mountainside road toward the hospital. A young but impressively efficient paramedic knelt next to him, calling out a blood pressure reading every fifteen or twenty seconds.

Sterling, New Hampshire, was small in many ways, but Zack could see Ultramed's influence in the emergency team's response. This was big city medicine in the finest sense of the term. Annie was still unconscious, although her breathing seemed less labored and her blood pressure was inching upward.

"Eighty over sixty," the paramedic said. "It's getting a little easier to hear."

Zack nodded and adjusted the IV which the young man had inserted flawlessly, and even more rapidly than he himself could have done.

Frank had stayed behind to tend to the family and contact a cardiologist. They would meet later at the hospital.

Zachary felt tense, but he was also charged and exhilarated. When it all came together, when it all worked right, there was no comparable feeling. *Come, Watson, Come! The game is afoot.* Zack loved the quote, and often wondered if Arthur Conan Doyle, a physician, had transferred the energy of his experience with medical emergencies to his detective hero.

After a brief stretch on the highway, the ambulance slowed and turned into the long, circular driveway leading uphill to the hospital. A large, spotlighted sign at the base of the drive announced: ULTRAMED-DAVIS REGIONAL HOSPITAL—COMMUNITY AND CORPORATE AMERICA WORKING TOGETHER FOR THE BETTERMENT OF ALL.

Zack smiled to himself and wondered if he was the only one amused by the hubris of the pronouncement.

The Betterment of All.

Ultramed Hospitals Corporation and Davis Regional Hospital could certainly never be accused of setting their sights too low. Still, although he had a few lingering concerns about working for a component of what some had labeled the medical-industrial complex, his conversations with Frank and the Judge, and his investigations of the hospital and its parent company, had provided no cause to doubt the proclamation, however audacious.

Ultramed-Davis, now a modern, two-hundred-bed facility, had a proud history dating back to the turn of the century, when the Quebec-based Sisters of Charity placed ten beds in a large donated house and named it, in French, Hôpital St. Georges. Over the decades that followed, brick wings were added, until, ultimately, the old house was completely replaced. The hospital's capacity grew to fifty patients, and eventually, to eighty. In 1927, the St. Georges School of Nursing was established, and before its closing in the early seventies, produced more than 350 nurses.

In mid-1971, the ownership and administrative control of St. Georges was transferred from the Sisters of Charity to a community-based, nonprofit corporation headed by Clayton Iverson, already a Clarion County circuit judge, and was renamed after Reverend Louis Davis, the pastor who had donated the initial structure to the town.

Over the years that followed, a succession of inadequate administrators, most of them using Davis Regional as a stepping-stone to bigger and better places, made a succession of unfortunate decisions, opting too often for projects and personnel additions that looked progressive but could not support themselves financially.

Gradually, but inexorably, community support for the facility dwindled, and benefactors became scarce. Older physicians began retiring earlier than they had planned, and a lack of financial inducements kept young recruits from taking their places. Bankruptcy and closure became more than theoretical possibilities.

It was then, with the wolves howling at the hospital door, that the Ultramed Corporation appeared on the scene. A subsidiary of widely diversified RIATA International, Ultramed assailed the hospital board with slide shows, brochures, stock reports, pasteboard graphs, and more financial information on the facility than even the most diligent trustee possessed.

Suspicious of outsiders and wary of losing control of an enterprise that had, for most of a century, been at the very heart of their community, a majority of the board opposed the sale, favoring instead another bond issue and one more stab at doing things right.

Clayton Iverson, citing what he called "the bloodred writing on the wall," knew the community had no sensible alternative but to sell. By his own spirited account, he worked his way through the trustees one by one, cajoling, arguing, calling in markers. In the end, Zack had been told proudly, the vote was unanimous. Unanimous, that was, save one. Only Guy Beaulieu remained opposed, though out of respect for the Judge he declined to vote at all.

Never one to relinquish power with a hook, the Judge extracted two concessions from the corporation in exchange for the sale of the hospital: a provisional four-year period after which the board of trustees could repurchase the facility, including all improvements, for the original six-million-dollar price; and the serious consideration of his son for the position of administrator.

As near as Zack could tell from his father's account, following an exhaustive series of interviews, Ultramed had selected Frank over dozens of applicants—most with extensive hospital experience.

That decision, for whatever reasons it was made, had proved brilliant.

Orchestrated by Frank, and aided by time-tested business practices and public relations techniques, the turnabout in the hospital was immediate and impressive. New equipment and new physicians underscored the corporate theme of "A Change for the Better," and the remaining opponents of the facility—mostly in the poor and uninsured sectors of the community—experienced increasing difficulty in finding a platform from which to voice their concerns.

In just a few years, Ultramed-Davis Regional Hospital had been transported from the backwater of health care to the vanguard.

"Hang on, Doc," the ambulance driver called over his shoulder to Zack. "We're here."

Zack braced himself against Annie's stretcher as the man swung a sharp turn and backed into the brightly lit ambulance bay. Alerted by

490

the ambulance radio, a team of three nurses dressed in blue scrubs and an orderly wearing whites was poised on the concrete platform.

Before Zack could even identify himself, two of the nurses, with tight-lipped efficiency, had pulled Annie's stretcher from the ambulance and sped past him into the emergency ward.

Zack followed the stretcher to a well-equipped room marked simply, TRAUMA, and watched from the door as the team transferred Annie to a hospital litter, switched her oxygen tubing and monitor cables to the hospital console, and began a rapid assessment of her vital signs. One nurse, apparently in charge, listened briefly to Annie's chest, then took up a position at the foot of the bed, supervising the evaluation.

"Excuse me," Zack said to the woman, who wore a white lab coat over her scrubs. "Could I speak to you for a moment?"

The woman turned, and Zack felt an immediate spark of interest. She was in her early thirties, he guessed, if that, with short beach-sand hair, fine, very feminine features, and vibrant, almost iridescent, blue-green eyes. Instinctively, and quite out of character for him given the situation, Zack glanced at her left hand. There was no ring.

"I . . . I'm Dr. Iverson, Zachary Iverson," he said. *Had he actually stammered?* "I'm a neurosurgeon due to start on the staff here tomorrow. That woman we just brought in is . . . I mean was . . . sort of like my governess when I was young. Mine and my brother Frank's."

"Now there's a name I recognize," the woman said, cocking her head to one side as if appraising a painting in a museum.

"Yes," Zack said. Several seconds passed before he realized that he had not yet finished explaining what he wanted. He cleared his throat. "Well. Frank said he would arrange for a cardiologist—a Dr. Cole, I think he said his name was—to come in and take over Annie's care. Has he arrived yet?"

"No," the woman said thoughtfully. "No, he hasn't, Doctor."

Her expression was at once coy and challenging, and Zack, often oblivious to women's attempts at nonverbal interplay, felt ill-equipped to respond with an expression of his own.

"I see," he said finally, wondering if he was looking as flustered and restless as he was feeling. His ego was goading him to be assertive—to remind the woman that, while he might have momentarily been taken aback by her, he was, at least until the arrival of Dr. Cole, in charge. He cleared his throat again and, unconsciously, stood more erect. "Well, then," he went on, with a bit more officiousness than he had intended, "would you please have someone call him again. I'll be in there with Mrs. Doucette. Just send him in as soon as he gets here. Also, could you order an EKG and a portable chest X ray."

"Certainly, Doctor," the woman said as he strode past her and into the room.

Bravo, his ego cheered. *Well handled.* He glanced back over his shoulder. The woman had not yet moved. "Could you call the lab, too, please," he ordered, wishing her eyes would stop smiling at him that way. "Routine bloods."

"Certainly," she said. "Cardiac enzymes, too?"

Damn her cool, Zack thought. "Yes, of course," he responded. "Have them draw extra tubes as well. Dr. Cole can order whatever else he wants when he gets here."

He walked to the bedside without waiting for an acknowledgment of his request, and forced himself not to look back.

Annie's eyes, still closed, were beginning to flutter.

"I'm Dr. Iverson," he said to the two nurses who were attending her. "How's she doing?"

"Her pressure's up to a hundred over sixty," one of them, a husky, matronly woman in her fifties, said. "She's moved both arms and both legs, and it looks like she's about to wake up."

"Good," Zack said, aware that a portion of his thoughts, at least, were not focused on the matter at hand. He slipped his stethoscope into place and checked Annie's heart and lungs. "Annie, it's Zack," he said into her ear. "Can you hear me?"

Annie Doucette moaned softly. Then, almost imperceptibly, she nodded.

"You passed out, Annie. You're at the hospital now and you're going to be all right. Do you understand that?" Again, a nod. "Good. Just relax and rest. You're doing fine." He turned to the nurse. "Dr. Cole's due here any minute. Until he gets here, we'll just keep doing what we're doing."

The nurse looked at him queerly, then glanced over at the door. Zack followed her line of sight and found himself, once again, confronting the enigmatic ocean-green eyes. This time, though, the disconcerting woman behind them stepped forward and extended her hand.

"Dr. Iverson, I'm Dr. Suzanne Cole," she said simply.

Her expression was totally professional, but there was an unmistakable playfulness in her eyes.

Zack felt the flush in his cheeks as he reached out and shook her hand.

"I'm sorry," he mumbled. "It was sort of dumb for me to assume . . . what I mean is, you weren't exactly . . . ."

"I know," she said. Her tone suggested an apology for having allowed him to dig such a hole for himself. "I'm sure it was this outfit that confused you"—she indicated the blue scrubsuit—"but I just finished putting in a pacemaker." She nodded toward Annie, who was now fully awake and beginning to look around. "You seem to have done quite a job bringing this woman back, Dr. Iverson. Congratulations."

It was nearing midnight. Zack Iverson sat alone in the staff lounge at the back of the emergency ward, sipping tepid coffee, sorting through what had been, perhaps, the most remarkable June the thirtieth of them all, and trying to slow down his runaway fantasies concerning Suzanne Cole.

It had taken several hours to ready a bed for Annie in the coronary care unit and to effect her transfer there. During that time, Zack had stayed in the background, watching Suzanne as she managed one dangerous cardiac arrhythmia after another in the woman, balancing complex treatments against their side effects, checking monitor readouts, reviewing lab results, then, suddenly, stopping to mop Annie's brow, or to smooth errant wisps of gray hair from her forehead, or simply to bend down and whisper encouragement in her ear.

Unlike what Zack had imagined from her cool composure during their initial meeting, she was actually quite tense and frenetic during critical moments, moving from one side of the bed to the other then back, checking and rechecking to ensure that her orders were being carried out correctly. Still, while she seemed frequently on edge, she was never out of control and it was clear that the nurses were comfortable with her ways, and even more important, trusted in them.

Who are you? his mind asked over and over as he watched her work. *What are you doing up here in the boondocks?*

The Judge and Cinnie had checked in twice by phone, and around ten, Frank had stopped by. He seemed restless and irritable, and although he mentioned nothing of the episode, Zack sensed that he was still quite upset by the Judge's outburst and thinly veiled threat. Citing the need to be near the twins during the violent thunderstorm that had just erupted, he had left for home after only half an hour. But before he left, Zack had managed, in what he hoped was an offhanded way, to pump a bit of information from him regarding Suzanne Cole.

Dartmouth-trained and a member of the Ultramed-Davis staff for almost two years, she was thirty-three or thirty-four, divorced, and the mother of a six-year-old girl. In addition, she was co-owner, along with another divorcée in town, of a small art gallery and crafts shop.

Zack had tried, with little success, for a more subjective assessment of the woman, but Frank, distracted and anxious to leave, had completely missed the point.

Now, as he sat alone, Zack wondered if it was worth waiting any longer for the woman to finish her work in the unit and, as she had promised, stop by for "a hit of decaf." The nurses had told him that it was not that uncommon for Suzanne, as they called her, to spend the night in the hospital if she had a particularly sick patient, and this night —with Annie and her pacemaker case—she had two.

Who are you? What are you doing up here?

The state of infatuation with a woman was not something with which Zack was all that familiar or comfortable. A bookworm throughout his college years, and a virgin until his junior year, he had had a reasonable number of dates, and a few short-lived romances after Lisette, but no prolonged relationships until Connie. He had once described his social life in college as a succession of calls to women the day after they had met someone special.

Connie was five years younger than he, but possessed a worldliness and sophistication that he felt were missing from his life. She had an MBA degree from Northwestern, a management-track position at one of the big downtown companies, a condo in the Back Bay, a silver BMW, friends in the symphony, and an interest in impressionist painters ("Pissarro has more depth, more energy in one brush stroke, than Renoir has in a dozen canvases, don't you think?") and foreign films ("Zachary, if you would stop insisting on plot all the time, and concentrate more on the universality of the characters and the technical brilliance of the director, this film would mean more to you").

Friends of his spoke to him from time to time of what they perceived might be a mismatch, but he countered by enumerating the new awareness Connie had brought into his life. Whether he truly loved the woman or not, he was never sure, but there was no questioning that he was, for most of their time together, absolutely infatuated with her beauty, her confidence, and her style.

Her decision to break off their engagement had hurt him, but not as deeply as he first thought. And over the months that followed, he had spent what free time he had flying the radio-controlled airplane he had built in high school, exercising himself back into rock-climbing shape, hiking with Cheapdog, and horseback riding with friends along the seashore at the Cape—but not one minute at a gallery or locked in combat with a foreign film.

"Hi."

Startled, Zack knocked over his Styrofoam cup, spilling what remained of his coffee into a small pool on the veneer tabletop.

"Hi, yourself," he said as Suzanne Cole plucked a pad of napkins from the nearby counter and dabbed up the spill. Was there to be no end to his ineptitude in front of this woman?

"It would seem you might have reached the limit of your caffeine quota for the day," she said.

She had changed into street clothes—gray slacks and a bulky fisherman-knit sweater—and she looked as fresh as if she had just started the day.

"Actually," he said. "I use caffeine to override my own inherent hyperness. I think it actually slows me down."

She smiled. "I know the syndrome. I'm surprised to find you still here, what with tomorrow being your first day in the office and all."

"I wanted to be sure Annie was out of the woods. She's been pretty special to me and my family. Besides, I just finished my residency yesterday. It'll probably be months before my internal chemistry demands anything more than a fifteen-minute nap in an institutional, Naugahyde easy chair."

"I remember those chairs well," Suzanne said, leaning against the counter. "There's an old, ratty, maroon one in the cardiac fellows' room at Hitchcock that I suspect would one day have a sign on it proclaiming: 'Suzanne Cole slept here—and only here. . . .' So, it's a progress report you're after. Well, the news is good. At least for the moment. Your Annie's awake and stable, with no neurologic deficit that I can identify, although you might want to go over her in the morning. In fact, I think I'll make her your first consult, if that's okay. You did say you were going to do neurology as well as neurosurgery, yes?"

"Absolutely. I actually enjoy the puzzles nearly as much as I do the blood and guts."

Her eyes narrowed.

"You sure don't talk like a surgeon," she said. "The ones I know have signs in their rooms like: 'To cut is to cure,' and 'All the world is pre-op.' "

"Oh, I have those, too. Believe me. Only as an enlightened, Renaissance surgeon, mine say: *'Almost all the world is pre-op.' "* He pushed a chair from the table with his foot. "Here, have a seat."

"Sorry, but I can't," she said. "I've got to go. Mrs. Doucette was my third critical admission this weekend, and I have a full day tomorrow. You ought to get some sleep, too, so you'll be sharp for my consult. Good night, now." She slipped on her coat and headed for the door.

"Wait," Zack said, realizing even as he heard his own voice that the order was coming from somewhere outside his rational self—somewhere within his swirling fantasies.

"Yes?"

She turned back to him. The darkness in her eyes and the set of her face were warning him not to push matters further. He picked up on the message too late.

"I . . . um . . . I was wondering if we might have dinner or something together sometime."

Suzanne sagged visibly. "I'm sorry," she said wearily. "Thank you, but no."

Zack's fantasies stopped swirling and began floating to earth like feathers. "Oh," he said, feeling suddenly very self-conscious. "I didn't mean to . . . what I mean is, it seemed like—"

"Zack, I'm sorry for being so abrupt. It's late, and I'm bushed. I appreciate your asking me, really I do. And I'm flattered. But I . . . I just don't go out with people I work with. Besides, I'm involved with someone."

The last of the feathers touched down.

Zack shrugged. "Well, then," he said with forced cheer, "I guess I should just hope that a lot of folks show up at this hospital with combined cardiac and neurosurgical disease, shouldn't I?"

Suzanne reached out and shook his hand. "I'm looking forward to working with you," she said. "I know we'll be terrific."

At that moment, from the far end of the emergency ward, a man began screaming, again and again, "No! I won't go! I'm going to die. I'm going to die!"

The two of them raced toward the commotion, which centered about an old man—in his seventies, Zack guessed—whom the nurse, the emergency physician, and a uniformed security guard were trying to move from a litter to a wheelchair.

The man, with striking, long, silver hair and a gnarled full beard, was struggling to remain where he was. Zack's gaze took in his chino pants and flannel shirt, stained with grit, sweat, and grease, and a pair of tattered, oily work boots. The old man's left arm was bound tightly across his chest with a shoulder immobilizer; the tissues over his cheek and around his right eye were badly swollen by fresh bruises.

"No!" he bellowed again. "Don't move me. I'm going to die if I go back there tonight. Please. Just one night."

"What gives?" Zack asked.

The emergency physician, a rotund, former GP in town, named Wilton Marshfield, released his hold, and the old man sank back on the litter.

"Oh, hi, Iverson, Dr. Cole," he said, nodding. "I thought you two had gone home."

"We were about to," said Zack. "Everything okay?"

He had known Marshfield, a marginally competent graduate of a now-nonexistent medical school, for years, and had been surprised to find him working in the emergency room. During a conversation earlier in the evening, the man had explained that Frank had talked him out of retirement until a personnel problem in the E.R. could be stabilized. "Plucked me off the scrap heap of medicine and offered me a salary as good as my best year in the office," was how he had put it.

"Sure, sure, everything's fine," Marshfield said. "It's just that ol' Chris Gow here doesn't understand that Ultramed-Davis is a hospital, not a bloody hotel."

"What happened to him?" Suzanne asked.

"Nothing as serious as it looks," Marshfield answered, with unconcealed disdain. "He just had a little too much of the hooch he brews up in that shack of his, and fell down his front steps. Fractured his upper arm near the shoulder, but there's not a damn thing we can do for that except ice and immobilization. Films of his facial bones are all negative, and so's the rest of his exam. Now, we've got an ambulance all set to cart him home, but the old geezer won't let us take him off the litter without a fight. We'll take care of it, though. Don't worry."

Suzanne hesitated for a moment, as if she wanted to comment on the situation, but then nodded and backed off a step.

Zack, however, brushed past the portly physician to the bedside.

"Mr. Gow, I'm Dr. Iverson," he said. The old man looked up at him, but didn't speak. His face, beneath the beard and the filth, had an ageless, almost serene quality to it, but there was a sadness in his eyes that Zack had seen many times during his years of caring for the largely indigent Boston Muni patients—a sadness born of loneliness and hopelessness. There was also no small measure of fear. "Are you in much pain?"

"Not according to him, I ain't," the man answered, still breathing heavily from his struggles. "I wonder when the last time was *he* fell down the stairs like I did and broke his arm."

"Who do you live with?"

The old man laughed mirthlessly, wincing from the pain. Then he turned his head away.

Zack looked to Marshfield for the answer.

"He lives by himself in a shack at the end of the old logging road off 219."

"Do you have a phone, Chris?"

Again, the man laughed.

"How did you get here?"

"How do you think?"

"A trucker found him sitting by the highway and brought him in," Marshfield explained. "Chris is no stranger here. He's a woodcutter. Periodically, he goes on a toot and cuts up himself instead of the wood." He laughed at his own humor and seemed not to notice that no one else joined in. "We sew him up and ship him back home until the next time."

Zack looked down at the old man. Could there be any sadder state than being sick or badly hurt, and being alone—of hoping, against hope, for someone to come and help, but knowing that no one would?

"Why can't he just be admitted for a day or two?" he asked. "Are there empty beds in the house?"

"Oh, we have beds," Marshfield said, "but ol' Chris here doesn't have any kind of insurance, and unless his problem is life-threatening, which it isn't, he either goes to Clarion County, if we want to ship him out there, or he goes home."

"What if a staff doctor insists on admitting someone who can't pay?"

Marshfield shrugged. "It doesn't happen. If it did, I guess the physician would have to answer to the adminstration. Look, Iverson, you weren't around when this hospital admitted every Tom, Dick, and Harry who came down the pike, regardless of whether they could pay or not, but I'm here to tell you, it was one helluva mess. There were some weeks when the goddamn place couldn't even meet its payroll, let alone buy any new equipment."

"This man's staying," Zack said.

The emergency physician reddened. "I told you we had things under control," he said.

Zachary glanced down at the old man. Sending him home to an isolated shack with no phone and, as likely as not, no food, went against his every instinct as a physician.

"Under control or not," he said evenly, "he's staying. Admit him to me as . . . malnutrition and syncope. I'll write orders."

Marshfield's jowly cheeks were now crimson. "It's your goddamn funeral," he said. "You're the one who's going to get called on the carpet by the administration."

"I think Frank will understand," Zack said.

This time, Marshfield laughed out loud. "There are a few docs beating the bushes out there for a job because they thought the same thing, Iverson."

"Like I said, he's being admitted."

"And like I said, it's your funeral. It's okay, Tommy," he said to the guard. "You can go on about your rounds. Dr. Social Service, here is hell-bent on learning things the hard way."

He turned on his heels and stalked away.

"Chris, you're going to stay, at least for the night," Zack said, taking the old man's good hand in his. "I'll be back to check you over in a few minutes."

The man, bewildered by the sudden change in his fortune, could only stare up at him and nod. But the corners of his eyes were glistening.

Zack turned to Suzanne. "Come on," he said, "I'll walk you outside. I can use the fresh air."

They walked through the electronically opened doorway and out onto the ambulance platform. A steady, windblown rain swept across the coal-black pavement.

"I guess I have a few adjustments to make if I'm to survive here," he said, shivering momentarily against the chill.

Suzanne flipped the hood of her trench coat over her head. "Do us all a favor," she said, "and don't make any ones you don't absolutely have to. That was a very kind thing you did in there."

"Insurance or not, that old guy's paid his dues."

"Perhaps," Suzanne said. "Yes, perhaps he has. Well, I'll see you in the morning."

"Yeah."

She turned and took several steps, then turned back. "Zack, about that dinner. How about Wednesday night? My place."

Zack felt his pulse skip. "I thought you didn't date men you worked with?"

"No policy should be without exceptions," she said. "You just made that point in there yourself, didn't you?"

"Yes. Yes, I suppose I did. But how about your . . . other involvement?"

She pushed her hood back from her forehead and smiled at him, first with her eyes, then with her lips.

"I lied," she said.

CHAPTER 4

LISETTE IVERSON stood by the glass doors of her bedroom balcony, wincing as half a dozen spears of lightning crackled through the jet sky over the Androscoggin River Valley. Far below and to the south, Sterling incandesced eerily beneath the strobe. A cannonade of thunder rumbled, then exploded, shaking the tall, hillside A-frame like a toy.

She tightened her robe and then tiptoed down the hall to check on the girls. Mercifully, after two fitful hours battling the ghosts of the storm, both were asleep. Lisette had never done well with thunderstorms herself, and felt no small guilt at having passed those fears on to her children.

God, how she wished Frank would come to bed, or at least talk to her. It was nearly one in the morning, and he was still downstairs in "his" den, staring, she knew, at the embers in "his" fireplace, and listening over and over to the album of morose, progressive jazz he favored when he was angry at her.

And as usual, she also knew, he would take his own sweet time in telling her why.

It was the job, the hospital, that kept him so tense. Lisette felt certain of it. For a year—no, much longer than that now, two at least—he had been a bear to live with. And with each passing week, each passing month, there seemed to be less and less she could do to please him. Silently, she cursed the day he had closed his business in Concord and moved back to Sterling, even if the little electronics firm was on the ropes.

To be sure, his success with Ultramed had given them more than she could ever have imagined. But as she reflected on the dashing dreamer she had fallen in love with and married, Lisette told herself the price they were paying was far too high.

For a time, she debated simply going to bed. If she did, of course, Frank would never come up. He would spend the night on the sofa in his den and would be in his office at the hospital by the time she and the twins awoke. With a sigh of resignation, she stepped into her slippers and headed down the stairs. There was no way she could outlast him. She cared, and he, for the moment at least, did not.

The situation was as simple as that.

GARFIELD MOUNTAIN
JUNIOR OLYMPIC TIME TRIALS

Sparkling like neon against the sunlit snow, the crimson and white banner said it all.

From his spot at the base of the main slope, Frankie Iverson squinted up at the giant slalom course—a rugged series of two-dozen gates marked with red and blue flags. *One more run,* he told himself. Just one more run like the last, and he would be on his way to Colorado.

The trip, the trophy, everything. After years of practice, years of frustration, they were so close now he could taste them.

"Next year will be yours," the Judge had told him during the agony and tears that had followed last year's race. "Next year Tyler will be too old to compete, and you'll be number one."

Tyler. What a joke. Why couldn't his father understand that it was the shitty way the slope had been groomed—the goddamn ruts that had caught his skis—that had caused him to lose by half a second. Not Tyler.

One more run.

"Hey, Frankie, you sleeping or what?"

Startled, Frank whirled. His brother, Zack, wearing black boots and a black racing suit, ambled toward him over a small mound of packed snow.

"Just studying the course, Zack-o," Frank said.

"As if you needed to. You could ski backward and there's still no one in this field who could catch you."

Frank jabbed a thumb toward the huge board where the times for the first run were posted. "You could."

Zack laughed out loud. "Make up three seconds on you when I've never once beaten you on a run? You've got to be kidding. Listen, all I want to do is stay on my feet and get that second place trophy. There'll be plenty of time for me next year when you're racing Seniors."

"Sure, Zack-o, sure. Lay it on any thicker and I'll slip on it. Since when did you get off thinking you could psych me?"

And psyching he was, too, the little worm, Frank thought.

They were just about two years apart in age, but Zack had hit a growth spurt just after his thirteenth birthday, and suddenly, over the

500

year that had followed, the competition between them had intensified in all sports—especially in skiing, where the gap separating them had been narrowing all winter.

Again, Frank glanced at the time board. There was a wide margin between Zack and the boy in third place. The final run was a two-man race, and his brother knew it as well as he did. He was being psyched, all right. Zack would be skiing second, right after him, and he was getting set to pull out all the stops.

"Listen, Frankie," Zack said, with that note of sincerity that Frank knew was a crock of shit, "I mean it. I'll try my best, sure. But I'll be pulling for you, too. Believe me I will." He reached out his hand. "Good luck."

Frank looked at his brother's hand and then at his face. There was something in Zack's eyes that made him almost shudder—a confidence, a determination he had never seen in them before. It was a look, though, that he knew well—a look he had faced many times in the eyes of their father. Frank hesitated for a fraction of a second and then pulled off his glove and gripped Zack's hand tightly.

"Go for it," he said.

"I will. See you up top."

Zack smiled at him, nodded, and wandered off to join a group of racers waiting for word that the second run was to begin.

Frank glanced over at the crowd of parents preparing to make their way to vantage points along the course. At that instant, the Judge, who was chatting with several friends, looked over. Frank smiled thinly, and his father responded with a hearty thumbs-up sign.

One more run.

Restless to get it over with, Frank crossed to retrieve his skis from the rack where they and those of the other competitors were lined up on end like pickets in a fence. He knew he was shaken by the brief encounter with his younger brother and by the look in his eyes. And that knowledge upset him even more.

Three seconds was a lot, true, but the way Zack had been coming on over the past few weeks, anything was possible. For a moment, Frank even toyed with the notion of asking him to back off, to wait his turn.

It wasn't fair, he thought. First that goddamn rut, now this. It was *his* year. The Judge had said so himself. Nothing was going to keep him from that trophy, that trip—nothing and no one.

He pulled his skis from the rack and ran his hand along the bottom, testing the wax.

Relax, he pleaded with himself. *Relax, but keep that edge the Judge is always talking about. That winning edge.*

It was then that he noticed Zack's black Rossignols, resting in the slot next to where his own skis had been. Trancelike, he set his skis back in their place and then took a coin—a dime—from his pocket.

This would be his year. Next year would be Zack's. That was the way it was meant to be.

He glanced about. No one was watching. Using the coin, he loosened the toe-binding screws on one of Zack's skis two turns—not enough to really feel different, just enough to lessen control a bit, to widen each turn a few inches, to preserve his three-second edge.

It was his year. His last chance. In fact, he was doing Zack a favor, ensuring that should he fall, the ski would come free and help keep him from a serious ankle injury.

But there would be no fall. No injury. Just a few inches at each gate. Just a few fractions of a second. Just enough. Next year was time enough for Zack. Then the Judge would have two Junior Olympians to boast about. It was the best way for everyone. The way things were meant to be. It was his year . . . his year. . . .

"Frank?"

The colors and sensations of that day faded as Lisette's voice nudged its way into the scene.

Frank rubbed at his eyes and then pushed himself upright on the sofa. The fire he had built against the chill of the summer storm had dwindled to a few smoldering embers. His mouth tasted foul from the two scotches—or was it three?—he had buried, and his head was pounding at the temples.

"Honey, are you all right?"

"I'm fine," he mumbled, pawing at his eyes. "Just great." It had been years since he had had that nightmare. Years.

"Frank, please, come to bed. It's after one-thirty."

"I'm not tired."

"You were sleeping."

"I wasn't fucking sleeping. I was thinking."

"Do you want anything? Some milk? A sandwich?"

"I told you, I'm fine. Just leave me alone."

It was going to be bad, he thought. He had fought the whole thing from the very beginning, but he hadn't fought hard enough. The last thing he needed in life was his brother moving back to Sterling. And now, thanks to the Judge and goddamn Leigh Baron, here Zack was, and already playing hero. He should have fought harder. Baron ran Ultramed, but Davis was still *his* goddamn hospital, and he should have fought harder.

"Frank, honey," Lisette said, "you say you're fine, but I know that's not true. You haven't said a decent word to me all night."

She tried to sweep his hair from his forehead, but he brushed her hand aside. Then he crossed unsteadily to the hearth, threw a log on the embers, and jabbed at it with the poker.

"That was quite a little show you put on this evening, Lisette," he said thickly. "Quite a little show."

"I don't know what you're talking about. Really I don't."

"Oh, give me a break. I saw you standing back there mooning over my brother. And I'm sure I wasn't the only one, either."

"Honey, that's crazy. I never . . ."

"Sure, like you never made love with him, either. Christ, it's a wonder you didn't rip your dress off right then and there in the kitchen."

"Frank, please. You've been drinking. You only say things like that to me when you've been drinking. What you know about me and Zack is all there ever was. Nothing more. And certainly nothing that didn't burn out years ago. I was excited about what he did for Annie, but so was everyone. Besides that I didn't say three words to him all night. Now please, come to bed. Let me rub your back or something."

"You go to bed. I'll be up when I'm ready."

"Frank, you believe me, don't you? I love you."

"There's only one reason, one explanation why he would have passed up all those big-time job opportunities to come back here," he said, more to himself than to her. "One reason. And that's to rub it in to me."

He splashed more scotch into his glass and downed it immediately.

"Frank, please don't have any more to—"

"He's a vindictive son of a bitch, Lisette. Beneath that mellow, do-gooder image of his, he's as vindictive as they come. And whether he admits it or not, he's got a score to settle for all those years he had to watch from the stands while everyone was cheering for me. He's got points he wants to make with Mom, with the Judge, with everyone in this damn town—even you."

"That's crazy."

"Yeah? Well, we'll see what's crazy." He stumbled against the side of the sofa and then dropped heavily onto it. "He can have this place. The hospital, the Judge, Leigh Baron, all of it except you—but only when I say so. Only after I've done what I've set out to do. Only after I've . . ."

His eyes closed and his head slumped to one side. In seconds, he was snoring.

Lisette took a blanket and drew it over him. It was the liquor talking. Nothing more. By morning it would be a wonder if Frank remembered anything of what he had just said. He loved his brother. Just as he loved her and the twins.

He just wasn't very good at showing it, that was all.

There was something tearing at him—something that had nothing to do with Zack.

Only after I've done what I set out to do. What in God's name had he meant by that?

Silently vowing to do whatever she could to get her husband through whatever it was that had him so on edge, Lisette turned and headed back up the stairs.

CHAPTER 5

THE CARTER CONFERENCE Room of Ul-
tramed-Davis, refurbished by Ultramed but originally donated to the
hospital by the paper company, was a large, all-purpose space, with
deep-pile carpeting, a speaker's table and podium at one end, and seating for close to one hundred. Metal-framed, full-color lithographs of
significant moments in medical history lined the room on either side,
and photographic portraits of past presidents of the medical staff filled
the rear wall by the door. Beneath each portrait was a small gold
plaque engraved with the officer's name, year of birth and year of
death. Beneath those photographs of past presidents still living, the
date of birth had already been engraved, followed by a hyphen and a
ghoulishly expectant space.

It was seven-thirty in the morning of Wednesday, July 3. The medical staff usually met on the first Thursday of the month, but because of
the holiday, the staff had voted to hold its July session on Wednesday
instead. The heated debate on the subject, typical for any group of
MDs, had taken up more than half of its June meeting.

Forty physicians, nearly the whole staff of Ultramed-Davis, milled
about the room, some exchanging pleasantries or bawdy stories, others
obtaining "curbside consultations" from various specialists. A few
merely stood by a window, staring wistfully at the brilliant summer day
they would never have the opportunity to enjoy.

Zack Iverson sat alone toward the back of the room, mentally trying
to match the faces and demeanors of various doctors with their medical
specialties (gray crew cut, red bow tie . . . pediatrician; forty-four long
sportcoat, thirty-four-inch waist, slightly crooked nose . . . orthopedist), and musing on his first two days in practice.

They had gone quite smoothly, with a number of consultations in
the office and several in the hospital. He had even spent a brief stretch
in the operating room, assisting one of the orthopedists in the removal
of a large calcium deposit that had entrapped a young carpenter's right
ulnar nerve at the elbow.

Several times each day, he had visited with Annie, who was progressing reasonably well in the coronary unit. He had also discharged old Chris Gow after a day and a half of good nursing care and after arranging for social services to help him get medicare coverage, physical therapy, and one meal a day at home. Contrary to Wilton Marshfield's dire prediction, there had been no repercussions from Frank or anyone else regarding the old man's hospitalization.

All in all, they had been two interesting and rewarding days—the sort that more than made up for medicine's liabilities as a career.

This day, however, was the one Zack had been awaiting. It would start with his first major case in the O.R.—the removal of a woman's ruptured cervical disc—and it would end with dinner at Suzanne's. He smiled to think of how misguided his apprehension about coming to Sterling had been.

"Okay, everyone, find a seat."

The staff president, a pale, doughy internist named Donald Norman, called out the order as he hand-shook his way to the front of the room.

Norman had interviewed Zack twice on behalf of Ultramed, and it was actually *in spite* of the man and those two sessions that Zack had decided to come to Davis at all. A graduate of one of the medical schools in the Caribbean, Norman had been subsidized and trained at Ultramed hospitals and was a company man right down the line. His portion of the interviews had consisted of little more than a mirthless litany of Ultramed procedural and medical policies, each accompanied by a set of statistics justifying the "guideline" as beneficial to the welfare of both patient and hospital.

While Norman hailed the streamlined corporate approach as "revolutionary and unquestionably necessary," Zack wondered if it amounted to a sort of gentrification of health care.

And he made no points whatever with the man by saying so.

To make matters worse between the two of them, Zack's spontaneity and relaxed, eclectic approach to medicine sat poorly with Norman, who, though no more than a year or two older than Zack, wore a three-piece suit, smoked a curved meerschaum, and generally conducted himself like some sort of aging medical padrone.

In the end, with Zack's decision still very much in the air, several of the other physicians on staff managed to convince him that Ultramed-Davis was far more flexible in its policies and philosophy than Donald Norman liked to believe.

Norman took his place at the front table and gaveled the meeting to order with the underside of an ashtray.

During the secretary's, treasurer's, and committees' reports, several latecomers straggled in, including Suzanne, looking lithe and beguiling in sandals and a floral-print dress. She was accompanied by Jason Mainwaring, who, Zack noticed in spite of himself, wore no wedding ring, although he did sport a sizable diamond on one little finger. The two took seats on the opposite side of the room and continued a whispered conversation, during which the charismatic general surgeon touched her on the arm or hand at least half a dozen times.

Zack spent a minute or two trying, unsuccessfully, to catch her eye, and then gave up and turned his attention to the meeting.

"Any additions or corrections to the committee reports?" Norman was saying. "If not, they stand accepted as read. Old business?"

One hand went up, accompanied by low groans from several parts of the room.

"Yes, Dr. Beaulieu," Norman said, taking no pains to mask the annoyance in his voice.

From his seat, five or six rows in front of Zack, Guy Beaulieu stood, looked deliberately about the room, and finally marched up to the speaker's podium—a move that prompted several more groans.

Zack, who had not seen Beaulieu in three or four years, was struck by the physical change in the man. Once energetic and robust, he was now almost pathologically thin. His suit was ill-fitting and his gaunt face had a sallow, grayish cast. Still, he held himself rigidly erect, as had always been his manner, and even at a distance, Zack could see the defiant spark behind his gold-rimmed bifocals.

"Thank you, Mr. President," Beaulieu began, with a formality that probably would have sounded unnatural and patronizing coming from most in the room, but coming from him, did not. His speech still bore an unmistakable French-Canadian flavor, especially his "th" diphthongs, which sounded more like *d*'s. "I know that many of you are becoming a bit weary with my monthly statements on behalf of those who are not being cared for by this institution, as well as against those of you who have slandered my name in this community. Well, I promise you that this will be the last in that series. So, if you will just bear with me . . ."

He removed a couple of sheets of yellow legal paper from his suit-coat pocket and spread them out on the podium. Once again, there were muted groans from several spots in the room.

Zack glanced over at Jason Mainwaring, who now sat motionless, staring impassively at the man. At that moment Suzanne turned and caught his eye. Zack waved a subtle greeting with three fingers, and she nodded in return. She seemed, even at a distance, to be preoccupied.

"I would like to inform the medical staff of Ultramed-Davis Hospital," Beaulieu read, adjusting his bifocals, "that I have retained the Concord firm of Nordstrom and Perry, and have filed a class-action suit against this hospital, its administration, its medical staff, and the Ultramed Hospitals Corporation on behalf of the poor and uninsured people in the Ultramed-Davis treatment area. I am being joined in this effort by a number of present and former patients who fall into that group, including Mr. Jean Lemoux, Mr. Ivan MacGregor, and the family of Mme. Yvette Coulombe.

"The charges, which include unlawful and callous discharge from the hospital, improper patient transfer, and refusal to treat, are currently under review by Legal Assistance of New Hampshire, who have promised a decision in the next two weeks as to whether or not they will join our effort. As I have said many times before, sound, compassionate medical care is a right of all people, not a privilege. The attitude of this facility has, over the past three years, become one of, 'Why should you get health care just because you are sick?' We intend to fight that policy."

Zack glanced around the room and catalogued myriad reactions among the physicians; few, if any of them, seemed sympathetic, and none of them appeared very threatened or upset. Some were openly exchanging looks and gestures of disgust, and one was actually circling a finger about one ear.

There are a few docs out there beating the bushes for a job because they thought the same thing, Iverson. Wilton Marshfield's warning against bucking the Ultramed system echoed in Zack's thoughts as he studied the sea of blank and disapproving expressions. Suzanne's, he noted, fell vaguely in the second group.

Beaulieu, too, paused and looked about, but then he continued as if unperturbed.

"In addition to the charges outlined above, we shall document a progressive and unethical blurring of the distinction between medical suppliers and providers, to the point where the care of patients throughout and without this facility is being compromised. We have evidence to back up our position, and every day we acquire more. It is my hope that those on the medical staff who have information which will further substantiate our claims will come forward and present such information to me or to our attorney, Mr. Everett Perry. I assure you that all such disclosures will be kept in the strictest confidence."

The man, for all of his "crustiness," as the Judge had put it, had guts, Zack acknowledged. Again he scanned the room; guts, yes, but not a speck of visible support.

"Finally," Beaulieu read on, "I would like to announce that I, personally, have initiated legal action against a member of this staff, as well as against the administration of this hospital, who are, I believe, responsible for the slanderous, inaccurate, and highly damaging rumors regarding my personal and professional conduct. I call upon any physician who has knowledge of this matter to come forward. Again, I promise strictest confidence. Remember, there but for the grace of almighty God go any one of you.

"I thank you for your patience, and would welcome your questions and comments."

Not a hand was raised. Beaulieu nodded in a calm and dignified manner, and then returned to his seat, apparently unmindful of the many annoyed and angry expressions that were fixed on him.

The staff meeting proceeded uneventfully. At the end of "new business," Zack was formally introduced and welcomed with brief, measured applause. Sensing that some verbal acknowledgment of the greeting was called for, he stood up.

"Thank you all very much," he began. "It feels great to be home again, and to be on the medical staff of the hospital in which I was born. As Dr. Norman noted in introducing me, in addition to my neurosurgical practice, I shall try to function as a medical neurologist until we are large enough, and lucky enough, to get one of our own. It is my hope to care for all those who need help in my area of expertise"— he glanced over at Guy Beaulieu—"regardless of their ability to pay.

"I would also like to thank our radiologists, Drs. Moore and Tucker, as well as my brother Frank, for their work in obtaining our CT scanner. It's a beautiful piece of equipment, and both radiologists have gone out of their way to become versed in its use. Sometime soon, the three of us plan to present some sort of workshop on the interpretation and limitations of the technique.

"Since my nearest backup is close to a hundred miles away, I'll be on twenty-four-hour call, except during my vacation, which is scheduled from August third through August fifth . . . three years from now. Thank you."

There was laughter and applause from around the room.

"Oh, one more thing," Zack added as the reaction died away. "I expected there might be some unusual problems arising from my decision to return and set up shop in the town where I was born and raised. So I'd like to make it perfectly clear that there is absolutely no truth to the rumor—started, I believe, by Dr. Blunt over there, who delivered me and was my pediatrician—that I won't go into the operating room without the one-eyed teddy bear I insisted on clinging to during his examinations."

Suzanne, with Jason Mainwaring in tow, caught up with Zack in the corridor.

"Zack, hi," she said. "Thanks for the laughs in there. Have you met Jason?"

"I think briefly, a few months ago," Zack said, shaking the surgeon's hand. "Nice to see you again."

"Same here," Mainwaring said, in a pronounced drawl. "That was a cute little speech, Iverson. I was especially partial to the line about the teddy bear."

"Thanks," Zack said, wondering if the man was being facetious.

"I even liked that other one. About your next vacation being so far away. You're a funny man."

"Thanks again."

"However," the surgeon continued, "I would caution you against makin' any more inflammatory statements about this Beaulieu business until you know all the facts. Y'see, Iverson, I'm the staff member Beaulieu alluded to in there—the one he's suin'. And noble as you tried to sound in your little pronouncement there, you and Beaulieu aren't the only ones who do charity work. I operate on plenty of folks who can't pay, too."

Zack was startled by the man's rudeness.

"Well," he said, "I'm glad to hear that. I only hope they get their money's worth."

"You know," Mainwaring countered, "I've always heard that only the most arrogant and sadistic surgeons elect to spend their professional lives suckin' on brain. . . ."

"Hey, guys, what is this?" Suzanne cut in. "This sounds like the sort of exchange you both should have put behind you when you climbed down from your tree houses and started high school. Jason, what's with you? Were you attacked in your crib by a mad neurosurgeon or something?"

Mainwaring smiled stiffly. "My apologies, Iverson," he said.

He extended his hand, but shielded from Suzanne the hostility in his eyes was icy.

"Hey, no big deal, Jason. No big deal."

"Good. Well then, we'll have to see what we can do about drummin' up a little neurosurgical business for y'all."

"Thanks."

"Meanwhile, you might try to steer clear of politics around this place—at least until you've been here long enough to learn everyone's name." He checked his gold Rolex. "Suzanne, dear, I b'lieve we still have time to complete our business. Nice to see you, Iverson. I'm sure you'll make the adjustment to this sleepy little place just fine."

Without waiting for a response, he took Suzanne's arm and strode down the hallway.

Andy O'Meara, red-cheeked, beer-bellied, and beaming, strolled among the tables of Gillie's Mountainside Tavern, shaking hands and exchanging slaps on the back with the twenty or so men enjoying their midday break in the smoky warmth. Over nearly twenty years he had come to know each and every one of them well, and was proud to call them his friends.

"Andy O, you old fart. Welcome back!" . . . "Hey, it's Mighty Mick. Way to go, Andy. Way to go. We knew you'd beat it."

First the cards and candy and flowers when he was in the hospital, and now this welcome back. They were a hell of a bunch. The very best. And at that moment, as far as Andy O'Meara was concerned, he was the luckiest man alive. Tomorrow would be Independence Day—the day for celebrating the birth of freedom. And this day was one for celebrating his own rebirth.

"Hey, Gillie," he called out, the lilt of a childhood in Kilkenny still coloring his speech. "Suds around, on me."

After three months of pain and worry, after more than a dozen trips to Manchester for radiation therapy, after sitting time and again in the doctor's office, waiting for the other shoe to fall, waiting for the news that "We can't get it all," he was back on the road, cured. The bowel cancer that had threatened his very existence was in some jar in the pathology department at Ultramed-Davis Hospital, and whatever evil cells had remained in his body had been burnt to hell by the amazing X-ray machines. The backseat and trunk of his green Chevy were once again filled with the boxes of shoes and boots and sneakers that he loved to lay out for the merchants along route 16, and the rhythm of his life had at last been restored.

"To the luck of the Irish," he proclaimed as he hoisted the frosted mug over his head.

"And to you, Andy O," Gillie responded. "We're glad to have you back among the living."

Andy O'Meara exchanged handshakes and hugs with each man in the place, and then set his half-filled tankard on the bar. It was his first frosty in more than twelve weeks, and with a full afternoon of calls ahead of him, there was no sense in putting his tolerance for the stuff to the test.

He settled up with Gillie and stepped out of the dim, pine-paneled tavern, into the sparkling afternoon sunlight. He prided himself on never being late for a call, and Colson's Factory Outlet was nearly a thirty-minute drive through the mountains.

He switched on the radio. Kenny Rogers was admonishing him to know when to hold and know when to fold. The country/western music, usually Andy's staple, seemed somehow out of keeping with the peace and serenity of this day. At the edge of the driveway he stopped and changed to a classical program on WEVO, the public station.

Better, he thought. *Much better.*

The tune was familiar. Almost instantly, it conjured up images in Andy's mind—softly falling snow . . . a stone hearth . . . a roaring fire . . . family. As he hummed along, Andy tried to remember where he had heard the haunting melody before.

". . . What child is thi-is, who laid to re-est in Mary's la-ap, lay slee-eeping? . . ."

He surprised himself by knowing many of the words.

"This, thi-is is Christ the Ki-ing, whom shepherds gua-ard and angels sing. . . ."

It was the Christmas carol, he suddenly realized. That was it. As a child in Ireland it had been one of his favorites. How strange to hear it in the middle of summer.

He paused to let a semi roar past. The noise of the truck was muted —almost as if it made no sound at all. Andy shrugged. As wonderful as it felt to be back on the road again, it also felt a little odd.

". . . Haste, ha-aste to bring him lau-au-aud, the Ba-abe, the so-on of Ma-ry. . . ."

He closed the windows, turned on the air conditioner, and swung out of the drive onto route 110. The green of the mountainside seemed uncomfortably bright. He squinted, then rubbed at his eyes and wondered if perhaps he should stop someplace to pick up a pair of sunglasses. No, he decided. No stops. At least not until after Colson's.

Settle down, old boy, he said to himself. *Just settle down.*

He adjusted the signal on the radio and settled back in his seat, humming once again.

Route 110 was two lanes wide, with a narrow breakdown space on either side. It twisted and turned, rose and dropped like an amusement-park ride, from Groveton on the Vermont border, along the ridge of the Ammonoosuc River Valley, to Sterling and Route 16. A scarred, low, white guardrail paralleled the road to Andy's right, and beyond the rail was the gorge, at places seven hundred feet deep.

Andy's restless, ill-at-ease sensation was intensifying, and he knew he was having difficulty concentrating. He adjusted his seatback and checked his safety harness. The guardrail had become something of a blur, and the solid center line kept working its way beneath his left front tire. He tightened his grip on the wheel and checked the speedometer. Forty-five. *Why did it feel like he was speeding?*

Subtly, he noticed, the trees on the mountainside had begun to darken—to develop a reddish tone. He rubbed at his eyes and, once again, forced the sedan back to the right-hand lane. Twenty-five years on the road without an accident. He was damned if he was going to have one now.

Ahead of him, the scenery dimmed. A tractor trailer approached, sunlight sparking brilliantly off its windshield.

Suddenly, Andy was aware of a voice echoing in his mind—a deep, slow, resonant, reassuring voice, at first too soft to understand, then louder . . . and louder still. "Okay, Andy," it said, "now all I want you to do is count back from one hundred . . . count back from one hundred . . . count back from one hundred . . ."

Out loud, Andy began to count. "One hundred . . . ninety-nine . . . ninety-eight . . ."

A blue drape drifted above him, then floated down over his abdomen.

"Ninety-seven . . . ninety-six . . ."

Hands, covered by rubber gloves, appeared in the space where the drape had been.

"Ninety-five . . . ninety-four . . . Why aren't I asleep?" his mind asked. "Ninety-three . . . ninety-two."

"Bove electrode, please," the low voice said. "Set it for cut and cauterize."

Another pair of gloved hands appeared, one of them holding a gauze sponge, and the other, a small rod with a metal tip. Slowly, they lowered the metal tip toward his belly.

"Ninety-one . . . ninety—"

Suddenly, a loud humming filled his mind. The metal tip of the rod touched his skin just below his navel, sending a searing, electric pain through to his back and down his legs.

"Jesus Christ, stop!" Andy screamed. "I'm not asleep! I'm not asleep!"

The wall of his lower abdomen parted beneath the electric blade, exposing a bright yellow layer of fat.

"Eighty-nine! . . . Eighty-eight! . . . For God's sake, stop! It's not working! I'm awake! I can feel that! I can feel everything!"

"Metzenbaums and pick-ups, please."

"No! Please, no!"

The Metzenbaum scissors sheared across Andy's peritoneum, parting the shiny membrane like tissue paper and exposing the glistening pink rolls of his bowel.

Again, he screamed. But this time, the sound came from his voice, as well as from within his mind.

His vision cleared at the moment the right headlight of his automobile made contact with the guardrail. The Chevy, now traveling at nearly ninety miles an hour, tore through the protective steel as if it were cardboard, crossed a narrow stretch of grass and gravel, and then hurtled over the edge of the gorge.

Strapped to his seat, Andy O'Meara watched the emerald trees flash past. In the fourth second of his fall, he realized what was happening. In the fifth, the Chevy shattered on the jagged rocks below and exploded.

CHAPTER 6

THE CAFETERIA OF Ultramed-Davis, like most of the facility, had been renovated in an airy and modern, though quite predictable, style. The interior featured a large, well-provisioned salad bar, and a wall of sliding glass doors opened onto a neat flagstone terrace with a half-dozen cement tables and benches.

Pleasantly exhausted from his three-hour cervical disc case, Zack sat at the only table partially shaded by an overhanging tree and watched as Guy Beaulieu maneuvered toward him through the lunch-time crowd.

During the summer Zack had spent as an extern at the then Davis Regional Hospital, Beaulieu had been extremely busy with his practice and with his duties as president of the medical staff. Still, the man always seemed to have enough time to stop and teach, or to reassure a frightened patient, or to console a bereaved family.

And from that summer on, the surgeon's blend of skill and compassion had remained something of a role model for Zack.

"So," Beaulieu said as he set down his tray and slid onto the stone bench opposite Zack, "thank you for agreeing to dine with me."

"Nonsense," Zack replied. "I've been looking forward to seeing you ever since I got back to town. How is your wife doing? And Marie?"

"Clothilde, bless her heart, is as good as can be expected, considering the filthy stories she has had to contend with these past two years. And as for Marie, as you may have heard, she grew weary waiting for you to propose and went ahead and married a writer—a poet of all things—from Quebec."

Zack smiled. He and Marie Beaulieu had been friends from their earliest days in grammar school, but had never been sweethearts in any sense of the word. "Knowing Marie, I'm sure he's very special," he said.

"You are correct. If she could not have you, then this man, Luc, is one I would have chosen for her. In an age when most young people seem to care for nothing but themselves, he is quite unique—consumed by the need to make a difference. He works for a village newspaper and crusades against all manner of social injustice while he waits for the world to discover his poems."

"Kids?"

"They have two children, and I don't know how on earth they manage to feed them. But manage they do."

"And they're happy," Zack said.

"Yes. Poor and crusading, but happy, and as in love—more so, perhaps—than on the day they were married."

Zack held his hands apart. *"C'est tout ce que conte, n'est ce pas?"*

Beaulieu's smile was bittersweet.

"Yes," he said. "That *is* all that matters." He paused a beat for transition. "So, your old friend Guy Beaulieu is a little short of allies in this place."

"So it sounds," Zack said, picking absently at his salad.

Beaulieu leaned forward, his eyes and his voice conspiratorial. "There is much going on here that is not right, Zachary," he whispered. "Some of what is happening is simply wrong. Some of it is evil."

Zack glanced about at the newly constructed west wing, at the helipad, at the clusters of nurses and doctors enjoying their noontime breaks on the terrace and inside the cafeteria.

"You'll understand, I hope, if I say that I see little evidence of that around me. Could you be more specific?"

"Your father spoke to you, yes?"

"Briefly."

"So you know about the lies."

"I know something of the rumors, if that's what you mean."

Beaulieu leaned even closer. "Zachary, I beg your confidence in this matter."

"That goes without asking," Zack said. "But I have to warn you of something. The Judge on Sunday, and you again this morning, suggested that at least some of your quarrel might be with Frank. You should know that I have absolutely no desire to take sides in that disagreement. Your friendship means a great deal to me. I don't know if I'd even be a surgeon today if it weren't for your influence. But Frank's my brother. I can't imagine lining up against him."

"Even if he was in the wrong?"

"In my experience, Guy, right and wrong are far more often shades of gray than black and white. Besides, I tried my hand at crusading during my years at Boston Muni. All it got me was a tension headache the size of Alaska. I should have bought stock in Tylenol before I took my first complaint to the Muni administration. I'll listen if you want to talk, but please don't expect anything."

"Thank you for the warning," Beaulieu said. "Even though I have a great fondness and respect for you, and even though, as you no doubt gathered, I haven't much support around this place, I was reluctant to share with you what I know, largely because of Frank. But then, when you said what you did at the meeting this morning—I mean about treating anyone, regardless of their ability to pay—well, I sort of took that as an invitation to talk."

Zack sighed.

"You thought correctly," he said finally. "I fight it tooth and nail, but when I'm not looking, the part of me that can't stand seeing people get screwed always seems to sneak to the surface."

"Yes, I heard what you did for that old woodcutter the other night."

"You did?"

"Don't be so surprised. This hospital, this entire town, in fact, has a communication system that would make the Department of Defense green with envy. You had best accept that fact and adjust to it if you're going to survive here. Drop a pebble in the lake and everyone—but everyone—will feel the ripple. That's why stories, such as those that have been spread about me, are so damning. In no time at all, everyone has heard a version."

"Like that old game—telephone."

"Pardon?"

"It's a party game we used to play. Everyone sits in a circle, and the first person whispers a secret to the one next to him. Then the secret goes all around the circle, and by the time it gets back to the one who started it, it has totally changed. It bothers me terribly to think that anyone would deliberately be doing anything to hurt you, especially making the sort of accusations the Judge says have been flying around."

"They are lies, you know, Zachary. Every last one of them."

Zack studied the Frenchman's face—the set of his jaw, the dark sadness engulfing his eyes. "I know, old friend," he said at last. "I know they are."

"So . . ." Beaulieu tapped his fingertips together, deciding where to begin. "What did you think of my little prepared statement this morning?" he asked finally.

"Well, the truth is, I thought you handled yourself, and expressed yourself, very well."

Beaulieu smiled. "Diplomatically put, my boy. But please, continue, and remember, my feelings are quite beyond being hurt."

Zack shrugged. "Okay, if you really want to know the truth, I kept thinking that all that was missing from the whole scenario was a horse, a lance, a shaving-bowl helment, and Sancho Panza."

This time, the older surgeon laughed out loud.

"So, you think I am tilting at a windmill, is that it? Well, my young friend, let me give you a closer look at that windmill. Richard Coulombe. Do you know him?"

"The pharmacist? Of course I know him. I called in a prescription to him just yesterday."

"And did you know that he does not own his pharmacy anymore?"

"The sign says Coulombe Drug."

"I know what the sign says. I also know that Richard is now an employee, and not a proprietor. He sold his store nearly two years ago to a chain outfit named Eagle Pharmaceuticals and Surgical Supplies. I do not know how that particular deal, with that particular company, was brought about, but I can guess now that it was no accident. Richard did not want to sell, but he needed the money to pay an enormous debt—a hospital bill and a surgeon's bill, Zachary—run up by his wife, now his late wife, Yvette, during a series of cancer operations."

Beaulieu chewed on a bite of sandwich as he gauged Zack's reaction.

"Did you perform the operations?" Zack asked.

The surgeon shook his head. "The Coulombes had been my patients for many years, but shortly before Yvette began having symptoms, the rumors about me began circulating. Like most of the other people in town, they decided, or were told—I'm still not exactly certain which—to go and see Jason Mainwaring, instead. They were also told that their insurance coverage was quite limited, but that barring complications, most of Yvette's bills would be covered."

"But complications there were."

"Four separate operations, all of them indicated and due to unforeseeable circumstances, as far as I can tell; but four nonetheless. Then there was a protracted stay in the Sterling Nursing Home. In fact, Yvette never did return home before she died."

"And, of course, there were more bills for that. I get the picture."

"Actually," Beaulieu said gravely, "you haven't gotten the picture at all . . . yet. You see, Ultramed Corporation not only owns our hospital, it now owns both nursing homes in town as well. Did you know that?"

"No," Zack said. "No, I didn't."

"The corporate name is the Leeward Company. They own nursing homes and rehabilitation centers all over the east and midwest, and about three years ago they purchased the two here in Sterling. But what not so many people know, including me until just a few months ago, is that Leeward is a division of Ultramed, bought out by them precisely four years ago. The bills for all three institutions—Ultramed-Davis and the two nursing homes—are actually spit out of the same computer. I'm not going to tell you who's in charge of that computer, but you can guess if you wish."

"I don't have to," Zack said, wondering why Frank had never mentioned the purchase of the nursing homes to him. "Coulombe's story is a very sad one, especially with the unfortunate outcome for his wife. But I see nothing evil or even immoral in it."

"That is because you are missing a piece of the puzzle," Beaulieu said. "A crucial piece. And remember," he added, "what I am about to reveal to you is just the tip of the iceberg."

"Go on," Zack said, wishing now that the man would not.

Beaulieu pulled a folded typed sheet from his jacket pocket, smoothed it out on the table, and slid it across to Zack. "As I mentioned before," he said, "I do not have too many allies in my little crusade. But I do have some. One of them has spent nearly six months traveling from place to place, trying to gather information for me. Just last week he came up with this. It's a list of the boards of directors of two companies."

Zack scanned the parallel lists of names, headed simply R and EPSS. Five of the ten names on each list were identical.

"What do these letters stand for?" he asked.

The fire in Guy Beaulieu's eyes intensified. "The R stands for RI-ATA of Boston, the megaglomerate that owns Ultramed. In a sense, they are our bosses, Zachary. Yours, mine, and every other doctor's in town."

"And the other?"

"The other, my friend, stands for Eagle Pharmaceuticals and Surgical Supplies—the corporation that bought out Richard Coulombe. Their boards of directors interlock."

Beaulieu illustrated his point by sliding the fingers of one hand between the fingers of the other.

Before he could respond, Zack saw movement at the corner of his eye. He slid the paper onto his lap at the instant a shadow fell across the table. He and Beaulieu looked up.

Frank, smiling benignly, stood not five feet away from them, holding a tray of food.

"Are you gentlemen having a heart-to-heart?" he asked. "Or do you have room at the table for one more?"

Carefully, Zack folded the sheet of paper and slid it into his pocket, although he sensed the move was a fruitless one. Frank had heard at least part of their conversation. Of that, he was almost certain.

A Bach fugue was playing on the small cassette deck by the sink. Barbara Nelms, staring glumly at the bathroom mirror, ran a finger over the furrows in her forehead and the crow's feet at the corners of her eyes. The creases had, it seemed, appeared overnight. Instinctively, she reached for her makeup kit. Then, just as quickly, she snapped off the tape, turned and walked from the bathroom. If she was bone-tired, if she was stressed close to the breaking point, if frustration and fear had aged her six years in six months, why in the hell should she try to hide it anymore?

The product of a perfectly uncomplicated unbringing in Dayton, Ohio, and four idyllic years as a business and marketing major at tiny St. Mary's College in Missouri, she had always prided herself on being a model parent, wife, citizen, and member of society. She was a registered Democrat, a voting Republican, an officer in the PTO three years running, a scout leader, a reader at church, a better than average pianist and tennis player, and, at least according to her husband, the best lover a man could ever want.

But now, after six months of haggard guidance counselors and harried school resource workers, of evasive, pompous behavioral psychologists and bewildered pediatricians, none of that mattered. She had dropped off all committees, hadn't picked up a tennis racket in weeks, and couldn't remember the last time she and Jim had had sex.

Something was wrong, terribly wrong, with her son. And not only could none of the so-called specialists they had seen diagnose the boy's problem, but each seemed bound and determined to convince her that it fell in someone else's bailiwick.

The violent episodes, occurring at first monthly, but now almost once a week, had enveloped Toby in a pall of melancholy and fear so dense that he no longer smiled or played or even spoke, except for occasional monosyllables in answer to direct questions—and then only at home.

Situational depression; delayed autism; childhood schizophrenia; developmental arrest with paranoid ideation; acting out for secondary gain; the labels and explanations for Toby's condition were as varied—and as unacceptable—as the educators and clinical specialists who had applied them.

The boy was sick, and he was getting sicker.

He had lost nearly ten pounds from a frame that had not an ounce of fat to begin with. He had stopped growing. He had failed to satisfy the requirements for promotion to the fourth grade. He avoided interacting with other children.

He had been given vitamins, antidepressants, Thorazine, Ritalin, special diets. She had taken him to Concord, and then to Boston, where he had been hospitalized for four days. Nothing. Not a single objective clue. If anything, he had returned from the medical mecca even more uncommunicative than before.

Now, as she prepared to drag her son to yet another specialist—this one a young psychiatrist, new in town, named Brookings—Barbara Nelms felt the icy, all-too-familiar fingers of hopelessness begin to take hold.

Toby's episodes at first seemed like horrible nightmares. Several times she had actually witnessed them happen—watched helplessly as her son's eyes widened and grew glassy, as he withdrew into a corner, drifting into a terrifying world he would share with no one. She had listened to his cries and had tried to hold him, to comfort him, only to be battered about the head and face by his fists.

In the end, there was nothing she could do but stay close, try her best to see that he didn't hurt himself, and wait. Sometimes the episodes would last only half an hour, sometimes much longer than that.

Always they would end with her son mute, cowering, and totally drained.

Perhaps this will be the day, she said to herself. Perhaps this man, Brookings, the first full-time psychiatrist in the valley, would have the answer.

But even as she focused on this optimistic thought, even as she buttoned her blouse and smoothed the wrinkles she should have ironed from her skirt, even as she went to her son's room to fetch him for yet another evaluation at yet another specialist's office, Barbara Nelms knew that nothing would come of it. Nothing, perhaps, except another label.

And time, she also knew, was running out.

The drive from their house to the Ultramed-Davis Physicians and Surgeons Clinic took fifteen minutes. For most of the ride, Barbara Nelms kept up a determined conversation with her son—a conversation that was essentially a monologue.

"This doctor's name is Brookings, Toby. He's new in town, and he specializes in helping people with attacks like yours. . . . We're going to get to the bottom of this, honey. We're going to find out what's wrong, and we're going to fix it. Do you understand?"

Toby sat placidly, hands folded in his lap, and stared out the window.

"It would make it easier for Dr. Brookings to do his job if you would talk to him—tell him what it is you see and feel when you have the attacks. Do you think you can try and do that? . . . Toby, please, answer me. Will you try and talk to Dr. Brookings?"

Almost imperceptibly, the boy nodded.

"That's good, honey. That's wonderful. We all just want to help. No one's going to hurt you."

Barbara Nelms thought she saw her son shudder at those words.

She swung her station wagon into one of the few spaces left in the crowded parking lot, locked her door, and then walked around the car to let Toby out. It was a promising sign that he had unbuckled his safety belt himself. Instantly, hope resurfaced.

Perhaps this would be the day.

The only other time she and Toby had been in the Ultramed-Davis Physicians and Surgeons Clinic was for a brief follow-up visit with Dr. Mainwaring. Toby's pediatrician worked out of an old Victorian house on the north side of Sterling. A directory, framed by two large ficus trees in the gleaming, tiled lobby, listed two dozen or so doctors, along with their specialties. Phillip R. Brookings, MD: Child and Adult Psychiatry was on the second of the three floors.

"Toby, do you want to take the stairs or the elevator? . . . Honey,

I promise you, Dr. Brookings just wants to talk. Now, which will it be? . . . Okay, we'll take the stairs, then."

Barbara took his hand and led him up the stairs, half wishing he would react, make some attempt to pull away. He was plastic, emotionless. Still, she could tell he was completely aware of what they were doing.

A small plaque by the door to room 202 read P.R. BROOKINGS, MD: RING BELL ONCE AND ENTER.

The waiting room was small and windowless, with textured wallpaper, an array of black-and-white photographs of mountain scenes, and seating for only four. At one side was a small children's play area, consisting primarily of dog-eared *Highlights* magazines, multicolored building blocks, and puzzles, none of which, Barbara knew, Toby would be interested in. She ached at the image of her son before it all began, huddled on the floor with his father, pouring excitely over his Erector Set.

No, Daddy, this way . . . turn it this way . . . See?

At precisely three o'clock, Phillip Brookings emerged from the inner office, introduced himself stiffly to her with a handshake and to Toby with a nod. He looked even younger than she had anticipated—no more than thirty-two or -three, she guessed, although his thick moustache made it hard to tell.

As so often had happened over the preceding months, Barbara found herself wondering if she had aged so much, or if doctors were actually getting younger.

"So," he said, taking one of the two remaining empty chairs, "welcome to my office. Toby, I appreciate your coming to see me, and I hope we can help you to feel better."

He wore a button-down shirt and tie, but no jacket, and Barbara's initial impression, despite his youth, was positive. If nothing else, he had started off on the right foot by not talking down to the boy. She glanced over at Toby, who sat gazing impassively at the photos on the wall.

"Here's the medical history form you sent us, Dr. Brookings," she said, passing the paper over. "You have the other reports I sent you?"

Brookings nodded and briefly scanned the sheet.

"I think," he said, "that if it is all right with Toby, I would like to speak with him alone in my office. What do you say, Toby? . . . We can keep the door open if you want, okay?"

He stood up and stepped back to the doorway of his inner office. "Are you coming?"

"Go ahead, honey," Barbara urged. "I'll be right here. Remember what I said. There's nothing to be afraid of."

Slowly, Toby rose from his chair.

"Wonderful," Brookings said. "Come in. Come in."

Silently, but with every fiber, Barbara Nelms cheered her son on.

He was being more cooperative, more open to this man than he had been to anyone she had taken him to in some time.

Perhaps, at last, he was ready. Perhaps . . .

She watched as Brookings disappeared into his office. From where she sat, directly opposite the doorway, she could see a roomy, comfortably furnished office with a large picture window, and plants arranged on the floor and hanging from the ceiling.

Go on, darling. Go ahead in. It's okay. It's okay.

After a brief hesitation, Toby followed Brookings in.

Then, after a single, tentative step inside the door, he stopped, his gaze riveted on the broad picture window across from him.

"Come in, Toby," Barbara heard Brookings say. "I'm not going to hurt you."

Barbara could see Toby's body stiffen. His hands, which had been hanging lifeless at his side, began to twitch.

Dear God, she thought, *he's going to have an attack. Right here. Right now.*

"Toby, are you all right?" Brookings asked.

Toby took several backward steps into the waiting room, his face chalk white, his eyes still fixed on the window.

"Honey, what's wrong?" Barbara felt her muscles tense. No one but she and her husband had ever witnessed one of the attacks before. Frightened as she was, she sensed a part of her was actually grateful for what was about to happen. At least someone else would know what they had been going through all these months.

Instinctively, she glanced about for any objects on which Toby might hurt himself.

Then, suddenly, the boy turned, threw open the outer office door, and raced out into the hall.

"Toby!" Barbara and Brookings, who had come out of his office, called out in unison.

The psychiatrist was across the waiting room and out the door before she had left her seat. Barbara reached the corridor just as he disappeared through the stairway door. Her pumps were almost impossible to run in. At the head of the stairs she kicked them off and skidded down to the first floor, falling the last three steps and skinning her shin.

As she limped into the lobby, Barbara heard the horrible screech of an automobile's tires and froze, anticipating the sickening thump of the car hitting her son. There was none. Instead, through the glass doorway, she saw him weaving through the parking lot, running as she had not seen him do in many months. Phillip Brookings was a dozen yards behind and closing.

Barbara raced across the drive, narrowly avoiding being hit by a car herself.

"Toby, stop! Please stop!"

The boy had made it beyond the parking lot and was sprinting across a stretch of thirty-or-so yards of lawn, toward the dense woods beyond. Brookings was now no more than a few steps behind him. With only a yard or two to go before the forest, the psychiatrist launched himself in a flying tackle, catching Toby at the waist and hauling him down heavily.

"Thank God," Barbara panted, hurrying across the parking lot. This was the first time, in all of his attacks, that Toby had done anything like this. Even at a distance she could tell that, although he was pinned beneath the physician, Toby was struggling. As she neared she could see his efforts lessen.

"Toby, stop that," she heard Brookings saying firmly, but gently. "Stop fighting me and I'll let go."

Barbara approached cautiously, expecting to see the familiar lost, glassy terror in her son's eyes. What she saw, instead, was a fierce, hot mix of anger and fear. It was almost as if he were snarling at the man.

Carefully, Brookings pushed himself away, although he still maintained a grip on the boy's belt.

As Barbara knelt beside her son, she realized that this was not one of his attacks after all—at least not a typical one. He was awake and alert. Whatever had set him off was in this world, not in the world locked within his mind.

"Toby, are you all right?" she asked. "What happened? What frightened you so?"

The boy did not answer.

"I'm going to let you go, Toby," Brookings said. "Promise me you won't run?"

Again, there was no response.

Slowly, Brookings released his grip on Toby's belt. The boy, still breathing heavily, did not move.

"What was it?" Barbara asked.

"Pardon?" Brookings's shirt and the knees of his tan trousers were stained with grass, and he, too, had not yet caught his breath.

"Dr. Brookings, Toby saw something out your window—something that frightened him. This wasn't one of his attacks." She turned to her son. "It wasn't, was it, honey?"

Tears glistening in his eyes, Toby stared up at her. Then he shook his head.

"Can you tell us what it was?"

This time there was no answer.

Phillip Brookings rubbed at his chin. "Mrs. Nelms, I don't know what to say. I saw Toby staring out my window, and I followed his line of sight. But there was no one there, nothing."

"Nothing?"

Brookings shook his head. "Just a big oak tree, a parking lot, and beyond it the emergency ward of the hospital. Nothing else. I'm sure of it."

The emergency ward. Barbara Nelms saw her son stiffen at the words.

"Toby, was that it? Was it the emergency ward?"

The boy remained mute.

"Dr. Brookings, what would you suggest?" she asked. "Can you help us?"

The psychiatrist looked down at Toby. "Perhaps," he said. "Perhaps with time I can. But I would like to insist on something before I begin."

"Anything."

"I want Toby to have a CT scan and a clean bill of health from a neurologist. As near as I can tell from reviewing the material you sent me, he has had neither. Correct?"

"I . . . I guess so."

"Well, if his attacks are some sort of seizure disorder, I think a neurologist should be involved, don't you?"

"Doctor, I told you when I first called, we're willing to do anything. Absolutely anything. Is there someone you can recommend?"

Brookings nodded. "There's a new man in town. Yale Med. Trained at Harvard hospitals. He's a neurosurgeon, actually, but he's doing neurology as well. His name's Iverson. Zachary Iverson. I'll give him a call and then get back to you."

Barbara stroked her son's forehead. There was nothing in his expression to suggest he had followed any of their conversation. For a moment, studying the sunken hollows around his eyes and the tense, waxy skin over his cheeks, she felt as if she were looking at a corpse.

"Please, Doctor," she said, "just one thing."

"Yes?"

"Do it quickly."

Brookings nodded, and then rose and returned to his office.

Barbara took her son by the hand and led him back to their car. Desperately, she searched her thoughts for any unpleasantness or difficulty he had encountered at Ultramed-Davis or in any other emergency ward. There was none. Nothing but a gashed chin when he was five and, of course, the incarcerated hernia operation last year.

But Barbara Nelms knew—as the surgeon, Dr. Mainwaring, had told her—that the whole hernia affair had been as routine as routine could be.

⋀CHAPTER 7

SUZANNE COLE and her six-year-old daughter, Jennifer, shared an isolated, narrow two-story north of town with a fat, yellow cat named Gulliver (". . . because," Jennifer explained, "he likes to travel") and a black Labrador retriever who seemed oblivious to any name.

The rooms in the modest place were cluttered and warm. Snow shoes, ski poles, tennis rackets, and even a pair of old stethoscopes hung on the smoke-darkened pine walls, interspersed with prints and original oils representing all manner of styles. There was a Franklin stove in the living room and a loom in one of the back bedrooms, as well as a battered spinet ("Mommy used to play a lot, but now she can only play 'Deep Purple' ") and dozens upon dozens of books.

The spaghetti dinner, Zack had been proudly informed, was largely Jennifer's creation, and she served it with a charm and enthusiasm that made almost as deep an impression on him as did her mother. She was a tall girl for her age, with an elegant nose, straight auburn hair that hung midway down her back, and Suzanne's magical eyes and smile. She talked of school and animals and ballet, and seemed quite pleased to show off her collections of rocks and stuffed animals.

In return, Zack had promised to introduce her to Cheapdog and to teach her to fly his radio-controlled plane. He even completed a relatively smooth, Italian-style thumb palm and transfer, although when he was finished, Jennifer had smiled earnestly and said, "That one could use a little more practice, Zack. I could see the coin."

By dessert—chocolate brownies with ice cream—what self-consciousness he had arrived with had long since vanished, and he found himself feeling more like a friend of the family than a guest.

If there was an uncomfortable edge to the evening at all, it was due to Suzanne, who seemed, at times, distant, distracted, and content to let Jennifer keep the conversation afloat.

But unwilling to find any fault with the woman, Zack read into her mood swings an introspection and vulnerability that only made her that much more interesting and attractive.

She was returning to the table with some coffee when Jennifer hopped up and announced that she was leaving to watch *M*A*S*H* and wash her hair.

"There's only one thing that troubles me," the girl said as she shook Zack's hand.

"What's that?"

"Well, it's your dog. I've heard of sheep dogs, but never a name like Cheapdog."

"Well," Zack said, "they're sort of the same thing." From the corner of his eye, he saw Suzanne stop and lean against the wall, watching. "You see, I was walking on the beach one morning in a place called San Diego. Do you know where that is?"

"In California?"

Zack nodded. "They have a great zoo out there and a killer whale who does advanced calculus and prepares his own tax returns. Well, there was this man on the beach—he was Mexican, but he was sort of . . . sleazy. Do you know that word? Well, it means, like, sneaky. Not all Mexicans are that way, by any means, but this guy sure was.

"Anyhow, there he was, with this big cardboard box, and in the box were a bunch of puppies—scruffy little mongrel puppies. He reached in and pulled this little fur ball up by the back of the neck. Like this. And he held him up for me to see.

" 'Señor,' he said, 'how would you like to buy this leetle fellow. I geeve you my word, señor, he is purebred, ol' Eengleesh cheapdog. His papers are een my safe at home. Buy him now, and I breeng them to you tomorrow. Si?' "

"That means yes," Jennifer said.

"Si."

"And you said? . . ."

"Si." The three of them said the word together, and laughed.

"And that's how Cheapdog got his name."

"Isn't there any old English sheep dog in him at all?" Jennifer asked.

"There must be some," Zack said, "because every time Princess Di or Prince Charles comes on the television, he stands up."

"That's silly." She thought for a moment, and then added, "I like that story." Again, she formally shook Zack's hand. Then she turned and raced up the stairs.

"Thanks again for dinner," he called out after her.

"I like that story, too," Suzanne said after the footsteps overhead had died away. "And I really liked the way you talked to Jen. Person-to-person, not grown-up to child. No condescension. And believe me, she appreciated it, too."

"Thanks. That girl doesn't encourage anything approaching kid talk, believe me."

Suzanne nodded somewhat sadly. "She's had to do a lot of growing up in a fairly short time. My marriage and divorce were a bit—how should I say—turbulent."

"Oh?"

For a moment, she looked as if she might want to expand on the remark, but then she shook her head. "Fodder for another evening," she said.

She chewed at her lower lip, rested her chin on one hand, and stared into her cup of coffee. There was a sadness in her eyes, but there was also, Zack observed, something else—a restlessness, perhaps; a tenseness in the set of the muscles in her face and neck.

"Is anything the matter?" he asked.

Suzanne hesitated, and then pushed away from the table and stood up. "I think we'd better call it a night," she said. "I have a really busy day tomorrow, and I have a lot of things to sort through before I go to bed. You've been great company—for both of us—but I guess I just need some time alone."

Nonplussed, Zack glanced at his watch. It was not yet quarter to eight.

"That's it?"

She shrugged and nodded. For a few seconds it seemed as if she were about to cry.

"I'm sorry, Zack," she said finally, "but I guess this just wasn't a good night for me to be charming and entertaining. God, it seems like all I ever do around you is apologize. Well, forgive me, anyhow. I'll make it up to you some other time. I promise."

She waited until he had stood up, and then locked her arm in his and guided him across the screened-in porch and down the wooden front steps. The subtle scent of her and the touch of her breast against his sleeve made his sudden dismissal that much more confusing and painful.

He shuffled along beside her, wishing he were less inexperienced in understanding women, and feeling totally inadequate and foolish for not knowing what to say.

At the camper, she once again apologized for cutting their evening short and promised him a rain check good for one after-dinner conversation sometime very soon. He reached for the handle and then stopped and turned back to her.

"Yes?" she asked, eyeing him appraisingly, as she had that first night.

"Suzanne, I . . . I know that something's bothering you," he heard himself say. "I only wanted to say that whatever it is, I hope it comes out the way you want."

He hesitated, expecting her to thank him politely for his concern and send him on his way.

She did neither.

"I'm afraid I've been guilty of not paying attention," he went on. "I guess I was just too busy indulging my own fantasies. Look, I just want you to know I'm glad we've met, and I'm grateful as hell we're becoming friends." He opened the door to the van. "If you ever do want to talk about whatever it is, I'm available . . . no strings attached. In fact, for a modest fee I'll even omit the coin tricks."

He moved to kiss her on the cheek, but then thought better of it and climbed up behind the wheel of the camper.

"Zack, wait a minute," she called as he began to back away. He stopped and leaned out the window. "There's a spot halfway up the hill behind the house where you can see almost the whole valley. It's really peaceful on an evening like this to sit up there and watch the lights of town wink on. If you'll give me a minute to check on Jen and get a blanket and some wine, I'd like very much to go up there with you."

"It's okay not to, you know."

She smiled in a way she hadn't all evening.

"I know," she said.

The soft evening air was filled with the hum of cicada wings and the chirping of peepers and crickets. For nearly an hour they lay side by side in the noisy silence, watching the mountain shadows stretch out across the valley. High overhead, a solitary hawk glided in effortless loops, its silhouette a dark crucifix against the perfect, blue-gray sky.

"The girls in the O.R. said you did a beautiful job on that woman's neck this morning," Suzanne said at last, sipping at what little remained of a bottle of chardonnay.

"You checked up on me?"

"Of course I checked up on you. Do you think you have a corner on the attraction-to-someone-you-just-met market?"

"No," he said, trying to ignore the sudden pounding that seemed to be lifting his chest off the blanket. "I guess not."

"Technique, high marks; speed, high marks; looks, high marks."

He grinned. "Well, I'm glad I made a decent first impression on the nurses. After nine years in various O.R.s, and all that time on rock faces, there's not too much that rattles me. This morning, though, I'll admit I was a little nervous."

"I can understand that. Doctors are *always* under a big magnifying glass of scrutiny, but never the way we are during the first few months at a new hospital. For a time after I arrived on the scene, I felt sort of like a new haircut. Everyone had to express an opinion. . . . The case you did is doing okay?"

"Pain free for the first time in a year, and moving all the parts that are supposed to move." Zack held up crossed fingers for her to see.

"That's super. You know, I'm curious. You seem like the type who would thrive on an inner-city madhouse like Boston Muni—all that action."

"Actually, I loved that part of it. But not just that there were so many cases and so much trauma to work on. I loved the patients—talking with them; getting a sense of their lives; becoming important to them; even growing into friendships with some of them. But I never was comfortable with the pressure in big teaching hospitals to become the world's expert in some little corner of neurosurgery."

Suzanne nodded. "And if you don't play it that way," she said, "then you end up being the world's expert at being passed over for promotion."

"Exactly. I also confess that I was getting a little tired of the political bullshit—the empire building and back stabbing; having to grovel before a department head or administrator just to get a lousy piece of equipment that the hospital would have been able to purchase out of petty cash if it weren't so damn inefficient."

"So you thought corporate medicine would be more stream-lined—more responsive to the needs of the hospital and the patients?"

"That's what I thought."

"You say that as if your opinion's already changed."

Zack propped his chin on his hands and stared out over the valley.

"I don't know," he said. "A few things have happened since I arrived here that . . ."

His voice trailed away. Throughout the day, he had more and more come to realize that there was no way he could discount Guy Beaulieu's claims. And if they were true—if Ultramed or Mainwaring or Frank had conspired, for whatever reason, to drive the old surgeon out of practice—then the situation in Sterling was more virulent, more frightening, more . . . unacceptable than anything he had ever encountered at Boston Muni.

He also knew that if his old mentor's concerns about the ethics and practices of Ultramed proved accurate, there would be no way he could walk away from the problem. He had returned to Sterling to practice the best possible neurosurgery in the best possible setting, and that was that.

"Hey, Doc," Suzanne said, "do you know that that last sentence of yours never quite made it out of the womb?"

He looked at her. "Fodder for another evening," he said. "I believe that's the established way out?"

"That's it, Charlie. 'Nuff said, then."

Suzanne rolled onto her side, resting her cheek on one hand. After a time, she reached over and ran her fingers lightly over his face.

"You really are quite handsome, you know," she said.

"Thanks. I have trouble believing that, especially having spent my life in the shadow of a man with Frank's looks, but it's nice to hear."

"It's nice to say."

Zack cleared his throat, which seemed to be getting drier and grittier with every passing moment. He was, at once, reluctant to touch her and even more reluctant not to.

"So," he managed, struggling to pull his thoughts from her perfect mouth, "what tale of crisis and resolution brought you to this place?"

Again, she touched his face, this time allowing her fingertips to linger on his lips. "I guess I didn't make the law of the mountain clear to you," she said. "As long as we're lying on *my* little overlook at the base of *my* mountain, I get to ask the questions. That's the law. Take it or leave it."

"But what happens to those unfortunates, like me, who don't have a mountain?"

Her eyes, and the very corners of that exquisite mouth, formed the smile that was, perhaps, her most alluring.

"In that case," she said, "you must adopt one. I'll send you the paperwork in the morning and have our social worker come by for an interview as soon as possible. Meanwhile, we'll save all that stuff from between the lines of my curriculum vitae until you get approved, okay?"

Zack shrugged. "It's your mountain."

"Exactly. It's my mountain. Do you think I'm too forward, touching you like this?"

"No. Not forward. Maybe a little tough to read, though, considering that a couple of hours ago you were trying to rush me out of the house and down the hill."

"Ah," she said, "but that was before you said the magic word."

"Oh, of course. The magic word. How stupid of me. Why, I've used that damned magic word approach so often, it's become automatic. . . . In fact, it was so automatic this time that that ol' magic word just slipped right past me."

She took his face in her hands and drew him toward her. Again, as at the dinner table, he saw a strange sadness in her eyes.

"The magic word, Zachary, was 'friend.' "

Her kisses, first on his eyes, then around his mouth, and finally over his lips, were as sweet and warm as the mountain air. For one minute, two, she held him, her tongue exploring gently beneath his lips, and then along his teeth and around the inside of his cheeks.

Finally, she drew away.

"Was that okay?" she asked.

Zack swallowed hard. "There are at least a hundred words I would pick before settling for 'okay.' "

"I'm glad. You look a little bewildered, though. I suppose I owe you some kind of apology—or at least an explanation—for being so inconsistent."

Zack ran his hand through her hair, then down her back and over the seat of her jeans. Her body was fuller than Connie's but tighter, and far, far more exciting to touch.

"You don't owe me anything," he said. "Shaw wrote that there are two tragedies in life. One is not to get one's heart's desire, and the other is to get it. At the moment, I think he was wrong about number two."

"Zack, out by the camper before you said, 'No strings attached.' Does that promise apply if we make love—right here, right now?"

"It applies." He slid his hand beneath her blouse and over her breast. Her nipple hardened instantly to his touch. "Whatever's going on, I just want to make it better."

"You're making it better," she said.

Again and again, they kissed. There was an urgency and hunger in her lips and her touch. Zack knew that it was the secret of her sadness that was driving her into his arms. He knew that, this night at least, she needed him rather than loved him.

But this night, at least, it was more than enough.

She helped him slip off his shirt and nestled her face against the hair on his chest.

"Slowly," she pleaded. "Just make it last. Please, just make it last."

Zack undid the buttons of her blouse, pausing between each one to kiss her lips and her wonderful breasts, then eased off her jeans. He worked his moistened fingertips over her nipples, then down her belly, along the edge of her soft hair, and finally to the tense nubbin of her clitoris.

"Touch me here," she murmured. "Two fingers. That's it. Oh, God, Zachary, that's it."

Moment by moment, what questions he had faded in the smoothness of her skin and in her craving for him. With every touch, every kiss, he felt himself drawn closer to her.

He brushed his lips over her ankles and along the softness of her inner thighs, and then he drew his tongue over her again and again.

She dug her nails into the skin of his back, pulling him even more tightly against her. "Don't stop. Oh, don't stop yet."

She was an angel—at once vulnerable and knowing, chaste and worldly wise. And making love with her was unlike anything Zachary had ever experienced in his life.

She drew his face to hers as she eased him onto his back, caressing him, then sucking on him until he begged her to let up.

"Now, Zachary," she whispered, her lips brushing his ear. "You're so wonderful. Please, do it now."

They made love—slowly at first, and then more fervidly; each immersed in the other; each focused on pleasing, rather than being pleased.

Darkness settled in across the valley. Far below them, the lights of Sterling flickered like so many stars, mirroring the expanse overhead.

"Zachary, what time is it?"

"Midnight. A little after, actually."

They were half dressed, bundled in the blanket against a slight, early morning chill. The connection between them had already transcended their lovemaking, and each minute, every second, it grew.

"Do you know," she said, "that in my entire life I have never come like that? What a wonderful rush."

He kissed her on the neck, then on the lips. "It must have been that chardonnay."

"Yes, of course," she said, buttoning her jeans. "How foolish of me to overlook that. Next time we'll have to try it without the wine. A controlled experiment. Just to be sure."

"My mountain?"

She laughed. "Your mountain it will be. You know, I keep saying it, but you are really a very kind and very sweet man." She kissed him lightly on the mouth. "I only hope you'll still respect me in the morning. Believe it or not, making love like this *is* a bit beyond my usual first-date fare."

"Not to worry," he said. "Doing what one wants in situations like this is a payback for all of the headaches and responsibilities of having to be a grown-up."

Her expression darkened. "Zachary, I'd like you to know what's going on—why I've been acting so weird all night. Well, almost all night."

"Listen, it's perfectly all right if—"

"No. I want to. Besides, by tomorrow night you'll know anyhow."

She rolled onto her back, took his hand, and guided it to her right breast. "The upper, outer quadrant," she said. "Fairly deep."

It took his fingers only a moment to find the lump—a disc-like mass, the diameter, perhaps, of a half dollar, and as hard as the sidewall of a tire; which was to say, too hard. His first impulse was to reassure her, to label the mass a cyst. But he knew better. There was, without a biopsy, absolutely no way to tell.

Suddenly the whole night—her distraction, her mood swings, their passion, everything—made sense.

"How long since you first felt this?" he asked.

He ached for what he now realized she was going through. If, at that moment, the lump were offered as an exam question with only one correct answer, he would have to call it trouble, all the way down the line.

And so, he knew, would she.

"A month. Six weeks now, I guess," she said. "There's been no change over that time. Mammograms were equivocal. A needle biopsy came back 'normal breast tissue,' and rather than go through that procedure a second time, I elected to go ahead with an excision, and, if necessary, a modified radical."

"When?"

"I'm going in tomorrow evening. Surgery's scheduled for Friday morning. And in case you couldn't tell, I'm scared stiff."

He held her tightly.

"I'm just grateful you didn't send me away tonight, that's all. You've made arrangements for Jennifer?"

"My partner in the gallery is going to take her. She has a son two years older than Jen."

"Good. It's going to be okay, you know."

Suzanne nodded grimly. "Just keep reminding me. I tell you, being a physician, I just know too goddamn much. And I'll tell you something else: no matter how much you read, no matter how many Donahue shows you watch, the prospect of what might happen just doesn't compute."

"It's going to be okay," he said again, forcing conviction into his voice. "You've got a friend who's going to be with you all night tomorrow. Will they be doing the excision under local?"

She shook her head.

"No," she said. "The anesthesiologist and surgeon both recommended general. And frankly, I was relieved."

"Who's the anesthesiologist?"

"Pearl. Jack Pearl."

"Good. He did my case this morning. He's a little on the weird side, I think; sort of like a character out of a Gothic horror novel. But he sure as hell knows what he's doing in the O.R. And the surgeon?"

Suzanne sighed.

"It's your friend from this morning," she said. "Jason Mainwaring. Whatever you might think of him, Zack, he's by far the best technician around."

"So I've heard. Well, I only hope his skill in the O.R. is more highly advanced than his skills in interpersonal relations."

"Oh, it is."

"In that case," Zack said, "we've only got one thing to worry about, right?"

⋀CHAPTER 8

FRANK IVERSON'S office was a spacious two-room suite on the ground floor of the west wing—the newest addition to the hospital. From his spot in one of three leather easy chairs, Zachary watched his brother's two secretaries go about their business with prim efficiency. One of the women was dark, with an air of sophistication and polish. The other was blond and wholesome. Both were young, well built, and remarkably good-looking—far beyond the run-of-the-mill in any setting, but near goddesses by Sterling's standards.

Gorgeous secretaries, a plush office, big-money business deals, a Porsche 911, a spectacular hillside A-frame—the man certainly had style, Zack mused. And while that particular style was not one Zack had ever really wished for himself, Frank had clearly come a hell of a long way from fraternity beer blasts.

Fifty percent identical. With each passing year, it seemed, the two of them were becoming less and less a validation of that genetic truth.

Still, there was a time, Zack knew, when their drives and their goals were not nearly so divergent, a time when the two brothers careened through their world along virtually parallel tracks, guided only by the beacons of early success: trophies, ribbons, medallions, and adulation.

It had become something of a game for him—a recurring daydream —to imagine his life had he *not* fallen that winter day, had the ligaments of his young knee *not* shredded.

Accidents. Illness. The violent, uncaring acts of others. The daydream, as always, led him to acknowledging how fragile life was—how totally beyond control. A patch of ice, the fraction of an inch, and suddenly, in one agonizing instant, the blinders were stripped away from his protected view of life; his unswerving track was transformed into a twisting, rutted path negotiable only one uncertain step at a time.

Zack's eyes closed as he drifted back to that day. He was in a perfect spot, racing after Frank. Three seconds was a lot, but nothing he couldn't have made up—especially with his brother being so uncharacteristically cautious on his second run.

And he wanted it. He wanted it more than he would ever admit to anyone—even, he reflected, to himself.

The colors, the packed snow, the sudden disappearance of the steady crosswind that had been blowing all day—it was a moment frozen forever in his memory. The conditions were perfect for an upset, for a demonstration to all that Zachary Iverson had suddenly come into his own. The Judge, their mother, and most of the town, it seemed, were gathered along the slope, anticipating his run.

Waiting beyond the red and blue pennants marking the slalom course was a wonderful trophy, a savings bond, a trip to the Junior Olympics, and a huge piece of the praise and newsprint that he had watched being heaped on his older brother over the years.

It was time. It was, at last, *his* moment, *his* run.

He checked the course below. No problems. A few final seconds to mentally chart his line, and he lowered his goggles and glided to the electronic starting gate.

Then, suddenly, he stopped.

Something was wrong. Something simply didn't feel right. His boot? The wax? No, he realized at the last possible second, it was his ski—his right ski. Somehow, the binding on it had come loose.

He backed away and made the necessary adjustment on the screw, cursing himself for not being more meticulous in his preparation in the first place. The oversight could have been ruinous.

But now there was nothing to stop him. It was his run, and there was nothing but two minutes of skiing between him and Colorado.

Nothing, that was, except a small patch of ice.

Zack shuddered and sensed his body recoil and stiffen as he relived some of the pain and helplessness of that fall, the bouncing and tumbling over and over again down the matted slope.

The loose binding, while never a factor, had certainly been an omen.

"Dr. Iverson, can I get you something? Some coffee?" It was one of Frank's bookend secretaries—the blonde, scrubbed and sensual. The prototypical farmer's daughter.

The impotence and anguish lingered for a moment, and then drifted away. Unconsciously, Zack rubbed at the still-hypersensitive scar that ran along his knee.

"No," he said hoarsely. "No, thanks."

He checked the time. Just four o'clock. Three forty-five, Frank had said; he had been quite specific about the time.

Zack had a consultation waiting and a small stack of paperwork in his office. Suzanne was due to sign herself into the hospital in less than two hours. The last thing in the world he needed at that moment was a meeting with Frank. However, the invitation had been couched in words that made it difficult for him to beg off, even for a day.

The fifteen-minute wait, while very annoying, was hardly surprising.

Frank had never been one to pay too much attention to the schedules of others.

"Excuse me," Zack said to the secretary, "do you have any idea how much longer he's going to be?"

The woman smiled blandly. "No, Dr. Iverson, I'm sorry, I don't. But it shouldn't be too much longer. Mr. Iverson is on the line with the Ultramed mainframe computer in Boston. He talks to it every day." She sounded very proud to be working for someone who regularly talked to a mainframe computer. "Are you sure you wouldn't like a cup of coffee? Or a Coke?"

Zack shook his head. "What I'd like," he said, standing, "is to reschedule this appointment for a time when he's able to keep it. Just tell my brother to have me paged when he's through, okay?"

"That won't be necessary, old shoe," Frank's voice boomed from the intercom on the blonde's desk. "I was just calling Annette to have her send you in. The door's open."

No explanations, no apologies.

Zack wondered how long the intercom had been turned on. The notion of being eavesdropped on did not sit well with him at all.

"Sit down, sit down," Frank sang as Zack closed the door behind him. "Are you sure you don't want the girls to get you something? A drink? Something to eat?"

"No, thanks, but go ahead if you want to."

The office was richly paneled. A floor-to-ceiling bookcase, complete with a built-in bar and sound system, covered one wall, and a huge aerial photo of Ultramed-Davis filled much of another. A computer keyboard and screen occupied only a portion of the massive mahogany desk that Frank had once proudly described to him as "a one-of-a-kind honey."

Frank himself, seated in a high-backed, brown leather chair, and dressed in a tan linen suit, silk tie, and custom-tailored shirt, looked as if he had just stepped off a page of *Gentleman's Quarterly*.

"So," he said, sliding a box of slim cigars across the desk, "how goes it?"

Zack slid the box back. "It goes fine, Frank."

"The office okay?"

"Perfect."

Zack's office, supplied and paid for by Ultramed for one year ("With the strong possibility of a second year, if all goes well"), was a neat, three-room space on the top floor of the Ultramed-Davis Physicians and Surgeons Clinic.

"Word has it you've been doing a hell of a job in the operating room."

"That's nice to hear."

"Nice for both of us. It's not too many hospitals the size of this one that can claim a full-time, Harvard-trained neurosurgeon. And, of course, I come off looking like some sort of health-care Iacocca for recruiting you."

"Frank, you didn't exactly beat down my door to get me to come."

"Nonsense. I just had some . . . some early misgivings, that's all. But the Judge and the Ultramed people helped me see the light, and now I'm really happy with the way things are turning out. You've been a real shot in the arm for the morale in this place."

"I haven't encountered any morale problems," Zack said, sensing the word was something of an introduction to the real business at hand.

"Well, we do our best to see that there are none," Frank replied. "And as you say, we do pretty well at it. But every once in a while, something or someone pops up that threatens to polarize our Ul-tramed-Davis family—turn brother against brother, as it were. And you know what they say about a house divided, right?"

"Right, Frank."

"So, Zack-o . . . Speaking of houses, how's your place?"

Oh, for crying out loud, Zack wanted to shout, *this isn't some sleazeball business adversary you have to play cat and mouse with. This is your brother. Just say what in the hell it is you want, and let's get it over with.* Instead, he folded his hands together, crossed his legs, and settled back in his chair. It was Frank's show.

"The house is beautiful, Frank," he said mechanically. "I don't know how you stumbled onto the place, but I'm certainly glad you did."

He wondered where Suzanne was at that moment, what she was doing, how she was feeling.

"Great," Frank said. "Remember what I said about the basement full of extra furniture we have. Just come by and take what you want until you get your own stuff, okay?"

"Sure."

Zack reminded himself that his brother, for all of his straight-up-the-middle-with-power athletic skill, had always been an expert at hidden agendas. It was an art he had studied at the feet of a master: their father. If Frank was operating true to form, this small talk was anything but casual.

"The rent's pretty decent for a place like that, yes?"

Zack laughed. Decent was far too tame a word. The rent for his tiny apartment in Boston had been three times what it was for the house, which had a huge, wooded lot, two fireplaces, and several times as much space as the apartment.

"Don't tell the realty company that owns it," Zack said, "but they're getting killed on this deal. I sleep with my lease under my pillow for fear someone will sneak in and take it away."

"Oh, we won't," Frank said calmly.

"We?"

Zack realized that the hidden agenda was about to surface.

"Ultramed-Davis, Zack. You see, Pine Bough Realty Trust is a sort of, well, convenient way for the hospital to administer some property it owns hereabouts. We're your landlord."

Frank beamed, obviously delighted with the way he had delivered the news.

"You know," Zack said, now consciously working to keep his cynicism in check, "somehow that little piece of information doesn't altogether surprise me. Not that it would have made any difference, Frank, but you could have told me when I rented the place that in addition to my salary, my office, my equipment, and my insurance, Ultramed was providing the roof over my head."

Frank shrugged. "This seemed like a more appropriate time."

"Tell me, is it customary for a hospital to have such a—how should I say—proprietary role in a community?"

"I would use the word *progressive.*" Frank smiled and winked. "You see, Zack, the bottom line of this or any other business is money. *Dinero.* The big D." As he became immersed in his rhetoric, he grew more excited and animated, his gestures more professorial. "That's what the administrators and boards of directors of hospitals all over the country are just beginning to realize. Fortunately, Ultramed recognized it years ago. Eliminate nonprofitable programs and deadwood; increase receivables and collections. Change the red ink to black, no matter how, and the rest takes care of itself. If it's real estate, then it's real estate. If it's other investments, then it's other investments. Colleges like Harvard and Dartmouth have some of the biggest stock portfolios and real estate holdings around. Why shouldn't hospitals follow their example?"

"I . . . I don't know why they shouldn't," Zack said. *But give me time,* he was thinking, *and I'm sure I can come up with something.*

The wedding of business and medicine was one with which he was simply not comfortable—at least not yet. He reflected on the new CT scanner . . . the incredible opportunity he had been given by Ultramed to set up a private practice. The marriage, he acknowledged, deserved, if not his blessing, at least his open mind.

Perhaps that was what his brother needed to hear.

"You know, Frank," he went on, "if I seem uncomfortable with some of this corporate-medicine stuff, you've got to remember that I've spent the last eight years in a hospital where everything was always in incredibly short supply. Everything, that is, except for the dedication of the nurses and the doctors, and the love—I guess there really isn't any better word for it—that they had for their patients.

"I'm grateful to be in a situation like this. Believe me, I am. But there are some parts of those years I spent at Muni that are hard to get out of my system. Frank, I tell you, there was something so pure about the kind of caring that went on in that grimy old place, something so . . . I don't know, holy, that many times patients seemed to get better when every medical fact—all the odds—said they shouldn't. Does that make any sense?"

Frank held up his hands. "Hey, Zack-o," he said, "that makes all the sense in the world. That's what makes you such a valuable addition to the staff here. So, you just do the doctoring and let me worry about the politics and the CT scanners and such. That way everyone benefits, right?"

Dignity, Zack was thinking, still immersed in his years at Boston Muni. *That's what it all boiled down to. The dignity that came from being cared for with love and respect: from being treated as something more than a credit or debit on a balance sheet.*

He flashed on the tears glistening in the eyes of Chris Gow at the realization that someone cared enough to stand up for him, regardless of the cost.

"Right?" Frank asked again.

"Huh? Oh, yes, exactly."

"Good," Frank said. "Then I can assume you'll leave this Beaulieu business to me?"

"What?" Again, Zack warned himself not to drop his guard too low. Frank was, and probably always would be, the fiercest of competitors.

"Beaulieu, sport. Hey, are we on the same wavelength or not?"

"Frank, you haven't said one word about—"

"Well, what in the hell else do you think we've been talking about? I've let that business with the old man and Wil Marshfield slide by because I knew that you hadn't had time to learn the system around here. But Beaulieu is another story. Zack, that man is on a vendetta because he thinks the hospital's to blame for his inability to maintain a surgical practice. Have you heard that kind of paranoid talk from anyone else around here?"

"No, but—"

"Every time someone new has come on the staff over the last few years, Beaulieu buttonholes him with wild claims and stories about how we're railroading him out of business and how we forced Richard Coulombe to sell his pharmacy in order to pay his hospital bills. Christ, I'm surprised he hasn't tried to tie us in with the fucking famine in Ethiopia. Let me tell you something, Zack. No one has to try and force Guy Beaulieu into retirement. He's doing a perfectly adequate job of that all by himself.

"And as for that Coulombe crap of his, ours wasn't the only debt the man had, believe me. He was in it up to here with everyone in town. Check it out yourself. Coulombe either sold that store or he spent the rest of his days in a courtroom."

"But—" Zack stopped himself at the last moment from breaking his promise to Beaulieu by bringing up the connection between Ultramed-Davis and Eagle Pharmaceuticals and Surgical Supply. He also found himself wondering if the former owner of the house he was renting had ever been a patient at the hospital.

"But what?" Frank demanded. There was a sudden hardness in his eyes, an edge to his voice.

"Nothing," Zack said. "Forget it."

With his thoughts focused on Suzanne and on problems at the office, he was willing to do almost anything to avoid a clash. "Forget it."

Frank shook his head. "You're holding out on me, Zack-o. It's written all over your face. Now, what's going on?"

"I said, *nothing.*"

Zack felt the skin tighten across the back of his neck.

Some of what is happening is simply wrong. Some of it is evil . . . Guy Beaulieu's words, his anger and his sadness, took hold. *Your old friend Beaulieu is a little short of allies in this place. . . .*

"All right, Frank," Zack suddenly heard himself saying. "You want to know what's wrong? I'll tell you what. I believe Guy, that's what. I listened to him, and I looked in his eyes, and I know he's telling the truth. That's what's wrong. I don't know if it's Ultramed, or that pompous ass Mainwaring, or what. And I sure as hell don't know why. But I think Beaulieu *is* being railroaded out of practice, just like he says. And if that's true, then it pisses me off. It pisses me off a lot, and it makes me want to do whatever I can to help the man out. There, is that what you wanted to hear?"

Frank laughed out loud. Then he lit up a cigar and sent a smoke ring swirling toward the ceiling.

"Let's just say it's what I *expected* to hear," he said. "You always were something of a bleeding heart, Zack—a sucker for anybody's cause. Vietnam, Timmy Goyette's supposedly-stolen Junior Olympics entry fee, women's rights, not enough mashed potatoes in the school lunches. Give the boy a sob story, and he gives you his guts . . . and his allowance. Remember all that? I sure do. So why should Guy Beaulieu and his paranoid stories be any different, right?"

"Frank, you can really be a bastard, do you know that?"

"Careful, boy," Frank said, launching another perfect ring. "That's your mother you're talking about. Besides, this time you're wrong. Dead wrong."

"What?"

"This is one cause you'd best steer clear of, brother. Beaulieu's on his way off the plank, and if you're hanging onto him when he goes, then you're going to get awfully wet. I promise you that."

He opened his desk drawer, withdrew an envelope, and slid it across.

"I've been keeping this letter quiet because I still hoped Beaulieu would back off. Now, I'm afraid, I have no choice but to present it to the ethics committee. There are people on the staff who wanted to do something months ago to limit or cut off his privileges, but I kept putting them off. Like the Judge said, the old guy did save my life. Here, have a read."

The letter was handwritten and carried no heading other than the date, June 17.

Dear Mr. Iverson:

I am writing to share with you some allegations against Dr. Guy Beaulieu by myself and several other nurses on the emergency ward. Over the past several months, he has become increasingly inconsistent and indecisive in his dealings with patients. He has been quite forgetful, at times issuing the same set of orders more than once, and at other times, neglecting to order certain studies which we would consider routine and basic.

In addition, on more than one occasion his speech has been slurred and his manner inconsistent enough to raise the question of drugs, alcohol, small strokes, or some combination of the three. Fortunately, his case load has been small enough so that no one has been harmed—at least no one that we know of. Still, we feel some sort of investigation and action is called for.

I would welcome the chance to meet with you and discuss this matter further. Meanwhile, I feel you should have a talk with Dr. Beaulieu.

> Sincerely yours,
> Maureen Banas, R.N.
> Head Nurse

Zack read and reread the letter in stunned silence, trying to match the charges with the eloquent, dedicated man he had listened to at the staff meeting and, later, over lunch. There was nothing in Beaulieu's manner, speech, or the content of his words that bore out the nurse's claims. Still, there was no way such charges could be dismissed.

Across the desk from him, Frank sat in smug silence, obviously savoring the moment.

"This is terrible," Zack murmured, trying, as he read the letter for a third time, to get a fix on the nurse, Maureen Banas. . . . *colorless, but efficient . . . distant . . . knowledgeable* . . . he simply hadn't spent enough time around her yet to have any real handle.

"Terrible, but true," Frank said. "I had hoped to spare the old duffer any more humiliation, but after hearing his little speech the other morning, and seeing the way he's gotten to you, well, it seems I have no—"

"Frank, does anything about this letter strike you as strange?"

Frank set his cigar aside and leaned forward.

"What are you talking about?"

Zack slid the letter back across the desk.

"Well, for one thing, this woman doesn't substantiate her charges with one specific example."

"Well, there's no doubt she has them. Zack, don't you think you're grasping at straws?"

"And for another, the whole damn thing is just too . . . too sterile."

"What?"

"Just look at it, Frank. Not one bit of sensitivity or poignancy. Not one indication that she understands the charges she's making could quite possibly send a man's life down the drain—a man who has practiced surgery in this town for thirty years. Christ, for all the awareness she's showing, she might just as well be writing to complain that a neighbor's poodle is shitting in her flower bed. The more I think about it, the more this letter smells. I think that woman should be spoken with, face to face."

"You don't think I've done that?"

"Well, then, *I* want to. It's the only way I'm going to even begin to believe all this."

"You go to her or anyone else about this business," Frank said, jabbing a finger at him, "and you'll be out on your ass quicker than you can say 'scalpel.' This is my affair—mine and Ultramed's. You really have it in your mind to fuck things up for me around here, don't you?"

"Frank, that's nonsense."

"Is it?"

For several frozen moments, Zack could only sit and stare at his brother. Despite his tan, Frank looked pallid, his expression a disconcerting amalgam of anger and—what? Fear? They had had their differences over the years, true, and from time to time, some magnificent arguments. But Zack sensed something far more powerful at work here.

"Frank, please," he managed. "Stop sounding like I'm your goddamn enemy. I'm not. I just care about Beaulieu and I want to see that he gets a fair shake, okay?"

A margin of color returned to Frank's cheeks.

"Okay?" Zack asked again.

Frank smiled.

"Sure, sport," he said, far too amicably. "I understand. I'll tell you what, why don't we just leave it that I'll keep you posted and you'll keep an eye on things . . . from a distance. That way I get to do what I'm paid to do, and you get to keep from taking a fall. I promise you, Beaulieu will get every break that's coming to him. Yes?"

Zack gauged the intensity in his brother's eyes, and then nodded. Their session had gone far enough.

"So, that's taken care of," Frank said, tilting back in his chair and folding his hands in his lap. His tone and expression gave no hint of their disagreement. "Listen, how about we have dinner sometime this weekend? I'll have Lisette give you a call."

"Sure, Frank. That'd be fine."

"Excellent. Oh, and by the way," he added, getting up from his chair as Zack stood to go, "tell that new squeeze of yours that we're all praying everything goes well for her tomorrow."

Now Zack felt the color drain from *his* face. "How did you—"

His brother patted him on the shoulder.

"Sport, if someone who works for me so much as farts anywhere in this hospital, sooner or later I get a whiff. That's worth remembering. Trust me on that one and you'll be doing both of us a favor. She's a terrific lady. I'm glad she's finally coming out of her shell. I hope things work out between you."

With that, he shook Zack's hand and ushered him out the door.

∿ CHAPTER 9

DISTURBED BY A CART clattering past the door of her hospital room, Suzanne Cole rolled onto her back, floating in the twilight world between sleep and wakefulness.

For a time, she struggled to complete a dream she had been having —a romantic, storybook dream, in which Jason Mainwaring, dressed head to foot in ebony armor, sitting astride a coal-black stallion, was jousting with a knight clad equally spectacularly in gold. Again and again, the men sped past one another, their lances exploding off their opponent's shield. With each encounter, one or the other came close to falling from his mount, but each time, the stricken knight recovered and swung about for another pass.

Suzanne herself was seated in the grandstand, wearing a flowing gown of pink silk and clutching a single white rose.

Who are you? she called again and again to the gold knight. *Who are you? What do you want from me?*

As the dream faded, the knight turned toward her and lifted the visor of his golden helmet. Like flashing neon, the face of the man kept changing. One moment it was Zachary Iverson, and the next, Paul Cole

—the pathologically self-possessed physiology professor who had picked her out of a crowded lecture hall during her second year in medical school and had swept her up in a whirlwind of flowers and parties and romantic weekends in the country.

Less than a year later they were married. If there were signs of the man's sickness during those months, she had missed them completely. Later, when the recreational drugs, and the erratic behavior, and the lies—"misunderstandings," Paul had called them—began to surface, she had chosen to ignore them, to rationalize them away.

By the time she knew that her efforts to hold their marriage together had been a mistake, there was Jennifer. The years she spent trying to accommodate Paul for her daughter's sake had nearly cost Suzanne her career, and perhaps even more than that.

Why? she pleaded again. *What do you want from me?*

"Dr. Cole, it's morning."

Why? . . .

"Dr. Cole?"

The nurse's gentle voice, and the touch of her hand, began to dispel what remained of the dream. The colors began fading into a sea of white.

How long had it been since Paul had last forced his way into one of her dreams? The arguments, the guilt trips, the hang-ups when *she* answered the phone, the missing prescription pads, the visits from the glib, condescending drug enforcement agents . . . *Why had she given the man so goddamn many benefits of the doubt?*

"Dr. Cole . . ."

Suzanne opened her eyes a slit.

"Hi," she murmured. Instinctively, she reached up and touched her breast, dreading the thick bandages she expected to find there.

"It's seven-fifteen," the nurse said. "Time for your pre-op meds."

Pre-op. Damn, she thought. It was not over at all. It was just starting. Why was this happening? Life in Sterling had been everything she had hoped it would be—so peaceful, so uncomplicated, so good for Jen. Now, suddenly, everything seemed to be unraveling at once. Why?

She opened her eyes fully.

"Seven-fifteen?"

"Uh-huh. You're on call for twenty minutes from now. This is some atropine and Demerol."

Atropine . . . Demerol. One to dry up secretions, and the other to help one not give a damn about the prospect of being disfigured, or worse. *What wonderful potions we doctors have at our fingertips,* she thought acidly. What wonderful potions, indeed. She turned onto her side and winced as the needle pierced her buttock. Then she rolled onto her back and smiled up weakly at the nurse.

"Nicely done," she murmured.

The nurse, a kind, elderly woman named Carrie Adams, patted her hand. "You're going to do fine," she said. "I've had a couple of cysts removed, and so has my daughter. The hardest part is the waiting to get it over with."

"I'll try to remember that."

Once again, this time in spite of herself, Suzanne reached up and touched her breast. It was all so crazy. This sort of thing happened to other people—to patients. She was trained to help them through their medical crises, not to go through one herself. She had bounced back so far, put so many pieces of her shattered world back together. Now this.

Helplessness . . . panic . . . rage . . . her emotions, held in check over the weeks since that terrifying moment of discovery, swirled about like windblown snow.

Where in the hell was the acceptance that the textbooks all wrote about?

"That Demerol should start to work in just a few minutes," the woman said, as if reading her thoughts.

"Good."

"And here are your earphones."

"Oh, yes," Suzanne said, taking the set and placing it on the bed beside her. "What's on today?"

"I don't know," the woman replied, "but Dr. Mainwaring's on channel . . ." She took a three-by-five card from her uniform pocket. ". . . three."

The system—tapes picked by the surgeons to be played in the operating rooms and broadcast to earphone receivers—was designed to reduce patient anxiety levels. Over the few years it had been in place, the innovation had received high marks from surgeons and patients alike. Suzanne flipped the dial on the phones to 3, and held one up against her ear.

" 'Greensleeves,' " she said.

"Pardon?"

" 'Greensleeves.' That's the music. A really beautiful version of it. Here, listen."

She passed the earphones up. The nurse politely listened for a few seconds, and then returned them.

"Very pretty," she said. "Well, I'll be back in a little while. Meanwhile, you just relax. Oh, by the way, there's an envelope for you on the bedside table. Perhaps you'd better read whatever's inside it before that medicine I gave you takes effect."

Suzanne thanked the woman, and then waited until she had left the room.

The envelope, with the Ultramed-Davis heading and logo, read, *Dr. Suzanne Cole.* She peeled it open, knowing it was from Zack. Throughout much of the evening, he had sat there with her, reading out loud from magazines and newspapers, laughing, sharing stories of his life, and, when there was nothing to say, just holding her hand. He had been as open, as tender, and as understanding as any man she had ever met.

She wondered if he realized the resentment she was feeling at his intrusion into her life. Silently, she cursed herself for using him the way she had. She had no intention of allowing a man close enough to ruin her life again—not now, at least. Possibly not ever. Zack had said they could make love with no strings attached, but she knew damn well that there were always strings. When the operation was over, regardless of the outcome, she would do what she must to put distance between them.

For a moment, the fear of what might be growing within her breast seemed pale next to the fear that she might never again be able to trust.

Dear Doc—

It's now 2 a.m. The sleeper they gave you seems to have worked, because you've been out fairly solidly for about an hour. I'm going to leave now, and hope that you don't wake up until a minute or two before they bring you down to the O.R. I just wanted to thank you for Wednesday night, and even more, for letting me share this evening here with you. I don't know if my being here helped you, but it has surely helped me. It's not much of a secret that I think you're pretty special.

I know how frustrating and frightening this is for you—partly because it's frustrating and frightening for me, too. Just know that whatever happens, I'll be with you as much and as closely as you want me to be.

If there's a good, working definition of "friend," maybe it's someone who helps us find the tools to get through this kind of shit when we can't seem to find them for ourselves. Regardless of what happens, you've got one in me.

It's going to be benign. That's all I can say. It's going to be benign, and everything's going to be okay.

Be strong. You have an appointment on my mountain as soon as this is over.

Zack

"I'm sorry, Zack," Suzanne whispered as she slipped the note back into its envelope, tucking it between the pages of the novel she had been reading for the past two weeks. "I'm sorry I wasn't stronger. . . ."

She settled back onto her pillow and slipped on the earphones. Her mouth had become uncomfortably dry from the atropine, but the Demerol, too, was having its effect, so she did not really care.

Carrie Adams and an orderly wheeled a stretcher into the room and helped her slide onto it.

Please, God, Suzanne whispered to herself as the fluorescent lights flashed overhead, *let it be nothing. Let it be benign.*

Jason Mainwaring met her in the operating room, his blue-gray eyes intent from between his aqua mask and hair cover. Suzanne pulled off her earphones. The same lovely piece she had been listening to filled the operating room.

"Welcome to my world, Suzanne," he said.

Suzanne smiled weakly.

"I wish I could say I was pleased to be here."

"I understand." He patted her arm reassuringly. "We'll take good care of you. Don't you worry."

"Thanks."

"How do y'all like my music?"

"It . . . it's beautiful."

"The most beautiful music ever written, I think. It's called *Fantasia on Greensleeves,* an' it's by an English composer named Ralph Vaughan Williams. I begin every single case with it, an' then go on to some other pieces of his. If you want, I'll make a tape of it for you."

"That would be very nice," she managed.

Jack Pearl, the anesthesiologist, appeared at Mainwaring's side. Together with a nurse, they helped her from the litter onto the chilly operating table. Then, in a maneuver so quick and painless she barely realized it was happening, Pearl slipped an intravenous line into a vein at her left wrist.

Next, a broad strap was pulled across her abdomen and tightened.

A final pleasantry or two from Mainwaring, and they were ready to begin.

Jack Pearl came into Suzanne's field of vision, held up the rubber stopper of her intravenous line, and slipped in a needle attached to a syringe full of anesthetic.

Please, God, she prayed once again, *let Zack be right. Let it be okay.*

"All right, Suzanne," Jack Pearl said. "This is just some Pentothal." He depressed the plunger, emptying the contents of the syringe into her intravenous line. "All you have to do now is count back from one hundred."

From the speakers overhead, Ralph Vaughan Williams's flowing fantasy filled the room.

"One hundred," she said thickly. ". . . ninety-nine . . . ninety-eight . . ."

Above her, the huge, saucerlike operating light flashed on.

"Ready," she heard someone say.

* * *

Takashi Yoshimura was one of seven Orientals living in Sterling, New Hampshire. The other six were his wife and five children. Though Japanese by birth, and, in fact, by birthplace, he had been raised and educated in lower Manhattan, and spoke both English and Japanese with a pronounced New York accent.

Like a number of the new Ultramed physicians Zack had met since his return to Sterling, Yoshimura, a pathologist who insisted on being called Kash, was young, well trained, and exceedingly capable.

It was just after eight in the morning. Yoshimura, diminutive, with close-cropped hair and Ben Franklin glasses, sat at his desk, with Zack peering over his shoulder. Before them, in a stainless-steel pan, was the fleshy, silver-dollar-sized mass that had just been removed from Suzanne Cole's right breast.

Zack watched in tense silence as the man maneuvered the tissue about beneath a bright light and magnifying glass. A floor above them lay Suzanne, adrift in the dreamless netherworld of general anesthesia. In minutes, the unimposing little pathologist would send word to the O.R. of his interpretation of the cells in the frozen sections of the specimen, and Suzanne would either have her incision sewn up, or a large portion of her breast and the surrounding lymph nodes removed.

If Kash Yoshimura was the least bit nervous about the awesome implications of this facet of his work, it certainly did not show in his face. He hummed a soft, almost tuneless melody as he scanned the surface of the mass, searching for any telltale dimpling or discoloration. Then, with a final, satisfied arpeggio, he used a scalpel to produce a thin slice from the core, and handed the pan with the exposed specimen to the histologist.

"Okay, George," he said to the tissue technician, "do your thing."

"Well?" Zack asked, after the technician had left.

"What do I think?"

"Uh-huh."

"You are, perhaps, familiar with the immutable medical law of eighty-five/fifteen?"

Zack shook his head.

"I'm surprised," Yoshimura said, "your being Harvard-trained and all. Well, simply put, the law states that every probability in medicine is either eighty-five percent likely or fifteen percent likely. Proper application of the law means one can never be wrong, as long as one knows whether the event in question seems remotely likely or not so remote."

Zack smiled. "I take it you scored well on your boards."

Kash Yoshimura nodded. "I did okay," he said.

"And the biopsy is eighty-five percent likely to be . . ."

"Benign. An adenoma, I would guess."

"Wonderful." Zack pumped his fist.

"At this point, you may be eighty-five percent enthusiastic," the pathologist cautioned. "No more."

"I understand."

Yoshimura reached across and patted Zack understandingly on the shoulder. "We'll have the answer in just a few minutes," he said. "Meanwhile, all I can tell you is that our mutual friend is in remarkably capable hands."

"Mainwaring?" Zack flashed on his initial, unpleasant encounter with the man.

Kash nodded. "I watched him work a number of times when I was a student and resident. He is a superb technician."

"So I've heard. He's a little short on tact, though. In the first five minutes after we met, he managed to say something snide about virtually every aspect of my life."

"Perhaps he finds a new neurosurgeon in town threatening to his ego."

"Perhaps. Where was it you trained?"

"Hopkins."

"Mainwaring was at Hopkins?"

"He was. No small fry, either. A full professor, if I'm not mistaken."

Zack was surprised. "I wonder what on earth he's doing up here in the boondocks," he said. "Especially the northern New England boondocks. That accent of his puts him well below the Mason-Dixon line."

The pathologist shrugged. "Beats me. Apparently, he doesn't deem pathologists threatening enough to insult. Aside from my reporting biopsies to him, we haven't had more than a one- or two-word conversation since he arrived a year or so ago."

"Actually," Zack said, suddenly anxious to learn more about the man Guy Beaulieu claimed was helping to drive him out of practice, "it was closer to two years. Did you ever tell him you watched him operate at Hopkins?"

"As a matter of fact, I did. Once, shortly after he got here."

"And what did he say?"

"Nothing, really. He glared at me for a moment with that steely look that I think surgeons practice in front of a mirror to use on nurses and anesthesiologists and the like." He grimaced. "I mean *some* surgeons," he qualified. "Then he just said, 'That's nice,'—something like that—and walked away."

"And no mention of that since?"

Yoshimura shook his head.

"How weird. Mainwaring seems very much the old-boy type. I'd expect him to go out of his way for someone from *his* college or *his* hospital—especially a prestigious place like Hopkins."

"Believe it or not," Yoshimura said without rancor, "there are still those about, even in our lofty profession, who are . . . uncomfortable with certain aspects of certain anatomies." He gestured toward his eyes. "Whatever the reason, the social circle Jason Mainwaring runs in certainly does not include the Yoshimuras."

"Well, I'd enjoy it very much if mine did," Zack said.

Kash Yoshimura eyed him for a second, and then he smiled. "I think we would like that, too," he said.

The histology technician announced his return with a soft knock on the doorjamb.

"Ah," Kash said. "This is the moment we turn our eighty-five/fifteen into something quite a bit more certain. Good sections?"

The technician nodded proudly, and set down a cardboard holder containing a dozen or so glass slides.

Zack was struck by the remoteness of the unfolding scenario from the woman whose quality of life, and even, perhaps, whose very existence, was at the center of the drama—a marked contrast to the immediacy and intimacy of surgical medicine.

Still, he knew, in the moments to follow, Kash Yoshimura would hold as much power, as much responsibility, as if he were the man in the operating room with the scalpel.

The pathologist slid the first of the sections onto the stage of the dual-view teaching microscope, and motioned Zack to the second pair of oculars.

Silently, Zack watched, barely breathing as the multicolored cells slid through the brightly lit field.

One by one, Yoshimura worked his way through the slides. With the fifth or sixth one, he had resumed his humming. Finally, he stopped, and looked over at Zack.

"You have an opinion?" he asked.

Zack nodded. "Uniform cell type, uniform pattern, no obvious foci of necrosis," he said. "I can't put a name on it, but I can say that it sure as hell looks benign."

Yoshimura nodded. "Should you ever tire of neurosurgery, Dr. Iverson, I would say you have quite a future as a pathologist."

He picked up the phone and dialed the operating room. "This is Dr. Yoshimura calling from pathology," he said. "You may inform Dr. Mainwaring that he has excised a totally benign, fibrous adenoma. Thank you."

Zack pumped the man's hand as if he had been the cause of the tumor being noncancerous, rather than merely its interpreter.

Before it had really even begun, Suzanne's nightmare was over. Anxious to be at the bedside when she awoke, Zack hurried to the recovery room.

One story above, in operating room 3, Jason Mainwaring received the news of the biopsy impassively, and then looked over at his anesthesiologist.

"So, Jack," he said, "if it's all right with you, we are ready to close."

Jack Pearl, a ferret-like man in his mid-forties, smiled at the surgeon from beneath his mask. Then he glanced down at the serene face of their patient.

"Everything is better than all right, Dr. Mainwaring," he said. "In fact, it's perfect. As always. Absolutely perfect."

Subtly, unnoticed by anyone else in the room, Jason Mainwaring returned the smile and nodded his approval.

At that moment, both men were focused on precisely the same thought: *Four hundred ninety-one down. Only nine to go.*

CHAPTER 10

OVER THE MORE than thirteen years that Zack had spent as a medical student and surgeon, Suzanne represented, without doubt, the most striking recovery from general anesthesia he had ever encountered.

He was already in the recovery room, waiting by the nurse's station, when she was wheeled in from the surgical suite. She was awake, smiling, and totally alert. Her jubilant thumbs-up sign to him made clear that she was also well aware of the results of her operation.

"That is the most amazing wake-up I've ever seen," Zack commented to one of the recovery room nurses as Suzanne, with very little help, transferred herself from the litter to her hospital bed. "It's hard to believe she was ever really asleep."

The nurse, an animated young redhead whom Zack knew only as Kara, beamed with pride.

"Oh, she was out, all right," she said. "Isn't it wonderful? Almost all of Dr. Pearl's cases come out of the operating room looking like that."

"Mine didn't," Zack said, recalling the prolonged, but quite typical recovery of his cervical disc case.

"Pardon?"

"Nothing. I'm just really impressed, that's all."

"Everyone around here is," the woman said. "Part of it may be Dr. Mainwaring, too. He demands that his patients be anesthetized just so, and Dr. Pearl is the only one he'll allow to work with him. I used to scrub before I got the job in here, and I tell you, they are quite a pair. Things have really taken a turn for the better at this place since they teamed up."

Across the recovery room, Zack saw Jack Pearl peering through an ophthalmoscope, examining the nerves and vessels on Suzanne's retinae while one of the nurses checked her vital signs. He was a slight, sallow man with a pencil-thin moustache and a broad, high forehead that dominated his nondescript eyes.

"What do you mean, 'a turn for the better'?" Zack asked, knowing he was fishing for some opinion on Guy Beaulieu. "I grew up in Sterling and then did an externship here. I always thought we were pretty fortunate with the surgeons we had."

The nurse eyed him warily, suddenly uncertain as to whether she might have said too much to a virtual stranger. Zack tried his best to appear only marginally interested in her response.

After a beat or two, she shrugged and brushed a wisp of hair from her brow.

"Ormesby's okay," she said, "at least for routine things. But I think it might be time for Dr. Beaulieu to retire, especially with all the trouble he's been having, and with someone as good as Dr. Mainwaring around."

"Is that the general feeling of the nurses?" Zack ventured.

Again, she appraised him.

"Dunno," she said finally, although her eyes told him otherwise. "But they like you. I can tell you that much. And we all like having a neurosurgeon on the staff. It makes Ultramed-Davis seem more—I don't know—special."

"Thanks, Kara. Thanks for telling me that."

The young nurse blushed.

"Well, I've got to get back to work," she said. "See you."

"See you."

Zack watched as the woman returned to her patient. Her opinion of Guy Beaulieu was, he suspected, typical of what he would encounter from most of the other nurses on the staff. Whether justifiably or not, the man's reputation at Ultramed-Davis was shot. And Zack knew that given the nature of medicine, gossip, and the intense microcosm of hospitals, there was probably nothing on God's earth that Beaulieu could do to reverse the situation.

Still, despite all the rumors and innuendoes, despite Frank's vehemence and the damning letter from Maureen Banas, Zack could not shake the belief that Guy was the victim of some sort of calculated effort to drive him from practice. The thought was so sad, so pathetic, that it almost defied comprehension. On some level, Zack realized, he was half hoping the charges against Beaulieu would prove true. At least then he could make some sense of it all.

Jack Pearl had finished his evaluation of Suzanne and was headed back toward the operating room when he noticed Zack.

"Morning, Iverson," he said.

"Jack." Zack nodded. "How goes it?"

"Did you have a case this morning?"

"No. I just stopped by to see how Suzanne was making out. She looks great."

Pearl glanced back at her. "Pretty routine business," he said.

"What did you use?"

For the fraction of a second, the anesthesiologist's expression seemed to tighten. Then, just as quickly, it relaxed.

"The usual," he said. "A little Pentothal, a little gas. Mainwaring likes his patients really light."

"I guess. She doesn't look as if she's even been asleep."

Again, tension flickered across Pearl's face.

"Well, she was," he said simply. He glanced at the clock over the nurse's station. "Got to go, Iverson. You have a good day, now."

"Yeah, Jack. You, too."

As the taciturn little man shuffled away, Zack realized that during this and all their previous encounters, Pearl had not once made direct eye contact with him. The trait was not that surprising, he acknowledged, given the nature of the breed. Although the exceptions were far too numerous for any generalization, many of the anesthesiologists he had known were introspective loners, skilled more in biochemistry and physiology than in the more subjective arts of clinical medicine, and committed to one of the specialties where conversation and interaction with patients—awake patients at least—was at a minimum.

Still, there was something unusual about Jack Pearl, something furtive and arcane, that Zack found both curious and disconcerting. He wondered if perhaps the man had a past—trouble somewhere along the line—and he made a mental note to ask Frank about him sometime. Then he turned and headed to Suzanne's bedside.

Though a bit pale, she was still smiling, radiant and wide awake.

"Hi, lady," he said. "What's new?"

"Oh, nothing." She feigned a yawn. "A little this, a little that. You know. Just another routine, humdrum day."

"Yeah, my day, too."

"That's quite obvious from those dark circles around your eyes," she said. "Hey, before I forget to mention it, thanks for your note. It meant a lot."

"You look fine. Are you in any pain?"

"Not really. At least not compared to what I would have been in if that biopsy had been positive."

"It *does* seem a bit easier to deal with this way," Zack said. "I thought I'd have the chance to break the good news to you, or at least to remind you of it, but you came out of the O.R. as if you'd never been asleep. It's absolutely incredible how light you are so soon after general anesthesia."

"I know. Jason said I would be. It's wonderful. I had my appendix out when I was seventeen, and I remember being totally out of it for a day. Jack Pearl said that if it was okay with Jason, I could go home this afternoon."

"That's great."

"Zack, God bless every woman who has to go through this madness. I know we're supposed to believe that there's some sort of grand, cosmic scheme operating in life, but cancer—especially breast cancer—just doesn't lend itself very easily to any philosophizing. I tell you, I'm so relieved, all I want to do is cry."

"Well, go ahead and do it. In fact, I'm pretty relieved myself, so if you're free tomorrow night, I could come over with a bottle of wine and a box of Kleenex."

Her eyes darkened.

"Zack, I . . ."

"Go ahead," he said.

"I really owe you for staying with me the way you did last night. . . ."

"There's a 'but' coming. I can feel it."

"Zack, Wednesday night was wonderful," she whispered. "I really mean that. But it's just not like me to start things in the middle that way. Do you understand?"

"I guess so."

"For weeks I've been so consumed with my damn lump, then suddenly you show up in my life and . . . Zack, I just need some time and a little space to sort some things out. You said the other night that you had no expectations. I hope you meant it."

Zack swallowed hard. "I hope so, too," he said.

She smiled thinly and squeezed his hand.

"Thanks at least for trying. Listen, I have the next week off. I owe Jen some quality time with her mother and my partner a few days of help in the gallery. I'll call you toward the middle of the week, okay?"

"Middle meaning like Tuesday?"

"Zack, please."

"Okay, sorry, sorry. Middle of the week is fine. Can I at least drive you home later?"

"I'll be fine. Besides, I don't even know if I'll be going home later. Zack, there'll be time. If it's supposed to be, there'll be plenty of time."

There was a sadness in her eyes that helped keep him from pushing matters any further.

"Sure thing," he said. "Hey, for what it's worth, I just ran into your replacement in Annie's room."

Suzanne smiled broadly, obviously relieved at the change in subject.

"Don Norman? Is he overwhelmed yet?"

"Hardly. Norman doesn't seem like the type to be overwhelmed very easily—at least not as long as there are guidelines and policies for him to follow. And Ultramed seems to have provided all the guidelines and policies he could ever want, so not to worry."

"I won't," she said. "And I agree totally. The man is conscientious as hell, but he *is* a little medical robot. Julia Childs with a stethoscope—strictly cookbook. Annie okay?"

Zack nodded. "When I stopped by, she was fighting with Norman about her sodium restriction, so I guess that's about as good a sign as any. Oh, get this: right in the middle of their little altercation he puffs himself up like he loves to do—you know, like this—and he says, 'Mrs. Doucette, pull-eese. Whether you know it or not, I am the Chief of Staff at this hospital. I certainly know what is best for my patients.' "

"Good imitation. Excellent. And what did Annie say?"

"Nothing too inflammatory. She just eyed him with this great Annie look, called him 'Tubby,' and suggested that he should lose weight so that he would be a better example for his patients."

"Oh, no."

"It was great. Norman turned ten shades of red, and looked for a moment as if he might haul off and pop her in the nose. Having been brought up by the woman, I can say that it's lucky for him he didn't. Even after cardiac arrest, my money would have been on Annie. Well, listen, I've got to go play doctor. If you change your mind about that ride home, give me a page."

"Sure."

"You know, I still can't get over it."

"What?" she asked.

"How light you are. The nurse I was talking to said all of Mainwaring's patients come out of the O.R. like that. I've got to ask him his secret."

"No secret, Doctor. Just good technique."

Jason Mainwaring, sans mask and haircover, appraised them from the foot of the bed.

"Well," Zack said casually, trying not to appear as startled by the intrusion as he was, "whatever it is, it's impressive. I'd like to scrub with you sometime to learn firsthand how it's done."

"My goodness," Mainwaring mused, "a neurosurgeon who doesn't know everything. What will the gods send us next?"

"Now just a minute," Zack countered, again feeling his hackles stiffen at the man's superciliousness. "I don't know if you're like this with everyone, or just with me, but I—"

"Hey, fellas," Suzanne cut in, "remember me? The patient?"

Mainwaring smiled down at her as if Zack were no longer there. "Is everything still all right, my friend?" he asked.

"Perfect, Jason. I can't tell you how pleased I am."

"That's fine. Just fine," he drawled.

Zack, arms folded tightly, stood back from the bed a step, wondering if he should say good-bye or simply leave. It was obvious that Jason Mainwaring, for all of his glistening reputation and surgical skills, was too threatened by him to let up even for a moment.

Unless he could find some way of reassuring the man that they were playing for the same team—and his experience with similar egos told him that possibility was highly unlikely—the two of them seemed destined to be enemies.

Well, so be it, Zack thought. It would only make things that much easier if, in fact, Mainwaring did prove in any way responsible for Guy's difficulties.

"Can I go home this afternoon?" Suzanne asked.

Mainwaring smiled, walked to the bedside opposite Zack and took her hand.

"If there's no major bleeding from that incision," he said, "and you still feel the way you do right now, I don't see why not. Listen, I've got an emergency exploratory in just a few minutes, and a gall bladder at two. Why don't I stop by after that—say, four-thirty? Then, I'll not only discharge you, but I'll even drive you home. Your place isn't very far out of my way."

Suzanne's eyes flicked toward Zack.

"Oh, Jason, I wouldn't think of—"

"No, no. It's settled."

Don't you think driving your post-op patients home is carrying bedside manner a bit too far, Doctor?

Zack barely kept the snide rebuke in check. He was already irritated with the man and his ways, and now he realized he was jealous of him as well.

Suzanne had made no secret that she and her surgeon had a friendship that, at times, went beyond the hospital. But she had also been careful to add that Mainwaring had a wife and children living somewhere in the South, who were, for whatever reason, as yet unable to follow him to New England.

There was, Zack reminded himself angrily, never a valid excuse for jealousy. Nevertheless, jealous he was. His reaction also reminded him that it was far more pleasant being threatening than feeling threatened.

"Well," he said, clearing his throat, but still unable to fully expunge the hurt from his voice, "you two seem to have everything pretty much under control, so I'll just get along. See you later, Suze. Nice job, Mainwaring."

Before either of them could respond, a nurse whom Zack recognized as one of the emergency crew rushed across the recovery room to Mainwaring.

"Doctor," she said breathlessly, "there's some trouble in the emergency ward. It's Dr. Beaulieu. He's—" She glanced at Zack and Suzanne, and stopped in mid-sentence, obviously unsure of how much more to say. ". . . um . . . Mr. Iverson would like you to come down right away if you can."

"Of course, Sandy," Mainwaring responded with urbane calm. "Tell Mr. Iverson I'll be right along."

"Thank you, Doctor. Hi, Dr. Iverson. Hi, Suzanne. Are you okay?"

"I'm fine, Sandy, thanks," Suzanne said. "Everything's all right."

"That's wonderful. I'll tell everyone downstairs the good news."
She hurried off.

"So," said Mainwaring, "I'll see y'all at four-thirty, yes?"

He gave Suzanne's hand a final squeeze and then strode out of the recovery room.

"Are you going down there?" she asked Zack.

"Uh-huh."

"Let me know what's going on, okay?"

"Sure."

He made no move to touch her.

"Zack?" she said softly.

"What?"

"I'm sorry I didn't handle that situation better. Jason comes on a little strong sometimes. He caught me off balance. He's really a decent guy. Just don't let him get to you, okay?"

"Sure."

"Talk to you later in the week?"

"Right."

He turned to go.

"I hope the trouble with Guy is nothing big," she called.

"You and me, both," he muttered.

But as he headed for the emergency ward, feeling not a little deflated, Zack could not shake an ugly sense of foreboding.

Nothing that Zack had imagined about what was transpiring in the emergency ward prepared him for the reality.

There was commotion bordering on chaos. The hospital's three-man security force was there, as were the director of nursing, Mainwaring, Chief of Staff Donald Norman, and half a dozen embarrassed patients and their families. The epicenter of the turmoil was behind the closed door of the family quiet room, where brief periods of strained silence separated angry, easily audible outbursts in English and in French from Guy Beaulieu.

"Damn you, Frank, get out of my way before I strike you," were the first words Zack heard. "That woman is my patient, and I have every right to care for her. Now, out of my way!"

"Guy, sit down and quiet down, or I swear I'll have the guards come in here and tie you down. I will not have you making a scene like this in my hospital."

"Your hospital! If it's your hospital, Mr. High and Mighty, then why don't you see that this is all a plot to take my practice away? You're in on it, aren't you? That's why. You're one of them!"

"Dammit, Guy, shut up. There are patients out there."

"I know there are. *My* patients! Now let me pass!"

Zack crossed to where Jason Mainwaring stood, leaning against a wall near the quiet room.

"What gives?" he asked.

Mainwaring glanced over at him and then looked back toward the source of the commotion.

"The old quack has gone beserk, that's what," he said coolly. "He's been unbalanced for some time, but at least he's had the presence and intelligence to limit his outbursts and paranoia to the staff meetings. This is disgraceful."

"Do you know what happened?"

Mainwaring's response was preempted by yet another outburst from Beaulieu, followed by still another, though more constrained, response from Frank.

Moments later, the door to the quiet room opened and Frank slipped out. He appeared a bit more ruffled than usual, but was still impeccably dressed, with not a hair out of place.

"Stay with him, Henry," he said to one of the security guards—a broad, neckless man with bad skin and close-cut hair, who looked to Zack like a mammoth fireplug. "If he starts yelling again, cuff him to the chair and shove a rag in his mouth."

"Mr. Iverson, I don't hurt people unless they hurt me. I told them that when I started working here."

"Look, Henry, if you want to keep on working here, you'll do as I say and keep that nutcase quiet until Chief Clifford and his men get here. Now get in there and do your job."

Shaking his massive head, the guard entered the quiet room and closed the door behind him. There were no shouts of protest from Beaulieu.

Frank scanned the cubicles filled with patients. "Christ," he muttered. Spotting Zack and Mainwaring, he approached them, shaking his head.

"This is fucking insane," he said, keeping his voice low. "And you know what? It's my fault. I should have done something about him way back when his craziness started. Well, Zack-o, if there's one good thing to come out of all this, it's that at least you get to see him in action firsthand."

"Exactly what's going on?" Zack asked. "What tipped him over?"

Frank laughed sardonically. "I keep telling you, brother, Guy Beaulieu tipped over a long time ago. This is just an example of how far. See that woman over there in bed five? Well, she's got some sort of bowel problem."

"Probably a ruptured diverticulum," Mainwaring interjected.

"Well," Frank went on, "Beaulieu's done some surgery on her in the past. On her husband, too, I think. This time, though, the woman and her internist apparently talked things over and decided that she might be better off with Jason, here, doing the surgery."

"I evaluated her right before I did Suzanne," Mainwaring explained, "and had her scheduled to follow in the O.R."

"Meanwhile, Beaulieu, the lunatic, comes strolling through the emergency ward, spots the woman, and without a word to anyone, begins examining her and issuing orders to the nurses. Needless to say, the poor lady, who's not too swift to begin with, was totally confused and absolutely terrified." Frank looked impatiently toward the ambulance bay. "Where in the hell are the goddamn cops? When you don't want them they're all over the place."

"Frank, you don't need the police," Zack said. "Let me talk to him. Can't you see where this might be upsetting and humiliating for him? I'll just get him out of the hospital and he'll calm down."

"He's out of the hospital anyway," Frank said acidly. "For good."

"What?"

"This was the last fucking straw. I told him about the latest series of complaints, and about that letter from Maureen Banas. And I suspended his privileges."

Zack's heart sank.

"Frank, is that when he went nuts?"

"What difference does it make?" Frank said. "Nuts is nuts. Just listen to him."

From within the quiet room, Beaulieu had again begun to shout.

"You ape, let go of me! Take your hands off me, goddamn it! Take your hands—" Suddenly, the surgeon's words were cut short.

Without waiting for Frank's permission, Zack bounded across to the quiet room and threw open the door. The guard, Henry, had balled a red bandanna in his fist, preparing to use it as a gag. Beaulieu was sitting, handcuffed to the arm of his chair. He was staring in wide-eyed terror, not at his tormentor, but at a vacant spot on one wall.

The right side of his face was starting to droop.

"Oh, Jesus," Zack said as he knelt by the man. "Guy, can you talk?"

Beaulieu turned to him slowly. His eyes were glassy and filled with tears.

"Head . . . hurts," he moaned.

His speech was thick and slurred. His tongue seemed bunched at the corner of his mouth.

"Did you hit him?" Zack demanded of the guard.

"Not even a tap. I swear I didn't."

"Undo these," Zack snapped, jiggling the handcuffs. The man hesitated. "Dammit, do as I say!"

"Do it, Henry," Frank said from the doorway. "What's happening, Zack?"

Zack turned slowly and looked up at his brother.

"He's having a stroke, Frank," he said hoarsely. "That's what. A cerebral hemorrhage, I would guess. I need a litter, a nurse, and an IV setup. And I want the CT scanner warmed up." He turned to the guard. "Tell me again, did you touch this man's head?" His voice was ice, his eyes fire.

"I didn't touch nothin' except his wrists," the man said defensively. "I swear, I don't hurt people unless they hurt me."

"Undo these. Quickly now!"

The guard did as he was told, and instantly, as if made of rags, Guy Beaulieu's right arm flopped off the chair and dangled down. Zack lowered him to the floor and cradled his head in his lap.

"I need that litter, please," he said, barely able to contain his anguish. He bent close to Beaulieu. "Easy does it, old friend," he whispered. "Easy does it."

Beaulieu's eyes opened, and Zack noted with horror and despair that the pupil of the right one had already begun to dilate.

"Okay, Guy," he whispered, stroking the older man's forehead and cheek, "the litter will be here in a second. Just hang on. You're going to be okay."

Suddenly, for a few frozen seconds, Beaulieu's eyes stopped their random drifting and focused on Zack's face.

"No . . . I'm . . . not," he said, forming each word with the most excruciating effort. "God . . . help . . . me . . . I'm . . . not."

Slowly, his eyes closed.

"Damn you," Zack hissed, looking first at the guard and then at Frank, Mainwaring, and Don Norman, who were clustered in the doorway. "God damn you all."

CHAPTER 11

OVER THE MONTHS since her son's attacks had first begun, Barbara Nelms's approach to housework had changed radically. Where once she had been meticulous almost to the point of obsession, now she cut corners wherever possible. She was never comfortable remaining out of range of the boy for more than five or ten minutes at a time.

With sitters unwilling to stay alone with Toby, and her husband drifting further and further into his work, the television set had become her closest ally. Only when Toby was engrossed in Saturday cartoons, or some of the programs on the children's cable network, did she dare spend any prolonged time doing laundry or preparing meals.

It was late afternoon, and Barbara had not even begun to think about dinner. All day Toby had been even more restless and remote than usual. She had read to him for a time and taken him to the store with her. She had pulled him around the block in his wagon and pushed him on the tire swing in the backyard.

Now, as she stared at the unwashed dishes in the sink and thought about the pile of ironing she had been avoiding, it was all she could do to keep from breaking down. Through the door to the living room she could see her son, lying on his back on the carpet, staring at the ceiling.

"Toby," she called out, "five more minutes and Robin's on. We missed him this morning while we were at the park. Why don't you go and get your bear, and I'll turn him on."

That the boy did not react was upsetting. When Toby was at his worst, his most distant, the prospect of watching *Robin the Good* usually brought a response of some sort. The actor who played Robin was overweight for the role and as patronizing to the children, as inane and vapid, as anyone she had ever seen, but his half-hour show, aired three times a day, was bright and quick.

"Okay, honey," she said, "you just stay put, then. I'm going to do some dishes, and then I'll turn on Robin."

Glancing almost continuously over her shoulder, she thrust her hand into the sink and snapped a nail off so low that it drew blood.

"Dammit," she said, sucking at the wound. "Dammit, dammit, dammit."

She ran cold water over her finger. Then, as much from frustration as from pain, she began to cry.

She snatched up the phone, dialed the mill, and had her husband called out of a meeting.

"Bob, hi, it's me," she said.

"I know. Has he done it again?"

"No. No, he's okay just now. But he's not acting right."

"He never acts right. Honey, I'm sorry I can't talk now, but I'm in the middle of an important meeting. Was there something special?"

Barbara blotted her bleeding finger on a towel.

"I . . . I was hoping you might be able to come home early. I'd like to put a nice dinner together, but I'm worried about Toby."

"Impossible," Bob Nelms said too quickly. "Honey, you just said he was okay. The people from Chicago are here. I've got a ton of stuff to go over with them. In fact, I was going to have Sharon call and tell you I'd be late."

"Couldn't you postpone them for a day? Just this once?"

"Sweetie, you know I'd come if I could. But they're only going to be here for a day."

"Please?" she whispered, fumbling through a cabinet for a Band-Aid.

"What?"

"Nothing. Nothing. When should I expect you?"

"Probably pretty late. How about you take Toby out for some pizza. I'll eat here."

"Bob, isn't there any way you could—"

"Barbie, please. Don't make things any more difficult for me than they are. I'll be home as soon as I can, okay? . . . Okay? . . . Doggone it, Barb, don't do this. . . ."

Slowly, Barbara Nelms replaced the receiver. Then she waited for her husband's return call. A minute passed, then another. Finally, she wrapped a Band-Aid around her finger and shuffled to the living room.

"Come on, my merry man," she said hoarsely, "it's time for Robin."

Toby Nelms let his mother lead him into the den and then sank down on the floor by the couch. He wanted her to get his bear for him, but the words to ask wouldn't come.

"Okay, Tobe," she said, switching on the television, "I'll just be in the kitchen. Call if you need me."

Stay, he thought. *Please stay with me.*

The cartoon that introduced Robin the Good's show appeared on the screen, along with a now-familiar voice that announced, "Hey, merry men and merry maids, get out your longbows and your stout staffs. It's time to travel once again to those days long, long ago—to Sherwood Forest and that friend of the poor, Robin the Good."

Toby watched quietly as his mother adjusted the color and then left the room. Moments later, she returned and set his tattered bear beside him.

"Enjoy the show," she said, patting him on the head. "I'll be in the kitchen."

"Thank you," Toby whispered. But she was already gone.

He stared toward the kitchen for a time, and then stuffed his bear between his legs and turned his attention to the television. Robin the Good, wearing a green suit and a hat with a feather, was dancing about and singing, while Alan-a-Dale played his guitar.

". . . We welcome all you boys and girls. But don't bring any diamonds or pearls. 'Cause I take from the rich and give to the poor. Then I go right out and get some more. . . . What ho, merry men and maids. Welcome to Sherwood, where learning is always fun, fun, fun.

Today we're going to do some drawing with Little John and take a ride on a camel with Maid Marian. But first, here's Friar Tuck. Tell us, pray thee, good friar, what letter we are going to learn about today."

A fat man with a brown robe and a bald place on the top of his head hopped onto the screen.

"Hello, boys and girls," he said. "What ho, there, Robin. Today, we're going to learn about one of my favorite letters. It's the letter that starts off a lot of our favorite words like *candy* and *cartoon*. It's the third letter in the alphabet, and it's called C. So here're Robin and Alan to tell you about it."

Robin the Good swung across the screen on a rope with leaves growing off it. Then he dropped to the ground as Alan-a-Dale began to play.

"Alas, my love, you do me wrong," Robin sang, "to cast me out so discourteously. Because today I sing this song about our friend the letter C. . . ."

Toby Nelms rubbed at his eyes as the color of the television set began growing brighter and brighter.

". . . C, C, is all our joy. C's for carrot and car and cat. C, C starts club and cloud. Now what do you think of that? . . ."

Robin the Good danced around a tree.

Seated on the floor in his den, Toby Nelms's body grew rigid. His shoulders began to shake. The sound of Robin's voice grew softer as the music grew louder. Overhead, lights began to flash past. A face floated into view.

". . . There's C for comet and C for crab; and C in front of the coat we wear. . . ."

". . . Now, Toby," the face said, "there's nothing to worry about. You're going to go to sleep. Just relax. Relax and count back from one hundred. . . ."

Robin the Good was singing and prancing across the television screen as Toby Nelms began, in a soft, tremulous voice, to count.

He was on one knee, crooning the final lines of his ballad, as the boy began to scream.

ΛCHAPTER 12

IT WAS, all would later agree, a magnificent funeral. Standing room only. The crowd, sweltering in the brutally humid summer afternoon, filled the pews of St. Anne's Church and spilled out into the vestibule. The priests conducting the mass were not only from the predominantly French-Canadian St. Anne's, but from the crosstown parish, St. Sebastian's, as well.

". . . Guy Beaulieu was not a *son* of Sterling," Monsignor Tresche was declaring in his eulogy. "He was one of its fathers—a gentle man, whose skill and caring hands have, through the years, touched each and every one of us. . . ."

Over the three days following Beaulieu's death, Zack had visited his widow, Clothilde, and daughter, Marie Fontaine, several times. Even so, he was surprised when Marie asked him to serve as a pall bearer. Although he would have preferred to remain less intimately involved with Guy's funeral than he had been with his death, accepting their request was the least he could do.

It had been at his desperate urging that Marie and her mother had put aside their biases against such things and had agreed to an autopsy.

". . . a man of vision and conviction. A humble man, who faced mounting personal difficulties with courage and dignity. . . ."

The priest droned on, but Zack, seated in the first row with the seven other pall bearers, heard only snatches. His thoughts kept drifting, as they had much of the time, to the agonizing scene with Guy in the emergency room, and to the equally unpleasant experience of viewing his post mortem examination.

As Zack had suspected, the man had died of a massive cerebral hemorrhage. There was, however, a major surprise. The arteries in Beaulieu's brain, and, in fact, in his whole body, were those of a man decades younger. The lethal stroke had resulted not from any crack in a hardened vessel but from the rupture of a small aneurysm—a pea-sized defect in one artery which, almost certainly, had been present without producing symptoms for many years.

The cause of that fatal tear, Zack knew, could only have been a sudden, drastic rise in blood pressure. That thought sent an angry jet of bile rasping into his throat, as it had over and over again since the autopsy. Guy Beaulieu's two years of difficulties at Ultramed-Davis, whether real or contrived, had loaded the weapon of his destruction.

The humiliating conflict in the emergency ward with Mainwaring, Frank, and the security guard had, in essence, pulled the trigger.

Frank, of course, saw things differently.

He had issued statements of shock and bereavement from the hospital, and from Ultramed, and had sent a basket of fruit to Guy's widow. But in the few minutes he and Zack had spent alone, he had made it clear that he considered Beaulieu's death nothing short of an act of Providence.

Unobtrusively, Zack glanced about the chapel. Suzanne, though dressed in sedate blue and wearing no makeup, sparkled in the midst of two rows of Ultramed-Davis physicians which did not include Donald Norman, Jack Pearl, or Jason Mainwaring. Several pews behind her, between the Judge and Cinnie, sat Frank, resplendent in a beige summer suit and appearing, as usual, composed and in control. The mayor was there, along with several other area notables, including the region's congressman.

Guy Beaulieu had once described himself to Zack as "just a plain, old, small-town Canuck, lucky enough to be born to parents who wouldn't let him quit school to work in the mills."

It was good, at least, to see that so many people knew better.

Later, as Zack and the other pall bearers shuffled up the aisle with Guy's casket, his eyes and Frank's met briefly. He felt so distant from the man—so totally detached.

Had they really grown up in the same home, played in the same yard year after year? Had they really worn the same clothes, shared so many childhood dreams? Had they really once been fast friends?

The hope of reestablishing a friendship with his brother suddenly seemed naive. They would make do, perhaps, tolerate one another, even work together. They would spend sterile time together at family functions. But they would never be close.

The open hearse was festooned with flowers. Zack, feeling overwhelmed by the sadness and futility of it all, helped slide the heavy casket into place among them.

"Excuse me, Doctor," a voice behind him said as he stepped back from the casket. "Kin I talk to you?"

Zack turned and was surprised to find himself confronting the huge security guard, Henry Flowers, who seemed ill at ease in a dark suit and solid black tie. Looking on, several respectful steps behind him, was a petite, plain young woman in a white lace dress—almost certainly the man's wife.

"Yes?" Zack asked.

The guard shifted uncomfortably.

"I . . . uh . . . I wanted you to know that I'm real sorry for what happened to Dr. Beaulieu," he said. "He took care of my wife's mother once, real good care, and he's never done nothin' bad to me. . . . Dr. Iverson, I never laid a hand on him except to grab his wrist. I swear it. I . . ."

His voice drifted away. It took several moments before Zack realized that the man did not know the results of the autopsy, and if he did, he did not understand them.

Zack reached out and put a hand on the guard's shoulder.

"You didn't do anything that caused Dr. Beaulieu's death, Henry," he said, loudly enough for the man's wife to hear. "He had an aneurysm —a time bomb—in his head, and it just happened to go off while you were there."

Relief flooded the guard's pocked face.

"Thanks, Doc," he said, pumping Zack's hand as if it were the handle on a tractor-trailer jack. "Oh, God, thanks a lot. If there's ever anything I can do for you, just ask. Anything."

He backed away, and then grabbed his tiny wife by the arm and hurried off.

Zack watched until the incongruous couple had disappeared around the corner. Then he turned and headed to his camper, feeling marginally less morose. At least one other who had shared those awful moments in the quiet room had been affected by them.

The procession to All Saints Cemetery was, according to the Judge, as long as any Sterling had ever seen.

Following the service, Zack accompanied Frank and their parents to the shaded spot where Marie Fontaine and her mother were receiving final condolences.

Marie, who seemed to have aged a year in just three days since her return home, accepted an embrace from Cinnie and a kiss on the cheek from the Judge. However, she barely touched Frank's outstretched hand before pulling away.

"It was good of you to come," she said coolly.

"Your father meant a great deal to all of us," Frank replied blandly.

She eyed him for a moment, and then said simply, "That's nice to know."

Zack glanced over at his parents, but saw nothing to suggest that they appreciated the tension in the brief exchange. Marie then turned to him, took both his hands in hers, and kissed him by the ear.

"Please stop by our limousine," she whispered.

Imperceptible to the others, Zack nodded.

* * *

565

Half an hour later, Zack sat across from Marie Fontaine and Clothilde Beaulieu in the back of the mortuary's black stretch Cadillac. The smoked-glass windows, including the partition separating them from the driver, were closed, but the limo's air-conditioning system kept the steamy afternoon at bay.

Marie's husband, a gaunt, bearded man whose quiet dignity reminded Zack a little of her father, stood outside.

"We wanted you to know how grateful we are for all you've done," Marie began.

"Your father was always very good to me."

"He was very good to everyone," she said. "That's why it's so hard to understand why nobody stood up for him while he was being murdered."

Zack's impulse was to correct her, but the intensity of her eyes told him not to bother.

"It upsets me a great deal to think that anyone might have deliberately set about to ruin him," he said.

"Not anyone, Zack. Ultramed."

"What?"

"Zack, we know Father confided in you. We know that even though your brother runs the hospital, he thought you would give him the benefit of an open mind. Was he right?"

"I told him I would listen and that I would respect his confidence, if that's what you mean."

Marie glanced over at her mother, who nodded her approval of Zack's response.

"That's exactly what we mean," she went on. "Several years ago, Father opposed the sale of the hospital to Ultramed. He just didn't believe an outside corporation should be given such a vital foothold in this community—at least, not with so little community involvement or control. If it weren't for *your* father's influence, we think he would have succeeded in blocking it. But that is neither here nor there, now. Did you know that shortly after they took over at the hospital, Ultramed took legal action to fire him?"

"No," Zack said. "No, I didn't."

"He was preparing to countersue them when they backed off. According to Father, they became frightened by a court decision in Florida that ended up costing one of the other corporations millions for trying to do the same thing to a pathologist who was working in a hospital they had acquired.

"Zack, Ultramed wants blind loyalty from everyone working for them—total acceptance of their policies. Father fought them at every turn. Less than a year after they dropped the suit against him, the rumors started. And within just a few months of that, a showy new surgeon was on the scene, snapping up chunks of Father's practice."

"That would be Jason Mainwaring," Zack said.

"Exactly."

"Have you any proof that Ultramed engineered all of this?" he asked.

"Only this." She reached beneath her seat, drew out a thick manila envelope and passed it across to him. "Mother and I talked it over last night. Father liked you and trusted you. And frankly, we have nowhere else to turn. This is all the information he had been able to gather in his battle against Ultramed. It doesn't prove they were behind his murder, but it does show something of how they operate—some of the things they're capable of doing to turn a profit."

"What am I to do with this?"

For the first time, Beaulieu's widow spoke.

"Dr. Iverson," she said, in a soft accent virtually identical to Guy's, "it was my husband's hope that the information contained in that envelope would convince the board of trustees, including your father, to exercise their option and order the repurchase of the hospital from Ultramed."

Zack stared at her in disbelief.

"Mrs. Beaulieu, are you forgetting that I *work* for Ultramed? They pay my salary, my office expenses, insurance, everything. To say nothing of the administrator at the hospital being my brother. What you are asking me to do isn't really fair."

My husband is dead. Is that fair?

Zack saw the response flash in the woman's eyes and then vanish.

"We are asking you," Clothilde Beaulieu said patiently, "to do nothing more than study the contents of that envelope and use it—or not—as you see fit. I assure you there will be no hard feelings if you return the material to us after you have looked it over . . . or even right now."

"We mean that, Zachary," Marie said. "We really do."

For a time, there was only silence. Zack looked first at one woman and then the other, and finally at the envelope in his lap.

A sucker for anybody's cause.

Had Frank's terse assessment of him been so irritating because it was so close to the mark? Suzanne . . . the mountains . . . the Judge . . . his career. Any clash with Ultramed and Frank was almost certainly destined to be a losing proposition for him. And there was much, so very much, at stake.

The envelope was a Pandora's box. A bomb that might be nothing more than a dud, or nothing less than a lethal explosion.

A sucker for anybody's cause.

Slowly, deliberately, Zack slid the dead surgeon's legacy under his arm. Then he reached across and shook hands with both women.

"I'll be in touch," he said.

* * *

567

Frank, Frank, he's our man. If he can't do it, no one can. . . .

Over the two decades since his graduation from Sterling High, not a day had passed that Frank Iverson did not hear the chant echoing in his mind. Cheerleaders dancing on the sidelines, each one hoping Frank would at least spend a few minutes with her at the victory celebration after the game. Grandstands jammed with parents, teachers, students, and reporters, all screaming *his* name, all begging him for one more pass, one more score. The Judge and his mother, proudly accepting congratulations from those seated around them.

Driving through the streets of Sterling toward his hospital, Frank heard the cheering as clearly as if he were standing on the field, staring across the line of scrimmage at the opposition, knowing that, in just a few seconds, his play would swell those cheers to a deafening roar.

Frank, Frank, he's our man. . . .

They had been days of glory for him; days of strength and independence. It felt so good to realize that after all the difficult, humiliating years that had followed, after all the lousy breaks and the goddamn patronizing, demeaning lectures from his father, a return to the stature and influence of those times was so close at hand. Two weeks, that was all. Three at the most.

He had done his part, and done it well. Now, all he needed was patience—patience and constant vigilance. Three years before, he had made the mistake of complacency, of trusting, and it had cost him dearly. There would be no repeat of that fiasco this time. Nothing would be taken for granted. Nothing. Besides, he affirmed as he swung up the drive to Ultramed-Davis, there were reasons aplenty for keeping his eyes open and his guard up. A million reasons, to be exact.

. . . If he can't do it, no one can.

CHAPTER 13

"Helene, I don't know how to tell you this, but I think it's time we moved Mr. Gerard Morris's fabulous woodland scene out of the window and more toward the back—like in the storeroom."

Suzanne propped Morris's huge oil against a display case and stepped back several paces, hoping that the change in lighting and perspective might thaw some of the feelings she had for the man and his work.

"The man's a legend," Helene Meyer called out from the back.

"In his own mind, he is."

"Suzanne, when are you going to come to grips with the reality that tourists don't come up to northern New Hampshire to buy abstract art? They want mallards."

"Paint by numbers," Suzanne muttered, remembering a tongue lashing she had received from the pompous artist for reducing the price of one of his "masterpieces" by fifty dollars.

"What?"

"Nothing. Nothing."

It was nearing three in the afternoon. Suzanne and her partner had been doing inventory nonstop since her return from Guy's funeral. Outside, muted midday sunshine filtered through a row of expansive, century-old sugar maples, turning Main Street into a gentle work of art that far surpassed anything Gerard Morris had produced.

Immersing herself in the inventory and spending time with Helene had helped lift some of the melancholy Suzanne was feeling, but memories of Guy Beaulieu kept her mood somber. Although she had not known the man outside the hospital, she had shared several patients with him before his practice dwindled, and more than respected him as a person and a physician.

Nevertheless, the stories that had been circulating about him of late were disconcerting, and Suzanne had gradually come to agree with those who believed that it would be in everyone's best interest for Guy to retire. Now, reflecting on Zack's opinion that the aging surgeon seemed quite capable and mentally intact, and with the realization that the man had died defending himself, she was having second thoughts.

First Guy Beaulieu, and then the old woodsman Chris Gow—in both cases she had backed off, siding with Ultramed through her silence. True, the corporation had plucked her from a situation that had seemed totally hopeless and had given her a chance. For that alone she owed Ultramed her loyalty. But still, there had been a time, she knew, when she considered herself a liberal, a champion of the underdog. There had been a time when she would have gone to the mat for either man, just as Zack had done. It was hard to believe she had changed so much over just a few short years.

As she hefted Morris's painting off the floor and replaced it in the window, Suzanne silently cursed Paul Cole for the chaos he had brought to her life.

"So?"

Helene Meyer, dressed in jeans and a blue-print smock, emerged from the storeroom with a pair of ceramic vases that they had taken on consignment from a MicMac Indian potter. She was a short, dark, energetic woman with close-cut hair and just enough excess pounds to puff her cheeks and arms.

"So what?" Suzanne asked.

"So where are Morris's ducks?"

Suzanne nodded toward the window.

"Good, good. You're learning, child. You're learning."

The White Mountain Olde Curiosity Shop and Gallery occupied the ground floor of a half-century-old, red-brick structure two blocks from the center of town. Three years before, when she received word that an uncle had died and left the place to her, Helene was working in a dead-end advertising job in Manhattan and competing with what seemed like several million other forty-year-old divorced women for any one of a minuscule pool of available men.

She took her inheritance as an omen for change.

Despite having "taken her act on the road," along with her two children, Helene had never given up on the notion that Mr. Perfect was, at any given moment, just one man away. Perhaps, Suzanne reflected, that was why the woman always had a smile and an encouraging word for even the bleakest situation.

"You okay?" Helene asked, setting the vases on a pair of lucite pedestals, and then reversing them.

"Huh? Oh, sure, I'm fine."

"You look tired."

"I always look tired."

"You always look beautiful," Helene corrected. "Today you look beautiful and tired."

"I'm fine. I'm just not sleeping too well."

The explanation was an understatement. Since her discharge from the hospital, she had been almost continuously restless and ill at ease, sleeping no more than an hour or two at a time and often awakening with an intense, free-floating anxiety. It was hardly the mood she would have expected, given the outcome of her surgery.

"You need some sex," Helene said.

"I don't need any sex. That's your cure for everything."

"Well, have I had a sick day since you've known me? As long as there are ski lodges and contra dances and Thursday night single-mingles at the Holiday Inn, I intend to stay healthy as a horse. Don't you think it's time you—"

"No. No, I don't. Now let's change the subject. Besides—"

She caught herself after that one word, but it was too late. Helene leapt at the opening.

"Besides, what?"

"Nothing."

"Oh, yes." She squinted across at Suzanne. "You did it, didn't you? The other night with that new doctor. What's his name?"

"Zachary. But—"

"Well, I'll be damned. No wonder you're so tired."

"I thought that was supposed to perk me up."

"Not when it's the first time in several years, it's not," Helene said. "You need to keep in shape for that sort of thing. Glory be. He must be something else, that's all I can say. Tell me about him."

"There's nothing to tell. He's a nice guy. I was frightened about my surgery and he was understanding, and things . . . things just . . . got out of hand. It was a mistake—just one of those things. We're not even going to see one another again outside the hospital."

"Glory be," Helene said again.

"You stop that."

Helene took Suzanne by the shoulders.

"No, you stop that," she said. "Suze, you're like my sister. Bringing you in as a partner in this place is the best thing I've ever done—except maybe for that furrier from White Plains. . . ."

She sighed wistfully, and Suzanne laughed.

"If I keep putting my two cents into your life," she went on, "it's because I love you. I know you had it rough with that jerk you were married to and all, but that's water under the bridge. He's gone. You can't keep letting him rule your life."

"I don't let him rule my life. I'm doing just fine, thank you"

"And you've got a great job and a great kid and a lot of interests and you don't need anyone messing things up for you again. I know. I know. You've said all that before."

"So . . ."

"So there's more. It's out there waiting if you'd just stop running scared and give it a chance."

"Helene, I'm perfectly happy, and my life is perfectly under control."

"Okay, okay. But if you ask me, you could do with a little less control and a little more—"

"Meyer, enough."

Helene held up her hands defensively.

"Just trying to help," she said.

"I know."

"So, this Zachary that you're not going to see again outside the hospital, tell me about him."

"Helene, I thought we—"

"Tall? Kind of a Clint Eastwood face? Great eyes? Dark brown hair?"

"How did you—"

At that instant, the door behind Suzanne opened. She whirled, and tensed visibly.

"Hi," Zack said.

"I thought so," Helene muttered. "Glory be . . ."

* * *

"I'm sorry to have popped in on you like this," Zack said, sipping the cappuccino Suzanne had made him. "I know you said Wednesday."

"That's okay. I needed a break."

They were perched on cherrywood stools on either side of a glass case that doubled as a sales counter and jewelry display. Following introductions, small talk, and a nudge that Suzanne had tried unsuccessfully to find annoying, Helene had gone off on "errands." Across the gallery, a dowager tourist and her diminutive husband were eyeing a Gerard Morris, entitled typically: *The Forest Is a Symphony. Life in Itself.*

"How's the incision?" Zack asked.

"No problem . . ."

The atmosphere between them was subdued, but not strained. And despite her efforts to pull away, Suzanne sensed that her connection to him, forged on the hillside behind her house and later in her hospital room, had not softened. Silently, she cautioned herself against giving off any encouraging signals. Helene meant well, but she simply didn't understand.

"I'm sorry about Guy," she said. "He was a nice man."

"Yeah."

Zack debated telling her about the envelope, but decided against it —especially since it still lay unopened on the seat of the camper.

"Are you off for the afternoon?" she asked.

"Nope. I'm due at the office in a couple of minutes. I . . . um . . . actually, I came by for a consultation."

She eyed him suspiciously.

"Seriously," he said.

She started to protest, but held back. Helene was right. He did have great eyes. *Damn you, Paul,* she thought.

"Annie?" she asked.

"No, thank goodness. Norman seems to be hanging in there all right with her. She doesn't care much for him, though. She says she doesn't trust him. No, I don't need advice from Suzanne Cole, cardiologist. I need it from Suzanne Cole, mother."

"Interesting," she said. "In that case, let me just change my expression from knowledgeable and unflappable to disheveled, bewildered, and exhausted. Okay, you may proceed."

Across the gallery, the dowager and her husband had shifted their attention to Morris's *Three Deer, a Stream, and the Cosmos,* a garish rendering with luminescent stars and tiny sparkles in the water.

"It's a consult I've got to do for Phil Brookings," Zack said. "An eight-year-old boy."

"Name?"

Reflexively, Suzanne picked up a pen and doodled *8 years* on the corner of a pad.

"Nelms. Toby Nelms. The kid hasn't spoken more than a word or two to anyone in five months. Brookings is ready to enter therapy with him, but he wanted me to evaluate him first. I think he's terrified at the prospect of spending hour after hour locked in his office with a kid who won't talk."

"That does sound awful—especially for a shrink. But the child doesn't exactly sound neurosurgical."

"Probably not, but he might be neurological. Apparently he's been having some sort of psychomotor seizures."

"Psychomotor?"

"Sort of a grab-bag diagnosis, meaning, I don't have a handle on what's going on. Some variant of temporal-lobe epilepsy is as close as I can come, based on what Brookings told me. During the first seizure, just before he stopped speaking, he destroyed his room. There have been a number of others since then."

"So why isn't it temporal-lobe epilepsy?"

"Well, for one thing, although there is this rage component like we see in temporal-lobe patients, there's also an enormous fear component. The kid acts as if he's absolutely terrified of something. And for another—and this is what's really disturbing—the recovery time is getting longer and longer with each episode. It sounds as if these seizures, or whatever they are, are associated with some actual increased pressure in the boy's brain."

"Cerebral edema?"

"Quite possibly."

"That's frightening."

"Until now, the swelling's been reversible, but as you know, at some point a vicious cycle sets in: edema causing high fever, causing more edema, and so on."

"Are there any triggers?"

"Triggers?"

"You know, something that sets off an attack."

"Oh, no. Not that anyone has picked up on. Brookings wants to put him on Dilantin or one of the temporal-lobe epilepsy drugs, but he wanted me to check the boy out first. I thought maybe you could give me some hints about dealing with kids around his age."

"Has he had an EEG?"

"I want to get both that and a CT scan, but according to Brookings, the little guy gets so agitated when he gets anywhere near the hospital that it's been next to impossible to get any kind of technically satisfactory study."

"The hospital?"

"Brookings swears that the kid looked through his office window at

573

the hospital and bolted. He had to chase him across the parking lot and actually tackle him."

Absently, Suzanne had scribbled the words *Nelms, psychomotor,* and *hospital* on her pad.

"I assume Brookings has looked for the obvious—a bad experience in the hospital, something like that?" she asked.

"Uh-huh. Repair of an incarcerated hernia a year or so ago is all. Your pal Mainwaring did the work. I reviewed the record. The boy was in overnight, but there were absolutely no problems."

Suzanne added *hernia* and *no problems* to her list.

"Was it done under local?"

"Something like Pentothal and gas, I think it was. Why?"

"No reason. Just throwing out thoughts. I had the same anesthesia, and I'm still talking up a storm, so I don't think that's it."

Across the room, the tourists were embroiled in a heated debate, the dowager gesturing toward *Cosmos,* and her husband toward *Symphony.*

"Any suggestions?" Zack asked.

Suzanne scratched lines under several of the words on her pad.

"Just one off the top," she said. "Don't see him in your office."

"What?"

"And do your best not to look like a doctor, either, or to call yourself 'doctor.' He'll probably know you are one, but there's no sense in making a big deal of it. Unlike most grown-ups, kids don't get impressed with our title. They just get scared."

"You mean, see him at my place?"

"Or even his place. Or better still, somewhere neutral. What about that plane you were telling Jen about? She's very excited about that. Is there any way you could put on a show for this child?"

"Excellent idea," Zack said. "Of course I could. That's perfect. I have just the place. The Meadows up at the top of Gaston Street. You know where that is?"

"Uh-huh. We've been there. That sounds just right. When are you seeing him?"

"Wednesday. Wednesday at one-thirty. Say, listen, that being Wednesday and all, why don't we meet up there at, say, eleven-thirty. We can have some lunch—a picnic. You can bring Jen and—"

"I can't," she said too quickly. "What I mean is, we already have plans."

"Oh."

"Zack, I'm sorry." *Why was she lying?* "Another time."

He smiled tightly.

"Yeah, sure. Another time . . . Well, thanks for the coffee." He cleared his throat and pushed off the stool. "I . . . um . . . I guess I'd better get back to the hospital."

"Zack . . ." she said as he headed off.

He turned back.

"Zack, I . . . I really am sorry about Guy."

"Yeah," he said, the hurt in his eyes unmistakable. "Me, too."

He turned again and was gone.

Stonily, Suzanne tore the sheet from her pad and balled it in her fist. Perhaps it was time she herself made an appointment with Phil Brookings. Sterling had been every bit the refuge she had hoped it would be. Peace and beauty, a good job, and time to spend with Jen. That was all she had wanted, and all she needed. *Why was this happening now?*

"Excuse me, Miss?"

The dowager, her husband hovering behind, stood by the stool Zack had just vacated.

"Huh? Oh, sorry," Suzanne said. "I see you're interested in Gerard Morris's work?"

"Yes. Is he local?"

"One town over. He's growing more popular every year."

Why had she lied to him about Wednesday? Jen *did* have plans with friends, but she was free. *Why had she lied?*

"Well," the woman said, "my husband and I are most interested in the work on the left. The one with those lovely deer. Could you tell me its price?"

"It's eighteen hundred."

"Oh," the woman said. "I see." She scanned Morris's mimeoed resumé. "Has he had any gallery shows outside of this area? Boston? New York?"

"No," Suzanne said, realizing that, despite her taste in art, the woman was no novice at buying it. "I don't believe he has."

Maybe Helene was right. Maybe it was time to stop running scared.

"Well," the woman said, "that being the case, don't you think the asking price for his work is a bit high?"

Suzanne eyed her for a moment, and then flipped the crumpled list into the wastepaper basket.

"As a matter of fact," she said, "I do."

For years people had called her the Witch of West Eighty-seventh Street. But Hattie Day had known better. They called her Batty Hattie and filed petitions claiming her cluttered apartment was a health menace and her family of cats against the law. But Hattie hadn't cared. On her infrequent trips to the store, children taunted her and even sometimes threw things at her. But Hattie had understood, and still loved them as much as she loved her cats.

For years, people had said that she was crazy. But because she had known better, Hattie had just smiled at them.

But now, since the terrifying events that had followed her trip to

Quebec, Hattie smiled at no one. Because now Hattie knew they were right.

It was nearly two in the morning. Exhausted, but reluctant to sleep, Hattie hobbled to her stove, lit a cigarette from the burner, and then put on a pot of tea. She was only sixty-two, but with her pallor, her long, unkempt hair, and her cadaverous thinness, she looked eighty.

She sank into a tattered easy chair and studied her hands. There was nothing about the bony, nicotine-stained fingers and the long, curving nails to suggest the wonderful music they had once made. The death of her parents in an accident had, in effect, ripped the violin from her hands—pulled her out of Juilliard and into a succession of mental hospitals. But over the years, she had made do. She had her apartment, and her cats, and her battered stereo, and more than enough records to fill each day with music.

But that was before Quebec.

Shakily, Hattie stubbed out her cigarette, hesitated a moment, and then limped to the stove to light another. The water had not yet boiled.

If only she had refused the invitation to Martin's wedding, she thought; if only she had stayed home where she belonged, none of this would have happened. But Martin, her cousin's son, was really the only family she had. And when *he* was at Juilliard he had stopped by often, bringing food and usually a record or two, and staying long enough to tell her about his studies. Once he had even brought his guitar and played for her—Bach, and several wonderful Villa-Lobos pieces.

Hattie smiled grimly at the memory.

The bus ride up to Canada had been easy enough, and the wedding had been beautiful—especially the chamber groups made up of Martin's friends. It was during the ride home that the dreadful ache in her leg had begun. The bus driver had turned her over to the ambulance people in Sterling, New Hampshire, and within an hour she was in the operating room having a cloth artery put in to bypass the clot in her groin.

They had called her recovery a miracle. After just a week in the hospital and two weeks in a nursing home, she had gone home. Martin had driven her back to Manhattan and had even gotten one of her cats back for her from the animal protection people. A miracle.

It was just a day after Martin had dropped her off that the frightening episodes had begun. Without warning, her mind would go limp. For an hour or more at a time she would sit, staring at nothing, unable to move or to focus her thoughts, knowing what was happening but powerless to control it. The colors in the room would become uncomfortably bright, all sounds unnaturally muted. Sometimes she could force herself out of her chair. Other times, she could only sit and wait for the terribly unpleasant episodes to pass. Twice she had wet herself.

She knew she was becoming insane.

Then, as if verifying her fears, some of the bizarre episodes had

begun exploding into horrible, vivid, distorted reenactments of her surgery.

The teapot began whistling. Hattie pushed herself upright, put a tea
bag into a chipped stoneware mug, and poured in the boiling water. On
the way back to her easy chair, she stopped and put on one of the
albums Martin had left with her—Elizabethan music and English folk
pieces, with Martin featured on his guitar.

Perhaps, she thought, it was worth calling Martin and telling him
she was going mad. She looked about for Orange, the cat he had retrieved for her. During the last of her nightmares, she had hurt it somehow—knocked out a tooth and cut its lip. Since then, the animal had
spent most of its time under the bed or behind the bookshelf.

Hattie sank heavily into her chair. For a brief time, Martin's playing
brought her some serenity and even some sweet glimpses into her dim
past. There was a set of dances that she felt sure she had once played at
a recital, and a lovely rendition of a song by Thomas Stewart. Next
came her favorite, a gentle and haunting flute and guitar duet of
"Greensleeves."

Bit by bit, her fears began to loosen their grip. Then, as they had
twice before that day, the colors in the room began to intensify.

No! Hattie's mind screamed. *Please, God, not again.*

The music grew faint, and gradually faded into the hum of traffic
passing on nearby Columbus Avenue.

No . . .

Hattie felt the unpleasant inertia begin to settle in. The glow from
the lamp across the room hurt her eyes.

Please, God . . .

Desperately, and with all her strength, she forced herself to her
feet, and grabbed her cigarettes, and stumbled toward the stove.

"Not this time," she said out loud. "Goddamn it, not this time."

She thrust a cigarette between her lips and shakily turned the
burner knob. The gas flame flashed on.

"Hattie . . . Hattie, just relax."

The voice, deep and soothing, seemed to be coming from everywhere at once. Then, from above her, Hattie saw the blue-gray eyes
smiling at her over the mask.

"Just relax now. There's nothing to worry about. Nothing at all. I
want you to begin counting back from one hundred."

"Please . . ."

"Hattie, count!"

"One hundred . . . ninety-nine . . ."

"Good, Hattie. Keep counting. Keep counting."

"Ninety-eight . . ."

"She's under."

"Ninety-seven . . ."

"Ready, everyone. Okay."

"Ninety-six . . . No, wait, please. You're wrong. I'm not asleep. I'm not asleep yet."

"Suction up."

"Wait!"

"Knife, please."

"No! Not yet! Not yet!"

Hattie Day screamed as the scalpel cut into the wall of her lower abdomen. Her screams intensified as flame leapt from the stove and ignited first her hair and then her robe.

"Snap, please. Now another . . ."

Hattie reeled across her apartment, knocking away pieces of fiery cloth. The rug began to smolder. She fell to the floor as the scalpel cut down her abdomen and over her groin. Flames seared her face and scalp. She retched from the smoke and the acrid smell of her own burning flesh.

"Retractors ready, please . . ."

The voice bored through the pain. The knife cut deeper.

"Sponge. No, over here. Right here!"

Her clothes now a mass of flame, Hattie Day lurched to her feet and plunged toward the window.

"Okay. Now, retract here."

Shrieking, and now engulfed in flame, the woman they all called the Witch of West Eighty-seventh Street hurled herself through the glass and out into the summer night, ten stories above the street.

CHAPTER 14

TUESDAY MORNING descended on Zack in the guise of one of his sneakers, set neatly and carefully on the side of his face by Cheapdog.

"Self-centered brute," he mumbled, working his eyes open one at a time. "The world has to turn upside down just because you have to take a pee."

Cheapdog responded to the rebuke by licking him on the mouth.

"Okay, okay, mop-face. You made your point." Zack scratched the animal behind one ear and made yet another in a long series of promises to get him a haircut. "I'm afraid I haven't been paying much attention to you lately, old boy. Thanks for being so understanding."

Feeling sluggish, and less enthused about a day at work than he had in some time, he pulled on a pair of surgical scrub pants emblazoned PROPERTY OF MUNICIPAL HOSPITAL OF BOSTON—NOT TO BE REMOVED FOR ANY REASON, let Cheapdog out into the backyard, did fifteen minutes of lackluster calisthenics, and finally started water for coffee.

Suzanne's striking change of attitude toward him was, he knew, one reason for his unpleasant humor. And as wonderful as making love with her had been, he wished now that they had played things differently.

But weighing perhaps even more heavily at that moment was Guy Beaulieu's legacy.

For most of the prior evening, Guy's envelope had remained unopened in the camper. In fact, at various times throughout the day Zack had actually considered returning it in that state. In the end, though, he realized that his decision to do what he could for the man had been made well before meeting with his widow and daughter, and in fact, even before the terrible events in the quiet room.

As he dripped hot water through his Chemex filter and scrambled two eggs with some chopped peppers, onions, and bits of leftover bacon, Zack mulled over his initial impressions of the surgeon's strange and bitter legacy.

It was after midnight when he had finally returned home from a long walk with Cheapdog and brought in the envelope. Too tired to read with much comprehension, he had spent two hours sifting through the material and sorting it into piles on the dining room table. From what he could tell, the Ultramed Hospitals Corporation, whether responsible for Guy's difficulties or not, had had a tiger by the tail.

There were dozens of newspaper clippings and official documents, plus computer printouts, a number of typed and amended lists of corporate officers and boards of directors, and several smaller envelopes filled with hastily scrawled, handwritten notes.

Beaulieu and his researchers had been thoroughly preparing themselves for battle. Still, despite their diligence, it looked to Zack as if the evidence they had accumulated of Ultramed's avaricious business practices was circumstantial and vague.

Zack felt certain that although the assorted documents might raise some eyebrows among the hospital trustees, they were lacking the one, essential ingredient that might turn that concern into votes: a flesh-and-blood example—even one—of the dangers of such practices—what Rock Hudson had been to AIDS, or the Challenger explosion to the dangers of space exploration.

Without such a rallying point, such an emotional linchpin, Zack knew that Beaulieu's efforts were ultimately as doomed as the man himself.

In addition to the evidence against Ultramed, the envelope contained a diary.

During the early morning hours, Zack had done no more than scan the small, spiral-bound notebook. Now, after clearing a space on the table for his breakfast, he opened it randomly. Not surprisingly, the writing, almost all of it in fountain pen, was meticulous and precise.

December 11th: Several patients cancelled today, including Clarisse LaFrenniere. Spoke on phone to her. She was reluctant to say anything. Had to beg her. Finally admitted that her son Ricky had heard at school that I had seen one of the girls in his class for a lump on her neck, and had undressed her and made her lie on my examining table, and then that I had walked around and around the table, touching her. No such patient exists in my records or memory. Made several calls to parents of any young girls I had treated. They admitted to having heard rumors, but denied any of them dealt with their daughters. They were all quite distant and embarrassed. I feel I may have done myself more harm than good by contacting them. Called Ricky and begged him to give me the girl's name. He could or would not. Finally, Clarisse took the phone from him, told me not to call again, and hung up. I will not stop trying.

Zack glanced at several other pages, some of which outlined more of Guy's efforts to dive beneath the murky sea of rumors. Others described clashes with members of the medical staff, the local newspaper, and even certain patients.

Taken as a whole, it was a chronicle of the agonizing disintegration of a man's life.

Allegations of malpractice, none of them substantiated or backed up with a suit . . . letters of complaint to the newspapers and the hospital, most of them anonymous . . . rumors of sexual misconduct . . . rumors of inappropriate behavior . . . patient defections . . .

Blow after blow, humiliation after humiliation, yet Guy Beaulieu had refused to knuckle under. On one page he seemed heroic, on the next, pathologically obstinate. As Zack scanned the notes, the fine line separating the two conditions grew even less distinct.

The chances that a man is in the right increase geometrically by the vigor with which others are trying to prove him wrong.

The maxim was one of Zack's favorites, and he had cited it any number of times over the years. But never had he felt it in his gut the way he did at this moment.

Still, there was more than gut instinct to consider. There was the incriminating letter from Maureen Banas, along with other damning evidence Frank claimed to have. There was also Guy's explosive and irrational behavior in the emergency ward on the morning of his death.

And finally, there was the lack of any really good explanation as to why the man might have been singled out for destruction in the first place.

Certainly, his widow's belief that Ultramed was trying to rid itself of a potential troublemaker was possible, but the response seemed absurdly out of proportion to the threat Guy posed—like shooting a fly with an elephant gun.

Zack retrieved Cheapdog from where he was lurking beneath the window of a neighbor's unspayed collie, and chained him on a long run in the yard. Then he showered, dressed, and headed for the hospital, wondering what he would do if he had to confront Marie Fontaine and her mother with hard evidence that Guy had been, in fact, irrational, unstable, and paranoid. Even with a negative autopsy, the man could have been in the early stages of Alzheimer's or struggling with nonanatomical mental illness.

As he was pulling into the small Doctors Only lot at the hospital, Zack flashed on another saying—this one from a poster he had tacked to the wall of his med school apartment.

Just because you're paranoid, doesn't mean they're not out to get you.

The emergency ward was in a louder-than-usual morning hum, with several private physicians doing minor procedures, and the E.R. physician of the day, Wilton Marshfield, huffing from one of four "active" rooms to the next, clearly upset that things were not proceeding at a more gentle pace.

Zack stopped by the lounge for one final cup of coffee, and was in the process of failing to confound two candy stripers with a thumb palm, when he was paged for an outside call.

"Zack, it's Brookings here, Phil Brookings."

"Oh, yes, Phil. If you're calling about that youngster, Nelms, I had to postpone his appointment because of Guy Beaulieu's funeral. I'll be seeing him tomorrow afternoon."

Zack glanced over at the candy stripers, one of whom was completing the more-than-passable thumb palm of a penny on her first try.

"I know," the psychiatrist said. "The boy's mother called me. She was, how can I say, a little concerned that you told her to meet you on the side of some mountain. I promised her I would check with you to see if . . . ah . . . if there was anything further I could do."

"Actually," Zack said, smiling at Brookings's discomfiture, "It's near the base of the mountain. Not on the side."

"Oh . . . I see . . . Well, I'll just give Mrs. Nelms a call and reassure her that you're not the, how should I say, the eccentric she thinks you might be."

This time, Zack laughed out loud.

"Phil, forgive me for being glib. The truth is, I probably *am* the eccentric she thinks I might be. But this time, at least, I'm just doing what I can to avoid the difficulty *you* had. It's a little tricky doing a detailed neurological exam on a moving target."

"I understand," Brookings said, although his tone suggested some lingering doubts. "I'll speak with the boy's mother and make sure they show up. And just in case, perhaps you should wear your sneakers. The kid is fast."

"Thanks, Phil. I'll be in touch."

Zack hung up as the candy stripers, still practicing, were preparing to leave the lounge.

"Here you go, ladies," he said. "One more. This one's called a finger roll. In it, this perfectly normal American quarter will be magically transported across the tops of my fingers and back without the aid of a crane, bulldozer, or my other hand."

Between the second and the third roll, the quarter slipped between his fingers and plunked into his coffee.

"Now, I suggest that you two stay away from this trick until you're old enough to work with hot coffee," he warned.

He stood proudly by the cup and waited to retrieve his coin until the bewildered pair had left the room.

"Me, eccentric," he muttered as he headed through the emergency ward. "That's ridiculous. Absolutely ridiculous."

A set of X rays, five views of a teenager's cervical spine, were wedged up on a four-paneled viewbox in the corridor. Hours later, when the tension and excitement had died down and there was time to reflect, Zack would be unable to explain what it was about those films that had caught his eye.

But in that one microsecond as he passed by, something did.

It might have been the widening of a shadow, or perhaps the slightly unusual curve in the lateral view. Or it might have been nothing more or less than the instinctive processing of the films against thirteen years of study and God only knew how many other C-spines in how many other settings.

Whatever it was, something made him stop, turn, and study the X rays in more detail.

The fractures of vertebrae C-1 and C-2 were far from the most obvious he had ever seen, but they were certainly present—and unquestionably unstable. If the spinal cord had not already been damaged, a sudden twist, or turn, or bump could be disastrous.

Either way, he certainly should have been called in on the case.

He checked the name and birthdate: *Stacy Mills, age 14.*

Next, he cut through the nurses' station, looking for Wilton Marshfield. The portly physician was hunched over a counter, hurriedly writing a set of discharge instructions. Next to the instruction sheet was a soft cervical collar.

"Hi," Zack said, moving close enough to verify that the instructions were, in fact, for Stacy Mills.

He looked past the man to bed 3, where a dark, pretty girl in riding jodhpurs and a lavender T-shirt was waiting with her parents. She was sitting on the edge of the litter with her feet dangling down, and she was rubbing gently at the base of her skull.

"Oh, hi, Iverson," Marshfield said. He glanced up only long enough to nod, and then returned to his writing. "This is one bitch of a morning, I'll tell you. . . . Saw you at Beaulieu's funeral yesterday. . . . Terrible business. Terrible."

"Wilton, could I talk to you for a moment?" Zack asked softly. Marshfield shook his head.

"Can't stop right now," he said, pulling a prescription pad from his clinic coat. "I've got to get rid of this kid, and then I still have two more patients to see. I'm getting too old for this pace, Iverson. Too damn old. Tell your brother he'd better hurry up and get this place straightened out so I can get back to my trout stream and my grandchildren."

"It's about that girl you're getting ready to send home," Zack said. "Stacy Mills."

Marshfield squinted over at the girl, and then picked up the cervical collar and the instruction sheet, and began writing a prescription for a muscle relaxant.

"Fell off her horse and strained her neck muscles," he said as he wrote. "Look, Iverson," he added curtly, "I'm sorry I snapped at you the other night. But please, just don't make any trouble for me today. I'm too far behind to—"

"Listen, Marshfield," Zack whispered. "I just looked at her films over there. She has a fracture. Two of them, I think. C-one and C-two."

The older man froze. In slow motion, his pen wobbled in his fingertips and then fell, clattering onto the counter.

"Are you sure?" he rasped.

Zack nodded.

"Jesus . . ."

"Come, let me show you."

Moments later, Zack led a mute, badly shaken Wilton Marshfield across to Stacy Mills and her parents.

"Hello, Stacy, Mr. and Mrs. Mills," he said. "My name is Iverson. Zachary Iverson. I'm a neurosurgeon."

He glanced back at Marshfield, who looked as if he were listening blindfolded to the final counts from a firing squad.

Inwardly, Zack smiled. If the man was waiting for gunfire, he was in for a pleasant surprise.

Hey, Wilton, relax, he was thinking. *As far as I'm concerned, this business of ours has never been a contest or a game. It's life. It's the real banana. And it's hard enough to do right even without the bullshit and the oneupsmanship. You did the best you could, and that's all we got—any of us. There's no way I would hang you out to dry.*

"Dr. Marshfield, here, has just made an excellent pickup on Stacy's

X rays," he said. "He spotted a shadow he didn't like, and wanted me to check it before he would consider sending her home. I'm afraid his suspicions were correct. Stacy, there is a small fracture—a broken bone right up here."

"I knew it," Stacy said. "See Mother, I told you it was killing me."

"Is it dangerous?" the girl's mother asked.

"It would have been," Zack said, slipping the soft collar into place, "if it had gone undetected. It could have been a blooming disaster. But everything is under control now. You're going to be just fine."

Mrs. Mills reached over and squeezed a stunned Wilton Marshfield's hand. Her husband patted him on the shoulder.

"Now, Stacy," Zack went on, "first of all, I don't want you moving your head around, okay?"

"Okay."

"Good. Then there are some things I must explain to you and to your parents about what we do for cervical fractures."

"Dr. Iverson, please," the girl's mother said. "Before you start, I'd like to get Stacy's aunt—my sister—over here. Would that be okay?"

"Certainly, but I don't see—"

"She helps me understand medical things. I'm sure you know her. She's the head nurse here. Maureen. Maureen Banas."

CHAPTER 15

ALTHOUGH OPERATING room 2 at Ultramed-Davis was newer than some of the dozens Zack had worked in, the ambience was no different. The sounds, the lighting, the tile, the filtered air—tinged with the unique mix of antiseptic and talc and freshly laundered gowns—provided sensations as familiar to him, as reassuring, as the mountains.

The stabilization of Stacy Mills's neck was proceeding flawlessly. Standing by the head of the table, Zack paused, savoring the sensations —the wonder of what he was able to do, and the bond he was feeling with the rest of the O.R. team. The sound system—Frank's brainchild, now installed in nearly all Ultramed's hospitals—was playing George Winston's magical treatment of "The Holly and the Ivy."

"All set?" he asked the scrub nurse.

The woman nodded.

"All right, then," he said evenly. "Stacy, this is the part I told you about. We're going to twist those four screws into place on your head. I've put lots of novocaine in each spot, so they won't hurt, but it will feel funny, and you might hear the grinding noise. Everything is going just fine. I know it's scary for you, but there's really nothing to be frightened about."

"I'm not frightened," the girl said. "At least, not too much."

"Good. And you remember what you have to do?"

"Don't move," she answered.

"Exactly . . ."

Zack checked the position of the cervical halo one last time, and worked the four screws farther into place through the small incisions he had made in the girl's scalp.

"Unless I tell you to, don't move."

From a spot several feet behind the O.R. team, Wilton Marshfield watched, his every breath a sigh of relief. Even though Zack Iverson had publicly gone out of his way to share credit for the pickup with him and had privately assured him that this sort of cervical fracture was the toughest of all to diagnose, he sensed that he would never be truly comfortable in the emergency ward again.

He had come out of retirement and into the E.R. as a favor to Frank Iverson, and because he was bored. Now, he knew, it was time to stop. And thanks to Iverson's brother, after forty years of busting his hump, of doing his best to survive first the knowledge explosion, then medicare and the paperwork crunch, then the malpractice crisis, and now the goddamn corporate-policy crap, he could at least go out as something of a winner.

"God love ya, kid," he said softly, as Zack tightened the apparatus in place. "God love ya."

"Okay, Stacy," Zack was saying, "that's one. Now, wiggle your toes the way I showed you. Good. Now your fingers. Good, good. We're almost there."

He stepped back for a moment and shifted his focus from the metal frame to the fine features and peaceful face of the girl/woman. Biology; organic chemistry; anatomy and physiology; boards and more boards; endless nights and weekends on duty or on call; countless meals of cafeteria food or nondescript leftovers in cardboard containers; countless hours in the O.R. and on the wards; scattered days, and weeks, and even months of consuming self-doubt—at moments like this one, the choices he had made in his life and the price he had paid made so much sense.

And when it was over, when the girl who loved to ride horses walked away from the hospital and from the split second that could have paralyzed her forever, he would take that moment and bankroll it in his mind as vindication for all the years and all the anguish, and as a hedge against those outcomes yet-to-be which would not bring smiles and handshakes and pats on the back—outcomes that, as long as they were unavoidable, were no less a part of medicine than this one.

"That's it, Stacy," he cooed as he tightened down the last of the screws. "That's it. You're doing perfect. We're all doing perfect."

With the elective surgery schedule now an hour behind, O.R. 2 was emptied out as soon as the last screw was in place and the proper position of the halo was verified. Zack accompanied Stacy Mills to the east-wing room where, for a few days, she would be observed for signs of spinal cord swelling or compression.

"Well, you just take it easy, Stacy," he said. "I'm going to go talk to your folks, and then I'll send them up. I'll be back to see you at the end of the day. Wearing this device won't be the most fun you've ever had, but like I said, it won't be forever."

"Dr. Zack," the girl called out as he was leaving, "in the operating room I said that I wasn't scared. Well, now that it's all over, I can tell you that I really was. I just didn't want to sound like a baby."

Zack returned to the bedside and smiled down at her.

"In that case," he said, "I've got something to tell *you*—something I've never told any patient before." He bent over her bed and whispered, "I'm always a little frightened and a little nervous when I operate."

"You are? Really?"

"The truth. I think it helps my concentration never to forget that it's always possible that something could go wrong. There, I said it, and . . . hey, Dr. Mills, I feel better already!"

"You're very silly, do you know that?"

"I hope so," he said.

As he was leaving the girl's room, Zack spotted Maureen Banas approaching down the corridor. She was in her late forties or early fifties, he guessed, with short, graying hair that looked as if it had been cut by an amateur. Although she carried herself with authority, the tension etched into her face and the lack of attention to ten or fifteen excess pounds hinted at a life that had, perhaps, not been an easy one.

"Congratulations, Dr. Iverson, and thanks," she said with an almost clinical lack of emotion. "Stacy is a very special child to a lot of people. We all owe you a great deal for what you did."

In that case, he wanted to say, *tell me about the nail you helped hammer into Guy Beaulieu's coffin.*

"Listen," he replied instead, "just seeing her moving those arms and legs and piggies of hers is enough to get me through six months of the usual neurosurgical nightmares. Besides, it's Wilton Marshfield you should be thanking. I was just the technician."

"Nonsense. I know he missed those fractures. Sticking up for him was a very kind thing for you to do, especially with the altercation you two had last week. Wilton's really a sweet old guy most of the time. But he misses too much."

He misses too much. The opening, however slight, was there.

Zack glanced past the nurse. The corridor was quiet. There might have been a more appropriate time and place, but one day after Guy's funeral, and only hours after reading his diary, thoughts of the man were too close to the surface for Zack to walk away from this opportunity.

"Sort of like Guy Beaulieu in that respect," he said. "Yes?"

Maureen Banas looked at him queerly. "I beg your pardon?"

"I was asking about your impressions of Guy Beaulieu. I was with him when he died, you know."

"Of course I know." Her strange expression had not faded. "I thought a lot of Dr. Beaulieu. To die the way he did was . . . was very tragic." She averted her gaze and peered around the corner into Stacy's room. "Well," she said, "I guess I'd better check on my niece and get back to the emergency ward. Thank you again, Doctor."

"Mrs. Banas, wait, please," Zack said.

The woman stopped, her back still to him, her posture rigid.

"Please?" he said again.

Slowly, she turned to face him. Her arms were folded grimly across her chest.

"Yes?"

"Mrs. Banas, I . . . I read the letter you wrote about Guy."

What little color there was drained from the nurse's face.

"Your brother had no right to go passing that around," she said.

"Why?"

The woman looked about restlessly.

"Dr. Iverson, I think I'd better go."

"Mrs. Banas, just a minute ago you said that you owed me a great deal for what I did for Stacy. Well, I don't usually call in markers like this, but I need to know about Guy—what he's been like these past two years; what he did that prompted you to write those charges. Please. It's terribly important to me . . . and to his family."

Maureen Banas's reaction was far from the anger or defensiveness Zack would have anticipated. She began to tremble, and quickly grew close to tears.

"I . . . please, I don't want to talk about it. Your brother said he would speak with me before showing that note to anyone. He had no right to give it to you."

"Look," Zack said. "I didn't mean to upset you. I'm just trying to get to the bottom of things—to the truth."

It took several breaths before the nurse began to regain her composure.

"Dr. Iverson, I've got three children, one of them retarded, and an ex-husband who hasn't sent a dime of support in ten years. I'm sorry I wrote that letter, but . . . but I had to. I had to. Now, you've got to leave it alone. For my sake. For my family. Leave it alone. I beg you."

"I can't, Mrs. Banas . . . Maureen, I don't want to cause trouble for you or for anyone, but I've got to know if that letter contained the truth about Guy. . . . Please."

The woman said nothing.

"What is it?" he asked. "Did someone pressure you to write it? Threaten to take your job away?"

The nurse bit her lower lip. Her eyes had filled with tears. She glanced nervously about. Two nurses were approaching down the hall.

"Come with me," she said softly.

There was a small sitting area at the end of the corridor—a colonial-style maple settee and two matching chairs arranged beneath a huge picture window that faced southwest, toward the mountains. Maureen Banas took one of the chairs and motioned Zack to the edge of the settee closest to her.

"Dr. Iverson, I meant what I said about my family," she began in a hoarse whisper. "If you speak of this conversation to anyone and I lose my job, you will have hurt a number of people who do not deserve to be hurt."

"You have my word."

"I . . . I'm terrified about doing this."

"Please . . ."

"At the beginning of the summer, I quarreled with Dr. Beaulieu in the E.R. We never got along all that well to begin with, but I think we more or less respected one another. It doesn't make any difference what we fought about. The whole incident was actually pretty mild. But there were a number of witnesses.

"A week or so later, there was an envelope stuck under my door at home. In it were ten one-hundred-dollar bills, a copy of the note you saw, and instructions that when I copied the note over in my own hand and sent it to Mr. Iverson, I would receive a second, equal payment."

"No hint of who the note was from?"

Once again, the nurse seemed close to breaking down.

"None."

"Well, did the note say what would happen if you refused?"

"It said that trouble would start happening in my life, and that I could count on being fired. Dr. Iverson, I know what I did was awful, but . . . but I had been doing so poorly with the kids, and the damn bills just keep coming in, and—"

"Please, Maureen. You don't have to explain," Zack said. "I understand that you did what you had to do. Do you still have the note?"

The nurse shook her head.

"I . . . I was afraid to keep it."

"Any sense at all as to who sent it? Do you think it was my brother?" Zack felt sick at the thought.

"I . . . I don't believe so," she said.

"Why do you say that?"

"Well, whoever wrote me added at the end that if Frank Iverson learned my note wasn't really my idea, he would be fired just as quickly as I would be. . . ."

She began to cry.

"You see why you can't say anything to anyone about this?"

"Yes, Maureen. I see. Telling me what you did was a very brave thing to do. I promise you that I'll honor your confidence."

"Th-Thank you."

She dabbed at her eyes with her uniform sleeve and then hurried back down the corridor.

Feeling more sadness toward the woman than anger, Zack propped his foot on one of the chairs and gazed across at the Presidential Range.

Hiking . . . climbing . . . camping . . . unique challenges in the office and in the O.R. . . . The projected life that had drawn him back to Sterling suddenly seemed so remote, so naive.

Guy, it appeared, had been right all along. Someone at Ultramed was committed to driving him from practice—and in the ugliest of ways. Zack was grateful that that someone did not appear to be Frank. But in the end, would it really matter? In Sterling, at least, Frank *was* Ultramed. And when push came to shove, it was hard to imagine him lining up against the company.

The situation was so crazy, so far removed from a patient needing help and a physician trained and ready to render it.

But for better or worse, Zack acknowledged, he was in it to stay. He had chosen this town and this hospital. And now, if he had to do battle with Ultramed to justify that decision, then battle there would be.

All he needed to complete the circle, to place himself once and for all squarely where Guy Beaulieu had stood, was proof—if not proof from Maureen Banas, then perhaps from the Ultramed system itself.

If Guy was right, if the policies and the climate created by the corporation were so ruthless and self-serving, if compromises were being made and corners cut in the name of profit, then somewhere there was the medical tragedy such a philosophy must inevitably bring. Somewhere, there was that emotional focal point that would translate possibilities and abstract concerns into flesh and blood.

And if such a tragedy existed, Zack vowed, sooner or later he would find it.

* * *

From his position at the nurses' station on West 2, Donald Norman, MD, propped Annie Doucette's chart on his ample lap and peered over the top of it at a Rubenesque young nurse named Doreen Lavalley. She was standing on tiptoes atop a small stool, stretching over her head for a bag of IV solution. The skirt of her uniform was at her mid-thigh and rising.

Doreen was the sexiest, most desirable woman in the hospital, at least to the Ultramed-Davis Chief of Staff. For months he had been cultivating her with small talk, friendly pats on the shoulder, an arm about the waist, and impromptu teaching sessions.

Since his arrival at the hospital four years before, Norman had gone out of his way to keep his reputation spotless and to portray the perfect, responsible family man and community servant. The powers at Ultramed rewarded such behavior just as vigorously as they punished actions that brought negative publicity down upon their house.

But after four consecutive yearly merit awards, he believed that the company would tolerate a few slips. And with his wife gaining weight and growing more involved with her school committees and steadily less involved with their physical relationship, Doreen Lavalley had become worth the risk.

Besides, Norman reasoned, Frank Iverson was rumored to have made it with half the decent-looking women in the hospital, and he had been made a member of the Golden Circle and had twice won the highest administrator's award that Ultramed offered.

Just as her skirt was about to reach the base of her panties, Doreen located the right IV solution and hopped down from the stool.

Donald Norman cursed under his breath.

"Morning, Doreen," he said, tugging at the small bulge that had materialized behind Annie Doucette's chart. "How goes it?"

"Oh, Dr. Norman, hi."

"Hey, I told you," he whispered, with a conspiratorial wink, "when no one's around you can call me Don. Listen, I'd like you to make rounds with me, if that's okay. Mr. Rolfe has some interesting findings in his chest, and that . . . that harpy, Mrs. Doucette, should still have her murmur."

The nurse glanced about.

"Well, I'm a little behind in my work, and—"

"Oh, come on," he urged. "I just have those two on this floor. It shouldn't take long."

"I . . . well, okay. As long as it's just two. And Dr. Norman, Annie's a nice lady. Really she is. Just give her a chance."

"It's Don, remember?" Norman said. "And as far as Annie Doucette goes, she may be a sweet old lady to you, but she's been a harpy to me." He checked the three by five file card he carried on her. "Besides," he added, "It's all academic. To all intents and purposes, she's out of here."

"You're sending her home?" Doreen asked with disbelief.

Norman shook his head.

"Not home," he said. "To the Sterling Nursing Home, provided they can clear out a bed. Remember, under the Diagnostically Related Group system—you know, the DRGs—medicare pays by the diagnosis, not the length of the hospital stay. Our job is to get patients out as quickly as possible."

What Norman did not mention, although they were certainly on his mind at that moment, were the Ultramed incentive points awarded for discharging patients before the end of their DRG period, and the even greater number offered for a transfer to a Leeward-owned nursing facility.

"I don't think Annie's going to like that idea," the nurse said. "She's very independent."

"Well, then," Norman said, tucking her chart under his arm and adjusting his tie, "we'll just have to reason with her, won't we? Bring your order book along just in case. By the way," he added as they started off, "I'm giving an in-service on hepatitis next Thursday evening. I hope you'll be there."

"Well, actually, I—"

"I think Flo Bergman, the Ultramed nursing director, will be up from Boston. I'd like her to meet you. With the Ultramed director of nursing and the Davis chief of staff on your side, there's no telling what opportunities might open up for you. . . ."

Annie Doucette flipped off the quiz show she had been trying to watch, settled back on her pillow and stared up at the ceiling.

The pains in her chest, little more than twinges throughout the previous day, had begun to intensify, and for the first time since the horrible night of her admission, she was frightened. There were gaping holes in her recollection of that night, but not gaping enough to erase the agony and the humiliation she felt, to say nothing of the disruption she had caused Cinnie Iverson, the Judge, and their family.

She should never have accepted their invitation to dinner, she told herself. Never. After twenty-odd years of doing her work proudly and well, of being the glue that held the Iverson household together, she had become nothing but a burden—an imposition and source of worry for everyone.

If only she could have just gone as her husband had, quickly and painlessly in his sleep.

She chewed two Rolaids from the pack her son had bought for her and tried to focus her thoughts on the sweaters for her grandchildren and the afghan for the church bazaar—unfinished projects waiting for her at home in her flat.

All she needed was a few more days—a week, maybe—in the hospital, and everything would be okay. She had not given in to the aches and pains and the passing years yet, and she would not this time. The rumblings in her chest were probably nothing more than indigestion, anyhow.

Annie closed her eyes as bit by bit the discomfort yielded to a gentle sleep. . . . *A week . . . That was all she needed. . . . A week to get her strength back. . . . Then everything would be okay . . . everything would be back to normal again. . . . It felt so good to nap. . . . So good to drift off . . . so good . . .*

"So, Mrs. Doucette, how are we doing this morning?" Donald Norman boomed.

Startled, Annie felt another, slightly more urgent twinge in her chest.

"*We* have felt better, Dr. Norman," Annie said, opening her eyes only after the last vapor of sleep had drifted away. "Oh, hello, Doreen, dear."

"Hi, Annie."

"And what seems to be the trouble?" Norman asked.

Annie debated whether or not to repeat what she had already told the nurses about the pains. Donald Norman had never paid much attention to her complaints, anyway.

"I'm getting some pains," she said finally.

Norman thumbed through her chart.

"Doreen, look. Here's the description I wrote of that murmur. Right here. A grade-two systolic. Let's listen and see if it's changed."

He slipped his stethoscope down Annie's nightgown, listened for a few moments, and then guided the nurse to the bedside with his arm around her waist and gave her a turn.

"Hear it?"

The young woman looked at Annie uncomfortably and nodded.

"Dr. Norman," she said, "Annie's been having chest pain on and off since yesterday morning."

"Of course she has," Norman said, as if he and the nurse were the only two in the room. "I would bet dollars to doughnuts that they started right after I mentioned her discharge from the hospital. It happens all the time. People get anxious. Did you order an EKG?"

"It's right there in the front of her chart."

"Good," he said. "Good work." He scanned the tracing. "Well, it shows nothing to be alarmed at. Just the same T-wave changes in the anterior leads. Here. See? Right here. I'll explain how they're different from other T-wave changes after we finish seeing these two patients." He turned back to Annie. "So, if everything else is okay, I think we should begin to plan for your discharge."

"I'm not feeling well enough to leave yet, Dr. Norman."

"I know, dear. I know." Norman took her hand to pat it, but Annie pulled away. "You're bound to be nervous at the prospect. That's why I've arranged for you to—"

"I wish to stay in the hospital for another week or so," she said. "Then I should be ready to go home."

"Mrs. Doucette, you didn't let me finish. I was saying that I'm in the process of arranging a bed for you at the Sterling Nur—uh, convalescent facility. A couple of weeks there, and you should be ready to go home."

"I won't go," Annie said flatly, sitting up in bed to confront the man. "You are not going to stick me in any nursing home. I shall stay here for one more week, and then I shall go to my own home."

"I'm afraid that's not possible, Mrs. Doucette."

"Well," she said, "I'll just speak with Mr. Frank Iverson, and we'll see what is possible and what is not."

"Feel free to do that if you wish, Mrs. Doucette. But Frank Iverson is not taking care of you. I am. And I am telling you that your hospitalization is about to run out and you will not be able to remain here for another week. That is the rule. In fact, it is one of the rules Frank Iverson is paid to uphold. Now, please calm down and try to realize that what I'm doing is in your best interests."

Before she could respond, Annie felt another stab beneath her breastbone. Under the sheet, her fists clenched.

"You're not a very good doctor, you know," she managed finally. "You not only don't take very good care of yourself, you don't take very good care of your patients, either."

Donald Norman glanced back at Doreen Lavalley, his face flushed with anger and embarrassment. The old woman *was* a goddamn harpy, there were no two ways about it. Not only was she jeopardizing a hefty set of bonus points for him, but she was making him look like a goddamn asshole in front of Doreen, as well.

"Mrs. Doucette," he said sternly, "we'll discuss this later. Meanwhile, lie back and get some rest. Doreen, come with me, please."

He turned on his heel and stalked from the room. The nurse looked down at Annie and shrugged helplessly.

"I'll be back a little later," she said.

"I want her to get some Valium," Norman ordered when they were out of earshot. "No, no, on second thought, make it Haldol, one point five by mouth every eight hours. Give her the first dose now."

Doreen Lavalley hesitated.

Norman smiled at her and patted her on the shoulder.

"Hey, Doreen, don't worry," he said. "This is absolutely routine stuff. Nobody *wants* to go to a nursing home, but some people have to. And listen, I didn't get to be chief of staff in this system by not caring about my patients. If anything, I care *too* much.

"Believe me, it's all for the best. The Haldol will calm her down, and by this evening she'll be a thousand times easier to reason with. You just watch. Okay? . . . Now, about my in-service talk next Thursday. What do you say we. . . .

Chapter 16

THE 1938 FLEET MONOPLANE cut through the warm midday air like an arrow, soared over the dense forest panoply and then across the broad, grassy field. It dipped and looped like a yo-yo, barrel rolling again and again, sunlight exploding off the hand-polished, crimson butyrate paint of its wings. At the far edge of the meadow it nosed upward, streaking toward a solitary puff of cloud in an otherwise flawless sky.

From his spot on a large boulder, Zachary watched intently as his fingers, through minute movements of the stick atop his radio control, choreographed the flight.

A stall, a spin, a roll out, a second pass over the field; Zack had built the Fleet as a high schooler, and although he had sometimes gone a year or more without the opportunity to fly her, he had kept the engine and the finish in perfect condition.

With a final, wide bank, he eased the model upwind and set her down sweetly in the grass. The plane was, as always, fascinating to watch, and this day, with any luck, she would be more than just a hobby. This day, she would be a tool to help him unlock the tortured silence of a young boy.

"Hey, Ace, that was a nifty piece of flying."

Suzanne, dressed in snug white shorts and a Dartmouth T-shirt, stood on a small rise, looking as if she might have just drifted down from the sun. She had a plaid blanket draped over one arm and a wicker picnic basket hanging from the other.

"You know," he said, squinting up at her, "about twenty minutes ago I started getting this funny feeling you might show up."

"Do we have time for lunch?" she asked, making her way down the slope.

Zack glanced at his watch.

"About forty-five minutes. I'm glad you're here."

Suzanne stretched on her tiptoes and kissed him lightly on the mouth.

"Me, too," she said. "Can I set this food out, or is Cheapdog lurking somewhere?"

"No, no. Mop-face and the Fleet out there are avowed enemies. Sort of like sibling rivalry. He's home digging up the yard."

She spread the blanket and set out dishes of fried chicken, smoked fish, and salad. Then she extracted a small portable radio, set it on the grass, and fiddled with the dial until she found WEVO. The announcer was thanking his guests for participating in *Midday Roundtable* and inviting listeners to stay turned for a special edition of *Music of the Masters.*

"You must think I'm a little crazy for the way I've been acting around you," she said as she poured lemonade. "I wanted to apologize."

Zack shrugged.

"No need," he said. "You've had a few more important things to deal with than me."

"Perhaps. Just the same, I've been acting like a jerk, and I'm sorry."

He reached over and brushed her cheek with the back of his hand.

"Fair enough," he said. "If that's what you need, then apology accepted. There, do you feel better?"

"Zack, I . . . I want to explain."

"Hey, I don't require any—"

"No, I want to." She studied her hands. "At least I think I do."

For much of the night she had sat with Helene, struggling to come to grips with the past.

"Nothing matters except the truth," her friend had said. "Nothing matters except how you really, truly feel. Right here, in your gut. I go out the way I do, see men the way I do, because I honestly know, in my heart, that I hate being alone. Otherwise I'd stay at home or join the Ammonoosuc Valley Quilters. Believe me I would. You don't have to do it my way, or anyone else's way for that matter, but your own, Suze. But—and it's a big but—you can't keep fighting your feelings. You can't fight who you are. If you think you care about the man, tell him who you are, where you've been. If he can deal with it, fine. If he can't, that's his problem."

It all had made so much sense while they were talking. Now, Suzanne was not so sure. There was more than a little to be said for living the safe life.

The meadow, abutting the low hills southwest of town, glowed verdant and golden in the dry afternoon sun. For a time they ate in silence, save for the deep, cultured voice of the WEVO announcer, who was extolling the virtues of an English composer whose name Zack missed.

"Zachary," Suzanne said suddenly, "the other night was the first time I've made love in more than three years."

"Well, you certainly haven't gotten rusty," he replied. "I would also guess that whatever the reason for those three years of celibacy, it wasn't a lack of offers."

She smiled at him wistfully.

"You're sweet. Actually, there haven't been that many. I haven't been able to trust any man enough even to be encouraging."

"If you're trying to make me feel special, you're doing a great job."

"You *are* special. . . . Zack, my husband—my ex-husband—did an incredible hatchet job on my life, and then left me for dead. The scars that formed just don't seem to want to heal. I don't put all the blame on him for what happened. I could have put my foot down when I figured out what was going on. I could have gotten out. But I stayed. I always told myself it was for Jen, but looking back, I realize that I simply couldn't admit to myself how blind I had been—how badly I had mis- judged the man I had married. And I couldn't accept that he didn't care enough about me to change."

"You were young."

"Twenty-three, if you call that young. And not a very worldly twenty-three at that. Paul was a Ph.D. Brilliant, handsome, charming as hell. Already an associate professor at thirty-five. Every woman in school had a crush on him. Unfortunately, what they didn't know— what *I* didn't know—was how sick he was inside. He was a sociopath, Zachary. A womanizer, a drug addict, and a glib, an unbelievably glib liar. He used me. In every way imaginable, he used me."

She searched Zack's eyes for any signs of judgment or revulsion, but saw only sadness.

"You don't have to share any more of this if you don't want to," he said, taking her hand.

"No, I'm okay. Much better than I thought I'd be. You're really very easy to talk to.

"For several years," she went on, "Paul stole prescriptions from the hospital, made them out to his women or his cronies or to people who didn't even exist, and signed my name. He had my signature down even better than I did. He hit up a dozen or more wholesale houses and worked his way through just about every pharmacy in the state."

"Jesus . . ."

Suzanne gazed off toward the mountains to the south and began rubbing at her eyes.

"Are you okay?" Zack asked.

"Huh? . . . Oh, sure. I'm fine. Fine."

She fished through her purse and put on her sunglasses.

"Where was I?"

"You were telling me about the prescriptions. Listen, if you want to change the subject, it's perfectly—"

"No, no. It feels good to be able to talk about it." She reached beneath her sunglasses and again rubbed her eyes. "Besides, there's not that much more to tell. Somehow Paul must have found out that the DEA people were on to me, because a week before they showed up at our door, he emptied out our bank account, sold everything we had of value, and took off. No note, no call, nothing. Jen was only two at the time. A year or so later, I heard that he was teaching at a medical school in Mexico. Somebody else said they saw him at an international conference in Milan. But by that time all I wanted was never to hear his name again."

"What happened to you?"

"Pardon?"

"I asked what happened to you. Suze, are you sure you're all right?"

"Is the glare bothering you?"

"No. Why?"

"Nothing . . . nothing. What did you ask?"

"Suzanne, let's just leave it for another time—"

"No! Now, wh-what was it?"

She continued to stare off at the mountains. The muscles in her face had grown lax and expressionless. Her hands had begun to tremble.

Zack studied her uncomfortably. He glanced at his watch. Barbara Nelms and her son were due in ten minutes.

"Suzanne?"

She did not respond.

"Listen," he said, shutting off the radio and putting it back into the wicker basket. "I think maybe you've shared enough for one day." He began repacking the leftovers. "I'm just happy you felt able to talk about it with—"

"You know, ridiculous as it may sound," Suzanne went on fluidly, "I'm not sure I know exactly what happened next. . . ."

Zack looked at her queerly. The lifelessness was gone from her face and her voice, and she was as animated as ever. He battled back the urge to again ask her if she was okay.

". . . One minute, I was suspended from the hospital, sitting in lawyers' offices, fighting with the child welfare people and trying to fend off the DEA animals, and the next I was here in Sterling, putting in pacemakers."

Zack studied her for any lingering sign of distraction, but saw none. It was as if a cloud had passed briefly across the sun and then had suddenly released it. He forced concern from his mind. She seemed, as she had claimed, to be absolutely fine.

"Did Frank have a hand in that?" he managed.

"I guess. One day he called, the next day he came down and interviewed me, and the next day, it seemed, the pressure that had been on me from all those sides began to disappear."

"Well, good for Frank." Zack felt his tension recede. "We haven't been getting along too well lately. I think I'll have to try a little harder."

"I'm not really sure if it was him or Ultramed," she said, "but someone got the wolves off my back."

"That's a horrible story."

"Except for the ending, it is."

"Call that part of it the beginning," Zack said.

"I hope telling you all of that helps you see why I've had a little problem with letting a man back into my life. And also why I feel obligated to support Ultramed wherever I can. Thanks to Paul, loyalty has moved ahead of just about everything else on my list of qualities that matter in a person."

"I understand."

She kissed him—once, and then again. The last drop of his worry vanished.

"So," she said, still cradling his face in her hands, "just be patient with me, okay?"

"Just once in more than three years, huh?"

"Yup."

He repacked the last of their lunch and pulled her down to him.

"As soon as we have a little time, I'd like to help you improve on that average."

She brushed her lips across his neck.

"In that case, just don't stop trying. My horoscope told me to be on the lookout for a tall, dark stranger who did coin tricks."

He ran his fingers slowly down the back of her thigh and over her calf.

"Thanks for the picnic," he said.

"Thanks for dessert. And listen, good luck with the Nelms boy. I hope this works out. If you get anywhere today, I think we should consider writing up our technique for some journal. We can title the article 'Pediatric Neurology Alfresco.' "

She pushed herself to her feet.

Zack walked her to her car and watched until she had disappeared down the hill. Then he returned to the field, absently humming a passage from *Fantasia on Greensleeves* by Ralph Vaughan Williams.

Toby Nelms looked chronically ill. His skin was midwinter pale, with several small patches of impetigo alongside his nose and at the corner of his lips. He was thin as a war orphan and carried himself with a dispirited posture, his gaze nearly fixed on the ground. But it was the listless, dull gray of his eyes that worried Zack the most. They were the eyes of utter defeat which he had encountered so many times in terminally ill patients—the eyes of death.

At Zack's request, Barbara Nelms hugged her son, promised to return for him as soon as she had finished shopping, and drove back down the hill to town. If Toby was frightened at her departure, his dispassionate expression hid the fact well. He had spotted the Fleet almost immediately, and had glanced over at it twice before she had even started to drive off.

Zack reflected on Brookings's account of the child's terrified dash across the clinic parking lot, and knew that, for the moment at least, he was making progress.

A tumor, a seizure disorder, a congenital, slowly developing vascular abnormality, a toxic reaction to something the boy was consuming without anyone's knowledge—Zack had balanced the possibilities against the psychiatric diagnoses and found all of them wanting. He had even made a brief drive around the boy's neighborhood, searching for a landfill or other dumping site where Toby might be sustaining a chemical exposure. Nothing.

"Hi, kiddo," Zack said, kneeling on the grass, two yards away from the boy. "My name is Zack." There was curiosity in the boy's eyes, but no other reaction. "I'm a doctor, but I'm not going to examine you, or do any tests, or even touch you. Please believe that. I would like you to learn to trust that I would never lie to you, and that I mean exactly what I say, okay? I'll say it once more. I will *never, ever* lie to you. I asked your mom to bring you here because I thought it might be easier for us to get to know one another outside the hospital."

At the mention of the word hospital, a shadow of fear darkened the boy's expression.

"Your mom will be back as soon as she finishes her shopping," Zack added quickly. "Meanwhile, we can lie around, or explore, or even climb up to that little cliff over there. This place is called the Meadows. I used to play here when I was a boy." He flashed momentarily on Suzanne. "I still do, in fact," he added.

Toby's eyes darted again toward the Fleet.

"I built that plane over there a long time ago," Zack explained. "It flies by remote control." He held up the control box for the boy to see. "She loops, and rolls over, and zooms up to the clouds. Go ahead. Take a look at her."

Toby Nelms remained where he was, but there could be no mistaking his interest.

"Go on. It's okay. I'm going back to the car for a second to get some fuel for her."

Only when he had reached the van did Zack turn back. The boy was kneeling by the Fleet, and was, ever so gently, running his fingers over the shiny, lacquered finish of her wings.

* * *

Too anxious to stay away for the last fifteen minutes of the agreed-upon hour, Barbara Nelms rolled to stop some distance downhill from the meadow and made her way quietly toward Zack's van, half expecting to find her son waiting there, in near hysterics, for her return. What she found instead, was a note, taped to the rear window.

Mrs. Nelms—
Take a peek if you want, but please, try not to be seen. No words from Toby yet, but we're getting there. I need another hour. Please call my office and ask my receptionist to do the best she can with my schedule. See you later.
Z. Iverson

From just beyond a small rise, she could hear the high-pitched whine of the model-airplane engine. Crouching low, she worked her way up. Near the crest of the hillock, she flattened herself in the tall grass and then peered over. Zachary Iverson sat alone, his back toward her. Her son was nowhere in sight.

Suddenly terrified at what she might have done by trusting a man who was little more to her than a voice on the phone, she began to scramble to her feet.

Then, just as quickly, she dropped back down.

The boy was there, nestled between the physician's legs, sharing the stick of the radio-control device.

"That's it, fella," she heard Zack cry over the noise. "A little more, a little more, and . . . now!"

The plane, which had begun a slow roll across the grass, shot forward and then up, climbing at a steep angle toward the treetops at the far end of the meadow.

"That's it. You've got it. Now ease off. Ease off. Terrific! Hold her right there."

Now well above the trees, the model banked smoothly to the south and began a lazy circle of the field.

"I did it! I did it!"

It took several seconds for Barbara Nelms to realize that the excited voice she had just heard was her son's. With a joyful fullness in her throat and tears in her eyes, she slipped back out of sight and hurried down the hill.

Zack and Toby Nelms lay opposite one another on the warm grass, a few yards from the Fleet, chewing on stalks of wild barley and watching a red-tailed hawk glide in effortless loops atop high, midday thermals.

"Now, just who do you suppose is working the radio-control box for *that* model?" Zack asked. "Whoever it is has sure built one quiet engine."

"That's goofy," Toby Nelms said.

"Of course it is. Anyone with half a brain could tell that's just a kite. Now, if only I could see the string . . ."

Once the logjam of silence—of fear and mistrust—had been broken, the boy's words had come with surprising ease, and even occasional spontaneity. Zack had been reluctant to test the progress they had made with any pointed questions, but now, with just a few minutes left in their two hours together, he felt comfortable enough to try.

"You know, kiddo," he began, "a lot of people have been very worried about you these past few months."

"I know."

"But you still won't talk to anyone?"

Toby shook his head.

"Not even your parents?"

The boy stared vacantly at the crucifix soaring overhead.

"They never help me," he said suddenly. "I scream for them, and beg them to stop the . . . the man from hurting me. But they never come until it's too late. They never stop him."

"What man?" Zack asked, at once repulsed and fearful at the thought of the boy being molested. "Who's been hurting you?"

Toby turned away.

"Hey, kiddo, I'm sorry. I didn't mean to say anything to upset you or frighten you."

For a few, anxious seconds, Zack feared he had pushed too hard and slammed the door he had, so gingerly, just opened.

"The man with the mask," Toby said without turning back.

"Mask?"

The boy shifted restlessly, and then drew his knees and elbows in tightly to his body.

Zack decided he had gone far enough for one day. He reached in his pocket for a coin. One good thumb palm and they would call it quits.

"He . . . he cuts it off," Toby said, in almost a whimper. "And . . . and then it grows back . . . and then he cuts it off again."

"Cuts what off, Toby? . . . Look, I know it's hard for you to talk about, but you've got to try."

He moved to put his hand on the boy's shoulder, but then thought better of it. He felt his heart pounding. *Don't stop now, kiddo. Don't give up on me now.*

"My . . . my peenie. And my balls, too."

"Do you mean he touches you?"

"No, he cuts it off. He promises he won't hurt me. He promises he'll fix my lump, and then he cuts it off. And it hurts. It hurts and I scream at him, and he won't stop. And I scream for my mommy and daddy, and they never come."

The boy began to cry, his shoulders jerking spasmodically with each heavy sob.

Again, Zack moved to touch him, but before he could, the child spun and flung his arms around him.

"Please, Zack," he cried softly. "Please don't let him do it anymore."

He promises he'll fix my lump. . . . Suddenly, the child's words registered.

"Toby," Zack whispered, still holding the boy tightly, "the lump you're talking about, is it your hernia? That place here you had fixed?"

The boy nodded, his body still racked with sobs.

"And the man with the mask . . . Is that the doctor?"

Again, a nod.

Zack eased him away, but continued to hold him by the shoulders.

"Toby, look at me. I think you've just been having nightmares. Bad, horrible dreams, but dreams that often go away as soon as you see them for what they are. The operation was perfect. All that's left is a little scar. The lump is gone for good."

"No," the boy said angrily. "It isn't. It grows back. So does my peenie, and my balls. But then he cuts them off again, and it hurts—worse each time."

Inwardly, Zack sighed relief. The boy's profound disturbance was rooted in a nightmare—the expression of pent-up fears surrounding a procedure now nearly a year in the past. Fascinating, but certainly neither difficult to understand nor as bad a situation as he had feared. At least Brookings would have something to work with.

"You don't believe me, do you?" Toby said. "It's not a dream. He cuts them off, and they grow back, and then he takes those Metzenbaums and cuts them off again."

Zack felt a sudden, vicious chill.

"He takes what?" There was no hiding the incredulity in his voice.

"The Metzenbaums. He asks for them from the nurse, and then he sticks them into me right here, and it kills me. Then he just cuts and cuts."

"Toby, think," Zack said urgently. "Have you ever heard anyone else say that word?"

"What word?"

"Metzenbaums, Toby. Have you ever heard anyone except the doctor in your nightmare say that word?"

Toby Nelms shook his head.

Zack released the boy and sank back on his hands. Something was wrong. Something was terribly wrong. Metzenbaum scissors were commonly used in surgery, but rarely, if ever, until after the initial skin incision had been made. Toby Nelms would have been asleep at the time they were called for. Anesthetized. There was no way he could have heard that term, let alone so accurately understood what it meant. No way.

But somehow, he had.

⚡ CHAPTER 17

BY THE TIME Zack had finished rounds and headed from the hospital to his office, evening had settled in over the valley. To the southwest, the silhouetted mountains were ebony cutouts against the deepening indigo sky. It was a quiet, awesome evening, perfect for a run by Schroon Lake or for a horseback ride into the foothills to watch the moonrise. It was an evening to celebrate the joy of living.

But for Zack, the magic of the evening was lost in reflection on the agonized struggles of an old surgeon and the desperate plea of the nurse who had condemned him; and in concern as to how much to tell the waiting parents of a child who was sinking deeper and deeper into a hell of dreams that were not dreams—dreams that cut and hurt and maimed.

As he crossed the parking lot, Zack noticed Frank's Porsche, tucked in its reserved slot. Early mornings, late evenings, weekends—for whatever his shortcomings and the failings of his past, the man had become a demon of a worker.

Soon, Zack knew, the two of them would have to talk.

There were things Frank needed to learn of and to understand about Ultramed, about Guy Beaulieu . . . and now, especially, about Toby Nelms.

The boy's condition was clearly on a downward spiral, and each passing day was a lost ally in the struggle to uncover the truth. With Frank's help, the odds of finding answers in time to make a difference would be considerably shorter.

But would he listen?

Over the years, the two of them had drifted far apart in many ways.

The disagreement over Guy Beaulieu had only underscored their differences. Still, Zack reasoned, they *were* brothers, and they each had a significant stake in Ultramed-Davis and in Sterling.

He glanced back at the Porsche. At seven that morning, when he had arrived for work, it was already there. Now, after more than thirteen hours, Frank was still at it. What more testimony did he need? The man had hitched his wagon to the Ultramed-Davis star. If there was a threat to the integrity of the hospital, he would listen.

Zack felt sure, at least, of that much. But he also knew that all he had were theories—gut sensations plus a few million questions. His brother was a company man. If there were trouble in his paradise, it would take more than suspicions to enlist his help—much more.

Barbara Nelms and her husband were waiting on one of the stone benches that flanked the entrance to the Physicians and Surgeons Clinic. Bob Nelms, clean-cut, fit, and hardy, had clearly borne less of the day-to-day strain of Toby's illness than had his wife. He greeted Zack with a firm hand.

"Pleasure to meet you," he said. "Barbara tells me you made some real progress with our boy. That's excellent. Excellent. Using that plane of yours was just a super idea."

"Thank you, but—"

"You know, I'm no professional, but I've been trying to tell Barbara all along that this was all just a nasty phase, and that when that kid of ours was doggone good and ready he would get through it. It sounds like you two made quite a large step in that direction today."

"Call it a baby step," Zack said.

Despite the machismo in Bob Nelms's words and manner, one look in his eyes and Zack knew the man was whistling in the dark. As a supervisor at the mill, he was used to accepting the burden of difficult problems and solving them. His thin-shelled denial would require delicate handling and constant awareness that Toby's condition was no less baffling and frightening to Bob Nelms than his impotence in the face of it.

As Zack followed the couple into the elevator, he wondered once again how much to share with them. It had never been his way to withhold information from his patients or, when the patient was comatose or a juvenile, from their families. But this was not information. It was the purest conjecture.

And even when he tested the explanation on himself, it sounded nothing short of phantasmagoric.

Mr. and Mrs. Nelms, I don't know how to tell you this, but I believe that your son was not asleep during his hernia operation last year. He appeared to his surgeon and anesthesiologist to be fully anesthetized. But somehow, at some level, he not only "saw" his operation from within his body, but, it would seem, he fully experienced the pain of it as well.

Now, in some perverted, distorted way, he is reliving that surgery in terrifying flashbacks, much like those described in LSD users. . . . No. I don't have any idea how that could happen. . . . No, to the best of my knowledge, such a phenomenon has never been reported with the anesthetics he received. . . . No, I don't have any hard evidence to back up what I say. . . . No, I don't know what could possibly be triggering the attacks. . . . No, I don't have any idea. . . . I don't know . . . I don't know . . . I don't know. . . ."

His suspicions were vague, fantastic, and virtually without proof. Disclosure of them to the boy's parents would almost certainly precipitate premature action by them against Ultramed, the hospital, and the physicians involved in Toby's surgery—action Zack was in no position yet to support, and which could well lead to a coverup of the truth . . . whatever that was.

"Mr. and Mrs. Nelms," he began once the couple was settled in across the desk from him. "I'm afraid I don't have very much to tell you at this point. Toby did not share a great deal with me. However, he did say enough for me to suspect that he is having very severe fright reactions, and that while these reactions are occurring he is completely unable to distinguish them from reality. In other words, in just a few seconds, apparently with very little warning, he is transported from wherever he happens to be into another reality—a very distorted, very terrifying reality."

"Are you saying he becomes insane?" Barbara Nelms asked.

"You've observed him," Zack responded, still feeling his way along. "What do you think?"

"But . . . but insanity is a condition, isn't it? A state of being. How can it possibly flick on and off like a light?"

"And what has the hospital got to do with it?" Bob Nelms added.

"I don't know," Zack said, wondering how many more times he would hear himself repeat that phrase.

"Well, what do you think?"

Zack tapped his fingers together, stalling for a few more seconds to sort his thoughts. As much as he hated deception, this simply was not the time to air his theory.

"I assume you are both somewhat familiar with epilepsy?" he began. "Well, most people think of epilepsy as an electrical disorder of the brain which causes periodic fits. The seizures we are most familiar with are motor seizures—that is, they involve the muscles and the extremities. But supposing the electrical explosion occurs in one or more of the cognitive areas of the brain—the thinking areas. What would result would still be a seizure, but it would be a sensory seizure rather than a motor one."

"Are you trying to tell us that Toby has petit mal or temporal-lobe epilepsy?" Barbara asked. "I've read everything I could get my hands on about both conditions, and quite frankly, Dr. Iverson, I don't think Toby's condition fits either one. He is aggressive like temporal-lobe epileptics, but only because he is absolutely terrified. And very little of his behavior resembles the detached, fugue reactions that I've read about in petit mal. And although the resting electroencephalogram is not that accurate in making either diagnosis, Toby's was normal the one time he had it done."

Zack felt his cheeks flush and cautioned himself against any elaborate untruths. Barbara Nelms was too desperate and too bright. She was tired of getting the runaround from medical and mental health professionals, and she had done her homework well.

"I don't know what to say, Mrs. Nelms," he countered, "except to point out that if Toby's case were straightforward and typical, someone would have diagnosed it before now."

"What about the hospital?" Bob Nelms asked again. "Didn't the boy say anything to you to explain why he seems so frightened?"

"Nothing specific," Zack lied. "But since that's the main clue we have, I do feel that's the direction our investigation should go."

Barbara Nelms slumped visibly.

"Dr. Iverson, investigations are fine, but you saw Toby. He's like a stick. His skin is getting infected. He gets bruises from almost nothing. He gets fevers with no evidence of infections. He's dying, Dr. Iverson. I swear, time is running out. Our son is dying."

"Barbara, don't say that!" Bob Nelms blurted.

His outburst hit a raw nerve.

"Don't tell me what to say and what not to say," she snapped back. "You're in that damn mill until seven every night. You don't see him."

"Doggone it, Barbara, I'm doing everything I can. You're the one who hasn't paid a bit of attention to anything but Toby these past—"

"Please," Zack said. "Please. I know this is hard on you both. But sniping at each other isn't helping anyone—least of all Toby."

The couple stopped abruptly and exchanged sheepish looks.

"We're sorry," Barbara said. She reached over and squeezed her husband's hand. "We never used to fight, even at home alone. But this has just got us all . . ." She looked away.

"I understand, Mrs. Nelms. All I can ask is that you both just do your best to keep it together, and give me a little time to do some reading and talk to some people. I'll work as rapidly as I can. I promise you that. And I'll plan on seeing Toby again next week. Same time. Same field."

"Meanwhile?"

Zack shrugged.

"Meanwhile, I don't think any specific treatment is indicated. Especially since I don't really know yet what's going on. I will tell you that I don't take my responsibility for my patients lightly, and I'm fully aware that we don't have all the time in the world. I'll do my very best to get to the bottom of things quickly."

He stood, hoping to bring the exchange to a merciful end before Barbara Nelms could hone in on the inadequacies in his explanation.

"Thank you," Bob said, standing as Zack did and shaking his hand.

Zack walked them to the outer door of his office and again promised to work as quickly as possible.

"Dr. Iverson, could you just tell me one thing?" Barbara Nelms asked.

"Of course."

"Are you holding anything at all back from us?"

Zack had to force himself to maintain contact with the woman's eyes. It was a technique at which, unlike Frank, he had never excelled.

"No, Mrs. Nelms," he said flatly. "No, I'm not."

The woman hesitated, and for a moment seemed poised to challenge the denial. Then she reached out and shook his hand.

"That being the case, then, thank you, Doctor. You will keep us posted, yes?"

She took her husband's arm and walked away with him, down the darkened corridor.

Zack watched until the elevator doors had closed behind them. He ached from his lies and from the graphic reminder of the power of illness over the lives of whole families. He also knew, from her parting look, that Barbara Nelms would never again allow him to hide behind evasions and half-truths.

He would review Toby Nelms's record again, and then contact the National Institutes of Health library in Bethesda for a complete search of the reported adverse reactions to the anesthetics he had received. Finally, he would meet with Jack Pearl and Jason Mainwaring.

Beyond those steps, there was nowhere to go—nowhere except another session with Toby himself and then the sharing of his suspicions with Frank. Something had happened to the boy during his hospitalization at Ultramed-Davis—something devastating. If nothing else panned out, Frank would have to realize that it was in everyone's best interests that he pursue the matter. He would cooperate, or face Barbara Nelms and her attorney.

"Frank, don't move, honey, please. You feel so good. I want to do a little while you're still inside me. Just a line. Okay?"

Frank's secretary, the blond one, was named Annette Dolan. She had moved with her child to live with her mother in Sterling, and had been working as a hostess in the Mountain Laurel Restaurant when Frank first spotted her and offered her a job. Her qualification for the position was, quite plainly, that she looked better in a sweater than any woman he had ever seen.

She was a mediocre receptionist, and a far-worse-than-that secretary, but she was sweet and polite to everyone, and had proved a wonderful, undemanding diversion, especially on those occasions when he was able to indulge her passion for cocaine.

"Go ahead, baby," he said, running his thumbs over her nipples. "But hustle. I don't have much time left."

For more than an hour, first on the oriental rug in his office, and then on the couch, Annette had screwed him as only she could—purely and passionately, without any of the head games he tolerated but hated in brighter women.

He cradled her breasts in his hands as she slipped one end of a straw into her nose and lowered the other onto the mirror that she had rested on his chest.

"That's it," he whispered as she inhaled the dust. "Get it all, baby. Get it all."

He glanced across at the Lucite clock on his bookshelf. Twenty after eight. Less than an hour until Mainwaring was due. Less than an hour until the beginning of the end. Annette had been the perfect appetizer for that session. Now, however, it was time to pack her up and ship her home.

Frank waited until she had wiped the last grains of powder off the mirror and onto her gums. Then he skimmed the mirror across the room and pulled her magnificent, glistening body close to his. Slowly, he toppled off the couch and on top of her on the rug.

She was beautiful to the eye and to the touch, but after an hour and a hundred dollars worth of cocaine, she held little excitement for him. All that remained was the mechanical need to climax. He grabbed her corn-silk hair tightly in his fists, buried his chest against her breasts, and rammed himself into her again and again until, in less than a minute, it was over.

If only Lisette knew how much he needed this sort of uncomplicated, unquestioning sex, everything would be much better for them, he thought. Much better.

He took a minute to stroke the woman's clit, her tight, flat stomach, and finally her perfect ass. Then he moved to the chair behind his desk and watched as she dressed. Once every week or two was perfect—just enough to keep the adventure fresh and the woman from becoming tiresome.

Absently, he thumbed through the papers on his desk—papers that included the application of the surgeon who would be Mainwaring's replacement. The whole business had gone down like clockwork, Frank mused, just as he had promised it would. He and Mainwaring had estimated two years, and precisely two years it had been.

Now, there was less than an hour until the final phase of their project would start. Less than an hour until the beginning of the end, until the beginning of everything good for him.

Frank wrapped up what was left of the cocaine and flipped the plastic bag across to the woman.

"Here you go, baby," he said. "Enjoy."

"You promised you would try some with me sometime, Frank. Remember?"

"Sometime, maybe. For now, you just get on home and enjoy it," he answered. "I don't have much use for that shit. There are enough other things I get off on. Like you."

And, he was thinking, *like a million dollars.*

Frank showered in the bathroom off his office, dressed, and cleaned up the last vestiges of his session with Annette Dolan. Then he settled in before the computer terminal on his desk. There were still twenty minutes before Mainwaring was due—just enough time to check in with Mother.

And, Frank noted, it was especially fitting that he should.

For at a time when his back was to the wall, when the absence of $250,000 he had borrowed from the hospital accounts and then lost in that foolish land deal stared at him every day like a gaping, black hole of doom, Mother had provided him with the answer.

Mother was UltraMA, the Ultramed mainframe computer housed in the home office in Boston. She was the fiber that held the expanding Ultramed empire together, providing it with consistency, rapid exchange of information, and a seemingly endless pool of physicians.

And in Frank's darkest, most desperate hour, Mother had served up both Jack Pearl and Jason Mainwaring.

Frank activated the terminal, dialed the network number, and flipped the toggle switch on his phone. In seconds,

> Good evening, welcome to UltraMA—
> Please enter access code

appeared on the screen.

Frank typed in the code and then, when requested, his own password. In a week or so his regional director would receive a printout of UltraMA users and would note on the appropriate evaluation form that at nine o'clock in the evening of that day, Frank had been hard at work in his office.

> Good evening, Mr. Iverson. We trust all is well in Sterling, New
> Hampshire. Do you wish to see your menu?

Frank typed *Y.*

Immediately, ADMINISTRATOR'S MENU flashed on, followed by a list:

609

1. Changes in procedures and policies manual
2. Ultramed current staff physicians and salaries (your hospital only)
3. Ultramed current staff physicians and salaries (your region only)
4. Available physicians (by specialty)
5. Promotions, reassignments, terminations (past 30 days)
6. National health news of note
7. Regional health news of note
8. Preferred suppliers and services (your region only)
9. Performance ratings (region)
10. Performance ratings (nation)
11. Golden Circle Administrators

As he invariably did when communicating with Mother, Frank began by affirming his membership in the Golden Circle and his position as the leading administrator in the northest region.

Leading administrator. Golden Circle. It was laughable now to think of how close he had come to not even applying for the Ultramed-Davis job. But with his electronics firm going down the tubes, the Judge refusing to help him out, and Leigh Baron insisting that he would get serious consideration in the search process despite his lack of hospital experience, he really had nothing to lose.

It had been a mild shock when he was finally offered the position. And although there could be no arguing his remarkable success with the corporation, it remained something of a mystery to him why Leigh had picked him over many more experienced candidates.

Frank scanned the regional and national rankings and then returned to the Administrator's Menu and summoned up item four.

The physicians of possible interest to the Ultramed system were listed by specialty and subspecialty, along with a detailed but straightforward summary of their education and work experience.

However, item four was hardly a typical employment bulletin board. Included with many of the names was a paragraph summarizing the professional and/or personal difficulties that had made that physician available.

Drugs, alcohol, sexual entanglements, financial improprieties, professional misconduct of one sort or anther—compiling the roster was the full-time job of an obsessively diligent investigator in the home office. Primary among her responsibilities was the weeding out of those physicians for whom there was little or no hope of rehabilitation. Those remaining on the list, many of them excellent practitioners, were of particular interest to the corporation. More often than not, they proved to be devoted employees, grateful for a second chance, totally loyal to the company and its policies, and willing to work for any salary that was reasonable.

Steve Baumgarten in the emergency ward had been recruited through UltraMA's unique bulletin board. So had Suzanne Cole, a real prize, who almost from the start had generated an income many times greater than her salary.

But for Frank, it was the one-two parlay of Jack Pearl and Jason Mainwaring that had made Mother worth her megabytes in gold.

For a time when Frank's back was to the wall, when he was becoming so desperate about the $250,000 that he was actually considering approaching the Judge for help, Jack Pearl's name appeared in item four.

The description of Pearl's problem, which Frank eventually had memorized, read:

> Holds patent on what he has claimed is revolutionary new general anesthetic. Texas license suspended pending investigation of alleged illegal clinical testing of the substance and falsification of information on experimental drug application. Physician with same name resigned 1984 from Wilkes Community Hospital, Akron, Ohio, because of alleged sexual involvement with a ten-year-old boy. Further information currently being sought.

Mildly intrigued, Frank had made a note to do some checking on the man, but had not put much energy into the project until, not a month later, UltraMA served up a brief item on a professor of surgery from Baltimore. Jason Mainwaring had been found to be an officer and partner in a Georgia pharmaceutical house, and subsequently had resigned his position due to charges of conflict of interest and illegal use of an unapproved drug.

It had taken trips to Maryland, Georgia, Texas, and Ohio; an additional twenty thousand dollars in Ultramed-Davis funds to gather information and secure the cooperation of a certain politician in Akron; and finally, a series of the most delicate negotiations with both physicians. But in the end, Frank had forged the key to his future. And now, within the next two weeks, the rest was about to become history.

For several minutes Frank scanned the electronic roster of physicians. He was amazed, as always, at how so many who held the ultimate ticket to success and prestige could have made such pathetic shambles of their lives.

A pediatrician from Hartford about to complete four months in an alcohol rehabilitation center; a gynecologist from D.C. who had resigned his hospital appointment amid a cloud of accusations that his examinations were too prolonged and included house calls; an oral surgeon facing revocation of his license for writing too many narcotic prescriptions for himself; Frank jotted down several names, along with a memo to himself to make some preliminary calls.

Ultramed and its parent corporation had the clout to make any physician's background difficulties disappear to all but the most intensive investigation. However, its administrators had been well warned against using that service indiscriminately.

Frank had just terminated with Mother when, with a discreet knock, Jason Mainwaring entered the office. He was dressed in a light cotton suit, monogrammed shirt, and white topsiders, and looked very much like the plantation owner he planned to become as soon as his pharmaceutical company had successfully produced and marketed Jack Pearl's Serenyl.

"Drink?" Mainwaring asked, setting his briefcase down and then striding directly to the small wet bar in Frank's bookcase.

"Sure," Frank said, quietly resenting the way the man, as always, stepped into a room and took charge. "Bourbon's fine."

The surgeon gestured at the huge aerial photo of the Ultramed-Davis complex.

"Nice little operation y'all have here, Frank," he said. "I think I'm actually going to miss it some. But home is where the heart is, right?"

"Of course," Frank countered. "Although I knew you had been up here too long when I heard a little Yankee accent creep into that drawl of yours the other day."

Mainwaring snorted a laugh as he scanned Frank's collection of cassettes.

"Mantovani, Mantovani, Mantovani," he said disdainfully, tossing them aside one at a time. "You know, the closest thing you have here to Beethoven is Mantovani."

"I like Mantovani," Frank said.

"I know."

Mainwaring thought for a moment and then snapped open his briefcase, removed two cassettes, and flipped them onto Frank's desk.

"I know I'm prob'ly tossin' pearls to a razorback," he said, "but here are some examples of *real* music for you. It's what I listen to in the O.R. Call 'em a good-bye present. This one's Beethoven's Third. It's called the *Eroica*. And this one's by an English composer named Vaughan Williams. It's a fantasia on 'Greensleeves.' Listen to these two pieces, and I suspect even you will appreciate the difference between real music and the Burger King brand you've been listening to."

"Sure thing, Jase," Frank said, dropping the tapes into his desk drawer. "I'll start my reeducation first thing in the morning."

"I won't hold my breath." Mainwaring settled in on the sofa Frank and Annette Dolan had so recently vacated, and motioned Frank to take the easy chair opposite him.

"I hate doin' business with anyone across a desk," he explained.

Unless it's yours, right? Frank thought. He hesitated, and then did as the man asked. There was no sense in making an issue of it at this stage of the game.

"So, Jason," he said. "I assume you're still satisfied."

Mainwaring took a file from his briefcase and opened it.

"With this kind of money involved," he said, "I won't be satisfied until our little anesthetic is in every operating room of every hospital in the world. But I am certainly pleased with the"—he consulted the file—"four hundred ninety-six cases Jack and I have completed. I must say, Frank, you've done all right. You promised me five hundred cases in two years, and you delivered."

"Like I told you when we first met, Jason, I know this town."

The key to the whole project had been the rapid takeover by Mainwaring of Guy Beaulieu's practice. And only Frank, and to some extent, Mainwaring, knew how skillfully Frank had engineered that feat. Details: that's what it all came down to. Attention to touches like the letter to Maureen Banas threatening his own position should she ever disclose to anyone, including him, what was being done to her. The sort of details he had neglected to attend to three years before.

"Pity about ol' Beaulieu," Mainwaring said blandly.

Frank could not tell if the man was being facetious or not. Again, he opted to avoid an altercation. In the morning, Mainwaring would be gone. And in a week or so he would be back to officially tender his resignation and to offer proof of a million dollars in Frank's Cayman Islands account and half a million in Pearl's, in exchange for the patent Frank now shared with Pearl and all future rights to Serenyl.

And that, Frank knew, was what it was all about.

He would, at last, have squared away the $250,000 shortfall in the Ultramed-Davis books, and there would be a nifty little bundle left over to build on.

"Well," he said dispassionately, "at least the old guy didn't suffer. When my number comes up, I want to go the same way. . . . So, I assume you have everything you need to conclude this business with your company in Atlanta?"

Mainwaring skimmed through his notes.

"It would appear so, Frank. Here's that, ah, little agreement you insisted upon."

He passed the document over.

Frank scanned the page to be certain it included Mainwaring's admission to having illegally used Serenyl on five hundred patients. It was Frank's insurance policy against any kind of deal being made behind his back. In the morning, the two of them would jointly place the confession, along with similar ones from Frank and Jack Pearl, in a safe deposit box at the Sterling National Bank, and upon Mainwaring's return to town, the three of them would retrieve and destroy the documents together.

"Remember, Frank," Mainwaring warned, "I don't have the final say in all this. My partners are still calculatin' what it's gonna cost us to go backward and do all the animal and clinical trials the FDA insists on, and—"

Frank laughed out loud.

"Jason, please," he said. "It costs tens of millions to develop and test new drugs that you don't even know are going to work, let alone work safely. You've got a gold mine here, and you know it, and I know it, and your partners know it, and even our little fairy friend Pearl knows it.

"After five hundred perfect cases without so much as one problem, the only money you're going to spend is whatever it costs to grease a palm or two at the FDA and to put together a few folders of bogus animal and clinical trials. So don't try to shit me, okay? It's unbecoming for a man of your class."

Mainwaring shook his head ruefully.

"There are a number of things I'm going to miss around here, Frank," he said, perhaps purposely intensifying his drawl, "but I confess you won't be among them. Be sure Jack has all the paperwork and formulas ready for me in the morning, y'hear? Assumin' my partners and our chemists give their okay, I'll be back in eight or ten days. Meanwhile, I shall assume that you or Jack'll let me know if any problems crop up."

"Of course, Jason, old shoe," Frank said. "But after two years and five hundred cases, I don't think you have to camp by the phone waiting to hear from us. Next to birth, death, and taxes, Serenyl is as close as life gets to a sure thing. . . . And you know that, don't you."

Mainwaring's eyes narrowed.

"What I know," he said evenly, "is that this little tête-à-tête has gone on long enough."

Without offering his hand, the surgeon snapped up his briefcase and left.

Not until the office door clicked shut did Frank's smile become more natural. In the interests of their deal, he had allowed the pompous ass to walk over him any number of times during the past two years. The son of a bitch even tried to tell him what music to listen to. Now, with the work completed and so successful, there was no longer any reason to defer to him, and Frank felt exhilarated that he hadn't.

After years of operating in the shadows of men like Mainwaring and the Judge, it was time to start casting some shadows of his own. His life had finally turned the corner. He was a rising star in a powerful corporation, and soon he would have the independence and prestige that only money could bring.

"God bless you, Serenyl," he murmured.

Softly at first, then louder and louder, the familiar chant worked its way into his thoughts.

Frank, Frank, he's our man. If he can't do it, no one can. . . .

Four miles to the north, Suzanne Cole screamed and leapt up from the couch where she had been dozing. A vicious, searing pain had exploded through her chest from beside her right breast. Bathed in a chilly sweat, she tore open her blouse and ripped apart the clasps on her bra.

The scar from her surgery was red, but not disturbingly so, and the tissue beneath it was not the least bit tender.

Still, the pain had been like nothing she had ever experienced before.

Desperately, she searched her cloudy thoughts for some logical medical explanation. Perhaps a neuritis, she reasoned—the single, violent electrical discharge from a regenerating nerve.

Yes, of course, a neuritis. That had to be it. No other diagnosis made sense.

Shaken, but relieved, she sank back onto the pillow. Then she checked her watch. Forty-five minutes. That was all she had napped. She needed more than that—much more—if she was going to catch up with the sleep she kept losing every night. It was lucky she had taken time off after her surgery. The strain of the whole affair seemed to have taken more of a toll on her than she had anticipated.

Slowly, her eyes closed.

Perhaps she should get up and take something before she slipped off again. An aspirin or even some codeine. At least then, if the irritated nerve fired off again, the pain would be blunted.

No, she decided. As long as she knew what it was, there was nothing to be frightened about. It had only lasted ten or twelve seconds, anyhow. If it happened again, she could handle it. For that short a time, she could handle almost anything. What she needed most was sleep.

Relax . . . Breathe deeply . . . Breathe deeply . . . Good . . . That's it . . . That's it . . .

Now, she thought, as she drifted off, just what was it she had been dreaming about . . . ?

CHAPTER 18

THE WHITE PINES Golf Club course, designed by Robert Trent Jones, was the pride, joy, and status symbol of its select shareholders. Sculpted along a narrow valley between two massive granite escarpments, the layout was short but exceedingly tight, and members still delighted in recalling the day in sixty-two when Sam Snead, playing an exhibition round from the championship tees, shot an eighty-six and lost two balls.

It was early Saturday afternoon, and for the first time in years, Zack was preparing to play a round of golf—his opponent: Judge Clayton Iverson.

Zack had originally planned to spend the morning meeting with Jason Mainwaring and Jack Pearl, and then the rest of the day not *between* the granite cliffs, but *on* them, climbing with a small group from the local mountaineering club. However, Mainwaring had signed out for a week to Greg Ormesby, the only general surgeon remaining in Sterling, and Pearl, too, was away until Monday morning.

And in truth, as much as Zack had been looking forward to making a climb, he was pleased with the chance to spend a few hours alone with his father for the first time since his return to Sterling.

Typically, the Judge's invitation to play had been couched in words that made refusal difficult. He had also intimated that there might be more on his mind than just golf. There would be, he had made it quite clear, just the two of them, although whether Frank was unable to come or had not been invited, he did not say.

Earlier in the day, after making rounds, thumbing once again through Toby Nelms's chart, and trying to locate Mainwaring and Pearl, Zack had spent an hour on the practice range. It had been a pleasant surprise to find that some vestige of his swing, developed over dozens of childhood lessons, remained.

Like most sports that involve doing something with a ball, golf had never held any great fascination for him. But the rolling fairways, perfectly manicured greens, and even the sprawling Tudor clubhouse with its shaded veranda and oriental rugs, had always brought him a certain serenity, especially on warm, cloudless, summer afternoons.

"So, Zachary," Clayton Iverson said as they approached the first tee, "just how interesting should we make it?"

He was dressed in white slacks, a gold LaCoste shirt, and his trademark—brown and white saddle golf shoes. Although he could hardly be said to be in shape, he carried his husky bulk with the easy grace of a natural athlete. Set off by a gnarled thicket of pure silver hair, his tanned, weathered face exuded confidence and authority.

"That depends on how badly you need money, Judge," Zack said, knowing that it was both fruitless and in bad form to argue with his father against a wager of some sort.

"Well, then, suppose we make it, say, a dollar a hole with carry-overs? I'll give you a stroke on the par fives and the two long par fours."

"Let's see . . ." Zack made the pretext of counting on his fingers. "Eighteen dollars. I guess I can handle that. Okay, sir, a dollar a hole it is. I assume you'll take it easy on me, as always."

The Judge set his ball on the tee and looked up at his son with a predatory smile.

"Of course," he said. "Just like always."

It was the most basic truth of the man's relationship with his sons, and almost a standing joke among them over the years, that he had never given them even the slightest quarter in anything competitive, whether gin rummy, at which he was a vicious profiteer, golf, or even business. Victories were to be earned, or not to be had; loans of even the smallest amounts of money were invariably accompanied by IOUs and were to be paid back in full, and always with some interest.

Zack knew that on this day, as always, not one punch would be pulled, not one edge given away.

The Judge's drive, to the genteel applause of a dozen or so onlookers, split the fairway and rolled to a stop well past the discreet two-hundred-yard marker.

Aware that he often felt less tension operating on a brain tumor than he did at that moment, Zack shanked his drive into the goldfish pond.

"I hope you don't have any pressing engagements, Judge," he said, teeing up another ball. "We could be here for a while."

"Slow your backswing and drop your left shoulder a bit," his father said.

Zack did as was suggested and hit a bullet that bounced almost on top of the Judge's ball and then rolled several yards beyond.

"Thanks for the help," he whispered, tipping an imaginary cap in response to the applause from the small gallery.

"Enjoy it," the Judge said as they walked off the tee. "At a buck a hole, that's all you get."

* * *

By the end of the front nine, Zachary was seven dollars behind and was getting blisters on the sides of both heels from his decade-old golf shoes. Still, the afternoon was warm and relaxing, and he was enjoying a seldom-experienced sense of connection to his father, born largely, it seemed, of casual snippets of conversation and brief flashes to afternoons, long past, like this one.

Clayton Iverson had asked about his new practice and shared a few anecdotes from the courtroom, but otherwise had given no real indication that there were any items on the afternoon's agenda other than golf.

Following a brief stop in the clubhouse for a beer, the Judge dropped off the motorized cart he had used on the front nine and arrived at the tenth tee pulling his clubs on a two-wheeled aluminum caddy.

"I need the exercise," he explained. "And besides, with me riding and you walking and chasing those shots of yours all over hell and gone, it didn't seem like we had much chance to talk out there."

"Very witty, Judge," Zachary said. "Well, just watch thee out. To quote the words of General Custer at the Little Big Horn, 'We have not yet begun to fight.' "

He led off the tenth hole with a decent drive, but his father's shot, sliced badly, flew far to the right and disappeared into a bank of tall rough. While they were scuffling through the heavy grass looking for the ball, the Judge waved the foursome behind them to play through.

"If we don't find it by the time those four have putted out, I'll drop one."

"Fair enough."

Zack wondered briefly about the amicable concession, which was out of character for the man.

"Zachary, tell me something," the Judge went on, still searching through the rough. "Have you encountered any problems with Ultramed since you started working at the hospital?"

"Problems?"

"Hey, you know what I'll bet? I'll bet my shot went a little farther right than we thought. Let's try looking over that way."

"Judge?"

"Yes?"

"What sort of problems are you talking about?"

Clayton Iverson hesitated for a time, apparently uncertain whether or not to continue the conversation.

"Guy Beaulieu came to see me a few days before he died," he said finally.

"Oh?"

"It was the second time he had been by in just two or three weeks."

"He was very angry and upset."

"He certainly was," the Judge said, now leaning on his club and making no attempt to look for his ball. "He was also quite determined to prove that Ultramed and Frank had railroaded him out of practice as a means of setting up their own man, this Mainwaring, in his place. He claimed to have evidence that such underhanded dealings are typical of the company."

"I know what he claimed. What I don't know is why on earth he kept coming to you when you made it clear to him how strongly you supported Frank and the excellent job he's done at the hospital."

They watched in silence as each of the passing foursome hit his approach shot. Three of the balls landed neatly on the green, and the fourth, hit by a grizzled old man whom Zack placed somewhere in his mid-eighties, landed in a sand trap. As he invariably did when around very old people, Zack found himself praying that the man's coronary and cerebral circulations were, at least at that moment, functioning as nature intended.

"The answer to your question, Zachary," the Judge said after the old man had hit, "is that Guy was convinced that Frank or no Frank, I would not want to see him go under for acts he never committed. Remember, he and I went back a hell of a long way. I can't count the number of committees and projects we worked on together over the past thirty years, struggling to pull Sterling up from the dying little mill town it once was. As often as not we were on opposite sides of the fence on an issue, but that never mattered. We both fought like hell, but we fought within the rules."

"I understand."

"So, I guess he believed that based on the way we handled our differences, and on my record as a judge, I would champion any cause I felt was just."

"And was he right?"

The Judge took a new ball from his bag and dropped it backward, over his shoulder.

"Of course he was right," he said. "You should know that as well as anyone."

"Sorry."

"Beaulieu's dead, but the issues he was fighting against, if, in fact, they are issues at all, remain very much unresolved—at least until the deadline to repurchase the hospital passes. After that we are all, quite literally, at Ultramed's mercy."

The buyback. Zack suddenly understood why Frank had been excluded from the afternoon. Silently, he cautioned himself against expressing any opinions until the Judge's position had become quite a bit clearer. Where Clayton Iverson and his scion were concerned, interactions and reactions had seldom, if ever, been simple and straightforward.

While Zack's schoolboy years, especially after his accident, had passed by quietly and, by comparison, virtually unnoticed, the relationship between the Judge and Frank had been a turbulent, volatile affair. The man had soaked in his older son's accomplishments like an insatiable sponge, and inevitably, when Frank's heroics were slow in coming, or worse, when he did anything outside of the persona the Judge had created for him, there was friction.

Thinking back, Zack wondered if either of the two ever truly appreciated the dynamics of those clashes.

If being Judge Clayton Iverson's second son had engendered certain problems for him, being his first had proven something of a curse for Frank.

He recalled the day when Frank, then a freshman or sophomore in high school, had received an A on a history paper. The teacher, in her comments, had noted that the writing style and content of the report were far beyond anything he had ever done before.

Suspicious of the sudden improvement, the Judge had confronted Frank in what he liked to call an eyeball-to-eyeball showdown. It was a technique that had seldom failed to uncover a lie from either of his sons, and on that occasion Frank was beaten decisively. After an hour of confrontation, he shuffled to his room and produced the senior's paper from which he had plagiarized.

The look in his eyes at that moment, a frightening olio of fear, hatred, humiliation, and anger, was one Zack would never forget.

The result of that showdown had been a zero on the report from the teacher and a four-game suspension from basketball by the Judge, although he subsequently rescinded his punishment after the coach pleaded that the team would suffer more from it than Frank.

That confrontation, and its aftermath, said much of both father and son. The Judge, feeling he had made his point regarding dishonesty in any form, never again brought up the incident.

For his part, Frank *was,* in fact, discouraged from further academic shortcuts, but only temporarily. Instead of responding to their father's leniency with change, he reacted with defiance. And one boastful day, not long after, he disclosed to his younger brother that he had dedicated himself to learning how to win in an eyeball-to-eyeball showdown. At first, he literally practiced before a mirror. Next came a series of what he called "test fibs." With time, even in the most critical situations he was able impassively to meet the man's piercing gaze and to hold it.

In the years that immediately followed, his conflicts with the Judge fell off markedly, due in part to Frank's mastery of his new craft, and in larger measure to his athletic accomplishments. Then, with Frank's repeated failures prior to Ultramed-Davis, their relationship again became strained.

Now, after four years of relative concord, a clash between the two men—possibly a monumental one—seemed to be in the making. And as always in the past, at the very heart of the matter were the Judge's expectations. Frank's performance had to be the very best, his conduct above reproach.

The foursome ahead of them finished putting and left the green. The Judge addressed his ball, but after several seconds he checked back down the fairway to ensure that no one was approaching, and stepped away.

"Zachary, you look troubled," he said. "What is it?"

"I'm not troubled. It's just that . . ."

"What?"

Zack shook his head.

"It's nothing, Judge. Go ahead and hit."

"You're worried that I'm taking sides against Frank. Is that it?"

"He *is* your son."

"And you think that because of that, I should turn my back on the possibility that he might be involved in something unethical, or even dishonest."

"I didn't say that."

"What, then?"

Zack stopped himself at the last moment from sharing details of Guy Beaulieu's legacy, of his encounter with Maureen Banas, and of his mounting distrust of Ultramed. There were still simply too many uncertainties to open those cans of worms before he had had the chance to discuss them with Frank.

"Judge," he said, carefully choosing his words, "Guy Beaulieu was trying his damnedest to bring down Ultramed. If Frank fell with it, that was no concern of his. I appreciate your commitment to doing what's right, but—"

"But what?"

Again, Zack hesitated. One slip, one misplaced thought, and the Judge would be off and running on another of his crusades.

In Frank's eyes, the two of them would be aligned against him and Ultramed, and any chance of enlisting his help, either in exposing the corporation or in solving the mystery of Toby Nelms, would likely be lost for good.

"Judge, Frank has his quirks and his faults," he said finally, "just like the rest of us. But considering the expectations and the pressures he's had to overcome since those days at Sterling High, I think he's done some things we should both be proud of. At the very least, we should be going out of our way to give him the benefit of the doubt in this business."

"So you think I'm being disloyal by wanting to know whether my son and the corporation he works for are making a profit at the expense of my community?"

"I didn't say that."

"And you think it's disloyalty to question whether Frank might have had a role in the destruction of a man's reputation?"

"Judge, please."

"I'm sorry, Zachary, but I've spent more than thirty years as a lawyer, half of them as a judge. As far as I'm concerned, doing what is right is far more important than any of that kind of so-called loyalty."

"I'm not arguing with that. It's just that from what I can see, this whole business isn't all that simple. Did you know that if it weren't for Frank's using his influence at the hospital, Beaulieu would have been suspended some time ago?"

The Judge looked shaken.

"No," he said. "I didn't."

"Well, it's true."

Of course, the story of Frank's intercession had come from Frank himself, but Zack saw no point in sharing that piece of information, or for that matter, his displeasure with Frank's behavior on the day of Beaulieu's death. He was enjoying the chance to play his brother's advocate. He also sensed that in arguing on Frank's behalf, he was, in some ways, making a case for their father's recognition of his own accomplishments in life.

The Judge seemed surprised and upset by his stand.

Again, he addressed his ball, although Zack could see from his stance and his bloodless knuckles that his concentration was broken. And suddenly Zack understood: his father had done something, or at least was contemplating doing something, that would not sit well with Frank, and now, all at once, he had doubts.

His swing was rushed and awkward. The ball, never really leaving the ground, skimmed across the fairway and slammed into the recently vacated sand trap. Clayton Iverson barely reacted to the horrible shot.

"You know," he said as they trudged toward the bunker, "from the day your mother and I first learned she was pregnant with Frank, we began to share visions of greatness for our children. I don't suppose that makes us unique, but I tell you, son, we spent many an hour by the fire that winter sharing our dreams. We even named Frank, and then you, after presidents—little-known presidents, but ones who did leave their marks on history."

Inwardly, Zack sighed. This talk was one he had endured many times over the years. Franklin Pierce, the only president born in New Hampshire, and Zachary Taylor, the much-maligned warrior who, despite four historically undistinguished years in office, established the Department of the Interior, were special favorites of the Judge.

"Believe me, Judge," Zack said, in what had become his standard response to the discussion, "both Frank and I appreciate the values and the drive you instilled in us."

He paused to chip his approach shot onto the edge of the green and then watched as his father, now totally off his game, took two shots to get out of the sand trap.

By the end of the hole, Zack had cut his deficit to six dollars, and following two ties and a disastrous seven by the Judge on the thirteenth, he had pared it by three dollars more.

"Judge," he said, motioning to the small refreshment kiosk by the fourteenth tee, "let's take a break. Anything that could upset you enough to play like this ought to be talked out."

"I'm not upset," Clayton Iverson said.

"Okay, you're not upset. You only went from shooting four over par for the whole front nine, to shooting eight over for the first four holes since you brought up this business about the hospital. Why don't you have a seat at that little table over there and let me buy you a beer."

The Judge started to protest, but then relented.

"Maybe I am a *little* upset," he muttered.

Zack left him at the wrought-iron table and returned with two frosted mugs and two bottles of Lowenbrau.

"So, what's going on?" Zack asked as he sipped at his beer.

"What do you mean?"

"I mean Frank, Judge. I know you helped him get considered for the job with Ultramed. Is that why you're being hard on him? Because you feel responsible?"

"Zachary, the mess your brother made of that damn electronics company of his wasn't his first fiasco. He just didn't have the patience for that kind of business. He was constantly trying to go directly from step one to step twenty. He was lucky the Ultramed opportunity came along when it did. I told him that when he—" Clayton Iverson stopped in midsentence.

"When he what, Judge?"

"Nothing. It doesn't matter."

"He asked you for a loan, didn't he?" Zack said.

Suddenly pieces of conversations he had had with his brother over the years began falling into place. Although Frank had never shared the details of his company's failure, he had made it clear that he felt their father was, at least in part, at fault.

"It was a foolish request. He was already in it up to here. It would have been throwing good money after bad."

"Frank didn't see it that way, Judge."

"Well, I did. I agreed to help him out of the hole he had gotten himself in, but only on the condition that he get rid of that company. The hospital job gave him a chance to get out from underneath that nonsense and to show everyone in town just what he could do."

To say nothing of bringing him back here, under your thumb, Zack thought angrily.

"So, he got the job, and he's done it well. What more could you want from him?"

"I could want him to bring the same values to his position that I bring to mine. That's what I could want. I could want him to stand up for what's right."

Despite the warm afternoon, Zachary felt suddenly cold.

"What's right?" *I'm the one with Beaulieu's evidence,* he wanted to shout. *I'm the one who confronted Maureen Banas. How can you be so damned sure of what's right?* "Dad," he said, "exactly what have you done?"

"You know, Zachary, I don't particularly like that tone of yours. You may be a big-shot surgeon, but you're still my son."

Zack sensed himself backing away from his father's glare. He couldn't remember the last time he had pushed against the man this hard.

"Sorry," he mumbled.

"Apology accepted. I think that thirty years on the bench more than qualifies me to tell when someone's handing me a line of bull. There was just too much smoke surrounding Beaulieu's complaints for there to be no fire. I . . . I didn't know until you told me that Frank had intervened on his behalf."

He hesitated, and then reached into the pocket of his golf bag, withdrew an envelope, and passed it over.

"Here," he said, "read this."

Mrs. Leigh Baron
Director, Operations
Ultramed Hospitals Corporation
Boston Place
Boston, Massachusetts 02108

Dear Mrs. Baron:

The contract effecting the sale of Davis Regional Hospital to Ultramed Hospitals Corporation is now in its fourth and final year. As you are no doubt aware, the agreement contains provisions for the reacquisition of the facility by the community-based board, of which I am chairman, provided the board meets no less than five months prior to the termination date of the contract and agrees by a vote of no less than 51% of its members to return to Ultramed the original purchase price—a sum currently held in escrow in the Sterling National Bank—in exchange for resuming control of the hospital.

Until recently, I had no intention of convening the board to consider such a vote. However, a situation has developed that greatly concerns me—a conflict between Dr. Guy Beaulieu, one of the first physicians to settle in Sterling, and your corporation. It was the late Dr. Beaulieu's contention that the hospital administration, and ultimately, Ultramed Hospitals Corporation itself, was responsible for machinations calculated to drive him out of medical practice. He further claimed knowledge of actions by your corporation, through Ultramed-Davis, which have been contrary to the best interests of our community. I know that he had conveyed his feelings to you on several occasions, and that he had, in fact, instituted legal action against both the hospital and Ultramed Hospitals Corporation.

Dr. Beaulieu's widow has contacted me and has requested that the board seriously consider Dr. Beaulieu's allegations before the end of our provisional period at noon on July 19. I have asked Mrs. Beaulieu to make every effort, in advance of that date, to supply me with details of her husband's claims and the evidence behind them.

Meanwhile, please consider this letter notification that I intend to convene the board at 11 a.m. on Friday, July 19, for the purpose of discussing our options. Also, as provided in our contract, I have commissioned a full, independent audit of the hospital, which I expect to be initiated within the next few days. As you know, according to section 4B of the contract, 15 percent of the hospital's profits over the past four years should have been funneled back into the community through the treatment of indigent patients, and another 3 percent through support of various civic projects enumerated in section 4C. Violation of that section, even if uncovered after the July 19 deadline, will nullify our contract with you.

Meanwhile, if you have any information or thoughts on this matter, I would welcome hearing from you.

Hoping for an amicable resolution of this issue, I remain,

Sincerely yours,
Clayton C. Iverson

Zack was incredulous. Beaulieu's widow and daughter had given him no indication that they planned to contact the board directly.

"Judge, just when did Mrs. Beaulieu call you?" he asked.

"Well . . . actually, she didn't call me. . . . I called her."

"And has she contacted other members of the board?"

"I, um, suggested she might want to do so."

"Oh, Judge, why?"

"Because ol' Guy might have been right, that's why."

"But Frank said he wasn't. Why couldn't you have just given him the benefit of the doubt?"

"I . . . I felt that if he hadn't done anything wrong, he didn't have anything to worry about."

"Of course he does. He's got to worry about how to explain to the people at Ultramed why his own father would be trying to sabotage their hospital. You don't even know what kind of so-called evidence Guy had, do you? . . . Well, do you?"

Clayton Iverson shook his head.

"I didn't think so. Well, I do, Judge. I know exactly what he had. Clothilde Beaulieu gave it all to me at his funeral. And I tell you there isn't enough proof of wrongdoing even to dent Ultramed. Circumstantial stuff. That's all he had accumulated. Just a pile of inferential lists, anecdotes, and newspaper clippings.

"I'll admit that I have some strong reservations about that company, but up till now there's no hard evidence—not one person that I know of—who was directly hurt by the corporation's policies. Why couldn't you have just gone to Frank? Talked to him? That's what I had planned to do. Did he even see this letter before you sent it?"

The Judge took a long swallow of beer and wiped the foam from his lips with the back of his hand. Then he smiled.

"I haven't sent it," he said simply.

"What?"

"The letter is being held by my lawyer in Boston until I decide what to do. I was thinking about having him send it over to Ultramed on Monday. I wanted to talk with you first. Now I'm glad I did."

Zack felt drained and exhausted—a yo-yo on the string of a master.

"You could have just told me what you wanted in the first place," he said. "You can't play with people like that, Judge."

"Nonsense. I haven't been playing with anyone. I needed your candid opinion, and I got it. I'm not committed to opposing turning the hospital over to Ultramed for good next week. I'm just reluctant to totally give up our leverage. You never know when you'll wish you had it. The truth is, it would take a hell of a lot more than anything I've learned so far to make me turn against Frank and send that letter. There, do you feel better?"

"What I feel," Zack said, "is wasted."

"Good. In that case, suppose we play us some golf."

The Judge set his beer down, took his driver from his bag, and wiped its head with a cloth.

"I'm pleased with the things you've told me about your brother, Zachary," he said. "I haven't made any secret of my disappointment with him over the years. But as long as he keeps acting for the benefit of our town, then he and Ultramed have nothing to worry about from me. However, if you learn of something, anything, that I should know, then dammit, you owe it to all of us to speak up. Clear?"

"Clear," Zack said numbly.

"Including anything in that material of Guy's."

"Right."

The Judge set his ball on the tee. Once again in control, he looked relaxed and confident.

"Okay if I hit first?" he asked.

His swing was loose, compact, and smooth as velvet. The drive was arrow straight and by far the longest of the day.

An hour later, Zack stood on the eighteenth green and watched as his father rolled in a twelve-foot putt for a birdie.

"Five straight holes for me," the Judge said. "That's eight bucks. I just love this game, don't you?"

CHAPTER 19

DOSE BY DOSE, microgram by microgram, the Haldol level in Annie Doucette's blood had been rising. The input from her senses, barely adequate to keep her oriented *before* the tranquilizer was started, had become blunted and distorted. Her periods of lucidity, even in the bright, noisy daylight hours, had all but disappeared.

Now, as the muted stillness of late Sunday evening drifted over the hospital, what little hold she had been able to maintain on reality had begun to slip away.

One moment, she was home, in her own room, her own bed; in the next, she was someplace else, someplace at once foreign and familiar. It was evening, it was morning. Desperately, she struggled against the madness. Desperately, she tried to focus her thoughts. Still, nothing was certain—nothing except the realization that somehow, she had wet and soiled herself.

Call Zack . . . Call Suzanne, her mind urged. *Tell them to come and clean you up. Tell them to get you out of this place.*

She turned to search for a telephone, but a wave of dizziness and nausea forced her back onto the pillow.

Lifting the sheet, she stared down at her legs. Foul-smelling, loose excrement was smeared over the insides of her thighs. So disgusting. So humiliating.

Must get washed . . . Must get showered before someone comes.

Annie peered through a gray mist toward the door of her bathroom. *Shower . . . Clean up . . . Then call—who? What was his name?*

With all her strength she struggled onto her side. There were metal railings along both sides of her bed. Using one of them, and battling the constant spinning, she pulled herself up.

How disgusting . . . How humiliating . . .

There was no guard railing at the end of the bed. With agonizing slowness she worked her way over the feces-soaked sheet. Then she dropped one leg over the low footboard and onto the chilly linoleum floor. The dizziness was becoming unbearable.

Still, she knew she had to get clean.

An inch at a time, she slid her other leg onto the floor. With every ounce of her strength, she tried to stand. Momentarily, her leg held. But then suddenly, it gave way, and for the briefest time she was floating in air.

She landed heavily and gracelessly, air exploding from her lungs with a loud grunt. There was another sound as well—a sharp, snapping sound coming from somewhere within her body.

An instant later, unimaginable pain shot through her from her left hip.

Second by second, the pain intensified. Then, a heaviness settled onto her chest. Slowly, the dim light in the room faded, and Annie felt a merciful, peaceful darkness settle in.

The night was heavy—overcast and humid, with not quite enough breeze for comfort. It was nearing eleven when Zack eased the Judge's Chrysler into the largely empty parking lot outside the Ultramed-Davis emergency ward. The Judge, hands folded stoically in his lap, sat next to him. His mother, grim and silent, rode in the backseat, working over the handkerchief she had balled in her fists.

Annie Doucette was in trouble.

Zack would have much preferred to evaluate the woman's situation before involving his parents, but a well-meaning nurse, unable to reach Annie's son in Connecticut, had noted that they were listed in her record as "employer," and had called them.

A fractured hip and new coronary were the only snatches a shaken Cinnie Iverson could remember to repeat to Zack from that conversation.

"Zachary, dear," she said now, as he helped her from the car, "do you think they'll operate on her tonight?"

"I don't know, Mom. It's doubtful, though. Especially if the nurse I spoke to is right about her having had a new heart attack."

"Her doctor—what is his name?"

"Norman, Mom. Don Norman."

"Dr. Norman. Did you speak to him?"

"He was in working on Annie. I didn't see any sense in bothering him."

"And did Frank say he'd be right in?"

"Yes, Mom. He's waiting for Lisette to get back from her sister's, and then he'll be in."

Cinnie gave her handkerchief one last squeeze and then stuffed it in her purse.

"Well," she said, "I just hope Annie's okay."

"Okay?" Clayton Iverson laughed disdainfully. "Jesus, Cynthia, what world do you live in? The woman's almost eighty years old and she just fell out of bed, broke her hip, and had a heart attack. How in the hell could you possibly think she'd be okay?"

"Sorry," Cinnie said. "There's no need to cuss," she added in a whisper directed more to herself than to her husband.

They entered the hospital through the emergency ward and took the elevator to the second floor. Annie had been moved back to the intensive care unit.

"Why don't you two wait in there," Zack said, motioning them into the small waiting room just outside the unit. "I'll be back as soon as I find out what's going on."

Anger and tension had knotted the muscles at the base of his neck and were gnawing at the pit of his stomach. To be sure, over the years of his training he had had patients fall out of bed, even when strict precautions had been taken. The risk was always there, especially with so many hospitalized patients being old and infirm.

But this situation was different. Since he was a consultant on her case, Annie Doucette *was,* technically, his patient; but even more than that, she was his friend. In some ways she had been as much a parent to him as had Cinnie and the Judge. And even beyond that, he knew, was the special, proprietary feeling experienced by every physician toward a patient whose life he or she had saved.

He was on edge, his physician's detachment and objectivity hanging by the thinnest of threads.

From the moment Cinnie had called him with the news, he had been reminding himself that, while it was reasonable for him to be upset, there was seldom, if ever, justification for a physician to lose objectivity—even when confronting oversight or negligence. In the microcosm of the hospital, explosions by physicians helped no one.

As he was heading into the unit, Sam Christian, one of three staff orthopedic surgeons, emerged. He was a tall, gaunt man, in his mid-fifties, who walked with a slight limp. Twenty-two years before, Zack and his mangled left knee had been one of his first cases.

"Evening, Zack," he said. He glanced into the small waiting room. "Judge, Cinnie."

"Hello, Sam." The Judge came out to shake his hand. "What's the story?"

Christian shrugged.

"She needs a new hip," he said matter-of-factly. "But until her cardiac situation gets straightened out, that's out of the question. To-morrow, if she's still—I mean, if she's settled down, I'll put some pins across the joint to stabilize it until we can do something definitive."

"Do you know what happened?" Zack asked. "Were the side rails up on her bed?"

Christian's expression darkened.

"You'd best talk to Don Norman about all that. But yes, apparently the railings were up. She went off the end."

"Oh, dear God," Cinnie gasped.

"Thanks, Sam," Zack said. He turned to his parents. "I'll be out in a little bit."

As he entered the unit he heard the Judge say, "So, Sam, level with me, now. Who screwed up here?"

Zack had seen Annie briefly during morning rounds. At that time, she was awake and responsive, but somewhat depressed and more le-thargic than she had been. He suggested that she try spending more time out of bed, and had actually offered to walk down the hall with her. She refused, citing a headache and lack of sleep.

The change in her over just fourteen hours, even allowing for her accident, was terrifying. She was disoriented and combative; her speech was thick and slurred. Her gray hair was matted against her scalp with perspiration and bits of feces.

From the doorway, Zack watched as Don Norman struggled to ex-amine Annie's chest. The portly internist had stripped off his suitcoat and rolled up his shirt-sleeves, but he was still wearing his tie, vest, and gold watch fob. Beads of sweat dotted his fleshy forehead and upper lip.

A young nurse stood off to one side, her face drawn and pale.

"Need an extra pair of hands?" Zack asked as Norman stepped back from the bed.

The man looked down at Annie and then shook his head.

"No, thank you, Doctor," he said. "I'm just about done."

"She okay?"

"If you mean is she going to die, the answer is no . . . at least not tonight. Since we got a line in and gave her some fluid, her pressure has come up. But she's extended her old coronary. There's not much ques-tion about that. And I guess you know that she's fractured her hip."

She's extended her coronary. *She's* fractured her hip. Norman's emotionless statement—his tacit implication that Annie was responsi-ble for her own misfortune—instantly rekindled the dislike Zack had developed toward the man during their interview many months before.

Still, there could be no arguing the truth in his grim assessment of her situation and prognosis. Pneumonia, stroke, embolism, heart fail-ure; while orthopedists could work near-miracles with hips in the oper-ating room, physicians and nurses knew all too well that immobilization of any sort was the deadliest enemy of advancing age.

Zack moved to within two feet of the bed.

"Is she making any sense?"

"Nope. Strictly word salad."

"Stroke?"

"I don't think so."

"Is there any evidence she hit her head?"

Norman shifted uncomfortably.

"I . . . I haven't really checked," he said. "As you can see, she's not the easiest thing in the world to examine right now."

"Mind if I try?"

"Try anything you want," Norman responded somewhat testily. Then he glanced over at the nurse.

Zack caught the look and warned himself against doing anything that would embarrass the man. He took Annie's hand. Instantly, she dug her nails into his palm.

"Hey, Annie D, lego! It's me. It's Zack. I need that hand for my coin tricks."

She looked up at him, blinking as if struggling to peer through a haze. Then, slowly, she loosened her grip.

"Do you recognize me?" Zack said, already speeding through a neurologic exam.

Annie did not respond.

"Well, you should." He checked her scalp for any telltale lumps, and her neck for any points of tenderness. "You used to wipe my runny nose and drag me back to the bathroom to wash behind my ears. Remember that?"

Although it remained uncertain whether or not Annie recognized him, there could be no doubt that his words had calmed her down. She lay reasonably still as he checked her eardrums and retinae.

"Well?" Norman asked. His arms were folded tightly across his chest.

Zack smoothed Annie's matted hair off her forehead. "There are no focal neurologic signs. Let's go out to the nurses' station and talk, okay?"

"Is it . . . . all right if I listen in?" the nurse asked, pausing between words to clear a huskiness from her voice.

"Fine with me, if Dr. Norman doesn't mind."

Norman hesitated and then shook his head.

"We haven't met," Zack went on. "My name's Iverson, Zack Iverson. I'm the new neurosurgeon on the block."

"I'm Doreen Lavalley," she said. "Annie was my patient up on four. I feel sick about what happened. We had her tucked in with the side rails up. She soiled herself. I think she was trying to get to the bathroom when she fell. We were all in with a post-op patient who had started hemorrhaging, and our routine bed check was delayed almost an hour, and . . . and we're just . . ." She bit at her lower lip and looked away.

"Go on," Zack said as they walked from the cubicle to the nurses' station.

For a moment, it seemed as if the young woman was going to cry. Then a flash of anger mixed with the anguish in her eyes.

"Dammit," she said, "I knew something like this was going to happen."

"What do you mean?"

She glanced over at Donald Norman and then turned again to Zack.

"We're short," she blurted. "That's what I mean. We're short a nurse on every shift on every floor except the unit here. It's been that way for more than a year. First they got rid of the union with all those promises of increased pay and benefits and staffing. Then, just slowly enough so that none of us could organize to complain, they began to cut back on nursing. I knew something like this was going to happen. I just knew it. . . ." Her fists were clenched in frustration.

"Who's 'they'?" Zack asked.

"The hospital, that's who . . . the administration . . . Mr. Iver—" She stopped in midword and looked sheepishly at Zack. "Oh, great . . . Way to go, Doreen. . . . Brother?"

Zack nodded.

"Sorry," she said.

"Don't be. Don, you're the chief of staff. Are the physicians aware that this has been going on?"

Norman's face was pinched and flushed. However, his indignation was directed not at the situation, but at the nurse.

"If Miss Lavalley has complaints about this hospital or the way it is run," he said, his back almost turned to her, "there are channels established for her to voice those concerns. She's worked here for enough years to know that—and also to know that airing her own distorted point of view in the middle of the intensive care unit is not one of those channels. Now, Doctor, if you'd care to share your thoughts on Mrs. Doucette with me, I can get on with the business of trying to save her life."

The woman tensed at Norman's rebuke, but said nothing.

Zack wrestled against the urge to defend her, and won a narrow victory. The issue at hand was getting Annie Doucette diagnosed, treated, and stabilized. The nurse's charges, disturbing though they were, could wait.

He thought about calling Suzanne in, but quickly tabled the notion. Annie's monitor pattern was regular, at least for the moment, and Donald Norman, as thin-skinned as he was thick-waisted, seemed hardly the sort to welcome any encroachment on his authority.

"So?" Norman asked impatiently.

"Well, there's no evidence for a stroke or for head trauma," Zack said, "but she's clearly disoriented. I guess if I had to put a label on what's going on, I would say she's sundowning—especially if her blood chemistries all come back normal."

Out of the corner of his eye, Zack saw Doreen Lavalley nodding in vigorous agreement.

Sundowning was not a medical diagnosis in the pure sense. Nevertheless, to anyone dealing with elderly, hospitalized patients, the disorientation and psychotic behavior stemming from unfamiliar surroundings and the diminished sensory input of evening were as real and reproducible a phenomenon as a strep throat.

"Excellent," Norman said, his expression and patronizing tone making it clear that Zack had added nothing to his assessment of the case. "Good job. Listen, Doctor, why don't you dictate a note, and I'll put a formal request for a consultation in her chart." He unrolled his sleeves and retrieved his suitcoat. "If there's nothing else, I'm going to see another patient. I'll stop back on my way out."

Zack, engrossed in Annie's chart, did not respond.

"What are you looking for?" Norman asked.

"An explanation."

"For what?"

Zack glanced up.

"Don, this woman's been here almost two weeks, during which time she's been totally with it. Don't you think it's a little strange that she should have taken this long to sundown?"

"On second thought," Norman said, "why don't you just forget about the consult. We'll discuss this whole thing in the morning."

"It's there, Dr. Iverson," the nurse said.

Norman shot her a withering glare.

"What is?" Zack asked.

"The explanation. Look on the med sheet."

"Give me that chart," Norman snapped. "Miss Lavalley, you don't know a good thing when you have it, do you? You just get the hell out of here. I'll deal with you tomorrow."

"You can deal with me tonight, Dr. Norman, because I've had enough. I quit."

"Haldol!" Zack exclaimed, slamming his fist on the page. "What in the hell is she doing on Haldol?"

The nurse's fury was not uncontained.

"Dr. Norman—excuse me, *Don*—" she corrected herself sweetly, "put her on it Tuesday when she complained about his plan to transfer her to a nursing home. He called her a harpy."

"Damn you," Norman hissed, his face now puffed and crimson.

"A nursing home? Norman, are you crazy?"

"Is *who* crazy?" Frank Iverson, hands on hips, stood just inside the unit door.

Zack rubbed at the grit of fatigue and tension that had begun to sting his eyes.

"This whole place, that's who," he said to no one and to everyone. "This whole place is crazy."

"Easy, Zack-o," Frank warned. "Just stay cool. How's Annie?"

Zack lowered his hand and looked up at his brother.

"She's crazy. That's how she is. She's crazy because for the last five days she's been receiving a major tranquilizer. Her blood levels have been rising and she's been drifting further and further from reality until it's doubtful she even knew where she was when all this happened. She lost control of her bowels and was trying to crawl over the end of the bed to the bathroom when she fell. The nurse, here, tells me they didn't get in to check on her as soon as they should have because there's been such a staffing cutback that they're shorthanded. What kind of a god-damn place is this, Frank?"

"I . . . I think I'd better get back to my floor," Doreen Lavalley said softly. "Mr. Iverson, my resignation will be in the nursing office tomorrow morning." Without waiting for a response, she whirled and hurried out.

"Don, what in the hell's going on here?" Frank asked.

"Your brother, that's what," Norman answered. "He barges in here, starts examining my patient without even being consulted, badgers the nurse into making some rash statments about the hospital, and then accuses me of causing the woman to fall." He turned to Zack. "You've been trouble since the day you got here, and don't think we don't all know it. This hospital needs team players, Iverson. You're a grand-stander. Ultramed-Davis ran perfectly smoothly before you showed up, and it will do just as well after you've gone."

"I'm not going anywhere," Zack said.

"Don't bank on it," Norman shot back.

"Easy, both of you," Frank said. "First of all, just tell me, is that woman in there going to die tonight?"

"It was touch and go for a while," Norman said. "But I've gotten things under control. She's a bit disoriented, but she's not in any imme-diate danger. We'll wait a few days to let her cardiac situation calm down, and then Sam Christian'll fix her hip."

"Zack?"

"What?"

"Do you think that's the way it is?"

"I think," Zack said wearily, still resting his head on his hand, "that Suzanne ought to be called in to take care of Annie. That's what I think."

"Over my dead body, you arrogant son of a bitch," Norman rasped.

"Careful, Don," Zack said. "That's Frank's mother you're talking about."

"Will you two please stop it? There are nurses and patients all over this place. Now, Don, tell me, did you have Annie on a tranquilizer or not? And for God's sake, keep your voice down."

Donald Norman was losing what little control he had left.

"First of all, Frank," he said, "I'll thank you not to tell me what to do with my voice. Second of all, I'll thank you and your brother, here, not to go questioning the therapy I choose for my patients. You may be the administrator here, but I'm the chief of the medical staff."

Frank stepped forward until his face was less than a foot from Norman's. His eyes were steely.

"Donald, one call from me, one"—he held up a finger for emphasis —"and you'll be lucky to have a job scrubbing bedpans. You should know that. And if you don't think I have that kind of clout at Ultramed, just try me. Now take that chief of staff crap and stuff it. Then tell me what in the hell you were thinking when you put Annie Doucette on tranks."

"Yeah, Don," Zack urged acidly, "tell him."

"Zack, will you please shut the fuck up for a minute and let me get to the bottom of this?"

Norman was visibly cowed.

"Frank," he pleaded, "I was just trying to follow policy. The woman's DRG payments are about to run out. I have a bed lined up for her at the nursing home. That's just what I'm supposed to do. When I told her what was planned, she went berserk. She demanded more time in the hospital. That was out of the question. You know the rules as well as I do."

"What rules?" Zack asked.

Frank ignored him.

"So you sedated her," he said. "Jesus, Don. She worked for my goddamn family. Couldn't you have just called me?"

"I . . . I didn't think to."

"What rules?" Zack asked again.

"Yes, what rules?"

The three men spun toward the voice. Clayton Iverson was just a few feet away, calmly appraising them all. His expression was non-threatening, but Zack could see anger smoldering in his eyes.

"Judge," Frank said. "You said you were going to wait out there with Mom."

"I got impatient."

"Well . . . well, good enough. I'm sure it's no great news to you that we can't always agree on everything in a hospital. Right?"

"Right."

Frank smiled cheerily, but Zack knew he was shaken.

"Don, here, tells us Annie's still disoriented, but that her condition has stabilized. Isn't that so, Zack? Listen, Judge, why don't you get Mom and bring her in. It's getting late, and I'm sure you both want to get on home."

The Judge confronted him in a brief eyeball-to-eyeball showdown, but Frank easily held his own.

"All right, Frank," Clayton said evenly. "As long as things are under control."

"Don's an excellent internist, Judge, and Annie's getting his best shot. Right, Zack?"

"Right." Zack nearly choked on the word.

"Don, come," Frank said. "Let's you and I go over some things before you call it a day."

Without waiting for an answer, Frank took Norman by the arm and led him from the unit.

"How much of all that did you hear, Judge?" Zack whispered.

Clayton Iverson looked over at Annie, who was clumsily picking at the restraint that was holding her to the bed.

"Enough, Zachary," he said. "I heard quite enough. I'm going to have that letter in Leigh Baron's hands tomorrow. Are you going to try and talk me out of it?"

Once again, Zack rubbed at the burning in his eyes. Even faced with this new reality, it was painful to accept that the promise of Ultramed-Davis—the sparkling physical plant and progressive approach to medicine—was no more than a veneer. Beneath the sheen, beneath the new equipment, the new specialists, and the intense public relations effort, the hospital had no soul.

"No, Judge," he said finally. "Tomorrow I'm going to give you a look at the material Guy had put together against Ultramed. You go ahead and do whatever you feel you have to do. I'm not going to try and talk you out of anything."

Zack waited until the Judge had left, and then called Suzanne.

"Zachary, do you know what time it is?" she said blearily.

"Gee, no," he said, "but give me a minute, and I'll see if I can find someone who does."

"That's not funny."

"Sorry. You don't sound so hot."

"I'm not. I have a splitting headache, and sixty milligrams of Dalmane had me barely asleep when you called."

"Sorry again."

"I've just got to get some rest. Was there anything special you wanted?"

"No," he lied. "Nothing special. I just wanted to see how you were."

"Oh . . . well, can you call me in the morning?"

"Sure."

"Thanks. I should go before this Dalmane wears off."

"Good—"

The dial tone cut him off.

*　*　*

The atmosphere in the shingled ranch Zack had leased from Pine Bough Realty was kept musty and comfortable by the lingering aroma of decades of hardwood fires.

It was after one in the morning. Seated in a frayed easy chair by the dormant hearth, Zack sipped from a cup of Constant Comment tea, absently scratched Cheapdog in his favorite behind-the-ear spot, and waited.

Frank had asked him to stay up to talk, and had promised to be right over. But Zack knew that his brother had never marched to anything other than Frank Iverson's time.

In truth, it made little difference how late Frank would be. Zack was too keyed up by the events of the evening to sleep. His feelings—disappointment, anger, frustration—were strangely akin to those of the dreadful night when Connie had finally leveled with him about her decision to break off their engagement and not to accompany him to New Hampshire.

"It wasn't supposed to be like this, Cheap," he said. "It wasn't supposed to be like this at all."

So much of him wanted to just pack up and run—load the camper and go back to Muni. For all of its underfinanced, stretched-to-the-limit turmoil, the place at least had heart. The bottom line there was never anything but sick or hurting patients and a crew of nurses, technicians, and docs determined to help them get well.

But even as he heard the crunch of his brother's Porsche on the gravel drive, Zack knew that he would stay. For Suzanne and the mountains; for Guy and Toby Nelms and all of the Stacy Millses yet to be in his life, he would see things through.

Frank's visit did not last long.

He was speaking even before the screen door had shut behind him.

"You really stuck it to me tonight, Zack-o," he said breathlessly. "You really stuck it to me."

"Have a seat, Frank. You want something to drink? Some tea? A beer?"

At that moment, Zack caught the odor of whiskey and noted the fine, red flush at the corner of Frank's eyes.

"I don't want anything except a little goddamn loyalty and help from my brother," Frank said, making no move to sit. "A good nurse has quit; my father, who also happens to be the chairman of the hospital board, is furious; and my chief of staff wants to shoot me, to say nothing of what he wants to do to you. That's great, Zachary. That's a hell of a night's work."

"Easy, Frank. Okay?"

"No, dammit! Not okay. Norman's right. From the minute you got back here there's been nothing but trouble. Playing Sir Lancelot all over the goddamn hospital, undermining my authority and Ultramed's policies, even flirting with my wife, for Chrissake."

"That's ridiculous. Frank, you've been drinking. Why don't we both just sit on this and we'll talk in the morning."

"I'll talk about it now," Frank snapped.

Having, perhaps, seen and heard enough, Cheapdog growled a soft warning and from somewhere beneath the shag of his face, bared his teeth.

Zack glanced over at the animal, but made no attempt to quiet him down. With Frank less than totally rational already, Cheapdog was some insurance against a major blowup. That the dog was basically a coward would remain his secret.

"All right," he said wearily, "so talk."

Frank was pacing, clenching and unclenching his fists and then rubbing his hands on the sides of his trousers.

"For years now, ever since you fell on that ski slope and I got to go to Colorado, you've been waiting for the chance to get back, to ruin me. Sitting in the stands all those years cheering and clapping with the others, and all the while hating my guts because you couldn't stay on your skis—"

"Frank, that's crazy."

Revising upward his estimate of how much Frank had had to drink, Zack could only settle back in his chair and watch.

"I told them things were going just fine up here," Frank ranted on. "I told them we didn't need any goddamn neurosurgeon, least of all you. Well, let me tell you something, Zack-o. Tougher nuts than you have tried to fuck with me. Where are they now?"

He whirled and leveled a finger at Zack's face. From the corner of his eye, Zack saw Cheapdog again stiffen.

"Now just listen, and listen to me good," Frank said. "Things are going to change around here or you're out. I've worked too hard to get this place the way I want it to have anyone screw it all up—especially someone with a twenty-year-old chip on his shoulder. So just back off. Let up on the staff, on the Judge, and on Lisette, or I swear, Zack-o, I'll come down on you like a ton of bricks."

Without waiting for a response, he spun on his heel and stormed from the house. Moments later, the Porsche screeched away.

Zack sat in numb disbelief. A twenty-year-past skiing accident; an innocent, unfulfilled high school romance. Was Frank merely drunk and tired, or was he truly crazy?

Let up on the staff. The warning would have gone unheeded under any circumstances. But now, there was not even room for dialogue or tact. An eight-year-old boy was drifting toward insanity and possibly death, and, consciously or not, someone at Ultramed-Davis knew why.

Zack glanced at his watch. It was after two. He picked up a book of crossword puzzles that were far enough beyond his ability to be soporific, and shuffled to the bedroom.

What he needed now, more than anything else, was some sleep; because warning or no warning, Frank or no Frank, he was going to get some answers—beginning in less than seven hours with Jack Pearl.

CHAPTER 20

THE SURGICAL RESIDENTS at Boston Muni traditionally spoke of exhaustion in terms of the Wall—the moment when a physician ceased to function with any creative effectiveness. Throughout training, one was either approaching the Wall, up against it, or, when operating solely on the gritty-eyed fuel of caffeine and nervous energy, beyond it.

At 6:45, when his clock radio switched in on the final two verses of an a cappella version of "Au Clair de la Fontaine," Zack could distinctly remember seeing three, four, and five o'clock flash on its digital display. His bedside light was still on. The crossword puzzle book with, perhaps, a dozen or so items out of one hundred thirty filled in, rested on his chest. The pencil was still wedged between his fingers.

Across the room, Cheapdog, quite ready to begin the day, was perched on his hind legs, his paws resting on the windowsill, the nub of his tail twitching at the prospect of joining some action in the backyard.

It wasn't supposed to be like this.

Zack's first thought of the morning was the same as the last he could remember from the night just past.

Boards of trustees . . . hospital buybacks . . . rules on length of stay . . . policies on who gets admitted and who doesn't . . . enemies . . . allies . . . realty trusts . . . Golden Circles . . . interlocking directorates . . . as if the stresses, pressures, and crises of day-to-day medicine weren't enough.

Perhaps, he mused, the real villain in the piece wasn't Frank, or the Judge, or Norman, or even Ultramed. Perhaps it was his own naiveté—his idealistic notions of illness and injury and the healing arts. Perhaps *that* was what needed overhauling.

Emotionally as well as physically drained, he shuffled to the bathroom to shave and shower, pausing to pull a quarter from behind Cheapdog's ear before letting him out.

The Wall, he knew, was just a few hours away.

Save for the lone librarian, the Ultramed-Davis record room was deserted. With thirty minutes remaining before his appointment with Jack Pearl, Zack had decided to give Toby Nelms's chart one last go-through.

Although he still felt numb and deflated from the madness of the previous night, the morning, at least, had gotten off to a decent start.

After getting Cheapdog settled on his run, he had chosen a route to the hospital that took him past a broad field of tiger lilies, lavender, and black-eyed Susans. For years Annie Doucette had allowed scarcely a day to pass without setting fresh flowers on the dining room table and mantel of the Iverson home. During her hospitalization, the family had done its best to repay her in kind.

Gathering up an armload bouquet, Zack had amused himself by composing cards he would have liked to have propped up by the vase in her ICU cubicle.

To Annie, with deepest apologies. Ultramed. . . . To Annie, my temporary patient: from Don, your temporary doctor. In repayment for your humiliation, heart attack, and broken hip.

In sharp contrast to the surreal chaos of the early morning hours, the unit had been bright and tranquil.

Annie, the Haldol largely out of her system, was fully oriented and even a bit feisty. Although she was sluggish from the analgesia she was receiving for her hip, she had talked in detail of her son and grandchildren, and of Zack's family. Of the thirty-six hours preceding her fall, she remembered nothing, except to reiterate her determination not to be sent to "any death-trap nursing home."

Donald Norman's cookbook cardiology had, for the moment at least, proven adequate, and while Annie's cardiac status remained shaky, it was not critical.

All in all, Zack had left the unit sensing that if anyone her age could make it through the ordeal she was facing, Annie Doucette could.

The record room librarian, an alert young brunette who was nearing the end of a pregnancy, seemed grateful to have company.

Zack signed for Toby's chart and brought it to one of several Formica-walled dictation carrels. The manila folder he set to one side contained the notes and the trickle of articles he had begun to amass on the more obscure complications of the two anesthetics the boy had received. None of those sources had offered so much as a clue to his bizarre condition.

Word by word, more meticulously even than on previous efforts, he picked through the chart. Family history—unremarkable; past medical history—usual childhood immunizations and diseases, nothing else of consequence; physical exam—normal except for an incarcerated inguinal hernia; operative and anesthesia notes—routine. Nurses' notes: "patient brought into recovery from O.R. awake, alert, and smiling; vital signs normal, no evidence for respiratory depression; pupils equal and reactive; lungs clear."

Remarkable. Absolutely remarkable. Zack read the notes once, and then again. Toby's total stay in the recovery room was less than thirty minutes.

He asked for Suzanne's chart. Her anesthetics and doses, when adjusted for weight, were virtually identical to Toby's; so were her recovery room nurses' notes. Total time in the recovery room: forty-five minutes.

The germ of an idea began to take root. Zack checked the time. Thirteen minutes until he met with Pearl.

"Excuse me," he called over to the librarian, "are these records completely computerized?"

"For the last five years, yes," she said, setting aside the romance saga she was reading. "I think they're working on the five years before that."

"Well, supposing I wanted to get, say, a list of all the gallbladder patients operated on in the last three years?"

"No problem. Cholecystectomy is one of our codes, 3982, I think."

"How about just the ones where Dr. Pearl was the anesthesiologist?"

The woman checked her manual.

"Dr. Jack Pearl. Physician 914. I can get the printout for you in just a minute, but it will take a while if you want me to pull the charts." She patted her belly. "As you can see, I'm walking for two."

"Your last month?"

"Last two weeks, I hope."

"Well, if it's too much trouble—"

"No, no. We both need the exercise."

"I hate to make it harder on you, but could I have the first few right away, and then come back in, say, an hour to check on the rest?"

"Sure. At this hour of the morning, this place isn't exactly humming."

She was already typing commands into the computer.

By eight-thirty, Zack had scanned nine charts out of thirty-one. He slipped the notes he had taken into his folder and promised to return for the rest. Despite his lack of sleep, he felt energized—keyed up and very sharp.

His idea had provided no definite answers. But now, at last, he knew he had some damn good questions.

* * *

If Jack Pearl had made any attempt to straighten up his office before Zack's arrival, he had failed miserably. The small, windowless space between the O.R. suite and the recovery room was cluttered with journals and scraps of paper, and smelled heavily of coffee and stale cigarettes. Half-filled ashtrays, one with a butt still smoldering, graced two corners of the desk, and opened, cellophane-wrapped packets of Kleenex were everywhere.

Pearl himself, sporting a wrinkled green polo shirt, was nearly dwarfed behind the pile of reprints, texts, and notebooks on his desk. The hand he extended was cadaverous.

Regardless of how skillful an anesthesiologist Pearl was, it was difficult for Zack to imagine his fastidious brother hiring such a man.

"So," Pearl said, his voice an annoying cross between Peter Lorre and, perhaps, Carol Channing, "I see you are an early morning person, too."

"Actually, I'm more a mid-afternoon person," Zack replied. "Thanks for making the time to see me."

"No big deal. You want some coffee? There's a machine right down the hall."

"No. Thanks, though."

Zack noticed a stained Mr. Coffee crammed to the side of one bookshelf, but saw no evidence of filters or coffee.

"So, Iverson, what's on your mind?"

Pearl, sniffling every twenty or thirty seconds, stubbed out what was left of the smoldering cigarette as he was cuing up a fresh one. He was a man in constant motion, wiping his nose, smoking, or fiddling with the papers on his desk. He was also, Zack felt, somewhat effeminate.

Though they had done one case together, and had spoken briefly after Suzanne's surgery, this was their first contact of any substance.

The office, for all its disarray, was somehow barren and sterile. There were no diplomas or certificates on the wall, no photographs or mementos on the shelves. Zack felt an instant, immense curiosity about the little man, but he had already abandoned any notion of small talk— even nonthreatening questions about his background. Nothing in Pearl's manner encouraged such an approach.

"I need to discuss a case with you," Zack began.

"Okay, shoot."

"It's an eight-year-old boy named Toby Nelms. Jason Mainwaring repaired an incarcerated hernia in him almost a year ago. You did the anesthesia."

"No bells," Pearl said.

"Here's a Xerox of most of his chart."

Zack passed the copy across and waited as Pearl flipped through it.

"Seems pretty cut and dried to me." Pearl hesitated, and then looked up, his brow pinched in thought. "Cut and dried. That was sort of a joke, wasn't it?" He thought some more. "Pretty good joke, too, if I do say so myself. Pretty good."

His laugh was a cackle. Zack smiled, but otherwise made no attempt to join in.

"Pentothal and isoflurane. Is that pretty routine for cases like Toby's?"

"Routine enough," Pearl said. "Why?"

"Well . . ." Zack rubbed at his chin and silently counted to five. "I have reason to believe that the kid wasn't asleep during his surgery."

Pearl's listless eyes flashed.

"That's ridiculous!" he snapped.

"Maybe, but I think it's true. He remembers details of the operation that there's no reason for him to know. And to make matters even more interesting, for the past six months he's been reliving the whole thing."

Pearl was ashen.

"What?"

"He's having flashbacks in which he reexperiences his surgery, only in a terrifying, distorted way. It's as if his preoperative fears have become fused with the actual procedure. Instead of having his hernia fixed, he has his testicles and his penis cut off, again and again. And each time, Jack, he feels the pain. Every bit of it."

"That's . . . that's insane."

"Is it?"

"Of course it is." Pearl took a nervous drag from his cigarette and then blew his nose. "He's lying, or . . . or he's been watching too much television."

"I don't think so, Jack. And neither do the boy's parents. They're *this* close to instituting some sort of action against the hospital, and, I assume, against you and Mainwaring as well."

"And you're encouraging them in this?"

"Hell, no. The opposite."

"Well, thank God for that," Pearl muttered.

"But I'm determined to get to the bottom of things. That's why I'm here. The kid's very sick from what he's going through. Very sick. In fact, he may be dying."

Pearl whistled softly through his teeth.

"Well," he said, "I can't help you much except to tell you that whatever is going on has nothing to do with his anesthesia. I've done thousands of cases with exactly the same stuff this boy got, and . . . and nothing like this has ever happened. Nothing."

"As far as you know," Zack corrected.

Pearl's expression was strange.

Zack tried to gauge the reaction against those he had anticipated. Anger? Arrogance? Confusion? Concern? Defensiveness? There was no real match. Something was going on, though. Of that he was almost certain.

The man was . . . was what?

"Look, Iverson . . ." Pearl ground out his cigarette and folded his hands on the desk. His fidgeting stopped. His gaze became more direct. ". . . I want to help you, I truly do. I want to help that kid. But there's really nothing I can say. He got routine anesthesia and had a routine operation. It's as simple as that. If you want to get to the bottom of whatever's going on, then you'll just have to head off in another direction, okay?"

In that moment, Zack understood.

His muscles tensed. The sensation was so familiar. It was being on the side of a steep drop, looking for the handholds and crevasses that would guide the traverse of a rock, and then suddenly seeing the perfect line across.

Jack Pearl's attempt at sounding concerned and accommodating had missed badly. He was frightened—absolutely white with fear.

The quieter and more composed he became, the more Zack knew he was squirming. Something *was* going on. His blade had hit a nerve. Now, it was time to give it a twist.

"Jack, I'm interested in something," he said. "Suzanne Cole was wide awake when she reached the recovery room. The nurse's notes in his chart say that Toby Nelms was, too. How do you do that?"

Pearl shrugged.

"I just pay attention, that's all. I monitor vital signs more frequently than most anesthesiologists, so I can keep the level of anesthesia right on the edge. A rise in pulse or blood pressure, and I just turn up the gas a bit. It's a matter of experience and technique."

"But why is it that you only seem to use that technique and experience on Mainwaring's cases?"

The anesthesiologist's hand flickered toward the pack of cigarettes and then drew back. Where minutes before he had been in constant motion, now he was rigid.

"That's nonsense," he said.

"The recovery room nurses don't think so. They tell me his cases always come out of the O.R. lighter than the rest of ours."

"Iverson, just what is it you're driving at?"

Easy, now, Zack warned himself. *One step at a time. No slips.*

"Look, Jack," he said. "I don't want to make trouble for anyone. I just want to help this kid."

"Well, throwing darts at me isn't helping anyone. You're . . . you're barking up the wrong tree. And frankly, your innuendoes are starting to annoy me."

Zack sighed. "Listen, just give me a couple more minutes and I'll be out of your hair. All I want you to do is look this over and tell me what you make of it."

With what he hoped was just enough theatrical flair, Zack slid the notes he had just prepared from his folder and handed them across.

Pearl scanned the sheet for only a few seconds before he snatched up his cigarettes. His hands were shaking and his heavy breathing blew out the match before it could ignite his smoke.

"Just what in the hell is this supposed to be?" he asked.

"You know what it is, Jack. It's a summary of nine of the gallbladder cases you've done the past two years. I have another twenty or so charts being pulled right now, and I suspect they'll confirm what this list already suggests."

Pearl looked ill. "Which is?"

"Which is, Jack, that despite having the same procedure, and receiving, at least according to your notes, exactly the same anesthesia, Jason Mainwaring's cases came out of the O.R. looking as if they had never been asleep, whereas Greg Ormesby's were normal. Look at the recovery room times. Mainwaring's cases were transferred out anywhere from one to six hours faster than Ormesby's. . . . They didn't get the same anesthesia, Jack, did they."

It was a statement, not a question.

"You're crazy," Pearl said, thrusting the chart back at him. "Those patients got exactly what I said they got. Now why don't you just take this . . . this garbage, and get out of here."

"Okay, Jack. But you know I can't let this thing lie."

Pearl's hands were again folded tightly on his desk.

"You do whatever you want, Iverson. I've got nothing to worry about because I haven't done anything."

For the first time since their session began, Zack began to have some doubts. A boy was dying. He had laid that on the table. Yet Jack Pearl, if he knew anything, had refused to budge. Could he have been that far off base about the anesthetic? About the whole situation? Or was the pallid little anesthesiologist some sort of monster?

Only minutes before, answers had seemed so close. Now . . .

"Have it your way, Jack," he said, rising. "You know how to reach me if you think of anything."

"I won't," Pearl said. "So just take your witch-hunt somewhere else."

"He's eight, Jack. Eight years old."

"Get out."

CHAPTER 21

FRANK IVERSON loved his Porsche 911 with a passion and intensity beyond that which he felt for any human being, including his children. The connection, he believed, was a spiritual one—man at his finest and man's finest machine, linked in style, flexibility, and speed. There were times, in fact, like this clear, windless Monday afternoon, when he felt certain the machine was actually sensing his mood and responding to it.

With a four-hundred-dollar Minuet radar detector scanning the road, and a mental map of favorite State Police hiding spots, he swept down route 16 toward the Massachusetts state line and Leigh Baron, nudging the Porsche through eighty-mile-an-hour turns with his fingertips.

The Ultramed managing director's call to meet her at the Yankee Seaside Inn, just over the border, had come this morning, only minutes after Frank had learned from Mother of his two-place leap in the national standings. Almost certainly, a promotion of some sort—probably to regional director—was in the offing.

The place for their meeting, a good hour north of Boston, had been chosen to accommodate Leigh, who would be attending a management seminar there—or so she had said. There were, Frank acknowledged excitedly, other possibilities.

Time and again, over the four years of their association, the spectacular redhead had hinted at an attraction for him. Perhaps now, with his stature rising in the company like a rocket, she was ready. And what an incredible prize she would be. Looks in a league with Annette Dolan's, money, power, and a brain to boot—the ultimate perk for the new Ultramed regional director.

Regional director. Frank beamed. The timing couldn't have been better. With Mainwaring's money as good as in the bank, and the nightmarish chore of juggling the hospital accounts to hide that quarter-million-dollar deficit nearly behind him, he would need the flexibility of offices in New Hampshire and Boston to set up some of the deals he had in mind.

Although the northeast region wasn't Ultramed's most lucrative, it was the fastest growing. He would be functioning in the center of the corporate spotlight. The company had set its sights on the prestige that involvement with established medical schools would bring, and there were ten of the world's most respected institutions in New England alone. In fact, only a year before, Ultramed had narrowly missed purchasing a major university psychiatric facility.

Success in getting the company's foot in *that* door, and he could pretty much write his own ticket.

And, Frank pledged, as he cruised around the Portsmouth rotary and south toward Newburyport, the first piece of business he would attend to with his newly acquired clout would be the removal from Ultramed of one Zachary Iverson. Since being taken to the cleaners in that disastrous land deal, he hadn't made too many mistakes in life. But allowing the Judge and Leigh Baron to pressure him into bringing Zack back to Sterling was easily the worst.

Frank screeched through a ninety-degree turn onto the ocean road. It might, he mused, even be worth making Zack's dismissal the condition of his accepting the new appointment. Leigh would agree or risk losing him. Making such a demand was certainly worth considering—if not now, then soon. In a matter of months, when his involvement with Ultramed amounted to little more than icing on his cake, he would have that kind of leverage anyhow.

And as the Judge loved to say, over and over again, leverage was the name of the game.

The Yankee Seaside, a two-story hotel laid out in a wide V above the rugged coast, was opulent but not garish. Frank stopped in the lobby men's room for a final check in the mirror—just in case—and then mounted the wide, circular staircase to the second floor.

The notion that Leigh Baron's call might have been social began to dissolve the moment she opened the door.

Suite 200 was a meeting room—richly appointed, with a fireplace and conversation area at one end, and an oval conference table with seating for ten nestled in the V. Huge plate-glass windows revealed a breathtaking vista of the North Atlantic.

Leigh herself was dressed for business in a lightweight burgundy suit and plain silk blouse. Her wonderful titian hair was pulled back in a tight bun, and she was wearing the tortoiseshell glasses that were sometimes replaced by contact lenses.

Still, there was no hairstyle nor manner of dress that could obscure her spectacular good looks. And there was no way, Frank promised himself, that they would not become lovers. If not that day, then before too long.

"Frank, welcome," she said, shaking his hand firmly, and warning him with her eyes against any other contact. "I'm pleased you could make it down on such short notice."

At, perhaps, five-foot-seven, she was shorter than he was by more than half a foot, but her bearing and manner neutralized that difference.

Frank felt off balance and edgy with the coolness of her greeting.

"You call, I come," he said, taking a seat in the conversation area, across a low marble coffee table from her. He gestured to the room. "Nice place."

"Thanks. We own it."

"Ultramed?"

"A subsidiary—Whiteside Travel Services."

"Whiteside Travel? I didn't know that was Ultramed."

"Not many people do."

There was a door across from the one Frank had entered, and in spite of himself, his mind kept flicking to the possibility that it led to a bedroom. It would fit her style, he was thinking: a stiff, businesslike greeting, followed by mention of his recent rise in the Ultramed rankings, then word of his promotion. Suddenly, just as it seemed they were through for the day, she would reach up casually and shake free her hair.

"So, Frank," she began, crossing her phenomenal legs and then consciously adjusting her skirt, "you're looking well. How are things going?"

"I'm doing all right," he answered cautiously. "My brother's been a bit of a pain, but it's nothing I can't handle as long as you and Ultramed back me up."

"We always back up our administrators, especially those with the sort of track record you have. I assume you saw the new figures we just posted in Mother?"

Frank smiled. Step two of the scenario was unfolding.

"I told you I'd make it," he said, feeling a surge of confidence.

"No, Frank," she corrected. "*I* told *you*. Remember? I want you to know how pleased we all are with the job you've done. Especially me, since I'm the one who first saw your potential and pushed for your appointment. Your success makes me look good."

And my promotion will make you look even better, he thought.

The scent of her, even at a distance, had begun to fill his head, making it hard to concentrate. He would be the best—the very best she ever had.

"Now," she said, "what's this about your brother?"

"Oh, nothing." He wished he had not brought up Zack until their business was concluded. "He just doesn't have, I don't know, the team attitude, I guess, to make it with Ultramed. He's been nothing but a disruption since he arrived in Sterling."

"What sort of disruption?"

Oh, Christ, never mind him. Just get on with it. A hundred miles from Sterling, and his brother was getting in the goddamn way.

"Hey, it's no big deal, Leigh. Like I said, I can handle it."

"Tell me, please."

Frank sighed.

"Okay," he said. "It's your dime. Zack's been constantly clashing with other doctors. He goes out of his way to undermine my authority, and he won't listen to anyone's reason. I tried to tell you he was going to be trouble."

"Yes, I remember."

"He always has been. I'll take care of it, though. Just as soon as we finish our business here, I'll take care of it." He gestured about the room again. "You know, this place sort of reminds me of a great little inn in Provincetown. I think you'd love it."

Her eyes hardened.

"Frank," she said, "I want you to listen to me, and listen carefully. At this particular moment, as far as you're concerned, I'm Ultramed. You work for me. If you want to continue working for me, you'll stop mentally undressing me and pay attention to what this meeting's all about."

"But—"

"It's not going to happen, Frank. Get that through your head. I have a husband I'm perfectly happy with. Understand?"

Numbly, Frank nodded.

"Good." She reached across and squeezed his hand. "Now just settle back and let's get down to business, because I'm afraid you have a problem to take care of."

Her voice was grim.

Frank sensed a dreadful sinking in his gut.

"What sort of problem?" he asked.

"This letter arrived early this morning by messenger," she said. "I assume, since you haven't mentioned it yet, that it will come as a surprise."

The moment Frank recognized the Judge's letterhead, an annoying whine began building in his head. By the time he had finished reading, the noise was a screech.

He scanned the document, and then read it again more slowly. It was, as Leigh had surmised, a total surprise.

An audit . . . When? . . . It was crazy.

Frank squeezed his temples, trying to quiet the noise as he struggled to concentrate, to understand what was happening, and why.

The whole thing was crazy . . . fucking crazy. . . .

The buyback threat he could deal with. The Judge was a bastard, but he was still only one vote. The board could be had. A member at a time, the board could be had. But until Mainwaring came through, an audit was out of the question. Absolutely out!

"Frank?"

. . . *It was Zack again. It was that goddamn scene with Norman that had pushed the Judge over.* . . .

Frank's teeth were clenched so tightly that his jaw ached.

. . . *Who in the hell did they think they were dealing with?*

"Frank, are you all right?"

"Huh? Oh, sure. I'm just furious, that's all."

"I'm not too happy about it, either. Any idea why your father wouldn't have spoken to you about this?"

Frank snorted a laugh.

"Only dozens," he said.

. . . *Regional director . . . Leigh . . . the flexibility . . . the leverage . . . the power* . . .

He had driven down with such high hopes. He would be driving back with nothing—nothing but headaches.

Fuck 'em, he thought viciously. *The Judge and his brother. Fuck 'em both.*

"Do you have anything to drink in this place?" he asked.

"Just coffee, Frank. You want that?"

"Yeah, okay. No, no, forget it."

He stood and stalked to the window, his fists opening and closing at his sides.

"Frank," Leigh said evenly, "you have to calm down. We've got to know we can count on you to take care of this. Ultramed has too much at stake right now to take any backward steps. The competition is just waiting for a screw-up that they can use to turn prospective acquisitions against us. So just stay calm. This isn't such a big surprise, if you think about it. We expected when your father insisted on a buyback clause that he'd probably make some sort of move like this. He's a controller. That's his style."

"Tell me about it," Frank said bitterly, still staring out at the Atlantic.

"The question is whether he's just playing his game, or whether he really intends to fight. Any ideas about that?"

Frank turned back to her.

"It's a bluff," he said.

"And that business about Beaulieu's widow?"

"Also a bluff. If Beaulieu had anything of substance, I would have heard about it long before this. It's the same sort of crap my father's been pulling since as far back as I can remember."

"Can you handle him?"

"You're damn right I can. There isn't going to be any goddamn audit."

"What?"

"I said I'll take care of it."

He cursed his slip, and silently cautioned himself to be more alert.

"This is just another of his little tests," he said. "I've taken them before."

They were underestimating him. Zack, the Judge, even Leigh. They were underestimating him badly, and they would see. They would all see. He was younger and stronger than his father, and he had learned the lessons of the man well.

"We're counting on you," Leigh said. "We want this whole business resolved before the board meets."

"It will be."

"Good. I'll be watching. It means a great deal to me to have you do this right. And it goes without saying that it means a great deal to you, too, yes?"

"When this is all over," Frank said stonily, "I want my goddamn brother out of Ultramed. I would fire him right now, but until this business with my father is resolved, I don't want to make any moves that might set off the Judge all over again."

"I agree. Above all, you've got to keep things cool. . . ."

Her tone softened.

". . . Listen, Frank, you deal with this smoothly and you'll have our blessing to get rid of your brother if that's what you want. In fact, prove you can handle your father, and you can consider your potential with this company unlimited." She smiled at him. "Unlimited, Frank . . ."

"I understand."

"Good." She stood then. "I want to be kept abreast of what's going on." She nodded toward the Judge's letter. "I don't like surprises."

"I understand," he said again. "There won't be any."

"In that case, Frank, you have a very bright future with our company."

A minute passed after the door to suite 200 closed behind Frank. Leigh Baron poured a weak bourbon and water from the room's well-stocked credenza. Then she turned to the intercom, inconspicuously placed on an end table.

"It's okay, Ed," she said. "He's gone."

Edison Blair, the CEO of RIATA International, entered the room from the inner office where he had been listening and crossed directly to the bar. He was nearing fifty but looked ten years younger, with close-cut, sandy hair, a lean, almost slight frame, and a deceptively boyish face.

His personal worth, estimated by various sources to be between twenty and thirty million, was actually closer to twice that, and was growing as rapidly as his young corporation.

"Unlimited potential. I like that little touch at the end," he said. "He thinks you were referring to yourself, you know."

"Of course I know. I picked up all the tools I needed to deal with Frank Iverson in Men 101. Take away his vanity, and he's got nothing. With men like him, you've always got to leave the carrot."

"I'll remember that. So," he went on, "what do you think?"

"Dunno. I have my doubts."

"I've only met this Judge Iverson once, but from what I sensed of the man, my money's on him."

Blair poured a shot of José Cuervo Gold Tequila, sniffed it once, and downed it in a single, quick gulp.

"I agree," Leigh said, "but I think it's worth waiting a bit before we play out our hand. Who knows? Maybe Frank'll pull it off. He's been a hell of a surprise so far—to everyone but me, that is."

"It's lucky we don't have too many more surprises like him working for us, Leigh. It's not exactly optimal business practice to carry an administrator who embezzles a quarter of a million dollars from you."

"Come on, Ed. He's made ten times that much for us already, and you know it. Our accountants haven't found so much as a missing penny since that one time. From the scrambling he's been doing, they think he's buying time to replace that money, and so do I. Either way, it's our ace in the hole."

"So we wait?"

"We wait."

"Leigh, I don't want us losing that hospital."

"We're not going to lose anything. You can count on it."

Edison Blair eyed her for a moment.

"I am," he said.

CHAPTER 22

DISAPPOINTMENTS AND hard times had dogged Jack Pearl most of his life. From as far back as he could remember, he had been different—an outsider.

For one thing, he was an insomniac, a pathologic insomniac.

As a youth, his parents would scold him for being in the basement at four o'clock in the morning, fiddling with his chemistry set. Later that same day, he would be reprimanded and sent home for falling asleep in class. His condition had led to threats of expulsion on any number of occasions, and he well might have been expelled were he not, thanks to an IQ in the 160s, the best student in his school.

Making matters even more difficult for Pearl during those school years was the gradual emergence of his homosexuality. And even within that subset he was a fringe player, preferring much younger boys and their photographs to any more threatening entanglements.

In college, no roommate lasted more than a few weeks with his bizarre biologic rhythms and deepening melancholia. His dormitory room walls were decorated with posters and photos of his special heroes: Napoleon, Dickens, Edison, Churchill, Kafka, and Proust, none of whom, according to the first of his therapists, had ever enjoyed so much as one normal night's sleep.

That an insomniac should have chosen anesthesia as his life's work was one of the few pleasant ironies in Pearl's life; that one should have developed Serenyl, the quintessential sleep-inducing agent, was the ultimate irony of all.

The Serenyl odyssey had begun years before, in Iquitos, a jungle village by the headwaters of the Peruvian Amazon, where Pearl had accepted a six-month medical mission appointment as a means of escaping yet another disastrous situation in yet another hospital. Within a few weeks of his arrival, he had developed an intense fascination with the drugs used by medicine men, and in particular, with a plant alkaloid used by the most mystical "doctors" in the region to induce a purgative state of deep hypnosis in their followers.

The moment Pearl first witnessed the incredible substance in action, the lack of direction and purpose in his life was at an end.

Two years of meticulously dissecting the active component in the alkaloid and modifying its composition led him to the synthesis of Serenyl—a structurally unique anesthetic, fully as remarkable as was its chemical forebear.

Now, for the first time since he conceived of its application, synthesized it, patented it, and adjusted its delivery and dosage in actual O.R. situations, Pearl's Serenyl was under attack.

It was five in the morning. An hour before, Pearl had given up trying to sleep and had brewed himself a pot of coffee. In the nearly twenty-four hours since his confrontation with Zack Iverson, he had slept, perhaps, two. Familiar feelings of loneliness and isolation—feelings he had been able to keep reasonably in check since moving to Sterling—had surfaced and were beginning to smother him.

The first glow of dawn was spilling over the valley as he wrapped himself in a blanket, padded across his dew-sliced yard, and settled onto a slat-backed chair. He wondered if a sleeping pill of some sort might be in order. With Mainwaring gone to Atlanta, the surgical load was light enough for his associate and their nurse anesthetist to handle.

He could call in sick and take a couple of hundred milligrams of Seconal. It had been years since he had taken a drug of any kind—he hated feeling the loss of control—but this might well be the time.

He had been thinking too hard, his mind poring over and over the evidence Frank's brother had thrown at him, frantically trying to assess the extent of the threat and to find fault in the man's logic.

Pinpointing even potential errors in Zack Iverson's reasoning had not been easy.

Pearl lit his fifth cigarette of the hour, searched about for a packet of Kleenex, and finally wiped his nose on the corner of the blanket. Why was it, he wondered, that every time life had started looking the least bit bright for him, every goddamn time, something or someone had come along to screw it up? *Why?*

Most aggravating of all to him was that this time, from the very beginning, he had seen the potential for trouble and had discussed his concerns with his partners.

He had warned them that Serenyl's marvelously diminished recovery time—the most distinctive of its many attributes—was also its Achilles' heel. The rest of the properties that set it apart from other anesthetics, injected or inhaled, were all unwanted side effects it did *not* have. He had even suggested using the anesthetic on other surgeons' patients, so that should questions arise, his technique, and not the drug, would be the focus of any suspicion.

But Frank and Mainwaring had been obstinate in their demand for absolute secrecy. In fact, both men had pooh-poohed his concerns and had laughed at the notion that anyone at Ultramed-Davis might be sharp enough, or interested enough, to put things together.

They hadn't counted on Zachary Iverson.

Pearl knew that he was drifting in over his head. Over a lifetime of turmoil he had developed something of a sixth sense about such things.

He should have been on the phone to Frank the moment Zack Iverson walked out of his office. But he had needed time to think—not so much about the gallbladder cases Iverson was reviewing, or even about the implications of the possible discovery of Serenyl, but about the chances that this child, this Toby Nelms was, in fact, suffering from a complication of his anesthesia.

Serenyl was the achievement of Pearl's lifetime—the validation of his entire chaotic and harried existence. It simply had to be flawless.

It was Mainwaring's promise, in writing, that Pearl would eventually receive credit for his work, that had brought him to Sterling. That Frank Iverson had arranged for him to be paid handsomely for his discovery when others had threatened to prosecute him for even working on it, was only icing on the cake.

Of course, Pearl acknowledged grudgingly, Frank Iverson had also smoothed over his past difficulties—most notably a dicey piece of business involving a politican's son in Akron. But without Mainwaring's promise, even the lure of escaping *that* mess would not have been enough to make him move to a place like Sterling, much less to share the Serenyl patent.

But share that patent he had.

And now, like it or not, Pearl knew that he had to talk to Frank about his brother *and* Toby Nelms. They had looked at every possible immediate complication of Serenyl—renal effects, liver function, pulmonary function—and had found none. It had been sloppy not to have been conducting a long-range retrospective survey as well.

But dammit, Pearl rationalized, the drug had persistently functioned so perfectly. . . .

Well, now he would simply have to make his partners understand that they had made a mistake; thank God it was not a fatal one. They merely had to go back and do the study they should have been doing from the beginning.

With just a little investigation, just a hundred or so calls to patients who had received the anesthetic, Pearl knew he could determine if Toby Nelms was a coincidence or a problem. Nobody would even have to know why he was conducting the survey.

And if there was a problem with Serenyl—if a second case like Toby Nelms was identified—almost certainly, he could fix it. He knew every molecule of the drug.

All he needed was the chance.

Pearl stood and paced nervously about the yard, mindless of the damp, which had already soaked through his cloth slippers.

He had a decent handle on Jason Mainwaring. In a sense, they were allies. The surgeon was a haughty, privileged bastard, but he was far more bark than bite. In fact, with his company's money on the line, he would probably demand that this loose end be tied up before consummating their deal.

Pearl stubbed his cigarette into the lawn and shakily lit another.

It was Frank Iverson he feared.

For as long as he could remember, wherever he had lived, whatever he had been doing, there had been Frank Iversons. They had pushed him in the schoolyard and called him names; they had sent flunkies to trip him and had stood laughing with their girlfriends as he clutched at the bloody scrapes on his knees and elbows; later in life they had loomed behind their desks, shaking their manicured fingers at him and telling him that there was no room in their institutions for "his type."

And however much *this* Frank Iverson's outward concern and intervention had helped him, Pearl knew better than to trust him. It was Serenyl, and Serenyl alone, that maintained the man's civility and support.

For nearly two years their work had gone on without a single hitch. It would take care and patience to convince Iverson of the need to hold off on the sale.

But what were a few weeks, Pearl reasoned desperately, or even a few months, compared with the importance of the anesthetic to medicine? In the end, even Frank would have to understand that.

Understand. Pearl shuddered at the notion. One of the more unpleasant constants in life had been that, where he and the things that were important to him were concerned, the Frank Iversons had never understood.

There were still several hours before Iverson would even be at his office. Until then, there was nothing he could do.

He badly needed to relax.

Glancing at his watch, he crossed the yard and entered the cellar of his rented bungalow through the metal bulkhead. The basement, dusty and unfinished, was illuminated by a single, bare bulb, suspended from the ceiling.

Pearl took a screwdriver from his toolbox, knelt down behind the oil burner, and pried out a loosened segment from the cinderblock wall. Creating the hiding place had been one of his first priorities after moving in.

He moved several dozen vials of Serenyl and the notebook outlining its synthesis off to one side of the space and withdrew one of two cigar boxes stuffed with photographs. Next, he carefully replaced the cinderblock and shuffled to his room.

Settling onto his bed, he undid his robe, and then, one at a time, drew certain photos from the box.

By the third one, Pearl's hand had slipped down the front of his pajama pants and begun gently to massage himself. Iverson had demanded, none too kindly, that he steer absolutely clear of any involvement with boys, or for that matter, with any men in the area. Without the photographs, he would have gone insane.

The ones he selected this morning were the very best in his collection—those he had taken himself.

In minutes, his growing arousal had begun to dispel some of the fears and loneliness. It would all work out, he told himself. Whatever words he had to find to convince Iverson, he would find.

He produced a five-by-seven in which three beautiful boys were frozen in a montage he had carefully designed. That afternoon in East St. Louis had been incredible—one of the very best.

Slowly, Pearl's eyes closed, his movements intensifying as his fantasies took flight.

Being different wasn't easy. It never had been. But as best he could, as he always had, he was making do.

And for once in his life, for once in his goddamned, troubled life, something was going to work out.

"Frank, come in, come in."

Judge Clayton Iverson's chambers, a huge, high-ceilinged room with dark oak paneling and three walls of immaculately, aligned tomes, was as somber and intimidating as was the man himself. On the wall behind the desk, surrounding a portrait of the chief justice of the Supreme Court, were dozens of framed photographs of the Judge in variations of the same pose with three presidents, half a dozen governors, and virtually every New Hampshire politician of substance for the past half century.

There was also, near the center of the display, a color photo of Frank, dressed in his purple and gold Sterling High School uniform, his left arm extended, his right cocked behind his ear, ready to throw.

The draperies were drawn against the midday sun.

Seated behind his massive oak desk, his thick, silver hair fairly glowing in the dim light, the Judge looked bigger than life.

Frank had feared it was an error not to have pushed for a meeting in some more neutral site. And now, as he sensed the awe that had always accompanied his visits to that room, he cursed himself for not having been more insistent.

Well, no matter, he decided. It was time for a new Iverson to take charge. He had set passing records on the fields of a dozen different rivals; his play had quieted scores of enemy crowds. He would meet the man in his lair, or anywhere else for that matter, and he would prevail.

"So, Judge," he began, matching, then just exceeding the firmness of the man's handshake. "How goes it? Mom okay?"

"She's still upset about Annie, but otherwise, she's fine. In it up to here in that garden of hers."

"She certainly does love that ol' garden. Lisette's been working on one, too, you know. You and Mom'll have to come see it. Speaking of Annie, have you by any chance seen her today?"

"Nope, tonight. I promised your mother I'd take her over."

"Well, you're in for a pleasant surprise. She's doing great. Don Norman tells me they'll probably operate on her hip before the week's out. Now Suzanne Cole is back on the case, so Annie's got the benefit of both doctors."

"That's good to hear, Frank. It's a shame, though, a crying shame that she had to fall like that."

Frank tensed. As always, the man had gone right for the jugular. No bullshit, no finesse. The key to handling him would be to stay cool and not allow himself to get rattled.

"No one feels worse about what happened than I do, Judge," he said. "But what's done is done. Now, our job is to get her back on her feet, right? And thanks to Ultramed, we've got one of the best physical therapy departments in the state."

"You didn't keep a tight enough rein on that doctor of yours, Frank. You're in charge. It's your hospital, just like this is my courtroom."

Oh, give me a fucking break, Frank thought.

"You're right, Judge," he said. "Your point's well taken. I've spoken to Don, and he knows his behind is on the griddle from now on. Also, he's making arrangements to pay for any expenses Annie runs up in getting home care after her surgery."

"Excellent, son. That's an excellent move."

"Our hospital's come a long way since Ultramed took over, Judge. I'll do anything I have to to keep it on the right track."

Clayton Iverson loosened his tie and ran his thumbs beneath the black suspenders that had always been part of his courtroom dress.

"I assume," he said, "that statement of purpose is your roundabout way of asking me to withdraw the notice I dispatched to your friend, Ms. Baron."

Damn, but the man was tough.

"Well, as long as you brought it up . . ."

The Judge swiveled in his seat, lifted the picture of Frank from the wall, and appraised it thoughtfully.

"Remember when this was taken?" he asked. "It was right before the state championship game against Bloomfield. The best game you ever played, I think. Six touchdown passes against the team people were calling the toughest ever in the state."

"Five," Frank corrected.

The Judge smiled.

"You're forgetting the thirty yarder in the third quarter that was called back for a holding penalty. On the very next play, you threw that forty-five-yard bomb to Brian Cullen. Three men hanging all over you, and you heaved that ball downfield like . . . like you were playing in the backyard."

"That was a long time ago, Judge." Frank was genuinely surprised and touched by the detail in the man's recollection. "You have quite a memory."

"Son," Clayton Iverson said, "you'd be amazed at how much I remember from those days." His tone was uncharacteristically wistful. "There was a toughness to you then, Frank—a determination to be the best. You had the whole world right in the palm of your hand. Somewhere along the line, though, you started backing off, making bad choices. No, not bad," he corrected, "*terrible.* Somewhere along the line, you lost that edge."

"But—"

"I'm not through. The worst part of it all is that the more you struggled, the less willing you became to listen to advice. You ran up against problems, and instead of plowing through them like you used to do, you tried to run around them.

"I want you to succeed here, Frank. I want that very much. But I'm not going to make it easy for you. I'm going through with that letter, and I'm going to try and find out just what went on with Guy."

"I've told you before, Judge. Nothing went on with Guy."

"I hope not, Frank. Don't you see? I want you to show up at that board meeting with a case for Ultramed that's so strong and so polished, no one on the board would even *think* about voting against you. This is one problem you're going to meet head on, son. And I pray to God you roll right over me."

Frank held up his hands in frustration.

"Judge, you're just making a mess of everything. Checking up on me and the hospital, auditing our books. The people at Ultramed are watching. If they see that I can't even reason with my own father, everything I've gained these past four years will be headed down the drain. Just the fact that I was the last one to know about your letter has already made me look like an idiot."

"Well, when Ms. Baron and her associates see the case you put together for their corporation, you will be a hero."

"But—"

"That's the way it is, Frank."

He swung back and replaced the photograph.

Frank felt an all-too-familiar anger and frustration begin to well up. He cautioned himself against any outburst, and reminded himself to meet strength with strength.

"Okay, Judge," he said. "You obviously have your mind set on this thing."

"I do."

"Well, then. I'd like you at least to compromise on one thing—the audit. We weren't scheduled for our general audit until next February. It will take me days to put everything together as it is, and it will throw my staff into chaos. Either cancel it or . . . or at least postpone it until next month."

The Judge shook his head.

"Farley Berger says it's got to be done in the next day or two in order for his team to have all the figures checked over by the meeting on Friday."

"But there's nothing in the contract that says the audit has to be done by the board meeting. Make it two weeks."

Clayton Iverson thought for a minute.

"Okay, Frank," he relented, "you want two weeks, you've got two weeks."

That's it, Judge, Frank thought exultantly. *That's it: that's all I need.*

"I'm going to beat you, you know," he said.

"I hope so, son," the Judge responded. "I truly do."

CHAPTER 23

For ZACK, the day had resembled some of those during his residency. Two consults on the floors; assisting one of the orthopedists with a back case; admitting a three-year-old who had fallen off a swing, hit her head, and then had a seizure; and finally, seeing half a dozen patients in the office. It was the sort of pace on which, ordinarily, he thrived.

This day, it was all he could do to maintain his concentration.

Six days had passed since his initial contact with Toby Nelms, and he was still unable to put together the pieces of the child's diagnosis. For a time after his abortive interview with Jack Pearl, he had tried, as an exercise, to give the anesthesiologist the benefit of the doubt—to concoct another explanation that would jibe with the facts.

He had cancelled his schedule for the day and driven to Boston for consultations with several anesthesiologists at Muni. He had also spent four hours in the Countway Medical Library at Harvard, reviewing every article he could find on Pentothal, isoflurane, and their complications.

By the end of his search, he considered himself qualified as one of the experts in the field. Always, though, his efforts brought him back to his original hypothesis, and back to a single word: *Metzenbaums.*

Now, in a few days, he would meet again with the boy and his mother. This time, Zack knew, Barbara Nelms would not settle for evasions and half-truths. The woman was desperate. She had every right to be.

It was just after four in the afternoon. From the west, dusky mountain shadows inched up the valley toward Sterling. Zack had just finished a detailed discussion of Menière's disease with the last of his office patients.

"I know exactly what you have," he had told the elderly man, who had come because of intermittent dizziness and a persistent, most unpleasant hum in his ears. "Unfortunately, I also know there is very little we are going to be able to do beyond teaching you how to live with it."

He had ordered some tests in hopes of coming upon one of the rare, treatable causes of the condition, had passed on the address of the national society dealing with Menière's, and had expressed his regret at not being able to do more. The man's disappointment was predictable and understandable, but it was nonetheless painful for Zack.

It's not going to get you, Toby, Zack vowed as he watched his crestfallen patient shuffle from the office. The practice of medicine provided more than enough of the frustration and heartache that came from having no answers. In Toby Nelms's case, the answers were there. And somehow, someone was going to supply them. *Just hang in there, kid. Whatever's going on, whatever they've done to you, it's not going to get you.*

Zack sent his office nurse home early, alerted the answering service that he would be on his beeper, and spread the boy's folder on his desk. Most of what he was rereading he knew by heart. After just a few minutes, he snatched up the phone and called Frank's office. There was no alternative but to share his suspicions with his brother and try to enlist his help in another confrontation with Pearl.

Frank was gone for the day, and his secretary had no idea where he was or when he would be back.

A call to Mainwaring's office gave him only the answering service, and the information he already had, that the surgeon was out of the state until the following Monday and was being covered by Greg Ormesby.

"Answers," he canted, drumming a pen on the edge of his desk. "There have got to be answers. . . . Where are you, Jason? . . . Who are you? . . . What do you know?"

On an impulse, he checked his hospital directory and dialed the pathology department. Takashi Yoshimura answered on the first ring.

"Kash," he said, "if you can do it, and if it wouldn't put you on the spot, I need a name. . . ."

Ten minutes later, Zack was on the line with a Dr. Darryl Tarberry at Johns Hopkins.

"Dr. Tarberry," he said after explaining how he had come by the man's name, and after listening patiently to ebullient praise of Kash Yoshimura and his work, "I *am* calling for a recommendation, but not for Dr. Yoshimura. Fortunately, we already have him on our staff. The man I'm interested in is Dr. Jason Mainwaring. Kash said you might have worked with him when he was at Hopkins."

For a few seconds there was only silence.

"Who did you say you were?" Darryl Tarberry asked finally.

From his recollection of the man, Yoshimura had guessed that Tarberry was in his mid-sixties by now. But from the harsh crackle in his voice, Zack wondered if he might be years older than that.

"My name's Iverson. Zachary Iverson," he repeated. "I'm a neuro-surgeon, and I'm on the credentials committee here."

Again there was a pause.

"Mainwaring's applying for surgical privileges at your place?"

"That's right."

"Well, I'll be," Tarberry said. "Where did you say that hospital of yours was?"

"New Hampshire, sir. Listen, I don't want to put you on the spot, Dr. Tarberry, but we would certainly appreciate any information you can give us."

"This call being recorded?"

Zack groaned.

"No, I promise you it isn't."

"I'm not putting anything on paper, now."

"That's fine."

"Mainwaring and his lawyers had this place tied up in knots for I don't know how long. Damn lawyers. Ended up costing the hospital a small fortune to settle even though we were one hundred percent in the right as far as I'm concerned. One of my colleagues got ulcers from it. I swear he did. I don't want that happening to me. I'm too damn old for that kind of nonsense."

"You have my word."

"Your word . . . Iverson, huh. That Swedish?"

"English. It's English," Zack said, staring upward for some sort of celestial help.

"Well, Iverson, I don't know all the details."

"That's okay."

"And as far as I'm concerned, we never had this conversation."

"Promise."

"Well," the man said, drawing out every letter of the word, "let me tell you first that Mainwaring may be the most ambitious sonofabitch

God ever put in a mask and gown, but he is one fine surgeon. Maybe the best I've seen, and I've seen plenty."

"Go on," Zack said. . . .

After fifteen minutes of prodding and cajoling, Zack felt he had extracted as much from Darryl Tarberry as he was likely to—at least over the phone. There was more to the story, he knew. Probably much more. But even so, a huge piece had fallen into place in the puzzle of Toby Nelms.

Zack was just finishing writing a synopsis of the interrogation when the door to his waiting room opened and closed.

"I'm here," he called out.

"What a coincidence. So am I."

Suzanne appeared at his office door, wearing a lab coat over an ivory blouse and ankle-length, madras skirt.

"Got a minute?" she asked.

"For you? Years." He set the Tarberry notes in Toby Nelms's folder and pushed it to one side of the desk. "Trouble with Annie?"

"No, no. Nothing like that. She's doing amazingly well. I think Sam Christian's going to do her hip tomorrow."

"Excellent. I'm so pissed off about what's happened to her. Everytime I think about what Don Norman did, I want to hunt him down and flatten that pudgy little nose of his."

"Zack, I'm as upset as you are about Annie, but I don't see how you can lay all the blame on Don. He didn't do anything with malicious intent."

"That depends on your definition of malicious. He was sedating her so that she wouldn't object to being sent to a nursing home, so that Ultramed could continue to rake in profits from her care. If that's not malicious, I don't know what is."

"Hey, easy does it, okay?"

"What do you mean?"

"That's your opinion. But it happens not to be everyone's. Couldn't you just let up on this place a bit?"

"Huh?"

"Zack, Frank just left my office."

"So, that's where he's been. I've been trying to reach him."

"He's really upset with you."

"I know. Is that why he went to see you?"

"As a matter of fact, it is. He . . . he wanted me to talk to you—to ask you to let up on your criticism of this place."

"He could have come and asked me himself."

"He says he tried."

"He was drunk. He threatened me. That's not what I would call the optimal approach. . . . So, now he's chosen to involve you. I can't believe this place."

"Zachary, I didn't come up here to pick a fight. I just wanted to do what I could to smooth things over between you two. I owe Frank a lot. I thought you understood that from all I told you of what happened to me."

"Sorry," Zack mumbled. "If I'm touchy, I guess it's that I just wish things were different between me and Frank."

"Well?"

"Suzanne, I can't help it if Frank thinks it's my fault that the Judge is pushing the board of trustees to buy back the hospital from Ultramed."

It was clearly the first she had heard of that development.

"My God, Zack, you can't let him do that."

"First of all," he said. "I have no more control over that man than Frank or anybody else does. And second, why not?"

"Well . . . well because," she stammered. "If the board threw Ultramed out, Frank would be ruined."

"Nonsense. He knows his job. He could do it just as well for a community corporation as he could for an operation like Ultramed. Better, probably. Suzanne, listen to me. Something's wrong around here. Something's terribly wrong."

"Dammit, Zachary, what is the matter with you? Don't you have regard for anyone but yourself? I come here to ask you to let up on a man who is partly responsible for saving my career, to say nothing of his being your brother, and all you can do is . . . is tear down his hospital."

"It's not *his* hospital. Look, I don't want to get into a fight. I have too much on my mind."

"Like what?"

Every instinct was clamoring for him to change the subject, to keep his theories to himself—at least as long as they were no more than that. He stared down at his hands. Darryl Tarberry's revelations about Jason Mainwaring were too fresh in his mind.

"Suzanne," he said slowly. "I have reason—good reason—to believe that human experimentation is being conducted at this hospital."

"Now that is the wildest—"

"And," he cut in, "I have just as much reason to believe that you might have been one of the subjects."

Suzanne listened in wide-eyed disbelief as he recounted his experiences with Toby Nelms and Jack Pearl, his brief study of the gallbladder surgery performed by Mainwaring and Greg Ormesby, and finally, his conversation with Tarberry.

"Apparently, a woman died of an anaphylactic reaction to a local anesthetic she received in Mainwaring's office. Mainwaring claimed it was Xylocaine, but there was plenty of documentation that the woman had received that drug on numerous occasions with no problems. A nurse of his, who was very upset with what happened, charged that Mainwaring had been testing something out that wasn't Xylocaine. Although investigators could never prove that was true, they did apparently discover that our friend Jason was part owner of a pharmaceutical house somewhere in the South."

"This is crazy!" Suzanne said. "Did that man you talked to at Hopkins happen to know what company this might have been?"

"He couldn't remember."

"He . . . couldn't . . . remember . . . Zack, this is exactly the sort of thing Frank was protesting. These are terrible, disruptive charges you're making on very little hard evidence."

"I'm not making any charges," he said, feeling his composure beginning to slip. "I'm sharing a disturbing theory with a friend whose clinical judgment I value and trust. I would think you'd be frantic at the thought that someone might have been fooling around with your body while you were asleep."

"Well, I'm not frantic, I'm worried—about you. Zack, you've only been here a couple of weeks. In that time, you've clashed with Wil Marshfield, had words with Jason, fought with Don Norman, upset your brother, fostered a move to buy back the hospital, and now, on nothing more than the flimsiest circumstantial evidence, you're accusing the finest surgeon and anesthesiologist on the staff of a terrible crime."

Zack pushed back his chair.

"Suzanne, listen to me—"

"No, you listen. How do you explain the fact that there hasn't been one other case like Toby Nelms's?"

"I . . . I don't know. Maybe it's a rare complication of whatever it is they're using. Maybe people have had episodes like his but they've happened in other places, or haven't been brought to a doctor's attention. Maybe there's some sort of sensory trigger involved that just doesn't happen to everyone. You told me yourself that you hadn't been feeling right since your operation."

"I've been tired. That's a far cry from having a psychotic seizure."

"What about that episode in the field?"

"What are you talking about?"

"You went blank."

"I did nothing of the sort."

"You did. It was as if someone threw a switch, and all of a sudden you weren't there."

"Zack, this is crazy. You've got to back off. You've hit this place like an earthquake."

"Suzanne, that child is dying."

"Maybe so. But it's not from something Jason or Jack Pearl did to him. One other case, Zachary. Just find me one other case like Toby Nelms and I'll listen. Even then I may not believe you, but I'll listen. In the meantime, I think you owe your brother, and all the rest of us for that matter, a little breathing room." She stood up. "Back off, Zack.

Please. Do what you can to keep your father from destroying what your brother has worked so hard to build, and give us all a rest."

She snatched up her handbag and, without waiting for a response, raced from the office.

For a time, Zack sat numbly, staring out the window at the waning afternoon. *A trigger, or a sequence of triggers.* Perhaps that was the key. Suzanne had no recollection of the episode at the Meadows during their picnic, but something weird had happened to her. A switch *had* been thrown. But what? A word? A sound? A smell?

Zack drummed his long fingers on the desk. He felt his thoughts darting out at the answer again and again, like the tongue of a snake. But each time not quite far enough . . . not quite far enough. . . .

Finally, he slid Toby Nelms's file back in front of him and opened it, once again, to the first page.

"They're not going to get you, kid," he whispered. "I swear, they're not going to get you."

Even among the best of the old New England inns, the Granite House was special. The slanting, hardwood floors, beamed ceilings, and oddly shaped rooms, each with a stone hearth, were rated by the guides as only slightly less wonderful than the cuisine and service.

Frank Iverson had chosen the spot carefully for his first encounter with the Davis Regional trustees; specifically, this night, a successful banker named Bill Crook, and Whitey Bourque, the rotund, often outspoken manager of the local A & P.

The evening had gone well—better than he had dared hope.

He had orchestrated the conversation beautifully, weaving accounts of Ultramed's successes and plans in with reminiscences of some golf games he had shared with Crook, and some interested queries about Bourque's daughter, Renée, one of the finest young horsewomen in the area.

Now, as they sat in the otherwise deserted Colonial Room, sipping cognac and smoking after-dinner cigars, he felt ready to nail the two men down.

There were twenty-one members of the board. Frank considered six of them to be all but in the bag—either because of their relationship with him or because of business they would lose if Ultramed was forced out of Sterling. Allowing for two no-shows at the meeting—and given the board's track record, that was a conservative estimate—he would need only three or four more votes to block the buyback regardless of the Judge's position.

And at least half of those votes were right there at the table, sitting, it seemed, in the palm of his hand. All he needed to do, ever so carefully, was close his fingers.

Unlimited potential . . .

Frank allowed himself the flicker of a smile.

Don't go too far away, Ms. Baron, he thought, eyeing the two men over his snifter. *I'm coming.*

"They sure know how to do it right here, don't they," he began.

Bill Crook, logy from the meal and the drinks, mumbled agreement. He was a slap-on-the-back Ivy Leaguer with a reputation for enthusiastically supporting the ideas of others while never coming up with an original one of any substance.

Whitey Bourque belched and dabbed at his lips with the corner of his napkin. Frank noticed the tangles of fine veins reddening his cheeks.

"Good beef," he humphed. "Nothing we don't have at the store, but good."

"Lisette always said yours is the only place in town to buy meat, Whitey," Frank said. "As a matter of fact, I think I'll have her stop by tomorrow and stock up our freezer. . . . So, now, before we break up and head home to our families, I want to be sure I've answered all the questions either of you might have about just what Ultramed has on the drawing board for our hospital. Bill?"

The banker thought for a moment, and then shook his head.

"Sounds like a pretty ambitious and exciting set of objectives to me, Frank," he said.

"And don't forget for a moment that Ultramed plans to finance every one of these projects with local money. Sterling National Bank money, if I have my way. Whitey?"

Bourque shook three sugars into a cup of coffee and drank it in one gulp.

"No questions," he said.

"I'll have details of our proposal for competitive bidding on our dietary service in your hands by the end of the month."

"That'll be fine, Frank. Fine."

"Excellent." Frank glanced at the check, and then handed it and his Gold Card to the waitress. "Bring us a few more of those little mints, honey," he said. He cleared his throat and turned back to the table. "So, gentlemen, I've enjoyed sharing this meal with you both, and I presume Ultramed and I can count on your support at the board meeting Friday."

The two men looked at one another, silently selecting a spokesman. Whitey Bourque was chosen.

"Well, Frank," he said, "all we can tell you at this time is: that depends."

Frank felt suddenly cold. "Depends on what?"

"On what your father comes up with these next couple of days. He called us yesterday, Frank, and asked us to keep our minds open on this business until he had checked up on a few things. I felt that considering how much help he was to me during last year's fund raiser for the new parish house, that was the least I could do."

"And I owe him for the way he stepped in when my boy Ted experimented with that damn dago red wine and had that accident," Crook chimed in. "He saved the kid's buns for sure."

"Gentlemen, please," Frank said, struggling to keep any note of desperation from his voice. "I'm not arguing against the good works the Judge does around this town. For goodness sakes, that's a given. And I'm proud to be his son. But it's apples and oranges. What we're talking about here is support for your hospital and the good works *we've* been doing. Renée's broken wrist, Whitey. Remember that? Or . . . or how about that coronary your mother had last year, Bill? People say that if it weren't for our new unit and our new cardiologist, she would have died."

"I . . . I understand," Crook said, staring down into his empty glass.

"Well?"

Whitey Bourque sighed.

"Frank, we're sorry," he said. "We'd like to help you out, but we gave the Judge our word we'd wait and follow his recommendation. He's the chairman of the board, and he's doin' all the legwork on this thing. All we want is what's best for Sterling. Since we're all too busy to do in-depth research of any kind, we're sort of counting on him to steer us in the right direction. I hope things work out. And whatever happens, I intend to help you and the hospital in any way I can."

"Ditto for me, Frank," Crook said.

"Well, then . . . I guess there's nothing more I can say, is there."

"You gave a good presentation, Frank," Bourque said, standing. "A damn good presentation. Your father'd be proud."

"Hey, what the heck. We'll work it out, Whitey. I'm sure of it."

Frank forced the words through a noose of anger and frustration tightening about his throat.

He walked the two men to the dirt parking lot, shook their hands amiably, and watched until their taillights had disappeared into the night. Then he turned and landed a vicious kick on the door of the Porsche, leaving a dent and a small scrape.

Heedless of the damage, he leapt behind the wheel and skidded from the lot, spraying a retired salesman and his wife with sand and stones.

From the moment she had heard the Porsche screech into the drive and the screen door slam, Lisette knew it was going to be another one of those nights.

With a mumbled greeting and not so much as a peck on the cheek, Frank stormed past her and into his den. She stood in the darkened hallway, waiting for the clink of ice in his glass. Frank did not disappoint her.

Now, as she brewed a pot of the herbal tea that Frank had once introduced to her as "the only drink I ever touch after ten," she battled the urge to bury herself in bed.

She set the pot, two cups, some sliced lemon, and some sugar wafers on a tray and carried them to the study. Frank was standing in one corner, his back to her, reading.

"Hi, what's the book?" she asked.

"Nothing."

He shoved the volume back into the bookcase and turned to her, but she had caught enough of a glimpse to know. It was his high school yearbook.

"Frank, are you okay?"

"Yeah, sure, I'm great. Do me a favor and just leave me alone, will you?" His words were already beginning to slur.

"I brought you some tea."

"I don't want any fucking tea."

"Frank, please."

"I said I don't want any goddamn tea!"

He swiped his arm across hers, sending the tray spinning across the room. Tea splattered on the wall. The fine china, a wedding gift from her mother, shattered.

Stunned, she stared at the mess.

"Frank, something's wrong with you," she said as calmly as she could. "You need help. Please, honey. I love you. The girls love you. For our sake, you've got to get some help." She stepped toward him, her arms extended.

"I don't need any help!" he screamed. "What I need is to be left alone!"

"Please."

She took one more tentative step forward, and he hit her—a swift, backhand slap to the side of the face that sent her reeling against a chair.

"I don't need you. I don't need my fucking father. I don't need goddamn Ultramed. I don't need anyone! I'm going to make it, and nothing any of you can do is—"

He stopped in mid-sentence and looked down at her as if noticing her for the first time. Instantly, the fury in his face vanished.

"Baby. Oh, Jesus, are you all right?" he asked, moving toward her.

Lisette backed away, forcing herself not to touch the burning in her cheek.

Then she turned and bolted from the room.

⋀ CHAPTER 24

LEIGH BARON stared thoughtfully at the receiver in her hand, and then set it gently in its cradle.

"Frank just lied to me, Ed," she said. "I don't like it. I don't like it at all."

As she sipped her coffee, she gazed out of her thirtieth-story office window, across Boston harbor to the airport. It was just after eight in the morning, and traffic was, as usual, badly backed up coming into the Sumner tunnel. She had spent the night in the city, working into the early morning on several impending Ultramed acquisitions and then catching a few hours of sleep on the fold-out in her office.

The RIATA CEO, still perspiring from his daily seven-mile run, scanned the list of the Davis Regional Hospital board of trustees.

"Which two did he meet with?" he asked.

"The top two on that sheet: Bourque and Crook. He told me just now that the session went well and that both men were as good as in the bag."

"Those were his words?"

"Precisely. The only problem is that Stan Ogilvie, our man on the board, told me last night that Judge Iverson had contacted all of them, and that Bourque and Crook had both given their word to go along with anything he recommended."

"So maybe Frank talked them into changing their position?"

"Possible, but doubtful. Ed, he's scrambling. I just know it. He refuses to admit that he's in over his head. No matter how big the writing on the wall becomes, he keeps thinking he's going to pull this off."

She filled two crystal goblets with fresh orange juice and passed one over.

"This is your baby, Leigh," Blair said.

Leigh nodded grimly. Three more New England hospitals were close to coming over, but all of them were holding out until the Davis Regional sale was final. Blair was watching her performance as closely as she was watching Frank's. And the genius behind RIATA Interna-

670

tional was hardly one to tolerate a failure of this magnitude from anyone.

"Well," she said, "I guess it's time I took a little trip up north."

"I think, my friend, that is a wise decision. You've done an excellent job with Frank Iverson—an amazing job, all things considered. But it's becoming increasingly clear that the man is limited. It would seem he has gone about as far as he can go."

"And then some," she observed. She sighed.

"What is it?" Blair asked. "Surely you can't be upset about pulling the plug on a man who's so blatantly put his own concerns ahead of yours or our company's?"

"No," she said. "But I can't help thinking that I'll miss him at all the regional meetings."

"Miss him?"

"Yes." She smiled wistfully. "Frank Iverson may be a little short on principles and a little long on ego, but he's been great visuals."

The pain, a gnawing, empty ache centered beneath the very tip of Frank's breastbone, had begun soon after his fight with Lisette and had intensified throughout the night. He had thrown up several times, and he suspected—although he had not turned on the bathroom light to check—that the last time had been blood.

A bottle and a half of Maalox had helped calm the burning some and enabled him to shave and dress and make it to his office in reasonable shape, but he sensed that it was only a matter of time before the searing pain resurfaced.

It was Lisette's own damn fault that he had hit her. If she had only been more patient, more understanding of the stress he was under, she could have been a wife, and not just another strain on his life.

Zack, the Judge, Mainwaring, Leigh Baron—as if he didn't have enough balls in the air without Lisette taking potshots at him; what goddamn nerve, telling him he needed to get some help when she should have been giving it to him. It was a miracle his stomach hadn't gotten fucked up long before this.

He snatched up the phone and dialed the hospital pharmacy.

"Sammy, it's Frank Iverson. What's the name of the stuff that's good for stomach troubles? . . . No, no, not that stuff, the pills . . . Cimetidine. Yeah, that's it. Listen, could you bring me up a week's supply? . . . I know it's a prescription drug, dammit. I don't need any lectures. What I need are those pills. . . . Good. And not a word about this to anyone, right?" All he needed was a rumor going around that Frank Iverson had a bleeding ulcer.

He slammed down the receiver and took another long swig of Maalox. It might have been a mistake not to have leveled with Leigh Baron about Bourque and Crook, but this battle was between him and

671

the Judge, and the encounter with those two spineless yes-men was no more than a skirmish. By the meeting, he would have more than enough votes to block the buyback.

He thought about calling Mainwaring for a progress report. If anything could help calm down his stomach, it was a few reassuring words from him. Two hundred fifty thousand back in the Ultramed-Davis account and $750,000 left over to build on. Just the notion of that kind of money was enough to ease the queasy sensation.

He simply had to calm down, ignore Lisette's behavior, and concentrate on the Judge and the board. The ultimate success, both within the company and without, was so close he could taste it.

He culled Mainwaring's Atlanta number from his Rolodex and was in the process of dialing when his secretary cut in on the intercom.

"Mr. Iverson, it's Annette."

Her voice instantly stirred up images of their sensual, uncomplicated, unselfish evenings together—evenings in sharp contrast to those he had been enduring with Lisette. Annette was the perfect low-stress woman for high-stress times, and Frank made a mental note to have her work late again as soon as possible.

"Yes, Annette," he said, "go ahead."

"Mr. Iverson, Dr. Jack Pearl is here to see you. He knows he doesn't have an appointment, but he says it's quite important."

Pearl. Frank could think of nothing the distasteful little fairy could have to say that he would ever possibly want to hear.

"Annette, ask Dr. Pearl if whatever it is can wait until later on this —oh, never mind. Have him just come on in."

Pearl, looking, as usual, as if he hadn't shaved in two days, entered Frank's office with a sheaf of papers in one hand and a cup of coffee in the other, and immediately caught his foot on the doorjamb and stumbled, sloshing most of his coffee onto the Persian rug.

"Oh shit . . . oh fuck," he mumbled, dropping to his knees and dabbing at the spill with a handkerchief that was far from virginal.

Frank was about to insist that he simply get up and leave the mess to housekeeping. Instead, he threw Pearl a towel from the bathroom and watched with some amusement as the physician crawled about the floor, alternately swearing to himself and clucking like some obscene, gigantic chicken.

"Enough, Jack, enough," Frank said finally. "Take a seat. I'll have Annette get you a replacement for your coffee—unless you want to wring that towel out into your cup." He laughed heartily. "Sorry, Jack, I was just kidding, just kidding. Seriously, do you want some more?"

"N-No, Frank. No, thank you."

"Okay, then. So, what is this matter of such earthshaking importance?"

Pearl shifted uncomfortably.

"Go ahead," Frank said. "I'm not going to bite you."

"There's . . . um . . ."

Pearl coughed and cleared his throat.

"There've been a couple of things that have come up . . . problems . . . with Serenyl."

Frank's eyes grew narrow and hard.

"What the fuck are you talking about, Jack?"

The anesthesiologist began to tremble.

"Well," he managed, "what I meant was, not problems, exactly . . . um, a . . . more like *potential* problems. I really needed to talk to you, Frank. You haven't been around."

"Business, Jack, I had business. For Chrissake, get to the point."

"I had a visitor in my office Monday morning, Frank"—his words began to come a bit more easily—"a doctor who is on the verge of figuring out that Mainwaring and I aren't using the anesthetics my operative notes say we are."

"That's impossible," Frank said, his mind already churning through the implications of discovery at this final stage of the game.

Awkward, certainly, he concluded; perhaps even expensive if some sort of payoff was needed. But not catastrophic. The testing was complete. The whole project had been designed to make Jason Mainwaring comfortable enough with Serenyl to buy it, and in that sense, the project was already a total success.

"I warned you this might happen," Pearl was saying. "I warned both of you."

"What are you talking about, Jack?"

"The recovery time. I told you and Mainwaring someone might pick up on it, but you wouldn't listen to me. And now, someone has." His word, initially stuttered and uncertain, began spilling out like a slot machine payoff. "And that's not all, either. There's this kid we operated on last January for a hernia, and . . . and he's been having these nightmares, and—"

"Okay, okay," Frank said, holding his hands up, "enough of this bullshit. I want you to slow down, calm down, go back, and start at the beginning. Got that? . . . Good. Now, first of all, Jack, exactly who are we talking about?"

"Well, Frank, it . . . it's your brother. Your brother Zachary."

Zack again! For Frank, the minutes that followed were the purest torture. He listened impassively, struggling to maintain his concentration and composure in the face of the grotesque little man and the fireball of hatred that was tearing at his gut.

He studied the notes Pearl had brought—Zack's review of the gallbladder cases and the hospital record of Toby Nelms. Then he insisted Pearl go through the entire story again, step by step.

Midway through that recounting, he excused himself for a few minutes, citing the need to get some papers signed and in the mail to Boston. Then he strolled placidly through his outer office and down the hall to an empty men's room, where he threw up.

Twenty minutes later, he had picked up the cimetidine and some more Maalox at the pharmacy and stood confronting himself in another men's room mirror.

As a quaterback, he had learned that plays seldom went exactly as the coaches had diagrammed them in the playbook. A lineman stumbles, and everybody's timing is thrown off; a halfback is thinking about a fight he has had with his girlfriend, and misses a crucial block.

The quarterback worth his salt always kept his head; always expected the unexpected. And it was in this area, Frank reminded himself —the instinctive, reflex ability to react and to adjust—that Frankie Iverson had been the very best.

This time, as in so many sticky situations on so many playing fields, his edge would lie in keeping a cool head. He had picked through Pearl's story a piece at a time, and realized that things weren't yet nearly as bleak as he had initially perceived.

When he returned to his office he was scrubbed, combed, and outwardly calm.

Annette Dolan, dressed in a short-sleeved pink sweater with a band of fine beadwork flowing over her breasts, looked even more alluring than usual.

Much work to do. Keep tonight open if you can.

Frank scribbled the words on a scrap of paper, signed the note with a smiley face, and set it by her elbow as he passed.

She glanced at it and, almost imperceptibly, smiled and nodded.

Now there, Frank thought, as he opened the door to his office, *was an understanding woman.*

The office was empty.

"Annette, did Dr. Pearl leave?" he asked over his shoulder.

"No. Just you," she said.

At that moment, the toilet in his private bathroom flushed. The notion of Jack Pearl sitting on his john was enough to start the acid percolating again in Frank's gut. He would have to get housekeeping to scrub the whole place down before he so much as stepped foot in there again.

Pearl emerged from the room wiping his nose with one hand and tugging at his still-open fly with the other.

"Hope you didn't mind my using your head, Frank," he said. "This whole business has really messed up my insides, and I've got the shits something awful."

Frank smiled plastically and vowed that after the sale of Serenyl was completed, sending Jack Pearl as far from Sterling as possible would rank in priority only slightly below dealing with Zachary.

"Okay, Jack," he said, "tell me what it is, exactly, that you want."

Pearl cleared his throat.

"Well, the more I've thought about the properties of the drug I built Serenyl from—the more I realize that it's possible your brother might be right about that kid."

"That's ridiculous."

"Why?"

"Jack, you and Mainwaring have done five hundred cases. *Five hundred!* Have you encountered even one problem?"

"No, but—"

"But what, Jack?"

"If the kid's problem is due to the drug, then it's some sort of delayed reaction. A flashback—that's what your brother called it. If he's right, maybe some others *are* having them, but they just haven't connected the episodes with the anesthetic. If I knew for sure that was going on, I could fix it, Frank. I know every molecule in that drug. I could do it."

"Jack, please," Frank said. "The whole thing is absolute nonsense. The kid is having nightmares from something he saw on TV—probably on that goddamn *Nova* show. They're always showing babies being delivered and people being operated on and shit like that, for Chrissake. It's a wonder more kids haven't gotten screwed up."

"Frank, we can check. A hundred or so calls, and we can see if anyone's having—"

"No!"

"But—"

"Jack, I've tried to be patient with you, but now I've just about had it. . . ."

Frank snapped a pencil in two for emphasis.

"Mainwaring's going to finish presenting Serenyl to his partners, and he's going to come back here, and he's going to give us each . . . half a million dollars, and we're going to give him the drug. That's how we planned it, and that's what we're going to do."

"But—"

"No fucking buts, Jack. If you don't want to believe me when I tell you that kid is just a coincidence, that's your problem. But I'll be damned if you're going to make it mine. Now listen, and listen good: if you say one word about all this to Mainwaring or anyone else, *one fucking word,* the Akron authorities will be here to scoop up what's left of you quicker than you can blink. I got them off your back, and I can get them back on. Clear?"

Pearl wiped his nose with the handkerchief he had used on the coffee spill and lit a cigarette. Frank Iverson had him between a rock and a hard place. It was a spot he knew well.

"C-Clear," he said.

"It had better be." Frank shook a finger at him as he spoke. "Because I'm telling you, Jack, I want that drug sold, and I want that money in the bank. Don't fuck with me on this one."

"I won't," Pearl said. "But . . ."

"But what?"

"Frank, what harm would it do to make a few calls? If there's a problem with Serenyl, I can fix it. I know I ca—"

Frank sprung around the desk, grabbed the anesthesiologist tightly by the shirt, and pulled him up onto his tiptoes.

"Dammit, Jack, I said no!"

He shook the little man like a terrier breaking a rat, and then slammed him back into his seat.

Pearl cowered before the onslaught.

"Okay, okay," he whined, shielding his face.

Why did his life always come down to scenes like this? Why?

"That's better," Frank said. He patted Pearl on the shoulder. "That's much better. . . ." He returned to his desk chair. "Hey, buddy, don't look so glum. Like I said, the kid is just a coincidence. That Serenyl of yours is just as perfect as you told me it was."

"What about your brother?"

"You let me worry about my brother. Just stay away from him. If he tries to confront you again, tell him to speak to me or . . . or to call your lawyer. Here . . . here's a name to give him. But unless you want a long-term vacation in Akron *after* your long-term stay in an ICU, that's all you give him, right? . . . Well, right? . . . That's perfect, Jack. Just like that little anesthetic of yours—absolutely perfect."

"Okay, Frank," Pearl said, stubbing out his cigarette and shuffling to the door, "you win."

The door opened and closed, and Pearl was gone.

You win. . . . That's right, Frank thought excitedly. *I do.*

He had handled the distasteful little pervert brilliantly. After tough go-rounds with Leigh, the Judge, and the two board members, it felt splendid to be back in control again.

All he had to do now was keep Zack at bay and off balance for another week. And whatever it took to accomplish that, he would do.

Meanwhile, some well-placed pressure on a couple of weak trustees, and the future of Ultramed—and of Frank Iverson—at the hospital would be secure. After that, he would be in a position to deal in a more definitive way with both his goddamn vindictive brother *and* Pearl.

. . . Frank, Frank, he's our man. If he can't do it—

The intercom crackled on.

"Mr. Iverson, it's Annette again. There's a Mr. Curt Largent on three. He says he's a neighbor of yours."

Major Curtis Largent, USArmy, Ret. was the way the aging war hero had painted his mailbox. Confined to a wheelchair by an errant piece of shrapnel during a battle for some village or church in Italy, Largent was the unofficial security guard of Frank's neighborhood, surveying the area for hours at a time from his upstairs porch and noting down in a book all suspicious comings and going, as well as virtually every license number of every car he did not know.

Twice over the years his vigilance actually *had* thwarted crime—in one case the theft of a bicycle, and in the other, the illegal dumping of some landfill off the end of the turnaround.

"Hello, Major, it's Frank Iverson." The last words of the cheer were still reverberating in this thoughts. "What can I do for you?"

Largent, despite a college education—engineering of some sort, Frank thought—still spoke with a pronounced down-east accent.

"Well, Frank," he said, "I called mostly 'cause I hadn't hud anythin' about yoah movin'."

"That's because we're not."

"Well, that's strange; that's very strange."

"What, Major? What are you talking about?"

"Well, I'm up he-ah on m' po-arch. You know, where I like to sit? . . . Well, down the street, right in front of yo-ah house, is a truck. And a couple of young bucks been loadin' stuff into it for more'n an ow-ah now."

"Are you sure it's *our* place, Major?"

"Do bay-ahs shit in the woods? Course I'm shu-ah."

"Do you see any sign of Lisette around?"

"Nope . . . Wait now, maybe I do. . . . Let me get my bi-nocs just to be certain. . . . Oh, it's her all right. She's with them cute little ones of yo-ahs, right by the truck, watchin' 'em load."

"Major, thank you," Frank said. "Thank you for calling me."

He hung up and dialed home. Twenty or more rings brought no answer.

Fifteen minutes later he brought the Porsche screeching around the corner and up the hill to his house.

". . . Fucking Lisette," he had kept muttering throughout the trip home. "Goddamn, fucking Lisette . . ."

Lisette, the children, and the truck were gone. Most of the house was still intact, but she had taken her jewelry, the microwave, the largest television, hers and the twins' bureaus, their toys, bicycles, and beds, and had left all the liquor bottles she could find smashed to bits in the kitchen sink, including the two-hundred-dollar bottle of Chateau Lafite Rothschild he had given her on her birthday and was saving to celebrate the Serenyl sale.

The note, carefully printed on Lisette's lavender stationery, was pinned to a pillow on their bed.

You will never hit me again. Please do not try to find us. I'll contact you when I'm good and ready. . . . Was it worth it?

Frank slapped the bedside lamp to the floor and then balled the note in his fist and threw it across the room.

"You'll see," he muttered angrily. "A million fucking dollars from now, you'll see what was worth it and what wasn't, you disloyal bitch."

He started for the liquor cabinet, but then remembered the mess in the kitchen sink and, instead, stormed from the house and drove off.

As he spun out of the driveway, from the corner of his eye Frank caught a glimpse of Major Curtis Largent, U.S. Army, Ret., sitting on his upstairs porch, rocking and watching.

The afternoon felt as close to normal—as close to the way afternoons once were—as any Barbara Nelms could remember. Sunlight was streaming through the bay windows in the living room and kitchen, bathing a house that was spotlessly clean. Stacked on the dining room table were the dishes she would use to serve dinner to the first company she and Bob had invited over in more than half a year.

Toby lay on his belly on the living room carpet, leafing through the pages of a glossy, coffee-table book on the history of aviation. On an impulse, Barbara had stopped and bought the book on the way home from the boy's outdoor session with Dr. Iverson. That impulse had proven to be inspired.

Over the days that had followed, Toby had spent hours quietly examining the photographs and paintings. And more importantly, he had not had a single seizure since then. Predictably, Bob had wanted to rush right out and buy a model kit to begin building with their son, but she had cautioned him to go slow, and for the moment, to leave well enough alone.

Even the psychiatrist, Phil Brookings, had been a help. Although he had declined to see Toby until after Dr. Iverson had finished his evaluation, he had seen Barbara herself for two sessions and was encouraging her to bring Bob in for some family counseling as well.

As she straightened out the bookshelves and polished the already glistening clock on the mantel, Barbara mentally ticked through the meal she had planned and the music she would choose. Perhaps after dessert and coffee, if she could nudge someone into a request, she might even play for them herself. It had been so long since she had allowed herself the luxury of such mundane thoughts.

"Toby," she ventured, "how would you like to help me put together the dinner we're going to make for Billy's mom and dad tonight?"

Toby continued to flip through his book, occasionally reaching out to run his fingertips over one of the planes.

"Okay," she said cheerfully. "Suit yourself. Just let me know if you get bored with your book. I'll be right in the kitchen."

It had been worth a try.

Minutes later, as Barbara stood by the sink washing vegetables, she heard a soft noise behind her. Suddenly tense, she whirled. Toby was standing by the kitchen door, the corners of his mouth crinkled upward in something of a smile. Barbara felt a surge of excitement.

"Hi," she said, swallowing against the forceful beating of her heart. "Want a job?"

The boy hesitated And then, ever so slightly, he nodded.

"Great! . . . I mean, that's fine, honey. I could really use the help. Here, let me get your little stool."

She put the wooden stool by the sink and handed Toby the peeler.

"Okay," she said. "Now all you have to do is scrape this over the carrots until they all look like this one, see? . . . That's it. Perfect. Listen, I'm going to the laundry room to fold some clothes. When you finish with the carrots, I'll get you started on the potatoes."

Normal. Barbara had never dreamed she would cherish the feeling so much. As she headed toward the laundry room she glanced at the wall clock.

"Hey, Tobe," she said, returning to the kitchen, "guess what it's time for."

She snapped on the twelve-inch black-and-white set that she kept on the counter to watch soap operas.

The cartoon intro for *Robin the Good* was just ending.

Toby stood on his stool, scraping the carrots, washing them in the cool, running water, thinking about airplanes, and looking over from time to time at Robin and his men.

"Now, maids and men," Friar Tuck was saying, "it's time to learn about our Letter of the Day. Today, it's a very special letter, because it's the only one that always has the same letter come after it. It's the letter that starts the words *quick* and *quail* and *quart.* Can you guess what it is?

"Q," Toby said absently.

"How many said Q?" the friar asked. "Well, if you did say Q, you're right! So now, without further ado, here's Robin and Alan to sing about what letter? Right, our good friend, Q."

Alan-a-Dale strummed his huge guitar several times. Then Robin the Good leapt onto a giant rock and, hands on hips, began to sing.

"Alas, my lo-ove, you do me wro-ong, I do not thi-ink that thou art true. For thou has ye-et to sing a so-ong, abou-out the le-e-ter Q-oo. . . ."

With the first few notes of music, Toby stopped his scraping and began staring at the tiled wall. The peeler slipped from his fingers and clanked into the steel sink. He rubbed at his eyes as the blue and gray tiles grew brighter.

It was beginning to happen. Just like all the other times, it was beginning to happen.

"Mommy . . ."

He called out the word, but heard no sound.

They were coming for him. The nurse and the man with the mask. They were coming for him again.

"Mommy, please . . ."

His eyes drifted downward toward the sink, toward the splashing water.

Stop them! his mind urged. *Don't let them touch you again.*

His hand closed about the black handle of a knife that lay beside the peeler.

Stop them!

As he lifted the knife, sunlight flashed off its broad, wet blade.

Over the half year since her son's attacks first began, Barbara Nelms had developed a sixth sense about them. It was as if something in the air changed—the electricity or the ions. There had been false alarms—times when she had raced through the house, terrified, only to find Toby sitting in the bay window and staring out at the lawn, or lying in the den, mechanically watching a show that held absolutely no interest for him.

But there were other times, especially of late, when she had found him thrashing wildly on the floor, or pressed into a corner, his frail body cringing from the recurring horror that was engulfing him from within.

Barbara was folding the last of the linen when she began to sense trouble. It started as no more than a tic in her mind—a notion. The house was too quiet, the air too still. Like a deer suddenly alert to the hum of an engine still too distant for any man to hear, she cocked her head to one side and listened. All she could hear was the soft splash of water in the sink and the sound of the television.

Robin the Good was singing his alphabet song—a series of absurd, ill-rhymed tributes to each letter, sung to the tune of "Greensleeves." It was a melody Barbara had actually loved before encountering the portly actor's version. Now, it grated like new chalk.

"Toby? . . ." she called out. "Toby, can you hear me?"

There was no answer.

"Toby, honey? . . ."

She set aside the sheet she had been about to fold and took a tentative step toward the door. Then she began to run.

She bolted through the deserted kitchen and was halfway to the living room when she heard the crash of a lamp and her son's terrified scream.

"Noooo! Don't touch me! Don't touch me!" he howled. "If you touch me there, I'll cut you. I will. . . . Stop it! Stop it!"

Toby was backing toward the far end of the living room, thrashing his arms furiously at assailants only he could see. It took several seconds for Barbara Nelms to realize that he was wielding a knife—a carving knife with an eight-inch blade.

Then she saw the blood.

Inadvertently, Toby had cut himself—a wide slash on the front of his thigh, just below his shorts. Crimson was flowing down his leg from the wound, but he was totally heedless of it.

"Toby!"

Barbara raced toward him, then slowed a step as his wildeyed fury intensified.

"Stay away from me! Don't touch me!"

"Toby, please. It's Mommy. Please give me that knife."

He backed into the hallway, still slashing at the air. His lips were stretched apart, his teeth bared in a frightening, snarling rictus. There was no sign that he recognized her.

His flailing sent a pair of framed photographs spinning from the wall. The glass exploded at her feet.

"Toby, please."

All Barbara Nelms could see now was the blood, cascading down her son's leg and over his foot, leaving grotesque crimson smears on the carpet. He was nearing the bathroom. If he reached it and locked himself inside . . .

There was simply no way she could let him do that.

The hallway was too narrow for any kind of attack from the side. Focusing as best she could on the knife, which Toby was slashing in wild, choppy arcs, Barbara ducked against the wall and dove at him. The point of the blade flashed down, catching her just at the tip of her shoulder and tearing through her flesh and the muscle of her arm.

Shocked by the viciousness of the pain, she dropped to her knees, clutching the wound with one hand and trying to hold onto Toby's T-shirt with the other. Blood gushed from between her fingers.

Again, the eight-inch blade slashed down. Reflexively, she pulled away her arm. The glancing blow sliced another gash in the skin by her elbow. Before she could recover, Toby had spun away from her and lurched into the bathroom.

"Toby, no!" she screamed as the door slammed shut and the lock clicked.

Woozily, she got to her knees and pounded on the door.

"Toby, open up! Open up, please! It's Mommy."

The only response was the shattering of glass against tile.

Through a sticky trail of her own blood, Barbara Nelms crawled to her bedroom and dialed 911.

"This is Barbara Nelms, 310 Ridgeview," she panted. "My eight-year-old son has locked himself in the bathroom. He has a knife and he's already cut himself. Please, please send help."

The walls had begun to spin.

She hung up and glanced at her arm. The larger wound, three inches or four, gaped obscenely. Beefy, bleeding muscle protruded from the cut.

The room began to dim, and Barbara knew that she was close to passing out.

She lay on her back and dialed the hospital.

"This is an emergency," she gasped, forcing hysteria from her voice as best she could. "Please help me. I must speak to Dr. Iverson. Dr. Zachary Iverson. It is a matter of life and death. . . ."

CHAPTER 25

THE AFTERNOON was oppressively warm and humid. Much to Judge Clayton Iverson's relief, several continuances and a no-show had led to the completion of the docket of the Clarion County Court far earlier than usual.

Returning to his chambers, he slipped off his black robe and tossed it onto the brass coat rack near his desk. With two unanticipated free hours before Leigh Baron was due at the farm, he was rapidly becoming obsessed with thoughts of a shower and a cold drink or two.

His white shirt was soaked through with perspiration, and his underwear felt as though it were glued to his body.

Over the summer, BTU by BTU, the courthouse air-conditioning system had been dying. Even worse, the chances of getting it replaced before several more summers had come and gone were, the Judge knew, remote. There was a time when he would have laughed at such inconveniences. But now, he could barely keep his mind off his own discomfiture and concentrate on the cases at hand.

Perhaps, he reasoned, in what had become a recurring internal dialogue, it was time to consider retiring.

Despite frequent promises to his wife and to himself to cut back—to travel more and work less—the pace of his life had, if anything, speeded up. Since buying the house in West Palm six years before, he and Cinnie had spent exactly two weeks there, and had finally leased it out. They had no real need for the rental income, but it had made no sense to leave the place vacant.

The Judge knew that with her arthritis worsening, and her childhood roots in North Carolina, Cinnie would jump at the chance to sunbathe away at least some of the grueling New Hampshire winter. They had friends who had already made the move south and sounded ecstatic about their choice. And goodness knew, his golf game could always use some attention.

Retirement . . . Such a soothing notion, he thought *. . . such a frightening reality.*

It was one thing to consider leaving the bench. He had done about as much as he could do, seen about as much as he could see in that position. But it was quite another to pack up and move to the land of oversized tricycles and afternoon tea dances.

The Judge sank into his chair and mopped at his brow with a towel.

For the time being, at least, Cinnie and her arthritis would just have to make do. Bum air-conditioning or not, he had yet to reach the point where the liabilities of giving everything up and retiring to Florida were outweighed by a few less aches and pains for her and a few more rounds of golf for him.

Besides, he reflected excitedly, for the foreseeable future he had business to attend to in Sterling—important business. In what could well become a landmark move in slowing the advancing juggernaut of corporate medicine, he had elected to spearhead the repurchase of Davis Regional Hospital from the Ultramed Hospitals Corporation, and then to supervise its reorganization and transition back to community control.

Meetings . . . politicking . . . bargaining . . . rearranging . . . bending . . . standing firm . . . winning . . . losing . . . Clayton Iverson felt an almost sexual rush at the thoughts of what the months ahead held in store.

It was an ironic harbinger of things to come that, even without knowing he had already made up his mind, Leigh Baron was making the four-hour drive from Boston "just to talk." It was also, he knew, probably not the last time Ultramed and RIATA corporate leaders would be dashing up to Sterling for a session with him.

It would be interesting to see the ploys they chose to try—interesting *and* amusing, for whatever they were, he had absolutely no intention of changing his mind.

Not that his decision to convince the board of trustees to annul the Davis sale had come easily. In fact, it had been one of the most difficult he had ever had to make. And the stickiest part of all was Frank.

Engrossed in thoughts of his son, the Judge packed Guy Beaulieu's folder and some related documents into his briefcase and left the courthouse for the drive home.

Zack was right, he acknowledged, as he rolled down Main Street and then out of town along the Androscoggin road, toward the turnoff to the farm; Frank *had* done an excellent job as administrator of the hospital. It wasn't his fault he was working for a company whose policies were so self-serving that they could ultimately cause catastrophes such as Annie's. Nor was it his fault, at least according to Zack, that the corporation had set out deliberately to destroy Guy Beaulieu.

Handling Frank just right through all of this would be a test . . . perhaps the hardest test of all. Still, the man was worth the effort. He had fallen on some hard times, true, made some bad decisions, but nevertheless . . .

The initial warning blast of the approaching tractor trailer entered Clayton Iverson's thoughts as nothing more intrusive than the familiar drone of a distant foghorn. He was driving by rote, looking without seeing. The second blast, far more desperate and insistent, startled him from his reverie with an ugly and terrifying suddenness.

The left side of the Chrysler had drifted far across the two-lane road—so far, in fact, that the solid dividing line was streaking along underneath the very center of the car.

The semi, a monstrous, red GMC was hurtling toward him, its air brakes screeching, its grillwork gaping down at him like the balleen of a whale.

In the clamorous, surreal, frozen moments that followed, the Judge processed countless minute details of the scene before him: the high, Slavic cheekbones of the burly trucker, who was staring down at him in wide-eyed terror and fury . . . his green baseball cap—its gold brim . . . the sun, glinting off the truck's windshield . . . the white script *Tenby's* on the crimson wind deflector above the cab. . . .

The horn . . . the air brakes . . . the face . . . the grill . . . the sun . . . the screeching tires . . .

With no conscious realization of what he was doing, Clayton Iverson whipped the wheel of the Chrysler to the right, spinning into one ninety-degree turn and then another before skidding to a stop on the gravelly soft shoulder.

Lurching and heaving from its efforts, the behemoth rig barreled past, shaking the Chrysler viciously in the vacuum of its wake.

The Judge glanced in the rearview mirror in time to see the trailer stop its pitching and level out as the trucker gradually regained control. Gasping for breath, he continued staring at the mirror until the crimson reflection disappeared around a bend.

Then he sat by the roadside, trembling mercilessly and waiting either for his heart and lungs to burst or for the adrenaline surging through his body to subside.

He had had more than his share of close calls on the road before, although none much closer than this one. And after each one, as now, he silently thanked his Higher Power for giving him reflexes quick enough to compensate for being one of the most easily distracted drivers ever set behind the wheel of a car.

He also paid brief tribute to his own foresightedness in purchasing one of the heavier models on the road.

After several minutes, his pulse had slowed and his shaking had let up enough for him to swing back onto the roadway. The rest of the drive, he promised, would be made at fifteen, twenty at the most.

The trucker, whoever he was, had earned a pass to heaven with his masterful driving.

. . . and masterful it was, too, he thought *. . .*

He fished a handkerchief from the dashboard pocket and wiped the drenching sweat from his face and hands.

. . . absolutely masterful. . . .

He savored a deep breath, then another. His pulse returned to normal.

Now, he thought, *where was he? . . . Ah, yes, Frank . . .*

It had been a joy to hear from both Whitey Bourque and Bill Crook of their dinner session with him.

One hell of a guy. Those had been Bourque's exact words. *Smart, well prepared, and persuasive as the Dickens . . .*

It was almost like the old days—the reporters, the TV people, the calls from friends every week. . . .

Judge, that's one hell of a kid you've got there. . . . One hell of a kid . . . Judge, can we get a shot of the two of you together? . . . What were you thinking when your boy took off and headed for the end zone like that? . . .

As far as the Judge was concerned, the moment Annie Doucette had tumbled off the end of her bed, the fate of the Ultramed Hospitals Corporation in Sterling had been sealed. But speaking to Bourque had helped him see that although the company had to go, there was no reason Frank had to go with it.

A few calls to select trustees had convinced him that the board would go along with him in keeping Frank on as administrator.

Now, he had only to convince Frank. . . .

The Judge had sped a hundred or so yards beyond the oversized silver mailbox marking the dirt drive to his farm before he realized that he had missed it.

"Damn you, Iverson," he cursed out loud.

He slowed, giving momentary thought to a U-turn or to backing up. Then, before he could talk himself into chancing either maneuver, he accelerated over the five hundred additional yards to the next driveway. Twice, trying turnarounds on that stretch of narrow road, he had backed into the drainage ditch. The last thing he needed at that moment was to spend a sweltering hour perched on the split-rail fence, waiting for Pierre Rousseau and his damn tow truck.

He had a date with a shower and a gin-and-tonic, and then with a lovely businesswoman who would try, unsuccessfully, to get him to reconsider his decision.

Leigh Baron wasn't all that tough, but she was bright and certainly diverting. And she would surely provide a decent warm-up for the encounters to come with the real heavy hitters.

Once again, he felt the scintillation—the rush—at the prospect of what lay ahead. It was hardly difficult for him to understand why generals gave up their commands so reluctantly.

Retirement? . . . Nonsense, he thought.

The game was on, and Clayton Iverson was right in the middle of it.

As he eased the Chrysler to a stop by his barn, stepped out, and surveyed his land and the mountains beyond, the Judge made a mental note to send a renewal off to their Florida tenant before Cinnie realized that the man's lease had run out.

The atmosphere in the intensive care unit was somber and extremely tense. A child was in trouble—serious trouble.

The nurses moved from one patient cubicle to another efficiently, but more quietly than usual, stopping from time to time at the doorway to number 7 to see if the nurse working on Toby Nelms needed any assistance.

Behind the nurses station, next to the bank of monitors, Zack checked over the latest set of laboratory figures with the boy's pediatrician, Owen Walsh, a soft-spoken man in his late fifties with close-cropped, graying hair, and deep crow's feet at the corners of his eyes which gave him a perpetually cheerful expression.

Across from them, in cubicle 7, Toby lay thrashing on a cooling blanket, totally unresponsive to his environment. His core temperature, despite aggressive measures, remained well above 104.

The fire/rescue squad had broken into the Nelms's bathroom and found the boy draped over the side of the tub, barely conscious, with multiple, self-inflicted slices and stab wounds on his arms, abdomen, and legs.

Barbara Nelms, conscious but in shock, lay in the bedroom, blood still oozing from the gashes in her arm.

Zack had arrived at the house in time to help with the first aid and the insertion of intravenous lines in both mother and child. Then he had accompanied the ambulance to the hospital and had turned Barbara Nelms, whose blood pressure had responded nicely to a fluid push, over to the general surgeon, Greg Ormesby.

Finally, after getting Toby up to the ICU and onto the cooling blanket, Zack had begun to repair his wounds, none of which involved tendons or vital structures. And, frightening as the lacerations appeared, Zack knew that they were of little importance compared to the fever and the deterioration of the boy's central nervous and cardiovascular systems—a constellation of signs that were almost certainly a reflection of brain swelling.

"Do you think Boston?" Owen Walsh asked.

Like many community pediatricians, especially older ones, Walsh was far more comfortable dealing with patients in his office than in the hospital, and was not comfortable at all with a critically ill child in the intensive care unit.

"At this point, I'm not even sure he could make it," Zack said. "Although I guess that's what we should be shooting for."

"He's been a patient there in the past, you know."

"I know, Owen, I know. And I know you're nervous about having him here. The truth is, I'm not so comfortable with it myself. But believe me, as someone who a month ago might have been called in to see this kid *after* his transfer to Boston, our fluids are just as good as theirs. So're our cooling blanket and our Tylenol and our steroids. And we've got a hell of a cardiologist in Suzanne Cole. So it's not like we're doing nothing. I think we should alert the people down there about what's happening and put one of the chopper teams on standby. But there's something we ought to attend to first."

"The anesthetic?"

"Exactly."

Zack had shared Toby's history with the pediatrician, withholding only his suspicion that some sort of secret anesthetic might have been used during his hernia operation.

"Can you explain it to me again?" Walsh asked.

"Sure. In a second."

Zack stood and peered across at Toby. Swathed in bandages, surrounded by the monitor, the clipboards, the intravenous, gastric, and oxygen tubings, and the large cooling blanket console, the child looked terribly frail and vulnerable.

"Any change?" Zack called out to the nurse attending him.

"Temp's down to 104, Doctor," she said. "No other change."

"Pupils?"

"Still equal and reactive, but sluggish."

"Thank you . . ."

He glanced at the monitor in time to catch several ominous, premature heartbeats.

"See if you can locate Dr. Cole, please," he said to the unit secretary. "Ask her if she can come down here."

He turned back to the pediatrician.

"Okay, Owen. Now, if what we're seeing is some sort of central, toxic reaction to an anesthetic, then as far as I'm concerned, the actual molecules of the drug, or at least their chemical imprints, are still there in Toby's brain, clogging up neuro pathways and periodically firing off messages without any warning or control from him."

"The seizures."

"Or flashbacks, or whatever you want to call them. Somehow, the messages these molecules are transmitting are violent ones—ones related to the surgery."

But why? Zack found himself asking for perhaps the millionth time. *Why do they happen when they do? Why not to every patient, or at least to more of them?* The answer, he felt certain, had to be some sort of neuroactivator—a trigger, or more likely, given the rarity of the condition, a specific sequence of triggers. No other explanation made sense. . . .

"Zack, you were saying?" Owen Walsh was looking at him curiously.

"Oh, sorry." Zack made a mental note to go over with Barbara Nelms the minute details of the events preceding Toby's attacks. He would also write down his best recollection of the minutes preceding and following Suzanne's bizarre episode. "Do you follow all this?"

"So far," Walsh said.

"Okay . . ."

Zack drew a sketch of several nerve endings on a piece of scratch paper, and used the diagram to illustrate his theory.

"So, what we might consider doing, is putting Toby back under again in a perfectly controlled, sensory-deprived situation. One of those isolation tanks would be ideal, but I understand that's just not possible with him being so sick. Anyhow, we just make things as dark and as quiet as we can, and we administer the same anesthetic he received originally."

"And what we'd be trying to do," Walsh said, "would be literally to wash out the molecules that are sending violent sensory messages, and replace them with molecules transmitting—what, blanks?"

"Precisely."

"You just thought of this?"

"Actually," Zack said, "there was some work done in the late sixties and early seventies using the isolation tank technique on patients who had become psychotic from recurring LSD flashbacks."

"You mean they treated LSD psychoses with LSD?"

Zack nodded. "A neurologist in Europe. Scotland, I think."

"Successfully?"

"Successfully enough to be encouraging."

This time, it was Walsh who stood and gazed in at their patient. The crow's feet by his eyes deepened with what he saw.

"Dangers?" he asked.

"Given the disaster you're observing in there," Zack said, "I don't see how giving the child some anesthesia can do much harm, as long as the anesthesiologist is standing by to intubate him if necessary."

"Will Jack Pearl go along with it?"

"That, my friend, may well turn out to be the sixty-four-dollar question. He and I haven't exactly seen eye to eye on this anesthesia business."

Owen Walsh nibbled at the edge of one fingernail.

"Perhaps we should present this to the boy's parents, and get their consent," he said.

"I can do that, provided his mother is still stable."

"And maybe your brother ought to know what's going on, too. He's a good man, and an excellent administrator, but he doesn't like surprises."

Zack felt the prickle of irritation and impatience. He reminded himself that one of the reasons he had opted to become a surgeon, while others, like Walsh, had chosen pediatrics or internal medicine, was the speed with which they went about making decisions. More often than not, the primary care people and the surgeons ended up at the same spot. They simply arrived there by different routes. He motioned toward Toby's cubicle.

"Owen," he said, "we don't exactly have a lot of time to play around with this thing. I can understand your reluctance, but we either do this or we don't."

Again, the man hesitated.

"Okay, Zack," he said finally. "You deal with Pearl and Barbara Nelms, and I'll take care of alerting Boston, getting the helicopter people on standby, and notifying your brother. We'll meet back here at, say, six-thirty."

"Six-thirty it is. And, Owen?"

"Yes?"

"It's the right decision."

⋀CHAPTER 26

ALTHOUGH CLAYTON Iverson deeply appreciated his wife of nearly forty years, and had actually endured a recent series of nightmares revolving around her premature death, the truth was that he had never had great use for any woman.

The oldest of five children, and the only boy, he had attended an all-male prep school and college, and had known no woman intimately before his wedding night, nor any other than Cinnie Iverson since.

Long before his wife had become pregnant, he had selected the names of his sons, and once suggested to her that, should the unimaginable come to pass, that they consider naming their daughter Ruth after Rutherford B. Hayes.

Despite his pride in describing himself as "an emerging liberal" on the subject of women's rights, the Judge still had difficulty taking women seriously in any business dealings of substance. And with no woman was that difficulty more intensely manifested than with Leigh Baron.

Evening had settled in around the farm, bringing with it a persistent, windswept drizzle. The Judge sat with Leigh in his study, sharing coffee and some of Cinnie's apple pie and talking in only the vaguest terms about Ultramed and its plans for the future.

It was nearing eight o'clock. The conversation with the woman was, in his opinion, becoming somewhat tedious. In addition to Ultramed, they had touched on the stock market (her ideas were innovative, but charmingly naive, he thought); children (she and her husband, who spent most of his work week in New York, had decided not to have any!); criminal justice (her notions about the issues surrounding capital punishment were rather simplistic and poorly substantiated); and sports (she had the temerity to compare golf to croquet, and to state that she would consider taking up the game only after she was physically no longer able to play tennis!).

"So, my dear," the Judge said, completely ignoring a question from her about the differences between putting greens in various parts of the country, "I assume that the powers that be in Ultramed didn't send someone as bright and charming as you are just to pass the time with this old north woods war-horse."

"No," she said, smiling at him curiously. "No, they didn't."

The Judge waited for her to continue.

"Well, then," he said finally, clearing his throat. "I suppose they wish you to lay some of the groundwork for tomorrow's board meeting."

"In a manner of speaking."

"Are you always this evasive and . . . and mysterious, Mrs. Baron?"

"Judge Iverson," she said, "exactly who do you think I am?"

"That's a rather strange question, don't you think? I certainly know who you are."

"Do you?"

There was a firmness in Leigh Baron's voice—a steely brightness in her eyes that Clayton Iverson had not noticed before. Still, the ploy of asking questions rather than answering them was an amateurish tactic, and one she would have to improve upon if her aim was to control their conversation.

"Okay," he said after some thought, "I'll play. You're Leigh Baron, vice president of the Ultramed Hospitals Corporation. Your division is, correct me if I'm wrong, operations."

"Judge, I hope this doesn't come as too much of a shock, but I haven't been a vice president at Ultramed since, oh, just a few months after I negotiated our arrangement with Davis Regional. We were restructured by our parent company. My formal title now is Managing Director. That translates into CEO."

Startled, the Judge pulled from his briefcase the Ultramed organizational chart Guy Beaulieu had compiled.

"Well, then, who's, um . . . Blanton Richards?"

Leigh smiled enigmatically.

"Judge Iverson," she said, "Blanton Richards hasn't been part of Ultramed for several years. I don't know who put that list together—Dr. Beaulieu, I presume; he was always putting lists together—but whoever it was didn't do his homework. I know how much you expect to be dealing with the good old boys on matters such as this, but I'm afraid that as far as Ultramed is concerned, *I'm* the good old boy."

"Now just a minute, young lady—"

"Young lady . . ." Leigh Baron's expression was not a little patronizing. "Judge Iverson, I appreciate the compliment—really I do. But I think it will make things easier for both of us if you understand that my young lady days are well behind me. I'm thirty-seven years old. I was second in my MBA class at Stanford more than a decade ago, I spent two years studying economics at Oxford, and I managed several smaller operations for RIATA International before I was brought into Ultramed. My income last year—not counting bonuses and stock options—was slightly over half a million dollars. Now, if that little misunderstanding is taken care of to your satisfaction, I would suggest we get down to work. You and I have some important business to attend to."

"Yes," he said, clearing his throat again. "Yes, I suppose we do. How about some more coffee first?"

The Judge suddenly felt edgy, and anxious to do something—anything—that would disrupt the woman's rhythm. What he had anticipated would be a preliminary sparring match with Ultramed had turned out to be the main event.

"No, thank you," she answered. "But go ahead if you want."

"I think I will."

He walked to the kitchen, poured himself a cup, laced it with a stiff slug of brandy, and took a long sip. The warm, velvet rasp had a calming, reassuring effect, reminding him that, although Leigh Baron had him back on his heels, this was the sort of game he loved to play—the one in which he held all the trump cards. He was still the chairman of the board of the hospital. And in the end, regardless of who Leigh Baron was, how much she earned, or what she had to say, *he* was the one who controlled the votes.

His next swallow drained the cup. He poured himself another before returning to the den.

"Okay, *Ms.* Baron," he said, with ever-so-slight emphasis, "what's your pitch?"

"No pitch, Judge. Simply put, I would like to know what your plans are for the meeting tomorrow."

He tried for a bemused expression, but sensed that he missed. He held all the cards. She knew that as well as he did. And yet she continued looking at him as if whatever he had to say really made no difference. He sought another taste of his brandied coffee, but realized that he had once again drained his cup.

"You have my letter," he said. "In it, I stated that it was quite possible the board and Ultramed would be able to work things out."

"Judge, we have reason to believe that the situation up here, at least in your eyes, has changed since you wrote that. I'd like to know what's going on."

"Nothing's going on. I've done what I was supposed to do as chairman of the board here, and sent you a letter. The meeting's tomorrow. We expect you'll be there to represent Ultramed's interests. At the end of the meeting there'll be a vote. *C'est tout.*"

He held his hands out, palms up.

Leigh Baron rubbed at her eyes wearily.

"Judge, that list you just consulted, was that compiled by Dr. Beaulieu?"

"As a matter of fact, it was."

"Then I can assume that you have all the other material he had been scraping together against our company."

"You did try to drive him out of practice."

"That, Judge, is ridiculous. Ultramed has grown faster than any company of its size in the field. We know exactly what we are doing. So does our parent company. If we wanted somebody out, believe me, they'd be out. Where did you get the idea that we would do such a thing?"

"Well, actually, it was from my—Actually, it's none of your business. You can find out everything you want to know at tomorrow's meeting."

"Your son Zachary was a pall bearer at Dr. Beaulieu's funeral. Is he the one who's taken up Beaulieu's cause?"

"If he has, then like I said, you'll find out tomorrow."

"If he has, then he's wrong. If Guy Beaulieu was being driven from practice, it was not by us."

"Perhaps," the Judge said, sensing a shift in control back toward himself. "If that's true, that should come out at the meeting also."

"Tell me something, Judge. You've already made up your mind, haven't you?"

"I wouldn't say that at all."

She flashed that same disquieting smile.

"You don't have to," she said. "Judge, if your board does vote to repurchase Ultramed-Davis from us, what were you planning to do about Frank?"

"Do? Why, keep him on, of course. If—and mind you, I said, if—we do vote to return the hospital to the community, we'll need him. He's done a terrific job. You told me that yourself."

"And I meant it, too," Leigh said, "with one slightly enormous exception. . . . Here, Judge, I think you'd better look this over carefully."

She removed a thin folder from her briefcase and handed it to him.

"While you're doing that," she went on, "if you could just point me toward your bathroom . . ."

"Huh?" He had already started scanning the material. "Oh, it's over there. Down that hallway and on the left . . ."

"Thanks."

Clayton Iverson finished reading the first page. Written by a well-established, highly respected Boston accounting firm, it was basically an explanation and summation of the material to follow.

Before going on, he went again to the kitchen. This time, he poured brandy into his cup but did not bother adding coffee.

By the time Leigh Baron returned to the study, he had reread the cover letter and begun to skim the lists of figures and transactions, all of which seemed to bear up the accountants' contention that almost three years before, Frank had embezzled nearly a quarter of a million dollars from the Ultramed accounts.

Whether it was the hour or the brandy or the acid anger welling in his throat, the Judge was having increasing difficulty concentrating on the specific financial transfer maneuvers, which were characterized by the bookkeepers as "rather superficial efforts to obscure the missing funds; efforts which any reasonable audit would uncover, and therefore ones which suggest Mr. Iverson's intention of making good the shortfall at some near date."

"So," Leigh Baron said. "Suddenly this all becomes very serious business, wouldn't you agree?"

"Why haven't you done anything about this before now?"

"Oh, come now, Judge. It's unbecoming for you to ask a question with so obvious an answer. Besides, as we've both been saying, Frank's done a terrific job for us. It's apparent that he just got a little greedy back there three years ago. He does have a way of being headstrong sometimes. But I guess you know that. . . . Well, I had actually decided that once the sale of Davis to our company was a fait accompli, I would write off the $250,000 as sort of a bonus for his good work. After all, anyone can make a mistake. . . ."

"Sure, sure. And now you're saying that I would be making a mistake to vote against turning our hospital over to you."

"You won't have left us much choice, Judge, other than to press charges. And believe me, the evidence against Frank is solid—absolutely rock solid."

In keeping with his overall outlook, Clayton Iverson had always reserved his strongest emotions—positive *and* negative—for men. But at that moment he hated the woman sitting across from him with more passion than he had ever hated anyone.

Who in the hell did she think she was?

The question echoed impotently, over and over again in his mind. She looked like some sort of high fashion model, and discussed issues with the naiveté of a schoolgirl; and yet, there she sat, smiling quietly as she viciously blackmailed him.

The life of his son and, by inference, the lives of his daughter-in-law and granddaughters, in exchange for a vote. He should have retired, he thought. He had clearly lost his edge. He should have stepped down from such dealings long ago.

His head was spinning.

"I . . . I need time to think," he said.

"I understand. . . . Unfortunately, you have only until tomorrow."

"I was right in wanting your company out of our town, Mrs. Baron. You're a very callous and self-serving woman."

"Let's not lower ourselves to name-calling, Judge. It's so unprofessional." She stood. "So, then. Tomorrow at one minute after noon everything will be"—she shrugged—"exactly as it is right now. Only more permanent. Yes?"

Clayton Iverson, his weathered face flushed, his eyes smoldering, could not respond.

"Oh, and Judge," she said, "there is one other thing. I would like to review that material Guy Beaulieu accumulated. I promise its return in . . . a few days."

"You can't have it," the Judge snapped.

"Judge Iverson, I know I don't have to spell it all out for you, but let me do it anyway. If you go along with our request, your son will be exonerated from all he has done, and we will complete our purchase of the hospital. If you do not, your son will probably end up in prison, and his family will be disgraced. Your influence in Sterling will be greatly diminished, if not destroyed, and we shall almost certainly end up with Ultramed-Davis just the same."

"This is insane!"

"Perhaps," Leigh Baron said. "Perhaps it is. . . . That material, please?"

"Dammit . . ."

"Judge Iverson, face it. It's going to happen. Our business arrangement is going to be consummated as it was laid out. Either easily and cleanly, or very, very messily. But it's going to happen. Now . . ."

Reluctantly, the Judge passed Beaulieu's folder across. Leigh Baron slipped it into her briefcase.

"As I promised," she said, "I'll return this in a few days. Don't bother to show me out. I know the way."

* * *

His face buried in his arm, Clayton Iverson sat alone in his study, listening to the soft spattering of night rain against the shutters. In all his business dealings, in all his years on the bench, never had he been manhandled so brutally or efficiently as he had by Leigh Baron this night.

Desperately, he struggled to keep his anger in check—anger directed as much at his son as at the Ultramed CEO. At this point, he reminded himself, he had only Leigh Baron's side of the story.

Before he made another move, before he spoke to one more member of the board, he and Frank had to talk. If Frank could adequately explain why he took the money, how he lost it, how he was planning on replacing it, perhaps they could work something out. If not . . .

Went to Frank's. Please don't worry.

Clayton Iverson set the note for Cinnie on his desk and walked, somewhat shakily, to the Chrysler, wondering if perhaps he had had a bit too much to drink.

His thoughts tumbled about as he tried to focus on what his options might be. He needed the fresh air of a drive as much as anything . . . needed to clear his head . . . needed to confront Frank. . . .

He put the car in gear, turned around with more difficulty than usual, and sped down the winding drive.

Frank would have an explanation, he thought. He would have an acceptable explanation for everything, and together they would find a reasonable way out.

But if there was no explanation . . . . if Frank had nothing to offer except greed . . .

The Judge sped through the turn onto the Androscoggin access road. A station wagon speeding south swerved sharply, narrowly avoiding a collision.

Clayton Iverson did not notice.

. . . Of all the ungrateful, inconsiderate things Frank had ever done, he was thinking, this was absolutely the worst. . . . Perhaps it was time he put his foot down. . . . Prison or no prison, disgrace or no disgrace, perhaps it was time. . . .

His eyes open, but unseeing, Toby Nelms lay twitching on the cooling blanket, jerking one restrained hand from time to time in what might have been an attempt to get at the breathing tube Jack Pearl had inserted into his trachea. His core temperature, despite the blanket, intravenous cortisone, and several doses of rectally-administered Tylenol, was still 103.

". . . Absolutely not," Pearl was saying. "There's absolutely no way

I am going to put a critically ill child under anesthesia for some off-the-wall theory."

"Jack, let me go over this again," Zack pleaded, making no attempt to mask his exasperation. "What I'm proposing is not off the wall. Just because it isn't a widely used technique doesn't mean that it's wrong. Hell, the problem hasn't been studied enough to be certain one way or the other. But there *is* the LSD article. Why do you think I drove all the way home to get it from my files for you?"

"No way," Pearl said.

Suzanne joined the two other physicians at the bedside. For more than an hour she had been battling one flurry of irregular cardiac rhythms after another in the boy. Now, for the moment at least, the situation seemed to have stabilized, but the dusky shadows enveloping her eyes were mute testimony to the tension of the struggle.

"So, where do we stand?" she asked, sipping tepid coffee.

Throughout the crisis she had made no overt reference to Zack's theories regarding Mainwaring and Pearl, although several times her expression had warned—or begged—him against any confrontation with the anesthesiologist.

"Well," Zack said, "we're right where we were before the arrhythmias started. Cerebral edema. Nothing more. Could be caused *by* the fever; could be the cause of it; could be both."

"Well, for what it's worth, his arrhythmias seem to be under control."

"It's worth plenty. Nice going."

"Thanks. So, have you two decided? Are you going to put the boy back to sleep?"

The two men exchanged glances. Then Pearl looked away.

"Well, Jack," Zack said, "go ahead and tell her. Tell her what we—tell her what *you* have decided. Look down at that child there, think about what I've told you, what I've shown you, and tell her."

"Zack, please," Suzanne said. She turned to the anesthesiologist.

"Sorry," he mumbled.

"Jack?" she asked.

"I refuse to do it," Pearl said simply. "The evidence that this child's anesthesia had anything to do with his present condition is flimsy enough by itself. Used as justification for a highly questionable maneuver, such as Iverson here is proposing, is absurd. I positively refuse to do it."

"Do what?"

Frank Iverson appeared near the foot of the bed. He glanced from one physician to the next and then, with some discomfort, at the thrashing boy.

"Do what, Jack?" he asked again.

"Frank," Pearl said, "earlier in the week I filed an official report and complaint about a visit I had from your brother, here. At that time, he accused me of any number of things, including improperly anesthetizing this child."

"Why, that's ridiculous," Zack said. "I never—"

"Zack, will you please let him finish. . . . Thank you. Go ahead, Jack."

"Well, now the boy's got cerebral edema—that's brain swelling—from God knows what. Maybe some form of encephalitis or something. Your brother has this theory that if this *is* some nervous system reaction to the anesthesia he received, my putting him under again with the same drugs might reverse the effect."

"And?" Frank said.

"And I won't do it."

"Why?"

"Why?! Well, because it . . . it won't work, Frank. That's why."

"Zack, has this been done before?"

"In analogous circumstances, yes. I brought in an article describing the theory behind it."

"Then, Jack," Frank said calmly, "what harm would it do to put this boy to sleep again as Zack is suggesting? You put critically injured and ill patients under all the time, don't you?"

"Well yes, but—"

"Suzanne, do you think this child would be able to handle being put to sleep?"

"I . . . well, his cardiac problems seem to have quieted down, and he *is* already on a ventilator, so actually, I don't see why not."

"But—"

"No buts, Jack. I'm sorry I didn't get over here sooner to discuss all this, but I was tied up trying to reach some people in Akron. Now listen. We're in the business of helping people. That's why we're here. If there's a chance that what Zack is suggesting will help this kid, I think you should try it. My brother's a pain in the neck sometimes, but he's hardly foolhardy. If he says he has evidence, then by God, he's got evidence."

Witnessing the bizarre exchange from his spot by the head of Toby's bed, Zack sensed an intense nonverbal interplay occurring between his brother and the anesthesiologist. He could also tell from Pearl's expression that the strange little man was no longer going to object to administering the drugs.

"What *were* the anesthetics again?" Suzanne asked.

"Pentothal and isoflurane," Pearl said.

"Ah, yes."

"Are you going to do it?" Zack asked.

"How long do you think we'll have to keep him under?"

"Eight minutes. That's how long they did it in the article."

Pearl glanced once again at Frank.

"Okay," he said unenthusiastically. "Give me a couple of minutes to get my equipment together."

"Good. I'll try and get this place set up." Zack leveled his gaze at the man. "Jack, whatever the kid got for that hernia of his, that's what he should get now. Understand?"

"He got Pentothal and isoflurane," Pearl responded with exaggerated firmness. "Now, are we going to do this or not?"

"Suzanne?"

"No objections," she said.

"Okay, then. Let's go for it," Zack said.

The eerie scene was one that nobody in the ICU that night would ever forget. Throughout the unit, all unnecessary lights were extinguished and every noncritical piece of equipment that produced a noise or vibration was shut off. Nurses sat silently and grimly beside their patients or by the nurses' station.

In cubicle 7, the only lights were flashes of Zack's and Jack Pearl's small penlights and the shimmering monitor readouts of Toby Nelms's cardiac pattern and blood pressure.

Toby himself, anesthetized first with Pentothal, and now with the gas, isoflurane, lay motionless and peaceful, his eyes patched and taped shut, his ears plugged with oil-soaked cotton and covered with bandages. His feet were encased in lamb's wool. Two thin cotton blankets covered him on top, and the water-filled cooling blanket lay underneath him.

Zack had checked both the new, unopened vial of Pentothal and the label on the isoflurane tank before okaying their administration. Now, watch in hand, he sat to one side of the darkened cubicle, waiting. Jack Pearl's willingness to administer the two anesthetics had dispelled some of his suspicions regarding an experimental drug, but doubt remained.

And even if this treatment was the right one, even if the anesthetics were correct, even if Jack Pearl was as pure and honorable a physician as Galen, Zack knew they might have waited too long. Cerebral edema was, all too often, a one-way street.

Five minutes, six . . . the time seemed endless. . . . Blood pressure, ninety and holding; pulse 120 . . . Seven minutes.

Zack watched the last thirty seconds tick off, glancing over briefly at Suzanne, whose attention was riveted on the monitor screen.

"Okay, Jack," he said. "That's it. Eight minutes."

He threw back the draperies to the room and motioned the nurse back in.

Her first move was to reinsert the rectal probe attached to the cooling blanket console.

"It's 103," she said.

Slowly, Toby began to stir, as concentrated oxygen washed the isoflurane from his lungs and bloodstream. Zack bent over him and checked his pupils. They were, if anything, more sluggishly reactive than before. Otherwise, a top-to-bottom neurologic exam showed no change.

"Anything?" Suzanne asked.

"Nothing."

Zack left the cubicle and circled the counter to where she was stationed.

"Satisfied?" she whispered.

"Not really, but I guess there's nothing more I can do."

Across from them, Jack Pearl had removed Toby's eye patches and was conducting his own exam.

"I really appreciated your restraint in dealing with Jack."

"It wasn't easy."

"I could tell."

"You still don't believe me about all this, do you?"

She shook her head.

"As I said in your office," she whispered, glancing first at the monitor and then at Pearl, "one other case, and I'll at least listen."

"I'm going to find it."

"You know, you are without a doubt the most headstrong man I've ever met."

"I'm the most headstrong man *I've* ever met," he said. "It's my finest attribute."

She looked at him coolly.

"Well, Zachary, that may be. But unfortunately, it's also your most frightening one."

She brushed past him and joined Pearl at the bedside.

Zack stood alone at the nurses' station, fighting the hollowness in his chest, trying to cling to the notion that for the moment, at least, he had done all he could for Toby Nelms—he had done his best.

"Dr. Iverson," the ward clerk called to him from her desk. "The call on line two is for you. It's Mr. Iverson."

"Zack," Frank said breathlessly, "I'm down in the E.R. We've got trouble. Maybe big trouble."

"What?"

"Auto accident. Two cars. Both drivers injured."

"Bad?"

"Dunno about one of them—apparently they're still trying to cut him out of his pickup. Marshfield's in with the other one right now."

"Let me just wash my face and I'll be right down."

"Make it quick, Zack. The guy Marshfield's working on is the Judge."

___⋀CHAPTER 27

THE EMERGENCY WARD was bedlam. Nearly every bed was full, as was the waiting room. Nurses, some of whom Zack recognized as having been called down from the floors, were hurrying between patients, the med locker, and the supply room. EKG and portable X-ray technicians were standing by their equipment in the hallway. Several blue-clad rescue team members were assisting the nurses while several more sat perched on countertops filling out forms.

Two of the rooms seemed to be the foci of most of the activity.

"The Judge is over there, in eight," Frank said as he and Zack crossed the lobby.

"What in the hell was he doing driving around at this hour without Mom, anyhow?"

"I don't know, Zack. You can ask him. He's all bandaged and splinted up, but he's perfectly with it. He must be. He's already told me that if we couldn't get a hold of his-son-the-neurosurgeon, he wanted to be transferred to another hospital."

"Frank, it's okay not to be snide right now, all right? Who's with him?"

"Not sure. Marshfield was, but I see him over there in trauma. The other guy from the accident has just been brought in."

"Well, do you want to call Mom now, or wait until we know what's going on?"

"The later the better as far as I'm concerned."

"Okay. Well, maybe you can call Lisette and have her go over and get her."

"Lisette's . . . gone."

Zack checked his watch.

"Well, when will she be back?"

"No," Frank said. "She's gone, as in: gone. It's a temporary thing. Listen, you go ahead in with the Judge. I'll take care of Mom. . . . And Zack?"

"Yes?"

"Too bad things aren't working out for that kid."

Without waiting for a response, Frank turned and crossed the emergency ward to where two uniformed troopers were speaking with a reporter from the *White Mountains Gazette*.

"Yeah, Frank," Zack muttered, flashing briefly on the bizarre, sub rosa interplay between his brother and Jack Pearl. "Too bad."

He was heading toward room 8 when the curtain drew back and the nurse, Doreen Lavalley, emerged.

"Oh, Dr. Iverson, I'm glad you were able to get down here so quickly," she said. "They called me down because I used to do E.R. work, but it's been a few years and—"

"I'm sure you're doing great. What's the story?"

"Well, I've been in there since just after they brought your father in. The rescue people found him sitting propped against a tree about fifty feet from the crash. They suspect he was thrown out of the car and then walked or crawled over there. He almost certainly has a fractured wrist. The rescue people also report there's a huge gash in his lower back, but nobody's had the chance yet to move him off the board to check it. Dr. Marshfield had to go in with the fellow from the other car. From a distance, at least, that guy doesn't look good at all."

Zack moved to a spot just outside the doorway to room 8. Through it, he could see his father, strapped to a transfer board, with his head and neck secured in excellent first aid fashion. One arm was wrapped and splinted, the other fitted just above the wrist with an IV line. A monitor was in place and chronicling a perfectly normal rate and rhythm.

"Did Dr. Marshfield have the chance to get any films?"

Doreen Lavalley consulted a scrap of paper.

"He got a portable shoot-through of his neck and a view approximately over where that gash is. I had the lab draw a blood count and chemistries."

"Blood bank, too?"

"Yes. I asked them to type him and crossmatch him for four units."

"Nice going, Doreen. I'm glad to see you're still working here."

"Just one more week," she said, somewhat sadly. "I've taken a job with the Visiting Nurse Association."

"Well, that's going to be Davis's loss."

"Thank you. I'll miss this place. At least the way it used to be, I will. I'll see if I can get those films."

If Clayton Iverson was relieved to see his son, he showed little evidence of it. Zack was not surprised. It had always been that way, and regardless of the circumstances, it would be that way this night.

"H'lo, Judge."

Zack leaned against the bed rail, assessing his father—the slight pallor about his lips, the deepened creases at the corner of his eyes.

The man was in some pain, and probably still bordering on shock. Reflexively, Zack reached across and increased the intravenous flow.

"Zachary . . ." The Judge spoke through teeth nearly clenched by the bandages pulled tightly across his forehead and beneath his chin to stabilize his neck. "Do you think you could get rid of this damn stuff?"

"As soon as I've seen the film of your neck, Judge. Apparently you weren't all that coherent when the police arrived. You could have hurt your neck and not know it. You in much discomfort?"

"Mostly my back—right through here. . . ." He motioned with his unsplinted hand at a spot just above his navel. "Does your mother know I'm here?"

"Frank went to take care of that."

"Have him tell her to wait at home, and that I'll call her later."

"Judge, just relax and let us take care of things. Okay? Now, what happened?"

"I don't know. I was on my way over to . . . ah . . . to talk with Frank and Lisette about some investments they're thinking of making. And just as I was passing by Cedar Street, boom. The next thing I really remember was the inside of the ambulance."

. . . to talk with Frank and Lisette? . . . Lisette's gone Judge. Who's lying? Frank to you, or you to me?

"Did you hit your head?"

"Not that I know."

"Zack?" Suzanne stood by the doorway, the X rays in her hand. "I came down to see if I could be of any help. The nurse said she'd be next door if you need her."

"How's the boy?"

"Not awake at all, but still reasonably stable. Owen Walsh is trying to arrange a transfer, but I don't think he's been able to find a bed yet."

"Well, I'm glad you could get down. Have you seen the films?"

It was only then that he noticed the tension in her face. Something was wrong in the X rays.

"Flip 'em right up there," he said, motioning her to the two view boxes on the wall beside the Judge's litter.

She illuminated the lateral shoot-through of the Judge's neck. Zack counted to be certain that all seven cervical vertebrae were displayed, and then checked the alignment and spacing of each.

"Normal," he said. "Perfect. Looks like we're in luck, Judge. We'll get a complete set of films, just to be certain, but I suspect they'll be fine. I don't see any reason not to remove this harness they've rigged up."

He reached for the restraint.

"Zack, you may want to wait on that," Suzanne said, snapping the second film into place. "There was a load of scrap metal in the pickup. The police wonder if maybe he fell on something."

"What is that thing?" the Judge asked.

Still constrained by the harness, he was forcing his eyes far to the left in order to see the X ray.

"It's a chunk of metal, Dad," Zack said, studying the piece, which was stubby, wedge-shaped, and pointed on all three corners. The longest, sharpest point of the three was directly between two vertebrae, the twelfth dorsal and first lumbar. "A pretty big chunk, too. I'll need a lateral view to know how deep it is. Are you having any numbness or tingling in your legs at all?"

"I . . . I don't think so."

"Well, just the same, I think I'll leave you strapped in for now."

"If you have to. Am I going to be all right?"

"Of course you are. But I'll feel happier when we know exactly where that metal is and we've gotten someone to take it out."

"*You're* not going to do it?"

"Judge, first things first, okay? Suzanne, can you send in the portable unit for a lateral view? Meanwhile, I'll go over the rest of him."

". . . Suction, I need suction!" . . . "Doctor, do you want another line?" . . . "His pupil's dilating" . . . "Christ, I asked for suction. . . ."

The snatches of exchange between Wilton Marshfield and a nurse came from the trauma room.

". . . He's vomiting again. Doctor, I think he's seizing" . . . "Get me ten of Valium for an IV push" . . . "Did you know that Dr. Iverson is in with his father?"

"Sounds like trouble," the Judge said. "Are you going in there?"

"If they need me, they'll come and get me," Zack said. "I'm not leaving you alone. Suze, while you're out there can you please check on what's going on? If that's the other driver from the accident, find out who he is."

Zack was completing a rapid exam when the curtain flew back and Frank entered.

"Oo-ee, what a zoo out there," he said. "Police, reporters, the works. What gives here?"

"He's got a chunk of metal in his back—see? It looks like it shot in there during the crash, but maybe he fell on it or rolled over it. I won't know exactly where it is until I see some more views, but it obviously has to come out."

"Well, Judge," Frank said, "even if it does, you got the better end of the deal in this one. Ol' Beau in there is a mess."

"Beau Robillard?" Zack and the Judge said the name in unison.

"Yeah, didn't you know? Public nuisance number one is right in the next room. That was his rust-bucket pickup you hit. If he's operating true to form, that scrap metal in the back of it was probably hot. Hey, Zack, remember how Robillard and his buddies used to follow you home after school and kick the daylights out of you?"

"Frank, that was junior high, for goodness sakes."

"He hasn't changed," the Judge said. "I see him in my court every other week, it seems. He's as nasty as ever. Nastier. I should have put him away the last time I had the chance. Was there anyone in the truck with him?"

"Nope," Frank answered. "The police say that while they were cutting him out of the cab he kept screaming that you ran the light at the bottom of the Mill Street hill."

"That's ridiculous."

At that moment, Suzanne reappeared at the doorway with the X-ray technician.

"Zack," she said, "Wilton asked if you could help him next door. The guy from the truck has a bad head injury. He's started seizing. His name's Robillard."

"Beau Robillard. We know. He used to beat me up in junior high."

"He's trash," the Judge said. "Petty theft, assault, disturbing the peace. Zachary, I don't want you going in there."

"What?"

"You heard me. Tell Marshfield you're tied up in here and you can't help him."

"Judge, I can't do that. . . ."

Zack paused, waiting for support for his position from Frank and Suzanne. There was none.

"Listen," he said finally, "I've got to go in and at least honor his request for help. Besides, you need more X rays and maybe a CT scan, and . . . and the O.R. team's got to be mobilized. By the time all those studies are completed, I should be done in there, okay?"

"I already told you how I felt," the Judge said. "Why are you asking if it's okay?"

"Zack," Frank said, "let me talk to you outside for a minute."

"Okay, in just a second. . . ." Zack felt shaken. "Please go ahead with a lateral of his thoraco-lumbar region and a shot of his wrist," he said to the X-ray technician. "On second thought, why don't you forget the portable. Take him over and get a really good set of films. Suze, can you go with him?"

"Sure. Owen Walsh'll call me if anything develops in the unit."

"You might want to go over him for pre-op clearance. I don't think they've had time yet to get a full EKG."

"I'll take care of that."

"Also, find out who's on for orthopedics, if you can."

"Zachary, I meant what I said about Robillard," the Judge said as Suzanne and the technician wheeled him from the room. "I never meant anything more."

Zack could only shake his head.

"Hey, listen," Frank said when the two of them were alone. "Just go in there and see Robillard, and do whatever you have to do. Leave the Judge to me."

"I know he's hurt and angry, Frank, but all the same, I can't believe he would talk like that. I just can't believe it."

"You've been away from here—away from the man—for a long time. Remember, buddy, we're not the only ones he keeps passing judgment on. Years and years of sentencing the same stiffs over and over again has done something to him. Listen, don't worry about him. I can handle things. Just go on in there and play doctor."

"Did you call Mom?"

"I have one of the state troopers going to get her."

"Okay. I'll be next door. Frank, thanks for your help. I hope things with Lisette get straightened out."

"Not to worry. Just get on in there and do whatever you have to."

The two of them left room 8. Zack entered the trauma room and Frank crossed the E.R. to the X-ray department.

The Judge had been moved, on the transfer board, to the X-ray table.

"I need a minute alone with him," Frank said, motioning Suzanne and the technician away.

"Judge, listen," he whispered, when the others were out of earshot. "I tried to reason with Zack about not seeing Robillard, but he just won't listen. I'm on your side on this one. One hundred percent. Just relax and let them take your pictures. I'll keep trying to make Zack see what's right."

The rescue team, nurses, and emergency physician cleared a path as Zack entered the trauma room. His programming in the evaluation of nervous system damage was in reflex operation before he reached the bedside.

Beau Robillard, lying nude on the trauma room litter, was disheveled, covered with cuts and abrasions, and even worse off than Zack had anticipated.

Comatose . . . respirations shallow, minimally effective . . . barely responsive to deep pain . . . right pupil, two millimeters; left pupil, five millimeters, sluggishly reactive . . .

"Was he ever awake, Wilton?"

"Absolutely," Marshfield said. "He was awake when the police found him, and moaning and incoherent when he arrived here. Then he seized."

. . . Some purposeless movement on the left side, no movement on the right. . . . Babinski reflex absent both sides . . . deep scalp laceration left parietal region . . .

"Could I have a pair of gloves, please. Size eight. Also, get set to intubate him. Number seven point five tube. Wilton, can I see his films?"

"We haven't had a chance to get them, what with your father coming in first and this creep looking a helluva lot better than he does right now. Do you know who he is?"

"Yeah, yeah," Zack said. "I know."

"When this . . . this thing here was a boy," Marshfield said, "He and his cronies beat up on my nephew so many times that my brother finally ended up having to send the kid to St. Michael's Academy. I'm telling you, he was really a creep. So were those two older Robillard boys."

Zack explored the deep scalp gash with his gloved fingers, and felt the distinctive click of bone fragments.

"Well, I don't care if he's the reincarnation of Jack the Ripper and Attila the Hun rolled into one," he said. "He's got a subdural or epidural hematoma expanding on the left. He needs Burr hole drainage, and quickly. Also, see if you can get Greg Ormesby in here just in case something's going on in his abdomen."

The nurse set a tray of equipment by Zack's right hand. He hunched over the head of the litter, positioned the steel blade of the laryngoscope against Robillard's tongue, and in seconds slid the polystyrene breathing tube through the man's vocal cords into his trachea.

"Hyperventilate him, please," Zack said, connecting a breathing bag to the tube and turning it over to the respiratory technician.

Burr holes! An hour in the operating room. More if there was trouble.

Zack backed away from the bed, a stranglehold of indecision tightening about his chest. Both Beau Robillard and the Judge needed surgery that, of those at Ultramed-Davis, he was by far the most qualified to perform. From a purely medical perspective, there was no dilemma, no doubt about the priorities of the moment. Without immediate intervention, Robillard would die. It was that simple.

But thanks to Judge Clayton Iverson, it wasn't that simple at all.

"Keep bagging him," Zack mumbled, rubbing at the ache that had suddenly materialized between his temples. "Be sure there are two teams available for the O.R. I'll be right back."

He glanced into room 8. It was still empty.

Please, he was thinking as he headed toward the X-ray department. *Let that chunk of metal be just below the skin. Let it be someplace where anyone with a scalpel and a little training can get it out.*

Suzanne was standing by one of the department's banks of view boxes, studying the films.

Even from a distance, Zack could see that the position of the metal fragment was trouble.

"How's he doing?" he asked.

"Okay. He's complaining of some heaviness in his legs, but I think you might have put that symptom in his head. Your mother's here. Frank's got her in the quiet room, I think. That metal's not in such a good spot, huh?"

"It's in near the cord, if that's what you mean. See right here how it's chipped the edge of the vertebral transverse process? Removing it should be reasonably straightforward, but it certainly won't be any smash and grab. The area's got to be explored to be sure there's no bleeding around the cord. Damn, but I wish this wasn't happening. That Robillard is going out. A Burr hole procedure now is his only chance, and not such a huge one at that."

"Are you going to do it?"

"Suzanne, I don't have any choice. Of course I'm going to do it. Did you find out who's on for orthopedics?"

"Sam Christian's the only one around, but he's in the O.R. over at Clarion County. Apparently he just started an open reduction."

"Damn. Well, listen, keep your eye on the Judge, okay? I'm going to call John Burris in Concord. He's an excellent neurosurgeon, and with that Beechcraft of his, he can be up here in an hour or less. Meanwhile, go ahead, call in the radiologist and get a CT scan of the area. See if we can assess the extent of bleeding. This day is really the pits, do you know that?"

"Zack?"

"What?"

"The Judge and Frank told me what kind of a person this Robillard is. If he's really as bad off as you say, maybe you should accept the inevitable and devote your energy to making sure your father's all right."

"Suzanne, I can't believe you're saying that."

"Really? Well, what if it were *me* lying in there with a piece of metal up against my spinal cord? Zack, this is your father we're talking about."

"Suzanne, that man in there's dying."

"You know, there are such things in this world as love and loyalty. They're allowed. According to some people, they're even worthwhile virtues to have. Even physicians are allowed to be human. That man you want to operate on steals and beats up on people, Zachary. That's what he does. The police say that the cab of his pickup was littered with empty beer cans. . . ."

Zack glared at her.

"I can't believe you're saying that. I just can't believe it."

He turned and stalked into the room where his father lay beneath the X-ray camera.

"Dad, how're you doing?"

"My back aches, and my legs feel a little heavy."

Zack tapped his reflex hammer against the Judge's Achilles' tendons, documenting once again through the reassuring flick of each foot that the ankle to spinal cord and spinal cord-to-ankle circuits were intact.

"Wiggle your toes, please. . . . Good. Other foot . . . good."

707

"What's the story?" the Judge asked.

"Well, your wrist is broken, but it will keep until Sam Christian gets done at Clarion County. However, that piece of metal in your back ought to come out soon."

"I thought so. You going to do it?"

Zack hesitated, and then shook his head, triggering a jackhammer pain between his eyes.

"No, Dad," he said. "I've got to do that man first or he's dead. Besides, we're not encouraged to operate on our own family if we can avoid it. I'm going to call John Burris up from Concord."

"I want you."

"Judge, please, don't make this any harder. You're quite stable right now. Robillard's dying."

"Let him die."

"I can't do that. . . ."

Clayton Iverson stared stonily at the ceiling.

In the silence, Zack became aware of others in the room. He turned. Frank and Suzanne stood just inside the doorway, watching and listening.

"Suzanne, please arrange the CT scan," Zack said, trying to ignore the disapproval in her eyes. "I've got to call Burris and then get into the O.R. I can see by your face what you want to say to me. Don't bother. I'm doing the one thing we are taught always to do—I'm doing what I think is right. . . . Judge, I love you, and I'll be keeping track of things. With luck, by the time Burris gets here I'll be done with what I have to do, and I can assist him. Meanwhile, just hang in there."

He turned and left, brushing past Suzanne. She followed him for several steps, but then, shaking her head in resignation and frustration, headed for the radiology office.

"Ma's here," Frank said, approaching the bed. "Judge, I'm sorry. I tried to help him see reason."

"Forget it, Frank," Clayton Iverson said. "Just leave me alone."

"But Judge—"

"Dammit, Frank, I said leave me alone."

Nothing felt normal or comfortable. The room, O.R. 4, seemed far too warm, the surgical team far too quiet. The blades and scissors and drill bits were too dull, the hemostats and needle holders unacceptably stiff or loose.

Zachary struggled to ignore his throbbing headache and his sodden scrub suit and to focus on the situation at hand. The circulating nurse, no longer waiting for his request, was mopping perspiration from his forehead and cheeks every two or three minutes.

They were nearly an hour into the Burr hole drainage procedure on Beau Robillard, and still there was no word that John Burris had arrived from Concord. Down the hall, in O.R. 2, a second surgical team stood ready.

"Valerie," Zack said to the circulator, "could you go on down to the E.R., please, and see what you can find out about Dr. Burris. He should have been here by now."

Beneath his green paper mask, Zack's jaw was clenched. He was right in what he was doing, dammit. He was a physician, a surgeon, not judge and jury. Why, then, was everyone acting as if his decision were some sort of mortal sin? Surely they understood that he wasn't choosing this man's life over his father's. The Judge was stable, perfectly stable. Beau Robillard was dying.

"Pressure's down a bit," Jack Pearl cautioned.

The words brought Zack's thoughts back in tune with his hands.

"Feel free to transfuse him a unit if you need to," he responded. "I've aspirated a fair amount through these Burr holes, but his brain's not showing any signs of reexpanding. If there's no action in a few more minutes, we're going to have to push ahead with a full craniotomy."

The circulating nurse, Valerie, reentered the O.R. through the scrub room.

"Dr. Iverson," she said, "there's a problem downstairs."

Zack shuddered.

"Yes, go ahead. . . ."

"I was told to tell you that Judge Iverson's feet have gone numb. He's unable to move his toes."

"Who's with him?"

The urgency in his voice bordered on panic. He glanced down at the persisting space between Beau Robillard's skull and brain surface, and begged himself to calm down.

"Dr. Cole and Dr. Marshfield," the woman answered.

"And where in the hell is—"

Zack breathed deeply and exhaled.

"Where is Dr. Burris?" he asked more evenly.

The eyes of everyone on the surgical team were fixed on him. There was, they all knew, little chance he could break scrub and leave the operating room without killing Robillard.

"The weather's gotten worse. Apparently there was a problem with Dr. Burris's plane," the nurse explained. "He's gotten someone to fly him up, but they lost some time."

"How much till he's here?"

"Twenty minutes."

"Damn," Zack murmured.

It would take another hour to complete the craniotomy—the open procedure he now felt certain was necessary. And even with the procedure, Beau Robillard's chances of survival as anything more than a vegetable were growing dimmer each second.

"Have them give Judge Iverson five amps of Narcan IV, and get him up to the operating room now."

"Five? But the usual dose is—"

"Dammit, I know what the usual dose is." He took a deep breath. "Sorry. I didn't mean to snap at you. The high dose is to help keep down the swelling in his cord. Also, please ask Dr. Cole if she can come up here and tell me exactly what's going on."

In truth, Zack had little doubt as to what was going on. An epidural bleed, not predictable at all from his initial exam, was compressing the Judge's spinal cord.

Had he missed something? Had there been a clue?

Uncertainty and self-doubt hardened around Zack's hands like cement.

With Burris less than twenty minutes away, could any significant change be effected now by scrubbing out on Robillard and going after the Judge's bleed?

Zack gazed down at the man for whose life he had chosen to be responsible. Having made that choice, did he even have the right now to renege on it?

The doors to the O.R. burst open, and Suzanne, dressed in scrubs, stepped inside.

"The Judge can't move his legs," she said. "Burris is about to land. A cruiser's waiting for him at the airport."

"Reflexes?"

"A flicker," she said. "It would seem, Doctor, that unless John Burris works a minor miracle, your father might well end up paralyzed from the waist down."

At that moment, Jack Pearl called out, "Dr. Iverson, his rate's dropping. I can't get a pressure."

"Give him an amp of epinephrine."

"Already done."

"Get ready for CPR."

"Pulse is dropping. Dropping more."

"Damn . . . Begin CPR."

"Doctor, he's straight line. . . ."

"Another amp of epi. Give him another amp of epi. . . ."

CHAPTER 28

IT WAS AFTER TWO in the morning. The fine, misty rain drifting over the valley for hours had sapped most of the warmth remaining from the day.

Zack lay sprawled on his living room floor, staring at nothing in particular. The only illumination in the room was from half a dozen candles and the red and green lights on his stereo receiver.

For the two hours since his return from the hospital, he had been listening to Mendelssohn and Mahler, talking almost nonstop to Cheapdog, and drinking—at first several beers, then beer plus shots of Wild Turkey, and finally, the 110-proof Wild Turkey alone.

"I didn't ask mush, y'know, Cheap? . . . Peace and quiet, some rocks to climb, a place to do my work without any hassles, the chance to make a difference. . . . Don't look at me that way. I know I said that before. So what? . . . You're the dog, so you just have to sit there and listen. . . . That's the way it is. . . ."

Zack could count on the fingers of one hand the number of major-league drinking bouts he had ever had, but he felt determined to add this night to the list.

Beau Robillard had survived his cardiac arrests on the operating table, only to experience several more arrests in the recovery room. Zack had called off the resuscitation after intensive efforts failed to bring back any functional cardiac activity.

In retrospect, given the extent of the cerebral contusion and hemorrhage Zack had discovered during surgery, it seemed that the die was cast for Robillard the moment the side of his head had connected with whatever it had.

Unfortunately, in the heat of battle, with no time to spare and a life on the line, there was simply no way for him to know that ahead of time.

". . . You know what medicine's like, boy? 'S like you come to rely on this wonderful woman who has promised you that if you treat her right, she'll always be there when you need her. . . . So you do. . . .

You study, and no matter how exhausted you are, you don't take any shortcuts. . . . And then, when you need her the most, when your own goddamn father's involved, you follow the system and use your clinical judgment, and do just what you're supposed to do, and *poof!* She's gone. . . . Gone! Damn women . . . Damn medicine . . ."

Zack had pronounced Beau Robillard dead just as John Burris was completing the removal of a jagged chunk of rusty metal from deep within the muscles of Clayton Iverson's back. Although there was no evidence that the fragment had pierced the dural lining of the spinal canal, apparently there had been some impairment of blood flow to the cord, because the Judge's paralysis had progressed and was now being regarded by Burris as total paraplegia.

Whether the condition was permanent or not, Burris would not speculate, although both he and Zack knew all too well that the prognosis following such a development was not good.

Word of Zack's decision, the Judge's paralysis, and Beau Robillard's death had spread through the hospital like wildfire. That Robillard's blood alcohol level had come back well below that of legal intoxication, while the Judge's was above the 0.1 cutoff, was a fact lost in the rumors and the stories of the accident, and the virtually universal condemnation of Zack's disloyalty to his father.

Suddenly, it seemed, there was not a soul in all of Ultramed-Davis who did not have a bone or two to pick with Beaudelaire Robillard, Jr., nor one who had not been helped at one time or another by Judge Clayton Iverson.

Throughout the hideous evening, which ended with a tense, one-way conversation at his father's bedside, Zack did not hear so much as one word of support from anyone for the difficulty of his position or the rightness of his decision.

With Suzanne and Owen Walsh watching Toby, and John Burris staying the night in the guest room at the hospital, there was no reason for him to stay around. And there was every reason to come home and get drunk. In the morning, he would in all likelihood pack up and leave. If only there were some way he could take off for parts unknown without bringing himself along.

With the heat turned off, and no fire in the hearth, the house had begun to absorb the chill of the night. Zack pushed himself up and shuffled to the bedroom for a sweater. He was surprised that although he had had more to drink over a shorter period of time than he could ever remember, he felt quite steady on his feet.

There was a certain irony that on this particular night he was unable even to do a decent job of getting drunk.

Returning to the living room, he laid a small fire, put on a slightly less morose album, and sipped another ounce of Wild Turkey. He could understand the Judge's stony castigation of him, and even his mother's.

They had every right to be upset. But Suzanne's reaction was a bitter pill.

She was a physician, to say nothing of being his lover. Even if no one else did, she should have had some compassion and understanding for his predicament.

He poured another ounce.

Years before, in the very beginning of his training, he had wrestled with the issues of making decisions in medicine, and had chosen to adopt the careful, objective, by-the-book approach over any of the more flamboyant, headline-grabbing tactics embraced by many of his surgical colleagues.

The decision had not been that difficult.

He was a second child, a plodder. He had done his best with what tools he had. Why couldn't Suzanne understand that? Frank was the buccaneer in the family. He was a scholar. Frank danced on the wind. He needed a system.

The room was growing stuffy and uncomfortably warm. If he closed his eyes for any length of time, it began to spin. His stomach felt queasy, his head like modeling clay.

Perhaps he had had enough to drink. Perhaps it was time to . . .

Zack fought the unpleasant feelings, crossed to the window and opened it a slit. The cool air felt wonderful.

Toby Nelms about to be shipped off to Boston . . . The Judge, paralyzed . . . The man he had chosen to treat instead, dead . . . He himself anathema at the hospital. Could things have possibly turned out any worse?

There are such things in this world as love and loyalty. They're allowed. . . .

Suzanne's words. He should have listened to her.

He was simply too stiff, too inflexible. Connie had told him that more than once, before she had checked out of his life. Now, Suzanne was trying to tell him the same thing.

Too many rules. Not enough person.

He gazed out across the glistening yard, past the low thicket, to the wall of jagged rock that he had named There, hoping someone, some-day, would ask him why he climbed it. The granite face, perhaps three hundred feet up and five hundred across, was the single aspect of the house that had most appealed to him when the Pine Bough realtor was first showing him around.

Sloping upward at seventy-five to eighty degrees, the face crested at a broad plateau with a better than decent view of the valley. The climb, though somewhat tricky, was one he had already made several times.

But always, he suddenly realized, he had climbed in the sunlight and with equipment. Always, he had done it by the rules. . . .

He negotiated a few heel-to-toe steps without any difficulty, and stood on one foot for several seconds. The alcohol would be no problem, he decided. Probably he hadn't even drunk as much as he thought.

Rules . . . systems . . .

Zack strode to the hall closet, pulled on his rubber-soled climbing shoes and his windbreaker, and stuffed a small but potent flashlight into his pocket.

It was time to stop being a second child. . . . Time to loosen up and shatter the mold . . . Time to break some rules . . .

"Because it's There," Zack cackled as he slipped out the back door and into the chilly night. "Just because it's There."

What in the hell other reason did he need?

The air held little more than a hint of the fine, black rain, but it was still cool and heavy. Several times as Zack crossed the yard and thrashed his way through the dense thicket, he swore he could see his breath. By the time he reached the base of the rock face, his climbing shoes were soaked through.

Climbing alone, at night, after a few drinks, in the rain . . . how many more rules could he think of to break? Perhaps, he mused, he should go up blindfolded as well. No reason to do things halfway. After a brief debate, he rejected that notion. What he was doing was quite enough for the moment—the first in a series of steps that would ultimately lead to his transformation as a person and a physician.

He moved laterally through the tall grass until he located a decent starting point, and then peered upward along the ebony granite. Above the rim, the heavily overcast sky was only slightly less black than the stone itself. It was going to be a hell of a climb.

And when it was over, when he had proven what he needed to prove, he would lie beneath the trees on the plateau overhead and watch as dawn floated in over the valley.

The exhilaration of the adventure coursing through him, Zack reached out and pressed his palms against the damp, cool stone. Then, with a final glance above, he was off.

Five feet . . . ten . . . twenty . . . forty . . .

The climb, even with the alcohol and the darkness and the rain, was a piece of cake.

Fifty . . . sixty . . . seventy . . .

Every time he needed a sound hold, his fingers found one. He was "zoned"—climbing with a beautiful smoothness and synchrony. If he had wanted to, he *could* have done it blindfolded. Below—now far below—he could see the candlelight flickering in the windows of his house. His street, the winding road toward the river, the occasional car, the night lights of town; with each new hold, each upward step, his vista broadened.

It was a magnificent climb, he told himself. . . . Absolutely magnificent . . . Connie was right. . . . So was Suzanne. . . . He should have been breaking rules like this long ago. . . . While it had been reasonable to operate on Beau Robillard—reasonable and medically sound—in the final, metaphysical analysis, perhaps it might not have been right.

Ninety feet . . . one hundred . . . maybe more . . .

Below, the steeply sloping rock had no features. Above there was only blackness. His progress was slower now, but steady still. The wind had picked up a bit, and a fine spray was, once again, spattering him through the night.

Minute by minute, Zack began feeling his breath becoming shorter, his grips not quite as firm. Foul-tasting acid started percolating into his throat and up the back of his nose. How much, exactly, *had* he had to drink?

Concentrate, he begged himself. *Use your adrenaline, your experience, and focus in. . . .*

The handholds became more slippery, smaller, and more difficult to find. He was traversing more as he searched for safe leverage, ascending less. His fingers were beginning to stiffen up. Behind him, nestled in the gloom, was his house—so tantalizingly close, so incredibly far. Without lines, descent in the dark and the rain was simply out of the question.

Then, without warning, he slipped.

His foot went first, skidding off the edge of a niche he thought was safe. Instantly, his grips gave way as well. He slid ten or fifteen feet, slamming his elbow against a small outcropping and skinning his knee and his chin. He reacted instinctively, using technique and years of practice to stem the fall.

Clawing and kicking at a shallow crevice, he was able to bring himself to a stop.

Then, gasping, he clung to the rock until, inch by inch, he was able to work himself to a more secure spot. His elbow and his knee were throbbing, but not broken. His lungs were on fire. Waves of cramping pain had begun to shoot from his stomach through to his back.

He looked below him. The rock face, what little of it he could discern, seemed almost smooth. It was ascend or find some way to strap himself in where he was, and remain there until morning.

Then he remembered the flashlight. How could he have forgotten it? He loosened his grip and gingerly reached down and patted his windbreaker pocket. The light was gone—probably lost during the fall.

At that moment, searing pain knifed through his gut and he vomited, retching again and again. Foul, whiskey acid poured through his mouth and out his nose, spattering onto his clothes and shoes and cascading down the rock.

For five minutes, ten, he could only hang on and struggle for breath.

He was in trouble. He had broken the rules, and he was in more trouble, more danger, than he had ever been in his life.

Gradually, his head began to clear, and his gasping respiration slowed. He was at least a hundred fifty feet up, he guessed; maybe more. Certainly, he was more than halfway. He could use his jacket or his belt to secure himself against the rock, but in the dark, there was no real spot he could count on. His only option was to climb, and to pray.

Once again, hold by hold, inch by inch, he started upward. The rain and the wind were real factors now, making every grip more treacherous, every ledge less dependable. The taste in his mouth and throat was abominable, the stiffness in his fingers, elbow, and knees worsening every second.

Still, he climbed.

It was all so stupid. He had taken on the cliff to . . . to what? He couldn't even remember. All that was clear was that he had taken a bad situation and made it much, much worse.

He glanced behind himself. His house was a toy, a shadow, vaguely discernible against the glow of a nearby streetlight. Peering up the rock face, through the rain overhead, he could almost swear he saw the edge of the plateau.

The pitch seemed steeper, the handholds even smaller. Zack scanned the rock face to his right, looking for a traverse that would set up the last segment of his climb. Damn, but he needed that light. It had been stupid, arrogant, and careless not to have tied it on.

Stupid, arrogant, careless . . . That thought brought the wisp of a smile. Before his great decision to break free of his personal constraints, he had been none of the three.

One limb at a time, he worked his way across the rock, searching with his fingertips for the changes that would, once again, guide him upward.

Almost there, he urged himself on. . . . *Almost there . . . Almost . . .*

Before he could adjust or even react, his right foot missed its plant and skimmed off the rock. His arms snapped taut. His hands, both with reasonable grips, held; but they were already stiffened and weak.

Straining his head back and to one side, he looked down. His feet were dangling a foot or so below the nearest purchase.

Oh God, was all he could think of at that moment. *Oh God . . . Oh God . . .*

Reluctant to put any additional pressure on his fingers by struggling, he lifted one foot, gingerly scraping it along the rock, searching for a ledge or a crevice. Below him, at a pitch that was almost sheer, the granite face disappeared into blackness.

Oh God, please . . . Oh God . . .

His foot caught the edge of a minuscule ledge. On a dry day, the tiny space would have been a virtual platform for him—more than enough. But now, there was no way to tell.

Desperate to take some of the pressure off his fingers, Zack planted the toe of his shoe on the ledge and carefully shifted his weight to the foot.

Hold, damn you . . . Please ho—

For a moment, the foot felt solid. Then, as he added more of his weight, it slipped off the edge, tearing his right hand free of the rock. For five seconds, ten, his left hand held.

Then, with a painful snap, his fingers gave way and he was falling, tumbling like a rag doll, over and over again down the sheer rock, screaming as he hurtled against granite outcroppings, shattering one bone after another. . . .

"Nooooo!"

His final scream, the howl of an animal, echoed in his mind, and then blended with another sound . . . a voice . . . Suzanne's voice.

"Zack? For God's sake, Zack, can you hear me?"

He felt a cool, wet towel sweep across his face.

Slowly, he opened his eyes. A cannon was exploding in his head. He was on the living room floor, soaked in fetid vomit. The lights were on. Suzanne was kneeling over him, concern darkening her eyes.

Nearby, resting on its side, was an empty bottle of Wild Turkey.

Across the room, watching intently, sat Cheapdog.

CHAPTER 29

"NEVER AGAIN. I swear it. Not a drop. Not ever."

Over the span of two and a half hours, with Suzanne as guide, Zack had wandered from the terror of his alcohol-induced hallucination, through a valley of tearful self-deprecation, across a brief stretch of cheery self-deprecation, and finally into an abysmal hangover.

"Never again?" she asked. "Do you want me to put that in writing? You can sign it and hang it on the wall."

Zack pressed against his temples.

"Write whatever you want," he said, "as long as the pen doesn't scratch too loudly on the paper. I just hope you can tell that I'm a total amateur at abusing my body like this."

"Oh, I can tell."

He did not clearly remember the shower, or the shampoo, or the first sips of tea, but he knew that Suzanne had taken him through each. Now, although his head still transposed each heartbeat into mortar fire, his thoughts had cleared enough at least to carry on a workable conversation.

He risked a deeper swallow of tea, and nearly wept with the realization that it was going to stay down.

"You've done an amazing job of putting me back together again," he said. "Thanks."

She smiled sadly.

"No big deal. Unfortunately, my ex-husband gave me a lot of practice."

"Great. I'm sorry."

"Don't be. It was bad, but like everything else, it came to pass. . . ."

"Have you been up all night?"

"Uh-huh. Helene's with Jen." She handed him a cool washcloth. "Here, wipe your face off with this. You want some aspirin?"

"Soon. How are things at the hospital?"

"No real change—at least as of half an hour ago. Toby's still in coma. His temp's around 102. Walsh thinks he'll have a bed for him at either Hitchcock or Children's by noon."

"And my father?"

"No change either, as far as I know. I think that neurosurgeon from Concord—what's his name?"

"Burris. John Burris."

"Yes, well, I think John Burris is planning to have him transferred later today as well."

"What a mess."

Suzanne pulled back the curtain. Across the backyard, the first hint of dawn was washing over the face of There.

"So," she said, motioning toward the granite escarpment, "the dreaded scene of your midnight climb."

"That's not so funny, Suzanne. I died on that rock. I really did."

"Well, I certainly hope so. Because from what I've been able to extract from your babble these past two hours, I don't think I would have much liked the guy who crawled up there in the first place. Confused, self-loathing, arrogant, the perennial victim—too close to Paul Cole for my taste."

"Hey, come on. I was just seeing things the way they are. There wasn't a single person in that hospital who had one encouraging word for me. Fifty thousand Frenchmen and all that . . . Well, those particular fifty thousand Frenchmen were saying that I screwed up. And don't forget, you were one of them."

"I know. I'm sorry for that. . . ."

"Don't apologize. You were right—all of you were right. I did screw up. By the time I got home, I couldn't stand who I was. And hallucination or not, when I went up on that cliff back there, I was honestly trying to break free of myself, to . . . to become more, I don't know, more flexible, more human in my approach to medicine. And to everything else, for that matter."

"I understand that."

"And?"

"And I was wrong for saying the things I did. Zachary, you have no reason to change. You're an excellent surgeon, a decent, caring son, and a wonderful friend to me. And I had no right to insinuate that you were otherwise. It was selfish and cruel of me. And it was wrong—very wrong. That's why I called in the first place—to tell you that. I felt so guilty for what I said to you at the hospital—for leaving the way I did—that I couldn't sit still. Then, when you didn't answer, I got frightened. That's why I drove out here."

"I'm glad you did," he said. "But there was no need to feel guilty. You were right."

"I was wrong, dammit! Stop saying that. . . ."

She took a deep breath to calm herself and rubbed at the shadowy strain that enveloped her eyes.

"Zachary, as I told you, Paul was . . . a very sad, very sick man, totally lacking in any center to his life, any perspective. He never, ever put me or Jen ahead of himself, or his booze, or his drugs, or his other women. Never. I still have trouble believing that I could have misjudged anyone so badly. That's why I've been so reluctant to get involved with you. But those things I said in the hospital last night—about loyalty, about what if it was me lying there—what I didn't appreciate until after you left was that I was really saying them to a man I was trying not to fall in love with, not to another doc with a terrible decision on his hands. I was punishing you for being the first man since Paul that I wanted to trust. I was wrong, and I'm sorry."

Zack stared down at his hands.

"Thanks," he said. "But you weren't wrong. The truth of the matter is that my father is crippled, and I probably could have prevented it."

"Zack, the truth of the matter is that you did what you thought was right. You didn't cripple your father; an automobile accident and a piece of metal did. Can't you see that? You did all you ever will be able to do. You did your best."

Zack could only shake his head. Hadn't he once said precisely the same thing to Wil Marshfield? Why couldn't he believe it now, hearing it from her?

". . . Doing what we do for a living isn't easy," Suzanne was saying. "Nobody ever promised us it would be. Nobody ever told us that everyone we took care of would get better, or that every decision we made was going to turn out to be the right one. Medicine isn't a board game with a set number of cards and answers. Every situation is different."

Zack looked over at her glumly.

"How in the hell am I ever supposed to trust my own medical judgment again?" he asked. "Can you answer that for me?"

"God," she groaned. "Listen, Zachary. Have another cup of tea. Then try a cold shower. Then, if you want to continue to castigate yourself, maybe you can try *really* climbing that wall out there. Do it with your hands tied behind your back, though. Put razor blades in your shoes. No sense in making it easy for yourself."

"Hey, there's no reason to snap at me like that."

"Yes, there is," she said, sounding close to tears. "There are plenty of them." She snatched up her jacket and purse. "I came over to make sure you were all right, to tell you I was sorry, and to let you know that I was falling in love with you. I've done all that. It hurts too much to stick around and watch you sink out of sight in your own little bog of self-pity. So if you'll excuse me . . ."

"Wait."

She turned back to him. Her eyes were dark and filmy, and as drawn and sad as he had ever seen them.

"What is it?" she asked wearily.

"I . . . I'm sorry."

"Don't apologize to me, Zack," she said. "What you're doing, you're doing to yourself. You've got nothing to apologize to anyone else for."

"I'm sorry for not listening to what you're trying to say. How's that?"

"Whatever."

"Suzanne, you don't understand."

"Don't I? You forget that I was married to the master of melancholy. Unfortunately for you—for us—I understand *too well.* I feel terrible about what happened to your father. I would no matter *who* he was. And I don't blame you for being upset—but it should be at the situation, Zack, not at yourself . . . at the vagaries of life and of medicine, not at the fact that you're not perfect. I'm sorry, but after all those years of Paul, I have no patience for this kind of talk. Life's too short. I simply have no patience for this at all."

She headed for the door.

"Suzanne, please. Don't go." He crossed to confront her. "I don't like the way I've been sounding, either. Really I don't. But I've never had anything backfire on me like this before, and . . ."

"And what?" She was keeping her distance.

"And . . . nothing. I understand what you're saying. Let's leave it at that. It's all beginning to sink in. And . . . and I'm going to be okay. Really I am. . . . Could you stay? Just for a bit?"

She eyed him warily. And then, for the first time all morning, she smiled. It was a tired, five A.M. smile, but it was vintage Suzanne Cole.

"Sure, Doc," she said. "I can stay for a bit if you want me to. You know, what goes around comes around. That definition of friend you once wrote for me cuts both ways: the one who helps you find the tools when you can't seem to find them for yourself."

She led him to the couch and laid his head on her lap.

"You've got to face it, Zack," she whispered, stroking his forehead. "No matter how much you want to take off, no matter how much you're hurting, you've got to go back into that hospital, pick up the pieces, and get on with business. There's too much at stake not to. Way too much."

"Way too much," he murmured.

Slowly, his eyes closed. His breathing grew deeper and more regular. In seconds, he was out.

"Please, Zachary," she urged softly. "Please don't run."

She lowered his head onto a pillow, brought his clock radio in from the bedroom, and set it for nine. A call to the O.R. would delay or postpone anything he had scheduled, and one to his office nurse would buy him time there as well. The next move would be up to him.

She was gathering her things when she spied a copy of one of her favorite pieces of medical writing: Davenport's classic treatise on the principles and art of clinical medicine. The slim monograph was wedged on the bookshelf between several huge surgical tomes. She opened it to a passage that she had read enough over the years to know nearly by heart, marked the page for Zack, and then slipped out the front door into the cool, hazy July morning.

Provided Toby Nelms was reasonably stable, there was still time to have a cup of coffee with Helene, to get Jennifer dressed and off to day camp, and to shower, before making rounds. She was nearing twenty-four hours without sleep, but as she so often told her anxious patients, nobody ever died from lack of sleep.

"Hello, Whitey? . . . Frank Iverson here. I'm glad I found you in. I know you're due to open in a bit, so I won't keep you. . . . Yes, well, I guess everyone in Sterling knows about it by now. Goddamn Beau Robillard. Never did a single decent thing his whole life, and now, he can't even die without hurting someone. . . . The Judge is doing okay, Whitey. John Burris, the neurosurgeon who operated on him, is sending him down to Concord early this afternoon by ambulance. . . . Well, I'm afraid you heard right. As things stand, he's paralyzed from the waist down. But Burris isn't making any predictions, and we're all hopeful as hell this is just a temporary condition. The Judge is tough, as we both well know. If anyone can beat this thing, he can. . . . Say,

Whitey, actually there're two reasons I'm calling. First was to touch base with you about the Judge, and second was to tell you that I spoke to Sis Ryder in dietary about next month's meat order. She's agreed to try allowing your place to handle the whole thing rather than going through the Ultramed purchasing office. Just to see how it all works out. . . . Oh, you're welcome. You deserve the chance. Oh, listen, there is one other thing. Needless to say, the Judge is in no shape to make that meeting this morning. . . . No, I'm afraid there's no way to delay the meeting. The contract calls for the sale to be finalized at noon unless there's a buyback vote by the board. I did speak briefly with him a few minutes ago, and he seemed content just to let each board member vote his conscience on this thing, and let the chips fall where they may. But Whitey, since you'll be running the meeting, there's one big favor you can do for me. I'd really appreciate it if that vote later this morning could be by closed ballot. . . . I know that's not how you usually do it, but don't you think that would be the fairest way? Do this for me, Whitey, and I promise you that dietary contract will be just the beginning. . . . Excellent, excellent. Hey, then, I'll see you at the meeting. And Whitey, thanks."

Frank replaced the receiver in its cradle, sipped his morning coffee, and then drew a careful line through Whitey Bourque's name on the block-printed list of business he had to attend to that morning.

Before becoming administrator of Ultramed-Davis, Frank had never in his life made a list of things to do. Lists were for morning people, for grinds and drudges; for catchers and linebackers, not for quarterbacks. They were for draught horses, needing to know in advance precisely where they would be clopping to and when, not for thoroughbreds.

However, four years of exposure to the efficiency and effectiveness of UltraMA's data banks, plus the pressures of juggling a dozen or more difficult situations at once, had changed him. Now, he began each day with a carefully drawn-up menu.

Frank liked to look on his emergence as a list-maker as one of the more visible manifestations of his adaptability and maturity.

And of all the lists he had ever made, the one for this morning was easily the most exciting.

He scanned the roster of members of the board to assure himself that everything was in order for the meeting. It had taken a hell of an effort, but with the Judge's influence virtually neutralized, he had used the promise of a closed-ballot vote, plus certain other inducements, to capture the additional members he had needed to block the buyback. The votes—six in all—had not come cheaply, but he had done what he had to do.

The sudden turn of events had him giddy. The whole thing was unbelievable—absolutely incredible: Zack teetering on the edge of

oblivion at Davis, waiting only for the smallest nudge; the Judge eliminated from attending the decisive board meeting.

He couldn't have scripted it better if he had tried. With Mainwaring
due back from Georgia any time, everything had fallen into place—
everything, that is, but one minor exception.

After brief thought, Frank took a black magic marker from his
drawer and eliminated *Call Lisette* from his list.

"Fuck her," he muttered.

The woman deserved neither the call nor the apology he had considered making. In fact, if there were to be any apologies, they would
come from her. She would see the truth on her own—come to understand what she had pushed him to do—or she would lose out. The
house, the car, even the children. She would lose out big. He had more
than enough friends in high places to ensure that she paid for her
desertion. This was simply not the day for dealing with a whiny, passive
bitch like Lisette. This was a day of triumph. If she didn't choose to be
available to share it with him, that was her problem.

He took his list and carefully added: *Check with A.D. re: tonight.*

Perfect, he thought. Annette Dolan was the ideal choice to help
celebrate the remarkable turn of events.

He keyed the intercom. Moments later, Annette knocked softly and
slipped into his office. She was wearing a tight plaid skirt and a beige,
short-sleeved angora sweater that seemed to be straining to cover her
breasts.

"G'morning," he said.

"Morning, yourself."

She stood primly beside his desk, her hands folded in front of her
skirt, her arms pulled tightly downward, lifting her breasts together in a
way that made them look even more spectacular.

"I . . . um . . . I have some Xeroxing I need done," Frank managed.

He passed some papers across to her.

"Twenty copies. No, make that thirty. You . . . ah . . . that's a
great sweater."

"Thanks."

"Do you think you might be able to wear it to work tonight? Say at
eight?"

"Oh, Frank, I don't know. My mom's not feeling too well."

"I'm sorry to hear that . . ."

He hesitated, and then reached into his desk and brought out the
diamond necklace he had planned to give Lisette for her birthday.

". . . because I was kind of hoping you'd wear this at the same
time."

Annette's eyes widened.

"Oh, Frankie, it's beautiful," she said. "It's the most beautiful necklace I've ever seen. You're so good to me."

"That's because you're so good to me. About tonight? . . ."

She ran her fingers over the piece.

"How could I say no?"

"I don't know. . . . How could you?"

He pulled her to him and kissed her, sliding his hand over her skirt and then up to her breast.

"Annette, honey, I don't want to wait until tonight. Just a little. Right here. Right now."

"Fra-ank, please," she said. "You've *got* to wait. I have work to do, and all that Xeroxing, and that door isn't locked. And besides, he might hear us."

"Who might hear us?"

"Why, your brother, of course. Didn't I. . . ?" She held her hand to her mouth and looked at him sheepishly. "Oh my. I was about to tell you."

Frank's expression darkened.

"How long has he been out there?"

"Just a few minutes. I'm sorry, Frank."

"Hey, no need to apologize," he said, giving her breast a squeeze. "Just wear that sweater tonight . . . and your necklace. Okay?"

"S-Sure."

"Perfect. Tell my brother I know he's here, and I'll be with him shortly."

"Okay. I'm sorry."

"Actually, now that I think about it, he couldn't have come at a better time."

The receptionist brightened noticeably. "Really?"

"Really," Frank said. "This will be the icing on the cake."

He patted her behind as she turned to leave, and followed it with his eyes as she sashayed from his office. Then he added another item to his list in the same, perfect block print as all the others: *Fire Z.I.*

He paused, studying the notation thoughtfully, and then drew a small happy face next to it.

CHAPTER 30

"DR. IVERSON, Mr. Iverson said to tell you that he knows you're here and will be with you as soon as he can. Are you sure I can't get you something?"

"No, no, thank you."

Zack managed to prevent himself, at the last possible instant, from augmenting his response with a shake of his head. Actually, the tympani that had been rehearsing in his brain had given way to the French horn section, and the tempest in his stomach had been downgraded to mere queasiness. Physically, it appeared, he was on the mend.

With a little assistance from Cheapdog, he had awakened well before the time set on his clock radio by Suzanne. On the coffee table beside him was a glass of water, a packet of Bromo Seltzer, and his old copy of Davenport, held open by his stethoscope and marked with a note from Suzanne which said, simply, *Be strong.*

Now, as he waited for his brother to decide that he had been kept waiting long enough, Zack withdrew the monograph from his briefcase and reread the passage.

Be diligent. Be meticulous. Be honest. Account for every variable. Acknowledge that which you do not know, and then, at the first opportunity, learn it. Believe in yourself.

That is our system.

Honor it, and it will support you like a rock. Honor it, and even the death of a patient will be no failure.

Zack had been especially grateful for those words when he'd arrived at the hospital that morning and been informed by his father's private duty nurse that except for his wife, the Judge was seeing no visitors, and that he had specifically included his sons in that group.

Even Annie Doucette, facing surgery on her hip in twenty-four hours, was less than cordial to him. After being barred by the Judge's nurse, Zack had gone directly to her room, hoping—naively, it turned out—to be the first to tell her of what had happened.

"I am not pleased with you, young man," she had said. "You save an old lady like me, who wants to die, and then let something like this happen to a man like your father. What kind of doctor is that?"

Zack had started to respond, but then had simply shrugged and left. Another time, perhaps.

Nor was the hospital staff any more amiable. Wherever he went, eyes were averted; greetings of any kind were mumbled or withheld altogether. Nurses and other physicians hurried in the opposite direction as he approached.

He had decided to stick things out at Davis, but reestablishing himself was clearly going to be an uphill struggle.

Be strong. . . . Be strong. . . . Be—

"Annette," Frank's voice crackled over the intercom, "would you please ask Dr. Iverson to come on in? And hold all calls—unless they're regarding our father's condition. Thank you."

Zack walked into his brother's office, wishing he were anyplace else.

"Have a seat, Bro," Frank said. "I was wondering when you were going to show up here again. Where've you been?"

"Oh, here and there. Mostly on the floor or on the toilet."

"I know."

Zack looked at him curiously.

"John Burris told me," Frank explained. "Apparently he called to give you a progress report on the Judge. He says you were obviously intoxicated and totally incoherent."

"Aw, he was just being kind."

"Zack, this isn't funny. Burris said something about it to one nurse, and already the whole hospital knows. Once they're lost, reputations around hospitals don't get found again very often. Ask Guy Beaulieu."

"Now who's being funny, Frank?"

"You know what I meant."

"Well, one of the reasons I stopped by was to tell you that I was sorry for causing so much disruption around this place. I see now that I've got to back off a little if I'm going to get by here, even though I've only been doing what I thought was right."

"Have you?"

"Dammit, Frank, you're an excellent administrator, but that doesn't mean you're on top of everything that's going on around here."

"For instance?"

"For instance, that sleazy anesthesiologist, Pearl, and his sidekick, Mainwaring. They're up to something, Frank. They're using something other than what they say they are in the operating room. I swear it."

"That's ridiculous."

"I have proof."

"Do you?"

"Well, not exactly. But I have some data about recovery times that are pretty damn suggestive. And I've learned some things about Mainwaring's past that even you might not be aware of. I'm telling you, there's a connection between that poor Nelms kid's seizures and whatever the two of them have been giving patients in the O.R. Frank, this hospital could be headed for terrible trouble. We've got to find out what's going on."

"No, we don't, Zack-o," Frank said simply.

"What are you talking about?"

"Well, first of all, we're not going to find out because there's nothing to find out. Those two men worked here for two years before you arrived, and there was not so much as a whisper of anything but praise for either of them. How do you explain that?"

"I . . . I can't really. At least not yet. But I'm right, Frank. I just know I am. Mainwaring's got a past that involves testing drugs illegally, and Pearl's hiding something. Couldn't you tell that from the way he behaved last night? He's so frightened of being found out that he was willing to put that kid to sleep with anesthetics he had never used on him in the first place. Something's going on, and dammit, I'm going to find out what."

"No, you're not," Frank said again. "You're not going to find out because you're not going to be stirring up any more trouble around here. And you're not going to be stirring up trouble because you're through . . . finished . . . fired. You're done at this hospital as of right now."

Zack stared at him in disbelief. Frank looked back at him, smiling placidly.

"Frank, that's crazy. I'm a physician on the staff. You can't fire me. Only the medical staff can do that, and then only after due process."

"Oh, really? Here, Doctor. Here are the corporate bylaws. You don't work for the medical staff. It's on page seven. Check it out. You work for Ultramed. And Ultramed can fire anyone they goddamn well please. And I'm Ultramed, and you're fired."

He held his hands out palms up. *"C'est tout, mon frère."*

Be strong. . . . Suzanne's encouragement was growing hollower by the moment.

"Frank, you can't do this."

"I can, and I did. You see, Bro, that's been your big mistake all along—not understanding that this is my hospital and that I can do whatever the hell I want to. I wanted Beaulieu out, and he was out. And now I want you out."

"Frank, you forget that even though you might not have wanted Beaulieu here, you didn't fire him. He was being systematically and deliberately driven out by—"

"By who?"

Zack hesitated, remembering his promise to Maureen Banas. Then he decided that she would simply have to understand. His situation was too desperate.

"It was Ultramed, Frank. He was being driven out by Ultramed. Just look at that letter from Maureen Banas. That's proof you don't know everything that's going on around here. Do you think she wrote that of her own free will? She was coerced, Frank, by that company we work for. By Ultramed."

"Was she?"

"Yes, she received a copy of that letter along with a note that—"

"That said if she told me about receiving it, both she *and* I would be fired?" Frank's gloating leer was at once disgusting and terrifying.

"Jesus," Zack muttered.

"Nice touch, don't you think?"

"Oh, Frank. You are really sad. Why didn't you just fire him like you're trying to do to me?"

"He was an obstreperous sonofabitch, that's why. I didn't want him making a big stink. I was just learning the ropes then, Zack-o, learning how far I could go. I know them now, and they tell me that it's okay to fire you, so . . . you're fired. God, I really love hearing that."

"You're crazy, Frank. Do you know that? You are absolutely nuts."

"Maybe," Frank said. "But I am also employed. Which is more than can be said for you."

"I'm going to fight you."

Frank shrugged.

"Do whatever you want. As far as the company or the medical staff is concerned, you're a drunken, disloyal troublemaker. I doubt that even your little cardiology fluff will stick up for you."

"Frank, Guy Beaulieu died because of what you did to him. *Died!* Doesn't that mean anything to you?"

"You have a good day, now, Zack."

"And don't you even care that it's possible some madmen are poisoning patients in the operating room of this hospital? What are you?"

"I'll be speaking with the folks at Pine Bough Realty. I'm sure they'll be more than happy to give you, oh, two or three days at least to get out of their house."

"Jesus. I'm coming to that board meeting, Frank. I'm coming, and I'm going to tell the board and Ultramed what's going on here. The Judge may be paralyzed, but he saw what Ultramed and its policies did to Annie. He's had time to review Beaulieu's evidence and to convince people how to vote. I'm going to be there to reinforce his position."

"Well, I spoke with him earlier this morning, and he's promised to keep hands off the whole affair."

"Frank, that's a fucking lie. I was just up there. The nurse told me the Judge won't see either of us."

Frank winked.

"Then let's just say that if he *had* spoken with me, that's what he would have promised."

"You crazy bastard, Frank. . . . You crazy, crazy bastard."

"I'll be happy to write you a letter of recommendation, provided the place you apply to is far enough away. Now, if you'll excuse me, I have a hospital to run."

"I'll be seeing you later at the meeting."

"Try it if you want to, Zack-o. The security guards will know exactly how to handle things if you show up there. And now, little brother, how about either you leave or I remind you of how much hurt you ended up with every time we fought behind the barn. I probably would enjoy that almost as much as I've enjoyed firing you. . . . You take care, now. Y'hear?"

Numbly, Zack wandered from his brother's office and through the busy corridors of the hospital.

The polished linoleum, the tile, the nurses bustling from one patient to the next in their starched whites, the framed prints in every room—how clean it all appeared on the surface, how perfect. The set of a movie.

Zack smiled grimly at the thought. Davis Regional had become a gleaming, movie-set hospital—Hollywood veneer with no soul. It was a nightmare. And now, a nightmare he could do no more than walk away from. He drifted into the intensive care unit.

Suzanne, wearing surgical scrubs beneath her lab coat, was in Toby's cubicle, moving about the heavily bandaged child in a way that could only mean trouble. At the foot of the bed, Owen Walsh, the pediatrician, watched, his perpetually cheerful expression darkened by concern.

"Hi," she said, glancing over only momentarily. "Glad you could make it."

She studied the monitor, and then emptied the contents of a syringe into Toby's IV line.

"Problems?" Zack asked.

Having just been fired from the staff, he found himself strangely reluctant to approach the bedside.

"These last sixteen hours have been like a crash refresher course for me in pediatric pharmacology," she said without looking up. "Every time his temp goes up, his rhythm goes crazy. What we're doing here amounts to nothing more than a holding action. I sure wish we knew what was going on."

I do know, he wanted to say. Instead, he forced himself to the head of the bed, where he made a quick check of Toby's pupils, eye grounds, and reflexes. While there was still no definite evidence of irreversible damage, there was certainly no sign of improvement.

"We've got the promise of a bed for him in Boston," Owen Walsh said. "But they can't transfer him until late this afternoon or this evening."

Take him away from this place, away from Jack Pearl, and you take him away from his only chance.

Again, Zack's thought went unspoken.

"Anything I can do in the meantime?" he asked.

"You can review the steroids he's getting." Suzanne checked the temperature reading from the rectal probe. "Back down to one-oh-two. And look, Zack—his rhythm's stable again. Damn, what's going on?"

"If you're able to leave," he said, "I'd like to talk to you for a minute."

Suzanne checked the monitor and Toby's chest, and then glanced over at Walsh.

"Just don't go too far," the pediatrician said.

"We'll be right outside in the waiting room, Owen," she replied. "Besides, you're doing fine here."

Walsh smiled. "She saves this child's life at least five times in one night, and she says *I'm* doing fine."

"Nonsense. I'll be back in a little bit. Hang in there."

As soon as the door to the ICU waiting room clicked shut, Suzanne threw her arms about Zack's chest and buried her head against his shoulder.

"I knew you'd come back," she said. "I'm so damn proud of you— of both of us. Listen, as soon as we get Toby off to Boston, let's go to my place for dinner. Helene's going to take Jen for the night, and I have a batch of shrimp in the fridge and—"

"Suzanne—"

"No, listen, it's my guilt for acting the way I did in the E.R. last night, and only shrimp sauteed in garlic butter will—"

He held her by the shoulders and moved her away.

"Suzanne, Frank just fired me."

"He what?"

"Effective immediately."

"He can't do that."

"Can and did. He even was kind enough to present me with a set of the corporate laws to prove he can."

He held up the book for her to see. Only then did he realize how totally drained she looked. Her face was pale and drawn, her eyes reddened with strain and fatigue.

"This is crazy," she said. "What reason did he give?"

"Actually, according to page seven here, he doesn't need a reason. But just to be fair, he provided a couple: being drunk while on call— technically, I was, you see—being a disruptive influence. Hell, I can't even remember everything he said. Listen, you look really wasted. Why don't you find an empty bed and crash for an hour or two? I'll watch Toby. Frank won't even know I'm in the hospital. And even if he finds out, he won't do anything about it. Owen's too panicked about being left alone to allow that. We'll talk later, after we get the child to Boston."

"No, Zack. I'm fine. Really." she said. "But Zack, we can't let him do this."

"You don't understand. This isn't a hospital the way we were trained to know one. It's a merchandise mart that hires doctors and nurses and technicians. And Frank is the president to that company—at least here in Sterling he is. He hires, and he can fire. Except with someone like Guy Beaulieu. In Guy's case, Frank didn't want the hassle Beaulieu was threatening him with, so he just took the route of destroying the man by rumor and innuendo. He admitted being responsible for all of that."

"To you?"

"He had already fired me. What did he have to be afraid of? He was actually boasting when he told me."

Suzanne sank onto the sofa.

"Oh, Zack," was all she could manage.

"Listen, Suze, this is my problem, and I'll work it out."

"No," she said suddenly.

"What?"

"No, it's not your problem—at least not yours alone. It's all of ours. The medical staff, I mean. We're going to fight this."

"Suzanne, I don't want anyone else getting hurt because—"

"No, listen to me. For years now, at least as long as I've been here, the doctors in this hospital have been acting like . . . like ostriches. This isn't the first time there's been a problem between Frank or Don Norman and staff doctors, Zack. It isn't the first time one of us has clashed with the system here and then suddenly found himself out. Don't you remember what Wil Marshfield said that first night? And I've been as much of an ostrich as anyone—so grateful for getting out of the trouble I was in that I've turned my back on any number of company decisions that might not have been in the best interests of our patients. I didn't feel committed enough to any one issue to make waves. But dammit, I feel committed now."

"Suzanne, I don't want you—"

"Please. You had the guts to come back and face the music. And now, dammit, I'm going to see to it that the medical staff gets behind you. It's time we stood up for this community—time that we stood up for our own. . . ."

She rose and took his hands.

"Zack, hang in here. Please. Do it for all of us. If I can just get us to present a unified front, I'm sure the medical staff can stand up to the corporation. And if we can't get Ultramed to listen, then . . . then we'll just take our case to the community."

"You think you could pull that off?" he asked.

"I'm tougher than I look."

He touched her cheek.

"That's not saying much, you know."

"Well, you just watch. Can you stand the heat?"

"Suzanne, I don't want to leave here. I don't want to leave you."

"Okay, then. It's decided. As soon as I finish with my office appointments, I'm going to start twisting some arms."

"It's not going to be easy."

She kissed him lightly.

"It's not going to be as hard as you think. Listen, I ought to get back in there. What are you going to do right now?"

"I think I'm going to try and get in to see my father. He refused to see me earlier, but I think it's worth one more try. I was planning on putting in an appearance at that board meeting later today, but Frank has promised to have the hospital security people ready for me if I do."

"Damn him. Zack, I think your brother and I are about due for a little meeting of the minds."

"You would do that?"

"Would and will. I have too many friends around here, and make too much money for this place for him not to listen to me. You must be strong. . . . God, Zachary, it feels so good to realize that all of a sudden I'm not afraid anymore."

"You were afraid of the corporation?"

"No," she said, kissing him once again. "Of you."

CHAPTER 31

Brief operative note (full note dictated): . . . Four-inch gash over T-10, 11, and 12 debrided . . . hemostasis attained . . . wound explored. . . . Jagged five centimeter by three centimeter piece of rusty metal removed without difficulty . . . dura appears intact. . . . No collection of blood noted. . . . Wound irrigated copiously, and then closed with drain in place. . . . Patient sent to recovery room in stable condition, still unable to move either lower extremity. . . . Tetanus and antibiotic prophylaxis initiated. . . . Preoperative impression: foreign body, low midback; postoperative impression: same, plus paraplegia—etiology uncertain, possibly secondary to spinal cord disruption or circulatory embarrassment. . . .

Seated to one side of the nurses' station, Zack read and reread the account of his father's surgery, and confirmed through John Burris's terse progress note and two much more detailed nurse's notes, that there had been little change in the Judge's condition since his surgery.

Dura intact . . . No collection of blood . . .

Zack chewed on the nub of his pen as he stared out the window at the Presidential Range. Something was off. The Judge's symptoms seemed out of proportion to the extent of his injury—way out of proportion. The pieces of this clinical puzzle simply weren't locking together.

Sheering forces snapping fibers in the cord, arterial spasm with enough interruption of blood supply to cause nerve damage—there were a number of logical explanations for the Judge's paraplegia, but none of them sat just right.

At one end of the Formica counter, a small plastic tray was piled high with pens and pencils, as well as a stethoscope and several other pieces of medical equipment. Zack slipped an ophthalmoscope, reflex hammer, and straight pin into his pocket and headed for his father's room.

It wasn't that he was questioning Burris's findings and opinion, he rationalized, it was just that . . . that a physician was taught never to completely trust anyone's findings or conclusions other than his own.

Now, if he could only get the Judge to allow him close enough to do an exam . . .

Cinnie Iverson was seated on a low, hard-backed chair in the hallway outside of her husband's room. She was, as always, dressed immaculately—this day in a plain blue dress, with a white cardigan draped over her shoulders. Lipstick and an ample amount of rouge failed to completely obscure her pallor. Her ever-present lace handkerchief was balled in one fist.

"Hello, Mom," Zack said as he approached.

She stood, and allowed him to kiss her on the cheek. Her expression was cool, but not angry, which was to say, as disapproving as Zack had ever known it to be.

"How's he doing?" he asked.

"The nurse is giving him a bed bath."

"Any change?"

Cinnie Iverson bit at her lower lip and shook her head.

"Mom, I . . . I'm sorry this has happened. You can't know how terrible I feel."

"I'm sure you do," she said quietly. "We all do. . . ." She hesitated, then went on.

"Zachary, I'm quite sure that in time I'll see things more charitably, but right now, with the Judge lying in there like that, you'll have to forgive me if—"

"I understand," he said. "All I want you to know is the same thing I came up here to tell him, and that is that I was only trying to do what I thought was right."

"I believe that. I don't think he'll speak with you, though," she added. "He's very upset—at everybody. And he's very depressed."

"He doesn't have to speak, Mom. He just has to listen. Who sent the flowers?"

He motioned toward an enormous vase of lilies, orchids, and birds of paradise that he estimated must have cost one hundred fifty dollars —probably even more.

"It just arrived from Frank," she said. "Whether you know it or not, you owe your brother quite a thank-you. He was very helpful in keeping us all under control last night. Very helpful."

"I'll . . . I'll thank him just as soon as I can, Mom."

"I just don't know what we would have done without him." She dabbed her handkerchief at the corner of one eye.

"I understand," Zack said, fighting off a wave of rage.

"I only wish Lisette were around. At least then I'd know he was getting a decent meal once in a while."

"He told you about Lisette?"

"He told me she and the girls are in Virginia visiting an old friend of hers, if that's what you mean."

"Sure, Mom," Zack said through nearly clenched teeth. "That's what I meant."

At that moment, the private duty nurse, an expansive woman with pendulous upper arms and thick ankles, wheeled her cart from the room.

"He's all set, dear," she said. "Sorry to take so long, but that husband of yours is a big man. . . ." She eyed Zack warily. "Still no visitors, Doctor," she said. "I'm sorry."

"Mom, I need to go in to talk to the Judge."

Cinnie took a moment to size up the exchange.

"It's okay, Mrs. Caulkins," she said. "I'll take care of things here. You go do whatever it is you have to." She waited until the woman had gone. "Zachary, I'll ask your father if your visit would be okay, but I don't expect him to say yes."

"Mom, it's important—very important that I speak with him."

She hesitated.

"Mom, please . . ."

"You won't say anything to upset him?"

"Promise."

"Well, then, I suppose you should be allowed to go in there and say your piece."

"Mom, thank you."

"And Zachary?" She continued to work her handkerchief over and over in her hands. "I know you didn't mean things to turn out this way."

"That's right, Mom," he said, knowing that she would miss the understatement—the sad irony in his voice. "I certainly didn't."

Muted sunlight, filtering through the nearly closed blinds, provided the only illumination in the room. The Judge, wearing a blue hospital johnny, lay on his back, staring at the ceiling. An intravenous line was draining into one arm.

"Hello, Judge," Zack said.

Clayton Iverson glanced over at him, and then looked away.

"Are you in much pain?"

There was no response.

"Judge, it won't hurt to talk to me. Believe me, it won't. . . . Okay, okay, suit yourself."

It might have been a mistake to have come. Zack could see that now. Merely going against the man's wishes was enough to warrant the silent treatment, let alone going against his wishes and achieving such disastrous results. He reminded himself that the Judge could be as petulant and inflexible as Frank.

Zack turned to go, but then he stopped. There were things he had to get out—if not for his father, then for himself.

"Okay, Judge, you don't have to say a word. I won't stay long. I just wanted to tell you that I feel very badly for the way things have turned out. I was only doing what I spent so many years training to do—using my judgment, and trying to do my best."

He pulled a chair over as he spoke, and sat down by his father's hand. The Judge continued to stare at the ceiling.

"Judgment, Dad . . . that's what you have to rely on, too, now that I think about it. Maybe in time, that will help you understand the dilemma I was in. . . .

"Judge, you're my father. I love you for that—for the things you've done for me, for the kind of person you've helped me become. I would never want to see you hurt. Never. I honestly believe that I would give up my life, if necessary, to protect you. But that's *my* life. . . .

"Anyhow, I guess what I really want you to know is that although I'm sorry as hell for the way everything turned out, given the information I had to work with last night, if the same situation arose again, I would make the same choices. That's the sort of person my parents raised me to be, and the sort of surgeon I was trained to be. I came up here to ask for understanding, not absolution."

He paused, hoping for some sort of reply. There was none. In that

735

moment, he decided to say nothing of what had transpired with Frank. Soon, the Judge would learn it all anyhow, but this was not the time to attack the man's myth of his quarterback son.

"Well, then," he said. "I guess that's that." He rose. "Oh, except for one other thing. I'm going to that meeting today to present Guy's case to the board. I don't expect to sway many votes, but I think Guy was right. I think we need to take a hard look at what we're willing to give up in exchange for a few shiny pieces of equipment and some black ink on the bottom line. So if you could just talk to me enough to tell me where that folder of his is, I'll—"

"It's gone," Clayton Iverson said flatly, still not looking at his son.

"What!"

"I said the folder is gone. I . . . I gave it to the Ultramed people to examine. They have it. Now please, go."

Zack sighed.

"You certainly underwent one heck of a change of heart there, Dad," he said.

"I asked you to leave."

"I'm going. I'm going."

As he turned, Zack's hand brushed against the instruments in his pocket. He hesitated, took several steps toward the door, and then turned back.

"Judge, I know you want me out of here," he said, "but . . . but I'd like to examine a couple of things on you if I could before I go."

Tentatively, he returned to the bedside, waiting for the man's outburst. There was none. He lifted the sheet off his father's legs.

"Thank you, Dad," he whispered, gauging the muscle tone of one calf with his fingertips. "Thank you for trusting me this much. This will only take a minute."

In fact, Zack's examination, carried out mostly with his touch and reflex hammer, took just over five minutes. Clayton Iverson watched him work in stony silence, although there was a spark of curiosity in his eyes.

By the time Zack had finished, by the time he had dropped down on a corner of the bed, shaken and mentally drained, the loose-fitting pieces of the clinical puzzle had been pulled apart and rearranged in the strangest of patterns.

"Mom, can you come in here, please?" he called out, after he had regained some composure. "There's something I want both of you to hear together."

Cinnie Iverson entered, took the chair next to the Judge, and held his hand.

Zack paced from one side of the room to the other, choosing each word carefully, suddenly frightened that the tendon and muscle activity he had detected were not true neurologic indicators at all, but rather the phantoms of his own hopes.

"Judge, Mom," he began, "have either of you ever heard of a conversion reaction?"

Cinnie Iverson shook her head. Clayton did not move.

"An older term for it was conversion hysteria, but I never liked that phrase, because hysteria implies craziness, and a conversion reaction is much more an intense, involuntary focusing of emotional energy than it is a sign of anything crazy."

"Zachary, what are you saying?" Cinnie asked.

"I'm saying that there are certain reflexes that disappear when the spinal cord is damaged, and others that show up. The pattern I'm finding now isn't consistent with that."

"I'm not sure I understand," Cinnie said.

"Judge, I know this may not make total sense to you at the moment, but I'm picking up signs—fairly strong signs—that your paralysis may be due to factors other than spinal cord damage—emotional factors."

"Emotional factors?"

Cinnie sounded incredulous. The Judge showed no reaction at all.

"I know it sounds far out," Zack said, "but believe me, it isn't. It happens all the time. One of my first cases on my neurology service was a man with psychologically induced blindness. There was absolutely nothing wrong with his eyes, yet he positively couldn't see. In fact, after hypnotherapy, much of his vision returned.

"Heart attacks in Type A personalities, gastric ulcers in situations of high stress—our emotions have power over every organ in our bodies. There's even a well-documented condition called pseudocyesis in which a woman who desperately wants to become pregnant has her periods stop, her breasts grow large, and her abdomen swell. Only a blood test or an ultrasound or X ray can prove she's not pregnant."

"And you think your father may be having one of these—what are they called?"

"Conversion reactions. Yes, Mom, I do. Judge, your neurologic findings simply don't jibe well with any other explanation."

The Judge looked away.

"But why?" Cinnie asked.

Zack shrugged.

"I'm not certain," he said. "Anger at me is the most likely possibility. There are other factors that could be at work, too, I guess: fear, grief, guilt. Only you can fill in the blanks, Judge. But whatever it is, is very powerful stuff. At the moment, even you might not know. Many times, though, as soon as the source of the conversion is identified, the symptoms begin to resolve."

"Are you sure about this?" Cinnie asked.

"No, Mom, I'm not. It's just that the other diagnoses don't fit with the operative findings and Dad's clinical picture, and conversion reaction does. I might be wrong. All I can do is hope that I'm not, and tell you what I think."

"Clayton?" she asked.

The Judge, tight-lipped, would not answer.

"Zachary," she said, "perhaps you'd better go now. We can talk about this again soon." She rose and kissed him on the cheek, her expression begging him to leave them be—to allow them the chance to digest what he had said.

"Sure enough," he said. "When is the ambulance due?"

"Any time now, I think."

"Fine . . . Dad, I—" He looked down at his father's pallid, emotionless face. "I'll be thinking of you."

As he reached the doorway, Zack checked the corridor for his brother or a security guard, and then headed for a room at the far end of the hall. If, as it seemed, he was running out of time within the walls of Ultramed-Davis, he would use what little he had left to make one last run at a clinical puzzle that was no less perplexing than his father's, and far more lethal.

"I knew it," Barbara Nelms said as Zack finished recounting his interview with her son and the theories he had developed as a result. "You are not a very good liar, Dr. Iverson. I could see it in your eyes that night in your office. I should have called you on it then, dammit. You know, holding out on me like that was a very cruel thing to do."

"I know, and I'm sorry. But I had no proof."

"Dr. Iverson, Toby is my son."

"I understand."

Barbara was propped up in her hospital bed by several pillows. Her right arm was in a sling and her left was fixed to an intravenous line that was infusing a potent antibiotic. Despite her pallor and the heavy shadows engulfing her eyes, her glare was piercing.

"I'm not sure that you do, Dr. Iverson," she said after some thought. "But I'm willing to give you the benefit of the doubt—at least for now."

"Thank you."

"You said that you held back information from me and my husband because you had no proof of your theories. Am I to assume that situation has changed?"

Zack hesitated.

"Dr. Iverson, please," she said. "Don't try to lie to me again. My son nearly stabbed me to death yesterday without even knowing I was there."

"Okay," he said. "Okay. The truth is, as things stand, I have no direct proof of anything. But the circumstantial evidence supporting my belief is quite strong—at least to me it is."

"Tell me."

Zack reviewed his impressions of Pearl and Mainwaring's gallbladder cases, and summarized his conversation with Tarberry at Johns Hopkins. He could see the anger smoldering in Barbara Nelms's eyes. In time, whether Toby survived or not, she would be out for blood. And where once that notion had been the impetus to have him lie to her, now it goaded him to share every detail. Frank had been given his chance to clean house, but he had ignored it.

"I wouldn't blame you a bit for being skeptical," Zack said as he concluded his account, "but that's the way I see it."

"Dr. Iverson," Barbara Nelms responded, her fury barely contained, "this is the first time since this nightmare began that an explanation has fit with the facts as I know them. I believe every word you've told me. Every word."

She turned and stared out the window. Resting on the rim of her sling, her fist was clenched. Slowly, her fingers relaxed. The tension in her neck and back lessened. When she turned back to Zack, the anger had given way to determination.

"Now then, Dr. Iverson," she said, "what can we do to save my son?"

Zack took a moment to sort his thoughts.

"Well, first of all," he said finally, "it would help tremendously if we could find the trigger."

"You mean the thing that sets Toby off?"

"Exactly."

"But how?"

"I want you to close your eyes, lean back, listen to my voice, and begin to tell me everything you can think of surrounding Toby's attacks. Everything, no matter how trivial it may sound."

"Are you going to hypnotize me?"

"I can. And I will, if it seems appropriate. But I believe all you'll need is a little help. Now, relax as much as you can, open your mind, and let it drift back to Toby's very first episode."

"He . . . he was in his pajamas. . . ."

"Good. Go on."

"It was before bed. . . . He was playing. . . ."

"Playing what?"

"I . . . I can't remember."

"Was he in his room?"

"Yes . . . No, no, wait. He ended up in his room, but I don't think he started there. He . . . he was in the den. He was watching television. Yes, that's right. That's exactly right."

"Good. Very good. Now, what was he watching?"

"The show?"

"Yes."

"I . . . I can't remember."

"Just relax, Barbara. You're doing fine. . . . Now, just open your mind to that evening and think about what he might have been watching. . . . See it. . . . Just relax, open your mind, and see it. . . ."

The muscles in Barbara Nelms's face went slack. Her breathing became deeper and more regular.

"That's good," Zack whispered. "That's very good."

Zack's words brought a strange, enigmatic smile to Barbara's mouth.

"I know what he was watching," she said. "Each time, I know what he was watching. . . ."

Λ CHAPTER 32

ZACK RACED down the corridor at nearly a full run, hesitating only to glance into his father's room. The bed was stripped, and an aide was washing down the plastic mattress cover. He bolted through the stairway door and vaulted down to the first floor.

A major piece in the puzzle had fallen into place—a piece that irrefutably connected Toby Nelms, Suzanne, and Jason Mainwaring. Now, Frank would have to listen.

"My brother in?" he panted to the buxom, blond receptionist.

Annette Dolan looked at him strangely.

"He is, but—"

"Thank you," Zack said, already on his way through Frank's office door.

Frank, behind his desk, working at his computer, looked up coolly.

"You don't work here anymore," he said.

"Frank, I've got to talk to you. I've learned something—something important."

"Mr. Iverson, I'm sorry. I tried to stop him," Annette Dolan said from the doorway.

Frank smiled at her emotionlessly.

"That's okay, Annette," he said. "I know how persistent my little brother can be. I'm sure you did your best to stop him. Before you get back to work, though, why don't you go on home and change that sweater. It's not appropriate for the office."

The receptionist hesitated a beat, her lower lip quivering. Then she turned and hurried away.

"Now, then," Frank said, glancing at his watch, "what on earth could be important enough to take you away from your packing?"

Zack moved to sit down, but Frank stopped him with a raised hand.

"Don't get comfortable, sport," he said. "Just say what you want to say and leave." He motioned to the computer. "Number six now, Zack-o. Six out of nearly two hundred administrators nationwide. Not bad, if I do say so myself. No, siree, not bad at all."

"Well, then you'd better listen to me, Frank. Because I've learned something that could bring this place crashing down about your ears if you don't do something about it."

There was no more than a flicker of interest. "Oh?"

"It's that anesthetic, Frank. The one I tried to tell you about before."

"Go on."

"I just came from speaking with Mrs. Nelms, the mother of the boy in ICU."

"I know who she is," Frank said.

"Well, I was going over some of my concerns with her, and—"

"You what?"

"Frank, just calm down and listen."

"No, *you* listen. Do you have any idea how much of a nuisance that woman will be if you fill her with all that human experimentation bullshit of yours?"

"Frank, it's not bullshit. It's really happening, and you'd better help me do something about it or this place will be crawling with lawyers, hospital-certification people, and police. I promise you."

"Don't you dare threaten me."

"Well, then, will you please listen, for Chrissake? Suzanne's life may be on the line here, to say nothing of that poor kid in the ICU. We don't have much time."

Frank toyed with a paper clip for a few moments, straightened it, and then snapped it in two.

"Okay, Bro," he said finally. "You've got five minutes."

"They're experimenting with something, Frank—Mainwaring and Pearl. They're fooling around with some sort of new general anesthetic, and they think it's working fine, only it isn't. The patients look asleep during their surgery and even think they *were* asleep afterward. But at some level, just below their conscious surface, they were wide awake, experiencing the whole thing—the cutting, the blood, the pain, everything."

"Sport, I didn't believe you this morning, and I don't believe you now."

"Well, you'd better. I have proof."

"Oh?"

"It's the music, Frank. 'Greensleeves'—the music Mainwaring operates to."

"What in the hell are you—"

"Mainwaring nearly always works to one piece of music. It's a classical version of 'Greensleeves'—you know, the folk song from—"

"I know the tune," Frank said testily.

"Well, according to Mrs. Nelms, every time her kid had one of his seizures, he was watching a children's show where they play that melody."

"That's your proof?"

"There's more. Last week Suzanne and I were together, when suddenly she went blank, totally blank."

"So?"

"Frank, that tune was playing on the radio. As soon as I shut it off, she snapped out of whatever place she was in, and kept on talking as if nothing had ever happened. I didn't put together what was going on until just now. She was on her way, Frank. I'm sure now that if I had left the radio on a little longer, she would have had a seizure just like the kid's. She was on her way to reliving her breast operation—probably in some bizarre, distorted way—just the way Toby kept reexperiencing his hernia repair."

"This is ridiculous."

"It's fact, Frank. Listen, you've got to help me find Mainwaring, or at least help me try and reason with Pearl."

"No way."

"That child is dying. We need to know what they gave him."

Frank picked up the phone and dialed.

"Chief Clifford, Frank Iverson here," he said. "That restraining order I asked you for ready yet?"

"Jesus, Frank, you *are* crazy," Zack said.

"That's fine, Chief, fine. So it's effective immediately?"

"I'm going to tell the board what's going on here, Frank—the board *and* Ultramed. And as soon as I find Mainwaring, I'm going to—"

"Chief, could you do me a big favor and send a couple of men around now? He's here, and he's refusing to leave. . . ."

"Dammit, Frank."

"Thanks, Cliff. . . . Oh, he's doing as well as could be expected. It's nice of you to ask. John Burris, the neurosurgeon from Concord, has transferred him down there. . . ."

"Frank, for Chrissake—"

"Hopefully, we'll be getting a new neurosurgeon in town soon, so that we won't have to send folks out who need our help. . . . Exactly. Well, thanks again, Cliff. When can I expect those men of yours? . . .

Excellent. You run a crack operation, Cliff. The best. . . . You bet. Take care now."

Frank laid down the receiver with exaggerated deliberateness.

"You've got about three minutes to get your ass out of my hospital," he said, "and less than a day to get it out of our house. I'd suggest you get home and start packing. And I promise you, if you so much as set foot in this place, or say one word to any of our patients, you will be in deep, deep shit. Is that clear?"

"Frank, you're making a big mis—"

"I said, is that clear?"

Without responding, Zack headed toward the door. When he opened it, a hospital security guard—if anything, even larger than the guard, Henry—was standing there.

"It's a little button right down here," Frank explained, gesturing to the base of his desk. "I never had to use it until now, but it just paid for itself. Tommy, would you please see to it that Dr. Iverson here is out of the hospital and off hospital property right away."

"Yessir."

"No stops."

"Yessir."

"It's not going to work, Frank," Zack said.

"I'll take my chances."

"What about that kid?"

"That kid will be better off having a doctor who doesn't get drunk when he's on call, sport. Now, I see by the ol' clock on the mantel that your five minutes are about up." He looked out the window. "Oh, and there are our friends from the constabulary, right on time."

"You are something, Frank. You really are."

Frank smiled broadly.

"Yes," he said, "I know."

"Greensleeves."

Curious, Frank fished through his desk drawer for the cassette Mainwaring had given him and popped it into his tapedeck. It was syrupy, spineless music—certainly far from being any sort of lethal weapon. Clearly, Zack had flipped over the edge, grasping at any straw in an effort to disrupt his brother's finest hour.

"No way, Zack-o," Frank murmured. "No fucking way."

He snapped off the tape and then watched through his office window as his brother was led across the hospital parking lot to his car by two policemen and the hospital guard. It was a scene he would carry with him forever. The days of sports trophies and star-struck coeds might be part of the past, but this triumph would do quite nicely.

As he followed Zack's battered orange camper down the hill toward town, Frank knew that the last obstacle toward his achieving every one

743

of his goals was all but disappearing. With the Judge out of the way, and Bourque having agreed to a closed vote, the final purchase of the hospital by Ultramed was a virtual lock. And with Zack out of the way, there was nothing to interfere with the satisfactory conclusion of his dealings with Mainwaring.

He felt at once exhilarated and exhausted. It had been a brutal game, but with time running out, he had just run in for the go-ahead touchdown and then recovered the fumble on the ensuing kickoff. Now, he had only to hang on to the ball and run out the clock. He glanced at his watch. The board meeting was less than an hour away. He reminded himself that no matter how exhausted he felt, this was not the time to let down.

"Loose ends . . ." he murmured. "Loose ends . . . loose ends . . ."

He called the guard room and ordered an extra man brought in to patrol the outside of the hospital, on the off chance his brother tried anything foolish. Then he phoned two fence-sitting board members to tell them about the closed-ballot vote and to call in favors he was owed. Finally, he called Atlanta and learned that Jason Mainwaring had left for New England the previous evening and was expected back in Atlanta the next day. Perfect, he thought. If the secretary's information was correct, Mainwaring had to be planning to conclude their transaction that afternoon.

Again, Frank checked the time. For the moment, there was nothing he could think of to do but wait. He returned his attention to the still-open hookup with UltraMA. Soon, perhaps within a day, his access code would be upgraded to that of a regional director and he would be made a party to some of Ultramed's most sensitive information.

Regional director, with a cool three quarters of a million dollars in the bank. Frank Iverson was within a cat's whisker of making it all the way back and then some. When she walked out on him, Lisette had made the biggest fucking mistake of her life. By the time the dust settled, he would have it all—the position, the money, the house and, goddamn it, the children, too. She'd see. He had handled the board, he had handled his brother, and he would handle her just as well.

Only when the knock on his office door grew persistent did Frank notice it.

"Who is it, Annette?" he asked through his intercom. "Annette?"

There was no answer. Then he remembered having sent the woman home, and cursed himself for forgetting that his other secretary was on vacation.

"Come in," he called out. "For crying out loud, stop that pounding and come in."

Jason Mainwaring, wearing his customary beige plantation owner's suit, entered, carrying his briefcase.

"Little shy on office help, aren't we?" he said, heading directly for Frank's liquor supply.

"You know me, Jason. Slice off the excess fat. Everything goes down to the bare bone."

Mainwaring ran his fingertips over the glistening mahogany surface of Frank's desk.

"Yes," he drawled. "I can see that philosophy at work all around me."

"I called Atlanta a while ago. Your secretary said she expected you back there tomorrow. You're welcome to use your house for a few more days if you want."

"Thanks all the same, but I've been here about two years too long already. My replacement lined up?"

"Ready to cut. He's due here next Wednesday."

Frank felt determined to keep his eagerness in check. He knew that Mainwaring wanted Serenyl at least as much as he wanted Mainwaring's million. If this was their last skirmish, he was damned if he was going to let the man leave with the upper hand. He crossed to his bookcase and poured himself a glass of tonic. Then he deliberately set aside Mainwaring's "Greensleeves" tape, which he'd been listening to, and snapped on a Mantovani in its place.

The surgeon flinched.

"Iverson," he said, "are you tryin' to bait me?"

"Hardly, Jason. I just thought that since this might be our last meeting together, I might see if I could change your opinion about Mantovani. This album's called *Roman Holiday*. What do you think?"

"I think we should get this business of ours over with. That's what I think." Irritably, the surgeon rose and shut off the tape.

Frank unlocked a drawer of his desk and withdrew a thick envelope.

"Here it is, Jason," he said. "Signed, sealed, and ready to be delivered."

"Just as we had it drawn up?"

"You were there."

"Well, then . . ." Mainwaring set his briefcase on his lap and opened it. "Our chemists have approved Dr. Pearl's work, and my company has authorized payment to you of the sum we agreed upon."

"That being?"

"That being the sum we agreed upon. Iverson, don't play games with me, or I swear, I'll be out that door."

"In that case, Jason, you'll be out two years of your life as well."

Frank was feeling glorious. It was the sort of scene he had watched his father play any number of times over the years. Now, there was a new Iverson pulling the strings—a new Iverson at the top of the heap.

Mainwaring hesitated, then flipped an envelope onto the desk.

"Barclay's Bank, Georgetown, Grand Cayman Islands," he said, somewhat wearily. "They won't release the money to you until they hear from me. But if you have doubts about the account numbers, feel free to call them."

"That won't be necessary, Jason. I trust you. Besides, I've arranged for my man at the Cayman National Bank to transfer the funds to accounts there as soon as he hears from me. So, if you'll just check over those papers, we can each make a call."

"You are quite the most distasteful man I have ever had dealings with, Iverson."

"Thank you," Frank said. "From you, I'll take that as a compliment. Now, if you'll be so kind."

He slid the phone across to the surgeon, then sat back as calmly as he could manage and waited. When the calls were completed, he dropped Mainwaring's envelope in his drawer and watched as the surgeon tucked the bill of sale and the patent rights to Serenyl into his briefcase. A million dollars, Frank was thinking. Just like that—a million dollars.

"I hope this means we're about to see the last of one another," Mainwaring said.

"We'll miss you, Jason," Frank replied with a straight face. "We surely will."

The surgeon stood and gave Frank's proffered hand an ichthyic shake. Then he whirled and was gone.

Frank walked to his bathroom, washed his face, and studied himself in the mirror.

"Funny," he said, straightening his tie and then winking at his reflection, "you don't look like a millionaire."

Judge, you're my father. I love you for that—for the things you've done for me. . . . I would give up my life, if necessary, to protect you. . . .

Lying on his stretcher, Judge Clayton Iverson watched the foliage flash past through the rear windows of the ambulance as he reflected on his son's words. They had passed through Conway five or ten minutes before, he guessed, so almost certainly they had split off from Route 16 and were heading southwest on 25, toward Moultonborough and the northern rim of Lake Winnipesaukee. Beside him, the paramedic, a woman with Orphan Annie hair and an eager, child's face, was carrying on a running conversation with the driver, pausing occasionally to check his pulse and blood pressure.

It was all so painful, the Judge acknowledged; so confusing. One moment, he was on top of the world, the next he was speeding through town to confront his older son with the facts of his dishonesty and embezzlement, and with the reality that, once again, the man had been given every opportunity and had failed. And even more distressing, Frank's perfidy had, in effect, ripped control of the Ultramed-Davis situation from the community board and handed it to Leigh Baron on a plate.

. . . Paralysis may be due to factors other than spinal cord damage. . . . Guilt, fear, grief. Only you can fill in the blanks, Judge. . . .

There was no cause for guilt, the Judge reasoned desperately. Beau Robillard hadn't done one thing of value his entire life. Clayton Iverson had been elected Sterling Man of the Year six times. Six! Besides, if blame were to be placed, it should go to Frank, not to him. If it weren't for Frank, there would have been no accident. If it weren't for Frank, there would have been no drinking, no lapse in concentration, no missed red light.

. . . Given the information I had to work with last night, if the same situation arose again, I would make the same choices. . . .

If it weren't for Frank, Zachary would never have been put in the position of having to make such a terrible decision. At least Zachary had had the guts to face him—to face him and to hold his ground. *Why hadn't he appreciated his younger son more before?* Explanations, but no excuses. That was the way of a real man. Frank always had excuses.

Now, because of Frank, Ultramed would have control of Davis forever, and with that control, a stranglehold on Sterling that even Clayton Iverson would be unable to break.

There was no sense lingering over the spilled milk that was Beau Robillard. That milk was soured to begin with. But the hospital was a different story. John Burris had told him that trying to attend the board meeting was out of the question, and in truth, he had wanted to get as far away from both of his sons as possible. But now . . .

If only he weren't so damned helpless. If only he could move. . . .

"Judge Iverson," the paramedic said.

"Yes, what is it?"

"Sir, you just crossed your legs."

"What?"

Clayton Iverson looked down at his feet. They were, in fact, crossed —his left ankle resting on his right. Gingerly, he lifted the upper leg and set it down on the stretcher. Then he lifted the other. His pulse began to pound.

"What time is it?" he demanded.

"Eleven, sir."

"Where are we?"

"Just outside of Moultonborough."

"Tell the driver to turn around."

"Excuse me?"

"Turn around, dammit. Turn around. I've got to get back to the hospital."

"Sir, we can't—"

"Do you know who I am? . . . Well then, I said turn around. I don't have time to argue. I'm paying for this ambulance, and I swear, if you don't do as I say, there will be hell to pay for both of you!"

"But—"

"Now!"

"Y-Yessir."

The woman knelt beside the driver, and after a brief exchange, the ambulance swung into a driveway and turned around.

"Use your lights and siren, and step on it," the Judge said.

"But sir, we're not allowed to—"

"The siren, dammit! I assure you nothing bad will happen if you do, but everything bad will happen if you don't. Quickly now, let's move."

The driver hesitated, and then switched on the lights and siren and accelerated.

Behind him, Judge Clayton Iverson crossed and uncrossed his legs again.

"Well, I'll be damned," he muttered. "I'll be goddamned."

CHAPTER 33

SHORTLY AFTER she had seen the first several office patients of the morning, Suzanne sent word to her nurse to try and reschedule as many of the rest as possible. It was, perhaps, the most killing aspect of private practice that a day's patients had no way to adjust to their physician having been awake most or all of the previous night. And, indeed, it was doubtful most of them would even want to try. They had waited days or even weeks for their appointments, and they expected—and deserved, as far as Suzanne was concerned—to have their physician be one hundred percent theirs for the short time they had together.

Normally, even after a grueling night she could rev herself up for her office work. This morning, though, try as she might, she simply could not hold her concentration together. A seventy-five-year-old lady who was taking double the amount of digitalis prescribed, had nearly slipped past her. A housewife had gotten cross with her for not seeming to take her complaints of fatigue more seriously. A pharmacy called because she had neglected to write the strength of a cardiac medicine on one of her prescriptions.

And, she knew, her difficulty was not simply one of fatigue. A child she felt responsible for and a man she was growing to love were both in serious trouble. Her thoughts kept ricocheting from one to the other. Twice, already, she had called the unit to check on Toby's status, despite knowing that she would be contacted by Owen Walsh or the nurses at the first sign of trouble. Twice, already, she had interrupted the workday of medical staff members to gauge their response to some sort of job action should Frank refuse to back down on his dismissal of Zack.

And overriding even her concern for Zack and Toby Nelms was her growing indignation at the treatment Guy Beaulieu had apparently received from Frank, and the mounting likelihood that unauthorized chemical experimentation was being conducted at the hospital. For more than two years, gratitude for her salvation from Paul and her legal entanglements had kept her from voicing any criticism of Frank's decisions or Ultramed policies. Now it was time to take a stand.

She buzzed her nurse.

"Janice, how are we doing with those reschedulings?"

"You're clear for the next hour, Dr. Cole," the woman said. "I haven't been able to reach Mr. Braddock or that new referral from Hanover, but I'll keep trying."

"Excellent. Listen, I'll be in the unit or on page if you need me. There are a few things I've got to get done."

She left her office and took the glass-enclosed walkway from the Physicians and Surgeons Building to the main hospital. On her way to the ICU, she passed the Carter Conference Room. Two dietary aides were busily arranging the tables for a luncheon meeting—almost certainly, she realized, the meeting of the community board and the people from Ultramed. There could be no better time to confront Frank with her concerns than right now. He would listen, and make some major concessions, or face the embarrassment and conflict of having her present those misgivings to the meeting.

Frank's outer office door was closed. Suzanne opened it and stepped into the deserted reception area.

"Hello? Frank?" she called as she tapped on the inner door. "It's Suzanne Cole. . . . Frank?"

"It's open, Suzanne." She was startled to hear his voice through the intercom on one of the desks behind her. "Come in." She opened the door and he rose from behind his desk.

"Well, now," he said, shaking her hand. "This is a pleasant surprise."

"Thanks, Frank. I'm sorry to barge in on you like this, but I need to talk with you."

He glanced at the Lucite clock.

"That would be fine, Suzanne, but this just isn't the time. You see, I have a b—"

"I know what you have, Frank," she said, taking a seat in one of the pair of oak-armed chairs facing his desk. "You have a meeting with the community board and the people from Ultramed. Before you go into that meeting, I think you should hear what I have to say."

"Oh, you do."

His buoyant expression chilled, perhaps, a degree.

"Yes. But first, I wanted to find out why you fired Zachary."

"Because I always do what is in the best interests of my hospital, and getting rid of a disruptive, drunken troublemaker was clearly in the best interests of my hospital. Speaking of which, would you like a drink?"

"Frank, listen to me, please. Two years ago you helped me out of a huge jam. I'm grateful for what you did, and ever since I've been here, I've done my best to support you."

"And I appreciate it, Suze. You've been great. Tell you what: as soon as this board business is taken care of, let's you and I do dinner on Ultramed and talk about some sort of increase in your pay."

Suzanne felt her irritability quicken.

"Don't patronize me, Frank. I came here to get some issues straight —to voice some concerns Zack has shared with me. And Frank, if you can't respond to those concerns, I intend to go in and raise them at that meeting."

I'm afraid I can't let you do that, Frank was thinking, rapidly sorting through his options. The votes to finalize the sale were almost certainly there now, but they were shaky. And of even greater concern were the clauses Mainwaring's corporate lawyers had forced into their contract, requiring legal reprisals or an immediate return of their investment should there be any deception—or even suggestion of deception—regarding the properties of Serenyl. *No, siree, baby,* he concluded, *I'm afraid I can't let you do that at all.*

He propped his elbows on the desk and his chin on his hands.

"Okay, shoot," he said.

"That's better. Well, I have two requests I would like your word on, Frank."

"Go on."

"First of all, I want your promise to allow the medical staff to determine whether or not Zack has been disruptive enough to be fired from the hospital."

"Done," he said.

"What?"

"You have my word. As soon as possible, next Wednesday's meeting if you want, we'll present our cases to the medical staff and let them decide. Satisfied?"

"I . . . I guess so."

"Good. Now, what's number two?"

"Well, number two has to do with some concerns Zack has raised regarding Jason and Jack Pearl."

"Ah, yes, the infamous anesthetic."

"You don't believe him?"

"Of course I don't believe him, Suzanne. But I am investigating his allegations."

"You are?"

Frank was hardly acting like the man Zack had described meeting with earlier that morning. And despite herself, Suzanne once again felt a spur of doubt regarding what she had been told.

"Absolutely," Frank was saying. "I have already contacted the members of the medical ethics committee, as well as Jason and Jack, and have scheduled a meeting for the first thing next week. Call them and check on that if you want. I'll be happy to have both you and my brother present if you wish."

"I wish. But what about Toby Nelms?"

"What about him?"

"Frank, if what Zack believes is true, that child might not have until the first thing next week. Is there any way you could try and reason with Jason and Jack, just in case?"

"Jason's away, but if it will make you feel better about things, you and I can meet with Jack at, say, five o'clock today, right here."

"Thank you. Would you mind if Zack comes, too?"

"If you insist. Suzanne, you're one of the best things that has ever happened to this place. I would do anything I could to keep you here and happy. But now, if you'll pardon me, there is a meeting room filling up with people. We can plan on getting together again at five o'clock."

By then, his thoughts continued, *I'm sure I will have come up with some more permanent way of dealing with both you and my brother.*

"Frank, I appreciate all of this very much," she said, rising.

In that moment, inexplicably, she began to sense that something was wrong—very wrong. The whole session had gone much too smoothly. There was too great a difference between the man Zack had described firing him and the one she was confronting now.

"Hey, no problem," Frank was saying, his hand extended. "I'm as committed as you are to making sure this place is the best."

Suzanne took his hand and, for just a few seconds, continued to hold it. There was an unnatural feel to it—a coolness, a tension.

"Frank, tell me one last thing," she said, releasing his hand but keeping her eyes firmly fixed on his. "Were you responsible for all those rumors and stories that circulated about Guy?"

Frank held her gaze unwaveringly. "Absolutely not," he said.

In that instant, Suzanne knew. The unflinching darkness in his eyes, the earnest set of his face—it was a look that had confronted her before. Many times before. *It was Paul!*

751

"Frank, you're lying to me, aren't you?" she said.

"Nonsense."

He forced calm into his voice, but beneath his lightweight suit, he had begun to sweat. There was no way, he reaffirmed even more strongly, that Suzanne Cole was going to that board meeting.

In the back of his desk drawer was a small revolver. Carefully, Frank eased the drawer open. Then he stopped. If Zack was right, there was an easier, far easier, means of regaining control of the situation. It was certainly worth a try.

"Suzanne, sit down, please," he said calmly, rising from his own chair.

Puzzled, she did as he asked.

"There's something I want you to listen to."

"Okay, but I don't see what—"

"Please."

"A-All right."

She followed him with her eyes as he crossed to his stereo, switched on the tape deck, and replaced the cassette that he had listened to earlier. After just a few notes, she recognized the music.

"Have you heard this before?" Frank asked, returning to his desk and opening the drawer another inch.

Suzanne did not answer. Instead, she began to stare at the large aerial photo of the hospital complex. The colors were growing more and more intense.

Get up! her mind screamed. *Get up and run!*

Her legs would not respond.

"Well, have you?" he asked again.

His voice was rumbling and muted, his face twisted in a strange, bemused smile.

"Well, I'll be damned," she heard him say.

Suzanne rubbed at her eyes. The sounds in the room—Frank's breathing, her own, gave way to the music, which itself drifted farther and farther away.

Then she heard the voice—slow and patient and reassuring.

"All right, Suzanne, now I want you to count back from one hundred. . . ."

"One hundred," she heard herself say.

"Go on . . . go on."

"Ninety-nine . . . ninety-eight . . ."

The blue johnny covering her was pulled away, exposing her breasts. She shivered at her nakedness and the sudden chill.

"Ninety-seven . . . ninety-six . . ."

"She's under, Jason."

"Excellent. Let's get started, then."

"No, Jason," she begged as russet anesthetic was swabbed over her

752

breast. "Please wait. It hasn't worked yet. The anesthetic hasn't worked."

"Turn the music up a bit. Fine, that's fine. Okay, then, knife."

"No, wait! Ninety-five! . . . Ninety-four! Please hurry, please work."

Overhead, the bright, saucer light flashed on. Gloved hands appeared just below Jason Mainwaring's sterile, blue eyes. Nestled in the right hand was a scalpel. In agonizing slow motion it drifted down toward her.

"Jason, no!" she screamed as the blade cut into the skin by her shoulder, releasing a spurt of crimson.

The pain intensified as the scalpel began slicing a slow arc around the base of her breast. But before she could scream, a gag was pulled tightly between her teeth and tied behind her head, and her arms were bound just as vigorously to her sides.

Soundlessly, praying for the relief of unconsciousness, Suzanne endured the agony of the surgical removal of her breast. And when the dissection was complete, she looked down at herself in wide-eyed terror. Where once there had been skin and breast tissue and a nipple, now there was only a gaping, bloody crater.

In that moment, amidst a final, silent scream, blackness mercifully intervened.

Fascinated by what he was observing, Frank set the stereo playing *Fantasia on Greensleeves* for automatic repeat and turned up the volume. For once, at least, his goddamn brother had been something of a help.

Suzanne lay semiconscious on her back on the rug, twitching and shuddering from time to time, and crying out as much as the handkerchief tied tightly through her mouth would allow. Frank loosened the sleeves of his suitcoat, which he had used to bind her arms, and then cut a bath towel into strips. It was probably overkill, he realized, even to bother tying her up. Mainwaring's syrupy music was doing as fine a job of immobilizing her as any truss. Still, at least until she could be removed from the hospital to some safe—and permanent—resting place, it was worth the extra precaution.

He rolled her onto her side and bound her hands tightly behind her. Then he laid her back and secured her ankles. Her eyes remained closed, but her restless movements had increased—almost in reflection to the intensity of the music.

Frank knelt beside her. Even under such difficult circumstances, she was a real beauty. Brains and looks—Leigh Baron without the hard edge. When Suzanne had first come to Sterling, he had made several carefully gauged attempts to start something up between them. Each time, she had politely but firmly refused him. It angered him that, after just a few weeks in town, his brother was already getting inside her pants.

Well, so be it, he thought. *The two of them deserved one another.*

And as soon as the board meeting was over, he would set about seeing to it that they got to spend an eternity together. He had tried to play it easy with both of them, but that appraoch had nearly blown up in his face. They had forced him to take off the gloves, and now they would see what kind of competitor Frank Iverson really was. He had always played to win, and now there was far, far too much at stake even to think of backing off.

He reached down and ran his fingertips over Suzanne's face and then down over her breasts. She really did have a phenomenal body. *Phenomenal!* Lisette, Suzanne—Zack was spiteful enough to be planning on screwing them both, if he hadn't done so already.

No way, Zack-o, Frank thought as he dragged Suzanne into his bathroom and set her on the damp floor of his shower stall. *No way you're ever going to humiliate me like that.*

He smoothed out his suitcoat and then combed his hair. The music reverberated through the tiled room. Behind him, reflected in the mirror, Suzanne continued to jerk spasmodically.

Perhaps, Frank thought, after the meeting, before he set about arranging an accident of some sort for her and his brother, he would take a few minutes to enjoy the favors she had denied him. To miss such an opportunity would be a shame.

Besides, he mused as he checked himself in the mirror, a moment before setting off for the board meeting, it would be a crime to waste such romantic music.

CHAPTER 34

"I'M SORRY, Dr. Iverson, but as I told you before, I'm under strict instructions from Mr. Iverson that no calls from you are to be put through to anyone at the hospital except him."

"But all I want you to do is to page Dr. Cole for me. Ask her to call me."

An hour had passed since Zack had been fired and ushered out of the hospital he had expected to work in for the rest of his professional life. He had driven home with the patrol car following him right into his driveway, and then had tried to reach Suzanne at her office. After a number of busy signals, he had gotten a tape saying that the office would be closed until one. He had tried his own office, but the line had already been disconnected. Now, after a fruitless call to the hospital switchboard and a no-answer try at Suzanne's home, he was giving the page operator one last shot.

"I understand what you are asking, Doctor," the operator said.

"And even when I tell you it's a medical emergency you won't do it?"

"Mr. Iverson was quite specific."

"What's your name?"

"Janine."

"Well, Janine, I appreciate that you have your orders, but how is Mr. Iverson to know if you just put this one call through for me?"

"You'd be amazed at the things Mr. Iverson finds out, Doctor. And if he does, it's my job. Now please, I've got to get back to my board."

"Janine, wait— Damn."

Zack slammed the receiver down and then snatched it up for another attempt. This time, he stopped before the switchboard operator could even answer. Frank had put an airtight seal on the hospital that no simple phone call was going to breach. Nor did it help matters that his decision to forsake his father's care in favor of the town derelict had reduced his influence around Ultramed-Davis to near zero.

Still, he had to get back into the hospital—to tell Suzanne of the trigger, and, he hoped, to enlist her help in confronting Jack Pearl. He had given up on even trying to speak at the board meeting. Frank would have him in a cell before he could get close to the door. But Toby Nelms was a different matter. Without cooperation from Pearl, without the man's willingness to admit what he and Mainwaring were doing, he felt quite certain the boy was as good as dead.

Perhaps, he began to think, the board meeting might be the key. With Frank inside the conference room, and his security people stationed nearby, there might be some other, unguarded way inside the hospital. He scratched out a crude drawing of the building as best he could remember it. There was, he was nearly sure, a delivery entrance outside the cafeteria—one that had to be open. Assuming Suzanne was in the ICU, he could enter the hospital through the kitchen and reach the ICU by a back staircase.

He checked the time. The board meeting, if not already under way, would be starting any minute. He could park on the highway and circle through the woods to the delivery entrance. Police or no police, it was worth a try.

He tied Cheapdog on his run and then lurched the camper out of the drive and down the hill toward the hospital, hoping that the time for Toby's transfer to Boston had not been moved up. As he drove he pictured the boy sitting cross-legged on the rug in his house, watching his favorite hero cavorting across the screen, urging him to join in a song extolling the virtues of the letter P.

"Alas my love, you do me wrong . . ."

How many others, Jack? he said to himself, practicing the words he would use. *How many other time bombs have you and Mainwaring planted in your patients?*

The hospital was located on the opposite side of town from Zack's house. Ordinarily, he took the highway bypass around Main Street. This day, lost in thought, he missed the turnoff and was well into town before he realized it. Traffic was heavier than usual, and it seemed, from the long line of cars at the corner of Birch, that the light was malfunctioning. After a moment's debate, he backed up a foot and made a U-turn, narrowly missing a two-tone Oldsmobile that was speeding past.

It took several seconds before he realized the driver of the Oldsmobile was Jason Mainwaring.

Zack began honking and waving, but it was several blocks before Mainwaring became aware of him and pulled over. They confronted one another in a small streetside park, circumscribed by an arc of slatted benches arranged about a marble pedestal and bust of one of Sterling's founding fathers. Several grizzled men sat on two of the benches, smoking cigarettes, watching the passing scene, and occasionally sharing surreptitious sips from a brown bag. They watched curiously as the two well-dressed men approached one another.

"Jason," Zack began, somewhat breathlessly, "God, am I glad to see you."

The surgeon looked at him strangely.

"I'm sorry, Iverson," he said after a beat, "but I've signed out to Greg Ormesby. If y'all need any surgical help, I'm afraid you'll have to call—"

"This has nothing to do with surgical help. Jason, we need to talk. I've been trying to locate you for several days."

"I've been at home in—"

"Georgia. I know." He glanced over at the old men, and then motioned to the bench farthest from them. "Please, Jason, what I need to speak with you about is pretty urgent and very private. Could we talk over there?"

"Well, Iverson, I'm afraid I'm in a bit of a rush. Why don't we get together, say—"

"It's about the anesthetic."

Mainwaring's color drained.

"I beg your pardon?" he said.

"Over there?" Zack again motioned toward the bench.

By the time they sat down, the surgeon appeared as composed as ever.

"Now, then," he drawled, "just what anesthetic are you talkin' about?"

"It's the one you and Jack Pearl have been using on your cases, Jason. The one that allows them to get out of the recovery room three times faster than anyone else's cases."

"I'm afraid I don't understand," Mainwaring said.

But Zack could see from his eyes that he did.

"I don't have time to play games," he said. "A child is dying, and I have reason, good reason, to believe that your anesthetic is at fault."

A minute tic developed at the corner of Mainwaring's eye. The hint of understanding disappeared from his face. This time, Zack felt certain, the man was genuinely surprised.

"Look, Iverson," he said, "I just don't have time for this nonsense. If you have something to accuse me or Jack Pearl of, then I'd suggest you do it through channels. I would also suggest you have a shitload of proof."

"Jason, please," Zack said, trying desperately to keep civility in his tone. "This isn't ethics or charges we're talking about. It's a child's life. Please listen."

Item by item, in a near whisper, he reviewed his investigation into the case of Toby Nelms. Mainwaring listened impassively. Only at the mention of Darryl Tarberry did Zack detect any reaction.

"So that's where things stand," he concluded. "The boy's mother is certain that at least several times he was watching this children's show when he had his seizures. It's a show that features a version of 'Greensleeves'—the same music you use in the operating room. If I could just get my hands on whatever it is you were using for anesthesia, I think I might be able to help that kid."

"Oh, you do?"

"It's a long shot, but right now, it's his only chance."

"Well, then," Mainwaring said, "it would appear that the boy has no chance at all. Because, y'see, Iverson, there is no mystery anesthetic."

Zack stared at the man in disbelief.

"Iverson, just who have you shared these charges with?" the surgeon asked.

"Jason, these aren't charges. A child is dy—"

"Who?"

"The child's mother."

"That all?"

"Suzanne."

"She believe you?"

"She was willing to listen. But I spoke to her before I learned about the trigger—the music. Now Jason, please—"

757

"I asked if she believed you."

"Not completely, but after I tell her what I've learned, I'm certain she'll—"

"Not completely," Mainwaring cut in snidely. "Iverson, I sure hope you have one hell of a lawyer. Have you mentioned this nonsense to your brother?"

Zack glanced at his watch. The board meeting was already under way.

"Mainwaring, this isn't nonsense. If that child dies, if anyone who received that drug dies, then it's murder."

"Don't threaten me," the surgeon said, shaking a finger at Zack. "Don't you ever threaten me. Now, I asked if you had shared this hokum with your brother."

"I did. Dammit, Mainwaring, doesn't any of this have an impact on—"

"When did you tell him?"

"Just a while ago."

"And his response?"

"Mainwaring, there's no time for this—"

"What was his response?"

"He ignored me."

"Just as I intend to do," Mainwaring said. "Now, if you'll excuse me." He rose.

"Mainwaring, you can't do this." Zack said loudly.

The grizzled observers' interest heightened, and one of them sputtered on the contents of the brown bag.

"Can, and am," Mainwaring said just as loudly. "Now you just quiet down, Iverson, or you'll have even more charges to deal with than you already do."

"Mainwaring, are you some kind of fucking monster?"

The surgeon turned and headed for his car.

"Well, are you?" Zack screamed after him.

Mainwaring, now at his car, turned back and shook a finger at him.

"Watch it," he said venomously. "Just fuckin' watch it."

The sun, which had been gliding in and out of hiding all morning, slid behind a dense billow of gray cloud, instantly cooling the air. Zack pulled the camper onto a dirt track off the Androscoggin road and worked his way upward through a forest still sodden by the midnight rain. He felt ill over his unsuccessful encounter with Mainwaring, and could not dispel his anger—not only at the surgeon, but at his own handling of the man.

Had he been too aggressive? Too abrasive? Would his arguments have been more effective if he had simply brought Mainwaring to the hospital and let him see Toby Nelms for himself? The questions burned in his thoughts as he picked his way uphill toward the north side of the hospital.

Only one thing was certain now. With Frank an enemy, and Mainwaring unwilling to expose himself to charges, Jack Pearl was all the hope the child had left. And without either of the other two men to back him up in a confrontation with the anesthesiologist, that hope was slim, indeed.

Through the trees ahead, Zack could see the top two floors of the hospital. The broad glass windows were, he noticed for the first time, tinted just enough to give them an ebony cast. The effect was cold and uninviting.

He moved up to the edge of the forest and flattened himself against a thick beech tree. To his left, just beyond an expanse of grass and past the corner of the building, was the patio of the cafeteria. A group of nurses sat laughing and talking at the only table in his line of sight. The entire north side of the hospital was deserted.

Cautiously, he picked his way along the treeline toward the corner farthest from the patio. He would have to dash across, perhaps, twenty yards of lawn to reach the delivery door. From there, he would walk nonchalantly through the kitchen, searching for a route to the corridor that did not take him through the crowded cafeteria itself.

Ahead of him the tinted windows of the hospital glinted ominously in the muted midday light. If there were faces behind those windows watching him, he would have no way of knowing. His heart was pounding in his ears, more so than even on the most treacherous climbs.

A crouch, a final check of the building line, and Zack bolted ahead. He saw the blur of movement and color to his right at virtually the same moment he heard the barked command.

"Stop! Right there, right now!"

Startled, Zack stumbled forward, slamming heavily against the brick facing and nearly falling as he spun toward the voice. Standing not ten feet away, brandishing a heavy nightstick, was the security guard, Henry, the pockmarked behemoth who had been present at Guy's death and again at his funeral.

"I been following you, Doc," he said, rubbing a hand over the side of his nearly nonexistent neck. "From that window right there, I been following you all the way across."

"Jesus, Henry, you just scared the hell out of me," Zack said, still gasping for breath.

His shoulder was throbbing viciously at the point where it had collided with the building. Gingerly, he raised his arm. Pain stopped it just below a horizontal position. He'd almost dislocated it. A first-degree separation at least, he guessed.

"Didn't mean to scare ya, Doc," the huge guard said, lowering his stick nearly, but not completely, to his side. "Just to stop ya."

"Henry, I've got to get in there," Zack said.

"Mr. Iverson left strict orders not to let you. That's why I was called in."

"There's a kid dying in there, Henry. A kid that only I can help. You've got to let me pass."

"Can't," the man said simply. "If I do, it's my job. No discussion, no excuses. That's what my boss said. I got three kids, and nothin' to support 'em with exceptin' what God gave me from the neck down. Jobs like this one don't come along that often to a man like me."

Zack started to argue, but then, just as quickly, stopped himself. He pictured the guard at Guy's funeral—his ill-fitting blue suit, his quiet, anxious little wife. The man was right. The job probably *was* a godsend to them and their children. And too many people had been hurt already. He would find another way to contact Suzanne, or perhaps a way to lure Jack Pearl outside the protection of the building.

"All right, Henry," he said. "I won't try to argue with you."

He turned and started back toward the woods.

"Doc, wait. . . ."

Zack looked back over his injured shoulder.

"How old's the kid?"

"He's eight, Henry."

"I see. . . . My Kenny's almost nine. . . . Doc, what in the heck happened between you and your brother, anyhow?"

Zack laughed ruefully.

"It's a long story, Henry."

"You know, he's not a very nice man, your brother."

"No, Henry," Zack said. "I guess he isn't."

"He doesn't think much of people like me."

"Perhaps he doesn't."

For a few moments, there was only the sound of the wind through the leaves overhead.

"Doc," the guard said suddenly, "why don't you just go ahead on in there and do whatever it is you have to do."

Zack eyed the man.

"You mean that?"

"Talking to me and my wife the way you did at Doc Beaulieu's funeral—that was a really nice thing to do."

"Henry, your job may be on the line."

"I'll find another one if I have to. You know, I really did think I was responsible for Doc Beaulieu's death. I'm big, and I'm tough when I have to be, but I'm not mean. I couldn't eat or sleep after he died—that is, until you talked to me."

"If anyone was responsible, Henry," Zack said, "it was my brother. He's the one who started all those rumors about Dr. Beaulieu."

"I believe it. You go on in there."

Zack started toward the door.

"You sure?" he asked.

"Do it for Doc Beaulieu," Henry said.

⋀CHAPTER 35

Forty-nine years.

Had Guy lived, Clothilde Beaulieu suddenly realized, they would have celebrated their forty-ninth anniversary in just one week. How strange that now, standing behind her chair, surveying the room of blank, bored, and patronizing faces, she should feel as close to her husband as she had at any time during those five decades.

He had stood in rooms like this one many times over the past two years, confronting these faces, or faces like them. And although she had never been there with him, Clothilde knew that she was feeling exactly as he had. She knew, too, that even though there was little or no chance she would prevail, he was, at that moment, by her side, and he was proud.

". . . For many years after my husband opened his practice in Sterling," she was saying, "he was one of only three doctors in town, and the only surgeon for almost a hundred miles. He was a kind and skilled and caring man, who did nothing—nothing—to deserve the kind of treatment he was to receive from the administration of this institution and the corporation whose philosophy it has adopted. . . ."

Seated across from the woman, Frank Iverson shaded in portions of the geometric design he was developing on a napkin, and checked the time. It would be a laughable irony if Guy Beaulieu's widow were allowed to drone on past the twelve o'clock deadline, rendering the vote of the board legally meaningless, regardless of its outcome. No, not laughable, he decided—perfect. It was all he could do to keep from smiling at the notion.

The Carter Room was set up in its conference mode—thirty chairs arranged around an open rectangle of sandlewood tables. At the back of the room, near the gallery of past medical staff presidents, a serving table was set with coffee, Danish, and bowls of fruit.

Hidden beneath the draping linen cloth of that table, awaiting the inevitable, several bottles of premium French champagne were chilling in sterling silver ice buckets.

The magic number was ten. Of the twenty-two members of the Davis Hospital board of trustees, nineteen were present. Absent from the group were a real estate agent who was vacationing in Europe; the CEO of the Carter Paper Company, who had never attended a board meeting since his first one years before; and Board Chairman Clayton Iverson. In the Judge's absence, Whitney Bourque had been presiding over the meeting.

Frank sat beside Leigh Baron at the corner of the arrangement farthest from Bourque. They were flanked by a trio of lawyers, two representing Ultramed and the third, the hospital.

Across from them stood Clothilde Beaulieu.

". . . Someone must realize that in a civilized society such as ours," she was saying, "the best available medical care must not be doled out as a privilege. The right to live one's life as free from disease as possible must be extended to all, regardless of their ability to pay. It was my husband's belief, and it is mine, that the Ultramed Hospitals Corporation has failed in that sacred obligation. By selecting only those who can pay for treatment, by influencing the therapeutic decisions of physicians who have studied many years to develop their craft, the corporation has reduced the delivery of medical care to the level of . . . of automobile mechanics. . . ."

Frank glanced over at Gary Garrison, proprietor of Garrison's Chevrolet Sales and Service, just in time to see the man smile and whisper a remark to the board member seated next to him. More irony. Garrison's vote was one of those that Frank had not absolutely locked up. Given enough time, it was possible that Clothilde Beaulieu could insult enough members on the board to make the vote unanimous.

Frank made his fifth head count of the session. When he had left his father's office, less than a week before, he was certain of only five votes, six at the most. Now, thanks in large measure to the Judge's absence and his refusal to use his influence on the board, he had eleven —one over the magic number. Gary Garrison would make twelve. And with the closed ballot Whitey Bourque had promised him, there might even be one or two more.

"You look concerned," Leigh whispered.

Frank smiled.

"No sweat," he whispered back.

"I hope so, Frank. We're counting on you."

"That's the way I like it."

". . . Over the past two years, Guy Beaulieu fought back against the attempts of Ultramed to drive him from practice. Unfortunately, as I said earlier, much of the evidence he accumulated is not available today. I have done my best without it to present our position to you. I leave you now with this petition, signed by sixty-seven residents of this area, requesting the return of our hospital to community control.

"I greatly appreciate the opportunity you have given me to represent my husband's interests this day. I know, just as he did, that the age of the country doctor making house calls and sharing the most intimate details of his patients' lives is all but over in this country. But I issue to you, in his name, and in the name of those on this petition, one final plea that you do what you can to stop the juggernaut of technology and profit from robbing medicine of so much of its dignity, compassion, and sacred trust. Thank you, and God bless you for listening so patiently to this old woman."

Several members of the board applauded lightly, and Bill Crook, seated on Clothilde's right, patted her on the arm.

Whitey Bourque, who had unabashedly checked his watch half a dozen times during the final few minutes of her speech, sighed audibly and tapped his gavel on the table as he stood by his chair.

"So," he said. "There you have it. Frank has had his say, and now Mrs. Beaulieu has had hers. Any other comments in the few minutes we have left? . . . Good enough. Well, in view of the seriousness of this repurchase matter, it has been suggested, and I agree, that we vote on the issue by closed ballot. Any objections? . . . Okay, then. You'll each find a ballot in your folder. Just mark whatever you think is right, and pass your vote over to me."

Across the room, Frank subconsciously nodded his approval. Beneath the table, his leg was jouncing in nervous anticipation. After immobilizing Suzanne Cole, he had called Annette Dolan and insisted that she stay home for the remainder of the day. Next, he had worked out an exquisite scenario for Zack and Suzanne, which would take both of them out of his hair for good and place the blame for their accident squarely on the shoulders of his brother.

He couldn't have scripted things better. First Mainwaring's million, now the vote, and later, a call to Zack and one final test of Serenyl—this time at the edge of the four-hundred-foot drop-off at Christmas Point. It would be the perfect ending to a perfect day. The game hadn't been easy, but he had met and overcome every obstacle. And now, at long last, Frankie Iverson was about to be on top again.

In the back of his mind, the cheerleaders' chant had begun to build. *Frank, Frank, he's our man. . . .*

With Henry checking the corridors and stairways ahead of him, Zack moved easily through the kitchen and up the north stairway to the ICU. The pain from his shoulder, while tolerable, was continuing to make its existence known, especially when he tried to raise his arm.

"Good luck in there, Doc," the guard said, barely able to contain his enthusiasm at the decision he had made. "I'll be around the hospital if you need me. Just have me paged."

Zack shook his hand gratefully.

"You've done a good thing, Henry," he said. "A really good thing. I'll page you if I need you. . . ."

Readying himself for the struggle ahead, he turned and entered the ICU.

The unit was virtually as he had left it two hours before, except that neither Suzanne nor Owen Walsh was there. Half of the glass-enclosed cubicles were empty, and what activity there was continued to center about Toby Nelms.

The nurses eyed him uncomfortably as he approached. Off to his right, he saw the unit secretary snatch up the receiver of her phone and then slowly set it back down again, as if unwilling to take sole responsibility for reporting his appearance in the hospital.

Bernice Rimmer, the nurse assigned to Toby's care, had actually been a classmate of Zack's from early childhood through high school. She was the mother of three children now, but still looked nearly as slim and buoyant as she had during her teens. She was also a nurse's nurse, tough on the outside, but with a core of honey—and smart. Her presence this day was, Zack realized, no less fortunate for him than his encounter with Henry. If any nurse would give him a break, it was she.

As he approached, Bernice, almost as if reading his thoughts, sent the aide who was working with her out of Toby's cubicle.

"Hi, Bernie," Zack said.

"Funny," she responded, "you don't look like public enemy number one."

"I'm not."

"Tell that to your brother. I never thought the two of you got along all that well, but this is something else."

She took a folded sheet of paper from her uniform pocket, smoothed it out on Toby's bed, and passed it over.

Zack was not surprised at the content of the memo, only at its viciousness. In essence, Frank had outlined a set of charges against him that would have made Attila the Hun proud, and had threatened summary dismissal for anyone not immediately reporting his presence in the hospital.

"Frank and I are having a few problems," he said.

"I guess."

"How's Toby doing?"

"About the same. His temp's staying around 101. Pupils are still equal. No change in his consciousness." She gestured at the memo. "You do all those things?"

Zack shook his head.

"Frank doesn't want to believe that the anesthesia this child received for his hernia operation is responsible for his problem."

"Is it?"

"Yes."

Bernice Rimmer studied him for a time, and then she gazed down at her charge, reached over, and stroked the boy's forehead. Finally, she looked past Zack to the unit secretary and shook her head.

"So, what do you propose to do about it?" she asked.

Zack started to thank her, but the look in her eyes stopped him. She wanted action, not platitudes.

He conducted a brief neurologic check of Toby.

"I need to have a few words with Jack Pearl," he said.

"He's in the O.R."

"That's okay. But before I see him, I need to go over some things with Suzanne. Do you know where she is?"

"No idea. She called a while ago to say she'd be down here shortly, but she hasn't showed. I think Dr. Walsh paged her once, but as far as I know, she never answered. He's gone to his office."

"Could you have her paged again, please? Also, try the E.R., just in case she's tied up there."

They waited several minutes for Suzanne to answer. Then, once again, Zack tried calling her at home.

"This is very weird," he said. "Does she fail to answer pages often?"

"Never."

"Hmm. Bernice, could you do me one more favor and page Henry Flowers, the security guard. Ask him to come here."

"You *want* security?"

"Not security—Henry. It's okay. And please thank the rest of the staff for holding off on reporting me."

Henry Flowers arrived at the unit in less than two minutes.

"How'm I doing?" Zack asked.

The massive guard shrugged.

"As far as I can tell, no one knows you're here."

"I'm trying to find Dr. Cole. You know her?"

"Of course. I just heard her paged."

"That was me. She didn't answer."

"So?"

"So I'd like you to start looking around for her, if you could. I don't think I'd last very long out there."

"Okay."

"Check her office in the P and S building first. Then maybe the cardiac lab."

Henry stroked his pocked cheeks.

"I saw her," he said thoughtfully.

"When? Where?"

"Not too long ago. I . . . I can't remember where, though, Doc."

"Try."

"Let's see. . . . I started my rounds on the front lawn, and then crossed through the lobby, and then . . ." Suddenly, he brightened. "I remember, now. I remember where I saw her." Then, just as suddenly, his expression darkened.

"Henry, where?" Zack asked.

"It was in the west wing," he said distantly. "She . . . she was going into Mr. Iverson's office."

Zack felt an instant chill.

"Henry, get me there," he said. He turned to the nurse. "Bernie, could you please find out who's on for anesthesia beside Dr. Pearl? Call whoever it is and ask them to stand by. Don't tell them it's for me."

With Henry resuming his role as scout, they left the unit and made their way down to the sub-basement, then across the hospital to the west-wing staircase and up. Zack flattened himself against the stairwell wall.

"Henry," he whispered, "I think my brother is in a meeting, but he has two receptionists."

"Yeah, I know. The knockout twins."

"Exactly. Talk to them. See if they remember when Suzanne left, or better still, where she might have gone. Also, find out if Frank was with her when she went."

Subconsciously, the huge guard straightened his tie, adjusted the lapels on his uniform, and pushed his massive shoulders back a notch. Then he slipped out the stairway door to confront the knockout twins.

Half a minute later, he was back.

"No one there," he said.

"No one?"

"Nope." He appeared disappointed. "Not the blonde. Not the dark-haired one. No one. I even took a chance because there was music playing inside, and unlocked the outer office door and listened at Mr. Iverson's door for voices."

"Music?"

"Violins. Pretty music, but it must be on awful loud to be able to hear it through two closed doors."

"Henry, I want to go back there."

"Okay, but—"

Zack was already through the stairway door. The guard shrugged and followed closely.

Just outside Frank's outer office, Zack stopped and listened. As Henry had said, the music coming from the inner office was quite audible.

It took just a few seconds for Zack to recognize the piece.

"Jesus, Henry, open this up, please!"

The guard did as asked.

The music, much louder now, brought a sickening tightness to Zack's gut. He knocked on the door and called out once, but knew there would be no answer.

"This door, Henry. Open it, please!"

"Can't."

"Henry, it's important. I think Dr. Cole's in there, and I think she's in trouble."

"No key. Only Mr. Iverson has a key to that door."

"Henry, we've got to get in there. . . ."

The guard hesitated.

"Please . . ."

"Well," he said finally, "I guess I can't get fired more than once, can I?"

He took a single step forward and then hit the heavy door with such force that the entire frame shattered. The door itself, crushed where his shoulder had made contact, fell to the floor like a playing card.

Fantasia on Greensleeves was playing at a near-deafening level.

Zack snapped off the tape, glanced about the office for a moment, then raced into the bathroom.

"Henry," he yelled. "Get in here!"

No longer mindful of being seen, Zack raced ahead as Henry carried Suzanne through the corridors of the hospital and up the stairs to the ICU. She was motionless, unresponsive, and soaked with perspiration. Her level of coma was deep, and her elevated temperature quite apparent.

Bernice Rimmer's surprise at their arrival lasted only seconds before she was in action, stripping Suzanne's clothes off, getting a blood pressure cuff around her arm, and ordering a Ringer's Lactate IV from one of the other nurses.

"She remind you of anyone, Bernie?" Zack asked. "She got the same anesthesia as Toby. You believe me now?"

"I believed you before," the nurse said, listening to Suzanne's chest. "You probably don't remember this, but I once asked you to cheat on a Latin translation for me, and you refused. I figured that if you were such an honest nerd then, you couldn't have changed all that much."

"Who's Pearl's backup?"

"The nurse anesthetist. She's in obstetrics."

"Call her, please. Tell her to meet me by the operating room doors in two minutes. Tell her it's a life-and-death emergency. Also, order some labs and blood gases on Suzanne—everything stat. And give her Decadron. Ten milligrams IV."

"Done."

"I'll be back shortly. . . . Get ready, Pearl, you bastard," he murmured as he slammed through the unit doors. "This crap has gone on long enough. I'm coming for you!"

CHAPTER 36

FRANK KNEW, as he watched Whitey Bourque separate the ballots into two piles, that the vote was going to be closer than he had wanted. He counted exactly ten ballots in one pile and nine in the other. By insisting on a closed vote, it had been his hope to minimize any influence the Judge might still have had on certain members. Now, it appeared, he had succeeded more in minimizing his own.

Fuck you, Garrison, he thought, watching the last of the ballots smoothed open. *Starting next year, it will be Fords for this hospital. Bank on it.*

"Well," Bourque said as he and the member seated next to him finished a cooperative tabulation of the votes. "I make it ten to nine. You get that, too, Charlie? . . . Good." He banged his gavel. "In that case, I am pleased to announce that the Davis—er, excuse me, the Ultramed-Davis board of trustees has, by a vote of ten to nine, approved the finalization of the sale of this hospital to the Ultramed Division of RIATA International."

Several members applauded; many others simply shrugged. Leigh Baron accepted the congratulations of the attorneys and then turned to Frank.

"That was close," she said.

Frank smiled.

"Hand grenades and horseshoes," he said giddily.

"Pardon?"

"Oh, just a little phrase my father drummed into my head."

"Well, Frank, it would appear that you are to be—"

"Excuse me, but I wondered if the acting chairman could delay the celebration long enough to listen to one more point of view."

Like the gallery at a tennis match, every head in the room swung, in unison, toward the door.

The Judge, a blanket over his lap, sat in a wheelchair just inside the room, pale but smiling grimly.

Whitey Bourque raced around and shook his hand.

"God, Judge, it's good to see you up like this. You all right? I mean, can you—"

"I can move 'em, Whitey. Not very much yet, but more every minute."

Somewhat painfully, he demonstrated by lifting his right foot several inches off its support.

Frank, too stunned by the sudden intrusion even to react, glanced down at his watch. It was eight minutes till noon. At that moment, he realized his father was watching him.

"Good to see you, Judge," he managed hoarsely.

The Judge nodded at him and then exchanged a prolonged look with Leigh Baron.

"I'd like to address the board, if I might," he said.

"Of course, Judge," Whitey Bourque replied. "Why don't you just let me wheel you up front."

"Judge," Frank said, "the voting's over."

"Is it?"

"I'm afraid so, Judge," Bourque said. "Ten to nine it was, in favor of Ultramed."

"Well, perhaps I can change a mind or two."

"That's not legal, sir," one of the Ultramed lawyers said. "The vote's done."

Clayton Iverson fixed him with a glare that would have melted block ice.

"Don't you dare tell me what's legal and what's not, young man," he rasped. "I was a lawyer and a judge while your mommy was still wiping your behind. Our contract with you people says that we have until noon today to repurchase this hospital by a majority vote of the board. That's what it says. No more, no less. And unless something's wrong with my timepiece, here, I make it seven of."

Ashen, Frank watched as his father was wheeled up to the chairman's table. He was desperately sorting through disruptions he could instigate that might carry the meeting past the deadline. But before he could light on a specific action, the Judge was speaking.

"I'll make this short," he began. "I had promised many of you that I would do the legwork necessary to ensure that it was to the benefit of our community to finalize our temporary arrangement with the Ultramed people. Because of my accident, and for other reasons which I have neither the time nor inclination to go into now, I decided to withhold my conclusions about this business and let the chips fall where they may. Well, I have come back at this time to tell you that my reaction was unfair—to you, my friends and colleagues, and to the city of Sterling as well.

"I have learned enough to appear before you now and tell you categorically that while we may have benefited in the short run from

769

Ultramed's involvement with our hospital, it would be a grave mistake to turn Davis Regional over to them permanently. My housekeeper, Annie Doucette, almost died because of a policy—an Ultramed corporate policy—that rewards physicians for transferring patients out of the hospital as early as possible, and rewards them even more if that transfer is to an Ultramed-owned nursing home. Patients who helped build this hospital are being shunted off to Clarion County because they haven't got enough insurance. There's more—much more"—he glanced at Leigh Baron—"but because of the time, I'm going to ask you to trust me on that. Now, we have three minutes until noon. If it is agreeable with Whitey, here, I would like to call for another vote on this question."

"Any objections?" Bourque asked.

"Yes," Frank said, standing. "I object."

"Well, I'm sorry, Frank," Bourque countered, "but you're not a board member, 'n' we don't have time for any outside objections."

Frank hesitated, and then sank numbly to his seat.

"Okay, then," Bourque said. "You all have a second ballot in your folders. I put one there knowin' that at least some of you were bound to screw up the first one."

A brief volley of laughter gave way to dense silence as the twenty board members marked their ballots, folded them, and passed them toward the front of the room.

Leigh Baron, her back to Frank, sat staring stonily at the gallery of presidents.

As the last of the ballots reached Whitey Bourque and was counted, the steeple bells of St. Anne's began tolling the noon hour.

Sara Newton, the nurse anesthetist, was a mousy young woman with braces that had yet to correct a striking overbite. She had been asleep in maternity, awaiting a delivery, and arrived at the doors to the operating suite only moments after Zack, breathless, bleary-eyed, and disheveled.

"Where's the emergency?" she panted, tugging at a kink in her bra.

"In the unit," Zack said.

His shoulder was throbbing from the dash through the hospital, and he had resorted to partially splinting it by jamming his thumb through a belt loop.

"The unit? Well, then, let's get going. Say, are you okay? You look a little pale."

"I'm fine. A little stressed out is all."

"That's right. There was a notice sent around that you've been fired."

"I've been rehired. Sara, I need Jack Pearl. It's a case he's familiar with. I'd like you to take over his case in O.R. 1 so he can leave."

The woman was astonished.

"Dr. Iverson, I can't do that."

"Listen, Sara," Zack said sharply, "I don't have time to argue. I know you're very good at your job, and if I thought you could do what I need, I wouldn't hesitate. But this is Pearl's affair. His and mine. And at least two lives are on the line. Now please."

"Wh-What can I do?" she asked, shaken.

"Get a fresh set of scrubs on and be outside O.R. 1 as quickly as you can. I'll signal you when it's okay to come in."

"Jack will never agree to something like this."

"You leave Jack to me. Now, please, hurry."

Zack raced into the surgeon's locker room and painfully undressed. He threw his clothes into his locker and pulled on a scrub suit, a paper hair cover, mask, and shoe covers, and he hurried past the sinks in the prep room and into O.R. 1. Greg Ormesby, the surgeon on the case, looked up and took several seconds to recognize who he was.

"Iverson?" he asked somewhat coolly. "That is you under there, isn't it?"

At the mention of Zack's name, all activity in the room came to an instant halt. Jack Pearl, who was hunched over his instruments, looked up and paled.

"Sorry to bust in like this, Greg," Zack said with forced calm, "but I need to talk to Jack, here."

"I'm busy," Pearl muttered.

"Well, whatever it is will just have to wait," Ormesby said. "We'll be done in half an hour. Now, if you please, Iverson."

Zack bent over Pearl and laid his right hand at the base of the man's neck.

"Jack," he whispered, "it's Suzanne. She's in the ICU right now, and she's having a seizure just like Toby's. She's reliving her operation and she's screaming out your name. Yours and Jason's."

Even wearing a mask and hair cover, the frail anesthesiologist looked ill. "That can't be," Pearl whispered back.

"I want you up there with me right now."

"You're crazy."

Zack slipped his fingers around the sides of Pearl's neck and applied just a bit of pressure.

"She's the second case, Jack. The one you were holding out for."

"I'm not going anyplace. Now let go of me! You're hurting me!"

Zack looked up just as Sara Newton appeared outside the door. He motioned her in with a snap of his head, and tightened his grip, digging his sinewy fingers into the nerves alongside Pearl's neck.

"Iverson, what in the hell is going on here?" Ormesby demanded. "Are you crazy? Somebody call security. Iverson, for crying out loud, there's a goddamn woman opened up on the table here. Can't you see that?"

"I'm sorry to do things this way, Greg," Zack said, raising the little anesthesiologist to his feet, "but there's trouble in the ICU that only Jack can help with."

"That's crazy!" Pearl cried out. "*He's* crazy! Ow! You're hurting me, Iverson! Let go!"

Greg Ormesby and the surgical team watched in stunned silence as Zack pulled the little man away from his console and gestured Sara Newton into his place.

"Iverson, stop this right now!" Ormesby shouted. "You're endangering my patient."

"Nonsense. Sara, here, is an excellent anesthetist, and you know it. She'll take good care of your patient. I'm sorry to have to do things this way, but I just don't have time to explain right now. I will, though, Greg. I promise."

"Oh, for God's sake. Will somebody call security? Iverson, this is madness."

Zack did not respond.

The pain in his shoulder partially numbed by his own adrenaline, he dragged Pearl through the scrub room and slammed him against the bank of lockers, pinning him by the throat so that he was up on the tips of his toes.

"Iverson," Greg Ormesby hollered, "I see now that what everyone is saying about you is true. I'll get you for this! I'll see you up on charges!"

"Okay, Jack," Zack said, ignoring the surgeon's bellowing. "This is it. Now tell me: There *is* an experimental drug, isn't there? . . ."

He augmented his grip with his injured arm, and hoisted the anesthesiologist up another fraction of an inch. Pearl's toes came off the carpet.

"Well, isn't there?"

Pearl, either too frightened or too obstinate to answer, did not respond. His face was violet. His eyes, now nearly level with Zack's, were bulging.

At that moment, a security guard burst into the locker room, and without a word, struck Zack with his nightstick—a blow that glanced off the side of his head and landed squarely on his injured shoulder. Crying out from the pain, Zack dropped heavily to the carpet, clutching his arm, as Jack Pearl slithered down the locker and, moaning, collapsed in a heap nearby.

The guard knelt on the small of Zack's back and raised his stick, preparing for another blow.

"Stop that! Right now!"

Startled, the guard came off Zack and whirled toward the voice. Zack reacted more slowly. He turned, and through tears of pain saw Jason Mainwaring, hands on hips, standing by the door.

"Mainwaring," he gasped, "it's Suzanne. She's in the unit, and—"

"I know. I just came from there." Mainwaring turned to the guard. "Everything's under control here now. You can go."

"But—"

"I *said,* things are under control."

"Y-Yessir."

The guard backed from the room, with Mainwaring's iceblue eyes helping him along.

"Okay, Jack," the surgeon said as the door swung shut, "give Iverson whatever he wants."

"Jason, I can't—"

"Dammit, Jack, do it! There are two people in deep trouble in the unit up there. I may have made some mistakes in this business, but I'm no murderer. If Serenyl's responsible for their condition, then I want Iverson here to get whatever he needs to help them. . . . Now!"

Pearl stumbled to his feet.

Zack tried to rise, fell heavily, and then tried again—this time with shaky success.

"Thanks, Mainwaring," he said. "I didn't think I'd gotten through to you."

"Just remember, Iverson, that just because I'm here doesn't mean I'm admitting to anything." He glanced over at the anesthesiologist, and then added in a voice too soft for the man to hear, "I'm no monster, Iverson. If Pearl's drug has hurt some people, I want to do whatever I can to help out. You remember that, now. You remember I did that."

"Yeah, sure, Mainwaring," Zack said. "I'll remember."

Frank sat alone to one side of the Carter Conference Room and watched as Whitey Bourque, the last remaining board member, wheeled his father away for readmission to the hospital. The re-vote had been an impressive fourteen to six in favor of repurchase.

As he neared the door, the Judge looked back at him and mouthed the words, "I'm sorry, Frank."

Across from Frank, Leigh Baron shared a final exchange with her lawyers and sent them off. Then she turned and surveyed the near-empty room and the vestiges of the meeting just past.

"Well, he beat you," she said finally.

"He beat you, too," Frank retorted.

"He's one of the hardest men I've ever dealt with."

"Tell me about it."

Leigh paced to one side of the room and then back.

"Unfortunately," she said, "that is, unfortunately for you, your father's actions have placed me in a rather ticklish position."

"Oh?"

"You see, Frank, three years ago you did a very stupid, very amateurish thing. You took money from us. A good deal of money."

Shocked, Frank stared up at her.

"I . . . I don't know what you're talking about," he managed.

"Oh, Frank," she said sardonically, "you disappoint me so." She crossed the room and laid the accountant's report in front of him. "We were a little worried about this vote today," she explained, "so last night I visited with your father."

"You what?"

"I shared the contents of that folder with him, and promised that it would be incinerated as soon as the sale of the hospital was complete."

"That's insane."

"No, Frank," she said calmly, "that's business."

"What kind of person are you? Do you know that you probably were the cause of his accident?"

"I know nothing of the kind. But what I do know is that your father made his choice, and now we must make ours. You can expect charges of embezzlement to be brought against you first thing next week."

"You can't do that."

"Can, and will," she said.

"I . . . I was about to put that money back. I have the cash. Right now. Right in the bank."

"Too late."

"You're an insensitive bitch."

"Oh, that's wonderful, Frank. So witty, so articulate."

"I'll . . . I'll double what I took," he said. "Five hundred thousand. I can have it in your hands this afternoon."

"Frank, you don't understand. If it was the money, you would have been buried three years ago, when we first became aware of what you had done."

"In that case," he said, suddenly seeing a crack of daylight and racing toward it, "if I go down, your company goes down with me, big time."

"What are you talking about?"

"I'm talking about some work that has been going on at this hospital—at *your* hospital. The testing of a new and unapproved anesthetic. It's work involving *your* administrator, and one of *your* surgeons, and one of *your* anesthesiologists, and it hasn't come out too well. If you need proof, stop by the ICU and check out a kid named Nelms. And I promise you that if I get charged with anything, I'll smear Ultramed's name until your stock isn't worth using as toilet paper."

"I don't believe you," she said.

But Frank could tell that she did.

"Like I said, just stop by the unit. I'm sure the child's parents and their lawyers would love to know that a multibillion-dollar company was responsible for their son's condition."

"You've been allowing this to go on without our knowledge?"

Frank felt the shift in momentum.

"Allowing it? Hell, I've been in charge of it. How do you think I was planning on coming up with that much money? In fact, the work is already done. I've been paid off. And fortunately—for all of us—only I know that it hasn't come out all that well. . . . Now, do we have a Mexican standoff or not?"

Leigh Baron spent several seconds sizing him up, but he knew that he had won.

"How many patients?" she asked.

"Oh, five hundred," he said, "give or take."

"I intend to check up on what you've told me."

"Feel free. Just be careful when you do. If this blows, it blows in your face."

"Frank, you're pathetic."

"Ah, ah. Now who's being articulate?"

"One word, Frank, if so much as one word about this . . . this stupidity touches Ultramed, I swear I'll bury you. What you've done is horrible."

Frank grinned broadly.

"No, it's not," he said with a wink. "It's business."

CHAPTER 37

THE ARTICLE, "Studies in the Reversal of the Delayed Toxicity of Lysergic Acid Diethylamine (LSD)," had been written by a Scottish neurologist named Clarkin, and published almost fifteen years before in the little-read British *Journal of Neuropsychology*. It was an anecdotal report, not a scientific study in the true sense of the word. Zack had stumbled onto the work during his first year of residency and had saved it because the notion of treating LSD flashbacks with LSD both amused and fascinated him.

In most of his cases, Clarkin had used a high-density, saline-flotation isolation tank. With no such device at hand, they would simply have to make do. And while the Scotsman's concepts were intriguing, the data presented were too scant to justify many of his conclusions. It was frightening to realize that with no other promising options, Clarkin's theories were all that Suzanne and Toby Nelms had going for them.

As he supervised the nurses' transfer of Suzanne to a water mattress—the first step in reducing her sensory input to the absolute minimum—Zack wondered about the neurologist and his work. *Was it a mistake not to try and locate him? Was he even still alive? Still practicing? Was he a scholar, or a fraud? Had he received acclaim for his theories, or scorn?*

But most of all, Zack wondered if he might be endangering his two patients by what he was attempting to do. Over the years of his training he had developed total, implicit faith in his clinical judgment. Now, having difficulty focusing past the pain in his shoulder, and with the nightmare of the past twenty-four hours so fresh in his mind, he was having doubts.

Be diligent. Be meticulous. Be honest. Account for every variable. . . .

Zack stared down at Suzanne, bound for the moment by four-point, leather restraints. Shortly after arriving in the ICU her coma had lightened and she had become combative and disoriented. Her symptoms were identical in many ways to Toby's, but were clearly evolving more rapidly and virulently—the result, Zack was certain, of Frank's vicious treatment of her.

Although she was groggy from Valium she had received, it was apparent that she was still locked in her psychosis, totally out of touch with reality. Her temperature had risen to almost 101.

Was there another way? He had been so sure of himself before the Judge's accident; sure enough to charge in and insist on applying Clarkin's anecdotal work to Toby Nelms. Now, even with Mainwaring's and Pearl's validation of his theories about an experimental drug, he felt himself on the knife's edge of panic.

Be meticulous. . . . Account for every variable. . . .

Zack rubbed at his shoulder. The swelling was increasing. Even the slightest movement of his arm was now sending numbing, metallic pain up into his neck and down to his fingertips. Fatigue and tension were battling for control of his mind.

Across from him, in quiet resignation, Jack Pearl was readying his instruments and syringes. Off to one side, Jason Mainwaring stood alone, watching.

As Zack finished placing patches over Suzanne's eyes and oilsoaked cotton in her ears. Mainwaring motioned him over. He looked uncharacteristically rumpled, gray, and drawn, and the concern in his eyes was, it seemed, genuine.

"Iverson, you know, I'm sorry this is happening," he whispered.

"You should be."

"I've never been one to make excuses for myself, but before you 'n' Pearl get started, there are two things I'd like you to know."

"Oh?"

"First of all, that woman you learned about from Tarberry—the one who died in my office . . ."

"Yes . . ."

"She died of a coronary, not any allergic reaction. She never got anything but plain ol' Xylocaine. And that's the truth. I had some . . . some enemies at the hospital who had learned about my involvement with a pharmaceutical company. They were determined to get me, and Mrs. Grimes's unfortunate death gave them the chance. I won't deny doin' some work in my office with an experimental local anesthetic, but Mrs. Grimes got Xylocaine."

Zack glanced over at Suzanne.

"Mainwaring," he said coolly, "I appreciate your coming back here the way you did. But don't look for any exoneration from me. What you two—*you three*—have done here was beyond stupid, and beyond wrong."

"I've never been one to cut corners, but our company was failing. We . . . we were desperate. Serenyl would have saved us."

Zack gestured toward the two comatose patients.

"Do you think they care?" he asked.

Mainwaring had no response.

"Zack, we're all set," Bernice Rimmer called over.

"Coming."

Throughout the ordeal the nurse had been a rock, quietly stemming the concerns of the rest of the unit staff, and promising to take full responsibility should anything go wrong. She was so quick, so efficient and compassionate. Zack found himself trying to remember what she had been like during their years together at school. The only image he could conjure was of a plain, soft-spoken girl, pleasant enough, but well outside of the in crowd. How meaningless all of that seemed now.

"All right," he said to the staff. "Before we start, I want you all to know how much I—how much all three of us—appreciate what you're doing here. I know you have questions about what's going on, and I promise that when things settle down we'll answer as many of them as we can. The plan is to put Suzanne to sleep with a new anesthetic in hopes of ending her seizure. After we're done, we'll do the same thing to Toby."

"Exactly what do you expect to have happen?" one of the other nurses asked.

"Ideally? Well, I guess we hope that whatever chemical molecules are poisoning their central nervous systems will be washed away, and they'll both just wake up. But it may take some time."

"Are there dangers?"

Zack looked over at Jack Pearl, who was drawing up the contents of one of his vials into a syringe.

"Well, Jack?"

Pearl shook his head.

"No," he muttered. "No dangers."

The nurse seemed satisfied.

"Okay, then," Zack said, feeling his pulse beginning to quicken, "let's go. Remember, no light, no sound, no movement."

The nurses began cutting the lights and equipment noise to a minimum.

Zack motioned Jack Pearl off to one side.

"Remember, Jack," he said. "Play this straight."

"Serenyl's not responsible for this," Pearl growled.

"Jack, don't start with me. Just do this right, dammit."

"It won't work, Iverson. You're crazy."

"You're absolutely right, Jack." His back to the others, Zack glared down at the man. "I am crazy. And don't you for one goddamn second forget that."

Together, they returned to Suzanne's bedside. The nurses settled down in the darkness as Pearl inserted a needle into the rubber bulb of Suzanne's IV line. Then he hesitated.

"Do it, Jack," Zack rasped. "This may be your only ticket out of hell. For God's sake, do it now!"

The anesthesiologist's hands were trembling so badly he needed both of them to hold the syringe.

"Dammit, Jack . . ."

Slowly, Pearl depressed the plunger.

Frank perched on one of the tables of the Carter Conference Room and watched as Leigh Baron gathered her things. She would, no doubt, stop by the unit to verify his claims about Toby Nelms. But then, with any luck, she would be out of his life for good.

His heartbeat continued to race, and there remained a persistent, sandpaper tightness in his throat, but that was understandable. He had narrowly dodged a bullet. Still, as he had learned countless times over his years as the quarterback, although his last-second victory wasn't a pretty one, a win was a win. And a win this most certainly was. His expectations of a regional directorship were gone, but the additional money in his bank account more than compensated for the termination of his association with Ultramed and Leigh Baron.

It was interesting, he mused, how suddenly unattractive the woman looked in defeat. The bridge of her nose; the shape of her hips; the stiff, unfeminine way she moved. It was absurd that at one time he had found her so desirable. He could do better—much better.

"Remember, Frank," Leigh said, snapping her briefcase closed, "assuming what you've told me is true, I don't want one word of it to get anywhere near Ultramed."

"Sure, baby. Sure."

Even her orders sounded different—groveling, hollow.

"Damn you, Frank," she muttered.

Before he could respond, she turned and was gone.

Gradually, the unpleasant tightness in Frank's throat began to subside. He was pleased to find he could breathe deeply again. He even managed a thin smile. He was on a roll. Another challenge had arisen and been dealt with. Still, he cautioned himself, this was no time to celebrate. Not yet.

Soon, though, he thought. As soon as Suzanne Cole and one Zachary Iverson had been dispatched, there would be all the time in the world.

He pushed himself off the table and headed toward his office, reviewing the plan he had devised. Removing Suzanne from the hospital was the only tricky part, and that could easily be accomplished with one of the hospital's laundry hampers. He had always been a "hands-on" administrator. It was hardly unusual for him to be seen carrying tools to a job, or moving a piece of furniture. So even if he *were* seen with the hamper, it was doubtful any questions would be raised.

The rest was elegantly simple: a call to Zack, a meeting at Christmas Point, and an accident. He had even thought to stop by central supply and appropriate some intravenous alcohol. Starting an IV line— especially one that needed to last only minutes—was no big deal. Once Zack was immobilized, either with an injection of Serenyl or the butt of his revolver, he would infuse enough of the alcohol to leave no doubt in anyone's mind what had happened—especially since he had already seen to it that Zack's drinking the night before was common knowledge around the hospital.

Inspired. Elegant. Simple.

Lost in thought, Frank hurried along the first-floor corridor toward the new wing, nearly colliding with the Judge's wheelchair as it was pushed out of the admissions office. Clayton Iverson eyed him grimly and then turned to the young candy striper who was transporting him.

"Kathy, dear, this is my son. If you don't mind, I need to talk to him. I'll send for you if I need you again. Thank you."

He waited until the girl had left, and then used his cast and his good hand to wheel himself past the doorway.

"I want you to know that it hurt me to do what I had to do in there, Frank," he said.

"Nonsense, Judge," Frank said. "I wouldn't have expected anything less of my father."

Clayton Iverson looked up at him in surprise.

"I'm pleased to hear you say that, Frank. Unfortunately, I wish that was all there was to it."

Once again, Frank saw daylight.

"Dad, listen," he said. "I just finished speaking with Leigh Baron. I know the spot she put you in."

"You do?"

"Three years ago, some people from Boston came to me with a once-in-a-lifetime chance to get in on a land deal. They were so goddamn smooth, so well organized, that I fell for their crap hook, line, and sinker. I borrowed the money from the hospital expecting to pay it back in a matter of a week or two. It . . . it was the stupidest thing I've ever done. . . ."

Frank knelt on one knee and forced a tremble into his voice.

". . . I was so frightened, so ashamed, I—"

"Frank, you should have come to me."

"I know that, Dad. I know that now. . . ." *Easy. Not too much. Not too thick.* "But . . . but you'd already helped me out of that mess in Concord, and—" His voice broke as he stared down at his hands.

"What did Leigh Baron say?" the Judge asked.

"Say?"

"About the money."

"Oh. Well, she was pretty reasonable, all things considered. You see, I've been working on some deals—a second mortgage on the house, the sale of that lot on Winnipesaukee—and I can get together at least part of what I owe. She understands that I meant to repay the money and that I'm probably out of a job, so she's promised to put the matter to rest providing I can come up with the full amount in the next few weeks."

"And can you?"

"I . . . I can try."

"How short are you?"

Frank struggled to mask his excitement.

"I . . . Judge, I want to handle this myself."

"And just how do you expect to do that with a wife and two children and no job?"

"I'll manage. *We'll* manage. I'll catch on somewhere. I may have made a stupid mistake, but I'm still a damn good administrator."

"The best."

"Thanks for saying that."

"And Leigh Baron has promised that if you replace the money, she'll be off your back?"

"That's what she said."

"How much?"

"Judge, please."

"How much more do you need?"

"A-About a hundred thousand."

"I see . . ."

"Dad, it's my problem."

"Nonsense. Frank, I'm very pleased with the way you're dealing with all this. I was angry as hell at you, but now I understand. You made a mistake, you admitted it, and you're trying to make good. That's all I could ever ask of you. I'll see to it that you get the money as soon as I get out of here."

"But . . ." Again, Frank stared down at his hands. First Mainwaring, then Leigh Baron, and now the Judge himself!

"No buts," the Judge went on. "You can pay me back when things get better. Believe me, it will be worth it not to have to explain all of this to your mother."

"Judge, I . . . I don't know what to say."

"Well, for starters, you can stand up and promise me that as the administrator of Davis Regional Hospital, you'll never let anything like this happen again."

Slowly, Frank straightened up, carefully monitoring every muscle of his face.

Who says you can't have it all? he was thinking. *Who says you can't have it all, and more?*

"You mean that?" he asked, with just the right mix of incredulity and gratitude.

"Frank, I don't think there's a single member of the board who wouldn't vote to retain you—that is, provided you'd agree to stay on."

Finally, Frank allowed himself a smile.

"I think I'll be able to manage that," he said. "Now, I think it's time you got out of that chair and into a bed. You look a little pale. What room did they give you?"

"I asked for the third floor. They gave me 301."

"Perfect. The best in the house. Come on. I'll wheel you up."

Frank pushed his father toward the elevator. As they reached the corridor to the new wing, he stopped.

"Listen, Judge," he said. "If you don't mind waiting here for just a moment, there's something I need to check on in my office."

"No problem," the Judge said. "Take your time."

The door to Frank's outer office was less than twenty feet away. Frank left the wheelchair against a wall, crossed to the door, and inserted the key.

At the same moment he realized there was no music coming from within, Henry Flowers entered the corridor from the stairway.

"She's not there, Mr. Iverson," he said.

"What?"

Frank felt a sudden, vicious chill.

"Dr. Cole. She's not there."

Frank threw open the door, revealing the gaping hole to his inner office.

"She's in the intensive care unit with Dr. Mainwaring and your

781

brother," the giant guard explained. "And you ought to be ashamed of the way—"

"No!"

"—you tied her up and—"

Frank shoved the man aside and bolted past him.

"Nooo!" he bellowed again as he slammed through the stairway door.

CHAPTER 38

"TWO MINUTES."

Seated beside Toby Nelms's bed, Zack mouthed the words and held two fingers in the beam of his penlight for Jack Pearl to see. Pearl nodded, and let up on the Serenyl infusion.

They had kept Suzanne anesthetized with the drug for nine minutes. Besides the cessation of all voluntary movement, the only sign of any change had been an almost immediate drop in her pulse rate from 120 to sixty. And although it was now more than twelve minutes since the anesthetic had been stopped, she had not awakened.

Rather than wait, Zack had decided to leave Bernice Rimmer in with her and to move on to Toby. The child, too, had responded to his anesthesia with a dramatic drop in pulse. Now, he lay in the eerie darkness, motionless except for the minute respiratory rise and fall of his chest beneath two thin blankets.

As Zack monitored the surreal scene, he struggled against the mounting foreboding that it was already too late for the boy, and possibly for Suzanne as well. Desperately, he tried reminding himself that he was too tired and in far too much pain to maintain any semblance of a positive, objective outlook. Perhaps it would take several hours to see any real change. Perhaps several days. And perhaps, he acknowledged, it was better, anyhow, to expect the worst.

"One minute."

He signaled with his flash, and glanced about the unit. Mainwaring . . . Pearl . . . Suzanne . . . Toby . . It was all so bizarre, so sad.

He had come back to Sterling with such high hopes, so many expectations.

"Thirty seconds . . ."

Never, he vowed. *No more expectations.*

He heard the doors to the darkened ICU glide open. Then there were footsteps.

"Fifteen seconds."

He turned and peered through the darkness, past Mainwaring, toward the doors. Just inside the glass, he could see the silhouette of a woman in a business suit. Barreling past her was Frank.

"Wake him up, Jack!" Zack whispered urgently. "Quick! Wake him up."

"What in the hell is going on here?" Frank bellowed. "Turn these lights on! Turn them on right now!"

Jack Pearl stepped back from Toby's bed. The plastic syringe slipped from his fingers and clattered to the floor just as the lights in the unit came on.

Frank, his fists balled at his side, stood beside the nurses' station.

"You've been fired," he snapped at Zack. "Get the fuck out of this hospital before I call the police."

"No way, Frank."

Frank turned to the unit secretary.

"Call security, and then call the police. Tell them that a physician who has been fired from this hospital is refusing to leave."

The woman did not move.

"Do it!"

Beneath his tan, Frank was livid.

One nurse rushed to close the glass partitions to other patients' rooms.

Zack stepped from Toby's cubicle to confront his brother.

"Frank, listen," he said.

"Shut up!" Frank shouted, looking wildly about.

Leigh Baron moved a few steps closer. Behind her, a wheelchair appeared.

"I tried to tell you, Frank," Jack Pearl whined. "I tried to tell you we should have waited. . . ."

"Jack, shut up . . ."

". . . We should have been doing a retrospective study. . . ."

"Goddamn you, Jack!"

". . . But you wouldn't listen. You wouldn't give me a chance to fix my Serenyl."

Frank stepped forward and punched the anesthesiologist squarely in the face. Pearl's head shot back. Blood sprayed across his face as he dropped to the floor.

Frank's fine features were twisted and distorted with rage.

"Get out!" he screamed. "All of you. You're fired! This is my hospital, dammit! You're all fired!"

"Frank, stop," Zack said quietly. "It's over. Stop and listen. You've done terrible things here—sad and very terrible things. . . . Frank, don't you see? Look around. Look at all these people. Don't you see that it's over for you now? It's over."

"Damn you!" Frank shrieked as he hurtled over a chair and leapt at his brother. "I'll kill you! I swear, I'll fucking kill you!"

The force of his attack sent both men smashing through the plate-glass partition of an empty cubicle. A nurse screamed. Zack's injured shoulder struck the floor, exploding with nauseating pain. Dazed, he rolled to one side, over a mass of broken glass that cut into his arms and back. He stumbled to his feet, staggering drunkenly. Before his vision could clear, Frank was on him again, snarling like an animal, his hands viselike around Zack's throat, driving him backward.

Powerless, Zack's arms went limp. The pressure of Frank's thumbs against his windpipe was inexorable, and he knew, as he listened for the snap of his own larynx, that he was going to die.

At the moment that his legs gave out, he soiled himself. The pain gave way, and he sensed himself falling, drifting. Then the back of his head slammed against the corner of the metal bedframe. There was a blinding, searing flash. And then, instantly, there was nothing.

The light, a soft, warm glow, washed over the darkness in waves. One by one, faces began floating through the void. Zack followed the images with a detached curiosity, pleased when he was able to spot an old teacher or relative or classmate among them. Gradually, the faces grew more defined—and more current. An anatomy professor at Yale . . . a Wellesley coed from—from where? . . . a climbing partner in Wyoming. . . . Then Annie Doucette . . . Toby . . . Suzanne . . . and finally, Frank, his face, pinched and crimson with hatred, spinning through the glow like a dervish.

I'll kill you. . . . I'll kill you. . . .

"I'll kill you. I'll kill you."

At first the voice was Frank's. Then, it was Zack's own, moaning the words over and over again.

"Iverson. Iverson, open your eyes. It's all right. You've had a concussion."

"Concussion?"

"That's right, Iverson. Look up here."

Zack's eyes fluttered and then opened.

For several seconds, the face above him remained blurred. Then its features grew more distinct.

"Ormesby?"

The surgeon nodded.

"You hit your head. You've been out for over an hour."

"An hour? Suzanne . . ." He struggled to rise, but quickly fell back.

"Easy, Iverson. Easy."

Ormesby put a calming hand on his arm.

Zack's thoughts began to clear. He was in bed, on a monitor, in the intensive care unit. An IV was draining into his arm.

"Did I have a seizure?"

"From what I hear, you did. Probably from the concussion. The CT scanner's warmed up and waiting for us right now."

"Don't need one."

"Iverson, you're the patient here, not the doctor. Got that? I've changed my mind about your being a nut case. Don't make me change it back."

Zack nodded meekly. His head was throbbing, and jabs of pain were beginning to spark from half a dozen other places on his body. The discomfort helped clear his mind.

"Suzanne . . ." he said. "Did she—"

"Right there, Iverson. Just turn your head to the right."

Through a brief, machine-gun burst, Zack did as the surgeon asked. Suzanne, wrapped in a blanket, her IV on a transport pole, waved at him from a chair not four feet away. She looked pale, but otherwise seemed none the worse for her ordeal.

"Hi, Doc," she said. "You come here often?"

"God bless you, Clarkin," Zack murmured.

"What?"

"Oh, nothing. How's Toby?"

"Still out, Zack. But he's lighter. I think he may be coming around, but it's hard to tell. The people from Boston are due here any minute to get him."

Behind Suzanne, near the nurses' station, Zack could see the Judge watching intently.

"Listen," Ormesby said. "I'm going to get them ready for your scan. Afterward, I have a few dozen stitches to put in you."

"My shoulder, I think it's—"

"We know. Sam Christian's already seen you. Now just relax, will you?"

"Where's Frank?"

"In jail by now, I would guess. You owe that big guard over there a hell of a thank-you, Iverson. Apparently everyone was sort of paralyzed. If he hadn't pulled Frank off you when he did, I think your ticket might have been canceled."

"Bless you, Henry," Zack rasped, rubbing at the soreness in his neck.

"Now, just stay put. I'll be back."

"Stay put," Zack echoed.

He waited until the surgeon had left and then reached over for Suzanne's hand.

She inched her chair closer to him.

"Sorry I can't get up," she said. "I get dizzy when I try."

"Why don't you go back to bed. We'll talk later."

"You okay?"

"I feel like shit, if you want to know the truth. But I'm okay. Fucking Frank nearly killed us both."

"Almost. But it's over now, Zack."

"What time is it, anyway?"

"Two. Almost two."

"Damn."

"What is it?"

"The board meeting . . . Do you know what happened there?" She squeezed his hand.

"I think your father wants to talk to you about that. I'll see you after your test."

"Sure. Meanwhile, stay away from the radio."

Suzanne smiled.

"Not to worry," she said. "Sooner or later, though, I'm going to have to, um, face the music."

She motioned to Bernice Rimmer, who brought a wheelchair over, took her IV pole and wheeled her from the room.

Moments later, the Judge appeared at Zack's bedside.

"You were right about my legs," he said.

"I'm glad."

"Zachary, don't feel bad about Frank."

"I do. Judge, he hurt a lot of people. He's very sick."

"I know. He stole a great deal of money from the hospital. Apparently this business with Jack Pearl and that Mainwaring was an attempt to replace it."

"Lord."

"I found out about it for sure yesterday, but I've suspected he was in trouble for some time. Frank never could put anything over on me. I . . . I just don't know where he could have gone so wrong."

Try at birth, Zack wanted to say. He looked at the bewilderment in his father's face, and knew that there was no percentage in responding.

"Judge, the board meeting," he said. "Did you go?"

"I went. They had already voted to sell out, but I had just enough time to turn things around. After the vote Frank had the temerity to ask me if we might keep him on as administrator. Much as it hurt me, I told him absolutely not."

"Great," Zack said with no enthusiasm.

"He should have known better than to try and hide the truth from me. He was always trying. He never could. I have no tolerance for his kind of deceit. No tolerance at all." He sighed. "I had such hopes for him. I gave your brother every chance, Zachary. Every chance. You know that, don't you?"

Zack closed his eyes, and instantly he was on the slalom run, tumbling over and over again down the snowy mountainside, his knee screaming with pain. The accident had eliminated him from competitive sports and, it seemed, from much of his father's interest as well. At the time it was the worst thing that had ever happened to him. Now, he could see, it well might have been his salvation.

"Of course you did, Judge," he said, looking away. "Of course you did."

$\wedge$ EPILOGUE

As if they could quantitate a miracle leaf by leaf, the meteorologists had proclaimed October 10 *the* peak day of the foliage season in northcentral New Hampshire. And in fact, as the day—a Wednesday—evolved, with acre upon acre of crimson, orange, burgundy, and gold sparkling beneath a cloudless, azure sky, not even those old-timers who always had a different opinion of such things could argue.

In the small, atriumlike auditorium of the Holiday Inn of Sterling, sunlight streamed through glass panels, bathing the hundred or so hospital officials, board members, and physicians in a warmth that made the northern New England winter seem still remote. Throughout the hall, there was an air of excitement and history. They had come together from communities across the northern part of the state, and had met for three days around conference tables and in back rooms, hammering out the framework of a new consortium of hospitals.

Now, in minutes, the fruits of those efforts would be presented to the gathering, and a new era in community medicine would begin. The hospitals involved—seven in all—would be banded together in a way that would give them enormous purchasing power without the sacrifice of one bit of autonomy.

Judge Clayton Iverson, his wife at his side, wandered about the milling crowd, exchanging greetings and handshakes with the other attendees, most of whom knew that he was about to be announced as the first chairman of the board of the consortium. His selection for the post had been virtually unanimous. The search committee had established experience and absolute integrity as the prime qualifications for the post, and through his handling of the Davis Regional-Ultramed disaster, the Judge had proven himself amply endowed with both.

Most impressive to the group had been the Judge's refusal to intervene in the trial and sentencing of his son Frank on myriad charges ranging from co-conspiracy in testing the unauthorized drug, Serenyl, to assault with intent to murder.

Then there was his handling of the surgeon, Jason Mainwaring. After demanding and obtaining the surrender of Mainwaring's medical license, the Judge had gotten the charges against the man diminished in exchange for the liquidation of his pharmaceutical company; from the proceeds a fund would be set up to aid those patients found to have been harmfully affected by the anesthetic.

And finally, there was the leadership role he had played in the reclamation of Davis Regional Hospital from Ultramed. Not only had the Judge supervised the transition back to community control, but, dissatisfied with the amount raised from the sale of Mainwaring's beleaguered drug firm, he had convinced the Ultramed directors of the sagacity of augmenting the Serenyl settlement fund with a multimillion-dollar contribution of their own.

Though he was constantly smiling, and seemed relaxed, in between handshakes the Judge continued to glance toward the doors at the rear of the hall.

"Do you see him?" Cinnie asked.

"No. You did speak to his girlfriend, didn't you?"

"Yes, dear, I did. I told her you had been selected, and asked her to try and convince Zachary to be here for the announcement."

"And?"

"And she said she'd try, but that she doubted he would come."

She drew him off to one side, away from the crowd.

"Clayton, please," she said. "There's still time. Please reconsider this, and let's go to Florida. Just for the winter."

"No."

"But why? Lisette has moved away with the girls, and Zachary almost never comes by anymore. We haven't had a Sunday dinner in I don't know how long. We have friends down there. I . . . Clayton, I don't want to spend another winter here. Please."

"Absolutely not. Zachary will come around. You'll see."

"I don't know. He's been so distant since that terrible business with Frank. I ask him why almost every time we speak, and all he ever says is that there are things he has to work out. He says he's not even sure yet that he's going to stay in Sterling."

"Oh, he'll stay. He's moved in with that Suzanne. Does that sound like he's planning to leave?"

"No," she said. "No, I suppose it doesn't."

"Take your seats, everybody. Please take your seats," the conference chairperson announced, tapping on her microphone. "This is what you've all been waiting for."

"He'll be here, Cynthia," the Judge said. "You'll see. His brother never appreciated the things I did for him, but in the end, Zachary will. He'll be here to share this."

"Clayton, please . . ."

"No. And not another word about it."

"Ladies and gentlemen, it gives me great pleasure to officially announce the birth of the Northern New Hampshire Community Hospital Consortium."

There was a burst of applause. Again, the Judge turned toward the rear doors.

"Face it, Clayton," Cinnie said. "He's not coming."

"Damn him," Clayton muttered. "The ungrateful . . . Damn them both."

". . . And as our first order of business, I would like to introduce to you the man chosen by our search committee to head our new consortium. He is a man of accomplishment and integrity, a man known to many in this room for his tireless work on behalf of his community and his hospital. He is a devoted man, dedicated uncompromisingly to the principles of fairness. . . ."

Six miles south of the Holiday Inn, resting on the deserted field known as the Meadows, the engine of a crimson model plane screeched to life. A young boy raced across the golden autumn grass, hand in hand with a young girl.

"Jennifer wants to learn, Zack," he said, clutching the radio control box. "Can I show her? All by myself. Can I show her how to fly it?"

"How about another quick coin trick first?"

"Oh, no—I mean, how about later on? Zack, she really wants to learn."

Zack leaned back on his elbows and breathed in the fragrant mountain air. Then he turned to Suzanne and brushed his lips against her ear.

"I think the kid's got a crush on your daughter," he whispered.

"So it would seem," she replied. "Toby, do you have a license to fly that thing?"

"A what?"

"Nothing, nothing."

"Can I, Zack?" the boy asked again.

"Sure, kiddo," Zack said. "Of course you can."

With Jennifer Cole watching intently, Toby Nelms eased back on the tiny control stick. Instantly, the Fleet shot forward, across the field and up into the perfect noonday sky.

About the Author

MICHAEL PALMER, M.D., is the author of *Silent Treatment, Natural Causes, Extreme Measures, Flashback, Side Effects,* and *The Sisterhood.* His books have been translated into twenty languages. He trained in internal medicine at Boston City and Massachusetts General hospitals, spent twenty years as a full-time practitioner of internal and emergency medicine, and is now involved in the treatment of alcoholism and chemical dependence. He lives in Massachusetts.